DOGTOOTH CHRONICALS

By Kirsty Fox

Bees Make Honey

First Edition Copyright © 2012 by Kirsty Fox
Published by Bees Make Honey, Nottingham, UK

ISBN 978-0-9573984-0-5

All rights reserved. No part of this publication may be reproduced, stored in a retrieval system, or transmitted, in any form or by any means without the prior written permission of the publisher, nor be otherwise circulated in any form of binding or cover other than that in which it is published and without a similar condition being imposed on the subsequent purchaser.

All characters in this publication are fictitious and any resemblance to real persons, living or dead, is purely coincidental.

Cover design by Dan Layton
Printed and bound in the UK by Lightning Source Inc.
www.beesmakehoneycc.com

Ta Duck

Many thanks to my superhuman editing, design & technical team...
Salome Jones, Tim Dedopulos, Mac, Eliot Earl & Dan Layton.
Thanks to my family for their love & support... Rhoda Fox, Ian Fox, Hannah Fox, plus extended family in Portland, SLC, Plymouth, Cornwall & Bucks.
Thanks to Notts Writing Group & the staff at Nottingham Contemporary, particularly Lucy Hamlin.
Thanks to all my friends for their support & inspiration over the years. In particular Ben Skinner-Watts, Kristel Taylor, Jenni East, Danny O'Shea, Mark Langstaff, Sam Morgan, Daniel Morris, Lawson Leefe, Emma Britton, Dan Layton, Ebon Benjamin, Claire Whittington, Phil Formby & Samantha Gallagher.

Very special thanks to Muriel & Douglas Thomas, without whom Bees Make Honey would not be possible.

(Special thanks to Ethel & Charlie Fox, without whom my dad would not be possible.)

THE CHRONIC PHASES
Phase One
In which their lives become interlinked & Wolfgang establishes his leitmotifs.

1.

Phase Two
In which Simian's holiday takes a turn for the worst & Sheffield is steeped in latency.

94.

Phase Three
In which the rain comes...

208.

Phase Four
In which they travel south in search of a better life & meet a few odds & sods.

341.

Phase Five
In which the North calls them home on a train & they learn a few tricks in self-sufficiency.

406.

Phase Six
In which they are stranded in the woods & Claudia meets a horse & a pig.

448.

Phase Seven
In which they search for Riddlehamhope & their wildest dreams come true at the foot of the Cheviot Hills.

501.

Phase Eight
In which Nikolai arrives & Charlie visits the house at Driskel.

593.

Phase Nine
In which they have a dinner party & Roxy finds a suitable conclusion.

655.

0

PHASE ONE

In which their lives become interlinked & Wolfgang establishes his leitmotifs.

WRITER'S BLOCK

Roxanne Ratcliffe, Next to Nowhere

The empty white page bleeds to an empty white world. I'm walking and yet there's nothing. The pale sky merges to the pale snowy landscape, except there is no landscape, no trees, no shapes. Just an expanse of white page, blank. Maybe here I am truly lost. Spinning around, I laugh. There is life in me, the cold air ripping out my insides, because inside there's blood and breathing, a nervous system bleeping away, monitoring reactions, movements, the feel of the snow that sinks softly beneath me.

    A figure emerges from the blank page. At first just a vague smear, getting larger and clearer until I can make out the laughter inside his eyes and the tiny flecks of cold moisture on his stubbly chin. He wraps me in his arms and the soggy wool of his grey coat. He kisses my forehead and his nose feels cold against my face...

* * * * * * *

2

AN IDEA

Wolfgang, Dreamscape

Beneath my feet the cold ground is hardened. There were ridges ploughed into the Earth long ago, when it was soft and giving. Now it is as concrete, desperate to trip me and crunch on my bones. I see a figure in the distance. I pray a gentleman, stood solitary in the centre of my vision. Either side of us cruel frosted fields expand towards the horizon. I strain my body to move towards him, but I'm heavy in slumber. His back is to me, my hand is stretched out, wanting to grasp his shoulder and turn him around so that I can see his face. But he is out of my reach, like the moon. *Remember the fox who jumped and took a bite from the moon?*

My joints have frozen up somehow, a kind of paralysis. I begin to move towards him but each step is painfully slow and he seems more and more far away. He is becoming just a stark silhouette, like the trees of winter. As this thought skips through my noggin, music reaches me from some past withered away. Some song I've forgotten, of dogs in winter. The feeling of being hunted.

And there are dogs, hounds, I see them now. He is a hound too. But he just stands there with his back to me like a human man. He is unflinching, unemoted, while the hounds gnash faintly, the cold clinging to their breath as it rises through the air like smoke. *How I want their gentle canines to caress my skin.*

I shout, or at least my mouth opens wide and performs a shout. But it is impotent, no sound. Some rat maybe ate my tongue... I shout again...

"Hounds! Come have me! Bring me to master!"

3

Someone punched my shoulder and I found myself adjusting to the darkness. The Kaiser was stood over me with a Scotsman's conviction.

"Stop fuckin shouting in yer sleep, I need peace," he said.

I sighed an enormous, weighty sigh; the room was stony cold, like a cell. *If only that jaguar were here I could read the cryptics in his fur and find out The Answer.*

"We all need peace, brother," I told the Kaiser. "Do you have a cigarette I may pilfer, sir? Is that within my rights?"

"What were yuu dreaming about?" He sat next to me on the bed, handing me a smoke and lighting it for me.

"Tobias, brother…" I said.

"Who?"

"The cat, sir. The black cat, friend of young Timothy… Such witchcraft and heathenism should not trouble my sleep, sir…I dream of the cold also, brother ape, always the cold…" I explained.

I could feel the Kaiser's impatience for my gobbled gook, though I could barely see his expression in the darkness. His eyes were just shading to visible; some sliver of light was creeping in somewhere, how so underground I'm not sure. Light is like liquid though, the way it seeps. Far off beneath the city there is some room with a ceiling entirely covered in lightbulbs. They all jangle against one another with the most joyous of sounds, like a child's laughter. And some tiny gap carries this light through cracks, where spiders wiggle. And somehow it seeps in and seeks him. The handsome authoritarian in his long black coat, tickling the rough-shod stubble across his jaw line, creating tiny points of light in the liquid of his eyes.

"Wolfgang. Stop calling me 'sir'," he said. His tone was powerful, every word was meant.

"Please accept my apologies, brother."

"Who is Tobias?" he asked again.

So pointed a question, I've spent millennia evading the pointed question.

"Tobias Roe? We'll know soon, brother, you and I. But not so much a person as an idea, sir..."

"I thought yuu said a cat?" he said.

"Exactly sir. An idea... an idea is surely neither cat nor person, nor both nor neither?"

He smoked silently in the darkness, staring into that black void of thought.

"An idea..." he murmured thoughtfully.

I should explain a little, for you also have pointed questions. Although I imagine him the Kaiser (I fictionalise all my people), he claims his name is Charlie, but also Bryn... Bryn McLarey... an actor and author of his own memoirs. And there is something else I ought to mention. As far as he is concerned, we haven't met yet, except in future memory.

* * * * * * *

THE JASON GENERATION

Claudia McLeod, North Yorkshire

Coffee an' cigarettes, they're just ma love affair wi' existentialism...

A little pretentious? I'd fit in a bit better if I were. I mean it ironically, I mean that I mean sommat totally maire obvious and justified. I'm addicted to coffee an cigarettes. I'm addicted t'the hollow hyped feeling they gimme. If ahm not a passive smoker does that mayke me an aggressive one?

Passive addiction, thas the bullshit, the difference between free student counsellin and serious rehab. Yar not real mother fooker, yar not a mess, yar not a healthy pile of shit, steamin off't pavement on a cold day. Yar a luke-warm cuppa tea. Moanin that they didn't giv ya the degree you wanted. A fookin scrap a paper tellin you what your brain is worth. Yar the drizzle on the window pane. Thinkin you can mention how you got dumped several months ago and that justifies you crying at the sight of the Dogs Trust ad. Yar not stuck wi' years of emotions crammed up in a little box waitin to explode. You only av one night a bein so drunk you don't know how you got home. You haven't woken up in your next door neighbour's spare bedroom cos you passed out in't wrong porch.

Sayin all this only mekks me reflect on my own patheticness. I'd love to be a passive addiction, a luke-warm cuppa. My neurotic little head is no better than yars, I jus deal wi' it worse. Soldier in't trench, been there fa months, rottin feet, pickin lice off his uniform, and sleepless nights because of *explosions*, not because of some drug binge. I watched the fun movies and this is wharra thought of. The joy of blackened, scabby-faced Orcs and righteous little heroes. A little death with my pizza, please, sum casual explosions, men rollin in't mud, gaugin eyes out. It's just plain good fun.

I'd looked in't mirror at the bags under me eyes and pulled out a little more cover stick. Naked wi'out black liquid eyeliner. It's not about vanity for me, it's about stage mayke-up. And when the rain falls and I cry it will paint stains down my fayce and I will look beautifully tragic, lyke a beaten up hooker. Heroin chic, crack-whore chic... little Twiggy in a sack dress.

6

I stood outside t'back door, the party cackling away behind me. I got out a cigarette an fumed away about the posh stuck-up girls in their silly fancy hause. Wi'their designer hedonism – champagne cocktails and charlie please – someday I'll open a bar called *Cocktails and Charlie*.

"Fookin stupid posh bitches..."

I stuck the fag in the corner of ma mouth lyke James Dean and searched my pockets fatha soggy matches I thought I still had. Swearin began. The moody little blonde havin a hissy fit, muscles tight and angry as though she's gonna beat the crap outtah hersel.

"Need a fucking light?"

I looked up. I were in a *Dawson's Creek* script, clearly.

On a beautiful stone balcony above me, Jody were leaning over looking down at me grinnin. Had he jus seen me kick the wall cos some girl asked me what ma Daddy does and I needed a fookin cigarette? Ma Daddy fooks lots of women. He's a grease monkey. He raised three kids by hissel. Women lyke that, they think that makes him sensitive so they let him fook them over. The girl were only pissy cos her mullet-haired boyfriend was hitting on me.

He dropped a lighter down and I fumbled ta catch it. I lit up (attemptin to regain my cool) and stuck the fag in't side of my mouth agen. I then began to climb the drainpipe up tu't balcony, pausin wi' one hand grippin to tayke a proper drag and then exhale over ma shoulder. On an up, the drainpipes on these big auld houses are great, not lyke crappy new houses.

Jody Jody Jody, wi'his slightly dopey (doped up) half-moon eyes that always seemed smilin, grinnin, laffin. All freckly, wi'a ridiculous long fringe... Unkempt rich-boy rebels and the biggest rebellion were not havin a coke habit... Jody my aggressive addiction. Same as any other, one day it would break me.

We'd only just met at this point, I think. Can I remember? No – I'd already sneaked in where he was workin after closin time and mayde him kiss me. But that seemed a world away. I still had the heebeegeebees over whether or not he lyked me as much as I lyked him. It's all very fookin romantic.

So we sat on't balcony and talked and laffed a lot. In some memories I wrestled him tu't ground and sat on his chest, but that might've been another time, or maybe I never did.

...Dog barkin at the ice cream van, another day, another daydream. He were already in the past and I were already lonely. I rubbed my eyes, I needed to clean t'house up, stray plates hidin under tables an that. I might've been a chic little mess, but I lyked a clean house. Cleanliness is next to godliness as Dr Morris used to say.

* * * * * *

FLOTSAM

Simian Thomas, Sheffield

My teenage years felt like a dreamscape that never really happened. Hot and heady, each off-focus image blurring badly into the next, a hellish paradise carved out by jutting peaks of hit-and-run emotion. My heart is quiet and bitter now – shrivelled up like balls in a cold sea.

My friends and I all hated the world back then – or *our* world at least. Having money and being 'privileged' didn't fit well with the wrath of adolescence. So we scratched its eyes out any time we could. All the toys and spoilings and expensive holidays cannot save the rich kid from being lost and angry at fifteen.

I was not born into this lifestyle, as the rest of them were. Nor did I, or my mother, earn it somehow through the nobility of hard work. It wasn't that kind of story. We were never really poor, but I once knew a world beyond the glossy bubble. The real world, maybe, and its bright reflection would glare at my fake world, sniggering. All my fears, problems, worries, amounted to nothing. They were laughable in the real world.

Just like the kids from the council estate, near my old school, we'd do anything to break our shitty reality. But we didn't have to mug people to support our bad habits, just ask for another handout. I recalled nights spent on a friend's private beach, full of spoiled brats tripping out. On one night I passed out and I still have no idea what happened after, but I'm still here and my mother doesn't know, and they were the only two things that ever mattered on the early road to self-destruction.

I still have scars from the night I went swimming in the sea and nearly died. The waves flung me against the rocks, where I clung with bloody hands and climbed out. I sat shivering there for a few hours until the tide went out and I could paddle to shore. Lucy was the only one who waited. The sight of her sat quietly on the beach, her white clothes a speck in the blackness. My will to live, suspended on that one spot.

I was an average middle class kid until the age of twelve, when my mother, in the aftermath of a messy divorce, got a massive inheritance. It was from some uncle of hers I'd never even met. I can't remember the exact sum, but it was enough for my mother to ditch her job and propel herself, and her only child, into the alien world of elite and privileged plastic. I always suspected the money wouldn't last, given she treated it like a bottomless pit. Maybe I was damaged by the lifestyle she flung me into, but no one gave a shit. I was just another rich kid on anti-depressants. Poor little me.

I first really met Lucy on a cruise ship, a horrible tacky cruise ship, I don't even remember where. My mother dragged me on so many they all blurred into one. Ditto skiing holidays and shopping trips to (yawn) New York. (I know you're feeling really sorry for my *'dangers untold & hardships unnumbered'* at this point). My teenage friendships (or enemyships) were shaped partly by school, and partly the social circle my mother contrived for us when she got rich. Upwardly mobile, sucking the proverbial dick, a social prostitute. I love you mum.

We were the children of this social circle and in the beginning my friend Calista was all I had in terms of someone I could relate to. We both hated everything and everybody, for no real reason, and spent hours slating stupid, boring people who didn't realise how stupid and boring they were. And I don't mean the rich or the poor or the middle classes. It was anybody who had no reason to exist and didn't even know it. This isn't as bleak as it may seem. These thoughts were fuelled by loving the world and loving life and hating people who didn't *live*. People who'd get a job they didn't like, because the money was good, and marry someone as dull as themselves because marriage was the done thing, and knock out a couple kids... and then eke out an existence driven by nothing. People who wasted their lives on materialism, or self-righteous morality, or something else that kept them from ever really *being*, and thought that happiness could be achieved in this way. If you can't even begin to fathom what I'm talking about, then you should stop listening now. You will only hate me for trying to tell you what you are.

Lucy was our arch nemesis to begin with. We called her *Sarah* because she looked like the girl out of the *Labyrinth* film. She was a bully, spoilt for friends and boys, very aware of her own prettiness and how to use her charms. We mocked her for being a brat, and she mocked us for being the gawky outsiders, but we were all growing. Cassie was studying art, reading about the Pre-Raphaelites and suddenly deciding having such very red hair was not a bad thing at all. She got into boys and sex and I'd see less of her, and each time we met she seemed ever more confident.

For whatever reason, Lucy and I ended up stranded in one another's company as we hid from our parents on the cruise ship. I began to realise that she just wanted to destroy everything and to sabotage everybody, and I fell in love with it. Probably because it was something I wasn't brave enough to do. Maybe she was a bad girl cliché, someone very bored who just needed to create drama. But she didn't really give a shit about money. She would have stacked it up and burned it for fun given half a chance. And for some reason she gave a shit about me, the puny, skinny, funny-looking boy who was unable to say anything polite.

* * * * * * *

THE ALMIGHTY

Bryn McLarey, New York City

There wus a small old man in the corridor watching me with mad eyes. I'd seen him nearly every time I'd left mae room, since we'd begun our stay at the greasy youth hostel off a side street next tu Central Park. He just wandered around all day in his dressing gown – loitering and watching everybody – and he had a huge white beard.

"Meybe he's God," I'd said tu Wolfgang, with mock intensity.

It made sense now tu me that he was God. Meybe this wus heaven, the mass maze of tunnels, full of nondescript features that blurred endlessly intu one another. Bunk beds and cable television in all the rooms, punctuated by communal showers (which this fellow seemed particularly fond of), constructing a rationale that in heaven there really is no vanity, no concealer, no liposuction, no airbrushing. Everything will be stripped away tu an infinite naked ugliness visible tu all – God will stare at your lifeless shrivelled up cock and tell yuu with his eyes that yuu are not a man.

New York City wusnae as cold as it ought tu have been, noo yet. It wus January. In a week or sae a blizzard would sweep in, bringing Times Square tu a halt. Frozen in winter-time, like Narnia in the power of the white hag. But we weren't aware of the impending weather – we just wanted some fucking sausages. The diner in the base of the hostel had 'sausage sandwich' on the menu. When we unwrapped our breakfast we were greeted with ugly sausage-meat burgers. Wolfgang sat gazing at it with tearful eyes.

"I knew I wasn't going to get a decent cup of tea, but

this..." He shook his head gravely. I leapt from mae seat and marched back tu the counter.

"Hey punk, you got any *sausages*? My friend's Deutsch for Christ's sake, he needs a fucking *Frankfurter*... else he's gonna die."

The Chef gave me an unperturbed New-York-gaze.

"We don't do hot dawgs... punk!" His top lip curled up on the last word, like a wolfie. "There should be a van down the block."

I returned tu Wolf with a grouchy shrug. He sighed heavily and looked bitterly around him at the other backpackers, most of whom weren't American, sae couldnae be blamed.

"Hey, whaddya say we head down Harlem way and try tu get beat?" I said more cheerfully.

"Get beat? What does that *mean*?"

"Ich wieß nicht."

Sae we returned tu our dorm (or doom as Wolfgang called it), tu amass thoughts and watch another half hour of the cartoon channel. With thoughts amassed we pulled on coats and made our way towards Harlem, with the attitudes of men trying not to look like tourists. But Harlem silenced even the devil in maeself and Wolfgang. We skulked through like a couple a bony stray mutts, wide eyes gazing around. "I forget," Wolfgang whispered, drifting back into his natural German tones out of nerves. "You don't get hurt for being a schmuck here, you get shot."

We sloped off downtown tu a grungy hip-hop bar near Little Italy and tried every different type of Bourbon Whiskey they had. I had tu remind Wolf that he needed to tip the bartender if he planned tu get served ever again.

The snow came and the sleepless, restless city came tu a sleepless, restless halt, sucking its teeth and stomping its hooves. We set off on an expedition into Central Park. An easy place tu get lost any day of the week due tu the absence of straight paths, and the existence of many banks, trees, and strategically placed rocks that all looked the same. In the blizzard, it wus impossible tu even see the skyscrapers on the skyline – it wus like walking out of the city and entering the wilderness. Hearing how cold it wus in New York, Wolfgang and maeself had purchased long black woollen coats. Being out of my usual uniform of wife-beater vest, leather jacket and ragged jeans had been troubling me. Now, as we staggered on intu the blizzard like two black shadows, I felt better.

We didn't talk. We couldn't talk. We lost the path and just wandered on, blistering cold winds ripping at the bare flesh of our cheeks. We'd bought black beanie hats just that morning. We pulled them lower over our eyes, laughing at the sight of each other, two black figures spotted with white like inside-out Dalmatians.

Then we saw Him standing there in the snow just staring upwards – the crazy old man. We hadn't thought that he ever left the hostel as he was always there, omnipresent... omniscient. He didn't stare at us nae, as though we were no-longer of importance. He just looked tu the snow-filled skies, the wind whipping his hair and beard intu a fury. I leaned right over to Wolfgang's ear, resting a gloved hand on his shoulder.

"Do you think he's causing it?"

Wolf's eyes glowed with laughter, but my own words sent a chill down my spine. It's easier tu laugh when you're an Atheist.

* * * * * * *

LOVE CRUMBS

Haydn Antoine, Derby

The pregnant woman glared lazily at us as we entered the building. She was sat at a table which was meant to be a desk, with a large open book which looked like the sort hotels have to list reservations. As we approached her, she didn't say anything, just looked at us while tapping the pen against the paper.

"Ah-ite," Rufio grunted to her, as though they'd already met, but I wasn't sure.

"What're your names?" she asked.

"My name is Rufio Gonzalez, 'is name is 'Aydn Antoine."

The woman, without asking about spelling, scrawled our names in the book – *Roofio Gonzarlez & Aiden Antwon* – and handed us two sets of keys. I motioned to the book, intent on altering her mistake, but she interrupted.

"Rent's due on the fifth of every month. Covers yer bills an all. Just bang on my door if you want anything," she said (in a tone which suggested if we did bang on her door for anything she would sneeze on us).

And so somehow, although the exactness still dazzles me, this woman, the evil bitch who I never knew the name of because she never let me dare to ask, managed to change my name, because she couldn't spell and Rufio didn't pronounce his aitches. If anyone sent mail with my real name on, I didn't receive it. My agency rang her for a reference and ended up deciding she was right and they were wrong, my name was Aiden not Haydn. My friends thought it was funny and introduced me to people as this ethereal alter ego.

15

"It's very Coen brothers, that," Claudia commented, when I explained it to her later.

Dresden House was amazing. It felt like it had been lifted from New York City and dropped in Derby. In the centre was a winding stone staircase with a wooden handrail with endless names engraved. Each floor greeted you with a door on either side from which sounds sometimes came, sometimes silence, yet always a sense of mystery, intrigue. Occupants grunted only a hello when passing on the stairs, leaving figments, images of themselves in my mind, which, in turn, invented them as people.

"This is well weird," I said to Rufio as we clambered the stairs to the top floor flat, lugging minimal possessions. (Our philosophy was that you don't need furniture and crockery if you have shit-loads of vinyl. Maybe I used one of his Prince records as a plate the odd time, I'm not telling.)

"*You* is well weird Blondie," he answered. "You not been around, you been livin in a cloud."

We bought cold beers and sat at the top of the great staircase dangling our legs between the rails like the girl in *Leon*, peering down and watching for people. A baby was crying somewhere and from outside came the demonically cheerful sound of an ice cream van playing the Match of the Day song.

"You want ice cream, Roofie?"

"I ain't climbin them stairs gen." He shook his head.

"Ever?"

"I'll be an 'ermit, you can bring me food... and tunes."

"I saw Nether Ed," Cookie mumbled hesitantly. She was sat crossed legged on a rouge cushion balanced on the top of the massive antique radiator. She'd already adopted our new digs as practically her own.

"You can't have," I said "I mean... how did you know it was him?"

"I just knew." She tapped her fag above the ashtray a few feet below her on the floor. Most of the ash missed and scattered on the bare boards. She chewed absent-mindedly on the glue of her pink hair extensions and watched my fingers play ballet across my laptop keyboard.

'Nether Ed nibbles his own toenails, some think that is quite a talent.'

"He was wearing a massive scarf, like not even a scarf, like a throw. It could've covered a chair," she said.

I nodded. I pictured him scratching his head and pondering the distinct horizon.

"He's got this quality... like a monk?"

I nodded furiously.

The door banged open and Rufio crashed in carrying a failing cardboard box of treats.

"Get that scutty bitch out!" he said, motioning to Cookie. "Why she always here?"

"You fucking love me! I bring The Maelstrom," she shouted.

"You bring the pigs is what you bring." He tossed a pack of love heart sweets into her lap and she squealed, dropping her cigarette. She scratched them open.

"Gosh, they're modern these days. *'Email me', 'dp me'!*" She threw one at me. It was orange and pink, landing on the keyboard in front of me... *'miss u'*.

"Miss you like a maelstrom." I broke it in half and love crumbs scattered on the keyboard. I ate the first half, placing it on my tongue like the body of Christ.

"You want a brew, yeah, Blondie?" Roofie asked.

I nodded.

"Yes, please!" Cookie squeaked unnecessarily loud.

"Shhhhhhhhh," I hissed, waving a hand at the screen to hint that I was trying to concentrate.

"I know you want a brew, Skag, anyfin fer free, you want," Rufio mumbled as he filled the kettle.

"How are you anyway, Roofie?" she asked adoringly. "How's it all going here?"

"Alrayt... not too shabby, not too shabby t'all." He made a Marlon Brando big chin face. She giggled.

"Haydee's being very studious," she said in a tone that wanted to get a rise out of me. "He doesn't even wanna get take out."

I lowered my glasses on my nose and peered over them at her... more giggles... I swear the girl was on laughing gas.

"That's cos I think we deserve Rufio's fucking awesome cooking tonight," I said.

"Yehman, I love the way you say 'fucking'," Rufio mimicked my over-pronunciation. "I ain't cookin nuffink in this kitchen, fuckin dirt-ee, man." He picked up a pizza box with three day old crusts rattling inside and chucked it at me. The corner met my shoulder.

"If I clean up then, will you make a shit-load of curry?" I asked.

Rufio nodded. "Yeh-man, you invite that prettee girl round and I'll make curry... you bangin anyone, Cookie? Whoo you checkin?"

"I'm trying to bang Haydn," she said.

"Lost cause, sweetart, he'll not bang you. Too busy pine-in fer that mentull girl."

"What if I get him battered and then take advantage of him?" she asked cheekily.

"I'm not getting battered tonight. I've got too much work on," I said.

Rufio pointed a backwards thumb at me. "See?"

* * * * * * *

SYNTHESIS

Roxanne Ratcliffe, Nottingham

"D'you think fucking intelligent people makes you more intelligent?" I'd asked Bobby with wry humour, as I collapsed next to her on the sofa.

She smiled, giving me the darkly flirtatious sideways glance that'd become her trademark – it made me nervous when it fell in my direction. I leaned over to the low table and picked up my Caipirinha, stirring the lime around with a straw, before taking a long sip.

"Damn, this cachaca really is much nicer. I never knew you could get the good stuff outside Brazil."

"So who's this 'intellectual' you wanna fuck?" Bobby was sat crossed legged, all made-up with black eyeliner and smoky shadow. Her almost black hair was dyed inky red at the time. She gazed absent-mindedly round the room at various people of interest. Nottingham had surpassed its turn of the century boom in pretentious cocktail bars. Bobby and I were only too happy to pour our hard-earned cash into them, provided there were plenty of people around to be verbally dismembered.

"I wouldn't call him an intellectual. I just haven't met that many people in my life yet that I can have such good conversations with... I dunno." I shrugged off a happy shiver.

"What about that bloke you met in Italy? Or did you make him up?"

She was expecting me to hit her, but I just shrugged and went quiet. I didn't like feeling like a silly little girl still longing for something she couldn't have. It made me feel young and foolish. Which we still were of course, but at nineteen you like to think you're a bit older and wiser. (Not much has changed).

She nudged me. She didn't like self-pity – it irritated her. She wouldn't pander to my mood swings like everyone else.

"Toby was different... He was more..."

"Spiritual?" She grinned, teasingly.

"Oh, fuck off then, you're such a fucking bitch," I said without emotion.

"What the fuck is she wearing?" she muttered quietly. A group of girls had hobbled in on heels too tall for their drunkenness. One was wearing a fuchsia pink dress two sizes too small for her. "Seriously, what's his name?"

"Hal," I said.

"Hal?"

"Well, Harry, but they call him Hal. I like the name Harry actually," I mused.

"Well, fucking stupid people definitely makes you more stupid. So maybe the same is true of the opposite. Just look at that girl. If she's ever had sex outside of a nightclub toilet, I'd bet my bottom quid he's some dopey Palais type, who at the age of twenty three still thinks he's on the verge of a career in professional football... or white rap." She drifted off to another train of thought. "Damn, why do all bartenders have such nice bums?"

We were sat in seats that overlooked the bar through a glass pane.

"What about Ian Wright?" I said, jumping tangent.

"The exception that proves the rule. He'll never make it in white rap either," she quipped.

"Do I have a nice bum then?" I asked.

"Mai Tai, honey," she said, giving me *that* look again. "The best."

A man approached us, staring like a coked up vulture. He sat down opposite smiling seedily.

"Can we help you?" Bobby said in a tone that offered an axe to the head of unwanted attention.

"Would either of you ladies like to join me for a cup of tea tomorrow?" There was something sinister in the tone of the question. Something that made me want to cover my entire body in a huge baggy jumper, and grow my fringe so long it covered my face totally so that he couldn't see me, so that he couldn't look with his poisonous eyes – eyes I would've happily cut out.

"I'm sorry, I only fuck professional skateboarders," Bobby said blankly.

"And her?" He looked to me.

"She only fucks people who've read *Heart of Darkness*," she said (murmuring to me), "That way you don't have to finish reading it, you can just absorb it through the skin."

"I'll be whatever you want me to be, baby girl," he slimed. I felt sick in my stomach, as though I was trapped inside his eyes.

"We'd quite like you to be absent. Or on fire. Or maybe both at the same time?" Bobby replied politely.

After a long, sinewy pause the man got up and walked away. I took a hard slug of my drink, immediately trying to erase his face from my brain.

"It is a trifle challenging," I mumbled.

"What is?"

"*Heart of Darkness*," I replied.

She beamed, nodding. "Maybe it's the way to skip all the hard work. Screw a literature student, a drama student... What does this Hal study? Assuming he studies?"

"Philosophy and Chinese."

"Damn that's hot... nearly as hot as a skateboarder who goes dirt-biking and surfing... so yeah, it's the way to become an intelligent well-rounded twenty-something. Have sex with certain individuals, absorb their freckles of creativity, philosophy, sense of understanding about the world."

"What about the skateboarders?"

"They're just for fun. They have nice bums." She sighed. "Oh, little Roxy, I shall never be as intelligent as you, and that's why. So are you gonna ask this boy out?"

"Of course not, I wouldn't physically be able to get the words out." I shook my head gravely.

"Oh, for fucks sake, wake up, honey. Wake up or have some balls." She delivered her usual level of patience for the meek and the shy.

I crumpled. I couldn't help it. It's the alcohol, the short sharp depression that clouds all of a sudden and goes as quickly as it comes. I went to the toilets. They were empty. I stared into the mirror, as though if I looked into my reflection enough I would know who I was. I looked very small and breakable.

I was on holiday with my parents in Italy, age seventeen, when I met Toby. I'd hated most of the holiday – I hated the Italian men that leered at me, I loathed the staggering heat, and I was bored of my parents bickering and fussing. I refused to go out during the middle of the day. They went off on trips to all sorts of places while I stubbornly stayed at the hotel, which was the only thing I did like about the holiday. It was a tall, narrow building, circling a courtyard of cobbles and café seating. Each room had a balcony facing on to it. I remember thinking the walls were the colour of crab shells, dashed with white and peachy-pink. It was shady and cool, down in this hollow world. Time and space evaporated, leaving a breezy calm, safe from the hot hustle of the city.

Toby had a balcony across from mine. I had seen him a few times and felt a little curious, but he was a few years older, with an air of nonchalance that I somehow found intimidating. I was bored one day, leaning on the balcony rail. He was sat reading on the other side, but he felt my eyes and looked up. Neither of us exactly smiled or acknowledged one another, we just locked eyes for a while. I remember he rubbed his stubbled chin in indecision, and then motioned to meet me in the downstairs café.

"What's your name?" he asked, once we'd sat down and ordered. He had a distinctively soft, Yorkshire burr. My first love affair with Yorkshire.

"Roxanne Ratcliffe." I always introduced myself fully at that age. I liked the sound of the two names together.

He gave my hand a gentle shake.

"Tobias Roe," he said.

"Tobias? Really? Like the cat?" I asked.

He smiled wildly. The speckles that patterned his watery irises collected into spider webs that bound us, silvery streaks of light scribbling out the rest of the world until there were just two people left. "*Tim and Tobias*? Y' remember those stories? Nobody else does. Ev'ryone calls me Toby, but Roxanne's such an enigmatic name I felt the need to match it."

He had a funny little habit of smiling slightly between each sentence, the corners of his mouth dimpled, more so when he was nervous.

"Roxy." I shrugged.

"Ah." He smiled again, brushing his stubbled chin a little nervously, trying not to look at me too much and failing.

"Don't you like the sun?" I asked him. He was, after all, taking refuge like me, every day.

"I love the sun. It's the heat I don't like. It exhausts my brain and I burn very easily."

There seems to be a little hole in my heart that could only ever be filled by Toby Roe. Some tiny, nuanced thing that I fail to put into words. He evokes the same emotions as the song *True Faith* by New Order, in which the echoey synths and nostalgic lyrics simultaneously remind me of who I was when I was young, and who I'll be when I'm old.

* * * * * *

JACK DOORS

Wolfgang, Sheffield

A woesomely tedious train of thought that begins with...

There are no polar bears in Poland.

There are no polar bears in Poland. Crazy, I went and checked, just to be sure...

Oh Bismarck flea, oh Bismarck flea, how lovely is your brain cheese?

People say I'm fucking cool, but frankly I'm still a virgin. People say I don't talk about real things. I speak riddles, my own riddled, riddling corpses. Inside I'm rotting but outside I'm smiling. A big ol' yellow toothed grin that spreads a little disease every time you look to me. I have the answers, yes, nestled in my cavities. Open wide, ignore the bits of leftover cowflesh caught in my molars. Take a good look beyond. No tonsils, I know, they were eaten by that rat that crawled inside my throat one night when I was catatonic on Ket. An easy meal he said, tramps on the street are easy pickings. He had those jaundiced eyes from too much dirt-cheap vodka, aged and matured to perfection in the sewers, the kind that eats alive those destitute enough to consume it... This is it, this is the answer. I am the answer. The world is eating itself.

For further profound thoughts that leave you in debt to my genius turn to page 42. *Do not under any circumstances* turn to page 237. There's a lady rotting in a bathtub. She'll make you afraid of your own en-suite bathroom.

    This is the trouble with the human race: they're afraid to look in my mouth. Unlike the rat race who take great joy (and a hearty meal) from what they find in there. The human race cannot face their own revulsion for themselves and others. This is why they will die, and the rats and the ants who strip the flesh from jungles and peoples, and the cockroaches, those nasty-cute little things. All these godly creatures will survive the next Ice Age because (and I cannot emphasise this enough) THEY ARE NOT AFRAID TO CRAWL INSIDE MY MOUTH.

There is some black mould on the bathtub. It is harmless, don't worry, you can lick it, it is not poison. Bacteria, there is she, her wiry hair grappling out towards you, her mouth parting in a grimace. She wants to smile but she has no joy. And you see each tooth is sharpened to a point. You're afraid. You reach for the Dettol. The black mould starts out as a slimy thing, but if you leave it to grow it will become soft and furry. Do not think you are alone in the house; there is always life, always breathing and growing, the bugs all nesting away in that elegant shag pile. *Anyway Bacteria and Dr Shipman are both dead, you know this. God rest their souls.* It's just a pity that Bacteria's green and yellow corpse is determined to spend her last rest in *your* bathtub. In your sweet little en-suite bathroom with a heated towel rail. She rather spoils the peace, and what of when your friends pay visit? What of those decorated internally with OCD, carrying little mini bottles of Dettol in their pockets, to ensure this stranger's toilet is clean enough for their soft rump? What will they think to her wiry hair and gnarling finger nails gripping the edge of the bathtub?

So you don't invite people around. You stay alone in the house with the bugs and the sweet little black moulds which are starting to gurgle and make cute noises.

There was a tap tap on your window this morning. A caw caw. You knew, you'd seen those big black birds playing on your neighbour's roof, rocking the television aerial like mischievous hoodies. Crows? Rooks? Jackdaws? Not sure how to differentiate. Wanted them to be ravens just for poetry. I think they're jackdaws, I have some memory of their mischiefs, and oh fuck (!) the window is ajar behind the curtains. What if Mr. Jack Daw comes inside and causes havoc in your bedroom? Hastily I pick up a cricket bat and smash everything in the room. Ha, Mr. Jack, ha ha. Nothing for you to destroy now. No mischiefs here for you now. Leave me in peace, leave me to my sweaty undeserved lie in, leave me to my dirty bath. Jack caws outside my window, outside your window. *'Put the bat down, Wendy, stop swinging the bat, Wendy'*. Shut up, Jack, just shut up. Fade to narrator.

You may wonder at jumbled narratives, you may wonder at what point we will get to the point. On what theatrical stage the characters' lives will begin to fit like a jagged, monochrome jigsaw puzzle. You may puzzle about when an anecdote becomes a storyline, and puzzled reader you will be rewarded – for patience, but most of all for wanderlust. Like the tired sigh of a bored young thing, flicking through travel brochures, no story shall stay still.

* * * * * * *

STRAIGHT LACED LASSIES

Bryn McLarey, Oxford

"The world somehow adjusted to people *like you*, but it sacrificed a great deal for it."

I laughed at her personal venom. "Don't be sae melodramatic."

"You stomp all over everything!" Juliette said.

It wus a domestic situation – I recall a mortgage having something tu do with it. The word still gives me the chills. It wus also the first in a long line of middle class, lefty women I stumbled into relationships with. Things were much simpler back in mae youth, with mae first girlfriend, Janine, stealing my fags, bleaching her hair tu death and screaming in unintelligible Glaswegian when I did anything untoward.

It's that look of disappointment that has punctuated all these later relationships. The joined up writing, the dull thump of a heavy lazy heart that no longer wants to be enmeshed in love because it just seems tuu much like hard work. Disappointment. I fingered mae signet ring and looked incredulous.

"Little something?" I asked Juliette (a reference to her mother asking the nieces if they're hungry for a snack). Her look of disappointment deepened.

"Seriously can we just go grab dinner somewhere, I'm hungry?"

"We can't afford to keep eating out every fucking night," she replied curtly.

Middle class women swear so elegantly. I usually get elegantly cursed at, at some point. They think use of the f-word might help penetrate my brain, which – given I've spent numerous hours in numerous pubs in numerous cities, surrounded by men who merge the word intu every other noise they emit as they spout utter drunken shite – is doubtless going tu be relatively ineffective.

Money. That's what it all comes down tu, and sex... or generally a lack of. Not necessarily a dryness on the part of the lady. I've been known tu keep the level of beer in mae system tuu high tu stay awake longer than a romantic slobber. But I needed the beer tu numb the word money. And spend the word money until it didn't exist anymore... I tried tu explain tu so many straight-laced lassies that mae way of overturning capitalism wus tu spend all of mae capital, and if they thought a joint-account wus a good idea, I generously taught them the pitfalls. We had sum good times sure, but they were blurred between the looks of disappointment.

"It's such a waste. What do you have to show for it all?" She reasoned.

I smiled darkly. "Tu waste and get wasted and not be saved by anyone. I had a good time. That's more valuable than a fucking mortgage, than poncey clothes, than a fucking Aston Martin I'm always tuu drunk tu drive."

"What if you end up lonely? With nothing but good memories you can't even really remember because every drunken night merges into the next and the next?"

"I'll always remember the nights yuu had a fucking smile on your chops." I shrugged casually. "And the rest is slops... neh matter."

She laughed a little bit then – this is because she still loves me and she's not yet bitter enough tu discard that. I put mae hand in mae jacket pocket, fished out sum change, receipts, and a scrap of paper full of scrawl. I dumped it all ontu the table, bits scattered. Finally I pulled out a second hand necklace, silver and green, a bit of costume jewellery as they say. I handed it tu Juliette. She stared at it.

"Pub change," I said. She'll probably assume I found it on a nightclub floor, but no matter tu me, it's part of the charm.

"Gosh, it's just my taste." She made that face I looked for every day.

"That's just what I said when yuu bought me a bottle of Black Sheep Bitter."

She laughed again and decorated me with kisses.

"I'll go to the shops and buy some nutritious ingredients for dinner. Yuu open some wine. We'll eat, we'll fuck and it'll be beautiful," I suggested.

"Oh really? When you say nutritious ingredients I hope you don't mean hash," she said.

Oh, these liberal lassies. "Why? Are you worried yuu might chill the fuck out?"

"Quick, Charlie, *go*. Before I sell you back to Scotland!"

No, no, I thought... You're stuck with me, pumpkin. At least until my pockets are empty.

* * * * * *

A TOKEN SILENCE

Roxanne Ratcliffe, Sheffield

It was time to meet Hal.

All I could hear was my own breathing inside my head and the fragile heartbeat of a captive animal, butterflies trapped inside the suit of a cosmonaut. I could see his face through the tinted transparent panel. He was a few feet away but it felt like a further distance, like my voice wouldn't travel.

I looked a bit like Zippy spinning through space. The room of the pub felt suddenly like a set. Not a film set, something more mundane, but everything was placed just so, to look casual and real, like the slightly screwdled beer towel on the polished bar top.

In times of disappointment I longed to hibernate, but my hibernation becomes a coffin. My dad once asked me why people my age were so fixated with the macabre. I suppose I'd always thought it a typical adolescent fantasy.

"You're dead, girl... How does it feel to be dead?" the man in my dream asks me. Fear takes a strangle-hold on my heart, squeezing it inside an iron grip. Mediated experience can never replace firsthand experience when it comes to fear, sex, or torture.

My brother was deaf from birth. Sometimes I'd wake and there was nothing, movement and vibration, but the sound was muted almost to non-existence. I could always hear electricity. When I walked into a room where a television was on standby, I could hear the static, hear it sat there thinking. Sometimes that's the sound in my own head, some barely audible white noise, twitching away. I fear it being the only sound left in my head. I fear that that was all that my brother David could hear, the sound of *my* fear, like some electrical energy in the atmosphere. He tried to look after me, regardless of his own issues. We spoke often with mere expressions. We drove our parents crazy as we would be silent and barely animate. They knew sign language, but this was something else. This was a mutual understanding of ordinary gestures, this was really tuning into another person, not needing to tap them on the shoulder in order to have their attention.

We got away with so much in this way, sat at the table for Christmas dinner. We talked silently of the relatives, of their evident walk towards death. Not physical, so much as mental. Their mundanity was increasing, and not in a noble way, in a pickety, repetitive way. They found our conversations amusing as they didn't hear the scathing words, and assumed David had little grasp of what they said. But David never misheard anything. He could lip read better than most of us can listen. He taught me to dance, because he could only feel music, not hear it. He'd sit in our room with his back against the large speaker and close his eyes. I romanticise the idea of him. We were too close – we shut out the world at the time.

Without you I must start all over, without you I must learn to function again.

It upsets me when people misunderstand me, but then they've not grown up with my silly little neurotics. And so I sat with Hal, in that pub, which felt like the theatre set for a kitchen sink drama. And it felt as though the audience watched me and took notes on my stage fright. Remarked softly to one another that a space suit was not really dating attire, the boots being a little clumpy and all.

* * * * * * *

MARMALADE

Simian Thomas, Sheffield

The marmalade cat licked its paw discerningly before giving us a vacant, green stare.

"Fucking spoilt beast!" Hex responded. "I give you

fucking ham and this is all I get in return?"

He'd bleached bits of his hair rather badly since I'd last seen him, with eccentric sideburns that emphasised his unattractively bony cheeks and nose. I knew well-enough he was probably trying to make himself look a bit like Wolverine. Anyone but me, he'd say.

"So what can I do you... for?" he said to Cassie.

"You can't do me at all." She instinctively picked up his trying-to-be-callous humour.

"Crack is good... I'm kidding. I don't have any crack." He chuckled to himself.

She blinked witheringly.

"Pills?" he asked hopefully.

"Not interested in designer yuppie drugs, more of a mushrooms girl," she replied. (This was a lie anyway, Cassie had a strong distrust for anything hallucinogenic.)

"Ecstasy isn't a yuppie drug. It's for ravers, party people... It's fucking new wave," he persuaded.

"Nineties crap," she said.

"I don't sell mushrooms, you fucking hippie."

"I'm not here to buy shit." She shook her hair.

He watched her transfixed. "Really?"

"Is your self esteem that low that any time someone comes to see you, you thinks it's to buy drugs?"

"People make friends with me for one reason and one reason only." He turned back to his cat. "Out for what they can get... *dry cured, breaded, slightly smoked, hand sliced!* None of that shit they scrape off the wall of the slaughter house."

The cat blinked at him, unfazed.

"I just find the fact that you talk endlessly to your cat highly entertaining."

"Okay, you don't want to get high at all? How about watching *The Never Ending Story*? Luck dragon is what I need."

"Do you ever watch proper films?" I asked, breaking my own silence.

"Don't pretend you *don't* love *Labyrinth*," Hex said.

"Yeah, but there is a *special* reason for that." Cassie rolled her eyes.

I glared at her but she ignored it.

"You know what Tim Burton said when someone asked him when he was going to make films about real things?" Hex gesticulated melodramatically. "He said *'all my films are about real things'*."

"That's different, Burton makes artistically justified films that comment on society and the treatment of outcasts." I waved a hand at his *Edward Scissorhands* poster.

"And they also relate to the boundaries of the imagination, which is exactly what *The Never Ending Story* is about."

"See, this is why we come to see you, Hex. *Good conversation*," Cassie said.

"Only achieved through reaching an artificial higher level..." He raised his hands and looked up to the ceiling, as though maybe he would be better off up there than down here with us.

"That's bullshit. You're the most amusing first thing in the morning when you're stone cold sober," she said.

"Have we ever slept together?" He tilted his head attempting to retrieve a memory from what must've already been a pile of mush.

"Only literally," she replied firmly.

"Ok, we'll watch it... provided you don't take anything to make it seem more amazing than it is," I muttered dismissively.

"You admit it's amazing!" he said.

"Anything's amazing if you're on smack."

"Do I take smack?" Hex asked.

"Too chic for you, mother-fucker."

"Will you just let me pour some Chartreuse in my eye?" he asked. "It's too late in the day to be sober."

"Your death wish is most endearing." Cassie flopped on the sofa next to him, rearranging cushions and crossing her legs as only teenage girls can do. The cat snuck in between them, to ball up in the comfiest spot. Hex poked at its ears so that it gave him evils.

"Ginger is your favourite, isn't it?" I said as I trailed his DVD shelf.

He looked deliriously at me and moved his hand without looking to stroke Cassie's hair.

"Yes..." He paused, dropping his chin to reassess himself. "Stem ginger biscuits."

* * * * * *

MOOMINS & DEITIES

Claudia McLeod, Sheffield

"I'm not shaar you ever get over anybody. It's always there, lyke a tattoo you wanna scratch off, then another one fooks you over, intentionally or not. You collect 'em lyke so many scars."

Roxy nodded heavily, so I continued.

"I don't regret them though, fook it, nobody died... It's not another notch on the bedpost when yaar fookin in love wi'em. It's another notch on't skin."

I paused uncertain'ly. I could see Roxy deluding herself tharrit might help to demonstrate this metaphor *literally*. The skin under your eyes is the most thin. I always felt lyke all Roxy's skin is lyke that, wafer thin. Maybe I just lyked to look at her and think 'weak', so I could tell missel I were a tuff cookie and feel good about it.

On the night we met, there were some sort of wake in a dingy rock bar that I'd never bin to. Someone in a band I knew had died the week before in a drunk-drivin accident. The bar had a cellar and candles ev'ywhere and people were lightin more and placing them around the stage. It were pretty fookin surreal and faar too overly meaningful. And there she was, just dancing by hersel, this little blonde chick wi' a round pale face.

"Lyke a lit'l Moomin girl," I said, pointin her out.

"That's Roxanne," Charlie said, unable to keep the smitten tone from his voice. She were only smitten wi' the music. He touched her shoulder to get her attention. She smiled at us both in a spaced kinda way. Charlie kissed her on the cheek and she wore it graceful'ly.

"I'll get some drinks," he said.

And so we jus danced away to *When Doves Cry*, spinnin around't room, smilin and enchanting people, treadin on their sadness wi'our own careless love. We necked the drinks Charlie bought furrus, eyes exchangin a look which knew we were forever bound by boath being unbalanced, teeterin gorgeously on the edge of sommat. Charlie watched us jealously. I felt his jealousy later. Although I didn't love her in the unhealthy way Charlie did, I still hayted introducin her to people, I hayted them gettin on soo well, I hayted them tekkin her photograph. It were a bit daft.

We sat later in quieter moments, talking wi' Charlie while she dripped wax into a bracelet on her skinny wrist.

"Doesn't that hurt?" Charlie said.

"Everything hurts." She din't look up.

Me an' her shared our despair for the cocaine culture growing around us.

Charlie scoffed. "A wee bit of charlie never hurt anyone," he said.

"It's not a wee bit," she said. "Some people I work with, it's like they've replaced their personality with it... I can't explain..."

She leaned over and dripped wax spots onto his arm, attemptin to form leopard markings. He maintained a stony fizzog, dark gaze steady. He watched the expression of concentration on her fayce. I could almost feel him holdin his breath. I felt suddenly stuck in this one-sided intimacy, so I left fa the bar. On the way I stopped to smirk at the moody black an white photo of a man who died too young. How we put the dead up on pedestals.

"Jeebs, Harry, what hav they done to ya? Keep truckin, honey, you were too good ta me." I blew him a kiss.

When I returned tu't table with drinks Roxy looked relieved. It's only safe to stir up affection in front of other people. Charlie probably just said sommat nasty – he had that look on his fayce.

"So, Roxy, how did you know Harry?" I asked.

She blushed and looked away and an unmistakable thunder cloud passed through Charlie's eyes.

"Hav I put ma foot in sommat stickeh?"

They both looked down. Charlie poked at the wax on his arm, which were stickin inta the dark hairs.

"Thas gonna hurt lyke fook, when it rips them hairs off," I suggested helpful'ly.

* * * * * *

CONFIDENT, STYLISH & CHARMING...
(A DEBONAIR)

Bryn McLarey, Oxford

In the very depths of mae pants is a bum... Not an arse, not a hairy, artistic arse... A hobo... mixing blue anti-freeze with gin... writing words on a page thinking they have some real meaning, honesty of voice because of *the state I'm in*.

The Mother Black Cap, the line between pretension and sincerity... I sit in the bath, swill full of bubbles and grease, eating battered sausage and chips off the side. Moments of impulse string together – get drunk, take a lick of some white substance (must ask Geoff what that wus), attempt tu shave the word 'debonair' intu the side of one's head (not sure that's strictly staying *in character* but Charlie'd appreciate the irony at least), buy 6 A.M. mutant greasy takeaway, long for the relaxing heat of a bath.

The bath is luke-warm. Sae are the chips. The chips taste leik they've been in the bath and the bath tastes leik it's been in the chips. I have a chip in one hand and a sausage in the other, when I realise on impulse I'd bought a pack of cigarettes and lit one and there it is. It's end turning tu a limp penis in the soap dish. (*Charlie has a soap dish, he just would*). I snatch at it, desperate for its filthy stinking taste in my filthy stinking soul. I gave up smoking when I became Charlie (*sounds like a sex change*)... I gave up battered sausage tuu. In grabbing the fag I dropped the sausage. It now bobs and floats somewhere around mae dick. I drop the chip and pick up the sausage. I drag on the fag again and then bite the sausage. It tastes of bath. I think this problem of only having two hands is repeating itself.

37

Impulse. I want tu lick you. Nicotine lung, the inside is yellowed leik the interior of a smoky bar, full of haze and pretty women. I drag mae torso upstanding from the tub. Standing ankle deep I catch sight of maesel in the mirror. I see Bryn, the black curls crawling from mae nipples to mae arse craic. The grey-blue scar of a seven year old tattoo. The eyes which fail somewhat to focus on themselves speak of the binge. I need tu fuck.

But to get one I must be Charlie again. I put on deodorant and fixed breakfast, the toast rack, the cafetiere, fetching the morning paper before it's quite ready. It wus my ritual. I put on the red sweater. (The one Juliette liked sae much which I hated because it reminded me of my Catholic school uniform.) How. How. How. To be Charlie... Firstly there was the shaven words in my locks. I already had a foppish hat ready for such mistakes, but how does one keep the hat on while making the beast with two backs? She wus noo the type tu go for a fully clothed fucking down a back alley...

I cleaned the flat up. Slowly I wus sobering, but how to explain the lack of presence in how long? I sullened maeself before another mirror. (*They're useful to have around for my doppelgänger.*) The drab of depression, of self-doubt, that's what Charlie has. Not the self-doubt that drinks itself intu the gutter. But the averted eyes, concealing enigmas. The careful murmur: 'I just needed to be alone for a bit...'

I phoned Juliette. I sounded meek and regretful. Time passed and she came around. The evidence wus all gone, the battered dick sat greasy in an outside bin. The blinds were closed, shutting out the grey truth of the daylight. I sat with the lamp on the side of my hair not shaven.

She sat down next to me and whispered fingers across my face.

"What's the matter?"

"I just needed to be alone is all."

"You already said that..."

Why do I trust one drug and not the other? You must read that sentence and assume one drug is love and that it's not Bryn's shallow justification of mixing things. Convolution. Politics.

"This duality," she said, "it fucks you... You forget which person you are with me."

I nodded.

She smirked then... "What the fuck have you done to your hair?"

Charlie must have taken over. All I wanted now wus tu enrapture her next to the red sweater and sleep, feeling safe.

* * * * * * *

ANOTHER ATTIC ROOM

Roxanne Ratcliffe, Dreamscape

Another attic room. I wonder if I could capture my life in attic rooms, just write the bits that happened inside them, as meaningful representations of something.

Toby Roe is sat in the corner, a spotlight angled away from his eyes so it falls on the edges of his face and torso. It sketches in light the muscles of his arms and hands poised around this old guitar. His nails are bitten away to nothing, finger-tips long hardened to thimbles from old blisters.

There are other people in the room but my awareness of them is vague, hesitant shadows, a presence from another time. Memories of the future.

"What d'you want me to play?" Toby asks.

A pause, stretching out into the night sky outside, which watches through skylights tipped ajar.

"An anthem for doomed youth, brother ape." Wolfgang must be speaking, all sentences littered with some wry term of affection, connection.

The darkness is inside of Toby's eyes, like the expanse of the ocean at night. He begins to play but I can't hear anything. My better ear is covered with a pillow and I view the room from this muffled space, my vision framed in sections. I can see his fingers work rapidly over the strings. And the movement of his eyes, long lashes blinking away invisible tears, in some way magnified by the loss of sound. The sound of strings far off in the distance, sounding like birds somehow... artificial birds...

Or *'the shrill demented choirs of wailing shells'*... maybe.

I stand on a chair to lean my upper body out through the window. Everything seems as it should be, the city lights spread out across my vision, and dark shades of neighbouring rooftops surround. Life continues – drunks piss in doorways, the warden on the nightshift dozes with the newspaper spread in his lap, a small dog barks as he smells a fox pass the gates of his suburban abode. I look back to Toby. His eyes tell me all this is lost already, that what I see no longer exists. He continues to play the song, any song, another song. I look to the other figures, mere shadows, Victorian silhouettes. Wolfgang's top hat is tipped down over his eyes. Bobby lounges like a grey lady, in layers of lace and voluptuous skirting. A small black dog lies in her lap, chewing away at the handle of her parasol. But Bobby is dead and I know that if I look again I will only see the remains of a mangled corpse dressed up like a puppet.

"Hey." A finger tip touched my nose and I opened my eyes to find a face pressed close to mine. I realised I'd been crying in my sleep. He smoothed away the tears with his fingers.

"Is Bobby dead?" I asked.

"Who's Bobby?" He kissed my cheek.

"Who are you?" I asked.

"Cuan."

Another attic room. We stared strangely at one another and the camera panned to a downward shot of our part-covered bodies laid close on the bed. The camera pulled away, afraid of the intimacy and horror inscribed within the image. It floated off out of the skylight tipped ajar and let the viewer ponder the city lights and reflect on themselves instead. The self is safe – at least it was before.

* * * * * * *

ATLAS OF BATTLES

Haydn Antoine, Derby

"Paddy Considine? Best fookin actor... ever," Rufio mumbled emphatically.

"See what I meant, bro? It's our building." I pointed up at the cracked ceiling.

"There no junkies in this building... jus busybodees and mad'eds. And it's not fookin hot. Fookin cold in middle of an 'eatwave. S'a fookin fridge, I open windows to let the hot in."

Patti leant and kissed Rufio on the cheek, tweaking his hair with absorbed affection. Rufio had only met Patti about a week before and they were already inseparable.

"*...It's the stairs Johnny.*"

"I love this film." I stared into the laptop screen, chancing on bits of information amongst the endless pointlessness – the deluge of unedited, unconsidered rubbish.

"Yeah, looks like it!" Patti said sarcastically running long fingers through poker-straight brown hair. She had a slightly Eastern European look about her.

"Blondie mentul. Eee can absorb everfing at once," Rufio explained.

"The bit where Paddy and Djimon face up... it's just fucking... IT. I nearly cry," I said.

"You nearly cry when I play *Purple Rain*, Blondie."

"Have you read Charlie Brooker this week? I forgot to buy the paper," I asked Rufio.

"Read it at work, free people in all morning, was borin man... He wont that gud today, anyways."

Patti pointed at the random dog that appears from nowhere in the film.

"Look, it's like Effi, ghosting... running in the snow."

"Shit, I haven't phoned Toby!" I glanced at the TV screen as I dialled. "I love kids, *look at them...*

"Hey Roe, how the devil are you...? Yeah... We're just watching *In America*, it's on TV, we watched that, yeah? ...shit, yeah you did... Roofie and Patti all coupled up, rubbing it in my face."

"Not my fault you need ta get laid," Roofie interrupted.

"Did you get the shit I sent, Toab...? I know, I know, you read my incoherent scribble okay...? So used to tap tap tap," I hit buttons on the keyboard as I spoke. "Yeah, we'll catch up, have a pint... Yeah totally, mate. It was blatantly not what he said! Yeah... obvs mate, obvs! We'll suss it anyways..." I leaned back in my chair, trying to evade the laptop hunchback.

42

"Yeah mate... Yeah man... Alright, laters... *Tschuß!*" I hung up.

"What's *tschuß*?" Patti asked.

"It's like *ciao*, but you're not such a wanker for saying it." I said, quickly.

"You sound like a wanker, Blondie. Maybes you make it wank." Rufio unslipped his arm from round Patti, and made a move to the kettle. "...Ad break and Blondie's ere, so we can't fill it wiv a quickun. Hav to mayke a cuppa 'stead!"

"You always call him Blondie. How would you feel if he called you Blackie? Or Brownie?" Patti joked.

"Blackie's a dog's name, and am not no dog. Brownie's a cake's name, and am not no cake. Blondie's a girl's name..." He gazed poetically out of the window as the first drifts of steam began to lift in the air and whisper across his profile.

"There is some brilliant sense of philosophy in that somewhere," I murmured.

"S' cos I is jealous of 'is Aryan beauty. Look how pretty ee is? 'Dolf would've kept him, as an example to us aw!"

"Have you seen *Too Fast Too Furious*?" Patti asked. Mutual nods.

"You guys remind me of the bit where the two guys have a pathetic scrap in the dirt... It's such a homoerotic film, I can't believe people don't see it."

I nodded, eyes back on the world wide dirtweb.

"*Scorpio Rising*," I mumbled.

"I do love Blondie more than you, Pattibaby, but that's cos we have a speciuw connection. I must repress my urges though, society frowns upon Brokeback Cowboys. We is hidin in the shadows waiting for a chance to be our reals..." He handed us both tea. "Shut up now the film is back on and Antwon needs to work!"

"You were talking, not me!" she said.

"I said shush, woman!" He sat down and she punched him playfully in the shoulder. Tea split in his lap.

"Hot tea on the crackers!" Rufio squealed.

"Shush!" I said. "I'm trying to work!"

* * * * * * *

THE NAMING OF DOGS IS A DIFFICULT MATTER

Wolfgang, Dreamscape

The naming of dogs is a difficult matter.

The Blonde Adonis takes a bite of his grilled cheese sandwich. He curses quietly, as a splurge of greasy, yellow, melted cheddar escapes the bread and makes a dive for his white, frilly cuffs. He looks to Tobias Roe for some kind of answer, but as always Tobias's face is blurred. I used to think I'd never seen his face because he'd not turned towards me. Again and again putting a hand on his shoulder to turn him. But he would seem to spin away. Not like he himself was turning away, like the Earth was turning him in some other direction. An axis only for him. Tectonic plates shifting under my feet so I lost footing.

But now he is a figure sat facing us, with all the nonchalance of a prince. I can see his clothing in such detail that it's as though my face is pressed close to the fabrics, to earthen corduroy and natural cotton. To the torso the clothes quietly conceal. He smells as though he has spent an afternoon in an allotment, wearing a cravat. But when my eyes crawl to his face, with the desperation of a Scientologist, it is a smear. The Almighty had taken his thumb and smudged out the face of Tobias. I reach up with my fingertips, like a blind man, staring with blind, blue irises which bleed to whites, reaching to touch the smear. To rearrange it back to a face. A grotesque face, a Francis Bacon, for I had not the touch of *Him*. I could not draw Tobias; only some misshapen interpretation of my own hope.

A hand reaches out and grabs my wrist, the grip so tightened that purple marks appeared on my skin. It is The Adonis who forbids me to touch Tobias, but his face is muted now also. Altered to resemble Amadeus himself, young and boyish, rosy cheeks bearing no weight. My cheeks are sagging already, my skin a jaundiced beige-grey. When I look to my reflection I see a sewer rat and hope he has good intentions. He does not.

My hands are yellow as greasy cheddar. I look at them because I feel suddenly intimidated by my companions. By their youth and curly locks, their ability to form sentences that don't sound like sentences I've said before. Sentences that don't betray a sense of self that I wait for quietly, wait to appear, to de-mystify. I want to point out that the smear of condensation on the window creates the illusion of the shadow of trees, a forest, and all the hidden excitement of such things. I don't say this because I've tried to say this before. I got part way through the sentence and realised their eyes were blank. They were listening to the drip, drip of that tap I cannot turn off. They were not hearing what I said.

So I stare at my hands and think of cheese. My fingernails are black and crusted with the disease that is life. Everything I touch collects, the mould, the chocolate, the stray hues of vodka that escape my mouth and dribble to whatever lies below. That is why I cannot touch Tobias. I would contaminate him with every filthy bit of rotten dead rat I'd squeezed my hand inside. That is why I cannot see Tobias, because then he would *see* me. And I would contaminate him with everything contained in my eyes. For they conceal nothing to someone that can read them. They will tell of all I've seen, of the furies, of love's coldest death. Of realising that there are only rats left and no dogs brutal enough to massacre them.

The naming of dogs is indeed a difficult matter.

* * * * * * *

THE STEED IS VANISH'D FROM THE STALL

Calista Siddal, Sheffield

I met Simian and Hex outside their school gates. The two of them hung on the corner with mutual awkwardness, while shiny overpriced cars zipped past collecting their precious little Henrys and Harriets.
"Shall we go for coffee?" Sim suggested.
"Won't it be full of rahs?" I asked.
"Yes. But I need a coffee."
"Caffeine dependency at sixteen, well done," I said.
He shrugged dismissively.
Lost amongst the moneyed bourgeois, I longed for bohemia. But it was rich bohemia nonetheless, safe from real squalor. Lord Byron slouched in an opium stupor on a beautiful chaise longue, a little blood dripping from the corner of his mouth.
We entered the café, which was full to asphyxiation with financially over-fed sixth formers. The bell catcalled as we entered and the eyes of Lucy (who I call Sarah) were

drawn to us, glancing us up and down with thick-lashed eyes that spilt spoilt poisons. As we used to take horse riding lessons together as children, Lucy knew me. She was always a brat, and now that she'd grown curves and sexuality, I suspected she was the princess of manipulation. A flick of dark hair and a pout of red lips affirmed my suspicions.

"Oh look, here come 'the Skinnies'," she said with icy wit.

Hex and Sim hesitated as though ready to bolt. (Oh, the wonder of the self-conscious teenager who simply wants the floor to swallow them).

I shot her a withering look. "Got an eating disorder, have we? Better go stick your fingers down your throat in the toilets, princess," I said quickly.

Hex and Simian shuffled to the counter.

"Are you planning to grow boobs and hips, Cassandra? Or are you going to look like a boy for the rest of your life?" Lucy asked.

"My name is not Cassandra, *Sarah*," I replied.

"My name's not Sarah. As if I would have such a common name... Well whatever 'Cassie' is short for. Castro? Casanova? A boy's name for a boy's body."

"It's Calista," Hex mumbled, barely audible.

"Well, Hector!" she exclaimed. "You have a voice box? I never knew."

Simian tugged my sleeve and dragged me away from her. We found a little table in the far corner.

"Why do you call her Sarah?" Hex asked.

"*Labyrinth*," I said. I put on a squeally voice. "*It's not faairr!*"

Sim put on his deep Bowie voice. "*You say that so often... I wonder what your basis for comparison is.*"

A snake escapes its old skin, and slithers away through a city dragged to the ground by the twisted arms of vines that creep, deceiving of their true power to erode and destroy, to find the weak point of collapse.

"So..." I paused meaningfully, searching the faces of my comrades. "We're going to this house tonight?"

They both looked back at me with the eyes of bush babies, wide as saucers. I sunk into the blackness of innocence inside them. Simian nodded. He'd rather confront the unreality of the house than the reality of his home.

"I'm gonna need some Dutch courage if we're gonna do that," Hex mumbled.

Sim turned to him.

"You need Dutch courage to get up the morning."

"Chartreuse... *'The only liquor so good they named a colour after it'.*"

"I like that you drink Chartreuse instead of, I dunno, alcopops... It's very Romanticist," I said.

"It's whatever I can steal from the liquor cabinet... not like I'd get served alcohol anywhere," Hex mumbled disparagingly.

'When you cut open the body the heart looks like a fist, a bloody fist,' the character said.

The house was in Nether Edge, which is a great title for a place of adventure. It was named so because it lay in a hollow of the valley, building up a hill and then suddenly, at the highest point, sharply dropping away all the way along the ridge. The edge is lined by an old stone wall. There are occasional gaps leading to steps into the woods below, and old fashioned looking lampposts growing out of the wall that look a bit Narnia-esque. I wished I'd known the place a hundred years ago and could've galloped horses through the trees to evade whoever was chasing me, forcing them over the edge to spin far off into the abyss (which is now just some dull housing estate).

But we were not going right to the edge today. The leafy suburb sought to deceive, appearing a peaceful haven to its leftist, middle class inhabitants. When night fell it became a labyrinth of shadows, avenues and roundabouts that all seemed to look the same. You'd hear the sound of footsteps on the road behind you, when you turned around there was no-one but the trees shivering with secrets.

The house was on a long road sketched with friendly-looking lights in windows and dogs on loose leashes sniffing the trees, the walls, and each other. It was halfway along in a large garden, practically swallowed by a miniature forest. Its grand gateposts were marked with writing long worn away. This house was larger and older than others on the street and echoed all the sweet clichés of The Haunted House of suburban legend. The windows were cracked and broken and boarded up and the grand front door was etched with the wounds of time. The middle window on the first floor drew your eye, as a single light bulb hung lonely from the ceiling. It was always glowing, through every day of sunshine and every dark night when the wind whipped the trees and rattled the windows.

There was never a person in the window, though someone must've lived there. I thought sensibly that it must be some eccentric, gradually restoring the beautiful old house. If you looked hard enough in the centre of the roof (nearly out of view from the street below) there was a tiny raised room, with windows on all sides like the top of a lighthouse. It was this room I wanted to be in the most, to stare across the city from this secret watching tower.

We crouched in the bushes and watched the house, a warm June night when the summer seemed stretched out before us. Hex shivered with nerves, his quiet voice uttering the dialogue of a thousand 'what ifs'.

"I tell you what, let's go and find the answers to all those..." I tugged both boys to follow me and flitted like a shadow to the window at the side, which was slightly ajar so that the stray cats could get inside.

* * * * * *

AN INTRODUCTION TO CLOUD 9

Roxanne Ratcliffe, Sheffield

Somebody was talking loudly. They'd been talking loudly for a while, but I'd only just recognised it to be real. The sun was soaking persistently through the curtains. The sounds of people in the house were disorientating. I couldn't tell if they were in the room that I was in. Someone was in the same bed as me... I thought it was a girl, but I wasn't sure. I hoped it was. I thought it was Charlie's house but then I remembered it was the day before that I'd woken there.

It went quiet for a while so I fell back to dreaming, but then talking woke me again... I peered from the covers at a stranger's room. My eyes fixed on the dregs of a bottle of Irish whiskey. The room was full of space and at the same time clutter. Someone else's space, someone else's clutter. The telltale signs of sleepless nights and rushed mornings – coffee cups and cigarettes and a stray tube of whitening toothpaste hoping to rectify the damage.

I realised it *was* a girl in the bed with me as I wriggled around to look at her. She did look familiar. She reminded me of Bobby, except that she was white and blonde. She was very pretty anyway, even in a drunken sleep with last night's makeup smeared, face squished against the pillow. I lay and looked at her for a bit in an unhealthy stalker type way. She woke. We know when we're watched, an instinct against being hunted. I'm fairly sure that Toby told me that. *Toby Toby Toby... Shut up...*

"Who are you?" I asked.

"Am'a manifestation a'ya wildest dreams," she murmured sleepily and yawned, adding, "in a non-sexual way." She had a deadpan Yorkshire accent, but more Northern than Sheffield, I thought. Leeds, maybe.

"Is this your house?" I asked.

"Yeah." She stretched, pushing her arm against the bed head.

"Can you make that man shut up?" I asked.

"Lee? Yeah, I've cut out his voice box afore, burr'ee jus keeps talking. He's lyke Chucky, he never dies."

It concerns me that the mundane can quickly develop a nightmarish quality, but then I know it's just in my head.

"What's your name? I'm sorry I never remember when I'm introduced to people," I bumbled sitting up.

She sat up, too, crossing her legs and straightening out a maroon football shirt. Damn girl looked pretty as hell even dressed like a slob.

"Claudia." She shook my hand with ironic formality, given our over intimate circumstances.

I nodded. "Roxy."

"I know. Fook knows Charlie's talked enuff about ya." She ruffled my hair to communicate a sense that she understood why Charlie talked of me. Hmm... Speak of the devil (or Kaiser) – there was a rap at the door and Charlie poked a nose in and then entered.

"Ratcliffe." He nodded. "Cloud..."

He sat on the bed and looked at us both with a silly kind of adoration.

"I'll mayke a brew... Tea or coffee?" Claudia pulled on a sweater and ran a hand through blonde bed hair.

"Tea, please," I said.

She nodded with a look I couldn't read and exited the room. The gentle silence that followed was faintly decorated with the sound of a kettle set to boil in the nearby kitchen.

Charlie peered at me carefully with that look of nurture that makes me cringe. "You should go home, Roxy."

I shrugged, trying to appear unfazed. "I know."

I'd treated my friends as a duvet for long enough. They'd kept me warm, hugged me regardless of how badly I needed a shower, soaked up my woes, let my tears fall and dry, fed me... Well... Duvets don't feed you, do they now?

Home was absence. Home was not home anymore now Bobby'd left for Leeds. Who could I talk to at two in the morning when I couldn't sleep? Who would make minty mochas for me? Home had people, but with the people was the absence of the feeling that I had everything to say. The television would glare blankly at me, hoping to suck away at my soul. Still, I decided that I should probably let the television and my housemates know I was still alive. But that was all.

I felt a small panic. "I'll go home and get clothes and have a shower... but please can I stay at yours?"

Claudia returned and handed me a cup of tea. My hand shook and a little spilt on it, dripping down to the carpet.

"Sorry, sorry..."

"Oh whatever, I've got red wine all over it anyroads." She shrugged.

Charlie sighed. "You can stay on the sofa. But Jenny is getting pissy about all this."

Claudia rolled her eyes to signify her lack of love for Jenny. "Oh, fa fooks sake, just stay here Roxy. We don't want to upset the missus. That's if you can put up wi' Lee. I barely can." She motioned to the loud talking still coming from the living room.

I felt weird. I barely knew this girl, but she was already a better alternative to home. I nodded thankfully, sipping the hot tea, letting it revive me. "What's the time, please?" I asked.

"Seven fort'y eight."

"Ah good, gives me time to go home and shower before Uni."

Charlie hovered scowling, as though he wanted to say something else. I looked at the light creeping in the curtains.

"I'm gonna head off, Rox," he muttered.

"Alright, let me know what you're up to later."

"I think I'll be busy," he said a little coldly. He left the room shouting familiar goodbyes to other housemates.

"Such a moody fooker!" Claudia smirked. She looked knowing. I feared everybody knew.

* * * * * *

A GLASGOW KISS

Claudia McLeod, Yorkshire

"I've always bin a bit of a tomboy. Me dad once said about that phase what teenage girls go through, when they wanna be trendy and wear skirts, but still wanna climb trees wi' the boys... I don't think I ever got over that phase." I shrugged and smiled.

"You wear a fair amount of make-up for a 'tomboy', Claudee," my housemate Maisie said. She thinks make-up is a waste a' time and money. Which it is, but then so are fags.

"Well, I've spent ma whole life bein told I look lyke a china doll. Least if I wear loadsa black eyeliner I won't look lyke such a pussy," I replied. "But I sure as shit don't enjoy spendin time wi' girly girls who phone each other up afore a night out to check what they're wearin."

Maisie giggled in agreement, but she's from a proper lefty, feminist background. It's a given for her to question behaviour.

"I don't think adoptin a stereotype helps women become more equal. I'm not gonna be dowdy and wear baggy jumpers, it's not me. I think it's about yar attitude to everythin," I said.

Maisie sipped her wine and shook her head, in wryness.

"What?" I said.

"It would be a bit difficult for you to be dowdy, with those boobs and that face!" she teased.

"Y'know someone actually suggested that I pose furra lad's mag, to up the profile a tha band?" I said.

"Really?" Maisie looked disgusted.

"Told them to fook rayht off. They want to sell me as a 'ladette', apparently stripping for't camera is part a the package."

"As if that gives off the right impression," she said. "I don't think the type of people who like your music would respect that."

Me dad were me role model in life. His attitude ta women was pretty good in some ways. But his path were littered wi' broken hearts, cause he were charmin and eligible and had three children. They didn't realise he were a commitment-phobe. They just thought he needed 'the rayht woman'.

I followed him t'town one afternoon when I were fifteen and curious of all the things I din't know about him. He was datin multiple women, which might seem shallow, but what I really learned of was *their* shallowness. Their hearts were only broken superficial'ly, cause they were of a culture desperate and impatient to fall in love. He wasn't sleazy, he didn't need chat up lines. They were jus flattered that he paid them attention.

I've never been flattered by that kind of attention. When men tell me on a casual basis how beautiful they think I am, it just narks meh. The repetition of the way they speak, the way they look as though I ought ta be soo grateful for their compliments. The way they assume the girl stood next ta me should sumhow be jealous of the attention I'm gettin. I once asked a hair dresser to dye my hair brown – she said 'you know how much money girls pay to have your hair?' Blondes don't have maire fun, they jus get hit on maire. Hanging out in a bar, or working in a bar, at bus stops, at friends' houses…

"Why a you always soo angry about ev'rythin?" Dad asked me one day, at the height a my teenage tantrum phase, which I've never quite grown outtah.

"I'm so pretty and clever, how lucky. I should be soo happy for missel," I said pithily.

He laughed. "Maybe it's my fault. I've taught you it's a disappointin combination."

"Where does he go all the time?" my eleven year auld brother asked me around't sayme time.

"He's out fookin women," I replied bluntly.

Malcolm nodded thoughtfull'y.

"What are you doin wi'ya life anyroads, Malc? I'd already taken up smokin at yar age," I asked with a shit-stirring tone.

"Is that summat to aspire to?" he asked sarcastically.

"It's a commitment to die young," I replied.

He shook his head wisely. "It's a commitment to die slowly."

It's a commitment to ugliness, to a stale smell, to a bad taste, yellow teeth and a greying fizzog. A man slimed up ta me in a nightclub one night, a few year later – he put his hand up ma skirt and said, "Fancy a kiss?"

I head butted him an broke his nose. A Glasgow kiss, I think they cahl it.

* * * * * *

AN IRRELEVANT OPENING TO A FANTASTICAL TALE

Simian Thomas, Sheffield

Over reliance on a snot rag is something I number amongst my small failures. I fear if a crisis ever happened, if I was faced with 'surviving something', zombies or an earthquake, I wouldn't do so well. In fact I'd probably help other people *not* survive, by holding them back, moaning that I had a slight headache and felt a bit dizzy. I'm all for adventure in theory, but a nice, safe middle class adventure. Nothing that gets me fully out of my depth.

"Let's get high and wait for doomsday!" Hex waved his pudgy hands at the ceiling from which lanterns hung. The only part of Hex that was pudgy was his hands, I should note. He had a bad heart, he told me once, and apparently it gave him funny fingers that didn't taper properly. All in all he was a visual hotchpotch, nothing quite coordinated, the stalkish frame with oversized feet, the pokey witch's nose. At this time, when we were all trying to start university, he seemed to want to be a cliché of the magic scene. He had tangerine hair.

Esme's house was elaborately decorated, as she was having an 'enchanted land' party. Being half rich girl, half thrifty bohemian, she'd trawled flea markets and charity shops to collect the most ridiculous objects – stuffed birds and fake plants – to go with the winter branches wrapped in fairy lights and twinkly things. Ordinarily I'd rather crawl into a spider-infested log than wear fancy dress. But something about the occasion reminded me of the masked balls in *The Labyrinth* and Herman Hesse's *Steppenwolf*. And so I'd donned an eye mask and my Jesus-shirt (straight-parted at the collar to show white hairless collarbones) and let Esmeralda smear my cheeks and arms with silver body paint.

Hex considered himself to be dressed as Cupid, in fairy wings with a bow and arrow, a joke added to by a box of Viagra amongst the tricks he was pushing that evening. For reasons of the varied stash of substances he harboured, he was greeted very warmly by all the party goers. Omar entered, his endless black curls for once worn loose, as he was dressed as Jim Morrison.

"Hector! The boy! How are you, man? Got some good shit for me, I hope? Have you seen Calista yet? She looks stunning. I think Jesse is totally *after that* tonight, God speed the boy."

I blew my nose loudly and looked bored. No point staying on the real planet tonight and alcohol would make my snivels worse tomorrow. Jesse entered then. He was impressively dressed as Mr Tumnus, his curly hair mussed around fake horns, cheeks rouged, beard twizzled and those electric blue eyes a-shine. He even had silver fluffies on and had painted his boots to look like hooves. I couldn't help liking Jesse. He was so calm and yet very present in a room. He never quite needed to raise the volume of his voice.

"Esme has gone cuckoo!" he exclaimed gently. "Have you seen how well-decorated the toilet is? It'll be a bomb site in no time."

Esme, herself, was already mashed, stumbling around hugging incomers, regardless of having met them before.

"Don't sit on top of the candles!" she called shrilly at someone, but who knew who.

I join the dots, I make the jump. I know it's all connected.

Sweat and tears ran down my cheeks, silver makeup pooled in my vision. I was talking to an elfin princess with raven hair and elongated lashes of pink. I fixed my eyes on the twinkly star which sat on her beauty spot.

"Do you want to kiss me, Simian?"

"How do you know who I am?" I asked vaguely.

"It's not that much of a devious disguise..."

I recognised her voice, the sweet churs of a fairy-bird in canary yellow. I fixed my gaze better.

"Lucy? Is that you? What are you doing here?"

"Esme is my cousin, didn't you know?"

Cassie passed in an emerald green dress and scarlet tresses. It was – I think – the first I'd seen of her that evening. She paused to glare at an old foe, but her hand was loosely coupled with Jesse's and she quickly disappeared, to peel off his fur and decorate his rouged cheeks with kisses.

I stumbled on a face I used to have, I'm not sure if it is a mirror, I peered through the layer of vacant dust.

The emerald witch kissed the fawn. In fantasy I can be immersed, lost, drowned in a sea of pearls and ribbons. Nothing is quite real. Nothing is pain. Nothing is a steady ache on a weighty heart. I sat down on the sofa next to the Pink Panther for a while, to settle my head. He flicked his whiskers and tipped his jaunty hat.

"Is there a pink cat sat next to me?" I asked Jesse, once he'd broken lips with Cassie. He was hunched over a tray rolling a joint. He looked up at me, blinking quietly and shook his head. I looked back at the Pink Panther and he winked at me. The floor in front of me fell away into green transparent waters that rushed inside my ears, a vertiginous tunnel of water spinning down, through that gap where everything is spun into mortality... There is a woodland glen where the water settles in a quiet pool. I can feel myself falling and I put out a hand. I don't want to spin that fast...

"Are you okay?" Jesse asked. "What did Hex give you?"

I'm back in the room, the clatter of laughter like cymbals in my eyeballs. The panther poked my funny bone ribs.

"Salvia," I answered.

He lit the joint and waved it at me.
"You want some?"
"That may not be a good idea."
He nodded agreeably. "It doesn't last long. You'll be out soon..."

* * * * * *

MECHANICS

Bryn McLarey, Sheffield

In the crane yard I wus lost tu the mechanics of mae insides – I clunked and churned, metal parts drew across one another scraping unevenly. Mae great escape from maesel is into machines, tu know the way the pieces fit together, gutting insides oot to make a sense of it all. I wus stealing cars at twelve years old, riding them out fae miles intu the night, driving on and on. Finding some wasteland or better still reaching some sickeningly beautiful glen as dawn snuck in.

    I'd stop the car and get out. Each movement in mae body was nothing but a mechanism. I climbed up and sat on the roof and she purred beneath me. She wanted her liver removed, tu find inside where her aorta may be severed in order tu cease existence. Mae eyes adjusted tu the light, picking out silhouettes until they became objects. I slid off the roof; the metal was cold tu mae skin. With the genteel precision of a serial killer I took the machine to pieces, spreading bits around in the dirt, mae hands bloodied with oil...

"YOU CANNAE BE MAE BOY BRYN!"

60

A hoarse vocal cord ripped out, echoing rapture through the red skeletons of tower cranes, which were laid out in rows of ordered chaos. Men climbed amongst them, hard hats tipped down over steady gazes. I scanned them fae the familiar face but he wus intentionally invisible. They guffawed at the common joke. They don't know the power of Dr Mabuse. I took a seat at the table ootside the staff kitchen. Stray mugs littered surfaces, all stained from oily hands and tea splashes never fully washed off. Here were layers of miniature histories, cigarette butts abandoned and florescent vests discarded on the backs of cheap, white plastic chairs.

A broad shouldered man strolled up. Lazy, arrogant nonchalance ebbed from the greased creases of age, which were etched intu his dirty face. His eyes twinkled at me, the twinkle mae mother once spoke fondly of. I stayed seated and expressionless – he grasped mae shoulder with a familiar strength, almost a shake tu get a smirk ootah me.

"Mae boy! How yuu doin? S'bin a while away since I last hadda peep attu!"

Grown up in Sunderland, lived in Glasgow for twenty years before moving tu South Yorkshire for the remainder, mae Dad's accent wus a thick hybrid, changing constantly in tone and idiosyncrasies. A voice that sought tu adapt tu its environment leik an animal, yet retaining an incomprehensibility tu all – no allegiance, no home.

I squinted in the sunshine at him. He wus squeezing out the corner of his t-shirt which wus dripping with sweat. Every time I saw this man I would try tu maintain that I tuu wus now a man, and that I wus tall enough and had guts enough tu punch him cleanly in the jaw. Only once, for he never hurt me or me mam physically. Just that once tu reprimand him for the lazy injustices of mae upbringing. But close up, contained within hus darkly buoyant gaze, I'm a boy again. If I looked at mae fist it'd be the size of a Satsuma.

"Pub?" I suggested, with no need for an answer – home tu the madman and the coward, a home fae mae daddy and maesel. In the passenger seat of his pick-up I stared through the hole in the floor at the road rushing beneath.

"What yuu up tu these days, eh?" he asked, after a short heavy silence.

I shrugged. "I work in a bar..."

There's no need for me tu mention having a degree, acting in the theatre, or being a bar manager, because I know he's just proud enough that I've got a job and I'm not a fucking skag heid.

"Oh aye, gud fer yuu. Ah worked in a pub one time, but ah got ther boot fer pissing all the stock up the wall. Neh surprises eh, wee Bryn?"

"Neh surprises, Papps. I worked with a fair few th'sayme."

The old engine grunted and groaned with the weight of expectations, of shaggy dog stories just waiting tu be told, of elusive truths swallowed down with a few pints of lager and a packet of dried up pig skin.

"Yer ever geyt an itch in yer bloodstream, Bryn?" he asked. I wondered if this wus sumthin cryptic.

"No. I dunno what yuu mean."

"Oh aye, neh body does. They think am spinnin' a yarn, but I've got it mae whole life, and it gets worse of the years... Beyond ma ken whattit tus, jus better drink maeself tu the grave before it kills me, eh?!"

* * * * * * *

DISASTERS OF WAR

Wolfgang, Belfast

'*We serve not King nor Kaiser...but Ireland*' – the mural read. A small black mongrel loitered near it, sniffing things. I looked at my Kaiser (whom I have served), trying to transfer some implicit irony. To let things speak by themselves, no need to utter, we brother, *we* have mutual understanding, brother of apes; we pick lice from one another's backs. Empathy, Darwin pondered, does not seem to have much porpoise to our evolution, to our survival. Why is it there? Why are we feeding children in Africa when we could be eating gourmet porridge ourselves?

Kaiser was watching the dog. He had not much interest in the mural or its profound words. We'd looked at rather a lot of wall paintings on that bleak Belfast day. And while I muttered the slogans and stacked them neatly in a corner of my brain saved for bumper sticker philosophy (or in this case bumper sticker politics, *if there is such a thing*), he was bored and numbed to them. The meaning of words no more that a stroke of paint, a colour, a 42nd shade of grey. I'm feeling very italic today I must warn you, little ape. *Very Italic.* Very ape.

"Boswell goes apeshit," I said.

Kaiser cocked a weary eyebrow. Though I'm not sure a cocked eyebrow can be considered weary. Kaiser wearily cocked an eyebrow.

"What?" he spat.

"I think it was Roswell actually, as in secret alien conspiring and so fourth... *But* in terms of my personal experience, there was a Boswell, a horse called Boswell, who to quote yourself was 'fully fookin mental'." (I tried at this point to ape the Kaiser's accent/dialect hybrid at the same time trying to add the Irish lilt to the hybrid. It does not sound right. I am Germanic not Celt, I fear.) "Therefore, it makes sense that *Boswell goes apeshit.*"

Sniff sniff. Said the dog. Kaiser lit a cigarette and stared off down the scuffed streets, knowing us to be tourists of poverty, poverty and a strange kind of war that cannot be described as a war.

"How have I not murdered yuu for your insane babblings by nae?" His lip was curled, in that self-awareness of performed irritation.

"You would've murdered me, brother, if you were only to spend a day in my head. It's much worse *inside* there, sir. There's no peace."

He smirked darkly. I wondered at his smirk. I wondered that he does not fear becoming trapped inside my head, with only a stack of bumper stickers for company, interspersed with torn out pages from books about philosophy and dread and Hegel. He wouldn't be able to cope with all that Hegel. I pointed suddenly to Kaiser (a page had fallen from that stack in my brain).

"*A constant companion and observer!*" I exclaimed in awe.

Instead of saying 'what' again, Kaiser made a rounding hand movement, meaning 'go on'.

"Boswell." I said.

"James Boswell," he said. "Samuel Johnson's biographer? He wus Scottish."

"Yes! The horse must've been named so after such a gentleman. The horse was not a gentleman though. Nor some genteel companion who quietly observed, he was..."

"...fully fookin mental," Kaiser finished, purposefully slurring his words together like a Scotch drunk, or a drunk Scotch.

"Which of us is the constant companion and observer? And which of us is fully fookin mental? And therefore the genius who must be biographified?" I asked.

He laughed so that his lips exposed his slight canines.

"If Boswell goes apeshit, then Boswell is both the quiet observer and the mental genius. We are both Boswell and Boswell is both of us, as wus the fookin pony, no doubt." He paused thoughtfully, waving his fag around, motioning to us both. "Have yuu ever wondered if we both exist, or if one of us only exists as a figment of the other's imagination? Doppelgänger? Alter ego?"

I made a shocked look, spreading my hands and spinning in a circle.

"Which is which?" I begged. "Can I not be real? I would like that. To be Mister Duck... to be Tyler Durden... to be Casper the friendly ghost..."

He laughed again, with the teeth. Then he tossed his cigarette butt and grasped my real shoulder, which was knotted with life's real tensions, and shoved me towards the pub. A proper grotty local pub, where we'd be tourists and they'd eye us with suspicion.

* * * * * *

PLATONICS

Calista Siddal, Sheffield

Don't wanna be real, don't wanna have feelings, just long red hair and a really pretty pistol.

I shared a bed with Simian again. He spoons in his sleep; not the worst friend I've slept next to. I took a shower and returned to the bedroom. He was gazing dumbly out of the window, the morning sun was orange inside his eyes.

"I had a dream. We were called Chassis and Phoenix. You were dating a footballer, and there were pink petals all over the bed, and you had a beautiful tiny little gun... and we had a pet horse called Harvey," he rambled. "Apart from that, everything was kind of *the same.*"

"Fascinating." I leant into the mirror to tidy my hair a little.

"Mum thinks I should just marry you and be done with it," he added.

This verified what I'd suspected was meant by the phrase *'the same'*. It was all about Lucy as usual, the great fucking void where a pretty bitch used to be.

"Why don't old people understand the complexities of inter-gender friendships?" he asked.

It was rhetorical, but I answered stubbornly. "Platonics." I like the phrase, it sounds like some other planet. "They're complicated. They often develop to other levels. Plus, like you say, she's a different generation. Most people got hitched to their first love back then."

"I don't want to have sex with you. It would make me sick," Simian said. A traditional deadpan insult.

I leaned over the bed and pulled open my bedside drawer, scraping away receipts and pulling out my mp3 player. There was no way I was gonna listen to Sim rattle on about Lucy on the way to town. He'd written her name all over his bony ankle and foot in biro.

"Can't you just punch the wall like a normal boy?" I said, but hugged him anyway.

"Like *Old Boy*," he said. "Can we get married, though?" he asked, a little pleadingly.

"Only if I don't have to have sex with you," I replied.

"Do you ever dream in the third person?" he asked.

"I've never thought about it."

"Do you ever dream that you're watching a film, but at the same time you're in the film...?" He shoved his bony ink-smeared foot into his sock and followed with shoes.

"Ready to go, you pathetic-weird-heartbroken-waste-of-air?" I asked.

A smile briefly passed his lips before dying in the voids of blue, melting black pupils. He nodded.

"Got bus fare?" I asked.

"Yup, let's go smell the plebs."

We left the house, entering the already greasy sunshine. Lucy watched from down the road as we exited the gate and paced off down the street, failing to avoid the cracks in the pavement. She watched our lips moving and the exchange of glances as we continued our ever-loving cryptics.

* * * * * * *

SHARROW LANE

Claudia McLeod, Sheffield

Fookin bo'hemia. I scanned the kitchen. The miss-painted cupboards and postcards wi' borin feminist slogans that mayde me wanna take up misogynism. They reminded me of that fookin woman who lived up ta every stereotype of the man-hatin lesbian, so that it dribbled out of her ears. I'm pretty sure these chicks think I'm one of them, y'know – a right-thinkin gal. I'd betray my gender every day a the week when I see them teeming into Collegiate Campus dressed up like entrants in a beauty pageant. No, I lie, I hated these fookin post-feminist-art-school bo'hemians maire...

Beazie lit a liquorice roll-up and dragged a hand through her scarecrow white mop. When I say white I reahlly don't mean white-blonde. She mus use extra fookin value toilet bleach. I mean what tha fook. Charlie smirked. I think he could tell what I were thinkin. He calls me a cynical, bitter witch. Hell he's jus the fookin sayme. He hates the English but walks among'um every day. And yeah, he puts ev'rythin he despises down as 'fookin English' and I say 'fookin southerners'... bear in mind *southern* is a state of mind.

He planted a mug a black coffee in front of me. It jolted as it met the table, a wave risin to spill over't side and spread a minor brown flood on't wooden top. The smell a tobacco in the early mornin mekks me dead sick'ly.

"Are ye okay, precious?" Charlie rasped Scottishly, restin his hands on ma shoulders. I scrunched ma nose at him. Addressing Beazie he said. "I know she looks a bit vicious but she doesnae bite..."

I only bite southerners, I thought. I could smell the toast were starting to burn in't toaster.

"Do you read, Claudia?" Beazie asked me.

What does she mean... ever? I thought. "Read what?"

"I mean, do you *like* reading?"

"Sumtimes I read The Sun, but mainly I just look at the pretty pictures."

She seemed to think about this, nodding. "I'm reading this book called *The Radical Absolute*. I really think you should check it out, with this stuff you seem to be into with your music."

Sounds like wank, I thought. "Mmm, yeah, I'll keep an eye out for tha. You read it, Charlie?"

"Fuckin A."

"Does that mean that you *have* read it, Charlie?"

He shook his head. I'm not sure he even listened t'question.

Burnt toast smeared with peanut butter... I betted ta missel that if I looked in the cupboard this girl would have Rooibosch tea... fookin Rooibosch. Smells like Burton-on-Trent.

Beazie put some *absolutely radical* music on and danced about tha kitchen. Roxy looked lyke a sleepy dormouse at the table across from me. I picked up her bony lit'l arm – she'd written an unreadable sentence all the way down it in smeared ink. Her eyes moved up to me from't tea stains lyke a cutesy bellikin.

"Our friend Simian does that, too. Is fashionable or summat? Some emo thing?" I asked.

She jus smiled at me sleepily and said nowt. She had such a precise face, the pug nose and the big eyes. But boyish enough to be attractiv'ly unpretty, I think.

"Have you heard that new band The Jasons?" Beazie asked. "They're fucking great."

"I mayke a point of ignoring ahl bands who use the pre-fix *'the'*... Apart from pre-nineties stuff," I said.

I waited fer Charlie to come up wi'a good nineties *'the'* band.

"Your band hus a clichéd format fa the name, Cloud. And if yuu left, wudnae they be called 'The Mistakes'?"

I sighed and rolled ma eyes. "They were simp'ly called *'Mistakes'* afore I joined, cause during sum drunken talk they all discovered they were unplanned babies. It were Jody that insisted that we became Claudia & the Mistakes. I din't wannit ta be an ego wagon, but he thought it were more memorable."

"It's pretty apt." Charlie chuckled.

"Trees scare me," Roxy said, outtah context. "They're soo big."

She tipped her head as though lookin up at them towering above her.

"Has she taken sommat?" I asked Charlie. Roxy never takes owt.

Charlie pointed upwards, and I laid back on the ground to stare up at the trees loomin over me. Sharp lines against the bright sky. A bird flew from one branch to another, the air whistlin briefly through its wings. I suddenly felt dead small and vulnerable. I closed my eyes and let the sun settle on my cheeks, reminded of the bit in *Easy Rider* which goes all weird cos they've tekken acid. Havin sex amongst grave stones. I wanted to see it agen because I couldn't remember it well enough.

"Ma coffee's cold," I moaned back in't room, tekkin a sip. Charlie smiled knowingly – I weren't sure why.

"I know someone called Simian," Roxy said, as though suddenly wakin.

* * * * * *

VAGABOND STORIES OF ODDITY

Bryn McLarey, Sheffield

'Nether Ed is dead inside, he regrets too much, soft regrets of the daisies and wallflowers he never summoned the courage to speak to.'

"I was thinking 'bout getting a ferret as a pet," Cuan muttered, with his usual forced eccentricity. We were stood on the back fire escape of the bar where we worked. We were smoking, and admiring the view. If yuu leaned over the edge of the railings, yuu could see junkie shit and used needles.

"Why a ferret?" I asked.

"I want something I can take to the pub with me, and dogs are a bit of a fuss. Ferrets are easy to hide." He crossed tu the other rail and peered down the sunny street over the back gate. "Hey, there's that crazy German bloke off my course." He stretched his lanky languid arm to point.

The man walked hunched over. He had a bird's nest of hair and beard, a long battered trench coat with patches on the sleeves. A snout poked out from all the fur, beady eyes well-hidden.

"What d'you say his nayme wus?" I asked.

"Wolfgang. How cool is that? He's fucking loopy, it's like talking to Hunter S. Thomson or sommat. But more..." He stopped completely and stuck the fag in one corner of his mouth, resting both hands on the rail. Eventually he took the cigarette in his hand again.

"You read any Günter Grass?"

I chewed at a black nail, reaching intu mae brain archive. "*The Tin Drum*?"

"Fuck yeah, that's the badger! I love his titles, titles are difficult, to have meaning y'know? To hold the whole book, but not be pretentious or clever-clever. *Dog Years*, *The White Terror*, *The Flounder* – that's wicked – you think it has that double meaning in German? Cause the book is actually *just about a fish*!"

I shrugged.

"What's 'the badger'?" I asked with the ironic tones of someone who thinks he is tuu old fae silly catchphrases.

Cuan laughed. "The bad boy! The best! Mai Tai...!" He screwed up a bit of his t-shirt tu mop the sweat on his forehead, "... my uncle is the badger. He calls himself 'Brock', the crazy fucker. He works as a cemetery attendant, looking after dead people."

A pigeon flapped haphazardly and landed in front of me. I watched it potter about the railing, admiring its ugly beak and polluted feathers.

"Fucking rank birds," Cuan said.

I nodded. I remembered the one that mysteriously dropped out of the sky and landed at the doorman's feet, stone dead. And then the half-dead one that the crazy Asian bloke brought intu the bar. He picked it up by the wing tips, stretching it oot against the light, leik it wus tu be crucified. And the one that used tu sit on the outside light every chill night, tu be warm. It would stare at me with an unnerving blankness when I took the bins out. They were leik us, the dregs of the street – vagabond stories of oddity that ended in a bloody mess of internal organs splattered on the pavement. We hated the pigeons, because they spoke of the aspects of the city we would leik tu sweep under a rug and forget. Flies hovering over junkie shit.

"You're thinking, my dear – and when you think you forget to speak." Cuan smirked at me.

"Flying rats..." I said, filling an uncertain gap with a well worn cliché.

"I really like to imagine actual flying rats," Cuan said. He stuck the fag in the side of his mouth again and scrambled through his pockets for a pen and a scrap of folded paper. He unwrapped it and rested it on the rail, scribbling an image. A rat who grew wings and decided tuu escape the city, flying intu the expanse of the bluest sky.

He laughed.

"My rat looks like Splinter!"

I leaned over the image.

"I think the tail would cause problems with the aerodynamics."

"Tie a knot in it sir, for he is a thief! Rat shan't visit party!" he gabbled.

"Yeah, I can see why yuu and this crazy Wolfgang character would get on well..."

He laughed and nodded.

* * * * * * *

BLINK & CLICK

Roxanne Ratcliffe, Sheffield

It's funny how I let the days go by... I'm so in love with humanity. I'm not so sure how to explain. Their capacity to surprise me, meeting people and coming to know them, being blindly amazed at how complicated and different they are from me. I think I'm just at that stage in my life where friends pass so quickly through my fingers. I used to hang on – you grow up feeling the need for that security. But part of the amazingness is only knowing someone for a few hours, or a few months, before they get carried off on some other drift, because their life is going somewhere else.

I began to photograph everybody, everybody I felt good or curious about. I wanted to collect these millions of photographs. It's just incredible to me. I'm obsessed with photographs of people. What's said in the closing and opening of the shutter, what is left unsaid. Where's the absence...? Some photographs I could just look at again and again, painting and repainting some sense of memory and time.

I stopped going home. I strayed from house to house. Other people's homes, other people's stuff, pictures on the wall, tea stains on the surfaces, socks drying on the radiator...
I was balled up on somebody else's sofa, in a borrowed t-shirt. I was watching my friend Benji ape around the room, making silly jokes that were cluttered with meaning.

"Oh, little Roxy! Don't make that face at me! You disapprove."

I hadn't eaten in a while but it felt good. The hollowness made me feel more true, like every moment was realised better inside of me. I laughed and made puppy-dog eyes at Benji. His housemate stared at me like I was of no use. What was his name? I was introduced but when I'm introduced I forget to listen to people's names. I'm too busy thinking about their face and how exciting it is. I like freckles because I don't have them.

Benji whacked up the volume, and the room reverberated with The Velvet Underground's bitter sweet howl on addiction.

I took a picture of the housemate. His hostility interested me.

"Why're you taking my photograph?" he asked.

I could only just hear him with the blaring music.

"I take everyone's picture."

"What?"

"I take everyone's picture," I said louder.

"Why?" He asked me in a tone that made me know that if I tried to explain he wouldn't try to understand.

"I like faces. I like to understand people," I said.

"I don't want my picture taken. Don't you know a bit of your soul is taken with every photograph?"

I handed him the camera. "D'you want a bit of my soul...?"

He held it in his hand as though I'd handed him a loaded gun, staring at me in disbelief. It'd started raining really hard outside. I jumped up out of my seat.

"Can I climb out the window, Benji?"

Benji always laughed at my tendency to do clichéd crazy stuff. His flat was on the second floor of a typical townhouse semi, and the flat below had a bay window which you could sit on top of. He hauled up the sash window as high as it would go and I climbed out and sat in the rain. I clung to the ledge, and my socks quickly got cold and wet. The raindrops slipped between hairs on my head to cause sweet sensations on my scalp. I grinned and peered back through the window. Benji's housemate took a photograph and his expression changed. As though he'd just discovered the wondrous power of having the chance to take a little bit of someone else's soul.

A car pulled up in the street below and Charlie got out. He peered up at me, shielding his eyes from the rain. He smirked. "Jump, Ratty, jump! I'll catch yuu, I promise!"

I smiled down at him, admiring the lazy arrogance of his stance, all dishy and dishevelled... I got my camera back from the other boy and took a photograph of Charlie. He shoved his hands in his pockets and smouldered away like a poser.

I said my goodbyes and scampered outside, with just a camera and the clothes on my back. I jumped and hugged Charlie and he hoisted me up and swung round, leaving me in uncontrollable giggles.

Once in the car my stomach rumbled, as loud as war. I wrapped an arm around it as though I could muffle the sound. Charlie glanced sideways at me knowingly.

"Have yuu eaten, lass? No, you havnae. Let's get sum breakfast."

I nodded. I stared out of the window into the wet blurry streets and Charlie sang to cheer me up. He actually had a powerful, gravely singing voice but he rarely bothered. Still he loved to embarrass me by howling out, "ROX-ANNE," all of a sudden.

I pointedly put the CD player on and thumped the volume up to drown him out. For seven minutes, I existed in a time warp – riding in a battered Volkswagen, with an analogue camera, listening to *Dark Side of the Moon*.

* * * * * *

THE SICKNESS

Simian Thomas, Sheffield

"Bite the bullet." Cassie said.

I bit the bullet. It hurt my teeth and left a weird bloody taste in my mouth. The iron in blood makes it taste like metal, and the blood in bullets makes them taste like the insides of a living being. She grabbed it back off me and replaced it into the barrel of the ridiculously over-decorated pistol.

"It was a fucking metaphor, you fool. I didn't mean it literally."

"I don't think in metaphors," I lied defensively. "You give me a bullet and tell me to bite it, you take me to a cliff and tell me to jump."

"Don't be so fucking self-pitying. Honestly, none of it matters as much as you think it does," she said with quiet exasperation.

"What am I supposed to bite the bullet over?" I asked, knowing the answer anyway. Sometimes denial is just the best place to be.

"Break it off! She makes you unhappy. You won't start learning happiness again until you give yourself the chance to start over."

"Happiness... *again*. I don't remember happiness being in my life, so I'm not sure how it can return," I said sombrely.

"Fucking Eeyore, man! Listen to yourself. You're so self-absorbed, no-wonder she can't stand you!"

Pistol whipped. I'm not sure which of my relationships is more damaging to my self-worth.

"I tried to break it off, but then I heard her voice and fell in love all over again," I mumbled.

"And you felt on top off the world for a full five minutes?" she asked.

"You never liked her anyway."

"For good reason."

"You don't know her like I do."

I listened to my own pathetic whinge and wondered where it all came from. I swear I wasn't always quite so neurotic.

"She's a virus and you're fucking diseased. It's a sickness, this fucking *thing* that makes people let others treat them like shit."

She put her uncle's antique pistol back into the glass case and locked it, then pulled a pack of cigarettes from the pocket of her long cardigan. She opened the window and climbed onto the balcony. She leaned her back against the iron carvings of the railings, which held her close to the house like a pocket. She tapped a heeled brogue against the opposite rail, staring intensely into the distance, with the determined wisdom of a teenager in the midst of a cat-fight with adulthood.

"What happened to you? Since when did you start smoking?" I wrinkled my nose at the smell, "and Marlboro lights too... how clichéd."

"We're all allowed bad habits." She gritted her teeth.

"Is it your new peer group?" I was looking for another nerve. We were like siblings, we couldn't help but pull the strings.

"What the little 'common people' you don't want to associate with? You hate these rich bastards too. Is anyone good enough?" Her voice was scathing.

I leaned on the window sill and felt hints of the breeze, but dared not go any further. I thought about how high up we were and it made me want to know what it was like to dive off. Not to kill myself, just to know the moments before impact with the ground. Maybe I should try bungee jumping...

"I'm not really a people person," I said.

"Go and be a hermit then – I'm bored with you."

'All I do is want. I want sex, I want intimacy, yet when it's there it sickens me, I feel repulsed and never ever satisfied. I want to drink, to fuck up my body, yet I drink and it just makes me want more fiercely, whatever I don't feel I have right then. I want to not be lonely, I drink to not be lonely, I fuck to not be lonely, I laugh to not be lonely. But all of it makes me feel more lonely. Intimacy, love, it just make you feel so much more. Worse and better all at the same time. And when that elusive spark is there, the moment passes so fast you fall on your arse and gaze dumbly at the sky.

Then it's gone, all of it, whatever it was. When love's not there you are numb. I am numb.

I beg you, Lucy. Just speak to me. Say you miss me, anything. It won't make me feel better, it will make me feel worse. I'm happier hating you. That's where we've always been and where we always will be. My beautiful rose strangling me with a stem of thorns, slicing open my Bambi white throat.

I am the crew of miscreants on the Black Pearl void of all feeling, I am Lestat with all of eternity stretched before me. Cut me open, let me bleed, just for the satisfaction.'

I read the solo page of diary I had with a scorn for my younger self. With scorn for the bits of me I wasn't rid of. I tore it up and ate it piece by piece, deciding to be a happier person. I phoned Cassie and asked if we could meet for coffee, I promised not to talk about Lucy.

"Only if you agree to go travelling with me," she said with decided firmness.

I nodded on my side of the phone. "Norway...?" I asked hopefully.

* * * * * * *

THE PHILOSOPHY OF BRIAN

Wolfgang, Sheffield

"Cursed is the ground for thy sake," said the Polish-Australian girl, as she looked up from the pages of Heidegger. She screwdled her nose a little, peering over spectacles.

"You don't much care for him, do you?" I motioned to the book.

She shook her head.

"Well," she said. "I do find it difficult to read in German. I mean it's dense enough without trying to fathom it in my third language."

I nodded. I stroked my beard with the thoughtfulness of a wise owl, but some sticky substance (I suspected Black Sambuca) had matted the left side, leaving it not so much enigmatically ruffian as a disgusting mess. There was also a small oil-slick of the anise liqueur spread, hardened, on the coffee table top. *A baby seal peers up from the pool with liquid eyes, (which speak of sickly premature death at the hands of man and his greed for intoxication.)*

I pointed to the table. "I recollect drinking this substance last night in a bar... but how did it get here?"

I waved a hand around the scruffy studio. The patent low winter sun was bulging inside my eye sockets, which carried heavily the weight of alcohol and lost sleeps.

She smirked. "You asked them to top up your whiskey flask at the end of the night. You said it was delicious. I beg to differ."

A rat-a-tat of gentleman's feet. Cuan entered with the wily grin of a young man who knows his victims.

"Well, look at this morose mother fucker right here! Hey Deutsch-bag, did you kip here last night, or what?"

I returned with a flat gaze.

"Hi," he said to the girl.

"Ah yes," I said. "Cuan, this is my new friend..." I faltered, "I'm sorry I've misplaced your name...?"

She smiled wryly, but it failed to conceal the tiny sense of disappointment. She doesn't know the more I like a person the more I forget their name. (I called Cuan 'Brian' for several months.)

"We didn't kip here, sir. I believe I was rather drunk and decided I had to rectify the fact that she'd not read any Heidegger forthwith! But I'd left the book here... so we arrived at seven when the cleaners open the doors."

"The cleaners were late though," the girl explained. "So we climbed in a window."

"Ah yes, indeed we did. I forget," I added. The presence of alcohol was still in my system, forcing me to lose the connections between the moments that form narratives.

"Fucking Heidegger!" Cuan shook his dishevelled curls.

"You've not read any to judge!" "That's because your book is in German and I only speak about three words." He glanced to the girl with a raised brow and she smiled. "All I know is only cunts spout on about Heidegger. All I know is that philosophy shouldn't be about being a condescending twat. Now, are you coming to the cafeteria? I need a stiff coffee."

'Noses screwdled like the pages of a book stuffed in an overcoat pocket. Hair entwines with other hair like love enmeshed. Undergrowth snatches ankles and captures better the beast that tries most desperately to struggle free. Conversations briefly satisfy the insatiable lust for filling the void left by the loveless. The void is the space left in a mother's stomach after the child is born. We can never fill that void because we can never take another being inside of ourselves. They will always be outside, be objective, not of our flesh, our greedy possession; our desperation to be understood from the inside out.'

I'd lost track of the people in the room as I hastily scribbled these words on a scrap of paper. They both just watched me for some time, exchanging more amused glances. I stopped and looked up, dazed by myself, the heady whir of whisky remnants escaping my body to inhabit a better place.

"*Kompt bitte!*" Cuan said.

I stumbled to my feet.

"If you write a book on philosophy I'll read it. Wolfgang the Deutsch-bag..."

* * * * * * *

ON THE CUSP & OFF THE CUFF

Roxanne Ratcliffe, Sheffield

On edge, on the cusp. It was once written in a school file that I had no beliefs and I wondered who'd decided, as I'd never been asked. There was a bit of me that liked Sheffield's bohemian side. But I didn't like the cliques and self-important types, nor the fashionable or the fashionably-unfashionable. I looked at them posing, and treating their friends and lovers as fashion accessories as much as anything else. Seeming to live their lives inside glossy magazine pages. It bothered me.

But I liked the non-existence, the never growing up or settling down. Never stop dressing like a teenager, never stop listening to music that is slightly offensive. So I put my Peter Pan boots back on, and stepped into bohemia. My vows against these fashionably-hatted types were made to the person who'd invited me that evening anyway.

But Claudia wasn't on edge at all, despite the clientele in the bar. She looked really happy and excited. My silent question mark on this subject reached Charlie. He was looking particularly rugged and stubbled, wearing a rotten leather jacket and speaking with a thicker accent so the posh kids couldn't grasp what he was saying.

"Jody," he said pointedly. "The ex."

And then I spotted Jody enter stage left where the band were faffing about after the sound check. He was an instant jester rolling into the spotlight that sought him. I couldn't catch his words from where we stood, but they were jokes rolled out with a Cheshire cat delivery. People smiled, he grinned and pulled his jeans up that were sliding too far down his back showing stripy boxers. He pushed ginger-brown hair from his face and his eyes shot a look to Claudia that said 'I know this is awkward but I'll joke us out of it'.

"Did you say Cuan was coming tonight?" I asked, remembering infatuation, but trying to keep it from Charlie.

"Yeah, he said he'd be down. His friend from school is back ferra wee while," Charlie said.

"Oh good," I said dryly. "Are you all gonna be blokey all night?"

"It's a girl. I forget her name, sumthin non-descript," he replied dismissively.

"Is she hot?" I asked.

"She's kinda pretty. But also kinda leik a wet blanket left ta dry on a broken radiator," he replied.

I smirked.

We fetched more drinks from the bar. I really wanted to speak to Claudia but she was pretty preoccupied. I looked over and she was sitting on one of the speakers. Jody was leant over her whispering something in her ear.

"The *ex*?" I said.

"Yeah." Charlie looked darkly self-knowing. "Ex-sex. Everyone knows ex-sex is the best."

I screwed my nose up, reminded of my own prudishness, and sensibleness. It's all just such a bad idea.

The cocky little lad who played guitar soon began rallying them together to start their set. Claudia and Jody left each other's personal space to sort the last bits of stuff out. More people were arriving and I scanned hopefully for Cuan. They started to play and Claudia shook off everything that wasn't attitude behind the mic and began singing. Her eyes and voice seduced the room.

I found the face I was helplessly looking for, slipping in the door with a tall skinny girl in tow. Cuan gave a wry glance to the hat-wearing punters poised in cool observation of the band and shot me a smile. They bought drinks and came weaving over. I'd forgotten to listen to the music cos my heart was wedged inside my mouth. I tried to keep it shut in case the butterflies escaped.

"It's a bit fucking hairy in here," Cuan quipped, grinning.

Charlie punched him lightly in the shoulder. "Lets hav a wee rumble, that'll scare em off."

The drink was going to my head, or maybe it was just Cuan. I didn't want to say anything. I might embarrass myself. He slid up beside me. He tried to introduce his friend over the noise but I couldn't hear her name.

"This is Charlie and Roxanne..." he told the girl. "*Foxy Roxy*," he said in my ear. But in a matey way.

I smiled shyly and glanced at his friend. She did look a little wet. If I wasn't careful I'd be left talking to her all night. I wanted my Claudia back – I wasn't in the mood for polite conversation.

The butterflies liquefy everything and turn it feverish colours. I stood in silence as the band played on. I let the music inside my brain, to find the emotive spot it hunted for. I digested the sound that collected in the air, the husky sarcasm uttered between songs, waiting, watching, time on its knees elapsed. The band finished and gave thanks. I waited for Claudia to come and find us, but she didn't appear.

"I'm gonna go see where Cloud is at," I said to Charlie restlessly.

He was occupied with rolling a cigarette.

"I wouldn't," he drawled, but waved me off.

I pushed past people to near the stage, coming across the drummer. She was very young looking, with pretty afro hair tied into ribbons.

"D'you know where Claudia is?"

She pointed to a side door leading off.

"I'd knock if I were you."

I knocked. The door opened by Jody's hand, but he was hugging Claudia and I realised she was crying, makeup smeared, hair mussed.

"Sorry." I stepped back to leave, but she reached out a hand towards me, beckoning.

I stepped nervously into the room, which was crowded with mic stands, amps and other such paraphernalia. It was a little cramped. I was sharing breathing space with Jody, who was tall and glanced guiltily down at me. Oddly I felt a rush of liking for him.

"Roxy?" he asked.

I nodded, he smiled holding out a hand to shake. Claudia began to wipe angrily at her face. She dug in her bag to find a pocket mirror and began to redo her makeup.

"I'll get us some drinks," Jody said.

He squeezed past me and shut the door behind himself, so that it was just me, the she-dragon and the uneasy gloom he'd left behind. I felt strangely special. Claudia ruffled my hair. I should've been comforting her, yet my presence had returned her to alpha female.

"Is Q-ball here?" she asked, eyes shrewd. (Q-ball is her nickname for Cuan). She pulled out eyeliner and began an artist's drawing of a face that never breaks.

* * * * * * *

THE CURSED

Simian Thomas, Sheffield

It was 3 a.m. We stood shivering outside typical student digs. We rang Hex's buzzer for his room, but there was no answer. A semi-familiar face came trudging across the car park from the all night garage. I dug around for his name, something I'd forget again tomorrow.

"Hi, Luke isn't it?" Cassie asked quickly.

He grunted agreement, flashing us a friendly but somewhat tired grin. "You here to see Hex? Grand timing." He sniggered with apprehension.

"He phoned me," Cassie said. "He seemed a bit wired, but he asked us to come over, and we were nearby so..."

Luke nodded. "Yeah. Wired, that's one way of describing it." He scrambled around for his key, and then rattled it in the lock for a bit until the heavy old door shunted open. The lights on the stairs flicked on as they sensed movement. We clambered up to the first floor and followed Luke down the long corridor to the common room. He pushed the door open with a creak. There were no lights on in the living room, but the orange street lights our eyes adjusted to flooded through the windows on the scene. On the main wall, which was painted with red gloss, words were scrawled in chalk capitals.

'LOVE IS DOOMED & WE ARE ALL DOOMED TO LOVE'

Hex was flopped face downwards on the sofa beneath it, as though his night's exploits were complete. Luke switched the light on in the adjoining kitchen and set out a couple of cleanish mugs on the breakfast bar. He rummaged through random cupboards and found a bottle of red wine.

"Ooh, Rioja. Far too classy for Helen. I'll buy her some Bock to make up for it."

I exchanged dubious looks with Cassie. Luke whipped through the draws for a wine opener and quickly opened it, beckoning us nearer and handing us both a cupful. We'd already had a fair bit to drink so I supped it cautiously, craving fatty, carby food for my body.

"He took some acid and watched *Old Boy*." Luke pointed at the crumpled torso, now entwined with slumber. "At least I'm assuming that's what happened from the evidence. That boy experiments on himself too much. He can't handle it. I thought I was a reckhead. He walked out into the Peak District at 6 a.m. the other morning, because he said he wanted to see the sunrise."

"I'm a bit worried about him," Cassie said, perching on a stool. "He's always been a bit mad, but since he moved out of his parents'..." She shrugged.

"You think he's better off at home?" Luke asked.

"Fuck no," I said. "It was them that did the damage. But he was kind of contained at home."

He was better before the cat died, I thought to myself.

"He was better before his cat died," Cassie murmured softly.

Luke sniggered a little (the reason I'd not said it). "Sounds about right," he said. "He should get a job, give him some purpose."

"He's kind of got a job," Cassie said.

Luke snorted. "Maybe he should put his entrepreneur skills to better use."

* * * * * * *

ALLOTMENT ENVY

Calista Siddal, Leeds

Nether Ed pointed silently at the place on the map that he used to live. He missed his city intensely. He wanted to be back among the Avenues layered with mushed up leaves, long fallen, long trodden. He'd always felt his loneliness to be a lack of having some kindred spirit to float along with. Now maybe, he thought he was lonelier without his place. Without the short walk to the woods, squirrels to chase amongst the great arching tree roots, soil in which to bury treasured nuts. The car fumes of the crowded city clouded his love for humans being. They bustled and hustled around him, stamping on toes and slow pigeons. Not the pigeons, he pleaded. The poor little wretches black from pollution and lame from poisons. He disliked mundane brutality with a passion, he longed for a better time. Fast death in the jaws of a skilful fox, snap snap.

"What are you writing?" Simian asked. He seated himself opposite in an identikit leather armchair, placing an identikit medium cappuccino on the table in front of him.

I looked up from my sketchbook, half concealing the page automatically. "Allotment envy. I saw a t-shirt that said 'allotment envy'. I felt the need to write something."

"Hmm, kitchen-sink profundity. I'm a fan," he said.

I flipped back a few pages to where I'd drawn him into a graphic depiction of a scene from *Planet of the Apes*. I'd titled the page in careful letters 'Simian Ape'. I very carefully tore it out and gave it to him.

"Freakish," he said. "Those words always feel like a command. I start to think about the meanings of the word ape, as a doing word, it's a struggle. Sometimes I actually think that I'm just a really clever monkey who convinced people that he is people." He held the page in his monkey paws like treasure, then carefully slipped it into his satchel.

"Have you got any further with the plans?" he asked tentatively. Tentative because he knew my response.

"Yes, I've continued sorting out everything all by myself. You *have* to come with me to STA travel tomorrow though. She keeps asking me for stuff I don't know about you."

"Like what?" he asked.

"I dunno, your date of birth for starters," I mumbled.

"You've only known me eight years. It's most acceptable that you don't know when my birthday is," he purred.

"I've no head for dates... It's February sometime."

"March," he corrected.

"March then. There's other stuff though. I can't remember it all, that's the problem. Do you know what jabs you're going to need?"

He squirmed. "Lots of unfortunate needles trying to make me faint? That's as much as I need to know."

I rolled my eyes. "You got the email I sent listing what you specifically need?" I pulled another notebook from my bag, in which I'd been attempting to stay organised for both of us. There was plenty I'd forgotten to write down.

"It's ages until I'll have to go through that. I'd rather not think about it." He slumped down in his seat, cradling the warm cup and glancing through the window to the wet street.

"But you should've printed the email so when you need it you have it."

"Can't you send it to me again when I need it?" he asked cautiously.

"Yeah, and I'll wipe your arse for you too, if you're struggling with that," I retorted. He shrugged carelessly. My insults fall on a deaf ego. "D'you miss Sheffield?" I asked, curious. He was always so scathing, always acting as though he couldn't escape quickly enough.

"Like a cat misses it's dirty, hairy, flea-infested basket. I can't find anything in Leeds. I would like to have suggested some amazing little independent coffee house to meet, but I don't know any. Do you?"

A bit of mascara must have got too close to my eye. I slid the edge of a finger through the lashes, distractedly.

"Um, I think James was talking about somewhere actually. I've found plenty of good hangouts in Huddersfield. But then it's a lot smaller."

I'd thought it would be best if Simian and I went to different universities, so I'd chosen little Huddersfield. I knew he needed to meet people himself. He'd never be happy with my crowd.

"Useful," he said doubtfully. "This James knows fucking everything."

I smiled wryly. "I'm sorry for branching out and making new friends."

"Oh, he's a 'friend' is he? I thought he was a *special friend*." He sipped his coffee, and made a face.

"You're such a prude, Sim. What difference does it make? It's just sex, everybody's doing it, in case you hadn't noticed," I said.

He manufactured detachment in his face, which just pushed me further, irritated by his general attitude to my sex life.

"Not everyone saves themselves for a princess and then returns to purity when she breaks their heart. Some of us have an appetite that needs to be sated."

"I don't want to know about your appetite," he said curtly, as though I were describing a weird food fetish.

* * * * * *

BONNIE PRINCE CHARLIE

Bryn McLarey, Sheffield

"Untrustworthy type (smelling rotten)...?" I leaned on the bar and read the crossword clue aloud.

Mae colleague Jimmy half laughed, and nodded toward a bloke sat in the corner of the pub with a lone pint. He looked leik a scruff, with lank hair and a beard that carried with it the remains of last night's dinner and possibly a small nest of birds. He wus watching out of the window at happenings on the street. I peered a little closer at him and then nodded at mae own affirmation.

"He's a friend of Cuan's."

Jimmy screwed his nose up. "Maybe Q has no sense of smell. How many letters is it?"

"Two words, three letters each, last letter G."

"Bad Egg," the scruff said, turning suddenly towards us. He'd felt so much farther away before. His eyes met mine with a dark twinkle and he half grinned a yellow-toothed grin, then turned back tu the window withoot a word. I looked down at the paper.

"Hot damn, the man is right," I said dryly, covering for our disconcertedness at him having overheard our conversation. "I think he's a hairdresser..." I whispered.

Jimmy stifled rude laughter.

"True story, he cut Q's hair." I addressed the scruff a little louder, "...you a hairdresser, mate?"

He turned back again and tousled a curl of greasy hair a little mockingly. "I am many things, sir. I used to work in a barbershop, but the manager fired me after I punched him." He had a European accent, but over-emphasised English words leik a toff.

"Fuckin weirdo," Jimmy murmured under his breath, keeping his eyes averted. He didn't like that I'd started up a conversation with the man. We got plenty of wacko customers bending our bartender ears with their boring problems and blatantly made-up life stories. It wus fun tu humour them on occasion though, tu see what gems of worldly weirdness you could turn up.

"Where you from?" I asked him.

"Latterly Sharrow, monsieur, but formerly East Berlin." He motioned a hand as if divulging the direction of each place.

"Oh aye, I've been to both. Porter Cottage?" I tried.

"A fine public house, indeed," he said.

"Assel?" I added.

"Also a most superb drinking hole. Though rather full of *Insel Affen* in the hotter months. I used to live on Oranienburger Straße actually, funny you should mention..."

He looked tu me curiously, with a face that wus suspicious of coincidence.

"I wus there a few years ago, mebees we encountered one another," I said. Looking at his expressions now I saw clearly he wus mad, or had consumed enough booze or drugs (or both) fae memory tu be eroded and tangled up by imaginings. Paranoia wus setting in, questions rolling in his beige eyeballs.

Had we met? Did I remember and he not? What had occurred? Was the purple monkey demon somehow involved in all of this? His brain seemed tu be chugging leik an aging train for a few minutes, which seemed like ages, as they were spent in conversational silence. The pretentious elevator-jazz Jimmy had put on filtered intu consciousness. The man stilled, took a sip of his pint and seemed tu return to the room.

"I rather like to think of myself as a 'bad egg'," he muttered cheerfully. "If you don't mind that is?"

"You may think whatever the fuck yuu leik aboot your aen self," I replied. Though the question rather evoked the nonsense of *Alice in Wonderland*. "I didn't catch your name, mate? I'm Charlie." I walked over and shook his hand firmly. I sat down opposite him, tu better peer at his weather-beaten-shit-beaten face.

He grinned the slimy grin, with a disconcerting nonchalance that comes from knowing a secret.

"My name is Wolfgang. But you, sir, are *not* 'Charlie'..."

I felt an ominous cloud of mae own paranoia setting in. Not that it mattered these days if people knew how much of a lie I'd been living, but yuu become so ingrained with tension at the idea of being found out.

"Oh, am I not? Who might I be then?"

I tried tu relax, to not let on that mae heart wus beating in mae mouth.

"Far away from little Bonnie Prince Charlie sailing on the sea to Skye... You, sir, I believe, are the *Kaiser*."

I raised a helplessly sarcastic eyebrow, thinking – *thank fuck for that, he knows nothing, he's just plain fucking crazy!* He glugged some more beer down, quietly and specifically watching my reaction.

"The Kaiser? They've not existed for a very long time I believe," I took out my rollies and tobacco, tu give myself something to occupy mae hands.

"Maybe not literally. But you're an Authority," he said.

I screwed my nose up. "What kind of an authority? An authority a fuckin what?"

He removed a pipe from his pocket, just leik mae Grandpappy wudhae done and began pushing tobacco inside it.

"May I join you for a smoke, sir?"

"Aye. If yuu tell me what I'm an authority for," I said.

"Why that information, sir, I'm not permitted to know..."

PHASE TWO

In which Simian's holiday takes a turn for the worse & Sheffield is steeped in latency.

COWARDICE IS A PRIVATE ROOM

Simian Thomas, Phuket

I hate the heat. Funny that, hmmm, let's go to Thailand. Let's soak up the vomitous heat. Let's mingle with people who want to layer up a beautiful, perfect tan, and then scratch it off back home as their skin dries to shrivelled fig brown. Let's mingle with bikini-clad-but-ugly-insiders who want to party on the beach. And shit, if they accidentally encounter some culture that's okay. Something to email their friends back home, presents to buy from street sellers. Generic gap year collectibles.

Also, I was scared of what I might find far away from the West. Scared of the people I would encounter, scared that the hostel would be dirty and insect-infested. No, no, Iceland was the way forward for me – that was my adventure. But Cassie bullied me. She didn't so much want heat, sun, tanned skin, as much as she wanted to be closer to the Equator... Malaysia and Indonesia were already calling us further south for her. The lines of longitude and latitude were being sketched out inside her soul, constellations playing dot-to-dot across the freckles on her pale skin.

We were a joke, our blue-grey pallor waiting for the sun to lick his dragon's tongue, expressive streaks of rouge painted over cheeks and shoulders. I could always find shade where there was none. I've always claimed invincibility from the fire in the sky. Dark alleyways find me, search for me, chase me. But every surface reflected the fire back now. If I'd dug a hole and buried myself alive it would still have found me. The rainforests sang provocatively of their deep green shade, tempting me towards them with a siren voice. But I knew in that longed-for shade the snakes and spiders waited quietly for my tender white feet. So I sweated and cooked instead.

The disgust and sweat was what Cassie searched for. It was real. I would gladly watch Michael Palin tell me how it is, watch him ad lib anecdotes on adventures in the Himalayas. Or walking through deserts with camels, listening to them make those unearthly noises as though they will one day enslave the human race. It was not enough for her; the Equator seeped into her dreams like some entity. The mosquitoes would have to feed on her blood before her thirst would be quenched. Watching *Pole to Pole* just made her restless and less satisfied with all the things she'd not yet seen, not yet found, not yet been bitten by.

I waited for the evening to come. Nine o'clock down on the beach, the hot sand mellowed to touchable. I lay and watched the haze. The exquisite turquoise ocean indigoed and the fleeting orange light reached inside my irises, reflecting my gaze back out onto the eternal flatness of the ocean. The vastness waited to be conquered, or waited to swallow, either would satiate something.

And the darkness there had a depth, a liquidity. As it sunk onto my body, I took a walk at the water's edge. Barefoot through the shallows, watching the water swell and peel away as my ankles moved through it... I knew that when I looked up I would've lost the world and there would only be darkness and me. And when this security failed me, I could turn, and the little sparks of light in the distance could guide me back to the safety of other naïve, young travellers.

"I'm surprised you're not afraid of encountering jelly fish." Cassie's voice.

I felt as though I'd been alone, her tone ever mocking... and true. I hadn't thought of jelly fish. I tried to suppress the tiny panic. One day as a child I saw one in the sea and refused to re-enter the water for a year, I think. Cowardice is a private room, but Cassie had a knack for knocking on the door.

I turned to find her in the darkness. Barely enough light to catch the edge of her face, hair mussy from the saltwater. Scathing words and scathing beauty, both fall to flatness often, and how can I explain why? To criticise each other is our security. The day she tells me she loves me – and that I'm the best friend she'll ever have – is the day I'll run away. Or at least shift uncomfortably in my seat and change the subject.

There's a jellyfish wrapping his beautiful tentacles around my shoulders, tickling my neck. I leap from my seat. Fucking wasps. Are there wasps in Thailand? Tell me there are no wasps in Thailand. Tell me that and I will go.

* * * * * * *

PSAMMEAD

Claudia McLeod, Ripon

I woke ta dry heat. A sliver of sunlight were streamin through tha window and the heat of it as it crept across the bed to touch ma body were unbearable. I was paralysed, though. I wanted ta roll away from its path lykah hero in an action movie, but my limbs felt lyke they were full a treacle. I could barely move my eyes. I knew I needed to sit up in order to snap out of it, but the heat was soo much. My mouth and throat felt lyke a furry sand animal ud jus crawled from inside – *what was that little gremlin creature called that used to crawl out of t'sand in Five Children and It?* I recognised the taste of stale beer on ma tongue and remembered neckin that last bottle wi'a grimace.

Nowt worse than a hangover in a heat-wave.

I sat up abrupt'ly, as though physic'ly rippin missel from't dozy state that my body were in. I gorra sickenin head-rush and my eyes clouded a bit. I reached fa tha glass a water by the side a my bed, but it were empty a'course. I vaguely recalled wakin at 6am and gluggin it down before fallin back into ma comatose.

Little bits a the night before began to worm into my conscious. Ma muddle of mem'ry returnin little titbits of torture. Some of them were stuff lyke '*ordering an absinthe cocktail*' or '*another shot of tequila*' others fell in't bracket of '*slobber'ly snoggin one a my mates and then walkin home alone cryin me eyes out, cause I never thought it possible to hate missel this much*'. By the time this particular mem'ry reached me, I were wrapped around the toilet bowl retching. There was nowt left in ma belly. I think ma body was tryin to vomit out some demons instead. *The Psammead... that was the name of the funny gremlin thing in the sand...*

I staggered tu't sofa and outta habit switched on the telly, even though the onslaught of chirpy images hurt me head. I forgot to turn it off as I remembered how hot I was and stumbled franticall'y to open tha window. (As though a second maire stuffy air would choke me.) My head reeled agen. The idea of gettin sum water came ta me. I moved too quickly to the kitchen an back agen, lyke a neon bouncy ball. I collapsed back on't sofa, settin the water down untouched. My auld boss's words returning from't first work day wi'a stinking hangover.

"Keep drinking water, Honey. I know it'll make you puke more. But it helps wash your system out"

I looked at the glass a water, but the effort of reaching furrit felt too much. My brain was heavy. I rested it on't back of sofa, burrit still pounded inside ma skull. Ma eyes rolled around, drawn to the bright telly screen, but they rolled away lyke ball-bearings. Unable to fix thissels on any one thing.

Malcolm appeared in't doorway lookin at me wi' that expression I knew too well. My lit'l brother, all disapprovin.

"Happy Birthday," he said flat'ly.

I made an inaudible alien noise.

"Ya should get some air," he said.

I thought this over afore managin to answer. "Too hot..."

"Be okay in't shade of woods. Can you get dressed?"

I were wearing only kecks and my Sparta Prague shirt.

"Cumon, jus put some trackies and flip-flops on..."

"I fookin stink," I said.

"The trees don't mind," he said reasonab'ly.

It felt lyke it took me hours to complete the mission of trackies and flip-flops. I moved in slow mo, stoppin to sit down all't time and stare at a variety of walls. But I find when I'm hung-over less time has passed than I think. Mal had mayde and drunk a brew by the time I got back. He handed me my sunglasses.

We had to cut down the back path ta get tu't woods. This was fairly open and the sun licked ma skin. But there were a lit'l breeze, so it were better than the stuffy hause. I've always found each moment is a tiny inch back towards recovery, once you start doin sommat. I already felt a bit better, though as ma queasy stomach were leavin me, my dull throbbin head was maire noticeable.

Mal kept glancin sideways at me as though I might faint. I pushed sweaty stragg'ly hair from ma face. We reached the stile, which was soo low I often frogged it. Now I jus stopped and looked at it as though it were undefeatable. Mal climbed halfway over and offered his hand. Slowly I completed the feeble task.

The woods were beautifully cool and still.

"Better?" Mal asked.

"Mmm."

"So, whaddya do last night?" my brother asked, wi'a tone expecting bad things.

"Shit."

"You did a shit?"

"Shit."

"You kopped off wi' Tom?" he said.

How'd he know? Was he there at t'time? I used to work wi' Tom. Hopefully I'd never hafta set eyes on him agen.

"Tosser. I were too pissed to think about it," I said.

"He said *you* kissed him," Mal added.

"What!" I spluttered.

"Can y' even remember?" he asked.

"Noo, but, exact'ly. I were too pissed to mayke any conscious decision to kiss anyone."

"He should know better either way," Mal said.

"Why? Cos he's a bloke and I'm a sweet vulnerable girl? He broke up with someone recently too. We're all in the sayme leaky fuckin boat."

Mal shrugged agreeably. He had strong principles about women, and not tekkin advantage of them.

"Ya not hookin up wi'him then?" he asked dubiously.

"Ugh, no. He hits on every girl he's ever friends with. Shit. I used ta think he was a sound bloke. Fucking creep."

"Good," Mal said. "That's what I wanted to hear."

"So you can sneak back and reassure Jody?"

"I'm just tryin to look out for you. Is that soo bad?" he said.

"It's okay, Malc. He's your buddy."

Mal looked distant. He always took everything upon hissel, tryin to resolve ev'rythin for ev'rybody, to be impartial and not tekk sides. He stared into the trees.

"You mekk ev'rything soo complicated, Claws. You two could work this out if you weren't such a bull in a china shop."

"But I am!" I said, breaking into hazy tears. I wanted to follow up wi' further desperate words, but I were choking on't last.

Mal hugged me as though he could suppress the tears. "Sorry. Sorry. I know you can't help it, rayht?"

I swallowed the tears back, my head wa thundering. "Can't help fookin ev'rythin up, no."

Besides, it were Jody's decision, not mine. He were the one who needed to get away from me, escape the chaos... I was the one left to face missel in the mirror every day. I couldn't break up with me.

"Cumon now," Mal said gently. "Stop hatin yersel. That's what causes it all in't first place"

"Easily said, wise owl," I replied.

* * * * * * *

A HASTY SLUG

Bryn McLarey, Sheffield

The doorbell rang again, piercing the scruffy ambience of Claudia's bedroom. She dumped her glass of wine on the table begrudgingly and headed out to see what delights awaited behind the panel of her front door. Her housemate Maisie and I waited quietly. She appeared again, no less disgruntled. There wus a weighty pause and then Cuan stumbled intu the room. He precariously navigated the clutter on the floor, swaying all the while, and then collapsed backwards ontu the unmade bed. He wus followed mock-sheepishly by the hairy German.

"I know my own disease!" Cuan announced, gaping at the ceiling.

Maisie giggled, but looked uneasy at the presence of his companion. Claudia lit up her seventh cigarette of the evening and tutted quite audibly.

"Ev'ryone come hang out in my room. I love bein matri-fookin-dee. I spose I should offer to fetch everyone drinks?" She sipped her wine and glowered at Cuan who grinned obliviously. "...And d'you *have* ta bring skanky tramps into ma house, Q?"

"What?" he said dizzily, tilting his chin up tu peer at the world for a moment. "He's not a tramp. He's an artist."

She arched an eyebrow and turned questioningly tu Wolfgang.

"D'you havva home?"

He grinned widely in the trademark fashion I wus beginning tu be familiar with, exposing as far as his beige canines.

"I have many homes, madam."

"Is this one'a yar hoames?" Claudia pointed down to indicate the house.

"Home is where one feels welcome, madam," he said, still smiling.

"...Is bein 'vagrant' an art project?"

She had that stirring tone she often gets when talking tu Cuan about his 'art'. But as Cuan wus barely capable of conversation, her scathery wus turned on the nearest victim.

"No, it's a craft, madam. Far nobler than art," he said. I laughed and he looked tu me. "I know you... we've met before?"

"Indeed we have, Deutschbag." I swapped tab from hand to mouth, and extended my hand tu shake his. It wus strangely cold again, leik closing palms with a ghoul.

He held out a carrier bag. "I come bearing gifts."

I took the bag off him curiously and waved that he should sit down in the chair next tu me.

"May I sit, my Lady?" he asked Claudia.

She rolled her eyes and waved a hand around in reluctant affirmation.

I pulled some small, dark bottled beers out of the bag and peered at them. "Duchess de Bourgogne..." I said reading the name. "What is it?"

"The blood of Christ mixed with wolf juice," he mumbled in wonder. "It's um, Flemish red ale. Rather bloody good."

"Is that what Cuan has had?" Maisie asked with concern.

"I realised!" Cuan exclaimed (possibly brought to by the sound of his name). He wriggled over in a heap and then sat up, and looked intu our faces like we were long lost children.

"Realised what, Screwball?" Claudia said impatiently.

"The idea of utopia and dystopia..." He held out two palms as if tu balance the two concepts. "As opposing forces... but... maybe they're the same...? Maybe we already live... in both!"

"What's 'dystopia'?" Maisie asked.

I'd meanwhile located a bottle opener and opened some of the beer. I clapped at Cuan's epiphany, tu which he gave a look of delight. I took a hasty slug.

"My God," I said, my taste buds dripping with earthly garden pleasures. "This is fucking fantastic."

Maisie stood and tiptoed over, tugging her floral hemline down over her tights. She poised next tu me, picking up a bottle and peering at it.

"It's six percent! *Is* this what Cuan drank?"

Wolfgang smirked unreassuringly. "No no, his state is nothing to do with me or 'the Duchess'. I found him this way. He was sat in the road. I asked him where he was going and he said he was late, and eventually he pointed at this house, so I rang the bell."

"And six percent, Maisie mouse, is not that strong," I said, condescending. "You wanna get some Brewdog in you."

She blushed slightly, retreating.

"Don't be a twat, Charlie," Claudia said. "I've seen the tears after a night on that Jaipur I.P.A. y' love, and thas only five point five?"

"Tears?" Wolfgang peered at me as if judging whether I wus capable of them.

"Tears of joy!" I added dryly.

Claudia finished her wine somewhat quickly and motioned for a bottle of beer. Wolfgang opened one and handed it tu her. "In return for your hospitality!"

She sniffed it, poured some intu her glass, sniffed it again and took a sip, paused, then nodded agreeably.

"Oh aye, very plum'y... tastes lyke perfume an port." She returned her attention to Cuan, who was still sat, staring into nothing.

"Why're you soo munted, Q-ball?" She sat next tu him and picked mysterious bits of dried grass off his brown sweater.

"You're very pretty," he said. "Have I told you that? Pretty like a Venus Fly Trap..."

"Thanks... Why are you soo munted?"

He paused in thought. "To better understand the English language."

"But *what have you consumed?*" she said.

"The English language... and some gin. You're very pretty, have I told you that?" he repeated.

"Lyke a plant what tempts insects to their doom. Yes thanks, y'have."

Maisie sipped her wine and giggled.

"What've you discovered about the English language?" Claudia asked.

"Language is all things," he said drifting off.

"Thas very profound," Claudia said wryly. She thought for a minute. "Here's one fa ya...the word jack," she poked him.

"Jack and Jill?" he said.

"It's a rayte versatile word in slang terms... just think 'jack shit' means nowt? The verb 'to jack' means ta steal. 'Jackass' means stupid, to 'jack up' means to raise sommat, but also inject drugs... 'Jack of all trades'. The jack in a pack a cards..."

Cuan gawped at her as though slowly turning this over.

"You've thought about this a lot," I said.

"Gottah occupy your mind somehow when you can't sleep, cos ya've tekken too many cheap drugs," she said with a bored sigh.

"That's not how I occupy mae mind when I can't sleep," I muttered.

Wolfgang's face switched between us in fascination as we spoke.

"Why have I not discovered you fine young cannibals before?" he said elatedly.

"She's mocking us anyway," I said tu him, pointing to Claudia. "She thinks me an Cuan are pretentious."

He nodded in agreement. "Exactly, it's pretence verses banality. But I think they're the same species," he mumbled.

"Fookin hell," Claudia said. "Not another one."

* * * * * *

MUCH ADO ABOUT NOWT

Roxanne Ratcliffe, Sheffield

Broken fingers stained violet like a pen leak, nails blackened like chipped nail polish. There's smoke everywhere, catching in my throat. It seems to have neither source nor destination, just creeps out of one dark corner and into another. Creeps from faces and bodies that emerge and then remerge with the space. Bloody faces from a pantomime, taut with the horrid realisation they've swallowed their own teeth. The smell of flesh burnt by fiction...

The faces smiled and laughed, some dancing to the music, and Cuan came pushing through the crowd with a loveable smirk. He handed me a bottle of beer, I watched my hand grasp the drink. It wasn't broken.

"Charlie's looking for you." He smirked some more. "I said I'd not seen you all week so if he appears we just ran into one another."

I sighed. It bothered me that he found it funny. At the same time it *was*. People are funny, how foolish they are to themselves. One of Cuan's shy friends appeared, hovering nervously at his shoulder. He was the size of a grizzly bear but seemed to want to shrink behind Cuan's slight, skulking frame.

"Hi," I said to him, smiling. I tried to think how to engage him so he didn't feel so second hand. He shrunk back further.

"I'm gonna sit down," I said.

Cuan nodded and turned to his friend, babbling something happily. I couldn't hear words over the music. I looked at my hand holding the bottle again and weaved to the sofas. They were already full with overgrown kids in each other's laps, laughing and smoking. I sat on a dirty step and leaned against a banister, swallowing cold lager down to invade my uneasy insides. Cuan appeared again alone and slid up right beside me tipping his face close.

"You OK?" He touched a strand of my hair. I gave him an inner beam, forcing out all the negatives in my body. I kissed his cheek and he blushed.

"Careful, he might see us." He glanced around.

"Shut up about Charlie, for fucks sake," I said grinning.

"S'alright for you, he won't start beef with you! He's bigger than me..."

I laughed. "Beef..."

"You sleep okay last night?" he asked.

I nodded and shrugged at the same time.

"Is that an actual yes?"

"Yeah," I said. Yeah is not an actual yes.

The smoke is in my eyes, clouding over my vision into darts and specks. Through these pieces of space I look at my broken hand again, the bottle dropping from the frail grasp. Floating in the smoke, bloody finger tips touching the cracks which peel open, and I fade back to the world.

Two men's faces, one rough and stubbled, scratched by rubble, the other a wisp, an ethereal.

"Roxy! Roxy?" Cuan turned to Charlie. "What's wrong with her?"

"Has she eaten today?" Charlie asked.

"I don't know. I only just ran into..." he began pathetically.

"Gimme a cut, Q. I'm neh stupid," Charlie said with deathly calm. "Has she eaten today?"

Cuan gawped a little, fishlike, thinking.

"Yeah," he said. "I made dinner."

I blinked at them. They both looked at me. I blinked at Cuan purposefully and he blinked back like a cat.

"Take her outside for some fresh air," Charlie said. "I'll get some water."

* * * * * *

SHARK MEAT

Calista Siddal, Phuket

We were sat on the white sand one day, trying to stay shaded beneath enormous fronds. We were discussing shark meat when two men approached us. They were both tall and looked a few years older than us. One was scruffily handsome, the other scruffily repulsive. Not that he was ugly. He was just really hairy and didn't look like he washed, and when he looked at me his beady eyes stared in an irritating way.

Anyway, he asked us for a light in a grim, rasping voice, smirking as he spoke so that all I could see was the slime on his yellow-brown teeth. I noted Simian had the same reaction to the man as me, repulsion, and he's not very good at hiding his feelings. This is generally why he never makes any friends.

"No... sorry," Sim replied in a nasally English voice. The adverse reaction he has to beggars.

The more handsome scruff studied us both with a cathartic stare.

"Fucking gap year brats..." he muttered, turning away.

"What the fuck is that supposed to mean?" I shouted after him. "All he said was, 'no, sorry'. Who the fuck are you to be such an assuming tosser to a couple of complete strangers?"

I knew this was a bit ridiculous, and I generally controlled these outbursts. Particularly in a foreign place, I felt it wise to stay shtoom as a survival technique. But hell, maybe I just fancied the guy and wanted to get a reaction.

He turned around and came to sit down next to me on the sand, moody eyes meeting mine.

"Ok, chick. Tell me why you ain't a gap year brat?"

"Oh, I am. Absolutely. It's the fairest way you could describe me." I threw him a pack of matches out of my bag.

He exhaled with half a laugh. His companion sat down crossed legged a little away from us, with the same silly grin on his face. Simian shot me a glare for letting them near us.

"What's your name, lass?" the man asked. His accent was English, but on the last word it slipped a little, as though he'd lived in Scotland sometime.

"Cassie," I said. "And this is Simian."

"Nice to meet you. I'm Charlie and this here fella is Wolfgang. He's Deutsch."

"Are you backpackers?" I asked, accepting the cigarette he offered.

"Well, we don't have backpacks," Charlie said.

"General vagrants, then?"

"Something along those lines." He nodded.

"You look like you could do with a wash," I said, breaking up the politeness of the conversation.

He grinned as though he was thinking something wicked. He probably should've given me the creeps, but I trusted something about him.

"You look leik y'could do with bein driven tu the middle ovva Glasgow council estate and left tu fend fa yerself." This came in a thick Scottish accent. He seemed to turn it on and off like a tap.

"I'd be fine. Don't let the plum in my mouth give you the wrong impression."

He raised an eyebrow, quizzically. "What aboot him?" He pointed the burning cigarette end in Simian's direction.

"He's not as posh as me," I replied.

"Don't mean nothing," Charlie rasped.

"What about him?" I motioned to Wolfgang, who looked liked he'd already survived an apocalypse.

"He'd eat his way out," Charlie replied with a deadly serious tone.

I imagined a Glasgow council estate devastated by one man's cannibalism. I flipped quickly back to the present, to the lapping water of aquamarine daydreams, to the red longtail boats tied idly at the shore. I studied each of the men with an even gaze. The trouble with wanting new experiences so as to be able to write better was that the wrong sort of people held so much intrigue. These two both fitted admirably into my thirst for story-telling.

"What brings you to these parts?" Wolfgang asked. His accent was indeed German, and his words were almost a little slurred, as though he might be drunk already. He looked wholly out of place amongst the nearby beach bums, wearing a badly stained vest beneath an old chequered shirt – the colours of which made me feel slightly sick. His skin was as pasty as our own.

I shrugged. "Just travelling around. General curiosity, I suppose."

He nodded and then looked at Simian.

"And you, young ape?"

Simian looked blank. He had no answer he wanted to give. "Um... Cassie wanted to come, and I was bored."

Wolfgang nodded, poking a finger in his ear to extract something disgusting that he discarded towards the sand. "And are you less bored now?"

Simian thought seriously for a minute. "Actually, I feel about the same." He looked a bit shocked, like he'd discovered something about himself. That paradise was not enough.

Wolfgang nodded, as though he'd already known the answer.

"What brings you two here? Given you're too old and pale to be gap year brats," I asked.

Charlie almost invisibly flexed his muscles a little, shifting position as though to cover it. I smiled to myself at this minute display of vanity.

"How old do you think we are?" he asked, attempting to lay on the charisma.

I looked at them both again. Charlie was easier to gauge. The dirt and rottenness of Wolfgang disguised plenty.

"I think you're around twenty-seven or twenty-eight... He's more difficult to tell, in his thirties somewhere I'd suspect."

"Pretty close," Charlie said. "Though Wolfgang tells me he's hundreds of years old, I'm not sure I believe him. And you two, you're what, nineteen? Twenty?"

"Twenty," I agreed.

"I wish I was twenty now, instead of when I was twenty," Wolfgang murmured with haphazard remorse.

"When were you twenty?" I asked.

He shifted his seat and stared out to sea. Slowly he looked back with a lonely expression, free of humorous teasing.

"I live my life in dog years. But each year is an actual year. I age one year in seven years. I can't remember exactly when I was twenty. It was a very long time ago, and frankly a lot happened that it's nicer to forget."

Charlie laughed loudly over him. As though to persuade us it was all a big joke, and not genuine lunacy (or simply genuine, how should I know?).

"Gosh," said Simian. "Would you look at the time? We've got somewhere we need to be..." He grabbed my arm and hoisted me up.

I smirked, picking my bag up and waving farewell to the two men, before he dragged me off down the beach, swearing skittishly under his breath.

* * * * * *

KAFKA'S PORRIDGE

Wolfgang, Dreamscape

In a library I sit alone, trapped. Half my face has mutated like the tree man, boil upon boil, gnarled and pretty as a hag's ass with piles. Some kind of antennae protrudes from my scalp and my eye is encased in armour. *Amour.*

I spazz around the room like a frustrated moth with beetle legs and stripy beetle juice, chewing rotten fruits left by my kin. The room is lined with dusty old shelves and dusty old books. I consume their words with a voracious appetite which seems wasted on the fruit, which rots and smells so that I feel like my very skin is rotten fruit. Coated in that green powdery mould which flakes off to the touch. So that my entire person disintegrates at the thought of you trying to give me a reassuring hug. I read and I read and I read, inside my biblioteque coffin, a box full of compartments for my selves. A leg here. A persona there. A yellow rotten toenail shelved next to a slightly damp copy of *A Midsummer Night's Dream*.

My confinement was never voluntary. They shelved me here. They placed me carefully inside the correct category so as to protect themselves. But now the door is left open and I could potentially escape. I sit and stare and a little panic begins to tiptoe inside my brain. It steps up into the little spotlight in the centre of the stage, rat ta tat, the music begins and the little panic begins a little tap dance. As I move towards the door, he rattles my frame until my limbs are not my own. I retreat back into the books. Inside the books I'm safe from everything except myself. And I cannot commit myself to suicide because I'm mad. And a true madman doesn't know that he'd be better off dead. It is almost Catch 22. Maybe only Catch 21 ½.

I am institutionalised by my own library. The world outside which once seemed so duly dull is now a fearful place. I don't think I'm ready yet. My beard is not quite long enough for starters, and its growth isn't helped by the bits of insect face that've mutated my skin. I hang sloppy little pods of gunk from shelves; they'd grow to beings themselves if only they could be impregnated by some other. People shrink with a little horror at me, at my webs and stripy juices... even my own kin. What can a poor boy do in the face of such things? I try to laugh off their horror but my laugh is a cacophony that echoes in hysteria. A mother's voice screaming down the phone in denial. It was so cold that day, I remember. I walked on dumbly in the cold. I watched her cry again and hope her tears will wash us all away again.

* * * * * * *

SUCKER PAUNCH

Bryn McLarey, Oxford

"Oh looky," Juliette said in that teasing voice. "There's an article here on 'How to tackle your beer belly'."

She waved it in mae direction, and I responded with a sour-humoured expression. "I strongly suspect that involves drinking less beer..."

"It may be just a bit of paunch now, but when you hit your forties it'll be a different matter," she said.

"I don't care. I'm not vain." I tried tu concentrate on the television.

"You spend an awful lot of time looking in the mirror for someone who isn't vain."

I pointed at the television, and exclaimed, half in jest, "Woman! Do you mind? I'm trying to fester my contempt for Jeremy Clarkson!"

She stood up and bent tu kiss mae cheek. "I'll still love you when your twenty-three stone anyway. I'm just thinking of your health... I'm off out now."

Something in her breezy tone made me suspicious. "Who did you say you're meeting?"

"I didn't say. Cameron, actually. Just for a casual catch-up," she said.

There's no such thing when it comes to exes.

"Oh," I said.

"You're okay with that, aren't you?" she said. She didn't want me tu be totally okay with it, as this would imply that I took her for granted.

"Sure," I left a dramatic pause, "but if he so much as casually brushes your thigh with his greasy mitts, I'll flush his head down the toilet in Yates." I guffawed slightly at the look on Cam's face at even entering Yates.

This seemed tu satisfy her. She picked up her handbag and fleetingly kissed me again.

"Have a pleasant evening," I said dryly, glancing her up and down tu note what was on show, and wus satisfied that the answer wasn't much.

The door clicked shut and mae Oxford flat was left in quiet, save for Clarkson's smug voice. I went tu the fridge and selected a bottle of beer, resting it sedately atop Juliette's magazine article as I dialled for the Chinese takeaway.

Nearly two hours later I wus napping in front of Newsnight with a full belly, when the intercom buzzed.

I answered drowsily. "Hello?"

There wus a distinct sob at the other end. "It's Ju, can you let me in?"

I buzzed her in, shaking sleep from mae body. I greeted her a few moments later at my door, deciphering in a few seconds that she'd had a few glasses of wine and wus crying. I gave her a big firm hug and sat her down.

"What's happened?"

She struggled back sobs, tu try to speak. "Um... he was late, so I had a few drinks... and then he wasn't very nice." She trailed off to blow her nose loudly in the tissue I'd handed her.

I kissed her forehead. "What did he say?"

She continued struggling to speak, gasping little bits of air and rubbing the tears off her cheeks. "Um... not much really, I can't remember." She snuffled intu the tissue for a bit. I puzzled over what to do to stop her crying. There's only sae much shoulder-rubbing and forehead kissing I can deal with before I get I bit impatient. Then I remembered something.

"You want some food?" I asked, waving my leftover Chow Mein in front of her.

She shook her head at first as if I wus being ridiculous, but alcohol makes a person emotional and hungry. So after a pause she took it and the fork I gave her, and began slowly eating some. The concentration of doing this – and the happy endorphins food gives – stopped her sobbing, and she sat there quietly eating.

I grant this is probably not a foolproof method to get a drunk person to stop crying. But there was one time I wus walking home from the pub back in Glasgow, when I happened upon a couple of first-year students who'd just been mugged. The girl was sat on the floor in hysterics, squealing that she wanted tu talk to her mum. After failing with the shoulder-patting, fae some reason I offered the girl the chips I'd been eating before I happened upon these unlucky pups. I thought she'd wail and throw them back at me, but instead she sat there quietly eating them. She soon sobered a little so that we could persuade her that waking her poor mother at 1 a.m. with little darling's tales of woe wus *a very bad idea*.

The intercom buzzed again and Juliette and I exchanged looks.

I answered it. "Hello?"

"Hi, is that Charles? Cameron here."

"I rather don't think she wants to speak to you," I said.

Jules shook her head furiously, looking as though she wus going tu break into tears again.

"Could I have a 'chat' with you then?" Cam said with a slight challenge in his voice. I raised my eyebrows. "Okay, I'll be out in a moment." I hung up, slightly bewildered, but mainly apprehensive that I'd have tu control maesel not to smack the smug cunt... preferably intu a wall. The battle between Charlie and Bryn wus beginning inside me.

"He wants to talk to me." I shrugged.

She looked apprehensive now. "What if he tries to hit you?" she said.

I laughed. "I'm more worried I'll break *his* nose."

"So am I!" she said. "Be careful... nice Oxford boys don't break peoples' noses!"

"Jaws...? Arms...?" I asked devilishly. "Are you more concerned I'll blow my cover than hurt little Cameron?"

She shrugged. "If you get arrested everyone will find out."

"I won't get arrested," I said as convincingly as I could.

I went downstairs, shoving mae keys in mae pocket. I had mind he might try tu barge in, so I stepped carefully outside and slammed the door after. It wus beginning to drizzle. I regretted that I'd not brought a coat. He had on a velvet blazer, which wus little more use. He wus shivering but the adrenaline kept him a bit warm. The sky wus only indigo, as it wus summer, supposedly. Charlie would think this a terribly awkward situation... Bryn would demand to know what he'd said to upset Jules.

"Yes?" I said politely.

"Is she okay?" he asked.

It struck me when I'd first met him, I'd felt the underdog to his middleclass arrogance. But the fact wus in this guise of mine, he considered me the toff.

"Well, um, yes, no thanks to you." I tried to keep any anger from mae voice.

"It's just *ridiculous*," he said. He waved his arms dramatically, as only a thespian could. There was a little malice lurking. "She's over-reacting as usual!"

He wus quite wild-eyed. I could feel the prickle of negative energy in the air. It wus strange. I felt the burning rage that envelops me, but I felt somehow apart from it. As though I could observe it, push mae head above the water and take a deep breath of semi-rational air.

"This is pointless. It's cold. I'm going back inside," I said, turning away.

"*She'll never love anyone as much as she loves me!*" he announced.

I clenched a fist and then let it free again. I gave him full eye contact tu show I had no fear of him, but I would not be dragged intu a fight, then I opened the door and stepped inside.

Mae parting shot – "Don't be such a bloody drama queen."

The door slammed behind me.

* * * * * *

NETHERLAND

Calista Siddal, Phuket

The bodies writhed in the sweat and heat, and love of their own sin. Flesh lost to darkness, flames on sticks dancing out of time, trying to paint the pieces of people. A rounded forcep, the apples of their grinning faces, the ugly swelling of their gurning mouths. I sketched them out in my head, hoping to put them to paper.

Charlie touched my shoulder. "Hey."

I turned absent-mindedly. He was looking at me quite meaningfully. Funny how when I feel so vague there's no flutter of nerves.

He handed me a drink and kept looking at me. "Lost in thought?"

I took a sip of the drink and then wondered on the possibility that it could be spiked. "Do you think if I took drugs, I'd be a better writer?" I asked.

I have a habit I can't help, of treating people a few years older as though they know stuff. They like this; they don't realise it's a test of sorts. The music was loud and I was unsure at first if he'd heard what I said. He motioned that we should sit down on the sand. I complied.

"You'd be tuu busy having fun to write," he said drolly.

We had to sit too close, in order to be able to hear one another. His body heat was at first unbearable.

"What about Lord Byron, and Hunter S. Thompson... and Jim Morrison?" I suggested.

"All the people you're talking about were fully fookin mental before they started taking drugs. Most people who take drugs to write think at the time they're writing something genius. When they wake up sober it's complete and utter drivel." He leaned towards me, waving a hand in the air, watching the reception of my face.

"I suppose I just feel sometimes that there are places in my writing I want to get to, but can't... my sanity or something is in the way."

Brief laughter flickered in his expression. "You see drug use as a kind of temporary madness?"

There was some glint then in his eyes, something I wanted, something I needed to snatch at. And now my nerves fluttered and my sense of detachment left, so I flattered him.

"How do you know so much about stuff? You don't seem the type who would bother going to university or anything?"

"University is not the only fountain of knowledge from which yuu can drink, pet." He paused. "Mind expanding drugs aren't the only way tu tap into your subconscious. I'm sure you know that."

"See, it's that whole term 'mind-expanding'?" I exclaimed.

He rolled his body around so that he was knelt facing me and put his hands on either side of my head. "Feel all the gunge and mouldy slops, half solidified inside there... growing and expanding inside your skull, pushing against the sides... trapped, throbbing..."

Nether Ed's head began exploding in slow motion, bits of brain slopping out all over the place.

Charlie leant to kiss me then, but a girl with an artificially expanded mind careered into us, giggling uncontrollably, her eyes rolling, swollen and vulnerable like fish out of bowls.

"Sorry!" she spluttered, dancing back towards the throng.

"Shall we go and sit by the water?" Charlie said.

We moved far down the beach and sat with our toes poking in the shallows, which crept up and then slunk away. My skirt soaked up some of the wet sand.

"Can I read some?" Charlie asked, pointing to the edge of my notebook, poking out of the small leather satchel bag I had in my lap. I handed over the worn book reluctantly. He had to peer so very hard to read any in the darkness. We sat in quietude. The sweaty music throbbed behind us like my heart inside my brain.

(The bloody fist)

The gentle waves were lapping, receding, crawling back out to a sighing ocean.

"I like the way yuu romanticise your dark places..." he said after a short time had elapsed.

"Why are they mine?" I asked.

"Well, I hope you'll romanticise mine. It'll make me a lot more palatable," he said with coy charm.

"It's a bit stuck in suburbia I think." I hesitated. "I suppose that's why I wanted to come travelling, even to disgusting tourist places."

"Ah, the classic feeling of the middle class kid coming of age and realising how small their scope of experience is," he murmured, a tad too condescendingly.

"Thanks, I like being told I'm a cliché," I replied.

"We're all clichés."

"And technically I'm upper class, not middle class," I added.

"You say that like it's a bad thing. Don't ever try to be middle anything... middlebrow, centrist, middle class. Be a maverick, else you'll die of boredom."

"Isn't that just rebellion for rebellion's sake?" I said.

"All rebellion is 'rebellion for rebellion's sake'. We only manufacture strong feelings on issues because our egos want us tu stand out, to matter because we know we don't matter. Humans are inherently selfish." He pronounced the words swiftly with such gusto, I could almost second guess he'd stolen this notion, or repeated it many times before.

"That's a bit harsh," I said.

"Yes, but it's survival of the fittest. How does being generous or rebellious benefit us in terms of evolution? It makes us stand out tu potential 'mates'. Intelligence is as much a commodity to attract the opposite sex as good looks." He paused, trying to read my expression again. "Anyway, I'm rambling."

"How come you hang out with that crazy tramp? How does that help attract mates?" I smirked.

He laughed. "I'm talking about humans in general, not maeself!" He scratched his jaw line. "I dunno about Wolfgang, I've known him a wee while now and he's just the most honest human being. He's a fucking nutter, but we all are. We just hide it better."

"Am I?" I asked.

"Time will tell," he replied.

* * * * * * *

THE FLOUNDER

Claudia McLeod, Sheffield

Drinkin coffee and watchin the pale entanglement of wrists. I spose it says sommat maire about *me* that I think relationships bring out the brittle emotions in us.

Cuan and Roxy mayde sense together – too much sense. There were a suicide pact in between their lovin glances. They were smitten wi' self-destruction. I wanted to mother them both. Burrah think I'm lyke the useless trailer-trash mom who's distracted by booze or sommat, and leaves the toddlers in the responsibility of a harf-blind sheep dog. They'd disappear f'days on end an I'd wonder if they'd found a lovers' rock to jump off.

Then they'd reappear, seemin exhilarated by the mystery of unspoken adventures. For all I knew they jus holed up in a bedroom and had loadsa sex, but that would be normal.

"What ya been up to?" I asked, tryin not ta sound nosey.

"We went to Castle Market yesterday and got some fish," Roxy mumbled happily. This accounted furra few hours at least.

"Did ya tape it to the neighbour's window, Q? I heard a rumour ya did that once," I said.

He giggled. "Have you heard about that?" he asked Roxy. "I don't like to tell the story myself of course. I'm too modest."

"If we sit in silence long enough you'll spill." I pushed the gauze down on my cafetiere and poured the coffee inta mugs.

He giggled agen as though he wont gonna be able to speak. "I had a bit of a disagreement with the lad next door. He threw a CD out of the window at me..."

"Why?" Roxy peered curiously at him.

"Oh, I think I just annoyed him. He said I looked like Kings of Leon or something. Which is unfair, because they're hairy, and I can barely grow a beard." He paused, aware he were ramblin, and then rambled on. "So he threw their CD at me... It was a bit shit, the album, I mean. Anyway, we had a running feud so my housemate had bought this fish he'd never remembered to cook. It was on the turn. So I climbed up and Sellotaped it to my neighbour's bedroom window. It was a hot day so within *hours* there were flies all over it laying maggots. It was absolutely putrid."

"Oh," Roxy said. "Was he very angry?"

"He filmed it for an art project, the pretentious sod," Cuan said.

"Did he get you back?" she asked.

"Well, we're kind of friends now. He's actually a real funny guy. I think he was quite impressed. He might be sneaky and be saving up some vengeance though..."

Roxy wrapped her hands around the mugga coffee and took a thoughtful sip. "We cooked the fish." she glanced ta me. "It was Panga... really nice."

Cuan sparked up. "There's meant to be a party in the woods tonight, you fancy coming?" he asked.

I cocked an eyebrow. "I'm not entirely sure I'm not too auld for that shit... What's Charlie up to? He mekks me feel young and fun in comparison."

Roxy scrunched her nose. "He's kind of avoiding us, I think."

"Well, I'll see if I can persuade him," I said. "And if we happen ta run into you in't bushes, so be it..."

* * * * * *

IN THE DOOM ALL DAY

Simian Thomas, Phuket

Hostelised insomnia. Are we asleep or awake? Words are exchanged – friendly words. Indeed sometimes the room murmurs to me. But they're restless and uneasy words. I'm exhausted but I cannot sleep, and neither can the city outside. The room is not a place to collectively sleep. It's a place to collectively sweat. We join our filthy, uneasy subconscious into one mass of gloop which revels in its own skeletal obesity. I think I've lost a pound in sweat already. Which given I lose my appetite in the heat should mean that I'll expire shortly. The bunks creak. Bodies shift. The incompatible sleeping habits of ten strangers are joining in holy matrimony with the consummation of grunting and the rearrangement of hair and body parts.

I am just a little scared by this close proximity to people talking in their sleep, living out dreams of rapture and torture, chases down dark alleyways. Words blurted and blurring to incomprehension, smeared across the ceiling, greased with human fat.

"Air conditioning? Twin room? En suite?" I begged Cassie, the first morning after a night of this.

She smirked. "That was a good night's sleep. Just you wait."

She was right. I began to appreciate nights when I didn't have to step over a naked body passed out on the dorm room floor to go for a pee at night. I began to appreciate sharing a bunk with someone who spoke of *'Mister Duck and the Bitch'* in his sleep, tossing and turning. It sure beat someone bringing back a one night stand and clamouring away for forty odd minutes, which happened one time.

What does one do in these situations? Pretend not to notice?

I left the room in disgust and went into the narrow corridor, the uneven floor marking my bare feet. It was even hotter, as there was no ceiling fan. I rested my torso against the wall. I could still hear the screams of joy. A small man was loitering at the end of the hall. He peered at me with narrow dark eyes.

"American?" he grunted.

"English," I replied.

I'm not sure what I hate more, listening to other people have sex or making small talk with strangers. He sauntered towards me, strung between arrogant nonchalance and a loose grip on gravity.

"Capitalism," he slurred, "... is built on a hierarchy of understanding."

"Iceland?" I said to Cassie the next day.

She nodded. "Right after Indonesia."

... Five countries away.

A girl is tugging my shoulder, waking me. I peer over at her and she cackles but I can't turn my body in the bed to look at her properly...

I woke the next morning not knowing if it'd been real. Cassie was hanging out with this Charlie character a fair bit. This should've given me some sense of freedom. Instead I felt trapped in a body that hated the heat, hated the dorm, hated the uncomfortable company of others. I feared getting lost amongst the scramble of streets and extraordinary buildings, I feared the pleasant jungle. I looked out to sea and longed romantically for it to somehow swallow me. I tiptoed towards it and as it moved towards me I tiptoed back coyly. In this way we danced back and forth teasing one another.

I looked down the narrow corridor again. Now there was a tall man, his head tipped so as not to scrape the ceiling, lank hair... and those stained teeth – rat's teeth. A rat would've be proud of them.

"Simian... ape," he acknowledged. I was fairly sure he wasn't even staying at our hostel.

"Wolfgang," I replied reluctantly.

"Don't stay in The Doom all day." He shook his knowing head. "There's a pet cemetery a few streets away, I show you?"

I nodded thoughtfully. "I'll get my camera."

He grinned.

* * * * * * *

LITTLE OWL

Claudia McLeod, Sheffield

Owlets. Little faces, big eyes in't dark, patterned on wallpaper. I looked around tha room. It were like a child's – not even an aulder child, a toddler's decor, or a mish-mash of ages. It did feel odd as twenty-sommats to be sat there. Wi' careful, mechanical precision I rolled a joint. Charlie and Cuan watched with blank fizzogs.

"Thas a nice shade a wallpaper, Q. What colour is that?"

He peered into the eyes a the lit'l cartoon owlets in't linin paper. He looked back at me and shrugged. "I'd go for cyan, but you'd have to check the B & Q colour chart to be sure."

"This is a pile a shit. What tha fook am I doin here?" Charlie said.

I nodded slightly ta the misplaced beats of music comin from Cuan's old stereo.

"You got somewhere better to be, Charlie-Brown?" Cuan asked, raising his eyebrows in mock space-monkey surprise. He were sat cross-legged on the single bed. The duvet was some sick floral design, all pastel shades, sommat to put in the guest room.

Charlie picked up a rough wooden box that looked like a drunk wi'a dirty hammer'd hacked it together. "What's this?"

"Cuban cigars, my friend," Cuan said, this time jus one eyebrow raised.

"Can we smoke some?" Charlie asked.

"Nadda, they're works of fucking art." He scrambled the box lid open and held one up. "Look how beautifully made that is. You think Duchamp put that much love into his urinal?" He ran it aneath his nose, absorbin the aroma.

"Besides you *have* to sip fine rum while smoking these badgers and I don't have any."

"Who's Duchamp?" I asked.

"The supposedly original *conceptual* artist. Though many suspect he ripped his ideas off a chick... They call that patri-art," Charlie muttered.

Cuan nodded. "Indeed, brother," he said in his Alex the Droog voice.

"Cumon, lad, let me smoke just one. Don't yuu ever practise the art of can?"

Cuan shook his head stubborn'ly.

"Charlie, how tha fook d'ya know soo much about art?" I asked, rummagin around the room for a lighter, tossin objects about wi' much disregard for their value to tha hoardin squirrel-boy.

Cuan's tone altered to a high pitched growl. "He's a tricksy one I tells you," he said as abstract explanation.

Charlie snatched the blunt from me and dug a lighter from his pocket, gruntin bad-temperedly. "Any chance we cun havva conversation with Cuan, not Schméagol or his seven fookin friends?"

"Where's our Roxy tonight?" I asked.

"...Roxy Disco." Cuan said

"Serious'ly..." I added.

"She's hanging out with that boy... Steve? Dave...? I think she's fucking him, whatever his name is." A flash a genuine doubt passed beneath Cuan's humour.

I took the joint off Charlie and took a drag, enjoyin the pause which only the music could fill, brain tunin int't wiring. I exhaled off ta the side. "Roxy dun't fook around, she's a closet prude," I said confidently.

"Yeah," Charlie drawled. "Has she fooked *you* yet? I bet she hasnae."

Cuan laffed and shuffled off outtah the room. Charlie nodded at me in a satisfied way.

"Why d'ya haffta push people's buttons all't time? What d'you have against ya friends?"

He let outtah belch a careless spite. "Someone's gotta." He took a cigar from't box and moved ta purrit in his pocket.

"Fookin put that back, ya cunt, else I'll start reducin yar shit-heap of a life to rubble," I said.

He shrugged careless'ly. Cuan returned wi' some bottles of beer.

"Okay, Charlie. Why are you so jealous and vindictive ahl the time? Whas wi' this great big chip on ya shoulder?" I asked.

He stood up. "I'm noo gonna hang oot like a fookin middle-class teenager with you twos, smokin weed and being melodramatic." He gev me an acidic look and left through slamming doors.

Cuan sighed a big sigh, openin bottles a beer wi' his eyes ta the floor.

"He took a cigar," I said, apologetic'ly.

Cuan smiled a strange weak smile. "I knew he would, but he won't enjoy it. It'll taste of his conscience. Silly bloke."

"Why're you always soo forgivin?" I asked a lit'l angrily.

He shrugged. "I get it. I've been in his shoes, besides Roxy is fucking adorable. I dunno why she likes me..." His eyes gleamed wi' uncertain happiness. His phone buzzed. He peered down at the message. "She misses me, why does she say she misses me?"

I belted him lightly around tha head. "Pull yersel together, ya big wuss."

He put the phone down on't side and relit the joint that were sat forgotten on the edge a the ashtray.

"Why don't you answer 'er?" I asked.

"I dunno what to say." He smiled that desperate smile that mekks me see a skull and a collection of muscles and nerve endings where a face ought to be.

I wrote a message ta Roxy missel sayin *'Cuan misses you, please come round'*.

"What are you doing?" Cuan asked.

I ignored him, nabbin the dregs a the joint. My phone buzzed up a message a moment later.

'Why can't he tell me himself?' Roxy asked.

I rolled my eyes in defeat. Maybe I'm just as bad. "She won't come round unless ya confess that you miss her..."

"Well, you'll keep me company, won't you?" he pleaded.

"Company?" I said. "Are ya a lonely O.A.P or sommat?"

He shrugged, and built a wall back up. "Okay, I'm off out then..."

"Why don't we go and meet them, an I'll seduce Dave fer ya, and gerrim out the way?"

"I think it's Steve," he said doubtfully. "But yeah, that would be very nice of you."

I messaged Roxy to ask where they were... "The Grapes. Fookin hell, not bin there since we did that awful gig in that upstairs box room. The acoustics were bollocks. Was you there that night?" I asked.

He didn't answer furra minute. He were fussing around for a jacket or sommat. "Um, no, I came to the Boardwalk gig. That was really good."

"Yeah, we were supportin someone then..." I gathered ma stuff together, wrappin myself up in a scarf and hat, ready for the onslaught a the blustery night outside. Cuan were still faffing so I pushed him bossily in tha direction a the door.

"Do I look okay?" he asked.

"You look lyke shit, Cuan. You always look lyke shit, it's how she lykes ya."

He looked at me strangely. "What d'you mean?"

"Ya look lyke a troubled genius, honey. Chicks dig that, apparent'ly."

* * * * * * * *

AN APOLOGETIC APOCALYPSE

Wolfgang, Bangkok

You can ask how many dead people I've seen, and I can ask you the same and you can say none, but the truth is that you don't know. How many street sleepers have you walked past, without checking their pulse?

I'm in the black. In the hole. Wormholes through time and endless darkness. Passages through immortality, crawling through the Earth. The body remains at death's door yet wanders on, fingertips scrabbling at the bricks and earth. The inside of my throat is exhausted from thirst and great (w)retching of breath. My throat is the tunnel. It swallows me and I wander through it, endless fingertips scratching the walls until they bleed onto me and I bleed inside.

Actually it's darkness.

The tunnels talk to me of the *city of the immortals*, of a death never reached, of a ring of sunlight climbed towards, but never touched... Skin turning to ash, washed away like silk spun down drains. The tunnels talk to me of the bottom of a whisky bottle. This is an entirely different conversation, and some might say a more comfortable slumber, but no more real. Death is the whole thing swallowed glass and all, waking up next to a pretty angular face, not a flea-ridden mongrel.

The Kaiser and I had left the doomed Phuket just before Christmas and travelled to Bangkok. We were inside the dirty haze of a Boxing Day hangover when we heard the news of a huge earthquake in the Indian Ocean, the repercussions of which one dares not remember too well.

* * * * * *

BUBBLES GO UP

Simian Thomas, The Indian Ocean

Underneath, the water is a different world. Below the surface I have a different body. It's lighter sometimes, but now it feels heavy. The water has hidden currents that suck you down and throw you away. I remember the black night sea again, but now it's insanely bright down here – the light stings my eyes. I'm attacked by objects, strange objects, the debris of everyday domestic life. A cup and a child's toy flee past me. Something wooden hits me hard in the shoulder, scraping away a patch of skin to sting and bleed into the salty water. Strangely I recall shark attacks and how they can smell blood from miles away. My limbs are flailing, my eyeballs roll in my head like a frightened horse. My mouth gapes open like a hideous blow up doll, wanting oxygen, instead breathing dirty water into my lungs – my heart is exploding inside me.

    I realise which way is up. Maybe once you jumped off a board into a deep diving pool, and for a moment you were unsure which way. For one millisecond you panicked very slightly, before following the bubbles upwards and grinning from adrenaline as you broke the surface. Yes, bubbles go up. Except, I think I saw something about whirlpools, when the whirlpool is about to start sucking, the bubbles go down.

The objects were above me, made of more floatable material than flesh and bone and panic. They were bobbing overhead. I kicked out towards the surface which was shadowy with these objects, in contrast to the luminosity of the water. My leg hit something that was sinking and I glimpsed the face of a child, bloated and yellow. I couldn't reach out – I was not a hero – it was gone.

The objects were blocking my way to the air. I felt such anger for them. They were dead objects that didn't need air, yet their advanced buoyancy disabled me. I snatched at them, trying to break between them, but there were so many riding the current together. I swung at something, a piece of wood, maybe part of a roof once, my fingers gripped it now and they felt air. Some other object hit my hands, like a baddie determined to stamp on my fingers until I fell from the roof top. It was all a blunt pain now. I held on grimly and pulled with every last bit of energy I had.

My gaping mouth tasted air, sucking fresh life into me. I looked like some horror movie creature coming back from the dead, Lestat crawling from the swamp. Some great hand reached out and grabbed my t-shirt at the back, which began to rip, but another hand grabbed my arm and I was pulled clean out of the water. I seemed to be rising up into the air, my consciousness failing.

I don't know how many moments later before I spluttered and coughed back to life, seawater pouring out of my mouth like vomit. I looked up at the man who, in my dreamlike state, looked like some mythic warrior –

brown weathered skin over slanting cheekbones, and narrow eyes full of immortal wisdoms. He spoke a few words in the language of the Gods to me, which was very possibly Thai.

We were stationary now, clinging to the rooftop of a building not swept down by the sea. I lay looking up at the sky and dreamed of Cassie. I saw her sinking slowly through that luminous water, red hair spread out in endless waves framing a pale white face, green eyes wide with wonder, yet blank with death. My body ached with self-hate. I'd always thought I would like myself more if I died young; I'd lost the chance to become a tragedy, to be deified by death so that everyone forgot what a pathetic cunt I was.

* * * * * * *

BUTTERFLIES & JELLY

Roxanne Ratcliffe, Sheffield

There was a faint thump-thump on the door. The front door it must've been, but so gentle, and me in the attic – how did I ever hear it? I was lying zombified on the bed, wide awake in a sweaty restless stupor. It's not just sleeplessness when it's hot. It is some frothy waking nightmare of extreme boredom, broken by my body attempting to slip casually to slumber before my subconscious roots out an image to terrorize it back to wakefulness. It must've been this heightened yet dumbstruck state that let me hear the soft thump, thump and feel not fearful uncertainty but a sense of calm.

Without hurry, I pulled some jammy bottoms on over my pants and, feeling conscious of my ugly white feet, pat-patted down the two flights of stairs to the front door.

"Is that you?" I asked the door.

"Yes," the gruff tone returned, coughing slightly over the word.

I unlatched it and peered into the meek early-morning light. Cuan's eyes met mine, but instead of a satisfied sense of safety, they slipped away with fearful hyper-consciousness. His collarbones were creeping towards his cheeks, his hands shoved in pockets. I wanted to hug him and cling on until he relaxed, but I was too nervous.

"Are you okay?" I asked. I could see in his eyes that he wasn't, something had tipped him over the edge.

"I just want to be more interesting," he said, with a sense of hopelessness. Not in a finite way of doubting self-perception, but in a confused way, in a mutilated brain worms way. He seemed to think for a moment. "Can we go somewhere?"

"Yes. Where?" I asked.

"Dirty hammer," he mumbled cryptically.

"I'll get dressed."

Cuan had been going through odd transitions in moods the past few days. He'd shown me the cellar at his Dad's house, where he stored an unimaginable collection of paraphernalia (or junk if you will). It'd seemed very personal, him showing me this stuff – the found photographs, the red spectacles, the flat footballs, the old film reel scrawled with the words 'John Carpenter's *The Fog*'.

He'd written on the inside of my wrist '*Butterflies & Jelly*', refusing to explain why, and then said quietly and forlornly, "I wish I could live down here... I wish at night

I could put myself away in a box on a shelf, I wish I could be an object... a collectable."

I hadn't even been sure if he was joking. He often did things like that. But he didn't smile – he just stood up and left.

When I've had no sleep, time elapses in a most peculiar way. We struggled on up the stony track. We'd been walking for an hour or so, but when you are in this lost state, every minute seems elongated and shrunken at the same time. It hazes around and you lose any sense of how far you've gone, of the exact sound of your foot dislodging a pebble from the path. My heartbeat ached next to my lungs, which sucked at the fresh, clean air. We'd not spoken for some time. I was glad, as everything he said unnerved me some.

He stopped and looked up the steep green hill to our left. He looked at me and smiled with a destabilised sense of awe, as though we'd only just met. "Up here," he said, climbing the stile.

I followed and we trudged up the steepening slope. He took my hand, loosely tugging me behind him. I grabbed the back of his jeans with the other hand, watching the grass pass beneath my feet as we clambered. At the top I raised my chin. The light turns the ordinary boy's world majestic. Grass lined with dry stone walls carved fields which fell away to the valley. Sheffield shined beneath us like lost treasure. In the fields, furry faces gazed at us with half-dozing eyes and ruminating jaws, disarming goofiness and fluffy bouffants.

"Llamas!" I said excitedly.

Cuan grinned. He'd somehow retained himself by bringing me here, mission completed, job done. 'If I can make Roxy smile I will be better.'

"Alpacas," he said.

I felt sleepy then. The day was gently warming. It would be a hot walk back. We found a suitable hillock and Cuan lay down, one arm draped over his eyes to shade from the light. I wriggled down next to him like a cat trying to get comfortable, pressing my cheek to his chest. He wrapped his other arm around my shoulders. I fluttered my eyes, taking a few last loving glances at the daybreak and the screwdled t-shirt. Then I slept, a deep satisfied sleep. His breathing slowly settled and his body relaxed, but I didn't know if he slept, too.

* * * * * * *

ALPHABET SPAGHETTI

Haydn Antoine, The Midlands

Yes, I regretted all the gushing... Once I was there actually speaking to her, I regretted all the gushing. Even though she couldn't possibly know, my face flushed with the thought that she knew.

We were sat as two professionals, her knee touching mine casually, unintentionally. It was strange circumstances in which I was interviewing Ms Claudia McLeod, in her friend's attic room, accessed through a hole in the floor with basic wooden steps. It was an artist's studio, but I was worried about the hole in the floor, worried I'd fall down it and make an ass of myself.

"I'm gonna write an article about this band – Claudia & the Mistakes." I'd pointed out the picture inside the CD case to Cookie. "Because *she*'s amazing."

"You're promoting a band because the singer is hot? How refreshing." She discarded it.

"Not hot, *amazing*. Well, she is hot, but that's not the point, I promise. She's just got incredible presence, and a great voice, and this song..." I flicked the CD player on a couple of tracks to *White Girl Blues*, and sat listening in awe, frustrated by Cookie's bored expression. She only liked folk music, or anything you needed to be stoned to appreciate. Crap, lame folk as well. The kind of crap, lame folk, which gives good folk a bad name.

Now in the same room as Claudia, all the intelligent questions I wanted to ask were failing me. I couldn't stop looking at her lips, they were a strange shape when she spoke. Had she noticed? There was so much energy around her. Her eyes were heavy and sarcastic and full of meaning.

I looked at the pages of my notes. "White Girl Blues. It's a great song, how did you come about writing it?" I asked carefully.

She bit her lip a little bit. When she spoke with that North Yorkshire lilt, every phrase was deadpan, the meaning of it left ambiguous.

"I were goin through a lot of really insignificant shit at that time. I've never appreciated how easy I've had it, I've always hated it, and mayde it into an obstacle. I were listenin to Jackson C. Frank and Robert Johnson a lot. But then also the Eels... I suppose they took effect. The soul a' the music, but also how it's bin ripped off."

I nodded, having little idea what to make of this. "Where's the band from?"

"Allover. Well am frum Ripon in Yorkshire. The rest a them are from't Midlands area – Cov, Derby, Loughborough. Thas why am kickin about these parts."

As I went to leave, I paused part way down the steps, so only my torso sat above the hole. I hesitated and fumbled my words.

"Are you tryin to ask me out?" she asked with a slightly ludicrous tone, the thick layers of mascara and eyeliner blinking me away like a pesky insect.

I coughed and shrugged. At least there was a hole in the floor to swallow me if she shot me down.

"I'm kinda seein someone," she said. "And when I say kinda, I mean seriousl'y... but then shit happens, people die. I'll keep ya number."

I gulped. "Oh... good."

I went down to the front door, through which her keyboardist was just arriving.

"Hi," I said "Jody? Isn't it?"

"Hi." He shook my hand. "Haydn, the music hack, I take it?"

I nodded and said polite goodbyes, quaking as I walked down the street. I ought to be past getting crushes on musicians. I know that loving a person's art and their public persona is quite different to the reality of knowing them. But then, if my life is an infatuation with music surely it's inescapable. I pondered this while grinning like an idiot to myself.

And yes, then all of a sudden it occurred to me: Was Jody the boyfriend? I got the train back to Derby, trundled home and then geeked it up on the internet for a bit. My suspicions were quickly confirmed, not through actual information, but what every web stalker/voyeur will be familiar with – the suggestive photo, or better several.

I rattled on about my day to Rufio, while he cooked up a pasta sauce and raised his eyebrows in readiness for mocking me.

"You like a weird lickle groupie, man! You gonna go whack one off to a photo of 'er now?" He spooned sausage and tomato pasta into my bowl.

"No. I, unlike you, am a gentleman," I said, wrapping fettuccine around my fork and promptly ditching half of it in my lap en route to mouth.

"They say clumsiness is linked to the emotions, gentle-Blondie. I know what you is like. You gonna proper dwell on this. S'not helfee." He shook his head dubiously.

* * * * * * *

A DAISY CUTTER

Bryn McLarey, Oxford

As I slide across the wet ground, the mud sloshes apart. As mae skin meets it, it's coated, a cold sensation that will dry and crack and rip around my leg hair, once heated. A small sharp stone also finds mae skin and carefully carves a neat cat-scratch reaching up to mae knee. It's a rainy Sunday morning – the best days, all somehow the saime, cold air ripping intu mae lungs tu be spluttered back out again. The pitch sae battered and churned that it's virtually all brown. Bogs emerging in front a'the goal mouths in which youngsters wrestle out an eternal flurry of feet. I make contact with the ball, badly though – a daisy cutter easily captured by the goalie.

We were lying in bed post-coitus one night and I wus thinking of mae muddy youth (I wus younger and thinner then). I wus all ready for a good kip and dreams of waking in the morning and hopefully fitting in more sex before breakfast. But there was that air of a question, and I suspected mae dear girlfriend had other ideas.

"Celtic or Rangers?" Juliette gazed up at the ceiling as though it wus a casual 'getting to know yuu' question, instead of one steeped in years of knuckle-headedness. I sighed. I'd known this sort of thing would be coming. Ju was an educated lass, with the curiosity of a fool-some feline.

And I wus lying in the mud, watching in slow motion the studs on the underside of a boot approaching mae face. Now I touch the faintest scar, a moon shape, the mark of a traitor. The rain you don't notice gets yuu wet, Amy used tu say, huddling on the touchline beneath an umbrella, worrying her curly hair might go frizzy. And young Bryn wondering if sex would be better than football, and maybe he ought tu pay more attention tu girls. They seemed tu leik him anyway, the only thirteen-year-old with roguish stubble. He hobbles over tu her grinning. She looks shocked at the amount of blood, but smitten all the saime, fumbling for a tissue which is drenched red in seconds.

"Does it hurt?"

Nothing hurts when your heart is pounding this hard and you're trying not tu go stiff. He wipes away blood with his sleeve. He wants tu kiss her but it feels a bit inappropriate. Duncan (the boy who did the damage) glares across the pitch. Bryn laughs and waves, the rain is gettin harder, diluting the blood. I can't remember how it all ended. She wudnae sleep with me anyway, but Duncan didn't know that.

"Are yuu asking me about mae opinions of football or sectarianism?" I asked returning to the present situ. A sensible bloke would simply have picked one and rolled over tu sleep, as though his answer meant nothing more than who he preferred tu win a sports tournament.

Juliette shrugged. "Well, both I suppose."

"Well, I used tu leik tu play football before I fooked mae knee. However, that shit they show on the telly all the time in *this* country is no fookin football. Mae Irish mate used tu say the Premiership is such 'a Tan thing'. But I think actually, if yuu wanna see the legacy of Thatcherism in this fookin country, switch on Match of the Day. They've turned the beautiful game intu Wall Street."

She lay there listening and smiling slightly, which I knew wus some affectionate thing, and it annoyed the shit out of me.

"You haven't answered the question though..." she said. "I wasn't asking for your contempt of the English. I know about that. And isn't it worse in Scotland? Only two or three teams have a chance at winning anything. Isn't that a bit boring?"

"Saime issue. Money. The English made football about money. The answer is Celtic. But you know very well that's just a euphemism for me tu tell you I'm a Catholic boy."

"Who made football about religion?" she asked.

"The church funded the original setting up of football teams. Saime in this country."

"So didn't the church make football about money?" she said.

"Don't be clever-clever," I replied with a curled lip, but she wus getting somewhere, so she didn't lay off.

"What are your opinions on Catholicism?"

"I think it's primitive and frightening... but I believe in God and I'm afraid of him. And maybe that makes me primitive, but I've done sae many bad things, and I'm afraid of what I'd be capable of doing if he didn't stop me."

The affectionate expression on her face wus gone and I knew I'd said enough tu shut her up, without really telling her anything at all.

"You're Protestant," I said.

She shook her head. "Agnostic."

"But your daddy is Protestant. He must be. He plays golf," I said in a tone of contempt.

"You have a lot of prejudices, Charlie," she said quietly.

"Of course I do, I'm a Weegie. That's all we have!"

* * * * * * *

MONGREL NEEDS HOME

Simian Thomas, Thailand

There was not always Cassie and nothing else. But she was the only constant in my life from the early years, as my mum was lost to the ideal life she thought she could buy. My dad seemed to think his job of being a bad male role-model was done with, once I'd reached double digits.

When I said we were going travelling my mum forbade me, saying it was too dangerous. If I wanted a holiday somewhere safe she'd pay for it. But the spoilt boy had been working and earning, because Cassie had bullied him to independence. So I left, telling her we were going sightseeing in Iraq, when in fact we were treading a traditional backpacker trail down through East Asia. A trail where we'd no doubt find ourselves and find a bunch of other stupid people also.

"I know Thailand's a bit of a cliché, but I really want to compare the effect of tourism there with the other

Eastern countries." Calista peered into one of a stack of guidebooks she'd spent the past few months digesting.

"Or you've spent too much time reading *The Beach*, and you're hoping to meet a dishevelled, brooding man like Richard who will take you to a secret, unspoilt paradise, doomed to become a living hell?"

Ironically Cassie may've still been alive if we had gone to Iraq. When it came to the normal danger of idiot humans she seemed to have a strange immunity. I, on the other hand, would likely be kidnapped, blind-folded and beheaded, for making the wrong facial expression. So it is in the life of a mongrel.

After the water subsided Charlie and Wolfgang found me somehow, amongst the human debris, by some fortuitous chance. Charlie picked me up and hugged my scrawny bag of bones. I've been a little brother figure to him since, I suppose. We all sat in silence for a spell and I accepted a cigarette under the circumstances, soaking up that alien feel of nicotine in my body, but morphine would barely have relaxed me. He noticed my ankle eventually, tugging at my trouser leg and peering at it. I'd repeatedly written in biro all down my lower leg and over the bones of my foot, *'she's gone she's gone she's gone'*.

He rubbed a sweating hand through unkempt black curls and looked disconcerted. "We may find her you know."

I shook my head. I knew she was dead, because it felt like I was missing a vital organ in my body. Charlie had repetitious dreams over the coming months that she was alive somewhere, suffering memory loss. He wanted to visit the temporary morgues set up in the temples to look for her body, but the smell of death in the air made us baulk. The heat was not preserving the corpses.

He asked if I wanted to go home and I realised I had nothing to go home to. I'd effortlessly lost touch with everyone I remotely liked and felt that my mum would only give me a big fat '*I told you so*' (as though it was obvious we'd get caught in one of the biggest natural disasters in recorded history). Definitely not what I needed at this point in my life.

There was not always Cassie and nothing else, but now there was and now there wasn't.

In the mean time we had a country to rebuild. It soon took us over like some greater force we had no say in. For every splinter and blister I gained clearing rubble from once idyllic beaches, a piece of me healed over a tiny bit, like the scars in the land. Life is strange. These two men were not friends I chose, nor friends I would've ever chosen. But by circumstance they were all I had in terms of a pathway through the wreckage. They felt like a couple of stray dogs left wandering the Earth, because whatever roots they had, or had ever grown had been severed in a bloody fashion. Now to stay in one place, to have a home made them feel like the trees that were planted in concrete. A slow death. Or so I thought.

"Where did you grow up Simian?"

"Sheffield," I answered without enthusiasm.

They looked at one another strangely.

"Neh shit?" Charlie said. "I thought you were fookin Southern."

"Thanks," I said. I have no patriotism towards the North. It's just the way people always assume I'm Southern.

"No, you don't see..." Wolfgang said, with the drama of a man who believed in mystical truths. "We lived in Sheffield, before we migrated to warmer climates. Don't you want to go back there some time?" He scratched at his beard and then became distracted by a bit of twig that was tangled in it. I watched him tug it out, not knowing whether or not I could muster a laugh at this ridiculous man.

"Eventually... Do you?"

Wolfgang grinned his slimy grin. "I'm sure the tide will carry us there in due course. We've both got a little unrequited love to be getting back to. Nothing like a 'wee dram' of self-loathing to make you feel like you're home!"

I stared at him dumbfounded that anyone would admit things like that. But then I was never sure he wasn't spinning some elaborate yarn. Charlie for his part looked like he wanted to punch the crazy German, so maybe an inkling of truth lurked.

"Good times to be had by all," I said.

"We can go back in spring meybe," Charlie said hesitantly. This seemed unspecific enough for all of us.

* * * * * * *

THE FURRIES & THE FURIES

Roxanne Ratcliffe, Mindscape

The frost is encrusted onto every surface. Broken fingers pull away some, afraid to touch, to feel that coldness, the morbidity of the ice; to be that cold is to be death. It's an absence, a gap, a furry void that can only be filled by some rabid Jim Henson puppet.

The sunlight mocks the coldness of the frost, hastening the departure towards an unknown death, cutting through tooth-like objects, stinging their nerves with its touch. When I tread it feels like snow. It makes that noise and gives slightly underfoot, the deception of secure footing, hinting at the loss of poise. The face that knows nobody will laugh at the joke she just made. The body falling, cold brittle bones ricochet off cold ground, tufts of grass and mud hardened to rock. A mirror's temperature is always at zero. I can only ever see my cold self, the hallowed self. The charcoal smears painted beneath the eyes, careful red lines drawn on the very edges of the lids, poetic tears decorate cheeks and leave subtle tracks behind.

'My fears are nothing to those you've faced, my tears are nothing, to those that've stained your face, I'll never be anything more than just a break in the storm.'

The kettle is the most important object you'll ever have. Steam rising to meet the cold air. Life. Hands wrap around the cup and its contents feed hope, dry tears, cure disease. I forgot to be funny. I forgot to say something sarcastic. I'd said something that made him smirk. But by the time that little bit of love had escaped his eyes and seeped into mine, I'd already forgotten if I was being deadly serious. If I should be upset that he'd laughed.

The snow isn't cold when you lie with someone laughing. When you go sledging and the dog chases you downhill wanting to join in. I look at my hands, bare in the cold. They've aged in minutes, red and white and cracked. With purple and yellow bruises where they're broken, where I'm alone.

Hunger is an emotion like lust (and maybe fear). I'm not always sure it amounts to want. Sometimes I think it's more about dread. The psychology of hunger deepens to a physicality. Like a drug addiction, the body rejects. A nauseous feeling sits in my empty stomach. It craves no company. It doesn't want its personal space invaded. When this occurs it gives off waves of doubt, of irritation. It's lonely and it craves not the loneliness nor the company, but both and neither at the same time.

It's only at crash time you realise that this was ever gone. The psychology is always there, but the physical rejection is forgotten. You start to think that it wasn't real because you have no need for it anymore. When it returns, it's both frightening and reassuring. It's not happy, but you don't want to be happy. You want to be devastated quietly on the inside.
You'd think I'd learn to take care of myself, so that I didn't end up in this place. I know the patheticness of it, of my growling hunger to be stable. To cope.

But you must understand that this is the default setting my body and mind returned to inevitably. It makes unhappiness feel somehow secure and familiar. I feel more akin to my body as it speaks to me. It does not possess me – I possess it. If I can endure this slow gentle pain it will make me stronger. Though I grow weaker every day.

Once you know (too well) the psychology of a person of our vile over-fed society – so vile and over-fed it could consider not eating as a choice – you start to notice that everyone seems to have an unhealthy relationship with food... or used to... or soon will. Besides the obvious calorie calculators, toilet-roll-snackers and the mortally obese, you notice all the more subtle nuances – the people too busy to eat, the person who'd rather spend their money on alcohol, the rugby players swapping tips on strange eating habits that boost muscle and performance.

Mainly though, just notice who notices your own eating habits. People project their own disorders and let others exacerbate them.

Cuan took hold of my wrist in one hand and little Nic's in the other. "Look how skinny you both are!" the skeleton said.

At times like this I want to escape from all the people. I feel their eyes as hot as fever. All my skin and inner splurge feels exposed. They can see too much. I feel like a Francis Bacon painting.

But then I miss the people I love, the same way I miss animals. I miss the clumsiness of their big paws. I miss the way they look at me like they wish they could make everything okay, like they don't understand that shitting on the carpet doesn't serve this purpose. I forgive my friends every mistake eventually, because they're just pets who don't know any better.

The nurse peers over her glasses at me and makes a disapproving face. "You're not crazy; you're just a silly little girl who is making herself crazy."

I am floating somewhere close to the ceiling among the clouds but the wrong chord is played on the piano. So myself and the fluffy things both drop into a heap. Luckily I hit the floor first so that I cushion the fall of the cotton wool. The nurse is still standing there with her clip board.

"I know," I say, almost happily. "But how do I stop?"

"Don't worry," my friend said. "You just haven't met the right person yet."

I nod. "That's just what they said to the dog when they injected her with death."

* * * * * * *

DOG PORRIDGE

Wolfgang, Sheffield

My heart is aflutter like a fleet fox. I was hanging around outside the Salvo with the Gentleman Hobo and his ugly, friendly Mastiff dog named Aphex. I happened to spot that Cuan boy walking past, hand in hand with a young lady. I like brevity most of all. I like to spike my porridge with dog hair in the morning to make up for the mutt that bit me last night. Some say crazy Jack is the best fucking actor that never killed himself. I grinned anyway, put my toke in my mouth and reached inside my plastic bag to fish out one of my cans of Tennents Super. I threw it to him as he approached with the reluctant girl.

She was a little angel waiting to suck on the poisoned wound and realise another life awaited. She tried not to cringe at the filthy scruffs, instead shrinking like a small violet flower in the hand of the goat man. Aphex wriggled with excitement and slobbered at them. He liked making friends – he liked new hands to dribble on. The fair maiden was not cowed by the dog three times her body weight (she was a little pea), instead she greeted him rather than us. Dogs are charmingly disgusting, not like me.

"Deutsch-bag!" Cuan held his lager can like a minor trophy. "Is this where you sleep?" He motioned towards the homeless hostel.

Gent Hobo shot me a glance. Straights are wary of scruffs and scruffs are wary of straights, *hobos prefer roll ups, gentleman prefer blondes etcetera, etcetera...* Actually he was possibly just noxiously paranoid, due to being on a downer.

"Goodness no, son – I'd have to pay – I'm a squatter through and through. Who is this *petit pois*? She's too pretty for you."

"This is Roxanne."

She smiled politely at me.

"Greetings, my name is Wolfgang."

"I've heard a little about you," she said quietly.

"Well, I do try to leave a little mythology behind. Speaking of which, that crazy Mexican fellow is doing a gig at the Red House tonight, Q-bawl. You think you might grace an appearance?"

"Hmm, yes, there's a distinct possibility. We could have a smoke out back and watch the stars."

Aphex lifted an uber paw and planted it possessively on Roxanne's arm. Cuan patted him on the temple.

"Have you ever met Ziggy, the three legged dog?" he asked.

"Everyone knows Ziggy. That mutt is more famous than the crazy Mexican," I said.

"It's most peculiar. Since I met Roxy, we've seen about seven three-legged dogs in the space of a month. It seems very odd." He pushed his fringe from his eyes.

"Seven is a good number," Gent Hobo muttered with the conviction of a wise man. "When you see nine, start to worry. Nine is a bad number."

"How's the writing coming along?" I asked. (I don't much like even talking of the number nine.)

A skinny, skag woman shrieked as she walked past us and sat down on the bench nearby. Aphex perked his flippy floppy little ears and we all glanced sideways at her, tapping a bruised wrist against the seat.

Cuan nodded to himself. "Yeah, I was actually trying to write a song, called 'dog porridge'. It's about porridge, but hopefully people will find some deeper meaning. But I think only the name is good. I blunted my fingers on a hot oven dish so I can't play any guitar at the moment. Will have to see how it is when I try to put some sounds in."

"I imagine blunt fingers would help with playing the guitar?" I said.

He nodded, peering for a second at the red raw tips. "It will when they scab up and go really hard. Well, hmmm, we should head off, I think."

"Yes quite. Improve the company you keep," I advised.

"Definitely, thanks for the beer," he said, and smiled charmingly.

"No trouble, don't go giving it away to any tramps now."

"Indeed. *Tschuß* be with you."

With that they turned and ambled off towards Devonshire Green.

* * * * * * *

CARNAL REFLECTIONS

Simian Thomas, Sheffield

The water was flat and dark and perfectly still. I stepped hesitantly forward and peered into it, until I could see myself. The surface was virtually level with the canal bank, so it was almost as though I were standing on it. I felt a strange sense of vertigo looking at my small face in the middle of that flat, blank expanse, which was both the water and the sky at the same time. I thought that if I fell in, I'd fall to the other side. Some parallel in which everything is the other way up.

If the sky ripped open… if the pink clouds fell…

I get a little lost in illusions. I withdraw. I'm an able chatterbox, and while maybe a little weird, I'm not exactly shy. People mistake quietness for shyness. The truth is sometimes I'm just rude and can't be bothered to say anything. I don't lack confidence to speak, and have an ample stack of conversation openers and many a quip to steal a smile from a new acquaintance.

"Listen to Mazzy Star. It'll change your life." I'd said that to the petite brunette with a blonde-tipped bob. She *was* shy, I think, but she also had this quiet confidence, a security in her own charade.

"Excuse me?" she'd said politely.

We'd just been introduced by a mutual friend and then kind of abandoned temporarily in one another's company. Usually in these situations I'd ask something more typical. But Roxanne was different, I could tell. As though she was bored with everything and would forget me instantly if I didn't do something odd. Or maybe that was my insecurity.

"Mazzy Star." I pulled out a pen and wrote it on her arm, because I was drunk and I can get away with things like that when I'm drunk.

"Okay," she said, humouring me. "Are they fashionable?" She didn't like fashionable (in principle), I reckoned.

"Oh no," I reassured her. "Not really."

"I'd like to recommend something to change your life, but I don't know that much about music."

"What do you know about?" I enquired, using her thinking time to take in her face properly. She had large pale eyes elaborated with shimmering colour and a strangely attractive puggish nose.

"Photography, I spose. And films, I watch a lot of films."

"Well, one photographer, one film," I said, trying to swallow my own enthusiasm. I've spent my life trying to appear laconic.

"Okay, Wolfgang Tillmans, but only if you like banality and penises."

"Who doesn't like banality and penises? I think the plural is peni though," I mused.

She giggled and scribbled the name on my arm, then sipped her drink and thought for a bit. The sweaty bar space and pounding music slipped into my consciousness for a while.

"*Lovers of the Arctic Circle*... hmmm, but only if you're a hopeless, tragic romantic."

"How did you know? Is it the hair?" I said.

She giggled again, and scribbled the film name on my arm too. We were still jabbering avidly when our friend returned. She looked bemused.

I didn't see Roxanne again for a while. But Sheffield had a smallness to it, a compact scene, that meant you ran into people sooner or later. Everyone you met knew someone you knew, or at least that was how it felt. Sometimes I enjoyed feeling part of it. Other times I longed for anonymity again. Probably what gave me my own travel bug. And curiosity, and being of a bored generation. Roxy was the same I think, pining for something more, yet having no idea what we were pining for.

Our meetings were always the same. We'd run into one another and talk slavishly for a while of the adventures we hoped to grow brave enough for. Then we'd promise to meet for coffee and never would because we both wanted to be nonchalant, and elusive, and sought after. And yet she was someone I wanted to talk to every day. I would think of funny things I wanted to tell her. Maybe it seems like infatuation, but it was 'friend infatuation', and she understood what I meant when I talked of that.

"I think," I said hesitantly one day, when we'd accidentally met in the park and sat outside the tea shop for a natter. "There are different types of attraction and we're attracted to our friends on some level. Not necessarily a sexual one. I think there's an emotional level, an intellectual level, a superficial level, and so on."

She listened quietly and intently, with her large eyes that absorbed light and ideas greedily.

"I think," I paused, "we only 'fancy' people who tick all the boxes, or most of them. But maybe we have a kind of crush on all our friends. Male, female, whatever."

I could see her flicking through her friends like pages, measuring them against this.

I never wanted to know Roxy properly. Maybe that was why I let the distance exist. I liked her mystery. I wanted to keep it. It was my fetish about her. The people I was truly and wholly attracted to were the ones who elicited in me the question *why? Why are you the way you are?* I would dig at their personality with my claws and chase them back and forth like a cat with a piece of string – unable to realise it was just a piece of string and nothing more.

I looked again at my reflection in the canal and tried again to cough up the fur ball that was Lucy. A ball of string digested and regurgitated so many times it was unrecognisable to how it really was in the first place. I tried to tell myself this was it. I wouldn't think about Lucy anymore.

* * * * * *

PINT OF BRAINS

Roxanne Ratcliffe, Mindscape

"Pint of Brains please," the Sandman requests.

It must've been something Charlie said, stuck in my head, churning. Was there really a beer called Brains? I think there was. The Sandman chuckles. He's sat on his haunches above the wardrobe, with his little bag of golden sleep, which is like the little bags climbers use to carry chalk. I beg him silently to throw me some, but he holds up his bruised and battered hands for me to see – he can barely grasp.

"I got in a fight last night with some meat-head. I nutted him and beat him with my fists, and then he hit me in the head and my brains fell out. So I can't decide who ought to go to sleep tonight. There's no fair judgement."

"Please," I murmur. "I'm so tired. I've got to work tomorrow."

He shrugs carelessly and smiles a little so I can see one of his teeth has been knocked out.

"Don't blame me, chicken. I just work here..."

"Well, you're not doing your job very well," I mutter plaintively.

"Depends what you think my job is, poppet. And besides, everyone deserves a good honest skive from time to time. Especially when they're hung over and a little bruised in the ribs."

"Other people are asleep though. Who let them sleep?" I ask, trying to catch him out.

"Other Sandmen. Or at least other strains of my personality with better work ethics. Motivation, self-esteem, empathy, that sort of thing. You got the worst of it, cherry pie. Like ladies who always attract bad men. Men who exacerbate their worthlessness. Are you one of those ladies, sugar-plum? Does that depressed little genius make you happy, d'you think? Or does he give you severe doses of insomnia, neuroticism and other such pathetic diseases belonging to modern man?"

I glance to Cuan, sleeping so beautifully beside me. Men look like boys when they sleep. Maybe they are.

"At least I'm eating," I say defeatedly.

"Only because you've not yet realised that he isn't. These disorders are contagious. Like heartbreak, like failure, like self-loathing and grumps."

I look at Cuan's bones. I love his bones, but does he love mine?

"You romanticise rhetorical death, you romanticise the tragic. Real people are dying from hunger and malnutrition somewhere right now, but you feel more guilt about *eating when you're hungry*." He peels a bloody nail off his finger and flicks it across the room.

I wince. "But I *am* eating."

"Today, yes. But all the days that will follow today? Tomorrow you'll feel bad because he could sleep and you couldn't. So you won't eat. There's a part of you that wants him to be more tragic than you. If his demons are bigger, you don't have to face your own. But there's a little competitiveness too. After all, your only talent is being pathetic. You may as well be better at it. He sleeps, you don't. He doesn't eat, neither will you. There's freedom in being the selfish nut-job who disappears and lets their friends worry. There's no freedom in being the one waiting and worrying by the phone."

I burst into helpless tears, pulling the duvet to my face.

Cuan woke and rolled over. He sat up and put the lamp on. I'd wiped my face hastily, and tried to smile. He gazed at me with glorious loveliness and touched my messy hair.

"Hey, hey, little Ratty, you okay? You were talking. Were you talking in your sleep?"

"I can't sleep," I said.

He shook his head. "I think you were asleep, you just don't think you were."

The lamp was lighting a different part of the room now. The bit where the Sandman sat was in deep, blank shadow. I snuggled down, hooking Cuan's arm round me. He switched the light off and I closed my eyes. Slowly I drifted to an abstract sleep, comforted by the bones around me. Cuan lay awake and spoke silently to the Sandman, who'd chosen his next victim.

* * * * * * *

BRAND NEW SECOND HAND

Haydn Antoine, Derby

"Where you been? Your mum callin you 'gen. She finks you not wanna speak to er," Rufio announced, before I was even through the door.

It was heavy and I was burdened. I gave it a further shove and set down two bulging carrier bags against the kitchen cupboards beneath the counter.

"Realised I was missing a few essentials," I said, half out of breath from climbing the stairs.

Rufio was wearing the furry badger hood Cookie'd made for him. He was bare-chested, save for some long blue beads with a cheap metal charm on the end, depicting Jesus on the cross (looking a tad depressed), and his tattoo of Greek letters on his arm. Which apparently said something clever-clever like – 'profound, spiritual statement'.

"You're very self-consciously eccentric, aren't you...?" I said, averting my eyes from his manly chest. This was the first time I'd lived with him. I'd always assumed the outfits that he DJed in, partied in and went to Uni in were all part of the hyperdrama that would fade behind closed doors. But no. "And how are you not boiling hot in that hat?" I glanced down at my own sweat drenched t-shirt.

He started rooting through my bags, pulling out objects – washing up liquid, the new Roots Manuva album, a toast rack.

"How the devuw is a *toast rack* essenshuwl?" he said.

I sighed, expecting the inevitable jibes on the way. "Where else am I meant to put my toast once it's toasted?"

"On a plate, you freakin Leicester-boi!"

"Leicester isn't posh you know. It's full of chavs," I said.

"Itus fuckin borin though. I never bin somewhere so non-descript in *all ma days*. I hates to break to you, but Derby got more goin furrit than Leicester."

I shrugged and took the toast rack off him. I placed it neatly in the centre of the kitchen table, which was already cluttered with newspapers and a very full ashtray. (Neither I nor Rufio smoke cigarettes, so the blame for that was a poltergeist named Cookie.)

"Wew, you almost make the place look civilised, Antwon," he mumbled. Then as though only just remembering added, "You left your mobile be-hind by the by. And that crazy bird you after called agen." He drifted off with casual drama.

"Claudia?!" I spluttered. True, we'd spoken earlier in the year, but it'd been strictly business.

"Yeah, that one. We 'ad a nice chat. I tried to pretend to be you, but she wont fooled. She's proper clever, that one."

"What did she say?" I asked, trying to contain my annoyance at his pranks.

"Calm down, geez. Giv 'er a bell," he said. He threw my phone to me. I fumbled to catch it.

I quickly headed for my bedroom as I searched her number. There was no way I could've handled Rufio making smoochy faces in the background while I spoke to her.

"Claudia? Hi, it's Haydn."

"I know," she said huskily. "Yar housemate'sa bittuva character, int he?"

I laughed, a little nervously. "That's certainly one way to put it. What can I do for you?"

"I'm in Derby furra few days. I wondered if ya fancied meetin for a drink?"

I was silent for a bit too long.

"...Haydn? Ya still there?"

"Yeah, that would be great. Can you make it this evening at all?"

"Uh huh, anytime after seven is grand owt."

"Ok, 7:30 then? Do you know The Blue Dog on Sadler Gate?"

"I think so," she purred thoughtfully. "I'll ask one-a-the natives to point me in't rayht direction anyroads."

"Brill. I'll see you at 7:30 then?"

"Okaay, look forward to it... Byye." She hung up.

I walked quietly out of my room, and paused outside the door. Rufio was still rooting through my carrier bags, finding homes for things. He tossed me the pack of johnnies I'd bought.

"Lucky you was feelin optimistic, Antwon. How'd it go?" he asked.

"I said 'brill'. Apart from that, pretty good. We're meeting for a drink tonight."

I sat down at the table and he patted my back.

"Where?" He was playing up the good friend.

"No fucking way I'm telling you," I replied calmly.

"S'alright, you got no originality. You meetin 'er at The Blue Dog, either that or Yee Olde Dolphin. But that's a bit outta the way for someone who not know the area. So I'm goin for the 'Dog."

I glared at him and said nothing.

"You should've suggested somewhere classeh."

"We're in Derby," I replied flatly.

"There's one cocktail bar at least! Wass it called? Wiv fake flame lights and shit..."

"Not exactly classy! Anyway, I feel like she's a pub person, so I'm going with my instincts," I said.

"So you's takin her to a pub full of emo kids, wiv an 'alf pipe out back!"

"It's either that or an old man boozer where I'll have to put up with men leering at her all night."

"Aw night? You *is* optimistic, Blondie. Aw the children will stare at 'er anyway. She'ull be used to it all if she's that pretty."

I stared into the middle distance and became increasingly flustered. "I should clean up, just in case she stays over. What should I wear?"

"You ever seen that film cawed *A Complete History of My Sexuaw Failure*? Cos you is lookin a lot lyke that bloke to me tuday," he jibed, giggling to himself.

"There's still time to look suave, Gonzalez. I'm not going dressed like this." I motioned to my ripped jeans and sweaty t-shirt.

"Do you fink she's *lookin* for suave?" he mocked.

"I'll go for preppy. If in doubt bruv, go for preppy!"

"Not in a rich boy way though! She's a Norvfern bird," he warned. "Go for Hip-Hop preppy."

"How does a white-ass Leicester boy like me do 'Hip-Hop preppy'?" I asked.

"Wew, Mr Hudson does it, and ee's a Blondie..." He shrugged.

* * * * * * *

BREWDOG PUNK

Bryn McLarey, Sheffield

We were sat in Cuan's attic room. I discovered he doesnae actually still live in his dad's house. He just has lots of shite there. He wus gradually accumulating shite here also. A large painting of a pig stared down at me, its big ears cocked as though trying tu eavesdrop. Roxanne wus sat crossed legged in what all who entered the room knew tu be the comfiest chair in the world. I felt a little old. The space reminded me of spaces from mae youth. I wondered if meybe I should've been a nine tu fiver by now. Goin home tu the wife and kids, instead of chasing the Lost Boys around. I grunted laughter in mae head, as if that would ever happen. But I paid a price for it.

Cuan had put on a 65 Days of Static album. I whacked the volume up and absorbed mae inner nerves in the music, mae organs collided and crashed like the riffs and clashes. Cuan and Roxy were busy havin a meeting of minds over photography. I usually found maesel digging intu these conversations, determined tu prove my own insight and disprove their unique sense of connection. Instead I wus slumped defeated, sneering at their enthusiasm and youth with jaded eyes. It felt grand.

"...Chris Marker says something in *Sans Soleil*, about how he doesn't understand how people remember if they don't photograph, don't film. Because it's so much a part of his life, it begins to *be* the memories almost," Roxy said, with wide young eyes.

Cuan scrambled though a pile of dog-eared pages and picked one out, adjusting his glasses.

"Here it is." He ran a finger over highlighted words. *"And what if we dare to forget? A life without photos or memento is a graceful descent into the quiet surrender of death. Photos are a taught face-lift at seventy that suddenly makes you look like a deathly twenty-five year old. Memories are a break block on life. A resistance to the future. Time caught in a visual calendar of panic."*

Roxy nodded smiling. I rolled mae eyes. She looked at me and reached over tu her camera which wus sat on its tripod and snapped before I could realise.

"Gosh," I said. "Now this precious memory can be remembered."

"I've taken many pictures of Charlie's sneers," she said.

Cuan squinted at me. "He's very photogenic. In a rough authentic way."

I made the V sign at him. "You two wudna last long where I'm from. Clever-clever, pseudo-fookin-intellectualism."

"Where are you from?" Cuan asked.

"Glasgow," Roxy put in. "I know cos Claudia told me. Why did you last so long, Charlie? You're quite prone to being clever-clever yourself. Or did your rough authentic-ness cross the divide where our pathetic middleclass-ness would've failed?"

I shook mae head, feelin a little leik a silverback gorilla in a zoo. "No, they didnae appreciate mae unique 'insight' where am from. Not at all. That's why I got oot. There's no such thing as a 'working class hero'. They just think yer fookin weird."

I thought about what animals do understand unmistakably communication-wise. I thought about grabbing Cuan by the scruff of his shirt and slamming him into a wall. I thought about destroying his brilliance. But violence doesnae destroy brilliance. Brilliance destroys itself. I knew this tu be true when I looked in his eyes some days and saw that blue-grey mist.

I wus sick annoyed with mae aen jealousy. I hated havin this animal inside me. A tightness in the chest, a miniature fury that morphed and manifested. That hid and pretended tu go away, and then returned with disconcerting laughter.

I suppose sum days I enjoyed the company. Relished the little fury and the justice I would've dealt if I were mad enough tu consider it justice. But after sae many nights unable tu sleep, with the saime restless thoughts haranguing me, I could easily cut out some part just tu be free. Tu be able tu look upon a world of opportunities. Just tu be able tu be foolish and fall in love again. Tu be blind tu Roxanne and the reasons she gave me tu be blinkered tu everyone else.

Sum days I resented her, aye. She damaged everything. One day a while ago I wus refreshed by the boy Cuan. His miniature anarchy. His way of twistin and divertin everything, confusing people who didnae realize he wus just playing Devil's advocate (be it with the woolly liberals or the closet fascists).

Now I could see nothin but poison in Cuan. And I felt when we debated the saime things we'd done in the past, I wus just humouring him. Just hoping if I wus patient he would disappear. And gladly he would. I'd noted quickly that Cuan knew himself tu be a one-trick pony, and hated the idea of people knowing him long enough tu be bored of him. He didnae have long-term friends. He flitted from group tu group. We were a temporary perch.

But I knew him disappearing would resolve nothing of the green-eyed Othello in me. I could play tug of war with the vain hope that one day little Roxy would be in love with me, but she never would. Instead she'd leave an invisible stain on any relationship I tried tu have, on any optimism that I'd sumtime be free of obsession. And this wus my biggest fear, that what I needed rid of in mae life wus not Cuan at all, but Roxanne Ratcliffe.

Roxy framed inside her lens an image of a bespectacled Cuan reading profundities, below the picture of the pig. The pig looked down at me with a knowing smirk.

* * * * * * *

A COUPLE OF DISGRUNTLED CATS & A DREADED TED

Wolfgang, Sheffield

"Run run run, fast as you can, can't catch me I'm a gingerbread cat!"

I chased the marmalade cat down the street. He bounded easily off in a monkey-like fashion, needing little swiftness to evade me, then stopped further up and looked disdainfully over his shoulder. Out of breath from a short burst of speed, I doubled over coughing and laughing at the same time. A woman in a house across the road tweaked her net curtains and little suspicious eyes peaked out. I waved at her joyfully.

They say the madman is truly free.
But who be madder?
Her or me?

It was bloody cold in Sheffield. The winds blew harshly betwixt the seven hills, and both the jutting buildings and stark trees drew themselves in various shades of charcoal in the dim afternoon light.

It was not rainy, but a sense of rain hung in the air. The day seemed rather ordinary, the ground unmagically waterlogged, without sugary frosts or mysterious fogs. But I enjoyed its ordinariness on my lonesome pondering walk between my favourite haunts. I began with the Victorian graveyard, where a bulky man ran his five dogs on the great lawn (beneath which the suicidal were once buried, when it was considered a sin to decide your own fate). A fearsome pack they were, of all the stocky fighting breeds we're wary of. But they careered about chasing one another playfully, tails a-wag.

I walked on up the road outside the cemetery and crossed the small roundabout, stopping to check in the portal of one of the houses where the front room was obsessively decorated with Mariner's kitsch. It always looked as though nobody ever sat in there, like it only existed as passing curio. On and up Psalter Lane, through a suburbia of grand old houses, and grand old trees that ruptured lines in the pavement. It curved on uphill to the Art School, a monument to Brutalism, a beautiful building uglified by a cynical grey sky.

Here I cut right, down a side road, and chased a ginger cat. At the end of the road round to the right again, the land dropped away steeply. This was Hunter House Hill. A joy to skip down (a gasper to walk up). The linear perspective of houses and cars framed a view of the city which was an unclarified smudge upon this day.

Another cat, this time a fluffy black and white specimen, was crouched on a bin.

"Bin cat!" I said happily. I reached out carefully, to try to tickle his chin. But he, too, scuttled off.

I like the beasties, but they sense the canine in me, the silent lupine howl. I continued my descent to Hunter's Bar, which bustled with human life. Children squealed in the nearby playground, curly haired women gossiped outside the Greek deli. I saluted the chap at the traffic lights selling the Big Issue, but he ignored me, not wanting to be associated with my lot no doubt. I criss-crossed the roundabout, dodging disgruntled drivers who seemed to think I ought to wait for the promised green man.

I considered now entering Endcliffe Park. But there were some dirty drunks sat arguing on the benches, and I recalled a run-in with them before, when they'd pilfered my Zippo and called me a hairy Hitler. I swiftly rerouted to the right of the park, up Brocco Bank, around a bend where the traffic growled. I waited a moment before flinging myself across the metallic rapids.

Through the iron gateway I entered the Botanical Gardens, where nature had been rebuilt and organised to make it palatable for the human race. With the tidy lawns, and the tidy flowerbeds, and an elegant hot house at the top, from which to draw the symmetry. The gardens were not without their little pleasures though. A kingdom reigned by grey squirrels – the clever, pretty vermin who know best how to exploit us. And hidden away, in a maze of this and that, was the Bear Pit.

This I now headed down into, through the pokey entrance into the bottom of a large, stone well-like structure. In the centre of this a bronze bear was frozen on his hind legs, in a mute roar against his entrapment by a race of civilised savages.

* * * * * *

RUFUS

Claudia McLeod, Derby

I stepped hesitantly int't coffee shop, scoutin for enemies. A crowd of mullet-haired teens were sat, mock-white-trash, trucker caps tipped over fashionable fringes. I mayde a noise somewhere between a tut an a hiss. Barely audible, yet sendin a mild vibration through the air which they would sub-consciously sense an wi'out knowin why, trudge home and throw out their hair-straighteners.

One a the girls (though they were all fairly androgynous) cackled knowing'ly at one a the boy's jokes. I clocked Haydn's housemate behind't counter, which were cluttered with overpriced paninis and jars of random almond-biscuit things. He were leanin nonchalantly over a newspaper, casually poising his muscular arm, so that his cryptic tattoo was displayed tu't room.

I approached. "Hi... Rufus?"

He turned his eyes up ta me wi'a lazy stare. "Rufio... but I forgives you, yeah, cos Rufus is a fuckin cool name."

"Rufio? Like in *Hook*? How tha fook wouldah forget that?"

He mayde a fist and lazily punched the air as he spoke. "*Rufio, Rufio, Roof! Ee! Ooh!* Blondie alwes calls me Roofie, innit. That's why you not know."

I puzzled that I'd not heard someone use the term 'innit' wi'out a bit a irony for some time.

"You Leo, yeah?" he said.

I realised he were skimming the starsigns. "Yeah, how'd ya know?" I was sure Haydn din't know when ma birthday was, unless he'd hacked me on the internet. I wouldn't purrit past him.

"Obvs," Rufio said. "You is *difficult*."

Obvs... That was Haydn's favourite word... favourite non-word.

"Are Leos difficult?"

"High maintenance. But not in a pussy way, in a contrary way. Being a fuck, for fuck's sake."

"Yeah, sounds about rayht," I said dryly. "What's gonna happen to me this week?"

"You gonna have sex tonight wiv an Aryan virgin, sorry – Virgo – pure in spirit, ready to be tarnished."

I nodded meaningfully. "Yeah, it scares me when them things are soo accurate."

He sniffed, gazing into the words on the page. "Don't be too aysty. Always jumpin feet firs' into the nearest puddle, you might 'urt sum-one."

"Can I gerra coffee please? Nowt fancy, jus black coffee."

"Whatever you want, bird," he smiled wisely.

He turned tu't machine and began the mechanical process of click, squash, wipe, attach. Then lined up the cup and pressed a button.

"Is you natural blonde?" he mumbled.

"Yeah, few highlights in there, but moastly, yeah," I said.

"Jeez, fink of the childrun you two would av."

"What – stupid...?" I asked.

He sniffed agen. "No babe, *pretty*." He turned placin the coffee on a saucer in front of me. "Lil Blondies runnin around, chasing rainbows and kittens and stuff."

He put a hand in his pocket and dragged out the keys to their flat, placin them carefully next to the coffee on't counter.

"Watch out for landlady, she's mentul. You two wud get on like an ablaze abode. And don't clean up. Freaks me out when birds clean up... Enjoy your coffee."

Wi' a cautious glance he moved onto the customer now waitin behind me.

* * * * * * *

BETWEEN THE COAST & THE SHORE

Simian Thomas, Dreamscape

But what about her cold blue eyes, floating inside the sea?

I'm clinging to a jagged black rock. So strange that the old trauma is the one coming back, the coldness of sitting on a rock just waiting for the tide to leave. Not the warm, choking ocean which chose to swallow the Earth. Not the dead children. Not the endless screaming that never seemed to stop (like the last girl in the *The Texas Chainsaw Massacre*). Not the thought of my friend's body strewn somewhere like a discarded bit of flotsam.

A blackness surrounds me fully, a cloak. There's nothing. I'm sure in memory there were little lights on the shore, a speck of white dress. Now there's nothing but the sound of my own breath shivering inside itself, and the lap of the waves placing an icy hand over mine, as if to offer cold comfort.

I know I'm bleeding, and stare harder in the dark, where the blood appears black. I'm too cold to feel pain and this calms me like a substitute for death. When you stop resisting the cold, it seeps gently inside you, into your bones. It numbs your fears, your fingers are brittle and if you were to move them they might just snap off, so you become stiller and stiller, crouching like some Victorian street urchin.

Time is immeasurable now. I know the tide is drawing out again. But maybe I've been here for hours, I don't know. I've almost stopped existing. But something in my body keeps trundling. Some trusty organ keeps saying *'now cumon lads, don't down your tools now, it's not this boy's time to go yet'*. Blood keeps pumping around my body like the steady tortoise who cannot yet see the finish line but knows it will come sometime. My eyes stare on into the black in front of my face. Then there is movement – a body emerges from the black water in front of me. Savagely matted, red hair and a white face with a mouth agape. And her eyes so very wide open. But when they look at me they look with a dead gaze, seeing past me, far-far past me.

I sat up in bed with a jolt, and water came choking out of my mouth like vomit. Then I looked down in the dark and knew that my bed covers were dry. I lifted up the duvet checking for corpses, then rolled over sobbing like a boy with a bruised knee. I drew bedding up around me and buried my head until it was my own real tears and snot choking me. Not the illusion of an ocean that had twice drowned me and twice discarded me back to the mortal world.

* * * * * * *

IN THE INDUSTRIAL HEARTLANDS, STOOD HIS RED GIRAFFE

Claudia McLeod, Sheffield

Sheffield were hot and vast in't summertime. Once the students were gone it were a ghost town moastly. We pretended to enjoy their absence, to enjoy not queuing furra drink at't bar.

Yet the loss of the foolish young-uns, cackling and squawkin and generally clutterin up the place, seemed to highlight the grubby underbelly a the city. The vacant-lookin homeless, and bored hooligans wi' nowt to do once the football season was over but drink and swear and intimidate.

We were sat out back at Dulos. I placed Charlie's pint down in front a him on the broken picnic table. He seemed a long way off. He mumbled thanks and took a slug, placin the glass carefully back on'ta wooden top next to the set of keys and the mobile phone which was hummin away on vibrate. It flashed '*Dad calling*', as it had done for the past ten minutes. The air smelt faintly of weed. Here on the cusp a the suburbs you could get away wi'it undisturbed. I could hear the landlord's deep, soulful laffter from back in't bar. Beneath a table nearby a scruffy little dog lapped water from an ashtray on't ground. He looked bored by the antics of his owners, who were listenin to a fuzzy radio playin nineties pop, and tekkin piss out of their friend's conspiracy theories.

The crisp coldness of the lager slid down ma gullet. "What does-eh want?" I asked, noddin tu't flashing phone.

Charlie looked at the phone, looked up at me and looked back at the phone. He raised a hand carefull'y and placed it on the large set a keys.

"What're they fa?" I asked.

He turned slightly in his seat, breathin int't warm night air. He motioned to the skyline above the shabby pub garden and the rickety fence. His eyes lit up wi' laffter, though his mouth never moved. Lyke every other angle of inner Sheffield at the time (regeneration bein the buzz word in scruffy cities), it were broken in't centre by a big red tower crane.

"The keys to the crane?!" I said, my voice for once broken wi' emotion.

He nodded smugly, tekkin another sip of beer and lightin a rollie. He let his eyes meet mine, to speak wi'out words the unthinkable adventure.

"Serves him right fa bein sae drunk by five o'clock that he's unfit tu drive home. Not that that would stop him."

A sense of bein twelve year auld agen, and feelin the need for mischievous revenge seemed to be flashin through Charlie.

"What're you plottin?" I asked, knowing all too well the answer. Another dull summer evenin were about to get a bit maire interestin.

* * * * * *

STEEPING IN THE HEAVENS

Wolfgang, Sheffield

Charlie was back smooching with Jenny again. I pondered upon his need for needy women. I'd portended to him once (like a wise old Billy Goat Gruff), that you should never go back to someone after a serious break-up. It'll all end in tears, as it already has. Besides it was his Juliette he really wanted back. Jenny was just a pale comparison. He'd even told her that once, the mean git. And still she returned like a faithful mutt for more emotional squalor. The vicious circle of love and doom.

Still I'm no gossipy neighbour, I've always left each to their own, no point meddling.

"No point meddling, is there Gent?" I said to Gentleman Hobo. He furrowed his brow and nodded wisely in affirmation.

We were rested against a tree in the park smoking the last of my weed. We were particularly placed so as to be invisible to odds and sods and dog-walkers on the paths below. But Aphex the Mastiff whined and whinnied and tuggled on his leash, for he could smell and sense those other mutts in the nearby vicinity. He just wanted to play. Though you wouldn't know it from the looks of apprehension on people's faces when they saw him bounding toward them, jaws open in a gleeful grin that let his great big tongue flap near his ears.

"We be rejects, Aphex," Gent would explain to him, in his grisly Cornish tones. But the Gent didn't really understand his dog's longing. He wasn't a friendly or curious person. He would've happily lived in a lighthouse out at sea with only crashing waves for company.

"He doesn't like being invisible, Jerry," he said. He always called me Jerry. He pointed at the dog in puzzlement. "Has to make a scene."

"Just as well, Gent, if it were just you shuffle-shuffling the streets, nobody would notice."

"I'd fade to nothing, Jerry," Gent agreed. "Nobody ud give me no money."

Aphex ran from side to side of the tree, to the extent of his lead, peeking over, trying desperately to get a better view. He never pulled hard though. He was too daft, or too devoted, to realise he could easily drag the Gent's bones any place he chose.

Gentleman Hobo shrunk down deeper inside his rags. He had no need to – it was a warm day. But when a person's been outside so many years, maybe their bones get cold all the way through. He scratched a bruisy scab on his face and coughed a little.

"What ails you, Gent?" I asked, with wayward compassion.

"Don't speak in tongues, Jerry. You know I hate it. I've no ale, you know I've none."

"There's a reason I speak the way I do, would you like me to tell it?" I said eagerly.

"I don't give a ruddy damn, Jerry. I never asked for your company, nor your funny talk," he said.

"*'Mine is a long and sad tail!*'" I announced. Then I glanced over my shoulder and remembered my tail had been forcefully removed some time ago. I rubbed my rump, which was still sore sometimes, feeling glummer.

Gent sighed and rolled his eyes, but Aphex sat and looked at me. My voice had hit a higher pitch, which pleased his flip-flop ears. He planted his big flumpy paws in my lap and washed my face with his flannel tongue. I pulled my head back a little and rubbed his chest and jowls.

"Many moons ago, Mr Aphex, before the language of the English had quite taken hold of my tongue, I was imprisoned at the top of a great tower. The Black Tower, twas known as. And in the top room of the tower there was a library. Now I know that seems awfully strange, that I should be imprisoned in a library of all things, but as was the way. A funny thing though. The tower was deep into the Baltic states, but the library was full of English books. And so through sheer boredom I began to learn the language well. Most of the books were quite difficult, but the easiest was a book for children named *Alice in Wonderland*."

I paused for meaningful impact, but the dog continued panting in my lap, listening as though he needed more.

"I read the book over and over, deciphering the language, and it gave me such joy. And so I moved on to more books and eventually I read the whole library. Of course, this isn't the whole story. I was able to read English but that barely helps one speak it. I returned to Alice when I had someone to teach me pronunciation. And I was in love with all the strange nuances, and yet, having moved here, you all toss words around like rubbish. Still, that is the nature of the proletariat. And, Aphex, now. I say that not snobbishly! For I count myself among the prols, we will *be* long after the others have perished."

As if his curiosity was satisfied, Aphex dropped away from me and again peered over the grand roots that anchored the tree to the earth. He wiggled his bum and thrashed his tail (a fine tail). He'd heard something, children's voices in the distance laughing and squealing maybe.

"Enough tall tales of tall towers," Gent grunted. He looked at the pale clear sky with suspicion. "There's a fair storm steeping in the heavens."

"How do you afford to feed such a monster?" I asked him, still gazing at the hulking frame of the dog.

"Butcher's bin," he answered. "And that woman that gives me cans of dog food. I hate the stuff. Tastes like paint..."

"What does paint taste like?" I asked, curious.

* * * * * * *

DOWN AT THE BOTTOM OF THE GARDEN

Simian Thomas, Sheffield

At some point we must become what we most despise. And so I found the soft rap of my knuckles upon Hex's door. I hadn't come to see how he was. I knew how he was. What vague curiosity and concern for his well-being I'd possessed in the past had long dried up to a breed of bitter exasperation.

I almost turned around and walked away again, but that sweet smell was there in the air. It had the tinge of sickly self in it. But it still promised a betterness, a level beyond, a beckoning illusionist in a top hat and tails.

The door peeked open a crack. It was dark inside, curtains were drawn. It smelt of a human sweating away in his own skin as well as the weed. Eyes squinted at me. At first I thought I must have woken the creature, but then our pupils met and I knew he was wide awake, too awake. He opened the door and motioned me in. I crept to the sofa in the darkness, feeling for the touch of the screwdled blanket that wrapped it, possessing mysterious sticky patches and so forth. My nose wrinkled – I'm a clean freak.

He switched on a small lamp and a tentative glow filled the room. He shrank from the light. I caught a glimpse of the hookah nose and beyond that a skeleton stripped of delights. He shuffled to the kitchen area to make tea, to retain seeming normality, to stem the seething dread. He was making normal movements, actions of domesticity. But invisibly he climbed the walls like a lizard, and scuttled across the ceiling to a dark corner from which to peer at me. His eyes widened and swallowed themselves inside a paranoid frame. They couldn't see beyond the frame.

He planted the cup of tea down in front of me on the table. A small wave rose to meet the rim and the tiniest dribble escaped over the side, sneaking down to the paper on the coffee table, painting a little ring.

Hex perched in a chair opposite, taking a sip from his own mug which he cupped close to his agitated torso. He let out a slow sigh and looked at me.

"Chill the fuck out, Hex. It's me," I said.

He smirked, something from a clearer, safer past remembered. Maybe just my tone of scorn.

"What's happened to you Simba? Since when did a posh shit like you use the phrase 'chill the fuck out'? It's that Scottish ogre you spend your time with."

His face relaxed as he spoke, the muscles formed words and smiles, the eyes shifted to soft focus. It was his turn to look me up and down. To note my vanity remained if all else had changed – the carefully pressed shirt beneath the vintage blue cord jacket.

"You come for weed?" he asked.

How did my eyes not falter in shame as I nodded casually? *People come to see me for one reason only*, Hex once said. Nobody genuinely wants to be friends with a schizoid.

I never intended to become a weed smoker. The very idea makes my nose crinkle. I think of scruffy, unwashed boys playing video games for days on end, eating out of takeaways boxes. I decided, though, when I was younger to just learn how to smoke without choking like a cat.

I think this was Cassie's influence – if you must be arrogant you must do everything with panache. When you're a teenager, you care too much what people think of you, so are easily led. We weren't so easily led. We knew we'd always be the outsiders. We didn't do things to make people think we were cool.

Yet the years had dribbled by and we ran with different crowds (well, she didn't obviously, she was dead). And yet I was the same socially inept boy. Could I bear to admit that I began joining in social smoking to make myself seem less uptight? I may also count innumerable acquaintances who spoke of their disregard for the drug cultures. For those who needed something extra to enjoy themselves. Yet adulthood brings new breeds of trauma, isolation, self-image. We think we've grown up but we have only grown older and become more tattered. And then some moment comes when someone offers out a little white powder, and we shrug off our morals and doubts. Stability is not something we aspire to.

Social smoking brought me a new kind of silence. I never felt a massive effect of the drug. It just felt like a space where strangers could sit around in relaxed quiet or idle chatter. Smoke filled uncertain gaps. I remained scornful of those who bought the stuff just for themselves and shut the door and smoked alone.

Then the gaps began emerging. I was alone too often and my own company was vile enough. I drank too much espresso and lay awake wishing my body would evaporate.

And as I sat out the back of that boheme little café after closing time, drinking coffee and enjoying the empty feeling it gave me. The sun was drowning in a blissed horizon, there was a sweet smoke filling the air, and a hand reached out and offered me a toke.

Level seven. The perfect point in the brain where the uppers and the downers meet. Once you've been to level seven you've forgotten everything else. You just want to go back there. It's not like the endless dance of spinning lights and colour, of fractured worlds. You're not floating near the ceiling waiting for the balloon to pop, and the uncertain drop that is inevitable. You're only just above the ground. If you stretch your toes you can touch back down. You've arrived here gently and you'll be barely conscious of your departure.

Espresso and marijuana. I even like the two words written next to one another. Hex dug around for a ready wrapped little parcel and placed it on the table.

"Shall we have one now?" he asked.

I shrugged and nodded. He began to search out a grinder and some rizzlas. I stood up and walked over to the window. He had floor length maroon curtains, I tugged them open a little. His flat was in the basement but the house was levelled on a hill so that French windows opened onto the garden.

"Can we sit outside?" I asked. "This room makes me want to vomit."

He smirked and nodded, collecting things together on a tray. We sat cross-legged on the grass. It was sunny and a little breezy also. Hex looked like living death in the sunlight, collar bones jutting at the neck of his t-shirt, reminding me of the description of Mister Duck, skin hanging off a coat hanger.

"It's good to see you, man," he mumbled without looking up. "It's just fucking mental about Cassie. I still can't get my head around it, I miss her soo much. Every day. I bet it was... just fucking dark, man. Darkness with a capital D."

I rolled my eyes. I didn't want this conversation.

"So yeah, Simba. Fucking good to see you..."

I couldn't wait to get out of there. I needed a coffee.

* * * * * * *

SAME SHIT, DIFFERENT DIMENSION

Claudia McLeod, Derby

"Lads wiv brollies, s'wrong int' it?"

Rufio was sat back to front on a wooden chair. He broadened out his shoulders to emphasise this point, then leaned forward agen, restin his weight over his arms so that he could peek nosily at what I were writin.

"Yeah. For once I agree. But I've issues wi' brollies in general."

"You got issues," he nodded, lookin up at me wi' those intense brown eyes that joked and were serious at't sayme time.

The cafe door clunked open and another metrosexual-lookin lad slipped in, pullin down his brolly so it dripped a trail on't floor. He ran a hand through his hair vacantl'y, tryin to catch his reflection in a mirrored panel behind the counter.

"Same shit, different dimension, ain't it?" Rufio mulled, watchin him.

I wrote this sentence down, irrelevant as it was to the lyrics I were mekkin notes on. He peeked over agen and frowned, stabbin a finger at it.

"Fookin copyrighted."

"Bullshit, Roofie. I bet it's from *Red Dwarf* or sommat. I like it though, it's got that Sci-fi philosophical thing to it. Reminds me of the deja vu comment in *The Matrix*."

Some teenagers in the café started laffin agen. Rufio looked narked at the regular custom of his workplace, despite bein off duty.

"Them cats always howlin." He shook his head.

Another lad came trippin through't door wi'a broken brolly. He stuffed it hastily in't bin, rufflin soggy blonde hair. My belly did a lit'l skip. He plonked hissel in the chair next to me, leanin over my writing wi' fleetin eagerness, mirrorin furra moment Rufio's body language. He pulled his silly over-sized coat off, havin already dripped on my pages.

"You remind me of the Cat actual'ly," I said to Roofie, who on a different tangent, was pointing at Haydn and sayin.

"Wannabe metrosexuaw. Not buy spensive nuff umbrella..." He then realised what I'd said and turned back to me. "What you sayin anyway? The Cat is gay!"

"What she actually means," Haydn put in, wavin at Kathy for some maire coffees, "is that the Cat reminds her of Prince and you also remind her of Prince."

I nodded. "But isn't Prince gay?" I asked.

"No no," Roofie said. "He's just a Kat, cat wiv a K."

"Obvs." Haydn chuckled.

I put some more words to paper, this time irrelevant to the conversation.

"Why you writin' in a book anyway Cloud? Get a laptop. You jus wanna look art-ee," Rufio said.

"I'm lo-fi. It means I can't afford a laptop," I replied.

A silence flitted b'tween us. Haydn kept shiftin his gaze back to me. Kathy brought over some coffees.

"Hi Aidey," she said self consciously. "How're you? Is the work going well?"

"Not too shabby, thanks," Haydn replied, notin my expression at her address. "A bit too much 'networking' and not enough writing... or sleep for that matter. But no rest for the wicked, eh, babes? How are you?"

"Oh, fine. Sounds exciting that, networking," she said.

"Ee means ee goes to bars and charms people and then shares some chimeney chenga wiv em. That's is job, fookin glamorous," Rufio said boredly.

Kathy nodded uncertainly, cleared our empty cups and removed hersel lyke an obedient maid.

"...She wants to bang you," Rufio said when she were out of earshot.

"You say that about every girl I speak to," Haydn said.

"Don't any of them want to bang *you*?" I asked.

"They aw do," he nodded, raisin a finger dramatic'ly. "They just don't know it yet."

"I see. And by the way, how do you survive the rain? I can't think it's good fa ya hair?" I asked.

"Nah man, makes me look like a French poodle, but I 'avva hood. Why would I need a brolly? D'ya fink Brant Bjork carries a brolly? Nope. D'ya fink Rufio Gonzalez carries a brolly?"

"I don't like my feet getting wet though," Haydn intercepted. "Don't your feet get wet?"

Rufio lifted a blue and black shiny trainer ontu't table.

"My treds is plastic. Space age Speedy Gonzalez, see?"

"Is Rufio Gonzalez your real nayme?" I asked. "Or is it just a DJ nayme?"

"Yeah-man. My grandpappy was Latino, and my mum wassa fookin hippy. Fuck knows where she got Rufio from. Took too much fookin acid in er yoof. She can talk ears of a donkey... I mean best not to ask 'er elws yull be there frever!"

I could feel Haydn's eyes too heavily.

"Stop looking adoringly at me," I said sharply.

He smirked and blushed.

"Yeah Blondie, not doin owt fer your bad boi image. Girls like guys who is aloof. Proper men who don't carry brollies."

"'*Girls like guys with skills... numchuck skills, bow-hunting skills!*'" Haydn muttered happily, more to himself than us.

"They don't like geek boys who quote jokes from geek films and geek TV, cos they not funny their sen." Rufio shook his head pitifully.

Haydn ignored him and carried on gigglin to himself. *"Got skills..."*

"Are you aloof, Roofie?" I asked.

"Not yet, maybes. But I bought these shades..." He dug in his jacket pocket and pulled out some chunky sunglasses, placin them slowly onto his fayce, an then flippin it round and caricaturising aloofness. "Yeah?"

"Now you're just waiting on a sunny day," Haydn murmured.

"You is too rule-abiding, Blondie. Truly cool peopuw can wear shades all the time."

"Are you truly cool then, Roofie?" I asked.

"Cooler than the cool side of the pillow," he nodded emphatic'ly.

* * * * * *

THE SAME THINGS CELEBRATED, WILL BE THE SAME THINGS BERATED

Wolfgang, Sheffield

"So you're a writer?" Beazie asked with disparaging enthusiasm. "Do you write poetry? I'm really getting into poetry at the moment. I think it's really making a comeback from being seen as 'uncool'. They have a night at The Runaway Girl. And you see a real fusion with performance art, it's *fascinating*," she paused. "So, do you write poetry?"

I waited to see if she would let me speak, trying to unsettle her with a yellow grin. But she was one of those extreme unjudgmental types, who adore befriending the homeless, or better a disabled person, or better a homeless, disabled person. She beamed patiently at me, in order to reassure me that I was a valuable interesting member of society, with something to contribute.

"I only write poetry when I'm hallucinating," I said hesitantly. "It's rather simplistic."

She nodded. "You should come along to the night and read some. It's a great platform for talent."

"I don't write things in order for them to be read aloud. It's a different kind of writing," I said.

"Oh, don't be nervous! You'll get such a buzz from doing it the first time. You could involve it in your coursework as well. They always mark live art highly, because it's the newest *thing*."

I looked at her with faux wide eyes. "Golly, aren't you young?" I said "You don't remember the sixties, I suppose."

"I'll help you practice, if you like?" she suggested.

I spotted Cuan skulking across the canteen. He made a fearful face when he saw Beazie talking to me. He came and sat down anyway, wanting to persuade me outside so that he could consume his daily diet of coffee and cigarettes. He dragged up a plastic chair noisily.

"Oh, hello, *Cuan,*" she said. "Gosh, I've not seen you for ages. Why haven't you been to the crit group? You really ought to knuckle down. You're so talented, you shouldn't waste it."

"I'm a talented waster," he replied, quick as a fox. "It's part of my art."

"Oh really?" she said. "I see."

"No, it was a joke. You've been brainwashed. You actually can't recognise a joke," he added bluntly.

"There's no need to be hostile, *Cuan*. Don't be afraid of expressing yourself. We're all artists here. We'll understand your medium, whatever it is. Do you do poetry? *Wolfgang* is coming to read at the poetry night on Wednesday. Isn't that exciting for him? You'll come and support him, won't you?"

"Is he really?" Cuan raised a slender eyebrow.

"Oh, there's my tutor. Back in a minute," Beazie said, springing up like a Jack-in-a-Box.

"Quickly. We must escape while we can," Cuan hummed.

"I was rather enjoying her company," I muttered. I gathered up my battered jacket and selection of essential carrier bags and followed him outside. It was raining so we stayed beneath the overhang. Cuan pulled on his gloves. They were worn through at the finger-tips and yellowed from clutching so many cigarettes and spilling so much coffee. He cradled his paper-cup of beige milky caffeinated pond water.

"You're not really reading at a poetry night, are you?" he asked.

I shook my head, watching the rain come down a few feet from us, dripping from the edge of the roof, forming pools and snakes on the concrete step.

"I might just get on the stage and growl at them for a bit, and see how that goes down."

"How's your dissertation coming along?" Cuan asked apprehensively.

"Well, I managed to cut it down to thirty thousand words. But then I had to add some more," I said woefully. It was difficult for me to write in a box.

"And what's the limit? About seven or eight thousand?" he asked.

I nodded. "Will you edit it for me? Tell me what needs cutting. Nothing does, it's all *essential*. But I'll take your word for it."

"I'm dyslexic, Mr. Wolf. You know damn well it would take me a week to read just a few pages of your stuff. I can't follow your cryptics. I get too confused." He coughed a little, half in laughter.

"I fear I'm destined to fail in the academic sphere, I cannot contort to fit the appropriate box," I mumbled, all glumsome.

"Fuck it, it's only art school," he replied quickly. "It's not like a real degree."

* * * * * *

FOUR STORIES BELOW

Haydn Antoine, Derby

'*Drop, drop, drop... tomorrow and tomorrow and tomorrow*'

Rufio spun a pen between his fingers. He was sat on the window ledge, which was the width of a bench seat, with his back to the wall. His body was folded into the frame of the eight foot window, beyond which the rain pounded the streets four storeys below.

He was dressed as theatrically as always, despite the severe unlikelihood of leaving the flat on a day like today. A cowboy's red neckerchief tied round his throat and a grey t-shirt tapered onto his torso. He had two belts around his skinny hips (because just one could pass as practical rather than accessory), with one massive buckle depicting a pistol clinking against another with two cherries on. His hand, which turned the page of his book, was defined at the wrist by a Thundercats sweat band.

He underlined something in the book.

"Why do you always do that...?" I asked. "Vandalise books."

"Tis my book," he grunted. "I read books in bout a day and then I just forget ev'ryfing in them. This way I pick up the best lines which define what I finks importunt. I'm leavin my mark beyind. Itus meaninfuw and powetic if you finks propleh bout it, Blondie."

"But you've ruined the book for the next person."

"Maybe I've made it bet'er by pointing out to them what they should take note of. You're so of the establish'munt, Blondie. They teach you bollox in posh school, you need to know."

"What did they teach of use in your school? How to hide a gun in your socks?" I asked.

This was a joke of its time as his hometown of Nottingham had fast-developed a worse reputation for gun-crime than Birmingham. One of Rufio's favourite quips to new people he met was *'itus not a good night out if you don't get shot'*.

"Equalit'y my son. How respect must be earned by a person, be they teacher or pupil or prime-fookin-minister. If you wanted to get an educashun at my school, you ad to be capable of thinking for your sen, filterin the shit out..."

"Why don't you use a pencil, then you can rub it out?"

He sighed and shook his head in mock despair. "I don't believe in pencils, Blondie. I don't believe in 'esitance or 'arf-measures. I don't believe in erasing my mistakes. I fookin own them, they are me."

"Is that why you always ruin the G2 crossword?" I glanced at my watch. "Shit, I need to put dinner on. Cloud'll be here soon."

"Isn't you just the loveliest 'ouse hubby?"

"She gets well-mardy when she's hungry, though."

"Hen-pecked. Hen-pecked and pistol-whipped, my son." He folded the corner of the page he was on to mark it, and placed the copy of *Brave New World* on the mantel next to the rainbow haired troll. "Nah, man. Cookie leavin 'er fookin tacky shit alover 'gen."

I rooted around in the bottom cupboard for some potatoes. "I kinda like it. Have you seen her life-size cuddly Zippy toy at her house?" I searched the draining board for a half-decent, clean knife.

"Yeah-man, s'fookin scary, wouldn't want to sleep next to that." He collected stray cups from around the room and squeezed them in next to the existing pile of dirty dishes. "Wouldn't want to wake next to er neevfer, mind. She's fookin scary nuff. She fookin shouts in er sleep and shit – 'as night terrors."

I nodded with passing concern.

"Thas why she just bangs blokes un never as a proper fella. So she can av sex but don't aff to sleep next to em cos she attacks em in er sleep!" he finished.

"Really?" I asked, unsure of whether I was being gullible or not.

He shrugged, running the tap into the sink, flashing fingers quickly beneath the water.

"Fookin 'ot water not workin gen. You gonna go speak to bitch land-lay?" He motioned downstairs with a thumb.

"Why do *I* have to? I set up all the payment of the bills. I set up wireless. I bought the TV licence..."

"Zackly, Blondie. You is a loverly 'ouse hubby, so regimented and wew organised. I can only bask quietly in the glory of your German efficiency."

I shifted my glasses up my nose, further realising I was reinforcing his mockery.

"She can't even get my fucking name right, Gonzo. I've been here what, six months? She's already ruined my life."

"You should see it as an opportunity, boy. A chance to av a new identity, to be reborn a phoenix. We could fake the deaf of Haydn Antoine, then you wouldn't get assewed by your ex-bird neevs."

I placed the wedges of raw potato into a pan and ran some cold water over them, then placed the pan on the stove and lit the gas with a match. "I'm not sure my mother would be too pleased."

"Yeah, she wouldn't assew you no-more neevs! I wouldn't av to be nice to er on't phone."

"Didn't you tell her she was a 'MILF' last time you spoke to her? And what pray did you tell her that means?" I asked.

"Nah, mate, she didn't ask proper. She's all confused by my blue colla lingo. She just laffs uncertainl'y when she not know what am sayin."

"Which is all the time," I said.

He gave a Brando big-chin nod.

I peeled open the fridge door and crouched down in front of it, inspecting the not-so-appetising contents. "I had some sausages. You know where they've gone?"

He shrugged. "Maybe Cookie ate them."

"Maybe you ate them," I said.

He held both hands up in innocence. I shoved and dragged green cheese and stale croissant out of the way and picked out a liquefied cucumber to toss in the direction of the bin. Finally I found the sausages at the back. I dumped them on the counter with some eggs.

* * * * * *

ALL THE CONVERSATIONS I'LL NEVER HAVE

Simian Thomas, Sheffield

Inside my eyes a beautiful pink sky was so slowly dimming. It called on the last days of summer and whispered that the leaves would soon fall.

I glanced over to the hairy ogre with the thick set forehead and bold black brows trying to brutalize the girlish length of his eyelashes. It felt sometimes like I was a little Tom Thumb sat in the protection of his large hands. He gave me friends – or, rather, returned them. I hardly used to see Roxanne much before, but it so happened in this smallness of worlds they knew each other and spent a fair amount of time together. Along with the delectable Claudia McLeod.

Sat with us also on this evening was the mythic Irishman, Devlin, whose exceptional gentility made me believe he might have killed somebody sometime. He had an extreme, unnerving calmness. Indeed he seemed to magnify the little jitters the rest of us tried to keep under wraps.

I sipped my coffee, which was not quite as good as it should've been. But given that we were sat on a roof terrace with an excellent view of the city falling away beneath us, and could smoke some, I was forgiving. (How gracious.)

Charlie passed me the joint. He was mid-conversation – they were all mid-conversation, vocal chords singing. I talked silently in my own head, because the only person I wished to speak to in that moment was not there, nor ever could be.

All the conversations I wished we'd had. All the conversations I had to remind myself I could never have. I tried to recall words I once wanted to say to Roxy, but never had the chance because she was so elusive. But I'd changed so much since then. The potential moment was lost a long time ago. I had no dialogue left, jokes turned bitter on my tongue. Granted if I'd bothered to listen to other people, I might've been inspired to speak myself. But my ears were empty, containing only white noise. Roxy spoke to me. I watched her lips move, but I couldn't read nor hear them. So I smiled apologetically and looked away.

I sat there like an awkward mannequin and filled my empty body with sweet smoke and bitter coffee and justified my selfish silence with the notion of grief.

I imagined Cassie sat there with us, spinning delighted energy around the space, poking fun at Charlie, making him smile warmly and telling breathy tales of our misadventures overseas. The strange truth is, if she weren't dead I probably wouldn't be sat here, but she might. I'd be shunning her new friends as I'd always done. The picture began to crumble like a biscuit in hot tea.

"Simian. How is it yuu've ended up the manager of a shop, given yuu have the social skills of a Camra member?" Charlie asked, breaking through the sound barrier.

"I wouldn't say a Camra member," Claudia put in. "They do talk. They're just a bit dull and faddy."

"No-one else was stupid enough to work there long enough to get promoted?" I proffered flatly.

"Aye," Charlie said. "Anyway, it's your round. Guinness for me, rum for Ratty, and Pale Rider for Cloud and Paddy."

"It's Devlin, you dumb jock," the mythic Irishman jibed.

I gathered my bones up and headed inside, just catching Roxy's sweet voice pleading quietly.

"Charlie, he's depressed, leave him alone!"

"He needs tu fooking snap oot of it," Charlie replied.

A part of me carried on past the bar and out of the door. But home was more fearful than a friend's honest exasperation with me. He was right after all. There's nothing quite so boring as insurmountable self-pity in a companion. Lord knows I've had it with my mother.

A fresh espresso, topped with fluffy clouds. I took small pleasure in the requited affection between myself and the drink, and then summoned words as a small gift for Roxanne.

"So you're going travelling next year, are you?"

She nodded hesitantly.

"Who are you going with?"

"My friend Bobby from back home," she nodded with tentative enthusiasm.

"Where's back home?"

"Nottingham. But Bobby's in Leeds at the moment studying. I miss her, she's the best."

I nodded, watching Claudia roll out of the corner of my eye and hating my own desperation.

"Where are you heading? Have you decided yet?" I asked.

"We're just going around Europe, nothing too adventurous. I'm not very good at saving money," Roxy rambled.

"I wish I'd gone to Europe. I'd love to do the Norwegian Fjords," I mumbled.

"Oh, you should come too, if you want. Bobby would like you, I think."

I shook my head slowly, my heart jumping into my throat. "I don't think that's wise."

Probably best not to verbalise my irrational fears. She looked wide-eyed at me, trying to read between the lines.

"Yeah, Scandinavia looks amazing. I'd love to go up into the Arctic Circle in summer, when it's twenty four hour daylight," she breezed on. "I dunno how far we'll get though, depends on money and stuff."

Claudia cackled loudly all of a sudden, at something Devlin said – he looked passably smug. She stood up out of her seat still aching with laughter, which echoed around the small terrace, rattling inside my brain. It somehow froze me to the spot, staring at her as she leant on the wall and looked over the city and tried to take a drag of her roll up, but had to stifle giggles again.

"It's not that funny," Charlie smirked grimly.

"Yeahrit'tis," she said.

* * * * * * *

HAIRY MCLAREY FROM DONALDSON'S DAIRY

Wolfgang, Sheffield

Like a monkey in front of the cameras, instead of acting out, he sways in the spotlight. And discloses nothing save for the fact that he is mad. Another booze hound falling out of a boozer, chased by news cats.

"Charlie's a published writer, don't you know?" Cuan announced.

It was the Kaiser himself who looked the most shocked. Clearly he had no inkling of Cuan's intrepid talent as a high tech nosey-parker.

"True story. Amazing what you can turn up on the internet these days. And oh, what have we here?" He produced in front of himself a slightly academic looking book, with all the feigned dramatic gusto of a Victorian magician, smiling as though he had won a complex battle of intellect over the Kaiser.

Myself, Roxy, Maisie (the Paisley Mouse) and Claudia all craned our necks over the pub table, moving half empty glasses out of the way to peer at the title *A Rat in the Boy's Club* by Bryn Charles McLarey. Roxy picked it up and examined it, scanning through the blurb on the back with a furrowed brow.

"Where did you get this from? Did you snoop through his stuff?" she said, with a tone that suggested Cuan possessed little morals when it came to snooping through people's stuff.

"Not literally," Cuan said still smugly. "Like I say – a little searching the net, a little tracking down of a valuable purchase item. I'm surprised no other cats have been curious enough... Has nobody ever wondered why he had such a rough childhood, yet often speaks like an English gentleman? Only a little snip of Glaswegian here and there when he's had one too many pints? He's not *ashamed* of his roots, he positively revels in them. He loves having more grit than us soft middle-class brats!" Cuan sat back with his pint and took a satisfied slug of ale.

Maisie whispered something in Claudia's ear and giggled. She had a crush on Charlie, handsome ruffian and all that. Paisley princess and the pauper. Cuan snuck a sideways glance, with a knowing smile.

One couldn't help enjoying Cuan when he was smug and clever and his whole being was electrified by humour. As though he'd been quietly waiting day upon day, while our Kaiser belittled him jealously. Now it was his time, he was rapidly reducing the mysteries of Charlie's cleverly moulded persona to so much rubble.

He pointed at Charlie, who maintained a half composed sneer. "This fucker went to Oxford." He left a dramatic pause for us to absorb the information, twirling a scruffy curl behind his ear with girlish panache (his mousey hair was getting a bit long, he'd ask me for a haircut soon). "Pretended to be an English public school boy, like an undercover cop, so he could write about it."

I'll never understand the term *public* school in this crazy country, so confusing.

"Well thas bollocks furra start," Claudia suddenly put in. "If anythin he pretended to be an English public schoolboy to gerrin a few posh girls knickers. He might've ended up wi' sommat intellectual, but I doubt that wa'tha plan."

"Oh, you know me tuu well, little Cloud," Charlie remarked with a sly grin. His anger at Cuan had quickly abated. After all, there was a yarn to be told here. And having a yarn to tell was the most important thing a person could have in the great scheme of things. The revelations of his early twenties merely left a large pool of question marks to make him interesting amongst his friends.

As if to reinforce this Roxy shrugged helplessly. "I feel so fucking boring in comparison to you lot!"

Cuan sniggered to himself, and said quietly (only audible to Roxy and those with rather brilliant hearing), "All people are boring. Some just create more elaborate costumes than others."

I swooned internally at his intellect, and the fact that, in all perhaps-ness, he was actually talking about himself.

"Does that mean you don't think I'm boring?" I asked Roxy quickly.

She smiled the wry, adorable smile which they all fall helplessly for. "You're far too mad to be boring, Wolfie."

I raised a dramatic finger, so they'd know I was trying to say something profound. "Maybe I'm mad because I'm bored with myself?"

Maisie cowered at the presence I inflicted on the space (or maybe just the smell of my rat breath when I spoke?). She was uncomfortable of me and failed to comprehend why the others accepted my company, like a slightly annoying tickle in the sinuses which makes one a bit snivelly. This was why she wouldn't survive the next Ice Age. Human fear of your own mucus is a major weakness in the battle for survival. I've muttered this many a time, I know.

"Did anyone ever read *Hairy McLairy From Donaldson's Dairy* when they were little?" Cuan asked.

I mouthed the title to myself.

"Rings a bell," Claudia said. "What warrit?"

"It was all in rhyme, about all the neighbourhood dogs joining together in a big impressive pack, and then at the end they're scared off by a big hairy tom cat..."

"Called Hairy McLairy?" I asked.

"Noo, I remember," Claudia jumped in. "Hairy McLairy was a scruffy lit'l mongrel terrier."

The moral? Even a pack of dogs can be dispersed by a big fierce cat.

"Why does it say you're name is Bryn on here?" Maisie pointed back to the book.

"Because thas mae name," Charlie said. "But it's a bit Celt to go through Oxford with."

"*You must know that a cat should have three different names,*" Cuan burbled "First they call him Bryn McLarey, second they know he's Charlie Brown, thirdly he is the Kaiser, because he has us all by the scruff of the neck."

"I'm confused," Maisie said. "I thought he was a dog, but now you're saying he's a cat again?"

Cuan laughed. "I was paraphrasing T. S Elliott. Besides, I *think* you'll find he's human. He looks vaguely human, doesn't he?"

"Why does everything become a riddle? I can't keep track," she murmured.

"I say what I mean, but do I mean what I say?" Cuan continued.

"Just shut up now, Q ball. You're giving me a fookin headache," Charlie said.

"Who said that?" Cuan rose in his seat and looked around as if there were no people anywhere near him.

Roxy grabbed his sleeve and pulled him down in his seat. She whispered into his ear, so quietly even I missed it. This seemed to calm him and he rested a resigned head on her shoulder. I got up and shuffled to the bar to get another round in, then returned with my hands full, planting drinks on the table.

"How come ya've money? Aren't ya homeless?" Claudia asked.

"Next student loan came in," I bumbled.

"You're a student?" she said, oozing incredulity.

"Fine Art at the delectable Hallam. How did you think I was acquainted with Cuan?"

"He knows ev'ry crazy fooker in this city," she said.

Cuan was flicking through Charlie's book again, reading excerpts, and giggling. "I loved it by the way, I read it all in like two days. And all these great reviews about it!"

"What about the 'great reviews'?" Charlie asked angrily.

"*A key sociological text?!*" Cuan exclaimed, slapping his thigh clownishly. "It's more like the ramblings of a jealous, paranoid narcissist..."

"Takes one tu know one, some might say."

* * * * * *

OLD KIDS

Claudia McLeod, Derby

I glanced at my watch and knocked on't door. It were quarter to midnight. Haydn wouldn't be home yet. He was getting a lift back from Birmingham where he'd been meetin a band (which generally meant gettin rat-arsed). Cookie opened't door, clearly not expectin me.

"Oh, hi, Aidey's not here." She glanced me up an down.

"I know. Rufio said I could come an wait ferr'im. Is that okay w'you? Or aya gonna turn me out ontu't mean streets of Derby?"

"There's no need to be sarcastic," she said airily, letting the door swing open and retreatin back through the barely lit room tu't sofa. I closed the door behind me and peered in the gloom, the television providing the only illumination. I dropped my bag next tu't coffee table, and took residence inna bean bag, realisin a lump of clothes next to Cookie were in fact a sleepy Rufio. He stirred to life and switched on a lamp.

"Crazy bird, ello. Forgets you is comin over. Got any rizlas on yer?"

I felt in my pockets. "Nope. Sorry, dude."

"No worries. Av some vino." He pointed to a half empty bottle of red wine on the floor. "Not no glasses clean though, aff to use a mug."

"Cheers," I said, strugglin up agen, and fumbling in't dark cupboard for somat to drink from. I sat back down again, tryin not to spill any, and took a satisfying sip. "Wow. This is pretty nice, not the usual shit."

"Wew, Blondie got paid, so we gets in the Mawlbec! How is you? How'd your gig go?" He picked up the wine bottle hissel and emptied the remains into his cup.

"Yeah yeah, went alrayte. Think they quite liked us, sold a few EPs. We were playin wi' the Whiskycats as well, who were fookin ace, it's their hometown."

"Oh, crazy fookin mosh jazz? Fink Blondie played em me," he said.

I laffed. "Mosh-jazz... that's one way to purrit"

Cookie was watchin an episode of *Skins* on telly. She looked over at me.

"Look how fash they are... Just like you, and drama queens, too." She folded her arms smugly.

"It's funny how you're so anti the whole self-image thing. Given you hang out wi' the two vainest men I know." I arched an eyebrow and waited til she looked at me, then blew her a flirtatious kiss. She actually giggled at that.

"True," she said. "Everyone's so vain these days. The nineties were so much better, everyone just raved and didn't give a shit. I don't fit in with the scene anymore."

What fookin scene? I wanted to shout, but am pretty sure listenin to a petty argument were not what Rufio had in mind. I thought maybe if I said nowt she might be quiet, but no such luck.

"I wasn't a cool kid at school," she said, as though she were gonna pour her heart out. I ignored the fact that she was contradicting hersel.

"Were you a 'cool kid' at school?" I asked Rufio.

"Nadda..." he said, poking a nose out from his hoodie. "Wew, I got bullied a lot. Too camp for 'um I sposes."

I couldn't imagine him bein bullied.

"How did you cope wi' it?" I asked.

He smiled. "I got worse. I just exaggerated my personalatee even more, carried on laffin. Laff til they tump you harder and laff some more. They can do nuffin to ya, less you let um. I fink that's how I built up a fanbase. I stood up for uvver peepew too, it's worse seein someone ewls get beat up than it is to take it your selwf."

We both looked at him admirab'ly, probably both recallin some point when we hadn't stood up for someone. Probably a friend even.

"A fanbase?" I said.

"Yeah," he nodded, flexing an arm. "By sixth form all the fookers who won't gonna make owt of their lives ud dropped out. And then I was *king*, cos I'd been a proper dude to peepuw, and they respected that. I've been the dogs bollox ever since!"

I laffed.

"What about you?" Cookie said. "Were you ever bullied at school?"

I sighed. "I *were* a bully at school, y'don't need me to tell you that. It were all a big game of surviving. I played the fookin game... sorry!"

Rufio tutted and shook his head at me gravely. "Was you part of the it-clique, Mc'Loud?"

I thought back to the parts a my life I'd smudged over.

"No, well, we had a bit'uva waar. There were the townie girls and then there were the 'alternative', which were my lot, grebs or whatever. I got in a fair few fights. I never beat up someone who din't deserve it though, but I was pretty nasty to some people unnecessari'ly."

"What's a 'greb'? We didn't have grebs, and by townie you mean pikey right?" Cookie asked.

"Southerners," I muttered. "Pikey means gypsy to me, how can ya not know greb? Scruffy, baggy jeans, would hang out at First Floor probably, afore the emos took over."

"Oh greebos," she said. "I was kind of a greebo, would you've bullied me?"

I laffed, thinkin yes. "I din't pick on someone cause of their tribe. It were purely on individual merit."

"Bless!" Rufio said.

There was the sound of a key rattlin in't door, which continued for quite some time. Then Haydn stumbled in a little drunk, not quite in control of his lanky frame.

"Heyy!" he said on sight. He sat clumsily on the floor next to me, wrapped an arm around ma waist and let his head drop in ma lap. I smirked and stroked his hair.

"Hey Aidey, Claudia was a bully at school," Cookie said triumphant'ly.

He raised his head back up to take in't information, tipped his face up to me and said in a slightly soppy voice, "I forgive you," then promptly fell asleep.

* * * * * *

THE MELANCHOLY DEATH OF THE BOY I NEVER WAS

Bryn McLarey, Glasgow

I look down tu bloody knuckles and it's leik the saime dream repeating itself over. Cold air ripped through mae lungs. I glanced back down the alleyway tu the dark shape of a man on the ground.

"*For fooks sake, wee Bryn. Keep yer fuckin temper fer once, ma boy,*" I muttered aloud tu maesel.

I slipped back inside the shite pub where the walls were bleedin self-hate fer young men like me. Who'd become old men an nuthin fookin changed, except that we cannae throw a punch sae quickly.

"Did I say punk?" I said tu mae auld mate, Billy. "I meant punch."

"Let's get the fuck ootah here afore hus maytes appear."

"Aye, Billy." I picked up mae jacket and tugged it on.

We swaggered oot the door intu the callous night. The city reeked nasty wisdom. The man I popped wus leant on the wall at the mouth of the alley, a little blood on his nostril. His face was crushed more from pishedness that oot I'd done.

"I'll get ma brother ontu you!" he howled, pathetic.

"Hear tha Billy? His fookin brother on yuu, yuu mean bastard."

"Serious, Bryn," mae Billy said. "Sortcha fuckin heid oot. I jus wan tu huv a laff tonight, y'ken?"

"Aye Billy, let's get some lasses. When they comin? We can go tu the nice pool bar and they can lean over the table in their pretty dresses," I said.

"Serious man, Bryn. When you gonna sort yer life out? The smartest man I know, and I know all this shite does nothing but get yu doon. Fookin women and pub brawls. Is that what you want fer the rest of yer life...?" Billy said.

I stopped and turned tu face him and we just looked at one another in the black street. And I knew and Billy knew, that I wus gonna leave him behind someday soon, tuu soon.

"I've applied to go tu Oxford," I said. Any of ye wud hadda snigger, but Billy knew I wusnae lyin.

"Shit, actual Oxford? They let scum like yuu in?"

I shrugged. "I think they huvva quota of scum they haffta let in. But anyway, les just enjoy ourselves while we still can." I placed a mock fatherly hand on his shoulder.

"Shit Bryn, bring it. Ah'll get the drinks toneet."

As we arrived ootside the bar, a taxi pulled up and I walked swiftly over, opening the back door. I pulled a girl out, squinting in the dark withoot ma glasses. I paused and looked at her, shaking ma heid.

"You're no mine." I go back in the car and pulled oot the second girl by the hand. She giggled, wrapping an arm around me. I half picked her up and swung her round, dropping slowly to kiss her with the sweetness of the man I pretend I'm not.

"Hey mae little Sheba, we gonna have sum fun tonight?" I asked.

"My name's no fuckin Sheba!" she said.

She giggled and we walked on in, Billy greeting the other girl, but lookin tu me with them sly eyes of gladness.

* * * * * *

JAM IN THE ATTIC

Roxanne Ratcliffe, Sheffield

It was Claudia's last day in Sheffield. We were out the back of the bar where we worked. We'd climbed off the fire escape and onto the sloping roof, so she and Charlie could smoke in the sunshine.

"What's the plan then?" Charlie asked.

"A few favourite haunts, a few favourite drinks," Claudia suggested.

Charlie gave a distant nod. Claudia flashed me a knowing look. She leaned over Charlie's shoulder and gave him a bear hug, draping long waves of blonde hair down his chest. She chuckled.

"Yar gonna miss me, Charlie Brown, I know y'are."

He smiled. "Aye, fooking top lassie, you know I know that. Dunno why you'd want tu leave us and move tu fucking Derby? For a boy. I hope he's worth it."

"Oh no, he's not worth it. But he mekks me laff and that's a start." She smirked. Was it possible that Claudia was actually really happy about something in her life?

"Fookin Derby though," he pursued.

"Sheffield isn't that pretty either, y'know. Derby has some good pubs," she defended.

Charlie leaned back and gazed at the sky. "Sheffield though, feels full of latent possibilities. Derby will always be a shitty little city with nowt tu offer."

"I don't care, I'm jus excited about brekkin the norm and livin somewhere new." She slopped some more of the unusual, expensive rum we'd bought her into a glass. "You're bein very quiet, Roxy. Whas on ya mynd?" she asked.

I smiled and shook my head. I just wanted to enjoy their joint company, to bask in the familiar exchange of cynicism.

"Anyroad," Claudia murmured. "Me an the lads are gonna go and have a last jam in the attic later. You rayte to tekk some pictures, Ratty?"

I nodded happily. The attic of the bar was dilapidated, slightly dangerous and very photogenic, and a couple of our co-workers also played instruments. So they sometimes got together with Claudia for a mess around.

"Always," I said. "I got given a shitload of film so I'm on a photography binge at the moment."

"I don't get why you don't use digital, it's sae much cheaper," Charlie said.

I opened my mouth to explain but paused too long.

"I'm gonna pop next door and get some bits tu cook us dinner. Any requests?" Charlie asked.

"You know me. Not too fussy so long as thes meat an carbs," Claudia mused.

"Roxy?" he asked.

"I don't mind, it's Claudia's night," I mumbled.

He climbed back over the rail and descended the steps into the bin yard. Then he slipped into the bar through the bottom fire escape, which was propped open to let some air in.

"...Funny how you've ended up working here after we've both left," Claudia mumbled.

"Yeah, more fun here though, the boss is less of a dick," I said.

"Have to wait and see who replaces me. It's notta great time fa this place, it's not trendy no more." She spoke with real glumness. She'd worked there a fair few years now. It was personal. I sighed. I didn't like being left behind. Things would be very different without Claudia. It felt like Bobby moving away all over again.

PHASE THREE

In which the rain comes...

NEVERLAND

Calista Siddal, Fiction

Nether Ed traced his fingertips across the fractures in the city, the fault lines that grated and rumbled like a stomach hungry for the old and the familiar. He liked the ever-changing notion of the place, but he feared the future a little. He was worried about falling down the cracks in the pavement and concerned for the futures of the ladybugs and bumble bees. Their wings a-flutter, flying above the world, asking why the sea was swallowing the green lands. Destruction of the coral reefs – he advised – is not good news. The sea is angry, she'll throw an almighty tantrum sooner or later.

He sat glumly, watching the paint peeling from the wall, listening to the groan of the dual carriageway, his fist propping up his troubled chin, propped up in turn by an elbow rested on a quivering knee.

If only I knew what to do – Ed pondered – If only I knew what to do.

That evening he asked his giant ladybird friend, Gilbert, to fly him to the Arctic, so that he might peer down and see what was afoot. They glided over the great white in silence. Gilbert's wings a pretty blur of red with flashes of gold and blue from the under-wings beneath, which were dowdy until they caught the majestic light.

On the way home Ed cried silently to himself, and Gilbert quickly chirped that he'd warned him the trip would be upsetting.

'I cry because I cannot help but feel the immense pain of all things,' Nether Ed responded.

* * * * * *

SOGGY SOCKS

Simian Thomas, Sheffield

Open doors let light in like water, seeping through slats to create an alluring shape, somehow sinister.

I wanted all the doors to stay open every day in the flat, so the sense of space was not lost. But mine was inevitably the first door to close. The light must be shut out, to be hidden from. We're safe above the city from expanding puddles, from ants seeking infestation in my skin. Now only the light threatens me, glowing at the foot of the door like John Carpenter's *Fog*. And the dust. *Dust is mostly human skin – Henry sucks up human skin. His stomach full, he wants to yak it back up.*

The stillness leaves a space for memory I don't want. The cracks letting light in remind me of water beginning to flood a building through its gills. My pretty little house swallowed up into *Waterworld*, Cosner with webbed feet sploshing down the stairs with a grim, green smile.

Repetitive news reels – water halfway up the red telephone box, dead animals and sewage, canoes roaming the streets. Nice weather for ducks, nice weather for frogs, a nice day for a white wedding. The bride sinks into a pool of white satin, hair spread out in endless waves, clutching a tattered bouquet, singing softly some sad song from another time.

Back to the dry world. Dry save for the pools of weak sunshine, the seeping light, the wind tapping insistently on the window pane with an elongated finger. Devastation. Over-used. The earthquake in Chile – three hundred dead – that's devastation. This was just a puddle, a spider drowning.

The summer floods in Sheffield brought a quiet, whinging misery. I lived on the side least affected, but a soggy atmosphere hung about. I stayed home a lot, letting a little agoraphobia creep in from time to time, only venturing out to work and the shop on the way home, and occasionally to Hex's flat.

But being outside left me edgy, constantly glancing over my shoulder. I cocooned myself in a gore-tex jacket during the haphazard down pours. They came often, and seemed relentless. Unthinkable previously, for someone such as myself, to choose practicality over the tweed and corduroy materials I so dearly fetishized. But I'd been beaten, so to speak. The weather was winning a battle of wills. Beyond the torrential rain there was drizzle and greyness. We waited for the day it would pass and some sense of summer would return, but the next week and the next came and went, with barely a smile of sunshine.

I'd retreat hastily each day to my top floor flat, to dry off. Stringing soggy socks and trousers about on radiators. The mundane becoming strange decoration that left behind an odd smell. I'd smoke marijuana to cover it and drink blends of Brazilian and Moroccan coffee to fill the air with a sweeter aroma. And then I'd consume books and films and newspapers, in order to abridge my uneasiness and the repetitive thought patterns, which rattled around my head like a toy train on a circular track.

When you start to read into events, you start to see patterns emerge. It was easy to collate the melting ice-caps and rising sea levels and think it evidenced our effect on the planet. A verminous species can't help but destroy their environment because there are too many of them, but I began to convince myself of other things. I had no scientific basis but my own vague and fallible memory. But I was sure there were more natural disasters that couldn't be shoved into the evidence box for 'climate change' than when I was young. The Earth was cracking open. We'd become too many, and when a species becomes too plentiful the human rationale is to cull it.

* * * * * * *

CHERRY-ANN & THE DROWNED RAT

Roxanne Ratcliffe, Sheffield

I cringed a silent inward cringe and squinted my eyes as though thinking. I was attempting to disguise the Claudia-like facial expression which tried to find my face. (I tend to absorb people's little idiosyncrasies so much they start to own me.)

I find it a personal insult when people I don't like hit on me. I s'pose I just hate embarrassment. But mostly I hate that they don't realise I scuttle from advances, not because I'm shy and fearful, but because I'm *not into them* and have no polite way of saying this.

Claudia's so used to the scenario she can brush people off like flies.

The flat-faced girl leaned on the bar, staring with the eyes of a hungry coyote. And all her chattering until there was nothing left but teeth and tongues and her over-emphasised laughter at my slightest joke. The laughter warps and distorts in my brain; it empties me out as it rattles inside of me. The basic thing I look for in another person is their capacity for silence and she had none. So intent on emptying out all her words in the hope that some would strike a chord, would seduce.

Off amid the hazy atmosphere of the low ceilinged room, with its scuffed architecture and nicotine stained walls, sat Cherry-Ann (a girl I did love, as far as I could love a girl). She was smoking and smirking, at the far end of the bar, about my obvious dilemma. She tossed her head a little. The top-heavy red curls danced above her penned-in eyes. She was all about illusion. About abandoning the real world for a labyrinth of stage props and smoke that seeped lovingly through mirrors. She loved me because I'd take her picture and she could only ever exist through a lens – the eye, or the eye of a camera.

In a much welcomed kerfuffle, Benjamin (an old friend, a ball of energy) came bounding into the bar, skipping up and hugging me. He sprinkled my cheeks with kisses not unlike a baby spaniel. He was drunk, or possibly pilled-up, or possibly neither. It was always hard to tell, and slightly irrelevant.

"Roxy! I missed you! Did you miss me?"

I gave him a wry smile.

"My house is flooded!" he gestured to the rain.

"Shit, really? How bad?"

It'd been pounding down outside all day. It'd left just a scattering of individuals holed up in the bar, sat in the nooks and crannies of sofas and scattered candles, nursing drinks for company. I looked to the grey-black windows which framed the sparkling torrent. Benji himself was soaked.

I ruffled his hair. "Drowned ratty," I murmured.

He smiled in that hyped way. "I'm gonna have to find somewhere else to stay. First it was the cellar but it's in the ground floor now. All the carpets are ruined."

"Where's your mum?" I asked. "She'll go mad."

"She's away down south. She *will* go mad when she sees the mess. She'll have flippin kittens! Have you heard the Owls stadium is totally flooded? It's like a swimming pool!"

A customer approached the bar so I left Benji to serve. The flat-faced girl took this opportunity to start up a conversation with him. He shifted awkwardly on the spot, rubbing at the soggy arms of his hoodie. When I was finished I returned to rescue him.

"Benji, come and meet somebody!" I dragged him around to where Cherry-Ann was perched kittenish on a bar stool, as though Edward Hopper ought to be painting her.

"Cherry-Ann, this is Benji."

She held out a delicate, long, white hand with perfect red nails and shook his. He gazed at her in delight, happily bumbling the first words that came into his head.

"Are you called Cherry because of your hair?"

A smile passed her pursed lips. "Or is my hair cherry because my name is?" she purred, casually wafting her cigarette smoke away from us. "Very pleased to make your acquaintance, Benji, and so dashing that you've saved little Roxy from having to talk to *that girl*."

Benji made an embarrassed face like he was unsure of casually disregarding a stranger.

"Why do lesbians always hit on you, Roxy? You must give off some vibe," she asked.

I scrunched my nose and shrugged.

"Whatever shall we do to pass this rainy night?" Cherry murmured. "I was meant to be meeting Johnston for a drink, but he got caught up in the rain at Snake's Pass."

"What do you mean caught up?" I asked.

"Well, he phoned me shit-scared because the water was coming up over the bonnet. He's got an old Mini. Wish I'd been there to film it. Is that shallow? A*nyway*, he's okay. He got home, but he's a bit shaken."

"Shouldn't you go and comfort him?" I asked.

"Gosh no, that's his girlfriend's job. Our relationship is purely sex and the exchange of intellect." She gave a little laugh that hoped to justify this. "Anyway, Benji, pull up a stool. Tell me about yourself. What's your favourite television moment?"

Benji bounced on the spot. "No one's ever asked me that! Oh wow, I don't know, television moment? Not programme, but moment?"

She took a drag, nodding emphatically in a hypnotic way that somehow dragged the deepest truths from a person.

I nudged him. "You want a drink?"

"Oh, yes. Rum please."

I begin to mix a rum and coke while still with an ear in the conversation. Benji scrambled in his pockets for a screwed-up five pound note.

"Oh, the houmous!" he said. "The bit of *Monkey Dust* when the werewolves eat the houmous! I like houmous a lot... I also collect animal t-shirts."

"A completely irrelevant, but most valid piece of information," Cherry nodded, stubbing her cigarette out. "What is *Monkey Dust*? I don't know it."

"Hey ho! Roxette!" the flat faced girl called from the other end of the bar. Her girlfriend appeared to have joined her, flapping a broken umbrella around to pool water on the worn, wooden floor.

I walked hesitantly over to take their drinks order. They both leaned on the bar and leered a little at me, while clinging still to each other. I glanced back at Cherry and she made a bemused face at me.

I listened to the water pounding down outside the window, rattling on the air vent. The echo sent a chill, musical vibration down my spine. Somebody would die tonight. I could feel it inside my skin.

* * * * * *

THE THRILL OF WAITING UP FOR THE END OF THE WORLD

Wolfgang, Sheffield

Dastardly devils dancing on the ceiling. No no Cecil, that's just in your head.

"Heid," Kaiser muttered. "H...E...I...D... Can you say that?"

"Heid," I said, though not quite the same for me. It comes out as a vampiric whisper. I opened my mouth as wide as I could and reached into my gullet. There was a hair stuck there at the back. I tried to pluck it out, dislodge it with my tongue. But it still feels a little like it's stuck there, along with a small disgruntled moth, but I don't mind him.

"It is nae what crawls in tu a mun's mooth, it's what comes oot a it," he enunciated.

I leapt in the air, dislodging the tea tray so the pot and the bats inside it flew all over the room.

"A thousand wee devils come oot a it!" I exclaimed.

I see them, little gargoyles with little wings all aflutter, playing now with the tea bats. And one of those wily bats is sending out those clever echoes. He knows there's a moth in my mouth. He fancies a wee snack to go with the tea. It's not tea without a nibble. I wrapped my hand over my mouth.

Rain was pounding the flat roof overhead. It disconcerted me, in its ordinary doom. Kaiser was not so affected. He sat nonchalant as a gentleman in an arm chair, admiring the books on the shelf (as though they were pretty ladies or special cakes). He altered his poise slightly and adjusted the collar of his long black coat, changing tack like good cop to bad cop. He was trying to teach me Scottish. Being able to speak English with the perfection of an Etonian, he couldn't fathom how we cannot all pick up accents like so many trinkets.

"Who is Cecil? You kept saying the name in your sleep."

I shrugged. "Maybe I met him in the trenches."

He rolled his eyes. "Are you okay, Wolfgang?" he asked. "See, I heard Kunsthaus Tacheles was being shut down. And though you're as mad as always, I think your dreams have got worse. You've some emotional attachment to the place, I assume? How long did you live there for?"

The bats all flit to the mantelpiece and one by one hang upside down off it. Then they stretch their fluffy gramophone ears and peer at me with beady eyes and wrinkled snouty-snouts. The gargoyles clamber the dresser where the crockery is so neatly displayed. They sit on their little haunches among the plates. Though their ears are tinier, they too perk up to listen and little specs of fire that must be eyes fixate and focus their heat.

"...Since I have an audience," I murmured thoughtfully, wondering if I would come out with a sentence worthy of sense. "Developers want to turn it into luxury apartments or some such. Can you fathom that? It is funny. F*u*nny with a capital U. I've been abiding here in Sheffield, watching how they're filling its charismatic sprawl with these little identikit boxes, for little matchstick dollies to live in. And... I don't know. I really believed nothing like that could ever possibly happen to my old home. It's like when someone breaks up with you and you've no idea why. And you're just stuck in this sense of disbelief. Like someone has punched you. And you're in the middle of being knocked out, but time has suspended itself. So you're hit and reeling but not yet found the floor...?"

The Kaiser's eyes were wide and warm as Charlie's. He rested a hand on my shoulder. "God damn, Wolfgang. That's the most honest sense you've ever made."

* * * * * *

NICE VICES

Claudia McLeod, Derby

I stared at the glass a whiskey an coke, the rim so far unstained by lipgloss or saliva. I wished I'd bought a pint. I glanced jealously at Haydn's pint as he purrit to his lips and took a long satisfyin sip of beer. I could feel in the corner of my eye a lad starin at me. The way yar mother taught ya not to stare... I wished there were an ashtray on't table. In previous times I've thrown stubs at people wi' such little self-awareness. Smokin ban had come in though. Made me itch in ma seat and stare to the door. It were a poor excuse for a summer outside, which didn't ease the ill.

The Blue Dog remained battered by its history as an ashtray. Fulla slightly smelly grungers and emos. The furniture and floors were worn out in a dusty familiar way, lyke a leather glove lost in a student's glove box. Through the dust, Rufio clattered intu't bar, his junk shop dynamic and comedy attitude standing out against the pale faces of artificial teenage angst. He clocked us and also the boy who were still gawpin at me. He approached the young'un at an angle and grabbed his shoulder.

"Av some self-respect goggle-og. Stop letting yer tongue roll out on da floor! I knows she's prettee an that, but she's no Jessica Wabbit, yeah?"

He shoved intu't seating next to me so that I were forced to budge up closer to Haydn. He kissed me on the cheek.

"Maybe ees checkin Antwon, I dunno." He unzipped his oversized turquoise and pink patterned ski jacket (though I should emphasize he's never bin skiing) and wrestled it off his shoulders. "How are you, babes?" he asked Haydn over ma head.

"Ahite geez, not too shabby."

Rufio nodded emphatic'ly, scratchin his black crop a pretentious facial hair. "Sorry am late. Went furra piss... and then a piss turned into a shit, an inevitably a shit turned into a wank, and 'fore I knows it I was doubled over in rhythmic ecstasy..."

I cackled loudly, so that everyone looked over at us.

"Really?" Haydn asked, playin the straight man.

"Nah, mate," Rufio shook his head as though disappointed in himself. "You want a pint, McLeod? You not touchin it." He motioned to my drink.

"That would be ace thanks, Roofie. Yurra fookin mind-reader."

"Aye." He picked my drink up, necked it and headed fa't bar.

"D'ya think we woulda lasted this long wi'out Roofie?" I asked. "I dunno what we'd talk about."

Haydn smirked. "How's work?"

"See, thas a married fa years, nowt to say ta one-another question."

"Seriously... how's the new girl? Have you made her cry yet?" he persisted.

"No, and am not tryin," I said.

"It'll come." He shrugged.

Rufio returned wi' three pints. "Got one free," he said, lining it up next to Haydn's other pint.

I took a long, satisfyin glug or two a mine, noddin happily. "You know wharrah read today in Vice magazine? 'Blondi' were the name of Adolf Hitler's dog, German Shepherd dog... His only true friend it said, he 'ad her killed when he killed hissel. Given yar Adolf obsession I thought that were pretty fookin funny."

Rufio stared at me agape. "No! Is dat true! You pullin my chain, bird?"

"It mus be true, it were in Vice magazine."

Haydn looked thoughtful.

"That's pure poetry, man," Rufio said, starin at't ceiling.

"Where did you get Vice? You got it with you?" Haydn asked.

"No, as my last copy mysterious'ly disappeared, am keeping this one. Gorrit in't random skate shop down't random street."

"Ah, yes, I knows it wew," Rufio murmured. "What was *you* doin in a skate shop?"

"Lookin for Vice magazine..." (I made sarcastic-quotations with my hands). "Obvs."

"You didn't get me a copy?" Haydn asked.

"I did actuall'y. I stashed it wi'ya porn so yull happen upon it next time ya lonely."

He nodded slowly. "How thoughtful."

"What you twos up to tonight?" Rufio asked.

"I'm gonna have a drink with Karl Cox and Dave," Haydn muttered. "Then I'm heading home to Wikipedia 'Adolf Hitler's dog'."

"Itus never one drink wiv Karl Cox and Big Dave. You may be in a serious gin stupor by the time you get tu Wikipedia."

Haydn mayde an agreeing face.

"True. I wonder if I've time to pop home first."

"Yull be fine, sweetie," I said. "Ya jus gettin separation anxiety bein away from your laptop for so long."

"You do look a bit pale and nak'd, Blondie. Don't you have internet on your phone?" Rufio asked.

"It's really slow. What are you doing tonight?" Haydn asked him.

"Am meetin da boys for a bangin night. Itus ma mate's birfday."

"Are you meeting them here?" he asked, turning to me. "It's amazing when they all dress up to go out, they look like the Michael Jackson *Beat It* video"

"No, we is goin tu Nottinum. My boys too fuckin hardcore for Derby, man."

"Are you staying at your mum's house?" Haydn asked.

"I'm not planning tu go ta bed. We wiw find some dirtee party, wiv sum dirtee girls and sum dirtee drugs... So Cloud-ma-cloud. What pray is you doin tonight?"

"Going hoam ta sleep, I think." I yawned.

Rufio nodded and polished his pint off. "Ri-ot, my chickens. Am off home to perfect the perfec afro!" He got up, patting my head, then leaned over and grasped Haydn's hand while patting his back in a manly embrace. He grabbed his coat and raised a hand in't air as he mayde his exit.

"...Rayht, time to go. Need a fag." I finished ma drink hastily.

Haydn sat lookin meek, starin at the one an a half pints still sat in front ayim. He let out a sigh and gev me doe-eyes.

I rolled my own eyes. "I'm goin tu't loo then. Sup up, lightweight!"

* * * * * * *

BLACK COFFEE AGAIN

Bryn McLarey, Nottingham

The Malt Cross smelt reassuringly of wood and leather and general musty-bookishness. It was an old music hall of unpretentious grandeur, now turned intu a café bar. A natural mecca for vegetarians, art students and the odd woodlouse. Claudia wus sunk intu the embrace of one of the cow-skin armchairs in our new favourite corner, leafing through the local rag.

"*Don't joke wi' a hungry man*," she read.

"I leik it," I said.

"Look at these fookin scenesters in't skinny-jeans, nu-rave-electro-luminous-cunts." She angled her body sae that she could peer suspiciously at them.

"You're a fucking scenester – you went tu an MGMT gig?" I said.

She gestured at the pixie-haired teens, who were congregated around one camp boy in a v-neck cardie. He wus speaking strung-together anecdotes, which were hopefully funny given their congratulatory bouts of laughter.

"Jody mayde me go. Am not that bad, am I?"

"You wudnae look outtah place. You've a sexy fringe. Fair enough it's no poker straight, but it would fit you in. With a little eyeliner, the odd bit of eccentric jewellery."

"Eusch!"

The crowd of youngsters left, leaving quiet behind them. Claudia seemed a little disappointed.

"What d'yuu want ta drink?" I asked.

"Coffee, please." She didn't look up.

"You need a shot of whisky in that?"

A brief glimpse of sorrow and a shrug. She'd had an abortion. She wouldn't talk about it of course. I tried. Meybe not hard enough, but I'm a useless bloke after all.

I ordered coffees from the bar downstairs and decided she should have sum cheesecake as well. A scruffy waiter brought them upstairs shortly. He had a swallow tattoo on his wrist and didn't fail tu leer a little at Claudia, as he placed everything carefully on the low table. She ignored the cake, stirring her drink with slow motions, watching the tiny silver spoon moving through the cathartic pool of black.

A couple sat down behind us. I hoped for a decent conversation tu eavesdrop on. Cloud wus understandably not much company being rather grey today. The woman wus chattering fast and I wus quickly tuu bored tu listen. So I just watched Claudia browse the paper, the flicker of her slanting brown eyes, which could almost be oriental, save for her fair hair and complexion. They were playing David Bowie in the bar.

"Bloody Bowie." I shook mae heid. Claudia loves Bowie. She said nothing. "What was he on with all that space shite? Acid?"

"Ev'ryone were on acid in them days. What's the relevance?" she asked.

"It wus just this young writer I met, a while ago." I was determined to press. "She wus asking me about other writers. Literature, poetry, lyricists. Whether it's possible tu write as freely and unselfconsciously withoot taking drugs?"

There wus a hint of intrigue in her eyes. She cannae help being strongly opinionated.

"It's a personality thing," she said a little dismissively. "Like Gram."

I nodded, remembering an old friend with a little sorrow.

"... And druggies are prone to writin. Ta gerrall a that crazy shit outtah their system," she added.

"Once a mind is expanded it can never go back to its original dimensions, as they say," I mused. "But is it more of a talent tu say you've written everything without the influence?"

"Or education, doesn't that 'expand' ya brain?" she said a little angrily. She has her own chip on her own shoulder about certain shite.

I nodded and shook mae head at the same time in disbelief. "Sumtimes talking tu you is leik talking tu maeself."

She sunk quickly back intu a black pool with a pithy reply. "Maybe we should meet other people."

Roxanne entered the scene in a bundle of ditzy rushing.

"Sorry I'm late," she said. She dragged a chair over from another table and faffed with her coat and bag until they were hung correctly from the back. "It's so fucking weird being back in Nottingham. There are so many people I forgot I never wanted to see again. She fumbled in her purse for money. "So how're you two?"

Claudia immediately shot me a look that required secrecy.

"We're super," I said wryly. "We've just been admiring the nu-rave babies and sae on. Muttering dismissively aboot those still young enough tu have the audacity to enjoy life. You want me tu get you a drink, Ratty? Since you don't have a job yet," I added quickly, standing up.

* * * * * * *

IN THE SAME WAY HE IS ME & I AM ALL MEN

Simian Thomas, Dreamscape

Got me a bone... but I'm still not a happy pup. A bone that keeps me stuck between rational wake and maddening sleep. I know where I went wrong, thinking if only I had someone to talk to, then I would feel like my thoughts had some value. Instead of dusty old junk stuffed in the attic.

You'd think after you'd spent years on some isolated outcrop of rock in the midst of obliterated lands, eventually fate would deliver somebody to bring the good times. But nothing happens. Love can explode Tinsley Towers. They'll fall in slow motion, dust chasing through the surrounding air. But loneliness is a brute without decorum or subtlety. He cannot be beaten by the most common love, the unrequited.

The ethereal mysteries of my coffee-stain crushes did nothing but crush me. My hopeful attentions seemed to induce some sort of cosmic fear in the object of my affection.

And so I chalked an outline of myself upon the concrete, for her to someday find. I knew the venom I felt was misplaced. She didn't deserve it just because she wasn't in love with me and my ego couldn't deal with the rejection.

"What brings you round these parts?" the screen siren asks me in a sultry whisper.

I like sleeping next to tram tracks. The sounds of them rolling on by, tunnels into my sleep and thus my subconscious. It's the sound of movement, the sound of not staying still and marinating in a comfort zone of discomfort. Roxy phones me and speaks quietly for a little while. It reassures me, makes me remember that I am not the only one stuck on this *filthy rotisserie of unrequited love*.

Claudia smiles wryly, the dream scraped from real events. She leans her back against the wall and sparks a cigarette. The changing light outside briefly turns her straight blonde hair all orange and curly. I see a fleeting glimpse of Cassie, like David Lynch's interchangeable characters.

"You watch alotta films?" she observes with the coolness of a laid-back 50s pin-up girl. "I don't understand people who don't. To me it's lyke if someone said they don't much listen to music."

She likes to swagger, a bit like a boy. She would've been Katharine Hepburn, not Audrey.

"Not everyone likes to be cultured," I say, twisting my body as I sit on the bed, so as to be able to peer through the gap in the curtains. The heat from the train tracks zips in my veins.

"What is cultured?" She gestures with her cigarette. (People who smoke like to gesture, like to laugh in the middle of an exhalation, also.) "I don't mind stupid films. It's the people who don't feed their brain with *owt*. That's what I don't understand."

"I'm glad we're connected," I say with disconnected sarcasm.

'Beware of enthusiasm and love,' he said inside the film. *'Neither last very long.'* (Better to steal Dylan's profound words than hope I have any.)

Claudia picks up the photo of me in Thailand with the two kids. "You're dressed like such a cliché here – gap year brat."

I take it off her too quickly and stare with abstract vanity at my own face. My hopeful expression beside the two kids who seem oblivious to the death and destruction. One is making a peace sign.

"Well, *my* clothes were lost in the waves. I had to borrow off that boy Greg."

"Was he hot?" Claudia asks coyly.

"I'm not gay," I defend. Though I had loved Greg a little bit.

"Really?" she purrs.

"I've had sex with girls and everything." A dry tone soaking the dry atmosphere.

She laughs mid-exhalation. "You *are* a bit queer though," she says through a perfect red pout.

"Thanks."

"What were it like?" Her tone drops in voyeuristic excitement.

"What was what like? Nearly drowning? Suddenly being in the middle of the ocean floating along with bits of buildings?"

"All of it." She leans in, trying to look intently at me. But I avoid her gaze.

"Best to reduce things back to the small when something so enormous has hit you," I say. "Quite literally."

"Where are we?" she asks, ignoring my sickening humour.

It being my dream, I suppose I should know, or decide.

"Berlin," I say. I've always wanted to go.

"Is that why am dressed lyke Katharine Hepburn?" she asks.

There was nothing so ugly as the squelch of the thoughts that clambered around my brain. I kept my empty, shallow anguish to myself. I suspected others wouldn't realise it was a cover for the darker depths, the things that did matter.

I hadn't spoken to my mum in eight months, I was pretending not to have noticed. My home city had been flooded to the nostrils in the middle of summer. I pretended there were no consequences. Deal with the small things, like my measly self-esteem.

I've got a bone, a juicy ol' bone to chew on. Only trouble, it's my own.

* * * * * *

A LOVE AFFAIR IN CONCRETE

Wolfgang, Dreamscape

I battle fisticuffs betwixt waking dream and sleeping wakeful. The sound of the bedroom door opening and an old love walking in as though everything was almost as it was. Except there's a trickle of reality in my heart that knows today is as much 'the good old days' as that far off yesterday. That the past is best left there on the shelf, where it lives.

I continue deeper into dream, though I surface from time to time, so it's not a peaceful slumber so much as a fine line teetered upon. I take in various land and cityscapes before I settle upon a building that's familiar and alien. Seeing the building has the same wrought emotional drama as seeing your old, dead dog returning to you in a dream. Oh, how you want to pat him and cuddle him, and play tug, because you know this may be your last chance.

I search out the courtyard in the building because it was always the absent hub. I used to sit in that grey, empty space, which was watched only by expressionless windows. I used to admire the quiet, only broken by passers-through and a palm-full of nattering smokers from time-to-time. But as I navigate the building I realise it's still populated, by young things and their laughter. All despite the great chasms, where it has been ripped asunder by bomb, or demolition team. I float through corridors and stairwells, impatient for my courtyard, though curious as to the changing nature of the place which mutates before my eyes between Classical, Gothic and Brutalist...

...And I realise, what I first considered to be my precious Art School on Psalter Lane (due for demolition) was somehow crossbred inside my subconscious with Kunsthaus Tacheles in old Berlin. The two here elastoplasted together like an Escher construct.

Oh, how I weep, for my love affair in concrete.

I float on, knowing the courtyard will still be, for one does not erase one's favourite traits, and I do find it, but it's not the same. It's full of life and laughter. Full of youngsters oblivious to the fact that the building they inhabit is slowly being destroyed about them.

Tacheles was always ravaged and halfway broken – that was its great appeal. But my Art School was strong and stout. When you rip holes in her, you are punching at my concrete Brutal heart. I fall like a wall impacted with a demolition ball. The sound echoes through the city like a warning drum.

* * * * * * *

CALMING EQUATIONS

Haydn Antoine, Derby

The wall separates us from words. Muffling bricks protected me some, but how much I wanted to be protected I wasn't sure. I was strangely glad of Rufio and Cookie sat with me in the living room, their desperation to eavesdrop reinforcing my own. They considered it not as nosiness or gossip-mongery, but as 'looking out for me'. I was glad someone was trying to, because I certainly wasn't.

I remained languid. The storm raged in the next room, and as children of divorcees the three of us did feel that slight tightening in the shoulders, but what is broken is broken. We could only catch Claudia's scathing words of violence. Jody's voice was just a murmur, their entire relationship no doubt.

"I DON'T WANT YA TO BE HAPPY. I DON'T WANT YA TO FIND SUM'ONE WHO'S *ACTUALLY GOOD FOR YOU!* THAT JUS BACKS MY STATUS AS THE BITCH THAT RUINED YAR LIFE."

Gentle murmurs, calming equations followed. Cookie opened her mouth to say something, but Roofie raised a finger to shush her. I put the kettle on to boil and if there happened to be a bunny in the pan we all knew who put it there.

"OH WHAT? SO I'M SPOSED TO FEEL BETTER THAT YOU'VE FOUND STABILITY AND I'VE MOVED ONTA SCREWIN SUM'ONE ELSE OVER...?"

The kettle hesitantly began to break the quietness in our room. The sun was slicing through the window at an acute angle, catching peoples' torsos. I wanted to smoke all of a sudden but then they'd know I was upset.

"I DON'T GIVE A FOOK WHAT MALC SAID! DON'T MAYKE A JOKE OUTTAH IT, AM NOT LAFFIN, NOBODY IS FOOKIN LAFFIN."

I pictured Jody trying hard not to smirk at this point. "DON'T MAYKE *THAT FUCKING FACE!*"

The kettle got louder and chundered haphazardly to its own climax. I poured the steaming water into three cups. The tea bags floundered on the surface. I opened the fridge and removed a half empty bottle of milk, removing the lid and giving it a reassuring sniff. I topped up each of the cups, then squeezed out each bag and tossed it in turn into the overfilled bin.

"You want sugar today, Cookie?" I asked.

"Sweet enough thanks, Hadee... unlike some."

It'd gone quiet in the other room now. I waited for Cookie to launch into a great lecture.

She took the tea and looked at me, looked at Rufio, looked back at me. "Are you actually okay with this? You don't think it's completely out of order?"

I shrugged, sipping from my mug (the mug is me), glancing briefly out of the window at the whispers of a breeze in the trees below. "It's not gonna help the situation if I kick off about anything. Me and Claudia are just casual at the end of the day. I've no right to possessiveness. How would that help?"

Cookie kind of just opened her mouth and gaped a bit. "Casual?! You're living together! You should get rid of her, she's trouble."

"Double bubble, toil and rubble," Rufio murmured to himself almost giggling.

"Roofie! Back me up!" she whined.

"Itus easy to preach from the outside of any relashunship, littuw Cookie. At this point in time Blondie is lookin out for his Johnson not is 'eart. He's not lookin for reason, let im be, he only stands to hurt his self. And maybe not, we not know... We av to see how the cookie crumbles..." He broke into giggles on the last word.

Quietness settled again and we noticed there was no sound left from the other room either.

"Gone quiet," Roofie pondered. "Problee avin a bonk." He stifled giggles again.

"Haydeee!" Cookie squealed. "You can't be okay with this!"

The bedroom door opened slowly and the two emerged. Jody gave me a guilty, apologetic look, hunching his shoulders over, hands shoved in pockets. A dark quietness had returned to Claudia's eyes. I leaned on the kitchen counter and sipped my drink and looked up at her quietly and meaningfully. She faltered and then shot Cookie a cold look to recompose herself.

"I need a fag... am goin outside," she said.

"You can smoke in here," I said.

"Ok, I need sum fookin fresh air then, and a fag to ruin it." She rushed off out of the door.

Jody hesitated, so I followed him out into the hall and pulled the door to.

"I'm really sorry, mate," he said sheepishly.

"Don't worry, it's not your fault," I said shaking my head and shrugging. I patted his shoulder and shook his hand simultaneously. "I'll see you next week at the gig if all goes to plan."

He nodded. "Yeah, we'll have a drink... away from the fucking women." He smirked beginning to descend the stairs.

"Yeah, mate. See ya later," I said.

He raised a hand as he turned away.

* * * * * * *

THE TRACKS OF MAE TEARS

Bryn McLarey, Oxford

I wus sobbin drunk. Yes, no fooking soddin drunk, but *sobbing*. Like a fookin cunt, like mae dad. I wus busy condemning the Jaipur IPA, and that fooking strong Brewdog they keep changing the name'a, sae yuu make the saime mistake agen. What fookin vile mix a'hops and fooking water had reduced me tu tears? I don't cry when I get drunk. At worse, I lose mah rag an start a fight with the nearest Begbie character in tha pub. At worse I decide MDMA, cheap speed and Jagermeister are a happy little mixture.

It starts with me wrapped around the toilet bowl pukking mah fookin guts up. Which is fair and familiar enough, but there's summat about really fookin vomitin which is sumwhat emotional, and I find maesel a wee bit tearful.

The thing that went fookin wrong though, wus that I hadnae time tu lock tha fookin door and the missus comes in. Me all teary eyed, though mostly from the great effort of turnin green and yakkin mae soul oot. Ah know there's sommat aboot a tearful fella tha makes women all motherly and she starts consolin' me. An tha room is fookin spinnin ta fook, an ah cannae handle the weird sense of pressure and gravity pullin me round. And am yakkin agen, almost missin tha bowl, and then am fookin cryin! And I cannae stop, sobbin leik a wee boy fallen off his trikey! Ah no it's her fookin fault, she reminds me of mah fookin mother.

I don't remember who, but a wise writer once explain'd sae fookin perfeckly why women love alcoholic men, and give them soo many fookin 'chances' that they never fookin deserved.

It's thae flood of verbal emotion that they didnae geht from a sober man. It's the profuse over-egged apologies thae they didnae geht from a sober man. It's the opportunity tu rescue, tu change a man for tha better. Men never admit that they're wrong, that they're sorry, that they love you and they will do *anything* fah another chance. Unless they're pissed ta' fook.

I wus sobbin because of the reflection of maeself – watchin maeself flailin round the bathroom, and ma girl tryin tu calm and console me. Her fookin empathy. As though I wus some fookin victim a anything other than mae own stupidity and lack a self-control. Tha wus mae daddy and mae mammy there in tha fookin mirror. The saime scene played over and over. His unintelligible sobbin apologies an he'd no even be sober enough tu know why he wus apologysin. Fooks sake.

I woke tu the dull day. Face slightly stuck ta the pillow with tears and a little bit of blood and vomit. Juliette had made me a brew. It sat steaming next tu me, and she wus still sat there with her head tipped, looking sympathetic. She tried tu rub mae shoulder and I shoved her hand away. Felt instant guilt for being a cunt. I couldn't put into words what I wanted ta say. She thinks it's male pride. That I wus angry she saw me cry. I didn't know how to explain.

"You were saying something about your dad last night..." she said hesitantly.

She looked so angelic in the soft focus morning light. I didn't deserve her.

"I wus acting like mae fookin dad last night. Can we say no more about it, please."

Not a request, a statement. Ya see? Men only 'talk' when they're pissed, only confess when they're pissed, even then it's garbled mulch. You want a man who is open with his feelings, dahlin? Date a fookin soak.

Meybee am givin up the booze for wee bit. Stick to class-As for a few weeks at least.

* * * * * * *

FAT UGLY LOVE

Claudia McLeod, Derby

I felt lyke I were gonna vomit. I thought it might be love though, is that fookin sickening? It were too much in my belly, my body wanted rid of it, this alien thing. It's lyke too many things mixed together, cheap red wine, tequila, bourbon whiskey and a bottle of beer. Then sum rancid chips and curry sauce that've bin sat in't takeaway all night.

I somehow managed to dress missel. I were goin to meet the band that we were meant to be touring with soon, so I needed to be a bit presentable. If I looked scruffy it should be in a chic way, so I smudged some grey eye shadow on and scraped my hair inta knot.

We stepped outtah Haydn's bedroom which led straight into the open plan room in't middle of the flat. Cookie were sat on't couch as though she'd been waitin for us to come out. She kinda scowled which were weird. Usually she's well happy to see Haydn. It must've been me. She'd decided I were a thorn.

"You want a brew Cookie?" Haydn asked absentmindedly.

"No thanks."

"What ya doing here?" he asked.

This were a nasty question, Cookie was always hanging out in their flat, though usually there was someone else as well.

"I wanted to talk to you, but it doesn't matter. I don't really think you'd understand," she whinged.

I mayde a face. It pisses me off when people a desperate to share their issues, but pretend they're not gonna. I stared at the kitchen wall which Rufio had plastered with pictures of 70s funk stars.

"Why wouldn't I understand?" Haydn looked wary as he turned his back on her to fill the kettle.

I leaned on't counter.

"Why do people just seem to want a girlfriend, or boyfriend, just as an accessory? I don't get it, it won't make them happy. It's like spending loads of money on clothes. You can show it off for a bit. Hang out in happening places looking cool, skinny hips and all. But y'know how it *won't* make you happy?"

I cackled. She honestly thought I was gonna stand there and pretend to assume she were talking about someone else. An cheek of it, s'not like I'm sum skinny molly-mawkin anyroad. There were a pause. Haydn didn't know how to handle the situation, not sure Cookie did either. I basked in the awkwardness, sparkin up. I chucked a tab into her lap.

"Av a fag, dahrlin. It's fookin cool to smoke, everyone knows that. And a line a fookin charlie an all. It's lyke Pete Docherty and Kate Moss, yeah? Only fookin together for the mutual fookin media opportunities. Only together cause they both wear skinny jeans. D'you recon if they got fat they'd stay together? You havta be fat *and* ugly *and* a bit smell'y to know *true true* love. In't that the truth? People lyke us, we're just in love wi' the image, wi' cuttin our wrists so people'ull look twice at us."

I stopped my rant abruptly.

Haydn stirred sugar into a black coffee and then handed it to me. He knew he ought to somehow take control an smooth out the situation. But bad feelin dun't get smoothed out, jus gets under-rug-swept. Cookie'ud lit the cigarette. She sat and smoked and narrowed her eyes at me.

I sipped my coffee an took a drag. "Think I might be sick." I said it as though I were just sayin it, but then I realised I meant it. I put the mug down hast'ly, splashin't counter an ran tu't toilet, droppin to ma knees and emptyin my guts into't toilet bowl, fag still in hand. I wretched rayht to the back of ma soul but I couldn't get the love out. It were stuck there. Fuck.

I washed my mouth out and brushed my teeth wi' Cookie's toothbrush. (Why the fook does she have one there, anyroad?) When I got back in't livin room, Rufio'd come out his room in silver pyjamas, his hair in an afro.

"Ah-ite geez!" he said to me. I think Haydn had said sommat apologetic to Cookie while I were gone.

"Listen yeah geezer?" I said to Roofie, putting on an awful London accent. "I don't mean nuffink by it yeah? No bad feeling yeah geez?"

He laughed and shadow boxed around me.

"Get a brew on, Blondie!" He punched Haydn softly in't shoulder.

Haydn shook his head. "You missed the round bruvv, yu'll have to get these in."

I looked at my watch. "We need to go, Haydes."

He nodded, reaching for his bag.

"Yo, Antwon. While you out, can you pop in Dave's and see if he has the Danny Breaks album? And can ya pick me some mix an aww?" Rufio asked.

"Is that a euphemism for drugs?" I asked boredly.

"Nah man, pic 'n' mix... prefs from Woolies, but I int fusseh."

"You know it's a bit exhausting being a slave to both of you?" Haydn said.

"Yep," Rufio said. "It's time to pick. Who gives better blowies?"

Haydn rolled his eyes. He whispered sommat in Rufio's ear. As he opened t'door he said ta me, "You gonna yak again on the way?"

I slipped on flip flops and sunglasses. We clattered down the seven flights of stone steps in't centre of Dresden house, where it were earthy cool, and then out intu't sunshine which settled lyke a wahm weight on us. We quickly steadied to an amble. It were an autumn heatwave. It felt alien to walk in sandals among fallen leaves and conker pods.

"Fook it's hot. Not sure I can be arsed to go inta town," I muttered.

Haydn ignored my contrariness an took holda my hand contentedly. He's big on hand-holding. Itas tekken me a while to come ta terms wi'this. In general I think he likes smug coupledom. I fookin don't, bein passionately cynical an that. After about five minutes I removed my hand from his.

"Too sweaty," I mumbled, wiping it on my top.

He smiled and kissed me on't cheek, and a few minutes later took ma hand agen when I were deep in thought and din't notice.

* * * * * * *

A HOOT

Simian Thomas, Sheffield

Roxy's eyes were the colour of bruises, yellowed and purple all at once, but it was just the natural tone of her skin in the dim light. Her lips were stained dark from the red wine she'd been sipping. Claudia in contrast looked healthy, the rosy apples of her cheeks lifting some hope in us, the hapless skinnies.

We were in my attic flat in Nether Edge. The two of them had come to visit me and I was glad of the company that dragged me from my selfish slumbers. I wanted to tell them I was better these days, less depressed and narcissistic. But this would've been a lie. More time had passed since the Tsunami and Cassie's death, but nothing had arrived to fill the crater in my psyche.

"Still on them happy pills, Simba?" Claudia asked. I think she was being ironic. What with me looking so drab, so desperate not to be drab, and yet still so drab.

"Yeah. I tried to phase them out but..." I shrugged. "Fuck it, been on them for years. Who knows what delightful personality traits exist beneath the yellow haze?"

"I don't lyke that shit. I couldn't deal wi' tekkin somat ta 'even me out'. Bein a wreck head is *ma'thing*," she said.

Being unable to face the real world is my thing. No, no, mental smack on the head. No good thinking that way.

"...Heard Maisie got engaged ta whassis fayce?" Claudia said, with some eye rolling. "Soo much fa bein a radical Fem-bot."

"Don't worry, I doubt it'll last. Freddie's a compulsive liar. She's daft to think he'll change," Roxy said.

There was a thunder clap outside. It felt surreally as though the house rocked, as though we were in a room perched in a tall tree, in the middle of a great forest. This thought was reinforced by the sound of an owl screeching, amid the wind whipping and whistling around the rooftop.

"Was that a fookin owl?" Claudia leaned off the chair towards the window, peering through the gap in the curtains at the branches swaying in the mean, black night.

"Yeah, there are owls living round here. I even saw one the other night on the gatepost. They're so soundless when they fly, just this white shape floating up like a ghost." I said, zombified by awe of the image inscribed in my mind. "Funny though, wouldn't have thought they'd be about in a thunderstorm."

"It's not the lyin that bothers me about Freddie anyroads. I've jus noo time fa anybody who sports a seventies moustache," Claudia added, turning back to us.

"Murderers, liars and sociopaths welcome. But strictly no moustaches..." Roxy said.

"I hope I never have to grow facial hair. It makes me look even more like a rather tall child," I said.

"Why would you *have* to grow facial hair?" Roxy asked.

"If I had no access to a razor. In a foreign prison or something. I've *had* nightmares about it," I said with endearing melodrama. They laughed and I felt slightly better about the world. "It would be awful!"

"Is that your worst fear?" Roxy poured more wine into our glasses.

"I think my worst fear would be to have chest hair like Freddie! You can even see it at the top of his t-shirt. I mean, crikey!" I said.

Claudia cackled. When the laughter subsided, she sighed comedically and remarked in emphasized Yorkshire twang.

"We av a good laff, when we're sittin bitchin."

"Aye, that we do," Roxy agreed.

"How's Charlie?" Claudia asked me slightly accusingly, as though I ought to be upholding the values of the 'old crowd'. Even though I'd been the last recruit, and probably the least enthused.

"I don't know – why isn't he here?" I asked.

"Anniversary... blah blah blah," she answered.

"Jenny's big on anniversaries. She celebrates them month by month." Roxy smirked.

"What did she do while they broke up for months? Miss those out?" I asked.

"They get included now, as though that bad bit never happened," Claudia said. "It's fookin ridiculous. She's purrim on such a leash now, wi' all this emotional shit about how she should be more important to him than *sum girls he gets drunk wi'*. She says his friendships wi' us are lyke adolescent friendships. And he'll never grow up while he keeps seein us. We don't even live in't sayme city anymore! We're not a sexual threat."

I nodded.

"I heard a snide rumour he'd been going to the gym as well. That got anything to do with her?"

"Imagine Charlie in a gym?" Roxy added. "It'll be funny if he's gone all macho and vain about it."

"I'd remark we're only bitching about other people's relationships because we're single. But Claudia, what's your excuse?" I asked.

She nodded, smiling. "The grass is always greyer on t'other side? I don't try ta change an improve the men I date, they try ta change and improve me."

"They've not done a very good job," I quipped.

"What happened with that girl you liked, at work?" Roxy asked. I baulked a little. I'd forgotten I'd mentioned that to her at all, probably the euphoria of infatuation had clouded my ability to be very private about these things.

"Oh, you know me. Always the bridesmaid, never the bride," I said camply.

We sat quietly for a moment and listened to the storm outside.

"D'ya 'member when we ended up at that stupid white-haired girl's house at lyke six a.m. Rox...?" Claudia asked. "She mayde us breakfast."

"...Oh yeah. 'Beazie', she calls herself. Typical art student," Roxy said.

"Why were we there?!" Claudia asked.

"You wanted to buy drugs, and Charlie said her fella would sort you out. But he was on a night shift. So we went back to wait for him, and he never turned up anyway."

"Oh," Claudia said, "Yeah." Realisation hit her that it was her own damn fault.

"And the moral is... don't take drugs?" I said.

The windows rattled, and the building shifted foot on its foundations, uncertainly. But this was just ordinary scorn poured on ordinary lives, in an ordinary storm, and nothing we couldn't weather.

* * * * * * *

A QUICK SHUFTY

Roxanne Ratcliffe, Nottingham

The rookie peeks suspiciously over the wall at the box.

"Can't hurt to have a quick look," he mumbles, with the conviction of the curious. He scrambles up the brickwork and hoists a leg over, dragging his remaining body parts after. He slides down into the alleyway to land with a thud. It's cool and dark down in this hollowed out world.

He examines the box. It's decorated completely with colourful sweets, stuck on with golden syrup. At first it looks appealing as though you could peel bits off and eat them. But on closer inspection he sees that dirt and hairs cling and ants scamper on the box. The rookie finds himself retching a little, but he gulps it back and opens the lid slowly, it creaks. He peers inside but it's gloomy. He moves around the object until the light falls in the right way. Inside the box is a mirror.

Inside the mirror, he is me.

"You want a cup of tea, love?"

My mum's voice woke me. She was knocking at my bedroom door.

I tried to extract my voice box from sleep mode. "Yeah... *pleease*."

I drifted drowsily between sleep and wake until my brother David knocked at my door and slid in. He was nearly thirty now, immaculately dressed as always, with his copper-brown hair in a side parting. He was carrying a mug which he perched on the bedside table. I sat up slowly and looked at him.

"Guess what?" he signed.

I felt apprehensive.

"I'm going to Cuba for a year," he signed. "They've a school for the deaf I can teach at."

"Won't they speak a foreign sign language?" I asked.

He nodded. "I'll have to learn the Cuban variant of Spanish sign language. But I already know some Spanish and I picked up French fairly quickly. So I'm not too worried."

He always paused thoughtfully between sentences. He had a lot of patience with everything.

I pulled my duvet back up to my chin. It was getting colder outside and my parents' Victorian semi was draughty. I rested the mug of tea on the tops of my bent knees. He tipped his head slightly and looked at me a little disapprovingly.

"What?" I signed, defensively.

"You look sad. You should be happy for me," he signed, but not in an accusing way. In a manner that said, 'I knew you'd react like this. Don't be so predictable'.

He'd always been quick to remind me when I'm being self-absorbed. Which was most of the time. My defence was always that there's no point worrying over other people's problems. I've no control over them. I protect myself in a shell, in which there is only a mirror and no windows.

"That's really great for you, sounds like a good adventure," I signed.

David raised an eyebrow. "That's if I manage not to be hammered on Mojitos twentyfour/seven," he replied.

"When will you be going?"

"In four months... February, I think."

"Last few months we'll be together as a family then," I signed.

"Good," he signed. "It's about time you got a proper job and settled down somewhere. Stop acting like a teenager."

He was just teasing, as usual.

"About time I joined the Rat Race?" I added.

He smiled and tapped my clock to point out to me that most productive humans were up and dressed already, making progress with their lives. When he'd left, I rifled through my stuff from Sheffield. I pulled out a picture Cuan had done for me – *Ratty in the Rat Race* – an image of me on the London Underground, with my camera and mousey ears, looking lost amongst rats in suits. I blue-tacked it to the wall.

I picked up my camera and trudged down to breakfast, spilling tea along the way. I'd always taken a lot of photos, I think for the same reason that I'd always stared in the mirror a lot. I was trying to make sense of what was in front of me. In uncertainty, I took a photo. I'm not sure what that meant at the end of the day – a shit load of photographs I suppose.

I had few friends left in Nottingham, so I had little to do except mooch around taking picture after picture. As though re-establishing a relationship with an old friend, searching for the particulars that were both different and the same. I'd returned with my tail between my legs, though it was defeatist to view it that way. Sheffield had many times left me heartbroken, and had begun to make me sad by reminding me of the happy times and friends I no longer had around.

This glumness greyed my view of the city that'd spawned me. Nottingham had prettier architecture and a whole new array of arty little haunts for me to sniff out. Yet compared to Sheffield's wide open spaces, the streets felt claustrophobic and cluttered with people. I missed always being close to a park, and better still a short bus ride from the Peak District.

But wherever I settled, it was the people that made home, home. While many old friends were long gone, there were always new gems to be found and a new self to be sketched out on a fresh page.

* * * * * * *

EVERY OTHER DRUG

Haydn Antoine, Derby

I always wanted to live inside media. To be inside a song or film or computer image. When everything is bad you can find some mediated level of understanding. Some sense that there is a great big world beyond you, and whatever silly Westernised troubles you have (even if they are a fucking shit-pile of cancer, breakups and addictions), you can philosophise them all away. Or at least forget them for a large chunk of your time.

    And if one thing doesn't fill the hole, I'm prone to trying several at once – a book and a film and some music that can I can whack the volume up on when I need to. In these spaces we can exist. And not alone either. Some days it's just easier to play someone a phenomenal song you've discovered, than try to talk about what you're thinking. A kind of mediated communication that they can interpret.

    And there is so much media – too much – you can't run out. Every other drug runs out at some point. Consumption, for me, is electronic, or at least paper. If my laptop crashed and my television expired, there's still always a radio somewhere (the most resilient of electrical objects) or a newspaper. If this consumption kills me, it'll be with square eyes and deaf ears at least.

The other drugs (namely alcohol) were hostile to this, though. Personified that morning, with explosive wrath, by my splitting headache and painful gaze. Thumping on the sides of my brain. I was doomed to silence and darkness, except the thumping wouldn't stop. The smell of Claudia's mid-morning cigarette made me nauseous. I leaned over the side of the bed and yelped out some vomit on the floor, which was scattered with worn clothes and an extension socket. Yuck. Claudia looked over at me disdainfully and then left for work without a word.

I crawled back under the covers and hoped for a hazardous sleep, but I found it hard to sleep without music. I tried some Nick Drake, but even that seemed to falter and echo feverishly inside my head, and I could smell the sick creeping around the room. I sprawled in uneasy silence. I tossed and turned and hummed a little and somehow my own vibrations settled me. I wondered at the giggle of the fly on the wall as I lay alone in a bed and hummed myself to sleep. I woke, still humming, bleary eyes peering at the clock. It was nearly seven. Rufio must have come back from uni as a door slam had woken me.

I dragged on some old jeans and stumbled into the main room. The light made me squint. Claudia was back also, though not so happy to see me. No kiss for my yak-flavoured lips.

"I wandered lonely as a McLeod..." Rufio mumbled. He poked me in the shoulder. "Brew for the bru?"

I collapsed on the sofa. "Yes, please. Sugar sugar, please."

"Ready for your fried brekkie yet, sir? Do you thee world of gud."

"That would be amazing. Do we have any food?" I asked gratefully.

"Wew... the bread is green, the eggs is fine, the bacon is edibuw."

Claudia sighed. "You shouldn't wait on him hand an foot cos he's been on the fookin binge. He's laid up here all day lyke a slob while we've bin at work, an that."

She switched the TV on and wacked up the volume. I closed my eyes in pain.

"Have you *just* come home to torture me? Because that's not very nice."

She tutted and examined her peeling nail polish. "We were *meant* to be goin ta see Yeah Yeah Yeahs tonight. And you were *meant* to be blaggin us some guest list tickets, cos we can't afford to pay. Though the amount you spent on booze an coke last night, ya wouldn't know it. *And* yar in noo fit state. So am slightly narked."

"Shit," I said. I stared at a spot on the ceiling. It began to move. "It's Tuesday."

"Yes it's fookin Tuesday. I don't spose ya've cleaned the sick up either."

Rufio, pan in one hand, spatula in the other, tootled around the kitchen area, giggling.

I fumbled in my pocket and dug out my phone. I hated using mobiles when I had a headache. It was like I could feel the microwaves entering my brain slop.

"...Yo Karl, bit short notice but can I get guest list for the gig tonight? Pretty please, I'm in major trouble with the missus!"

Claudia cuffed me around the back of the head. My brain reeled a little bit.

"Dude, you're an absolute legend... yeah... wicked...I'll get some in, no worries... yes mate, I was properly wrecked, tried to chat up a lamppost... ha... nice one... byeee."

I collapsed from the effort of conversation, then slowly looked up at the ceiling again.

"A'ya actually gonna be okay to go?" Claudia asked, trying to maintain the scathing tone, but a hint of concern was creeping in.

"No probs, babe," Rufio murmured. "Fried egg sarnie'll sort im out. Then ass-prin un pepto bismaw if that faiuws."

She looked at me questioningly. I nodded. Anything to bring back my capacity for consumption. Without it I was just a blank tape.

* * * * * * *

JOINING THE DOTS

Bryn McLarey, Sheffield

Disappointment – the ugly face of. And this time it's mae own. Disappointment in the routine, trapped in a life of stability, comforts and empty promises. Committed tu personal growth, as though there wus a butterfly inside Bryn's grey-black cocoon, just waiting to be set free. There wus no butterfly. Just a big, ugly goblin caterpillar, who wus happy with his sins.

"Have you thought about writing another book? Your first one was published. Surely the hard work is done. You just need a proposal for another?" Jenny asked one night over a candle-lit dinner.

I am *the Bothersome Man*. I lie between the train tracks and wait for the train tu come, tu maim and bloody mae eligible facade.

"That book wus everything I had to say," I replied. I'd hated the book ever since Cuan had preyed on it. In fact, I'd hated it before. My life's work amounted tu those

502 pages. Of which each word I'd poured over again and again, until I wasn't sae much reading them, as tattooing them inside mae brain.

She sighed. "Well, no need to be defeatist. Maybe you should pursue the acting for a while and see where that takes you and possibly another book will come from your life experiences. When are you going to let me read your book anyway? Are you worried I'll know what goes on in that funny brain of yours?"

"I don't have a copy," I said (truthfully). "And it would only upset you, because there's a lot about Juliette in there."

"Don't be silly! I don't have jealous feelings about Juliette. You've not seen her in years." She paused, pursing her lips in thought, then lifting a forkful of food towards them and chewing slowly, while watching me eat, less gracefully. "And I don't believe for a moment that you've not even kept a manuscript," she added.

"I burned it," I said (a little dramatically). I remembered the destruction and the cathartic sense of satisfaction it'd given me, as I watched the flames lick the pages and eat the words.

"What a childish thing to do," she chided.

I grinned manically like a demented arsonist who thoroughly enjoyed his work.

"Please don't make that face. There's nothing to be pleased about." She was smiling, despite herself. She set her knife and fork down in the centre of her plate, which wus still cluttered with discarded bits of food (mostly spinach, but a few appealing scraps of pork fat and potato). She sipped the Orvieto.

"Have you any auditions lined up, in the bigger theatres?"

I nodded without enthusiasm. I'd mostly been working at a little independent theatre, helping the technician and more recently running the bar. They paid me what they could afford tu pay me.

"Why have you ended up doing the bar work again? I thought you were past that," she asked, a little impatiently. She thinks bar work holds me back, because it leads tu me socialising with people younger than me. Or people with similarly destructive vices ta mae own.

"Because they don't know what the fuck they're doing with the bar and it could be key ta keeping them going! I hate tu see a bar run badly." I scoffed the last of the food on mae plate, and then peered at her leftovers, tu see if she might offer them.

"You could have just *advised* them on it. Rather than taking up the reins without even being offered a proper contract or management pay." She picked up both our plates and carried them tu the kitchen counter.

"I tried that. They were still ballsing it up. And besides, they can't afford to pay me as a manager. They can barely afford to pay themselves. It's a tiny bar and I'm not managing any people. I'm just bartending." I slugged down more wine, tu drown my routine sorrow.

"That's all very noble and socialist, Charlie, but it hardly helps pay the bills," she said, running the tap and flashing fingers beneath the water.

"It's just mae bread and butter salary. The other stuff pays better, but it's irregular. I can't count on it, but together it's enough to get by on okay." I helped maeself tu more wine. "You want more wine?"

"Just a splash. Aren't you tired of 'just getting by'? What about the future?" she asked.

"I always figured the smoking and the drinking would kill me off at about forty-five, and I wouldn't have tu worry," I said.

I knew there were other questions hanging in the air, waiting tu rear their ugly little faces and ruin the peace.

Questions of mortgages and children. As if I'd want tu pass on all my fuck-ups to another bastard generation.

* * * * * *

ALL THE CONVERSATIONS I COULD ONLY EVER HAVE WITH MY CAT

Simian Thomas, Sheffield

I can hear a radio, although I know I'm alone in the flat. I lie in sleep paralysis and stretch my ears. It's only a murmur, but tonally it sounds like Radio 4. I'm aware this is a sonic dream, but my sense of reason still drifts amongst the fairies and tells me someone else is here.

My eyes are open to the bedroom but they can't move. I think it's my dad in the flat and this fills me with dread. It'll be so embarrassing if he walks in my bedroom. I've not seen him in maybe thirteen or fourteen years. He might not even recognise me. He used to listen to Radio 4. It was his only redeeming feature, so far as I can remember.

There's a cat now, in the room. I can't see it as it slinks outside of my eye line, but I can hear its hearty purr. I feel the soft weight as he jumps on the bed near my feet and stalks the length of it behind my torso to my head. He sits near my ear, the purring louder, and I can almost feel his whiskers brush my skin. It's Hex's cat, I somehow know, though Hex's cat is dead.

I wake and I'm in a different room. It looks familiar and I know it ought to be Hex's bedroom at his parents' house. But things are rearranged and there's a view of the sea even though it's miles inland. I hear a lovely burbling sound from the next room. I untangle myself from the bed clothes. I'm wearing pants the pattern of my grandmother's wallpaper. I slip through the door that's ajar letting light in, and then I'm in the study. And Hex is pottering about, talking to his cat in that child-like, carefree tone. The one that can only be used when no other human is around, just the perked ears of a ginger feline.

I woke. Whenever I woke after having watched Richard Linklater's brilliant film *Waking Life* – in which a boy keeps waking into another dream and another, until he starts to wonder that maybe he'll never wake – I was filled with a cocktail of joy and disappointment.

I was alone. The flat was empty of noise and optimism. I thought I ought to go and visit Hex, just for the sake of seeing how he was. I should go to the cat shelter and take him a cat. But I was worried for a cat living in that dirty hovel. Maybe a cat shouldn't be relied upon to give mental stability.

I knew that Cassie would suggest that *I* go and live with him. But I was worried, in a cowardly manner, that if I lived with him I'd realise that he needed to be sectioned. Cassie would reason that he wasn't mad. It was just the drugs and the isolation. He just needed some counselling and support of friends.

I drank a mug full of coffee. I showered and dressed for the bright, pondering autumn and descended stairs to a leaf-littered street. My shoes rustled happily through it, shuffling along until I reached the flats where he lived. There was a happy, burbling noise coming from the garden, which his French windows faced on to. So I followed the noise down the alleyway to the back.

His curtains were open, the windows flung wide and he was sat squinting in the sunlight on a step, smiling to himself.

"Hi Hex," I said.

He looked up, and smiled wider. "Simba, I've not got any stuff in I'm afraid. The piggies took it all."

"I'm not here to buy. I just came to see how you were," I mustered.

A black cat slunk up next to Hex and peered suspiciously at me, as though he was a bodyguard. Hex stroked him and burbled under his breath.

"You got another cat?" I asked.

Hex shrugged. "He's kind of adopted me the way they do. I dunno who he belongs to."

"What do you mean the piggies? The police raided your flat?" I asked.

"Yeah. I think a neighbour complained about dodgy visitors. I only had a bit of weed luckily. Not enough for them to prove it wasn't just for personal use. I'm thinking of going clean."

I felt an inkling of disappointment. I hadn't saved him from himself. The cat probably had, appearing like a guardian angel.

"What will you live on?" I asked dubiously.

He laughed and his face looked warped with happiness. "I've got lots of money in the bank. I've never really spent it on anything. It's just built up over the years."

"Are you going to get some help, some counselling?" My voice sounded weak.

He looked at me accusingly. "Are you?" he said, as though offended, but then he broke into a grin again. "I might enrol again, then I'll get free student counselling. I can't be doing with the shrinks my parents sent me to. They're part of the disease."

"Are you going to study Psychology again?" I sat down next to him.

"Nope. Psychology courses are full of depressed people who don't know what to do with their lives, that's the irony! I might do zoo-keeping, how cool would that be?"

"Wow, you really thought this through," I said, disappointed in my own lack of motivation.

"No, it was just an epiphany. Did you ever finish your degree?" he asked.

Those years had passed him in a haze I supposed.

"No, I hated Leeds, I couldn't stay there. So I took a gap year and worked, and then Cassie and I went travelling. And the rest is history, as you know."

I looked to the cat for his response and he gave me a Cheshire smile.

"It's never too late to have aspirations, Simian." Hex shook his head wisely.

* * * * * * *

BADGER'S PARTING GIFTS

Wolfgang, the Peak District

"Mozart was a fucking living Opera, that's how mental it is. Why did I never know that?" Cuan stood atop a jagged tor, waiting for the wind to blow him off.

Dregs my friend, dregs. The bottom of the wine bottle, tannin stains and bitter tongue. All my friends feel familiar to me because I am dregs. I am the stain of tannin on pure white teeth.

I boiled the kettle again. I was in everyone's way, but my quest was too important. I missed the times when we just loitered and chatted. They were pure. Now you expect something of me that I'm not sure I can provide, some sort of ship, friend or other relation. In my haste I made tea instead of coffee. Now I felt as though I was drinking from a great trough of nothingness instead of pure intense inspiration. I scribbled notes on a page like an avid composer. My hands moved in tourettes-like motions in their desperation to transfer brain language, to eye, to page. I've filled the pages. I faltered and they looked at me, waiting.

"That girl is ridiculously skinny." I pointed as a distraction, then picked up a newspaper and began writing in the margins and spaces. Marginalised writing, so meaningful, yes. So in keeping with my philosophy. The ball-point pen ripped the page a little, engraved through to the table, then ran out. They looked at me again, expectantly. I decided to draw blood and use my blood as ink on the pen nib to write radical phrases in the margins of the newspaper.

"Does anybody have a razor?" I asked.

I hoped for some contamination, some strange ink poisoning. For all my veins to show violet beneath my skin, like some beast. And then I should fall upon the exposed areas of rock atop Stanage Edge, slice my arms and write the truth in blood and ink on the damp, open ground. Some sort of ritual, bloody sacrifice of my own words. At this point they couldn't fail to be important, for they would've become too much. I rested.

The bar flies gathered, a few at first, then they swarmed and slowly, painfully, carefully, covered my face. Drinking whisky from my pores and beer from my saliva. They drained me to a dried up piece of fruit with hallowed eyes that look but cannot see. I raised my arm, but the muscles were dry as a wino's mouth. I shuddered. My force was gone. I'm a shell, a piece of dry brown seaweed picked off the beach. Tossed back into the wind to land with crumpled crisp packets and ripped up dregs of Tesco carrier bags.

I'm the dregs, my friend. Of your soul. Of the words you wished you were able to write if you could only accept that dark matter inside your fucking heid. Floating dark matter. Have you ever looked at it? Cut it out and done a little autopsy? Are you afraid of what will be there? Afraid they will know that you're jam? There was some anger around me, some negative energy, maybe they think I'm writing about them. Opinions are dangerous and perverse. You don't have any, that's why you're afraid. Sat there, turfing out your brains, raking them for some kind of substance.

Beyond the dregs of my psychosis, the future was beginning to clarify in the broom cupboard of my mindscape. The black and white jigsaw puzzle clicking and joining. Nobody seemed quite aware yet that their world was falling to pieces. That the things they took for granted would soon fall away like forgotten tears. I tried to mentally prepare myself. Like knowing death is near. Like speaking of what is beyond. Badger threw away his walking stick and danced off down the long, long tunnel through the Earth. I watched as he turned to a speck and disappeared into the darkness, unafraid.

* * * * * *

PIGEON ENGLISH

Simian Thomas, Sheffield

I'm dreaming in Technicolour of a world like ours filtered through cinema-scope. The people are almost absent, mere shadows upon the periphery. I can't be sure that they're human at all. Maybe some other similar species in some other parallel. They've built things as we build things, and they're buildings of grandeur and rich earthy colour that're falling to pieces – bit by tiny bit.

I turn around inside the backroom of what we'd call a bar. Away from the paint peeling thoughtfully off the wall. Away from the drips from leaking pipes that would add to the damp, and slowly rot the place into a grave. The wall is missing at the back. I puzzle if this is intentional. But I'm quickly distracted by the view of the woods behind, which I enter. Twigs snap under me, feet rustle in dry leaves. The trees look like silver birch but as with everything on this other Earth, their beauty is magnified. They gleam in the light that sneaks down from the canopy and bounces off surfaces, creating so much colour that even the greys seem to glow.

I walk down a woodland path. But I'm aware that I'm not far into the wild. Civilised streets and buildings lie only a little way to my left. I can hear the bustle, the voices of people, though with no exact words reaching me. There's some sort of fuel station, and from this source a fire whips into the woodland. It's spread within moments to everywhere around me. The flames are fantastically beautiful though, so vivid and yet so unreal. I float up above the flames, a dark shape flying in the smoke, which smears and fades the scene into theatre, like dry ice. I can hear voices calling for help below, and I fly to seek them out, to seek out these creatures so alike to us.

I woke then, and cursed the dull, drizzly morning. I cursed the Earth's dim light which painted everything a different shade of grey. I saw Wolfgang in the street that day. I'd not seen him in months, since I didn't seek his company. Did he even have a phone through which to be sought?

He was shuffling along like a lost beggar, pawing something in his grubby hands and peering sadly at it. I paused and said his name as he passed, but he seemed not to hear. He appeared shrivelled, though his stature was broader and taller than mine. I hesitated, hovering in the drizzle, realising I'd no real appointment to anything that day. So I turned and followed him as he ambled along. All I could see from the back was his long tweed coat, patched up on the sleeves, and the mop of wild hair sprouting just above his collar.

He was muttering away in a confused mixture of German and English. He reached the top of Sharrow Vale and turned left off the roundabout down Cemetery Road. He entered the General Cemetery in front of the old dilapidated church and trundled over the weed-strewn cobbles to a patch of grass sprouting eagerly skywards. Here he knelt and placed the object in front of him. I stood above him and saw that it was a dead pigeon.

"Are you okay, Wolfgang?" I asked, more intrigued than worried.

"I'm very sad," he said, without looking at me, as though maybe I was just a voice in his head. "That was no ordinary pigeon. That was Brian. He taught me to speak English."

* * * * * * *

DROP THE DEAD PONY

Claudia McLeod, Ripon

"Blimey, put some clothes on. You look like a skag addict!" Dad teased wi' his own-brand humour. It were a runnin family joke (yawn) that I tell him he's too fookin liberal and should act lyke a proper Dad. So he comes out from time ta time wi' such phrases.

It were a blindin hot day already, despite it bein afore nine a.m. So I were wearin a vest top that exposed the tattoo between my shoulder blades, fa which ma Dad likens me to Amy Winehouse. I lit a cigarette and glared at him through blackened lashes. He grinned and returned to his paper.

"Happy funeral day," I said flatly.

"Indeed," he said wi'out lookin up. "You'd think you'd try to dress a bit maire appropriatel'y."

The funeral in question were that of our first pony, Bailey, who'd stumbled on to a daft age afore Dad decided his quality of life were low and quantity a vet's bills were high.

"Oh, fook off," I said wi'out emotion.

He laughed as ma brother Malc wandered in, a little dazed from sleep.

"Whassup wi'you today?" he asked me as he filled the kettle and waved a cup in my direction, ta which I nodded.

"She's jus narky that she's glum, and has to pretend to be narky, soas we don't know she's glum," Dad said.

"Story a my fookin life," I retorted. I'm prone to imply blame on me Dad for my mardy nature, reinforced by his geniality. But he's too used to this (and too genial) to be bothered.

Malc wrestled in his pyjama pocket and brought'outta scruffy photo which he handed to me. A picture a me as a kid all goofy grins and angelic blondeness, wi'my arms around Bailey, a tuff but cute Dartmoor pony the colour of Bailey's liqueur, hence the daft name. I stared at it furra bit.

"It were a simpler time," I muttered eventually, proppin it on't window sill.

"You were a fookin nightmare, Claws. It weren't a simpler time for us."

This came from my baby brother, who were always so damn mature furris age. Soo calm and considerate, just lyke Daddy. I sat down at't kitchen table in front a the coffee Malc had mayde.

"Sorry. Anyroads, now I'm a nightmare fa some other jobsworth," I said.

"Speaking a which, have you spoke to Jody since you wrote his car off...? To maybe say sorry?" Malc asked.

"I didn't write off his car. It warra minor prang."

"You drove into a ditch," he said.

"Exactly. A ditch is much less bad than a wall, or a tree. I were jus bein dramatic anyway, you know that."

"Yeah, I know." His tone had risen slightl'y in exasperation. This was the most mad Malc ever got. I've reacted worse over losin my keys.

"Where's Melissa?" Dad asked. "I thought she came back from't pub wi'you two last night."

"She's at her mam's," Malc said. "They fell out agen."

"She's a twat. Still, 'least she expresses emotions. Even if they are blairy, whingey ones." I glared at them.

"As if you don't love me maire." Malc prodded me.

"I don't even *like* my sister, so you win hands down," I said.

"Learnin to share the spotlight was tuff on you."

Melissa came to live wi'us furra bit at age thirteen. Not that it lasted long. Me an Malc were jus jealous that she had a mum who gave two shits about her. Sommat she liked to remind us of.

"Is she comin round?" Dad asked.

"Why don't you phone and find out. She'll do owt for you," I said.

He jus smiled amiably and rose from his seat, stretchin and rubbin his neck. He reached for the house phone.

"Man, wish I'd got maire sleep, this heat is proper... Hiya Cheryl, it's me. Is Mel up yet...? Oh right, kay then. How's the new job goin...? Oh, well it's always a bit lyke that int it... uh huh... sure. Oh well, best of luck wirrit all, byyee."

Malc and me look expectant.

"She's on her way already," he said.

"Joy. So what time *were* you up this morn?" I peered at the dark rings a worry I'd forgotten to notice.

"Oh, I barely slept. Got up at 4.30 and did some work. Best to get stuff done stead of lying awake thinking bout it. I were chattin to the Mays yesterday anyroad, and they've got a real difficult filly at the moment, so they want me to girra hand with that too. So that helps. A few months time though, if things don't pick up, it'll be difficult. Prolly gonna have to sell Geoffrey and the Morris Minor."

Malc and me exchanged looks. Things'd been different when we both lived back'hoam. We all pitched in and ev'rythin would be okay, sumhow. I never realised til I went to secondary school that havin a self-employed, single dad who were both a mechanic (specialising in vintage cars) and a hoarse-trainer warra bit unusual.

But he'd always been dead set about livin the dream. Sheer graft and skill had paid off so far. Raisin kids hadn't been cheap or easy, afterall. But sumhow this were a different time. The economy was failin, people wont putting their hands so deep in pockets anymaire.

"Are you gonna have to sell the house?" Malc asked quietly.

Dad shrugged. "Eventually, if things don't get better. I'd rather not get to tha point where the vultures from't bank are tekkin away the roof over me head forcib'ly..."

The backdoor swung open and Melissa swooshed in. She laid her expensive handbag on the kitchen table and removed her oversized sunglasses to study our glum faces.

"Oh, he was auld, get over it. Dad, I'm totally overdrawn again. Any chance you could lend me some money until pay day? Pretty please!"

I slid from the table and rinsed my mug out, placin it next to the sink.

"Wow, Claudia. Crack-whore chic is pretty hard to pull off. But you've done so well," she swiftly added.

"Mel, if she hits ya, don't cry to me. You're all adults now apparentl'y. And sweetiepie, I'm strugglin fa money. You'll have to deal wirrit yissel like ev'ryone else. You know that whole actions and consequences thing yer sposed to learn?" Dad said, returning to his gentle humour.

Melissa rolled her eyes. "Mam's broke too. What's going on with everyone these days? Mal? Can you help?"

Malcom chuckled. "For once Claudia's the one wirra decent salary."

"Oh, for fucks sake," Melissa said, not even botherin to look at me. "So what are we doin today? Having a wake? I mean you sold the horsemeat, right?"

"We were jus gonna spend some time together. Go out forra ride before the midday sun gets up. Sound alreet?" Dad asked.

"We could go up t'ridge. That were Bailey's favourite spot to duck his head and eat grass and refuse to budge," Malc murmured.

"Oh, please. Drop the dead pony. Can we talk about sommat more cheerful?" Melissa said.

* * * * * *

RAIN & REVELATIONS

Bryn McLarey, Oxford

Bloody knuckles I conceal in pockets. A man passes me in the cobbled street, sidestepping puddles, his black burglar hat pulled down over his eyes. I slip quickly through the pub doorway and guitar strings greet me, a voice shivering a sad song.

I shook off a wet duffle coat. I didn't understand how these plum boys were arsed ta carry a massive coat around all the time. I know it kept me warm and dry, but where the fuck do you put this woollen monster when you get intu the pub? Mae friend George wus up in the little wood-panelled booth at the back of The White Horse. I ducked mae head to join him.

He looked me up and down. "I think maybe you ought to buy a waterproof coat, Charles. One that doesn't soak up the world."

I smiled a charming smile. "Less poetry in that, my good man."

He wus sat below the mirror with a young lady, who looked a bit familiar. She smiled a little boredly at me as though tu be polite. She wusnae like the other Oxbridge types, I could see that in her eyes. She projected the kind of sophisticated intelligence I'd only ever seen in women on the television, and even then rarely. And she had a light, modest beauty tu her.

"Charlie, this is Juliette," George said, as brief introduction. He headed off tu the bar to get a round of drinks. I pushed mae glasses up mae nose, imitating nerves.

"Hello," I said.

"What do you study?" she asked politely, tu fill the awkward silence in the small space.

The rest of the pub wus crowded as usual. Conversations ricocheting off the walls and ceiling, as the lunch throng stuffed hearty food and ale into their over-privileged mouths.

"Um, law, yes law at The University," I wusnae sure why I wus lying even more. I just knew she expected a boring answer, so I gave one. It wus always a big game.

"And you?" I asked.

"Philosophy and ancient history," she said.

"Oh, how fascinating!" I exclaimed "Better than dull law!"

She smiled mischievously. "I dunno, I hear the bestiality cases are pretty funny."

Instead of laughing knowingly, at the way she undermined the culture (this wus the sort of thing the chaps said, not the ladies by gum!), I pretended tu be very slightly taken aback.

"Roland Barthes? Does he count as a philosopher...?" I asked, feigning ignorance.

"He's difficult to pigeon-hole. He's a linguist as well," she said.

"Fascinating," I said again.

George returned, looking a little possessive over his female friend.

"So, are you and Cameron broken up for good now, Jules?" he asked casually, probably looking to catch her on the rebound.

"Yes," she said bluntly. As though tu imply that this conversation wasn't on the table. I shifted the salt and pepper around idly. Charlie likes ta fidget and arrange things tidily.

"You know Cam, don't you, Charlie? Lives with Jeremy in Jericho..."

"Oh, yes, charming fellow," I said, picturing the pretentious, self-satisfied thespian. "Obviously has good taste!"

I beamed a little goofily at Juliette, but she seemed only bemused. She wus beginning to look at me quite intently, as though a penny had dropped.

I pretended tu listen to George as he nattered on for a bit about the controversial and amusing antics of Jeremy and Cameron, back when he'd shared dorms with them. And how Cam wus from Stratford upon Avon, and that wus why he wus such a bloody drama queen. Juliette seemed irritated, but kept looking at me, when she thought I wudnae notice. I lined up the beer mats so that the pattern connected, then I rearranged them so that it connected in a different way.

"Where are you from, Charlie?" she asked, interrupting.

"Oh golly, we moved around a lot for my father's work," I said, making good excuse of the eye contact. "I lived in the country in Buckinghamshire for many years, then we lived in Lewes, in East Sussex, for a while when I was a teenager," I drifted off, glancing in the mirror tu see her hair from the back. She had a slender neck. I hoped ta nibble it sumtime.

"Where in Buckinghamshire...? I have some extended family there," she pursued.

"Near Winslow?" I proffered.

"Oh yes."

George made a show of looking at his watch. "Golly, look at the time. I've got to get back to work."

"George, I needed to talk to you. That's why I suggested I join you for lunch," I said, a little irritated.

"Really sorry, Charlie. I'll give you a ring later?"

I shrugged in agreement. He gave Juliette a peck on the cheek and left.

"Fancy another drink?" she asked, maybe a little coyly.

Fancy more than that, I thought. "Yes, that would be lovely."

"Same again, is it Bryn?" She extracted herself from the snug and left for the bar before I could answer.

I looked at her again in profile form, leant on the edge of the pub bar, lips moving. I mentally stood her next tu Cameron and remembered mae first introduction to a pub-full of Oxford inhabitants over a year ago, when it hadnae occurred ta me tu be anything other than my crude Weegie self. I'd met Cam several times since, and he (along with many others) had forgotten ever meeting a Scot, named Bryn.

She returned with a pint of Young's Bitter for me and white Bordeaux for herself and sat down. She didn't look at me now. She just waited for me tu speak. I shifted uncomfortably, wondering which way to play it.

"Why are you pretending to be something you're not?" she asked eventually.

"I don't know what you mean." I performed mae spectacle adjustment and floppy hair flick.

"It took me a while to realise why I recognised you. You're Scottish, aren't you?"

The curtain dropped from mae charade and I replied as only Bryn could, in mae thick mother tongue. "Oh, is *that* why you were starin at me? Thought I wus gonna geht laayd."

She laughed, and her eyes lit up with secretive delight. She shot a glance around the pub as though I'd just confessed I wus a fugitive.

"For the record, I lied about studying law an ahhl. Ah'm doin classics and English. Am surprised we havnae crossed paths?" I said, feeling I should get the other lie off mae chest also. Juliette wus a sucker for the truth.

"I'm not studying at Oxford University is why," she said. "I'm only in this city at all for bloody Cameron."

"I'd better come up with a damn good reason for you tu stay then," I said with all the enigmatic intensity I could muster.

The scene dissolves in mae memory. It's replaced by rain-soaked, potholed streets where the drizzle is always in mae face, and mae socks squelch inside mae shoes. And there're always another few streets tu go tu the pub, or some other home.

* * * * * * *

A STORM IN A TEACUP

Simian Thomas, Sheffield

I admired the orderly lines of clothes in the shop. When I'd started working there it'd looked like a junk shop. It's hard to make second-hand individual items (rebranded as 'vintage') look neat and ordered. But particularly that day I felt I'd conquered the monster. The belts curled next to one another, the hats tilted in symmetry on the old hat stand. I felt equilibrium had been reached and allowed small satisfaction. Before reminding myself the reason it looked so unspoiled was due to a lack of customers cluttering up the shop with their actions and noise, moving things around willy-nilly.

The sole other employee that day was Jess, who came tumbling through the door with a squeal, carrying our coffees from the shop a few doors down in a clumsy, panicked fashion. Her hair was littered with chunky, white hailstones. She handed me the drinks and forced the door shut against the gale that seemed to be blowing in, rattling the metal racks.

"It's like the end of the world out there!"

She tugged her pea green cagoule off and hastened to the back room to find a place to hang it up to dry. She came back via a full length mirror – brushing hailstones from her artificial strawberry-blonde locks and rubbing beneath her eyes from where the rain had run her mascara.

She wandered back to where I was still standing, staring through the glass fronted shop at the angry weather. She took her coffee, and we stood side by side in quiet horror as the harrowed sky inflicted upon the city a merry onslaught with every weapon it could muster.

The wind was making a mockery of all human life. It snatched brollies from hands so that they whipped into the road, where drivers curb-crawled in fright at the minimal visibility through their windscreens (which instead appeared to be cinematic frames for disaster movies). It seemed to be raining and hailing simultaneously, both varied from minute to minute in size and demeanour. The street was drenched, the puddles ankle-deep with drains choking in surprise. Pedestrians who tried at first to side-step sodden pot-holes soon gave up, too confused by the wind and hail to be particular about where they stepped.

A woman opened the shop door and bustled in, in a similar fashion to Jess, with gasps of indignation.

"Eh loves. It's hell out there. Mind if I shelter for a while?" she asked breathlessly. The three of us forced the door shut again, as it buffeted back at us. Flimsy as it was, I had to lock it shut this time, so it didn't blow open again.

"Yeah, that's fine!" Jess said. "Don't think we're gonna get no customers today."

As she pulled a stool over for the woman to sit on, there was an almighty thunder clap and the shop actually seemed to shake as though with a ground tremor.

"That'll be that big tree down!" the woman gasped. "I said to meself it were gonna go, when I saw it! I 'ope nobody's hurt."

"It really *is* like the end of the world out there," I said in awe.

This was to be the first of the Great Storms which wreaked havoc across the country, and then seemed to reproduce itself with terrorising regularity. The religious freaks began saying it was The Rapture. But Jesus never came. Only twisters, and lightning, and horror came.

* * * * * * *

DOGGEREL

Wolfgang, the World

The little bearded man known as Tobias Roe was at odds with society. He could see himself too easily becoming his parents. Arguing about mortgages and convincing themselves that because they used a chiropractor, they hadn't very quietly and gradually become that alien of things – 'conservative'.

It was easy to idealise, when you were young. But now your bones creak and you have to worry about pensions and providing a future for yourself. The wilderness absolves this very quickly. The wilderness tells you that you'll die when you are no longer physically able to hunt and gather. Your demise won't be drawn out into a pitifully banal tale of incontinence and hip replacements. There'll be no hospital bed and sense of doom. Just the sky and the land, which will suck the last of your sprite out through your irises. Through the little specks amongst the colours that join so easily with the wind, once the moisture on your lenses has dried to glass. It might be a slow, lonesome death of starvation or illness, but it's noble nonetheless. And it's not so slow or lonesome as living in a flat by yourself, with a special red button to press should you take a fall.

I read a book written by young Toby Roe and it stuck with me. Whether he really ever wrote a book I can't say. For it echoed so much of Farley Mowat, Jack London and H. Mortimer Batten, it may've only been an amalgamation of these that I'd somewhat dreamed into being. For all those books and pictures seemed to merge. Seemed to speak in turns of the character Nether Ed who Cassie had written of. Which in turn reminded me of Cuan's little skeletal scribbles.

Indeed it could've *been* young Cassie Siddal who dreamed us into significance. She had all the freckles of a Greek goddess of stories and trees. I think it's funny that the term *Raconteur* is so very masculine. It describes a ballsy chap stood in a pub, surrounded by eager faces that laugh and listen (*with that bird man on his shoulder*). The pages of Lissy Siddal's stories are half finished and read only by educated squid. In fact it's not peculiar at all that the word raconteur is so masculine. It's just very bloody French. But then I would speak ill of the *cheese-eating surrender monkeys*; it was a Frenchman that stole my wife, after all.

At some stage in youth we all reach a certain wall, one that is too high to be scaled with the merest of tools our upbringing has laden us with. I'm off track, I think I was trying to justify lunacy somehow, but I've forgotten how. I'll come back to the wall presently. Firstly, know that the jolt you experience as you transcend dream to wake – that's your death inside the dream. That's your soul leaving the dream to return to your waking life. You'll feel that same jolt when your soul leaves your body, this I am sure of. But when it comes to death and the great beyond, that's all I am sure of...

I felt that that was so profound, I pondered if I was already on page 42... Had all of it passed so quickly?

... And Toby Roe, he'd long put aside the path written for him from university into a steady job. He was walking in the wilderness amongst the wolves and bears who, like man in his hungriest, barest form, could turn at any time and take his life. As dangerous and fearful, some might say, as crossing a busy road every day, so bored with your routine that you barely pay attention to the traffic. Never lose your fear of the big metal beasts (Toby would advise), for all their gleaming beauty and hypnotic yellow gaze, they're predators. And push come to shove, if that Toyota is hungry, you're lower in the food chain. But like the wolves, most of the time you're pretty safe. He'd rather quaff petrol than human blood.

Most of us are too acclimatised to our society and comfort zone, to do little more than daydream of the wilderness. But Toby's comfort zone had become the wilderness. He was inside the changing seasons, the routines of the migrating creatures, the multitude of insect life which held the planet's eco-system together. But he'd once had the guts to leave humanity to their lot and go into the unknown. Now, he felt it time to summon up those guts once more. For all his disillusion with the human race, they were just animals, and he had more than a little affection for a few of those animals he'd left behind.

Back to the wall. You may know the wall already. You may've conquered it, or it may have cowed you. We've all been cowed, or will be. No one can be sure of their breaking point until they're broken. To be cowed is not to be conquered though. The cowed can get back on the horse they fell off. So it would be, with the (*apologetic*) apocalypse we were walking blithely into.

I have spoken... and it is so.

* * * * * * *

WHEN ALL SNOW HAS LOST ITS MEANING

Claudia McLeod, Ripon

I walked on intu't snowscape and let missel get utterl'y lost. I vowed never to let the snow lose its romance. I missed it mostly, living soo many years in inner cities where it would snow at night and be brown sludge by morning. Out in the countryside it fell deeply and thickly, and merged the white sky intu't rest a the world. When the sun peeked through the ground glittered with a million tiny, lit'l points a light.

It began to fall agen, settlin in ma hair, on ma eyebrows, on ma shoulders. My boots squeaked slightly as they trod it down underfoot. I carried on through the fields that were edged wi' trees, all sense of place and time leavin me in a great cathart'ic wave. And then I let missel cry wayve upon wayve of grief, arrivin in tremors through ma body. Tears an snot quickly merged wi' snowflakes. I wiped ma face on ma sleeve burrit was already damp and cold.

Eventually, as the fallin snow eased, I crouched among the roots of a tree. I thought about the missin part in ma body. The lit'l life that never were. Burrit blurred and merged with all the other death and grief.

"*You can scribble me out if you want,*" I mumbled tu't deaf landscape. "*I once wanted to always be maire important to you, but I understand I must fall by whey side sumwhat.*"

But the scribblin, it's lyke death int it? Me dad had the sayme address book since I were a kid. What of all those people that moved house, numbers changed, lost touch or died. Scribble it out. I waited fa the first Christmas card not signed from both grandparents, that gap, that space.

So if you cross me out, am I dead? If I stop existin to you, how do I exist?

In fookin truth you'd already stopped existin in ma life. You were already jus an imaginary photograph, a distant concerned phone conversation. I'd already scribbled you out and I had to face that fact. That death maykes grief easier, yes it's harder, bigger, maire painful. But it's a full stop. I can think of yar picture and know that I will never ever see you ever. There's no danger I will one day run into you in't street someplace, wi' a better parent. We won't have to face weird joy at seein each another, and then wonder bitterly at the choice of severance. My choice.

In the snow I thought of you, of followin yar footprints in the hope of findin my own. Of the look a confused wonder you might have at this powdery white stuff. That look is the rewind button, returning to zero, knowin not bitter cynicism but uncertain awe. Love is the first snow you ever saw... and fallin flakes settlin perfectly on every surface recalls sommat of this. Look at their faces when they see the snowfall, stripped to childhood. They'll cuss the inconvenience tomorrow when it maykes them late for work.

So I'm sorry I let you down. I'm sorry you were too inconvenient. I'm sorry you didn't fit well wi' my plans. I'm sorry that you died alone wi'out me there to cradle you and tell you how much I loved you. I'm sorry I scribbled you out.

* * * * * *

THE LAST DISCO

Haydn Antoine, Derby

"No mate! Thatull be my sevenf shot of tequila!" Rufio exclaimed loudly over the pounding music. "Number seven!"

"It's lucky," I replied, clinking his glass and knocking back my own. He drank his and sucked on the lime wedge, before tossing it over his shoulder. *Lime but never salt* was Rufio's mantra. Proper Latinos know how to drink quality tequila. It was his birthday and he was doing a DJ set. A bad combination because folks buy you drinks on your birthday. The slickness of his mixing was at risk.

I stood next to him behind the decks, sipping a bottle of beer and gazing into the throng, enjoying at least the sight of other people having a good time. I was feeling increasingly sober and yet increasingly reckless with each drink. One of the downfalls of booze being a depressant. I would never have this problem on charlie – it made me feel like the best version of myself. But I'd overdone it too much, so I was trying to stay off it. I could see the boredom growing in Claudia, I was frightened she'd ditch me. She had little patience for cokeheads.

Despite his own level of squiffiness, Rufio was still astute enough to notice my lack of glee.

"Wassup Blondie? You look in a proper grump."

I made an exaggerated shrugging gesture, no point trying to have a conversation with any depth when the music was this loud. I spotted Patti lurking across the room and waved her over.

"Heey guys," she said dreamily. "I feel proper zonked tonight, how are you guys? How are you?"

"Not as zonked as when you got a roofie in yew!" Rufio quipped.

"Ah, roofie-jokes, always funny, never inappropriate," I said.

"What did he say?" Patti asked.

I shook my head to indicate that I wasn't going to be a translator.

"Oh, I love this song," she squawked, skipping back down to the dancefloor.

The loose cannon that I've never been. The successful socialite, the cad, the gadabout. What would my brother say? I was still irritated by his visit in the last week, when I was quickly more drunk than my girlfriend.

He'd said to Claudia, "Good work. You got him on the Pale Rider early!" (Pretending he knew anything about strong ale... the Grolsch-quaffing Rugby twerp)... to which my lovely Cloud replied –

"Uh huh, maykes him easier to molest."

Later in her absence he'd said, "Christ, Haydn. She's a bit *Northern,* isn't she?" I wanted to punch him squarely on the jaw, but I knew I was already too drunk, more's the pity.

"Reckon I can splice Sonic Yoof wiv Brant Bjork, or will I lose em?" Rufio asked, gesturing to the young things on the dancefloor.

"Fuck it, it's your birthday. Let's not feel we have to resort to Calvin Harris just to keep the kids dancing. They're all wasted anyway."

Rufio gave his Brando nod and slid out a fresh record from the casing, giving it a showman's flip before placing it on the second deck.

"Guerrilla rock revolutionaries," he said with comical lowered brows and a serious demeanour.

I smiled with the inner joy that came from being buddies with such a relentlessly happy soul.

"Followed by Enemigo Publico... (I kid yew not, that is the translation!). I got it aw down, wiv the usuaw finalee..."

"Not *Purple Rain.* You can't do it every time, they'll get bored!" I insisted in his ear.

He gave me the sign to zip it, shaking his head. "Blondie, I am the beast of cupid! Do yew know how many platonic friends have drunkenly bonked each uvver cos of me playin *Purple Rain* at the end of the night? They is lonely. They need a littuw push in the right direction."

"But you'll make Barney the bartender cry. His girlfriend just dumped him, you know," I added.

"Wiv a name like Barney, ees lucky tu av ad a bird at aw! Try tellin im that to cheer him up! Whoops..." He quickly changed song and the bluesy cords of *Cheap Wine* rumbled through my body. I'd finished my beer, I pointed at it and pointed at Rufio.

"Just water, please, Blondie," he said firmly.

"Cowboy the fuck up!" I replied (with his own call to arms).

"Yew may not take my job seriously, Antwon, but I do," he returned.

I weaved to the bar, avoiding another meaningless exchange of sozzled words from Patti.

"Ay up, Barney, how are you doing mate?" I said above the racket.

"I'm getting totally wrecked, people keep buying me drinks!" His eyes were full of sadness but still smiling.

"Cool, cool. Can I get a pint of water for the disco jockey, another beer for me and a shot of tequila for yourself."

"No no, mate! You buy me a shot you have to do one too, thems the rules!" He plonked down the bottle of tequila and two shot glasses.

"Jeez," I said. "This is how it all goes wrong. Generosity!"

He nodded, clinked my glass and necked his shot, slipping the ten pound note neatly from my grasp.

Meanwhile Rufio joined in on the mic with the opening words to his next selection, *Bring the Noise*.

* * * * * * *

ARTFUL DODGING

Bryn McLarey, Sheffield

It doesnae cheer me tu read of teenage suicide. It's no gud ritual attention-seeking. You cannae much appreciate attention when yer dead. Better tu wait for doomsday when the true believers will be in God's presence for all eternity. An the rest a yuu mother fookers will burn in hell, cause humanity is pure evil.

But am no bastard, I wusnae born out of wedlock me. Yuu blaspheme, middle-fookin-class and littering yer aen speech with trinkets of fook and piss and shite. I misjudged the situation, aye. I wus an obnoxious cunt I know, I know... I didnae mean it like *that* but you took it like *that* didn't ye?

Sumtimes yer just a cunt fa sayin the truth. But am addicted tu it, can't stand it. Like I can't stand losing ye. I read in the newspaper today, with dread, of the children hanging themselves in the woods in Wales. I fear I'll see them all in mae dreams. Tuu young, tuu young, so foolish. They didnae even have tu wait tuu long for *The Rapture*. I wait, yes, not long now.

Jenny had left me for someone more mature. Someone with a 9-5 job. Someone with financial security. Someone who'd perfected their 'water cooler lean' over the years, sae as tu seduce female co-workers with unhappy love-lives.

Our flat wus empty and echoed with female disappointment. We still had a few months on the lease and I could just about afford it on mae wages now. And she wus decent enough tu offer tu help me out if I cudnae (the bitch).

But the rattling emptiness wus getting ta me. The sound of mae aen breathing. The dishes and litter piling up, because what wus the point in tidying if there wus only me there tu make a mess again?

I left the house intu the frozen late morning, the frost pinching mae nose and cackling at me. It wus Saturday. Wolfgang would be begging in the town centre near the Cathedral. I popped mae collar and strode purposefully down the street. My mouth belched steam intu the cold air leik a chimney, mae eyes scanned the prettily frosted lawns with aching cynicism.

I crossed the cityscape, reaching the Cathedral by pushing rudely through the flocks of shoppers and pushchairs that writhed and flowed en masse like maggots on dead flesh.

Wolfgang wus there sure enough, looking a bit like an aged vision of the Artful Dodger. He wus wearing a long coat that wus tuu big for him, with the sleeves rolled up and a brimmed hat perched precariously on his heid. He wus crouched against a wall, a posture exposing that his trousers were tuu short for his legs, revealing yellow socks with unsightly patches of beige. In addition tu the one on his head, he had two hats for begging, one on either side – a tweed farmer's cap and a stripy woollen beanie. He also had a cardboard sign with a small essay scrawled on it, finished in larger letters with – *PLEASE HELP!*

A lad wearing a neon tracksuit and a baseball cap tipped back on his head stopped in front of Wolfgang, chewing gum like a ruminating cow.

"What's wiv all the hats, maate?" he asked rudely.

"A gentleman can never have too many hats!" Wolfgang beamed.

I sidestepped some groping teenagers and 'accidentally' barged intu the lad.

"Oh, sorry, son. D'yuu mind? I need a quick *word* with this piece of junk," I said in a less than polite tone.

"Whatever." The lad skulked off in the direction of Argos.

Wolfgang grinned at me.

"What can I do for you, boss?"

I held out a hand and dragged him tu his feet, he reached down tu collect his hats and sign, shoving them in oversized pockets.

"Jenny's ditched me. D'yuu want tu come and live at the flat?" I asked.

"I don't have any money," he said.

"Doesnae matter. It's just tuu fooking quiet with nobody there."

"But I have a home," he said, seeming confused.

"You've a paper castle with no heating," I replied. "It's getting pretty fooking cold, Wolfgang..."

He shrugged with exaggerated nonchalance. "Can I bring the ferret? Cuan gave me his ferret. It's pretty smelly."

"You're pretty smelly," I replied.

* * * * * * *

A HUNDRED LASHES

Claudia McLeod, Derby

"Another fookin cuppa tea!" I exclaimed.

Haydn slipped in't bedroom door carryin two mugs. He stopped and grinned at my ungratefulness, shruggin carelessly.

"Literally, Aidey, including coffee I've had lyke twelve brews today. I'm gonna piss all night."

I were huddled in bed under't covers wi' just the flicker of light from the television screen. Pages were discarded on't bed and on't floor, sometimes there's no real creative spark found in the cloudsa self-pity, jus frustration. I can't write, and pickin up a guitar maykes me lose my temper and want to smash the thing. I'd pretty much moped since he'd left several hours ago.

"You don't have to drink it." He handed't mug to me. I rested it on't tops a my knees.

"Course I'll drink this one. It's got maire love in than the ones I mayde missel."

He had a new coat on. It were very shiny and hooded, gold and cream. I dunno how I ever let myself be smitten by someone that dressed this way.

"That coat is worse than t'other one. What exactly are you tryin to achieve, the eighties pimp look?"

He unzipped it and dumped it on the chair.

"It's fun. It's easier for girls to create a look and be a bit ridiculous. I don't mean to be taken seriously. I just like watching films and stuff and taking looks."

"Oh aye, what 'look' is this?"

"*Back to the Future II*! You know the bit with hover boards and shit."

"Yar problem is that you think Vince Noir is actually cool." I pulled back the covers on one side a the bed. He stripped to t-shirt and boxers and climbed in.

"Shit, it's cold." He shivered.

"Always cold in my bed, only ice here," I mumbled.

He pulled the covers up to his neck, huddling next to me. It were true, he felt warmer than I did.

"Are you watching this again? What's with your obsession with this film?"

He peered at the still image of the little blonde girl in the red rain mack playin wi'a stripy ball near a pond.

"It's one of the best films I've ever seen. But I'm not obsessed wi' the film, I'm obsessed with her."

I'd watched the openin sequence to the film that day as many times as I'd mayde myself a mash.

"Why...? She looks like how you would've looked when you were little," he said.

"Maire that she looks how my daughter would look," I let my voice drop to a whisper. "Would'uv looked."

Little Christine was hauntin me. We wanna be haunted. We wanna find hidden meanin in it all. Angsty songs I once sneered at started ta mekk sense in my despair. I stopped bein able to write my lyrics, everyone else's entered my head. Scattered pages lay scribbled on, tears'd smeared the ink if Haydn were to look closely enuff. Had I wanted him to find my black hole...? I spose.

The film stayed paused. The girl frozen in play, unaware a'her loomin demise. The room were quiet and dark and hollow. I could hear Haydn breathin and the cogs in his brain turnin ev'rythin over, fittin together the pieces. I looked at his face, his eyes, his blonde lashes. I looked away and looked back agen, chokin on the words. Unable to get them out lyke the first time I tried to say 'I love you' to anyone.

"I had an abortion last year..."

He continued lookin at me very intensely. He'd slipped his fingers into my hand. I'm always interested in men tryin to fathom this whole thing. Whether or not it might be beyond their comprehension. Not the loss, not the guilt, the fact that a bit of you is gone, *physic'ly*.

He waited and I waited and we both knew the only thing that could break the tension was me cryin, my face breakin open. And him smotherin me in his arms so that am choking on tears and skin.

* * * * * * *

CAPPUCCINO IN THE RAIN

Simian Thomas, Dreamscape

The sky opened up and let the rain out. We were quickly drenched, but I liked the feel of it. We retreated to a cafe and I sat in the window, I rested my head against the pane, feeling euphoria as it continued pounding the pavements outside.

"It's always raining!" Lucy whined insistently. "It's been raining for days, when will it stop?"

"So?" Simian said. "It's only fucking rain."

"It makes my hair frizzy!" she whinged.

"It makes your voice frizzy," he said, mussing her hair until she hissed.

"I just want a plain day so we can go shopping properly."

I yawned without covering my mouth and she gave me a repulsed look.

"It can't rain all the time," I murmured, not letting my eyes stray from the window.

Sometimes I remember things from Cassie's point of view. As though when she died I inherited it, and forgot my own. It must be raining in the waking world, because each dream merges with the relentless sound.

Here the rain, and everywhere. Inside and outside, every bit of rotting wood choked with water, wax jackets leaking, wool soaked.

'*If we don't try, we don't do; if we don't do, why are we here on this Earth?*'

Irony has cost us much. We know too much, the post-cold war generation, the Jason generation. We've stared oblivion in the face and now nothing is shocking and everything is amusing. Grand statements seem silly. They've lost their truth. Blood in the dirt is just another everyday image.

I've nowhere to hide from the rain so I accept it, into my skin. The coldness takes me, but not in a deathly way. I remember liking torrential rain hammering the streets when I had a café to escape to. Maybe I still like it, the absoluteness. No gentle pit pat, no scattering of showers. Just rain and rain and rain, seeming eternal.

Simian's tears can cure cancer. Unfortunately he's never cried...

Charlie and me crouch down for a moment. We watch the dark doorway that frames the electric streaks of white light catching on the rain. We wait for Cassie to appear in the doorway. She doesn't. We pretend we're looking for something else instead.

"You'd do anything to save these fuckers, wouldn't you?" I say to Charlie.

"*Shenandoah*," he says, pausing to think. "*Mes fils.*"

"We're not all boys."

"None of ye are. What I mean is – look after your aen," he says.

Shenandoah, I think, remembering the train. One of those freight trains that carry people like cattle, used in the Holocaust, too.

'This train carries people to where they don't want to be. It is a sad train. Burn it.'

No fire for the rain soaked wood surrounding us. A figure appears in the black doorway, silhouetted by the back-lit rain, a cinema image, nothing more. He can't see us crouching there with the other debris.

He pauses but stumbles in. Light glints on a shiny surface – a gun, a knife, a Rolex, all worth dying for. Charlie doesn't wait to find out which. A silent shot is fired, the impotency of the silent gunshot, the pretence. Adrenaline draws me to the fallen man, a tiny trickle of blood seeps from his nose, like a cokehead spiked with WD40. Charlie grabs my collar and drags me on. My sons may see death but they may not feel it.

I recall the café again, two girls' faces watching the rain outside, exchanging poisons. The goodness of when all that we cared about were personality clashes and the tender balance of espresso, milk and froth. Cassie only took up smoking to annoy Lucy, didn't she? Charlie shakes his head, no she didn't.

"Where in the world are you?"

A voice down the phone, an umbilical cord wrapped in those twirling wires.

We shadow across the pier, fleeting white faces and hands in the darkness, cardboard boxes limp with water. I want a streak of fire to come chasing down a line of petrol, I want Gabriel Byrne to point a gun at me. I want to know this is just a dream of a film in which I'm the hapless protagonist.

"Who was the first person you killed, Charlie?"

His face seems suddenly too close. I can see the detail of rain deflected by eyebrows, eyelashes blinking away the floods. There's innocence to the privilege of this unusual closeness.

"Bryn McLarey," he says without pause.

"Who was he?" I ask. When I speak the rain gets in my mouth and simultaneously spits back out again.

He shifts his gaze back blankly.

"He wus me."

* * * * * * *

THE YOUTH OF NATURE

Wolfgang, Sheffield

The real world is tough for the whimsical. I went for a stroll one day and found myself into the moorland, clambering the mighty rocks and sinking bogs, and laying in the heather getting sheep poo stains on my knees. Some might say I got a little carried away, straying a little far from home. After a few days I realised I was meant to be at work, and that it was likely I was now unemployed again.

I pleaded to my employer, how captivated I was with the moorlands, to no avail. They didn't appreciate my brave tales of bivouacking beneath the stars and nightly howls of wild things. They insisted wild wolves were extinct on this isle. And those silver ponies I'd glimpsed in the fog, with ornate horns protruding from their foreheads, were '*nowt, but the visions of a barmy man*'.

The younglings peered at me with wide eyes, and I looked back wearily and wished I had the stamina of a toddler and the attention span of a matured Homo Sapient, instead of vice versa. "Upon a whim, young things, I lost my employment," I advised them, foreboding of the whim.

"Yuu don't work anywhey," the Kaiser told me. "You're a hustler."

"Isn't a hustler a pimp?" I asked, puzzling the word, puzzling the place of Americana amongst romances of the Peak District in all its bleak, audacious beauty.

He wrinkled his nose as though he couldn't be bothered to explain the intricates of the English/American language.

"Not really. It has several meanings, but I mean it in terms of a blagger."

"What's a blagger?" I asked.

"Somebody with a knack for getting things for free, instead of grafting away in order tu be able tu afford tu live," he said.

He was attempting to look busy reading a script he needed to audition for, but I could see his eyes glazing over at it.

"I graft at being a blagger," I said.

"Exactly," he muttered. "That's hustling."

"I'm confused," I said.

"Good, can you drop it now?"

"Drop what?" I quipped, holding my hands out to show him they were empty.

He ignored this, instead asking, "D'you know anything about this play? *The Lady's Not for Burning?* Taffy says I should go fa the role of Thomas. I think he's typecasting me as a drunk who thinks someone ought ta hang him." He waved the book at me.

"Ah, yes. I played the role of the dog in it once. Didn't have any lines though."

"Not even a woof?"

"I emitted a low growl during act three, but the director chastised me for making up lines and affecting the ambience," I said, with woe.

"Did they fire yuu?" he asked wryly.

"No, no, too late to find a replacement. Besides, I was an excellent dog." I paused in thought. "You know when you envision the glory of nature in fiction... say the Garden of Eden? Or if you should envisage another planet similar to ours, unspoilt in youth?" I queried.

"Yes?" he said.

"Like... a paradise?" I said.

"Yes?"

"Don't you think it's always conjured to look like an Amazonian rainforest, or the crystal clear waters of a Canadian mountain lake?" I suggested.

"Yes. It reflects the paradise we already have," he said quickly, second guessing (wrongly) what I was getting at.

"It would never be conjured to be like the moorland, and the grey, drizzly peaks," I furthered. "Doesn't that make them even more special?"

"Has this got *anything* tu do with *The Lady's Not fa' Burning*?" Charlie asked.

"The heathenism and witchcraft of the Celts created the Peak District," I informed him. "I think I have a Celtic heart and that's why I'm drawn here."

"You're Germanic," he replied, adding "Teutonic..." to try to sound knowledgeable.

"'*Germen*' means seed or offshoot of the Celts," I corrected him. "At least that's the version of the story I wish to believe!" I beamed.

He shook his head dubiously. "Hearsay."

"All knowledge is hear, say," I announced, beaming still.

I could tell he was pondersome of how good an idea it'd been to invite me to abide with him – could he abide with me?)

"Will yuu be helpful? Or will yuu shut up?" he asked.

"Apologies, sir, what query you about the aforementioned play?" I said.

"Well, I think I should go for the role of Richard. He's the boring 'good guy', right? Like Benvolio, utterly boring and utterly necessary," he said.

"Are you trying to learn to be a boring, good guy?" I arched an eyebrow (beneath my mane and thus without significance).

He coughed a smokers' cough and laughed.

"I tried that one before. No, it's just more challenging tu play a dull role and bring them out."

"Wouldn't it be more a challenge to play Jennet? The accused witch?" I suggested.

The Kaiser rolled his eyes. "I think I'm a little burly to pull that one off."

* * * * * * *

DREAMS OF THE LUCID LIVING

Calista Siddal, the Afterlife

I'm walking down a passage in time, trying to conjure old familiar memories. The surface of the tunnel is like a white powder that crumbles when touched. It forms a perfect circle ahead of me, followed by another and another, stretching away in a series of engraved rings. It makes a beautiful sound as the soles of my brogues take quick steps forward. Not quite the squeak of snow, nor the crunch of sand, but some finite place in between. I pick up sounds now, not dully like the human ear, but as though they are digitally re-mastered and wired inside my mind.

There's someone inside the tunnel ahead and I feel a quiver of excitement, for I've meandered for many moments without meeting a single soul (time is now incoherent to that measured by those in the waking world). This person is too large for the passage. As I come to a bend I see them bent over, raven hair draping like a curtain. Different strands of it appear indigo and purple in the light, which has no source but seems to emit from the walls, looking in turns translucent and opaque.

I feel a strange reassurance in the familiar face of Lucy. Her lips are the colour of the Undead, as though painted by blood. Her pallor is paled from the healthy brown glow of our teenage years.

"Hello, Lucy," I greet her in a friendly manner.

"Lizzie Siddal!" she gasps.

"It's Calista... Cassie," I explain patiently, folding my hands in front of my dress.

"I was told you'd be here, Lizzie. I was asked to wait for you, but I didn't believe that I would find you *here*. Still I'm glad you've arrived, for it's so very cramped for me. I've lost all feeling in my spine."

She pushes at the walls and a little powder crumbles off, but they don't give.

I smile politely, ignoring her getting my name wrong as she always has done.

"I have something for you Lizzie." She reaches in her pocket and brings out a bottle, part full of crystal clear liquid. The bottle is as big as my torso, but I take hold of it awkwardly anyway.

"Thank you, Lucy," I say. "How is everybody? Do you still hear from Simian?"

She looks disconcerted. "How should I know such things? I can't very well be here and *there*. Thank you for coming, but I must be gone."

She disappears strangely fast down the passage, given that she's crouched over. I try to follow her, carrying the bottle – which feels lighter and smaller with each step, oddly.

The passage dips steeply over and I skid to a precarious halt. There's a cavernous opening below, and beyond that an abyss.

I sit down on the edge and peek over, the wind blows gently below. I look at the bottle and the enticing clarity of the liquid. The label, written in old hand says

'*Laudanum*'. I shiver in horror, debating whether to toss it into the abyss or leave it here. Worried it should hurt someone far down below, I leave it. With great care I roll onto my stomach and slip through the opening. I cling to the rings of white with my finger tips, fumbling blindly with my feet until they find a foothold...

* * * * * * *

A GAME OF CAT & MOUSE

Bryn McLarey, Sheffield

I wus always concerned that the word *malevolent* wus just 'male' and 'violent' shoved together in a lazy fashion. But meybe there wus a notion of the word volatile lurking in the middle. And I always loathed the simplicity of misogyny meaning 'hatred of women'. I preferred tu consider it the fear of female power, the reason men have struggled always ta dominate. The all-seeing matriarch will one day have a great big mardy that will cause the self destruction of the planet.

"Hey, Charlie! I didn't know you were working here." Maisie appeared through the narrow doorway. The pokey little bar was made to feel smaller and more idiosyncratic by the old theatre posters plastered ta the walls and sloping ceiling.

She wus followed closely by that other girl, Josie, who always seemed to regard me warily. Maisie's cheeks flushed a little and a light bulb went on in mae head, reminding me she probably had a bit of a crush, and for once I wus in an excellent position tu take (un-gentlemanly) advantage.

"Hiya Maisie, Josie. How are yuu both?" I let the Scottish lilt work its gravelly charm.

"Good thanks." Maisie nodded.

"Have you heard Claudia's moving back to Sheffers?" Josie asked, clearly knowing that I hadn't.

"Really?" I said. "Nice tu hear it through the grapevine, eh? I fookin texted her t'other day to ask how she wus and she dinnae answer. Probably in a huff. Is Haydn coming with her?"

"Noo..." Josie said, leaving a dramatic pause.

"I hear he's a nice chap, so doubtless she fooked that one right up!" I said.

"He's got a job in London and Claudia doesn't want to go with him," Maisie added quickly.

"I see. She moving back in with you lassies then?" I asked.

Josie nodded. "And Roxanne."

"Roxy's movin back? Nottingham didn't last long," I said.

"Yeah. She's been offered a job doing events for Art Sheffield."

"Events organiser? Thes good money in that."

Josie scoffed. "Probably not if the Art's Council are paying. It's good experience though, I'm well-happy for her."

"Yuu twos havin a bevy then?" I asked, considering mae options.

"Two rum and cokes, please," Maisie said.

I nodded, lining up glasses and filling them with ice and spent limes.

"Might join yuu for a drink or two when I clock off. If that's alright?" I said coyly.

I knew I'd geht finished pretty early. The shite weather wus not encouraging much custom.

"Yes!" Maisie said happily. Josie rolled her eyes and turned tu her friend so as tu block me out of the conversation a bit.

"What's Freddie up to tonight, Mayz? Not seen him in a while..."

Maisie shrugged stubbornly, without an iota of guilt. "He's being an idiot as usual. I've texted him three times and he's not answered. He didn't even come over to mine last night like he promised. He phoned me at 4 a.m. to say he wasn't coming!"

"Well, you do know how to pick em," Josie said cynically.

"There you go, ladies," I placed their drinks in front of them. "Enjoy."

"How much?" Josie asked, lifting her bag up.

"These are on me," I replied.

"Oh, thanks, Charlie," Maisie said, beaming in a whirlwind of rosy cheeks and a flirty tug of the hemline of her pink skirt.

Josie sighed and stalked off tu find a seat. I flashed Maisie a charming smile and resumed filling the glass washer up with dirty glasses.

* * * * * * *

LOONEY TUNES

Roxanne Ratcliffe, Sheffield

"I don't want to go out, it's too hot," Simian mumbled.

"You mayde it here?" Claudia suggested, unsympathetically.

"My flat's too hot. It's cooler here, the windows face the other way."

We were in the middle of a monster heat wave. I'd never seen green little England so pale and wilted.

"You jus wanna sit in't doom all day?" Claudia asked.

"I'm going to move to Iceland," Simian announced.

"It'll be rainy and freezing agen in a few weeks," she added.

"You said that last month."

"It's gorra break soon," she said. "There'll be a great big thunder storm, I can feel it."

In the faded afternoon, which sat surreally among the storm ravaged lands, the toasted grass tickled my feet through gaps in my sandals. We crossed through Endcliffe Park, once contrived by landscaping, roughly designed in levels so that little middle-class brats named Oliver and Jemima could ride their trikeys up and down. Mummy could push them up that one last steep bit of slope and then they could sit at the top, feeding the ducks and smearing their faces with ice cream.

But the park'd had an almighty scrap with the weather through the past winter. The statue of Queen Victoria still towered near the entrance, looking grumpy and bored. Beside that, the little bridge over the stream was speared at an angle with part of a fallen tree that had crumbled a lot of the brickwork. The old pavilion had become a nest of debris, captured from the wind, with graffiti daubing out the ominous warning – *THE END IS NIGH*.

In the baking heat, there were council workers out, turning ever redder beneath the afternoon sun. They'd only just begun the reconstruction project on the park – repairing phone lines, clearing trees from roads, and rescuing houses flooded with sewage had been the priority up until then. They toiled slowly and laboriously, unable to make much progress given the temperature, stopping at regular intervals for sandwiches, lucozade and ice lollies.

We walked up into the wooded part of the park, where it was cooler and shady. The natural part of the landscape seemed to have fared better. The tree roots held land together more securely through the onslaught of floods, thunderstorms and what'd been dubbed 'The Robin Hood Twister' – a small tornado which had lifted a vintage Mercedes from Fulwood and dropped it in a run down part of Hillborough. We sat on the dry, baked ground and stared quietly into the middle distance. There was something about the horror of the destruction in broad daylight that left us without very much to say.

I'd brought my camera. It seemed important to document the changing landscape, to put a frame between myself and the Earth's torment. But now I held it in my hands impotently. I felt that to raise it and search out an artistic composition would trivialise things.

Wolfgang appeared from the bushes as though he'd been loitering there, waiting for somebody to prophesize to. He sat down next to me, a pungent odour materializing in the air, reminding me of dead animals and bad eggs.

"*'All she wants is constant affirmation. Everything outside of herself is ruled out. But Art, my friend, cannot be ruled out!'*" he announced.

"Who?" I said. "What are you talking about?"

I wanted to decipher if he'd read my thoughts, or if it was just the tune of the loony.

"It's a quote from Günter Grass," he explained. "I think he was talking about *woman* in general, but for me it's Mother Nature."

"Whoopedy doo, Wily Coyote is back on't scene," Claudia said flatly.

Simian sat between us trembling.

"Look at them wastin their time," Claudia said of the workmen. "How long til it's wrecked agen?"

"If it ain't broke, don't fix it," Wolfgang said, as though in agreement.

"It is broke," Claudia answered gloomily.

* * * * * *

THE DEAD SPACE BETWEEN MYSELF & THOSE I WILL NEVER SEE AGAIN

Wolfgang, Sheffield

'Dreaded ted is in my mind
He's fucking with me, fucking with me.
A dogged, toothed tail of chronology
Of spiders drowning in the dead sea.'

I was going to eat some fruit today to improve my skin. Instead I sucked on a joint until it drew a tiny red line in the centre of my bottom lip. The dry dirt inside my lungs chokes and cloaks the city in a poetic fog, that hopes itself to be like Gotham. Stylized to spread maggots and dread of the *voodoo girl*, with the discothèque eyes, who cannot love anymore because it makes her bleed. Through tiny little holes until she disintegrates.

There's no sugar today so I must drink my coffee straight. The bitter taste of gutter water brings the Twins to mind and they hasten God's arrival. He debates whether Mugabe should live another day, live to spread the disease of political cleansing. I shall strike down upon thee with great vengeance for not choosing me. Me. God created the ladybird, not the reaper standing grim. He strikes not old Robert in the decrepit bitter shoulders that carry corpse upon corpse, he strikes a child who's been starved because his mama doesn't want to vote for me.

I sip my coffee and suck another roll up, which has lost the sweet taste it never had. I stare into dead space, that most treasured thing. It's a tangible loneliness when surrounded by others. It's sitting across from a lover in a café and realising that all the things you want to say are clogged in your throat, and in the space between your lips and their eyes. So you sit in silence and the silence slowly kills whatever connection you thought you had.

But this is *precious*. Don't sob into a tissue about it. It's the reason humanity (no matter how sheep-like) can never be eternally brainwashed into a perfect society. Loneliness is the gift of individual thought. I am not you, I cannot eat you. And if I did it would not make me less lonely. They're just cookies sweetiepie – they're not love.

I looked at Cuan today and I realised with quiet horror that something seemed to have died. He was a cartoon when I met him. If you threw him at the wall he'd bounce back, and if you threw him harder he'd bounce back happier. Now he's like the stripy ball sat in the cellar for seventeen and a half years. Not popped, not punctured by the fang of some excited dog, just a bit flatter. He's bitter, but there's still humour wry and hiding. I worshipped him. I put him on a pedestal. And then in my sleep I took a chisel and carved him and made him more like me.

Dreaded ted is made of stone, so his great paws and elongated claws cannot actually come pounding down upon my shaky frame. But he's there at my shoulder. The wuthering heather of dark torrents in his fixed gaze. His gaze fixed on me, waiting to strike, waiting for Medusa to rewrite her spell. There's something that glows about you, which makes no sense. But maybe it's part of the manic and not the bottom of the whisky jar. But there's something manic about running around in the bottom of a whisky jar. I know, I've been there. I tried to tell you this but then I realised that your madness was your own and I shouldn't contaminate it with mine, the way others have done to me.

If I eat today I shall feel better, I know. I sit and stare at the apple on the table. It's bruised in a way a human can never be. I can't bear to nibble around the bruises. Nor do I want their sloppy taste in my mouth. So, instead I watch the apple rot. Together we could've been better. I would've eaten Mr. Apple, saving him from the slow death of time, and he would've fed my skin with a polished glow. With rouged cheeks that chase away the sallow, that tell of sustainable living. I don't. I watch him rot instead and suck on the dregs of joints so that the red line in the centre of my bottom lip turns black.

I sometimes find the news reels overwhelming. I can't compromise between atrocities in Zimbabwe and a local Nana whose entire three generations of kin have been wiped out by the storms. Further to that, I can't compromise these with watching a friend disintegrate, unable to hold out a hero's hand.

Just last night we were running along a rainbow you and I. Afraid only of falling off the edge, and the romantic tumble towards Earth...

* * * * * *

WOLF LIKE ME

Claudia McLeod, the Isle of Mull

The light were perfect. Perfect for what I don't know – Roxy to have tekken loadsa photographs if she were wi' us. Or some silly water colour painter to sit mesmerised, blandly tryin to imitate sommat soo breathtaking. It was mid-evening. Low early-summer sunshine pannin out the flatness a'the sky an't sea, wi' the green land beginnin to fade ta dusk.

It were exactly what you chose to go to Scotland for. I was exhausted from all the drivin, but here was some reward. Some promise that this wouldn't be a week of rain an bickerin. I had ta ignore the views moastly though, as I sped down't single track road, which dipped and rose and then hair-pinned. We met a car in front, drivin atta sensible speed. I growled impatiently in time wi' my car engine.

"Please, don't tail-gate," Haydn begged quietly. "I know you're determined that we should both die young and beautiful, but please spare others. They might have kids in the back."

A fleetin chance came of a straight wide road and the car slowed to let me overtake. I nipped past wi'out glancin to the man's disgruntled fayce.

"There's sommat cathart'ic about brekkin't speed limit in a Volvo, in't there?" I said, clingin to another bend in't road.

"Oh, that's pretty," he exclaimed, peerin back to a view we were quickly losin. "Can we stop?"

"If it warrup to you we woulda stopped eight times already," I said wi'a driver's exasperation.

"Yes, we would. I appreciate these special moments," he said.

"It's alrayht for you, ya can look at't view anyway."

"Well, it's better than staring into the jaws of imminent death."

I hit a bump and the car hopped excitedly in't air. It landed heavily, but eagerly continued on its way. Haydn were purposely quiet furra moment and then finally said what I'd been waiting fa him to say the past six-odd hours.

"So, is there any chance you'd consider moving to London?"

"No," I said, definitely, defiantly.

"Any wiggle room in that?"

I could hear him thinkin his way through this conversation. Tryin to work out where there might be a weakness in my opinion of 'movin to London'.

"Ev'rybody moves to fookin London," I growled. "For their career, or whatever. They're all fookin unhappy as well – speak to them. They spend stupid amounts a time commutin, crammed on't underground lyke cows. They no time for friendships cause they haffta work soo much to afford to live there *and* spend so much time commuting. It's really fookin lonely, and hectic and stressful."

Haydn thought for a bit.

"It could be a good opportunity for you, there's so much going on," he said a little pathetically.

"That's what ev'ryone thinks when they move to London. It's funny, if there are so many good opportunities goin around, why have *all* my friends had to compromise and do sommat they either don't lyke much, or could've done back hoam?"

Silence flowed and ebbed lyke the landscape swallowed and freed from't tide.

"You know I have to do this, don't you? You know I *am* going to take the job?" he said quietly and insistently.

I swallowed hard. "Yeah, course I do. I'd kick yar ass if you din't do it. You'd be stupid not to tekk it."

"You won't move... not for me?" His voice shivered on the last word.

We reached a small headland wi' space to park on the grass. I whipped the steerin wheel and sped to a halt. The overwhelmin beauty of our surroundings soaked through my irises, framed by the windscreen.

"Don't ask me to. It will only break yar heart when I say no," I said.

"Is that a no?"

A sense of mass dread and fear washed over me. I kept very still and silent, frozen in metaphorical headlights, not darin ta move, to give my position away. I could sense that Haydn had a few tears in his eyes. He looked away from me, over't sound.

"Where does that leave us then...?" he whispered.

"Nowhere, obviously," I replied, maybe a little harshly.

"You don't want to see how things go long distance?" His voice was mousey now.

"We all know how that'll end up. You'll just keep hoapin that eventual'y I'll change my mind and move down to London."

I sensed him nod despairingly.

"Can we just forget about this til we get home?" I asked politely.

"Okay," he murmured, gulpin air, and tryin to regain composure. "Will you stay in Derby?"

I laughed. "And hang out wi' Rufio and Cookie? Noo, I'll go back ta Sheffield. There's some people movin outtah Maisie's house soon, I think."

"Oh," he said.

"I did move to Derby *for you*. It wasn't fatha fantastic nightlife, or the grouchy locals," I informed him, tryin to mekk missel seem a tad less selfish.

"Oh," he said. As though this hadn't occurred to him. "But London's too far."

I sighed, knowin the whole week would be lyke this.

"It's not *too far*, if you were movin to fookin Alaska I'd probably come wi' you. It would just compromise ev'rythin I believe in, about how I want to live ma life."

I got out of't car, and walked to the edge where the green land dropped away a few feet, to rocks and pebbles and then the lappin waves. I gazed across the view and savoured the feel of sunlight and sea breezes. I took a photograph. Haydn gor'outtah the car and loped over, hands stuffed in pockets, sunglasses blankin out his expression. I took another photograph of him framed against the view.

"Please, don't," he said.

"I'm sorry," I said, forcin the words out. I hugged him and he clung tightly to me, and I held back the tears.

* * * * * * *

BLINK & YOU WILL MISS ME

Roxanne Ratcliffe, Sheffield

A broken future, fractures and uncertainty. My fingers scrabble for a grip in the cracks. I lie awake at night and listen to the cats screaming on the rooftops, their furry furies... tearing imperfections into one another. Demonic hisses that waft like winter breezes through bushes.

The civilised world trembles. We get on with it, because you get used to anything eventually. The Plague, the Blitz, the Troubles, the Cold War... The Weathers. Things are different, but somehow still the same. If it was stormy, or extremes were forecast, you slept under the bed in cocoons of blankets. The weather presenters looked increasingly stoical, like war correspondents. It was their turn to predict the horrors of tomorrow. Sometimes I just sat and cried for little reason, because it was real and I was in it.

We were sent aid and support when the Gulf Stream first began to tear holes into our country and those surrounding it. Some areas were evacuated, and refugee camps sprung up, either in local sports stadiums, or in nearby safe spots like the South of France. But the Thermohaline Circulation Shutdown was causing more far-reaching problems than our little crisis. Gradually the governments of the world were switching off aid to other countries and trying to look after their own. It was impossible to cope with the scale of it, impossible to restrain the devastation.

The cats bristle. A paw is hesitantly extended. The claws are out and we wait. When I hissed at you – sweet, docile kitty – you hissed back in fright, and slashed at my cheek. I have fleeting moments of bravery the same as you. Animals have the same social struggle when they inhabit our society with us. They must face the outside, meet the drizzle with conviction. Look into the face of creatures they meet and decide on fight or flight, or friendship. We humans are supposed to be more doglike. Being pack animals, seeking company. But we're a finite balance between other animals. We crave both company and loneliness, the open parkland and the shadowy undergrowth. The familiar home and the mysteries of the far off horizon.

The far off horizon looked red. I wondered if that meant a better day tomorrow. I wondered if Mother Nature would hold back. What comes out of us when we stop holding back? Tears, an orgasm, a fart? All just icky bodily fluids. Mucus, sweat and spunk, it's not something to be shared with other people.

There was a girl on Cuan's art course who painted a fierce caricature of herself putting a tampon in. It was splashed with layers of red liquid. She wanted us to believe it was menstrual blood. We giggled at the exhibition.

"Art students go to great extremes to not appear dull," Cuan had said quietly, as wry explanation. "They have a great fear deep inside, that they are not unique, special, little snowflakes. That they're just fucking ordinary..."

He glanced around the room with weighty apathy for his peers, and then raised his voice just above appropriate volume.

"They are just fucking ordinary."

I was transfixed by a half reflection in a mirror behind the bar. I was lost in my grief-riddled train of thought, lost in images half-composed, of headless people, of incomplete objects. Of a pair of pointy ears poking above the bed. I know you only at a glimpse, a scrap, an excerpt. I know you only as handwriting on a postcard from Cuba. Seven sentences to sum up a rum-drenched paradise. Seven sentences were all I had left of my brother, David.

Not a hair out of place, he modelled himself on a Wall Street banker. He said if he looked clean-cut people took him seriously. If he had messy hair, they thought he was mad and ignored him. The barmaid maintained a patient face as David ordered our drinks in broken half-formed words. I wasn't even old enough to drink at the time, but nobody ever asked when I was with him. They were too embarrassed having to communicate with a deaf person, and if I kept quiet, they maybe assumed I was deaf, too.

We sat in a corner, curtained by the torsos of people standing nearby. He wrote on a piece of paper.

'If a tree falls in the woods and David's around, does it make a sound?'

I giggled. He liked a philosophical joke at his own expense. I still had that bit of paper stuck on my wall years later for people to ponder.

Cuan was astute enough to 'get it'. Unfortunately he had a habit of trying to be too astute. "You're drawn to people you think are much cleverer than you," he'd said, looking at it one day, completely out of context of the earlier conversation.

I looked at him for a bit, picking at his curly hair.

"Are you saying you're cleverer than me?"

He shook his head.

"I'm saying that *you think that I'm cleverer than you*. It's the same with your brother. You protect yourself with clever people."

I sighed, his little notions could be tiresome. But then that was his intention, to poke holes, to get a reaction.

"Am I not intelligent enough to look after myself?" I asked.

"No, I'm not talking about intelligence. I'm talking about cleverness, like a fox. You do know you're intelligent. You just don't think you're clever."

"I'm too tired for your riddles today, Q."

He thought for a bit, and carried on as though to himself.

"Most of your friends aren't emotionally intelligent anyway... just clever."

"*Emotionally* intelligent?!" I said in annoyance.

He grinned sheepishly and I instantly forgave him.

"They kinda overreact to stuff," he said gently.

I stared into the mirror image of us lounged on the bed, him watching my face with haphazard intimacy.

"You may not have emotional outbursts, Cuan. But keeping a stiff upper lip and sulking is no less an 'overreaction'."

His kissed my cheek.

"I know. I count myself amongst your friends."

* * * * * * *

IDIOSYNCRATIC PUNK ROUTINE

Haydn Antoine, East London

It's funny how tragic events can create a chain reaction for something better. Using the word tragic in the new world context seems like an overstatement. So, admittedly, I am talking about a break-up. Still it knocked me sideways, and I hovered for a bit in a strange sense of disbelief. But then things began to domino around me. Though it was my hand tipping the pieces, it felt out of my control, because all I could do to plug the holes in my body was work like a fiend.

I'd left a lazy, nonchalant boy behind in Derby. With few distractions to my routine I was suddenly efficient. All my friends were mere acquaintances and all my lovers were merely casual. Such is the London lifestyle when you first arrive. It was lonely, fucking lonely, just as she had told me it would be – living in a shitty little basement bedsit with only spiders for company.

But I had a shiny Mac Book to accompany me all over, as I spent the day dashing here and there, and moments of rest sat in cafes setting up the e-zine I was determined to make a success of.

The job I'd moved south for was not all it was cracked up to be – but this too, was a blessing. I could do it with half my brain and knock out articles that kept them happy and topped up my quivering bank balance. I also got taken out for drinks and food so often that I barely spent any money feeding myself, as I could go a day and a half before I got so hungry that it broke my stream of conscious.

A biscuit here, a coffee there. At the cafe I most often frequented, I befriended a charming Albanian named Aleks. He'd slip me a free latte or muffin from time to time. He was a budding musician of course, and it was an exercise in mutual back-scratching. Luckily he was talented.

It was in this particularly boheme hole that I did my best work, a typically idiosyncratic East London hangout. A sparsely redeveloped warehouse space, part deli, part cafe, part bar. The upstairs was lit mostly with candles and furnished with worn out, decadent objects probably rescued from charity shops.

In the ambient gloom I could absorb myself in work, whilst keeping an observant eye on the trendy local urbanites. It was here that I spawned my internet baby: 'The Chronicals (a Media-Junkie's Survival Guide)'. It was birthed, so to speak, from the sense that I was balanced in a precarious position, surviving in the unknown, when bad things were happening and there was a growing dread in the population.

We'd banished a government who'd thrived on a climate of fear they'd created in order to justify their phoney war and later breaches of human rights. The new dread came from the people, not the Man. The human grip of control on the planet was slipping, Greenland was melting, each ice floe too quickly becoming part of the expanding ocean.

And yet we still danced, we still drank, we still smoked and charmed ourselves into living in the present.

Not because we were callous, but because we were wise. Because music still mattered and cinema still mattered and booze still mattered. Because it was all that was keeping us sane. I never set out to be the catalyst for a new generational attitude, very modest I know. I just planned to put the name Aiden Antoine on the map, for the same reason we all do (hacks, artists, etc) – an inbuilt fear of insignificance and powerlessness.

> The Chronicals (A Media Junkie's Survival Guide).
> Home Page.
> About.
>
> The most fantastic film I ever saw was in my dream. I dreamed Steve Buscemi was the director. It was a combination of crude traditional animated drawings merging to hyper-cinematic images of landscapes that left me awestruck in their visual grandeur.
>
> Upon a hill sits a building. It looks like something from Ancient Greece, all ivory coloured pillars and huge doorways. Inside there is a Senate of sorts, but these people are drawn with sparse mockery. As though Steve Bell is scrawling his cartoons on the walls of a cave. Outside this building the scenery is, in contrast, very real looking, almost

photographic and yet layered in intense colour that harks back to graphic novels. The Grecian temple is sat on top of a bizarre urban structure like scaffolding, which creates a stable foundation, as this is inbuilt into the great hill.

All around it the land drops steeply away, in jagged crags and gullies, and far down in the valleys is the sense of a destroyed world. A post-apocalyptic landscape, dreadfully beautiful. I can't fathom much of a script. The film simply paints civilization destroyed. And yet the people inside the great temple still chatter on with their Punch & Judy politics, with expensively educated diatribes, as though any of it matters anymore.

When I woke up I was upset that the film hadn't really been made. I even pondered trying to make it myself, but it would've needed a huge budget to justify the visual power in my head. And so I've written it here for you to imagine. And maybe collective imagination is far greater than a mere piece of faux-political cinema.

Welcome to The Chronicals (a Media-Junkie's Survival Guide). Because you need us... and we need you.

I was trying to perfect this passage as Aleks came around collecting dirty mugs and replacing failing tea lights. He peered over my shoulder at the home page to my site, curiously pursing his lips as he read.

"Hmm... We should definitely have a drink sometime." He paused, and then looked at me with a slight gasp, deciding it had come across as though he was asking me out. "Oh, no, not like that! I know you straight, boy."

I laughed. "Sure sure, what time do you finish?"

* * * * * *

THE ROAR OF THE WARRIOR

Bryn McLarey, Sheffield

At the turn in the road I stopped abruptly. There wus a tree stretched across the road, but it wus only a small tree. My eyes focused quickly on what wus beyond it. That quaint, pretty little theatre that I'd poured my soul into wus wearing another tree, like a strange contemporary hat a lady might wear tu the races. I sighed with a sense of numb acceptance, and phoned the owner, Taffy.

"Yuu alright, mate?" I asked, when a quivering voice answered.

"Not really," he answered.

"Where are you, buddy?"

"In the Byron..."

"Christ, have I not taught yuu *not* tu frequent shite pubs?" I said.

"It's the nearest place with decent Scotch," he answered.

His usual excuse wus it wus the nearest place he wasn't afraid tu go in. Taffy wus a slight man who hated conflict of any sort.

I took a detour tu avoid the worst of the storm damage and strolled down the avenues tu Nether Edge crossroads. On a further corner stood Byron House, a local pub that ought to have oozed charm, but to me seemed to lack something. Taffy wus sat at the bar. His wild hair stuck up in tufts. His face rested on his arms close tu the glass of whisky.

"Are yuu nursin it? Or is it nursin yuu?" I quipped.

He gave me a faint smile, followed by a weighty pause as I drew up a stool and ordered two more Scotch.

"What'll I do, Charlie?" His voice wavered in the South Wales accent – the reason for his nickname. His real name wus Takeo (ironically meaning warrior), but I'd been so struck by the novelty of an East Asian with a Taffy accent. His eyes were lined and weary with people not getting his name right. The theatre staff tended tu refer tu him as Tarquin, or more mysteriously Shergar, after the missing race horse.

"You'll drink whisky and worry, Taffy," I told him. "Not much different from yesterday."

"There'll be no insurance money," he said glumly, cupping his slightly tubby, slightly square face with his hands. "With all the so-called 'acts of God', they've written storm damage out of insurance policies."

I nodded.

"I'm ruined, and it's not like I had much in the first place. It's such a tragedy, such a *beautiful* building."

"You just have to get on with it," I said firmly. "Get an ordinary job tu keep yourself going and hope things'll settle down. The Arts Council might just give yuu money tu fix the damage."

"You think they might?" he asked painfully.

"If things settle down," I said dubiously. "You just need tu try tu hang ontu the land if you can afford not tu sell it. Not that anyone is buying right now."

"I've debts," he whined.

"Everybody has debts Taffy, but the banks aren't allowed tu forcibly take things off you at the moment."

"What can I do to earn money? I've only ever worked in the theatre, but nobody is going to the theatre anymore," he asked.

I patted him on the back. "In this scenario, you take anything yuu can get. You work in the fookin sewers if needs be. We both gottah make ends meet."

"You've always done all-sorts," he said. "You know the right folk to get you sorted in employment."

"I'll help yuu where I can. You've got plenty of skills – y'do a lot of handy-work and cleaning, and serving booze," I said, feeling as usual like I wus breathing hot air intu his deflated self-image.

"It's awful. I know I'm a pessimist, but it's just *awful*," he said.

"Where's your missus?" I glanced about warily.

"Out walking the dogs. She's sick of me feeling sorry for myself. It's only been a few hours since I found out. Shouldn't I be allowed a little time to grieve...?"

"Of course you should, Taffy. Course you should."

* * * * * * *

ALL ABOUT THE BREW

Simian Thomas, Sheffield

It was no surprise that the economy was flatlining. The shop I managed had closed down. The only parts of the service sector still doing well were pubs, supermarkets and local grocery stores (which benefitted from people's fear of straying too far from home). My mum had moved out to Spain with her new beau in the passing months, hoping to escape. She'd asked me to go with her, knowing I would say no.

I went to work on repair projects, my experience in Thailand all of a sudden becoming relevant. The surreality of that exotic disaster zone was echoed in the grey local cityscape as I trampled between bricks and cement blocks, standing knee deep in a shitty puddle. I was still grimacing at the stench of death, which seemed to remain long after the removal of the latest victims. I was wearing waders that were too big and rubbed at my aching feet, but they protected me from the sinking ground. I peered down at an innocent-looking rat paddling past my leg. It reminded me of the birds and rodents swimming in Alice's tears.

I'd stood too long and now my ankles were suckered in the Earth. "Shit!" I exclaimed behind a protective face mask. I tossed a last brick into the wheel barrow, which was rested on higher ground.

"You okay?" one of the other workers asked – a girl with soggy brown hair tangled up under her hard hat. She had a freckly face, smeared endearingly on the cheek with black muck.

"Think I'm stuck," I mumbled, trying to slowly remove my foot.

She held a railing next to her, and reached a gloved hand out. I grasped it thankfully and was surprised at her strength as she pulled me free.

"What's your name?" she asked brightly, in a typical Sheffield burr. She reminded me of old photographs of the women working in the second world war, dressed up as manual labourers, with resilient smiles.

"Simian," I answered after removing my mask.

"I'm Pip," she replied. "What've ya been asked to do?"

"Collect bricks," I answered without enthusiasm, "and then clean them."

She nodded. "Done a lot of that already! I hate knockin the cement off. It reahlly mekks my wrists ache. D'ya want some help? Less boring when you've got company."

"Yes," I said. "Good idea. What were you asked to do?"

"I was helping salvage furniture to go to the Refuge. But my supervisor's fooked off fer lunch now, soo am at a loose end."

"You not going for lunch?" I asked.

She shook her head. "I can only afford one meal a day, reahlly. Be nice if they brought us sum sandwiches once in a while, wun't it?"

"Yeah," I said. "I've got a flask of tea if you want some. Help warm us up."

"Oh, ace!" she said. "It's all about the brew, to keep ya goin."

* * * * * * *

A JERRY HAT TRICK

Wolfgang, Sheffield

"*Underneath the sea... far away from land... that's where I will be... shaking on the sand... rattling in my withers... dithering on my deck – I'm just a neerrrvvous wreck!*" I sang to myself, a silly song which I so cherished for its phonetics. I was pretty sure some of the words were wrong – I'm not sure that ships have withers, I think that's only horses.

"To what place or state and what is the likely future of...?" the newsman asked the politician, who shook his jowls and interrupted bombastically.

"You cannot hold the government to account for acts of God!"

The newsman pursued him into a corner hastily. "Are you scape-goating God here? The fact is the government neglected to put in place stringent enough measures to help backtrack the effects of climate change. Do you agree?"

"The present government is not responsible for the years of politicians *and the general public* putting their heads in the sand," the politician defended.

"But before you came to power, *your party specifically* funded scientific research, which denied that humans were responsible for climate change. Do you still agree with that scientific research...?"

I flicked the television off, or maybe just zoned out. (It's torturous to continue watching the authorities chasing their own tails.) I shuffled over to the kettle, which I filled a little and set to boil, scuffling through the cupboards for the dregs of some instant coffee granules. It was quite time I achieved some paid work, so I flicked through yesterdays local paper and found the advert for 'Protect & Rebuild'. A noble title for what essentially consisted of shifting rubble and fallen trees, and praying not to happen upon any undiscovered corpses, secret victims of the Weathers.

"To wither is to weather... to whither be not known," I mumbled to myself as I precariously dialled the phone number on the cordless house phone.

It buzzed with interference and strained for contact. I poured boiled water into a grubby mug, watching the murky swirl rise (like the tide of dissent).

"Protect and Rebuild, South Yorkshire. How may I help?" A lady's voice answered, somewhere far off at the end of a wire.

"Hello, I'd like to apply for the work," I said (maybe a little too enthused).

"Okay, name please?"

"Wolfgang," I said.

"Sorry?"

"Wolf-gang," I enunciated loudly and clearly.

"...And your surname, sir?"

I glanced madly around the room until my eyes settled on a book. "Hesse," I said quickly and firmly.

"How's that spelt please?"

"H...E...double S...E," I explained, aware behind me of the back door being unlocked and the Kaiser entering.

"Do you have a work visa?" she asked.

"Yes."

"What is your experience?" she asked.

"I've experience as a manual labourer," I said.

"Okay, lovely. If you could report to the Sheffield City office at 9 a.m. tomorrow, please. Bring your documents with you, do you have safety boots?"

"Yes," I said.

"Lovely... we'll provide a hard hat. You know where the offices are?" she queried.

"Yes," I repeated.

"Okay, 9 a.m. tomorrow then. Thanks, bye."

I hung up.

"What manual have you ever laboured over?" Kaiser asked with cruel wryness.

"You're speaking nonsense," I replied quickly, opening the fridge, selecting a carton of milk and giving it a sniff.

"I see you worked out how to use the talky stick and get yourself a job?" he said.

"One must be part of the Plan," I said patriotically.

"It's balls. But I don't care sae long as you bring some money in."

"What are '*safety boots*'?" I asked.

He laughed. "I've got some. I'll lend yuu them. Might be a bit big though." He peered at my feet, which were gaffer-taped into old boots full of holes.

"D'you ever take those off?"

"Not if I can help it. But it will be nice to wear dry boots. I think my feet might be rotting," I mumbled happily.

"Well, I don't want tu be around when you take those off. The smell will no doubt kill me." He filled the kettle a little and set it to boil again. "Have you used the last of the coffee again, you geriatric scrounger?"

I maintained an innocent smirk and sung the ship song again to myself.

"Can you cut that oot, it's fookin annoyin," the Kaiser interrupted. "And it's not *withers*, it's *riggin*."

* * * * * * *

AN EMBODIMENT OF THE ACT OF SELF-CURSING CONTAINED IN THE EARTH

Haydn Antoine. East London

A dreamscape expanded in white. White is every colour of light whipped together. I was trapped inside my box in London town, snowed in. After so many meek, mild winters that snivelled through to spring, we were finally getting the icy brunt. Of course we were ill-prepared, with grit shortages and footwear suitable for fashion but not so great on snowy, icy pavements.

My basement flat had snow covering the small windows, which peeked over ground level, and my door seemed to be frozen shut. I phoned work, frustrated. I almost wanted to demand that someone come and dig me out, but I wasn't sure who I could ask. I bounced around a little panicked, full of cabin fever, but then it occurred to me, this was a damn fine opportunity to sit down and gets loads of work done on my own shit – with no distractions.

I made myself a pint mug of strong instant coffee and arranged my notebooks and laptop on the bed (I didn't have the luxury of a table). I was all ready to be constructive, but there were thoughts nagging at the back of my head from the night before. I'd accidentally caught sight of a picture of Claudia on a friend's profile page, looking very drunk and depressed.

"I get *the furies*," she'd warned me once, when we'd just gotten together.

"What do you mean?" *Female deities of vengeance in Greek Mythology...?* My private education was betrayed inside my head.

"I just mean I get irrationally angry about stuff all't time. In case you hadn't already noticed."

I sighed and gazed into the middle distance, sick of my brain going over the same terrain. I checked my emails. I hadn't got internet in the flat, but I was easily able to hack the neighbour's WiFi given his password was 'password'.

I had one sat there, that I'd not yet had time to read, from my friend Toby Roe. He'd been in Canada for several years now, doing environmental research, specialising in the behaviour and conservation of wolves. I'd been with him years earlier when his fixation with the canine had birthed. As soon as he'd finished university he got a rescue dog. I recalled meeting him shortly after.

Toby was drinking Guinness in his local. A brown and white collie dog was poised upright with its forepaws on a wooden bar stool, gazing at him with handsome admiration, tongue lolling out on one side. I rested one hand on Toby's shoulder, the other on the back of the dog.

"Two flies are hovering over a piece of pooh in the street and one says to the other '*Is this stool taken?*'"

Toby smiled wryly, the dog grinned and dribbled a bit.

"Big, isn't she? How's all the boundless adoration going? Must be good for the ego," I asked him.

He quietly and neatly got the bartender's attention and ordered two more pints and I slipped through to pay for the round. He sipped his stout thoughtfully, mulling the question.

"It's funny, dogs are so openl'y besotted. Humans are so much more reserved, playin it cool."

I thanked the bartender, as she gave me my change and she made eyes at me, before walking off into the back room.

"She checked you out," Toby remarked.

"Openly besotted?" I asked.

"I wouldn't go that far. She in't doing little excited wees, and lickin ya face…"

We'd stifled laughter as the girl had walked back behind the bar.

The email said he was finally coming back to live in England for a bit. There was a sense of purpose within the tone of it. I anticipated the wisdoms he'd bring home. Toby was unlike any of my other friends, being unconcerned with Narcologics or being a music anorak.

I was playing a track that sampled The Doors *Unknown Soldier* at this point. Like a small miracle the sound of the gunshot in the song coincided with a firework going off outside.

I popped up on my feet like a meercat and scampered through the mess to the window, which was still white. I pondered why someone was setting a firework off in the snow, at 11 a.m. on a Tuesday… Surely bored yoofs were entertained enough with snowball fights and other novelties that had been rained off for so many years. I tapped the window, in the hope that some of the snow might be dislodged, but I was pretty sure I was actually buried in a polar tomb.

I returned to my bed and trundled on through the email, but found it a little ambiguous. Toby likes ambiguity.

For the first time since I had gotten to London, I suddenly felt a stab of anxiety. It wrapped a fist around my heart and squeezed it, until it beat too hard and thumped inside my brain. I'd slaved over work and meeting people, and all the while there was a lining on my psyche of loneliness, and edging sorrow. Now alone, buried beneath the restless, everchanging city, I was a prisoner of my own thoughts. The box which was supposed to be my home was closing in on me.

What if I was trapped here for days, with no food in the fridge? Would anyone in this ruthless sprawl even notice my absence if I quietly disappeared?

They were questions easy to rationally answer, but my feet were not firmly planted on the ground. They were six foot beneath it.

>Narcologics.
>The Origin of Aiden.
>
>Inside my mind I'm not sure what damage is done. In the dark tunnels and twisting nerves. I look in the mirror and see the snide face of paranoia setting in. I'm not sure which bruises are from living the ordinary life with the fucked-up family and the boy's desperation to be liked and be good at stuff. And the sibling rivalry. The fact that Joseph got bought a new bike and I got Scrabble at Christmas back when we were ten and eight.
>
>I'm not sure which bruises are from booze killing off brain cells. Or falling out of a taxi drunk, my skull meeting concrete, and the concrete winning. I'm more inclined to think my head hurts because my brother was the bad boy. My brother ran away from home. My brother was the one they worried about. Little Aiden was always quietly happy to be alive. Little Aiden was always contented with his lot. Little Aiden accepted with gentle maturity the bad things that happened.
>
>Little Joseph was cocky and arrogant and got on everyone's nerves because he liked to brag

about how good he was at everything. Little Joseph hated that little Aiden did better at school. So he told him he was an embarrassing geek and kicked him in the knee cap.

My knee cap throbs. But I'm pretty sure that's to do with that shitty comedown after the drum 'n bass weekend in Birmingham. I fell out of a friend's cabin bed, while trying to fight off the zombies in *Resident Evil*. I'm not sure which bruises are from the drugs warping my perception. Making me feel like an acceptable person because I live the fast, fleeting lifestyle that rolls with the punches, and sure as shit rolls a spliff if things get a little heavy.

I lie in the fuselage of a plane buried nose-down in the sand. I feel an oily liquid dripping over my hair, slipping inside my ears to contaminate my bruised mind, which only wants to rest and sleep.

I stopped writing abruptly, I was pretty sure that on reading back, this bit of writing wouldn't even make The Chronicals, despite wanting to have an article in it titled 'Narcologics'. It would be too gooey and personal. My brain relaxed into a relieved sense of failure. I lay down on my bed and closed my eyes, and slept a sleep that I didn't deserve, but wanted badly.

* * * * * * *

THE BARGUEST & THE PADFOOT

Claudia McLeod, Sheffield

"Can y'just leave now please?" I repeated agen.

The mad drunk took a step away from't bar and swayed somewhere above the abyss. His mouth strove to form words agen but they melted to nonsense. Sommat about trying to get on wirris dad, wet socks that won't ever dry.

His disjointed figure and face that drifted 'tween threat an despair blurred like all the others into't shadows of the bar. Into't noises the room spoke when there were no one there. Eyes remained in the darkness, chasin reflections in't mirrors, tryin to fix on an object, slippin away. Losin the focus of sobriety.

I hayte it when you call me chicken, it maykes me think ya think am ready for slaughter.

I took the till up to the office, to begin again the nightly robotics. I wacked a playlist on, printed off some fresh till sheets, and then I laid things out in order and began to purrem in their place. Hail pounded the window pane. I weren't sure if it were part of the music to begin with – *rat ta tat tat*, knockin repeatedly like the doubts I had about ev'rythin. I thought about Haydn's ability to be so resistantly happy whatever happened, not lyke me.

I noticed it then, a whiff of cigarette smoke. The smell seemed so much stronger since it were banned in pubs. Smokin weren't allowed upstairs at all an there was no one that'd be havin a cheeky one, save for me. I looked at ma hands but they held only the £20 notes I'd lost count of. I sniffed the air lyke a wary fox and there it was the smell, too strong to be ma clothes or hair. I continued ta count but I checked nervously over my shoulder, tryin-ta swallow my irrational paranoias. Tryin-ta swallow the big nothing that haunted me.

The yellow light painted the scruffy objects in't room, papers strewn, hoards a rubber bands, faded blinds that concealed the street below which continued always the conversation a the city.

I cursed softly, 'memberin I'd left the change-box downstairs. I listened to my feet fall along the corridor. The boards moved quietly under'um, doors creaked and slammed softly, steps seven – eight – nine.

Down in't bar I rooted out what I were afta.

"I can smell smoake upstairs. Like someone's smoakin," I said to t'other barstaff, busy cleanin up. "It's reet freakin me out."

Only puzzled shrugs from ma colleagues.

I mayde my way back tu't office. Back upstairs the corridor stretched out towards the door I'd left ajar, the door I hesitantly pushed open. The mad drunk is sat in the office smoakin, he looks around at me and speaks agen. Words I can't mekk out, like smothered voices on faraway telephone lines. All I can see are his eyes – slippin... driftin in and out of blackness... hallowed... death inside somewhere. Hidin in the knot of an auld gnarled tree. Smoake drifts across the room, dissolving the ghoulish boggart. Lingerin in't air like a poison, whisperin sweet-nicotine-nothings to me.

There were noo man. The room were empty, save for the sad objects that stunk familiar, The Cinematic Orchestra still playin from the computer. Hail still patting the window pane. Yet there on't desk, stubbed out in an auld tip tray which had since collected stray paper clips and pennies, was the dregs of a fag end.

* * * * * * *

THE BIG THAW

Roxanne Ratcliffe, Sheffield

I spin around taking pictures, unable to focus on one thing. Unable to stay still long enough. The photos can only document the labyrinth of lights through bleary eyes. They cannot paint purely the stark realism.

I'd sold a couple of my photographs to *The Archive of the Weathers*. This drove me further into a sense of purpose in spending my free time out with my camera.

After weeks of blizzards and ice and chaos, South Yorkshire suddenly began to thaw. Amid sheets of depressing drizzle, the ice and snow, once deathly white and ever expanding, was turning grey and dripping away. Only little winter islands remained tucked in corners. The parks and fields, already water-logged beneath the snow, couldn't absorb the big melt. It sat in huge puddles and swelled choking streams.

I set out, on my day off, for low laying farmlands to the south of Sheffield, armed with wellies and head to toe waterproofs. As I got off the bus in a suitably rural area the rain began to come down harder. I'd fashioned a waterproof wrap for my camera by cutting up an old cagoule bag, so that I could still look through the lens. It had to be gaffer-taped into the bag each time, to minimise leaks. I had to snap and hope, as there was no way to fiddle with apertures and so on.

I was restricted where I could walk, so I let the lines of higher ground dictate my route through the landscape. I wondered a little foolishly late whether my path back might be cut off if the rain continued.

But the sodden landscape was addictive to capture. Diagonal rain spewed across the frame, the hills beyond smeared away in a fast receding background. For a while I was trapped between two high hedgerows with only the vanishing point of the track ahead to photograph. I needed to keep wiping the front lens again and again, as too much water blurred things completely. As the rain kept on, I was beginning to think that maybe I wouldn't get any really good shots. Maybe it was time to turn back. (Although the allure of analogue photography is the latent potential of the photo that develops. You never really know which will be the best shots.)

Finally an opening appeared in the hedgerow, from nowhere. I climbed the wonky tractor gate which was slumped precariously in the mud and tiptoed along the edge of the field. It had rows of regimented puddles eventually expanding into one huge pool, which connected to another in the next field and so on.

There was a river nearby, as I could see a current flowing in parts. But where the puddles ended and the river began wasn't clear. The rain was clearing some and a little more light peeked from the bleak sky. I picked a nice angle created by another gate, fences, and trees, and tried to gain a secure enough foothold to photograph it properly. As I snapped this I spotted something in the next field, almost out of sight. I carefully trod along the boundary until it came into view and then picked a spot accordingly to get the best picture. I had to walk away and around again to avoid wading straight through. But within fifteen minutes or so I was successful.

Out in the flooded field stood a very old Ford truck, part-submerged in the water. The headlights peeping above the surface and the bulbous shape of the bonnet made it look like a curious hippo.

I took the photograph and then peered at the image in front of me again. I waited a little, hoping the light might improve and the wind stop unsettling the water, so that I might get a better reflection. But still waters were not typical of these times, and the light dulled further instead. I tried to take another picture, but my camera seemed not to want to. Had I finished the film already? I couldn't remember. I had more film with me, but it was drizzling again and I didn't want to risk opening the back of my camera.

I headed home with a quiet little hope that that one image would be good enough all by itself.

* * * * * * *

THE NEW FLUXUS

Simian Thomas, Sheffield

I was becoming wary of associating with Charlie in the middle times. I'm often confused that our friendship survived at all. I suppose if I'm Freudian about it (it is best not to be), I know I always rejected proper masculinity. I preferred the company of women, or slightly effeminate males like Hex. But I suppose we are drawn to our fears and doubts, like moths enamoured with lightbulbs that burn to touch.

Charlie was becoming increasingly politicised during the onset of the Weathers. He'd always been dubious of radicalism before that. He'd postulated (during many drunken arguments) that it came from the core of the human ego – the desperation to matter, to effect things. It was a theory he'd stolen arrogantly from an enigmatic chap named Cuan, who I'd had little real contact with, but heard a great deal about.

The frail human is shaken by circumstance though. When things appear good they're happy with those who govern their civilization (albeit with healthy cynicism). When things are bad they can return to savagery at the drop of an illusionist's hat.

Now Charlie personified the anger of *The People*, which was happening in knock-on effect worldwide. Experiencing his company consisted of listening to a barrage of rants, about the effects of the Thermohaline Circulation Shutdown (which was causing the dislocation of the North Atlantic Drift). He questioned why it'd happened so very quickly, and listed every damn thing we'd inflicted on the planet, from oil drilling to the casual destruction of coral reefs and wetland bogs, which had all contributed.

Having established the scale of devastation and a brief outline of the reasons for it (mainly obvious), I'd begun shutting off from the news channels to some extent. Ignorance provides a certain peace of mind. Besides, the phonelines and electricity grids regurlarly went down. I was becoming used to reading by candlelight to get through the evening. But Charlie would continue listening to radio shows and rattled on in maniacal form, showing every symptom of over-exposure. He seemed unable to fathom why we weren't all ready to storm parliament and overthrow the government.

We'd agreed to meet one night in an old air raid shelter in Crookesmoor which someone had turned into an illicit drinking den. Probably on the cheerful logic that if things got too bad they could hole up in there and drink themselves to death (the only food on offer being crisps and pork scratchings).

Roxy, Claudia and I sat staring boredly at Charlie as he managed to turn every conversation around to the global situation. Wolfgang shrunk back in a shadow created by the candlelight, muttering and giggling to himself. The madman embraces the maniacal, it is his brother.

"The gov'ment can't do jack-shit anymaire, Charlie. Apart from damage limitation. Whas the point?" Claudia demanded in annoyance.

"Apathy has killed this country for tuu long." He was speaking in harsh rasps.

I muted his words and instead studied him visually, as an Expressionist piece. The apples of his cheeks painted rouge by the lighting. The yellow and black streaks highlighting and shadowing his features, as they metamorphosed through his emotions. The tiny lines of scarlet that painted his brain inside his eyeballs. I felt suddenly sick of everything and everybody, my stomach a maelstrom of doubts, fear and hopeful denial.

Or maybe it was just the taste of cheap wine.

* * * * * * *

KIND OF BLUE

Haydn Antoine, London

This is the winter of our discontent...

I set this as an opening sentence for my contributors to write a series of articles on. For this was certainly the darkest, iciest winter I could ever remember. Although there were glorious days also, when I bent my plans so I could walk in the snowy park. The winter sun glowed, casting blue and yellow shadows across the white. I followed the footprints of beasties – birds, dogs, foxes, squirrels. No doubt the odd heffalump, too. There was something about the snow that made me want to run and laugh, to be reckless and carefree. But I had nobody to do that with and this made me solemn. I blinked snow from my eyelashes and looked at the world in the fisheye lens of my eyeball.

I wrote an article about Ray Mears' recommendations for surviving lost in the snow. I couldn't imagine if a person was in this situation they would happen to be carrying a shovel with which to hollow out a makeshift igloo, though.

The man in the next door flat had a spade-shaped parcel delivered a few days later. I wondered wryly if he'd read my piece.

"Shouldn't they be called 'blogs' not 'articles' if it's an e-zine?" Aleks gazed into his coffee, rubbing his hands together near a candle, as the heating in the cafe was not so good.

"I don't really take blogs that seriously. It's like a person's autobiography before they've cut all the crap and boring bits. I think of this as experimental journalism, of a sort. If that doesn't sound too pretentious? I don't know how to push the content in the direction I want, though. I know things are a bit heavy these days. But I don't want it to be some sort of nagging prophesy of doomsday."

He nodded, listening with a calm gaze. "I don't think you need to manipulate it too much." He gestured as though holding a baby bird. "It will come into fruition gradually and then you can frame it however you please."

A girl named Florence that I'd been seeing arrived at this point, presenting herself so as to be central. I was already getting the ick on her. No drama queen could quite replace Claudia. But she was a regular in the cafe so difficult to avoid.

"Aleks*ander!* I have the perfect boy for you," she announced coyly. She glanced at us both and the lap top screen and rolled her eyes a little, so as to disregard whatever she was interrupting. "Let's forget all this boring shit, Lady Flo is in the flow, let's go kooky tonight and get totally bitched!"

Aleks shook his head. "I work til midnight tonight and I'm back in at 7 a.m. I'm too old for not getting at least five hours sleep."

"But the boy! He's so lush."

"I'm too old for chasing boys. How old is he?" He looked bored by her matchmaking.

"He's about nineteen, lovely bottom." She tossed her black curls and spread perfectly manicured hands out, her bracelets jingling.

Aleks shook his head again. "That's too young. I don't go in for immaturity, I'm not into it."

She waved a hand dismissively. "Aidey, then. You'll come out to play with me, won't you, sugar plum?"

I laughed at her silly phrases. "Sorry, I have to work, bills to pay."

"Oh, put it on credit. For fuck's sake, sweetie, you only live once. And Florence needs some arm candy!"

"No, no. Fraid you'll have to find someone else tonight."

She sighed dramatically, collected her handbag and bustled off, tutting. Aleks gave me a bemused look.

"You do attract the moggies, don't you?" he teased.

I shrugged. "She's okay, she's just a party girl."

"You've not seen her angry. If you keep rejecting her she'll get angry."

This was the winter of my discontent. If only Claudia were here. The queen of cats to see off unwanted attention. It was tough to resist though, too many pretty ladies, too little to lose. I was in the downward spiral, the disorientating blizzard of a broken heart that turns gentlemen into skirt-chasing fools.

> 'I join the dots, I make the jump, I know it's all connected...
>
> 'This is the winter of my discontent. Not because of the government, who will always be lying shits. Not because my boiler broke again and my landlord treats us like disgruntled cattle. Not because I've fallen over a lucky seven times on the icy hills of Shufflefield. No, this is banal and ordinary. That is my discontent, that I don't live in Fairy Land and ice skate to work every day, where I carve ice sculptures that leave jaws agape at their wondrous beauty. That I can't build a giant music box, for my ice carving of the fairy queen to spin inside to the chimes of avante-garde music. Survival for my species (the geek, not the human – they must perish) won't happen through whinging or dreaming. Yet all we do is whinge and dream.'

I watched Aleks skim through the bit of writing, he smirked knowingly.

"I like this one, who is this? Someone you know?"

"It was written by a bloke called Simian Thomas. I don't know him. He must've found out about it all himself," I mused.

"I can see you two getting on," he said.

"How so?" I asked.

"He still uses the term 'avante-garde music'," he giggled.

* * * * * * *

STRANGERS IN THE STATIC

Claudia McLeod, Sheffield

Roxy were out and I were worried. I sat on't wide window ledge in my bedroom, my body folded intu't frame a the window, starin out at the sparklin torrent of rain which came and went in great bursts. Night was arriving in purple and ev'rythin went quiet and still furra moment save the wind, which seemed ta rock the trees in slow motion. I watched the street below. Waitin furra small figure to come hurrying t'wards house. But it were empty and another brattle shook the stillness. I thought sadly of a storm way back in't past. One that I'd delighted in, instead of worryin about all the people I knew who might be out.

Afore this other storm, I were sat in the attic of number 42. It were maybe five years earlier, 'fore I dropped out of Uni. I were workin at my computer when there was a mighty thunder clap outside. There'd been a heat wave during the week which were on the cusp a breakin grandly, the way they always do eventually. My skylight was wide open, temptin a downpour. A delayed flash came, so bright it seemed to reach inside t'window and fill the room. It was followed by another brattle, and my stereo playin The Pixies album kicked into the whiney intro of *Where is my mind?*. The air'ud been stuffy and wahm but now a chill ran through me.

I stood up to close the window some as the pit pat of rain began. I pulled it down and watched the water begin streakin and spottin the glass. A face appeared at't window and I stifled back a yelp of fear. It were you a'course, a manic grin spreadin at yar crafted prank. You'd been three doors down at a mate's house, likely jammin in't cellar, when you'd thought to climb over the roof-tops and scare the shit outtah me. I let you in, grabbin at you as you dropped down onto the bed in dirty trainers. Yar messy ginger-blonde fringe was wet and mattin, my anger at bein surprised easily mutated into lust. I kissed you.

That boy was not Haydn of coarse. It were Jody. And yet the rude tangle of two bodies is the sayme. In my dreams lovers merge indiscriminately. I don't want them to. It gives me belly-wark ta think that it's all the sayme. That each new love in't special and unique. Jus a different shade a muck beclartin ma mem'ry. I remembered the thunderstoarm wi' equal nostalgia and dread. As I 'membered the glimpse a love in his eyes muddied always by the tone of doubt in his voice. Which mayde me know that it would end bitte'ly, and I would hayte us boath for ever havin met. And each new love would always be tainted by ev'rythin that came before.

There was a flash a light'nin in the present thunderstorm and the wind rattled the window close to ma head. But I hugged the sense of fear in a burst of breathy adrenaline that drove back tears for loves lost in't past, and missin friends in't present. I stood up and went over to the landline, as the network on my mobile was down agen. I dialled Roxy's number, but there was just a hiss of static and strange ghostly voices on the phone. As though wires were crossed. I purrit down, and waited a bit, hoverin wi' my hand on it. There was a knock at the door.

"Yeah," I said, coverin the shake in my voice.

Josie and Maisie came in. Josie went and peered outtah the window, tuggin anxiously at irratic brown hair. Maisie sat down on't bed pokin at a hole in her jeans.

"Is Roxy still out?" she asked softly.

"Yeah," I said cynic'ly. "Same shit, different day."

I dialled her number agen. This time it rang a few times and then there was quiet, and the sound a wind.

"Roxy?" I said, my voice unusually deep.

The wind howlin, then...

"Hi...tsssssssssssssssssssssssssss...Claudia?"

"Where are you?"

"Tsssssssssssssssssss...I'm okay...tsssssssssssssssssssss." The line went dead.

"I'll make tea," Maisie said decisively.

We nodded. She left the room and Josie and I looked at one another glumly. The house shook agen wi' another thunderclap. It was dead dark outside now, vast and unforgiving.

My deep cynicism for all things can only be smashed by you, and these words frighten me more than anything. Because beyond my deep cynicism I'm not sure there is a person left anymore. What if you were to find a hollow?

* * * * * *

RAGNAROK

Bryn McLarey, Sheffield

There wus barely a crack of light in the room, but cement dust wus falling somewhere abouts, and the smell of it cloaking mae nostrils spelt doom. The rat-runs and hovels, belonging tu the stupidest intelligent species, were falling apart. It took a lot. They were well-constructed, with modern engineering and measured skill. The age-old pattern of brickwork held together, despite gaping holes beneath the structures, despite a never-ending onslaught. Mae flat, fae one, wus holding out. But the cement dust wus falling and unearthly horrors were manifesting in the world ootside.

I could see, in mae mind's eye, the tower block where mae mother lived. I felt her pain and fear. I felt her utter powerlessness in a world that'd only ever dealt her a shite hand. Only ever kicked her in the teeth in return for her good deeds. I wus angry with maesel that I'd spent so much a'mae life thinking about mae dad. Because he wus the one who made me grind mae teeth. He wus the one for whom there were not enough swearwords tu express the venomous wrath. Now as our little island soldiered on through the night, leik a punch-drunk boxer, I only worried for mae mam. Shivering in that shitty little flat she'd refused tu leave. Even when Ah'd gotten the money from mae publishing contract and offered tu buy her a small place, somewhere nice, she'd refused. She'd always earned every pitiful penny she had. So I pissed away all that money on a Master's degree, and little more of value.

Ootside mae flat, sommat pounded the ground in rapid progression, leik a giant running past. The attic of the building rumbled again, as though a barrel wus rolling around. The streetlights ootside the boarded up window occasionally flashed on and mae little light would almaist flicker fer a wee moment, but die sae fast, if I blinked I missed it. I huddled in the alcove, a steel colander on mae heid as a makeshift helmet. I spooned cold baked beans straight from the tin, and slugged from a bottle of Lagavulin I'd been hiding for a special occasion. It wahmed mae viens and filled mae body with a sense of awe that I'd once believed had sumthin to do with God or Jesus. Now the awe had more tu do with fear, and death and oblivion. Meybe they're one and the saim. Any myth's existence in our minds and power over our shaking hands, is inarguably an existence nonetheless, albeit beyond reach.

Mae torso throbbed with mae heartbeat, confused at having tu comprehend annihilation at the same time as trying to digest cold beans. Every song in mae heid spelt the end of everything now, every cynical joke rang tuu true. I rattled mae spoon around the bottom of the tin can. I adjusted mae colander. I slugged mae whisky. I prayed fae the flat black waters tu swallow me gently.

* * * * * * *

A SEMI-COLON

Wolfgang, Sheffield

'One day the rain is gonna come and wash all the scum off the streets.'

The rain came... but I realise now it doesn't choose. It's not some sort of judgement day, when those with black unworthy hearts will be washed into some vortex portended by that Hawking fellow. Into the full stop where everything is obliterated and must begin again.

We're not quite ready for the full stop. What we have on our hands is some sort of semi-colon, used for dramatic porpoise at the tail end of a paragraph. Dirty sock water came gushing through the ceiling. It emptied out the rooms, people flailed in its maelstrom. I sat myself in the eye of the storm where everything is deathly quiet and calm, smoking and gazing up at the little round iris of a clear blue sky. Pacific.

This was to be the Brutalist of the Great Storms, the storm to shake the remains of normality to ruins...

The rain left behind strays and ghosts. Hallowed faces begging next to the carcass of a city. Among the dead I fall to my knees and weep. Not for any loved one of my own, but for the other loved ones, the ones who should've lived. The unloved ought to be the scum washed away...

Or not. It's always knocked me backwards to realise for every scumbag rapist, there is someone who loves them. They fucked the girl in the mouth until she vomited on their dicks and then they beat her to death. Afterward they went home to Mama and she made them tea, and told them they were good boys.

It's only when the entire human race is wiped out that *they* will be gone. The pit-bull terriers will play happily in some eternal sunshine, because there's no man left to drive them to rabid fights. No man to beat them a little bit every day for 'their own good'. Maybe I shall breed myself a race of pit-bulls, who themselves may pick and chose who shouldn't survive the next Ice Age. For no God can chose fairly. It's only the base instinct of the feral that can choose the natural order.

In the aftermath, I found myself searching for the precious. Not for emeralds scattered like broken glass on the streets, which climb inside the gaping holes in my bear feet. I searched for innocence, but only the sort weathered by storms. A kind of slowly decaying innocence that itself possesses a sense of brutality, and only by this careful breeding can it survive.

In oddity, most of these *Lieblings* were already part of my papered history, already written into my haphazard plot. We sought each other. When a person comes to realise their family is dead or missing, they turn strangely to others, to pack formation, a body of protection. I sniffed out the being I knew best the habits of.

Kaiser was sat in what was once his favourite pub. The building was barely standing save for the bar room. He was sat smoking, drinking the last of the Guinness as all the ale tasted sour, having no-one to care for it. He poured me one as I entered, and fetched some Irish whiskey from the shelf to fortify the stout.

He handed me a cigarette. "I'm guessin nobody's gonna fine us fa smoking in a public house no more."

I grinned. "Where are your friends, Hairy McLarey? I sense you'll be the first they come to. Man of action."

"Oh, they'll be here," he answered, staring off as he sipped his pint. "It's just a matter of time."

PHASE FOUR

In which they travel south in search of a better life & meet a few odds & sods.

A WET BLANKET LEFT TO DRY ON A BROKEN RADIATOR

Roxanne Ratcliffe, Sheffield

Over a week of storms and floods had taken its toll on Sheffield. Just like the rest of the country (so we'd heard on the radio), which had turned to vast mires in which surviving buildings and life thrashed in astonishment.

There was no big disaster movie to be made of what had happened, just a slowly building nightmare blown in on a wet northern wind. The city looked like something from the Blitz in part. Roofs lay on pavements, chimney pots in gardens and multiple trees blocked main roads. People sought to escape sewage floods and dead bodies, huddling together in the remaining structures, lighting campfires and waiting for the worst to blow over.

The great hospital up on the slope of the cityscape still stood guard. A stony shadow that retained a stiff upper lip despite damage to the west wing. People set out to carry the wounded there, as traffic couldn't get through.

When the structure of the urban landscape first began to really fall to pieces, people clung to mobiles, to speak to loved ones and far off families. But days passed without electricity and batteries died slowly, beeping feebly. We were alone. I'd lost contact with my brother in Cuba a while ago, Mum and Dad were okay last Tuesday, but one of the last radio broadcasts we'd heard described Nottingham taking the worst hit from Cyclone Lorna. Those that survived had been evacuated south.

Claudia hugged me. Our housemate Maisie was dead. We'd buried her in a shallow grave in the pissing rain, our hair and tears plastered to our faces and muddied bodies. Josie had been missing for six days. The weather seemed to have finally settled a bit. There was sound outside, like the world was getting back to its feet. We'd been sharing a house with two panicky young men, sleeping under a sturdy dining table in case the roof fell in, rationing what clean water we had.

"We should find Charlie," Claudia said.

I nodded. Charlie would have some sort of plan.

"How?" I asked.

She shrugged.

"We'll use our noses."

Claudia had found a proper backpack, so we began searching the present house for useful objects: matches, candles, a hammer –

"It's a bit heavy, what's the use?" I asked.

"It'ull protect us," she answered darkly.

– a maglite, some batteries, a metal coat hanger, a tin opener, gaffer tape, string, a sharp knife, a pack of soap, waterproof clothes…

"Where are you going?" one of the men asked us.

"To find our friends," I answered. "You can come if you want."

Outside we immediately happened across a makeshift rescue operation, and were asked for help to carry a person on a homemade stretcher to the hospital. The blokes with us volunteered, and Claudia quickly dragged me away.

"Gettin side-tracked will slow us down," she said.

We reached the main road, and started walking down it towards the city centre. There were people looting the chemist's shop. Claudia went in politely and selected TCP and bandages, while arguments raged between others for painkillers and insulin. At a newsagents an elderly Asian bloke stood, leaning in a doorway, watching the chaos.

"You want some bread?" he asked.

We stopped, a little taken aback. He waved us in and packed our bags with loaves, and bottles of water and juice.

"Why don't you keep it for yourself?" I asked.

He shrugged and smiled weakly.

"My wife and children are dead. I've nothing here now."

I tried not to cry as we continued down the road. My eyes fixed on a building, its cement shell cracked, exposing the brickwork. Why cement over red brick in the first place? Parts of the roof and walls were torn away, exposing networks of beams and wires, innards left unprotected, the side of the building opened up like a doll's house. Inside the building nothing was left, nothing but memories and lost potential.

"This isn't the way to Charlie's flat," I said hesitantly.

"I think he'll be in't Red Deer if it's still standin," Claudia said.

"Really? He hates it since it got taken over, and they replaced all the Scotch with Malibu and Archers."

"I just havva feelin," she said. "And if he's not there, it'll be another pub."

The roundabout at the bottom, with its circle of underpasses, was swallowed into a strangely architectural pool. We turned off left to avoid it and cut through the council flats, passing the empty playground where Cuan and I had once played on the swings when walking home drunk. A washing line previously suspended from a balcony lay on the ground, the washing wet and mucky.

"Euyh! A rat!" Claudia said, leaping away.

I looked to the bedraggled animal, a pathetic paw rested on my frozen foot. I realised suddenly it was a half-grown cat, so wet that it was barely recognisable. It mewed, looking off into the distance as though its mother might appear.

"It's a cat," I said quietly.

She took my arm.

"Leave it. It's just another mouth ta feed."

I picked up the scrap of life and held it in front of her.

"You have to put it out of its misery, then. It won't survive."

She pushed it away.

"It's probably carryin diseases!"

She walked on up the slope. I shoved the cat inside the front of my coat and followed her.

* * * * * * *

NOW THEN, NOW THEN

Simian Thomas, Sheffield

My chin was buried. I was watching the raindrops settle on my Gortex jacket as I turned off the main road onto the side street, once cluttered with university students, now empty and wary. And so I was looking at the tiny puddles of water on my arm when the rain shower stopped and a beam of sunshine struck me at an angle, like a message from the heavens. I turned with cynical affirmation, knowing in the sky above me (rubbing in the *badness of everything*) there would be a weak rainbow, feigning hope.

I stopped and turned, squinting at it in the alien sunshine, realising that once upon a time in exactly the same spot, Roxy had photographed Cuan beneath a rainbow. I'd seen the picture stuck to her wall, and the deathly joy in his gaze to camera that said *'If you believe that I'll make everything better, you've another thing coming to you.'*

I turned my back on the rainbow and rounded the next corner hesitantly, wondering if the pub would still be standing – and it was, just about. The familiarity of my hand pushing open the creaking door, as though it were any other day. The Red Deer had always been bright inside, an antidote to fashionable ambience and low lighting, but the electrics were down, of course, and blinds were drawn on the windows. I could see candles but with my eyes still adjusting I could make out little in the gloom. So when Roxy leapt to hug me I nearly thrashed out at her.

"It's me, Simian!" she said.

"Sorry, I couldn't see."

I peered into the room at the spectating shadows – Wolfgang lurking in his patched up trench coat like a hungry, mangy fox, Charlie stood leaning with the usual arrogance, Claudia and Roxanne sat on low stools close together. I trembled like a cat in a second hand mog shop, waiting to be picked, fearing the future.

"Is this us then? Is this who survives?" Claudia asked.

Charlie took a long drag on his roll up, slanting his eyebrows in an enigmatic frown.

"Aye, well... We'll wait til tomorrow, see if anyone else turns up."

"Anyone heard from Cuan?" Claudia asked.

"He said he was going to Stanage Edge, to wait for the storm to carry him away," Wolfgang announced.

We all looked sceptical. This could easily be one of his overactive delusions. Roxanne broke down loudly into tears and I found myself staring in horror at this utterly human reaction.

"Now then, you're better off withoot that mentalist," Charlie said quickly.

"My brother's probably dead, isn't he?" Roxy sobbed.

"My brother's likely dead an all," Claudia wrapped a caring arm around Roxanne's shoulders. "We can't dwell on it."

Roxanne peeked inside her jacket and pulled out the limp body of an animal, a lost kitten that had found its last rest close to her heart.

"It's dead," she said to Claudia.

* * * * * * *

DUST OF AGES

Bryn McLarey, The Midlands

We'd left Sheffield in gloom, begrudgingly migrating south, which wus rumoured tu have fared better. No surprise, given it had more protection, more bunkers, more sandbags, more vehicles fashioned for road-clearing. I'd heard of an anarchist group that'd been growing in number over the past few years, and I thought that meybe it would be beneficial for us tu align ourselves with them. Safety in numbers and all that. I supposed they would have an alternate plan for the future tu the government.

We couldn't yet be accused of being *at one* with nature. We were at odds with everything – fumbling over the first shelters we built and fires we made, delighted tu find the occasional old barn which looked as though it could house us for the night without collapsing while we slept. Our initial determination quickly faltered tu a stumble in tune with our uncertainty. What part of the human just picks themselves up and carries on, not out of sheer guts or pluck, but because there is no other choice? The small country suddenly felt like an infinite expanse. The green and grey pastures rolled endlessly on and on.

And we were afraid.

I wus, I suppose, the muscle of the group and *I wus afraid*. I feared robbers or rapists or who knows what else might be lurking in this lawless, God-forsaken land.

We'd walked for several days now. I suspected we'd crossed two counties nearly.

"I think we're in Leicestershire." I surveyed the deserted landscape. "The arsehole of the Midlands."

Roxy nodded, but then she would agree. She'd had many a run-in with Leicester boys over the years. In fact I'd probably adopted the prejudice from her. The skies spoke of their own niggles with the world, the grey wash bleeding to white and feint blues and yellows, before returning to grey. They'd been kind tu us sae far. Aside from the hollow, bone-chilling cold, they'd only inflicted drizzle. As unwelcome as these two companions were on our journey, they were better than the alternative. Our supplies of food were dwindling, and it occurred tu me that we should probably start thinking about alternative food sources.

"So, what do we ken aboot huntin and gatherin food?" I asked.

They all stopped in a long line, looking bedraggled in layers of hoods and jackets. We gazed at the empty fields, wandering what could be gleaned from the big nothing that lay about us. I put on mae glasses, which I had tu spare for occasions, but there wus little more tu focus on.

"Not be much at this time of year," Roxy said quietly. "These look like livestock fields, but who knows where all the sheep and cows are."

Our stomachs rumbled through the sparse, boggy terrain, explaining in no uncertain terms our unstable future. Ragged clothes and the rattle of bones, energy sapping away with each step. Running on empty. Inside mae hefty boots and several pairs of tough socks mae feet were wrinkled from the damp and bleeding from the walking.

"We'd best keep goin fer now. I'm not planning tu starve tu death in Leicestershire of all places." I set off again decisively. I pawed the Stanley knife in mae pocket and wondered whether, if I set eyes on a big old cow, I'd even be able tu slay the thing.

* * * * * * *

AT THE END OF THE DAY

Haydn Antoine, London

A florescent-vested skinhead was knocking on the door asking who a car belonged to.

"I dunno, try next door," I mumbled, bleary eyes peering at him.

"Sorry, mate. I've not woke you av I?"

I shrugged, feeling self-conscious in my cow-print pyjama bottoms. I'd only bought them to entertain Rufio and try to look a bit more like Drazik from *Heartbreak High*.

Just as this thought jumped in, the bloke's two colleagues appeared – also vested skinheads, though one was at least foreign (Eastern European, I think), and so in theory they couldn't be BNP.

"That your car mate?"

Already had this conversation, I thought. This fellow had a coarse Belfast accent.

"Hey, nice trousers... Moooo!"

I tried to look humoured.

"Cheers, boss. I dunno who the car belongs to."

"Alright, geez. We'll let you get back to bed." The Londoner winked. "Give the missus one from me."

"Moooo!" said the Irishman.

I shut the door, ignoring the banter that continued outside. I wondered what they were doing. Clearing debris I suppose and sandbagging. It was a bit late for me. My flat had already flooded twice. The carpets were still squelchy and the bottom of the furniture and walls were fucked, the wallpaper tide-marked with a beige horizon. I returned to my bed but couldn't sleep, so I got my laptop down from the high shelf, where I stored it to stay safe from more flash flooding.

London was in chaos, like the rest of the country, but more centralised into a vortex of contagious panic. Everyone was demanding that somebody do something, something to save us. We were London. London picks its chin off the ground and gets on with it. London forms a solution to a problem this big. It doesn't sit marinating in a ravaged pig sty of expanding sewage. But that's exactly what we seemed to be doing, knee-deep in shit and sinking fast, still standing there demanding that the State pulls us free. Moutains of household waste and wreckage were forming at the ends of streets, and children were clambering on them searching for something to eat, or build a new home with. Football stadiums were filled with the destitute and the homeless. People slept nose-to-tail like sardines, under pitiful gazebo-like tents. In this context, the morning awakening seemed ever more surreal.

> Sunday morning banter from vested skinheads... glad someone is still enjoying themselves. There's nothing very Yokel in London. So many nationalities crammed in, I don't know how racists survive. Just stay holed up in Dagenham with a baseball bat and a St. George tattoo?
>
> I wonder how they feel about all this. Are they managing to blame foreigners for the weather somehow?
>
> I remember a story in the paper a few years back about a real rabbit crossing the track of a Greyhound race. Only one of the twelve dogs in the race deviated and went after the real animal, instead of the stuffed one. I'm sure that says something vaguely profound about social conditioning?

My landline rang, jolting me from idle scribbles.
"Hello?"
"Hi Haydn. It's Toby." A hazy familiar voice.
"Fucking hell. Brilliant. Where are you?" My heartbeat leaped in happiness that he was even alive.
"Huddersfield... or there abouts. Think you can make it up here? I have a plan of sorts."
"I thought the North was fucked!"

"Oh my naive lit'l Londoner, the North will never be broken. We have soul and stuff."

"That's very patriotic, Toab, for a practical foreigner," I teased. He'd been audacious enough to call me a Londoner after all.

"I'll always be a Yorkshireman," Toby said, and there was great big smile in his voice.

* * * * * * *

FRAGMENT

Wolfgang, Dreamscape

When I sleep cold, I dream coldly also. I can hear the sound of boots scraping snow from ice – an aching screech that rattles in my riggin. Big, hefty boots, made for hiking and kicking and stomping... now they scratch snow from the disturbing dark smudge beneath the thick ice set on the edge of the lake. Thick enough to walk on... or die beneath.

The Adonis stares down with the face of a child. We are as children when we witness horrors, the underdeveloped brain slowly fathoming the image. There's a body beneath the ice, his stricken expression pushed close to the surface – Roman nose and hefty brow show he was a well-built chap.

I wrestle my eyes from the image, praying silently (like the faithful) that he died quickly. I study instead my co-witness, who continues to stare at the face beneath his feet, transfixed by death's immutable visage. Flecks of snowflakes sit on his eyelashes and redden his nose. A dark scarf is pulled around his chin, his lips parting a fraction to gasp the icy air, and then let it escape back out as an ethereal spirit forming and then dispersing. His blonde locks are covered with a woolly hat, and greying with time. Still, his slightly bearded face and eyes (as blue as the sky and the ocean used to be) give clues of a Nordic race in years past. Long forgotten at the bottom of a sock drawer.

I avoid altogether now looking back at the dead man. For a sudden fear grips me that I'll think he is moving, and have to cut him from his icy tomb, only to find it was my eyes playing tricks as they do. I study the landscape made savagely elegant by the ice and snow. I fear the thaw that will come and free the body, to bob at the edge of the lake, turning green and putrid. I can only hope wild dogs find him before we do.

The Adonis mouths something to himself, as though testing the sounds that his lips might make.

"Looks like Hugo," he muses, brow furrowed, leaving a hefty pause of disbelief. He shakes his head to himself as though to dismiss that it was. He smiles towards me, a fresh conversational tone destroying horror with chit-chat. "It looks a lot like a fella my brother used to play rugby with..."

* * * * * *

ROUGH SLEEPERS

Calista Siddal, Yorkshire

We lay close on a wonky sofa bed. The others had gone to bed and Jesse had switched off the main light, leaving just the artificial Christmas tree lit up, casting spiky, coloured shadows across the ceiling. The old gas fire was on low, purring away. He hadn't wanted us to come here, mumbling that we'd know how poor his family were. I liked the house though. I liked the chintz and tastelessness. He'd hate me for saying that, but the house felt honest, more honest than my father's minimalism or my mother's antiques. I burrowed further under the covers, wrapping a stray arm across his chest, feeling the strange sensation of cold skin and body warmth mixed up. I wanted to stay awake longer and talk and stare at the ceiling, but sleep was stealing me.

Days like this reminded me of the meaning of the term 'blustery'. Fast moving clouds altered the brightness mode. The sun came blinding for a moment, turning the stark trees into gloomy figures. The rows of houses clambered the hills towards the skyline. For a moment the brightness turned them to hazy shadows, tiny glints of light sparking off skylights and shiny bits of rooftops. And I knew it was morning, and I knew the night was over. Moments were passing in a haze, waiting to be snatched at, waiting for happiness. Waiting to crawl out from the covers and know that he'd left for work already – and worse that he'd already left me in his head. It's my all over.

Simian Thomas, The Midlands

I woke at daybreak. It felt natural. The bleep of a desperate alarm clock abandoned on a pile somewhere with the rest of the civilized world. The sky was hazy, strangely painted in yellow and purple as though bruised. It felt in the chill, uneasy breeze like a post-apocalyptic world. I was reminded of the descriptions of the dead world in *The Chronicals*, but there was life here. Little had really died except the status quo.

I could hear rustling in the undergrowth outside our shelter. My ears perked up like a cat hearing the tell-tale signs of breakfast time.

I was lying near the opening, keeping as still and quiet as possible, wondering what animal would venture near our den. Surely it would smell us and stay well away, unless it was attracted to scavenge from us... A fox? What would fox taste like? I waited, swallowing my breath.

The creature boinged into view. A victim of the years in which we stood in parks and cooed at his fluffy tail and big liquid brown eyes set in a small skull, that cute little nose sniffling. The squirrel could see me, I was mere inches away. He peered at me with his tail a-twitch. I knew how fast he was, how the natural odds were stacked in his favour. But it was precisely these odds that made him too bold. For a tiny moment his attention wavered, and I snatched.

I yelped in surprise, having hold of the animal's tail. I was suddenly standing. I panicked then, knowing that a reaction from the squirrel would involve teeth and claws. I kept swinging it round, so my momentum would stop him being able to go on the offensive. And then he was limp – neck broken – a feeble scrap of nothing.

A row of faces peered at me from our shelter made of sticks and tarpaulin. I stood staring back at them, like that skinny child in the famous photograph, holding the toy hand grenade.

"I caught a squirrel," I said, in anguished disbelief.

Claudia cackled loudly and the others, too, joined in laughing.

* * * * * * *

BABY STEPS

Roxanne Ratcliffe, The Midlands

States of panic, of shock, of anxiety. The symptoms of modern life – depression, intolerance, phobia. Those feelings of intense helplessness, both perceived and real. As in my worst dreams I pulled back, and viewed things as though they weren't really happening to me. They were happening to *Roxanne Ratcliffe*, not Roxanne Ratcliffe. The characters followed the script and learned their dialogue, they worked together and looked out for one another, sometimes they fell out and had rows – it was inevitable.

The weaker characters began to prove themselves, developing survival skills that seemed not to come easily. Everyone evolved as people, because you either lived or died. Those were the choices. A sense of dumb luck hung over our heads – like a cloud that was half pink, half grey. I imagined it floated above us as we hiked down through the last scrap of Yorkshire, then on through Nottinghamshire, which materialized, like my grief, in the shuddering scale of devastation. We trod through the remains of a yacht which the winds or the floods had discarded in the middle of a barley field. The residue of excess clashing with agricultural wasteland. We were followed sometimes by homeless dogs and people, forlorn and feral. I hid any semblance of empathy under a threadbare woolly hat and eventually they would abandon us.

We continued on down through Leicestershire, shadowed, if not by beggars, by all the other guilt and grief and utter painful hopelessness. I was at least heading in the vague direction my family might have gone if they were still alive. Claudia was travelling away from any hope of finding her brother and dad. But she was adamant that we should stick together. We stayed close enough to sources of water to have a drinking supply, but far enough away that we wouldn't be flooded out while asleep. Sometimes we chewed at bark and grass, we were so desperate for food.

Though the old anxieties were irrelevant now, they haunted me like a mist in my mind. My irrational fears were present here in numbers. The massing silence, the looming shadows and the massing, looming sense of loneliness led by the loss of so much *life*. Even the loss of superficial reassurances like television or music to block the quiet. Even the purring of a cat to help pass the evening. Even the flick of an electric switch to reassure that the shape you see is no bogeyman. All that was left was the nervous noise in my head, and the million suggestive rustles and creaks of the woodlands, and ruined villages. I wasn't entirely alone, no, and I hoped this stayed so. I always crave company in some form, any feral dog or mischievous goat will do, or people. But only those I know I can trust.

One night in the past, after a few drinks in town, two of us had taken a short cut through the great cemetery. It was a safer, but darker, alternative to Frog Walk, which was dubbed '*rape alley*' by the local students. I remembered being there in that all consuming darkness, and the blurs of booziness, with only Claudia to steady my jitters (a stone guardian angel above an open grave). The path was lined densely with trees and head stones, and the night had such depth, I could barely see my own hands. The girl ahead of me was a pale glimpse of features that merged with shadows. In my head, as though playing from a car's old tape player that hymn from my lost childhood, which made me cry softly for my parents, Bruce Springsteen's *If I Should Fall Behind.*

* * * * * * *

LOCK 101

Simian Thomas, Leicestershire

A row of figures stood by a canal, dirty peasant faces, thin with exhaustion. It'd been difficult to think through the hunger, but staring at the water I found a memory in its gloomy, looming facade. I set my rucksack down hesitantly, carefully undoing the straps, for it was threatening to fall to bits. I rummaged through the stowed objects, which might or might not someday be of use. The only thing that had so far (except food and clothes) was the little compass which hung around my neck.

Finding the worn paper wrapped in a plastic cover, I crouched on my haunches and examined it. Charlie watched over my shoulder. He was suffering badly for his large stature, muscles stringy, torso looking increasingly like a cage that trapped his eyes, heavy with responsibility.

I read aloud softly, the title of the paper.

"Inland Waterways of England and Wales."

I peered at the various shaded lines, which signalled broad canals, narrow canals and navigable rivers. I traced a line down carefully with a finger.

"If we can travel south on this, *I think* it will join the Grand Union Canal further down and that will take us towards London."

Charlie took it off me and looked more closely at it, mouthing the names of places that would likely be nearby if his sense of direction was in tune.

"Why've yuu only just told me yuu had this?" he asked, his voice numb and detatched.

"I forgot about it," I said glumly. "Do you think we can still travel on canals? The water level will be higher won't it?"

He shrugged.

"Worth a bash. Just need tu find a fuckin boat."

Roxanne had been stood, staring hard into the water for some time.

"There's fish," she said.

"Anybody know owt about catchin fish?" Claudia asked.

"I remember hearing that if yuu tickle a salmon's belly yuu can hypnotise him and then catch him easy. But then I always thought if you're close enough tu tickle his belly, can't yuu just spear him anyway," Charlie rasped, thick with useless humour.

"Does anyone have any kind of netting?" Roxanne asked. "It's loads of little fish, I'm sure we could get a few."

We all shook our heads, making mental notes to salvage some sort of netting in the future.

Wolfgang rummaged through his pockets and brought out one of his many hats (a navy beanie), he shuffled around for a bit and found a suitable stick to poke through either side. Then he crouched quietly on the bank, staring into the water, still as a heron... Splash!

It created a fair kerfuffle in the water, and by all accounts a woolly hat is not so very streamline. He whipped it back out again and let water drip from the soggy bottom. We all peered inside where three tiny fish flapped pathetically. More pitiful morsels. The fish in the water had fled. Wolfgang shrugged exaggeratedly, muttering to himself something that sounded like a Latin quotation. He put the fish he'd caught in his pocket, checked my compass and then pottered off down the waterway, watching the water until he found another area where there were lots of fish gathered.

We followed him, having little else to do, and I was so caught by watching the eccentric trying to catch tiny fish that I didn't even notice at first a narrowboat tied up ahead on the canal, part concealed by bushes that teetered on the bank. A man was sat at the back and he watched us approach. Wolfgang still didn't seem to have noticed him and continued his comedic fishing. The man laughed audibly. I fell instinctively to the back of the group as we got closer. The fellow was a little scary looking, with a scar defining one of his cheek bones, and piercing green eyes. He was wearing a wax jacket, but it was oddly lined at the collar with a whole fox fur, complete with a face frozen in the impotent snarl of death.

"Good day, sir," Wolfgang announced dramatically, unperturbed by the frightful face that looked back at him. The man just nodded and said nothing. He looked well-fed and healthy and clearly had little inclination to share his secrets.

"May we barter a ride on your boat?" Wolfgang continued.

The man shrugged.

"What have you got that I would want?" he asked, leering at our female companions. Claudia glared back at him and Roxanne shifted closer to me, shrinking to a shadow.

"What're you running the boat on?" Charlie asked. "Can't imagine diesel and the like are tuu plentiful these days."

The man chuckled and nodded.

"Running a bit low, boy. That much is true. Got to find me an animal big enough to pull this thing. Are you offering yourself?"

"Think it'd be quicker for me to walk than tug your boat. So if we *could* get you a horse, that would pay for our passage?" Charlie asked.

The man shrugged and nodded. I remembered a children's story (perhaps by Roald Dahl) in which a bear fur and a crocodile handbag came back to life and attacked the humans that wore them. I stared at the fox and imagined his revenge with a kind of bitter glee. We walked off away from the boat to discuss our options, while the man meaningfully pulled out a proper fishing rod and flicked it out over the water.

"Where exactly d'we get a hoarse from, Charlie?" Claudia demanded quickly. "And it would need to be t'size uvva Shire to be strong enuff. Not that I wanna gi' that man the responsibility for lookin after a livin creature."

"This isn't really the time for worrying about animal rights, sweetie," Charlie replied with a sarcastic smile.

"In that case we'd better offer you fa't job after all," she said.

"Well meybe we should offer you up in exchange for our travel," he retorted.

"Go fook yissel Charlie. Don't even fookin suggest it as a joake. I'll rip yar fookin throat out." She spoke softly with eyes fired up.

"Calm down. Please stop arguing. Any sensible ideas?" Roxy said.

"Sumtimes farmers keep their own stash a' diesel kickin about." Claudia squinted towards the nearest remains of buildings.

"Why don't we just kill him and steal his boat?" Wolfgang grinned.

We all stared at him. We knew this was a kind of joke, but the world we were now living in was (in part) that ruthless and that brutal, that a joke like this suddenly became more realistic.

* * * * * * *

JETSAM

Claudia McLeod, Northamptonshire

I woke as tense and exhausted as I'd felt when I'd laid down eight hours afore. Despite the length of sleep – on't first mattress available since Sheffield – I'd bin driftin in and outtah conscious the whole time, uneasy dream-thoughts mergin wi' the claustrophobia a'tha cramped cabin. The loud engine had been going since early hours, but now suddenly stopped. Water lapped peacefully against the sides a' the boat so it rocked us lyke a cradle. But as I peeked suspiciously about in't gloom, I realised only missel and Roxy still slept – boxed in together 'tween a cupboard and a wall.

"Rox!" I hissed, pokin her. She twisted her neck to look at me, her face reflectin my own uneasiness. We wriggled from our makeshift bed, and sat adjustin feebly to waking life. I could hear Simian's hackin cough outside. He'd been coughin for days now.

"Do you think he has any tea in here?" Roxy asked grumpily.

I snorted in humour, but she probably weren't jokin. We'd managed eventu'ly to loot some diesel fa Gaz the previous day and were now waterborne and headin south.

"Girls!" Charlie called from't deck.

"We're definitely not girls anymore," Roxy said wi' glum acceptance.

We emerged into bright grey daylight at back a' the boat, joinin Simian, Charlie and Wolfgang, who stood gawpin. I scrambled ontu't narrowboat roof furra better look and tiptoed the length ayit – Gaz stood at't front, holdin the boat steady wi' a pole.

Beyond him was a landscape entirely submerged in water, as far as the eye could see. Where the moss swamps started, lakes ended, and canals began, that were not clear. The only navigable objects were the odd bittah fence or tree stuck outtah the mass gloomy waterscape – a hundred shades a grey-green and grey-blue.

"Fookin hell," I said quietly.

Gaz turned to peer up at me, wi' his hateful squinty eyes and the pawky smirk. Lyke the demon boatman, ready to ferry our souls to hell. A pathetic'ly soggy hell at that.

Charlie shifted up next to me.

"If we run aground in the middle of all that, we're proper fooked," he said.

"It's alright," Gaz said. "I know the way. Some of us don't need sat nav," he added charmlessly. "The water comin from over there will create a current though, so I'll need you lot to help me steer, to stay on the canal line."

"What happens when we get to a lock?" Charlie asked.

"I don't know," Gaz admitted. "Might be submerged... we'll see. TIME TO SWAP, FOLKS! I NEED TO OPERATE THE TILLER," he called out so they heard at't back.

I moved down and took the pole from him at the front, an then Roxy, Wolfgang and Simian joined me, cramped inta't pokey space.

We left Charlie and Gaz to their macho posturin' far off at't back. Simian sat down. He coughed agen, lookin a little green in the fayce. He were restin over the side a'tha boat, lookin at the water which lapped innocently.

"Yar not a fan a water, are ya?" I said dryly.

"I've nearly drowned twice in my life. What do *you* think?" he replied.

"Twice?" Roxy said.

He nodded, to indicate that he weren't gonna give detailed notes on either. Roxy peered at the murk and slime surroundin us, seemin to leach itsel onto the underside, as though wantin the narrowboat as another birrov'its furniture.

"It doesn't even look good for drinking," she said.

The engine kicked back inta life wi'a primal howl that drowned out our idle ramblings.

"KEEP HER STRAIGHT NOW!" Gaz called as the boat began slowly to move.

I concentrated my attention on a line ahead, usin the few landmarks assa guide. I stuck the pole inta the water agen, this time it sunk much further, unsteadyin me. I could feel the slight tug of an undercurrent way down beneath us, where nobbut trouts and porriwiggles thrived.

"GETTIN DEEPER!" I called.

"SHOULD DO," he answered.

* * * * * * *

THE BODY IN THE GUTTER

Bryn McLarey, Milton Keynes

A throbbing pain. My neck wus twisted from the blow, not made better by the further kickin. The ligament's unhappy state wus causing a regular jarring pain with mae slightest movement. The rest of mae back wus clenched in empathy – the histories in muscles and nerves suddenly remembered. The repetitive strains from a bygone era or tuu... from when I enjoyed a rumble, or from when I racked eighteen gallon barrels of ale, night after night.

When I lay totally still, the pain centralised at the top of mae spine, leik a headache ball. I could almost feel it reaching up towards the back of mae skull. This wus the pain of Milton Keynes, no doubt. The concrete, double-glazed abyss. The city with no soul and little more history. I wus bleeding from a cut on mae forehead, but I cudnae feel it. Numb tu lesser pains – the little niggles.

I'd thankfully had the nous tu stow mae spectacles away in their tough case before anyone aimed a bat at me. They were safe in mae pocket somewhere, but it left me with vision leik a Van Gogh painting. The starry sky was a series of purple-black and yellow smudges and smears. I wusnae sure how long I'd been lying there, as my eyes fought optimistically tu bring the street intu focus.

There wus the lurking shape of a dog, I realised. I wondered if it wus one of my attackers' semi-feral hounds that I'd seen frothing on the end of a chain (not six inches from my nose) shortly before... They were long gone, I thought.

The lone dog came trotting down the street. In mae simplistic vision he looked at me with hungry eyes and morbid curiosity. I couldn't move, not much anyway. I didn't want tu jerk pathetically leik a fish and give away how vulnerable I wus. I stared him down, mae eyes enlarging him superficially.

He knew I wus fooked. He came sniffing around me, hot smelly breath, and damp whiskers. He absentmindedly licked the blood on mae face. Not affectionately. Just like he might lick a carcass. But something startled him and he moved on, paws padding away across tarmac still damp from the day's rain.

I shifted mae torso round, beneath the now clear sky, tu look behind me. Just a blob, with hair twitching in the breeze. I fumbled now for mae glasses – still safe. Pain shooting through mae neck making me grit mae teeth and swallow hard.

It wus a woman that came intu focus beyond the magic lenses. She looked a bit leik a bag lady, or a cat lady – Tim Burton hair, layers of dirty clothes, braised red cheeks.

"Your friends?" She pointed up intu the nearby flats. She held her hand out and heaved me up with a strength I hadn't anticipated. I repressed a whimper of pain.

I followed her intu a doorway and up several flights of steps, stopping for breath, I leaned on a railing and stared out over the city. It wus the same purple-black as the sky, here and there pock-marked by old metal drums with fires inside. There wus an uneasy pattern tu them I realised. They marked out the territories of the gangs that ruled this new dystopia. I wus breathing heavily from the painful climb, mae pupils wide in the blackness. The woman looked at me, with a wearied expression that knew my conceited male ego had left me bruised and bloodied.

"It's best not to venture out at night alone," she said, her lips forming a grim line that knew it stated the obvious. "If at all."

* * * * * * *

FERAL HUMAN MEETS TAME JACKAL

Wolfgang, Milton Keynes

"Gaz is my ex-husband," the woman explained. There was a cruelty in her voice, an insinuation that she'd been done very wrong, but somehow it was inflicted by the self. Some people believe they deserve what they get, no matter the ifs and buts.

She'd seen him drop us off at nightfall, with that dirty smirk carved into his face. A face of gaping chasms that split open with silent laughter. Gaz was the other type of cruelty. The type that thinks *other people* deserve what they get.

I'd known nothing of Milton Keynes, save the Kaiser's prejudices dished out coldly into a chill twilight. The Boatman had dropped us off in leafy, benign-looking suburbs. There was no sign of life. No sign that this was a city. The rain had stopped and clouds cleared exposing us to the limitless bounds of space. As we walked towards the deserted centre, there was an atmosphere to the place that I knew felt wrong. It was almost like it was so quiet because people were hiding. But while we found an old bus shelter to hide out in and take stock of our situation, the Kaiser stomped off to 'find food', deaf to the warning signs.

"I dunno what it were like before." The woman shrugged. She had a south west accent, I was pleased to be able to discern. Somewhere quaint-sounding, like Dorset, I supposed. Dorset had to be the home of Dormice, I'd always thought. But there was a gravellyness over the quaintness which scraped away any nicety. Gaz had been from somewhere else, I mused. She noticed my thoughtfulness and eyed me suspiciously. Or had I been thinking aloud again?

"He dumped me here, like he dumped you here. He knows it's not all like this place, civilisation and whatnot, destroyed by them criminals," she said.

She'd shuffled into the bus shelter and announced gruffly that it wasn't safe for us to stay there and then guided us to the flats. Now we sat in near-silence, drinking weak tea, while she slowly divulged our situation.

"He wasn't always such a..." she paused self-consciously, "you know... C. U. N. T. Our daughter was killed..." She stopped, staring into her tea and we all swallowed, knowing we were being told something too personal. But maybe she felt the need to justify the wickedness. "She were mauled to death by feral dogs. Gaz always hated animals, said I was soft on 'em." She stopped again and listened. We all heard it, as though it mocked her and her stoical grief. Dogs barking outside, many voices, in frenzy.

"That'll be your friend," she said bitterly. "Nobody else dumb enough to be around."

I frowned puzzling the words, as though it was the Kaiser creating this frenzied barking in his ravaged soul.

"Gaz said he'd show me just what dogs were good for. The gangs all have dogs. The more dogs they got, the better. Gaz trades with people, up and down the waterways. He knows what goes on."

Claudia broke our silence, with impatient gusto.

"Can we go an help Charlie?"

She was already on her feet, but the woman had locked the door with a key that sat in her pocket.

"You all go down, they'll take everything you've got. Your pretty young faces, everythin. They won't kill him. They never kill what they can steal off."

The silence that filled the room now, ached with guilt, ached with the pain of being the person who stands by and does nothing. All we could hear above the steam creeping off our weak tea, was the hounds and the men baying for the blood that already tarnished the filthy tarmac.

* * * * * * *

THE LIST OF THE LIVING

Roxanne Ratcliffe, Hertfordshire

We lived for a time in an old school block, long since abandoned as a place of learning. The Brutalist concrete architecture still stood mostly solid to the elements. There were a few broken windows which we'd blocked off with scraps of wood and suchlike, salvaged from an old skip in the courtyard behind the former wood and metal workshops. The building was full of spacious, airy rooms that made the most of natural daylight, and various furniture and objects left abandoned which could be made use of. But it remained very draughty, and after making some makeshift chimneys, we spent a lot of time huddling around wood fires in corners, desperately trying to fill cracks in the rooms with old newspapers.

A kind of commune had formed in the building. Each group attempted to support one another and put up with screaming children – who, bored and hungry, ran around being a nuisance, tiring quickly and wailing at the unfairness of it all. Food was the greatest challenge and had to be consumed secretively. There are only so many people you can share meagre rations with, and only so many times you can let a parent guilt-trip you into feeding their sprogs when they made less effort than you in finding food.

One day we walked a few miles in search of something to eat. We found a house reduced to rubble, and obviously dangerous to enter. We had one hard hat between us, salvaged for such missions. Being the smallest, I volunteered to crawl in and have a look.

This may've seemed a silly risk, but the most dangerous buildings were the ones most likely to have been vacated quickly, and least likely to have already been re-entered for looting. We also had a flashing whistle (a nineties rave throwback I suspected) to alert friends if the scavenger got in trouble. I'd already become very adept at such missions, sliding myself through little gaps and checking how secure things were, like some sort of abstract potholing.

After a time, I found a trap door which lead to a cellar. Once down inside it was solid and safe, and oh the delight, a boxy little room, stacked to the ceiling with tins and packets of food. Some poor soul had stashed it all away, knowing they might get trapped in their house by the Weathers, and then probably been killed when the building fell. Leading out from the room was a tiny corridor, which I scrambled down, shoulders hunched so as to not knock my head on the ceiling. It lead to the back of what had been the garden, to another overgrown trap door leading up, which I forced open and stuck my ratty little head out, to the surprise of my friends waiting in the garden.

"There's a room full of tins and stuff!" I exclaimed.

Charlie grinned widely.

"Thank goodness fa the hobbit."

They gathered around the mouse hole in a circle and I peered up at them.

"Shall I bring out what we can carry and then we can come back another day if we hide it well?"

They nodded, unzipping their bags in readiness. I crawled back and forth for the best part of a half hour ferrying goods to them. We loaded ourselves up like mules and re-covered the trap door with twigs and debris, setting back off home with a spring in our step.

"You're gonna love this," Charlie said in gallows tones. "Our tin opener's been nicked."

Claudia shrugged diplomatically.

"We can't really hide all this anyroads, we're gonna haffta do some barterin."

"What do they hav that we need, apart from a fookin tin opener?" Charlie asked. "I dinae wanna live among a bunch of thievin gypos anymore. They pretend tu be communists but it's more leik *Lord of the Flies*, they're dog eat dog and they dunna wan tud mit it."

"Well then, we should plan our next move and use this food to see what we can exchange ta help us out. We could do wi' better weaponry if we're travelling," Claudia suggested.

"This is daft, we have it good here," Simian said dubiously. "We've a roof over our heads, and fire, and protection. Surely something like this is the future for us?"

"Sommat *like* this," Claudia said, "but this is too many people. They're maire of a drain than a blessing. Thes always another head poppin up tryin'ta be a leader."

"But aren't you gonna miss that Tyrone fellow yuu're always disappearing off with?" Charlie asked, with a mock innocent tone.

She laughed.

"It's jus sex, I'm sure he'll miss me maire."

My shoulders were already aching savagely, the food getting heavier with each step. I felt weary to the idea of moving on again, though it did feel right. We were less spirited on entering the school, as eyes quickly fell on the loads we were carrying. We returned to our room at least, to slightly reduce the number of hungry mouths. Charlie cleared his throat and began to barter.

As a nation were walking backwards through supposed human progress. The only form of communication and media that seemed to still survive was radio, if batteries were working. And so we'd huddle around it hoping news would get through between the fuzz.

We'd not cared too much for a while, given it only spoke of cities and towns reduced to ruins and predicted weather patterns too late to warn us. Vast bits of time were filled with bland propaganda, for without a solid country, it was all the government had going for them. But a new narrative was developing fast, that there was action now. Beaurocracy had been thrown out, but so too had democracy it seemed. So as we gathered round that evening with pale, expectant faces. We held our breaths and listened with awe, or horror, or some other emotion that has yet to be named. For when a country tries to turn its chaos into order, there will be collateral damage.

What were meant to be authoritative announcements, came through the airwaves full of stutters and hesitations due to the interference –

'iiissssssssssssssssssssssssssssss...zzzzzzzzzzzzzzzzzzzz...the s..rime minister today announced the total rebuilding...ff greater and central London...developing away from the Thames and out...shopping centres...the underground system...sports stadiums....ssszzzz...necting together to fform a completely sheltered city. Top engineers and experts in various fieldszzzrrr...working on ways to reinforcesh such a development...sssoo that itiss protected from the most violent weathers, initially the development will be abzzle to howwse....psssteemillion people, but will continue to spread outwardsz aiszz farass practical...the governmentas had to desciide

tufff measuuuss on who will qualify for accomoddasshhon in the build, those with relevant sskill towards its success will be able to 'pay' forthere entree in kindssszzzvvv through manual labour...other occupations qualify iff deemed vital for the success of a new socciety, the liisst goess as follows though any individuall may apply for citizzenship iff they feel they can contribute something vitall...

...the under twelves are conssiderredsss conditionable to a new society and arre the future of our racce so all automaticcallee qualify exccept those who have committed crimmees, thossezzzz.....ver twelve qualify if they have the occupationzzzskilss of...builders, plasterers, brick layers, skilled labourers... plumbers, engineers, electricianssszz... architects, carpenters, machinists, farmers, butchers, bakers, game keepers, huntsmen, fishermen....sstsss... doctors, teachers, medics, scientists, physicians, policemen, soldiers...other people may qualify if they offer a monetary donation to the cause and for further donations their family may qualify also, subject to background checkzs on criminal history and violent or anti-soczzial behaviour...'

A happier atmosphere had entered our area of the school with the aroma of cooking smells, but as more gathered to listen, an air of indignation threatened to spill over. These were after all, the liberals and socialists of a previous time – able to read aptly between the lines that gaped in the brave new world being built inside a bubble. Skilled labourers would be accepted, but what would be the later cost to them? And mainly it seemed the big plan hoped to save those with money from the big bad world. A burr of conversations erupted about who in the room qualified for the sheltered city, and whether or not they'd be willing to accept the rules of admission.

"We have seen the crumbling of a country...!" one man announced dramatically. "But *this* is the demolition of the welfare state! Did you hear any mention of what will happen to *pensioners?*"

There was a doubtful shaking of heads, but murmurs of the poor signal and bits of interference.

"They're throwing thirteen year old children out on their ear!" he continued. "I doubt a few old biddies who're a drain on their resources will get admission."

"I havnae seen yuu out feeding the elderly?" Charlie retorted, unable to shrug off the man's self-righteous attitude.

"*I have my children to think of!*" the man replied even more self-righteously.

"How auld are they?" Charlie asked.

The man held one son close by the shoulder, who was clearly young enough to be saved. His daughter looked older, she shrugged off her dad's hand with slight venom.

"Will you let them take Toby?" she challenged him.

He was silent.

"I'm fairly sure moast people over sixty a dead already," Claudia said darkly.

I shushed her, picking up something further from the radio transmission.

'It is as yet unknown how many have died as a result of the Weathers, upon entry to the new Sheltered City, citizens will be compiled in 'The List of the Living', everyone else will be listed as 'Missing, presumed dea....ttttttttttsssssssssssssszzzzzzzzzzzzzzzzzzzz'

* * * * * *

SMOKING SPIDERWEBS

Claudia McLeod, Hertfordshire

In't bottom a the coffee cup the sugar crumbs sit half in, half outtah black liquid – slowly dissolvin into the mire which dirties ma clothes, and hair, and face. For once I dream. In one dream am sold inta sex slavery by Gaz the boatman, in another I'm cast in a modernised *Mad Men* as a cheated wife, smokin a cigarette and lookin ever-existential. The dreams aren't separate, though the narrative that connects them is blurred, interrupted slightly by the woken world stirrin, the shared bed creakin.

    I woke to the exposed concrete and indoor winds a'tha commune, peerin at the rows of mekkshift beds, lyke some Victorian poor'ouse, and the pale half-starved fayces... a refugee camp.

    "Made you a coffee," Roxy whispered, floatin in lyke a grey ghost.

    "Job's a goodun," I mumbled.

    I sat up and rolled a cigarette from papers and tobacco swapped fa some tinned sausage and beans we'd looted. We left the sleeping quarters an went ta one a'tha colder, empty rooms where nobody'd be mardy about me smokin. I flicked through the stray pages a mem'ry over all the other times Roxy'ud suffered the cold wi' me when I smoked. I changed my frame of reference agen, in tune wi the architecture and Roxy huddled shiverin, likenin us to Russian peasants in the Soviet Bloc. She rested 'genst the window and admired the stark views outside, a chintzy auld blanket around her shoulders. It were always coldest wakin up, havin bin laid still so long. The blood took a while to pump back round. Afta'a moment's thinkin, she said.

    "Wolfgang's next door. I can hear him."

I nodded and we moved tu't next room, first peepin in ta check there were no parents around to lecture me on my vices. They mayde me feel like a teenager agen, which were quite nice (as my bones felt auld) – if a little patronisin.

Wolfgang was with Simian and a bloke named Dave, smokin spiders' webs wi' his share a'tha rizlas.

"Why?" I asked.

"Someone once told me they were hallucinogenic," he explained. Dave, being prone towards harpin on about the adventures of youth, was also in on the experiment. Simian was loiterin in amusement.

"How long should it take to work?" Dave asked in his Brighton drawl.

"How long is the ladder to Heaven?" Wolfgang replied.

"Yeah." Dave laffed. His laffter escalated from a chunter inta full blown fits, though this was no indication of a mussweb high. It was typical ayis drug-addled brain.

"I don't understand your issues with these Southern Englanders," Wolfgang said to me, grinnin in'tween long drags. "They're a barrel of fun rolling down a hill."

"It's not *all* Southerners, Wolfie," I explained patiently. "It's the smug-Londoners and the people who think livin in the South Hams is a dream existence."

"It's grim up North, but they know how to make pies," Dave chipped in.

"And thas a bit annoyin." I waved my fag at him. "And not using sparklers on hand-pulled beer. All that pretentious bollocks about it 'fectin the way it tastes, when all it affects is the fobbiness."

Dave gev an exaggerated shrug of innocence.

"I'm a cider man. I don't even know what you're on about, darlink."

"Typical Southerner, playin fookin innocent in't face a'tha evidence!" I joked.

"I like this bird," Dave said. "She's a good larf."

"Laff," I corrected and he chuckled agen.

Charlie barged in at this point, his expression and body language tellin me he'd finally flipped and wanted outtah the commune. It'd bin weeks since we'd decided to leave.

"There you all are," he said grumpily. "Dave, out! I need a word with this lot."

"We're all friends 'ere," Dave said grinning. "I'll keep your secrets, you've been good to me. Well the German has anyway." He winked conspiringly.

Charlie glowered, but seemed beaten on the issue.

"It's time tu go," he announced to us. "We should feast today and build our strength up, an prepare tu leave tomorrow."

"The Man has spoken," Dave said.

Wolfgang giggled.

"Where?" I asked.

"The Outerlands of the Bubble. I'm curious tu see what's going on there and we can get a bigger picture of what's happening elsewhere." He seemed calm and thoughtful now.

"...And I know the quick way to get there," Dave said happily.

"You coming with us?" Roxy asked.

He shook his head.

"Me mam's here. I gottah do the best for her, as long as she's alive."

"What's the quick way?" Charlie asked.

"It'll cost you the location of your food source. I'm guessing there's still more there. You can't carry it all...?"

Charlie nodded in agreement.

* * * * * * *

A BOTTLE & A FRIEND

Bryn McLarey, The Outerlands

The Outerlands of the Bubble were leik a giant shanty toon, built from rubble and part remains of buildings that'd withstood the Weathers. People came and occupied a small space (a fookin rabbit hole), and survived on a strange mixture of good neighbourship, and distrust of strangers. The unspoken rules seemed tu be, if you knew someone's name and they said hello tu yuu in passing, it wus bad form tu rob them. In fact you ought tu be sharing your loot, offering them a cup of rotten Tetley from a soggy box you'd 'found'.
    People were there for many a reason. Sum were hoping tu get approved for the Bubble (or at least get their kids in), others came because there were other people, and they only knew how tu survive in a big filthy community. They could scrounge off whatever got smuggled out of the inside. They could sift the great rubbish heaps for things they could sell or use, and they could guilt trip their neighbour intu sharing their pet goat's milk (in exchange for keeping a lookout tu make sure nobody tried tu steal the goat). There were still bars and gambling dens for people tu waste away in, if they had anything left tu waste.
    Smelling even more pungently of these dirty beasts and their toilets in the ground, it made the commune seem less like hell by comparison. We rolled up with our sacks of tins and were surrounded by the fookin vultures in minutes, trying tu barter their shit and shoving grubby-faced children towards us tu beg with doe eyes.

"Stand tha fuck off," I said.

They half ignored me, but moved off a wee bit.

"All we want is a tin opener, lots of tobacco, clean water and a bottle a' whisky."

Some ignored this, still calling out what they had.

"Why the fook would we want *dandelion seeds?!*" I asked. "Soas we can grow our aen wee patch of *weeds?*"

A short fellow pushed forward with a rusty tin opener.

"Five cans," he haggled.

"We only have ten between us. You can have one can, cause we can open them with knives, it's just more hassle." I held a tin of baked beans just out of his reach.

"Done," he said, handing it tu me.

"I can get tobacco... and rizla," a woman said.

"Meet back here in an hour?" I suggested.

"Done." She scuttled off.

"Bottle of Paddy." A child held out some Irish whiskey. Someone else in the crowd tried tu snatch it, so I grabbed his wrist and twisted a little, then kept a hold.

"Where did you get that, young lady?" I asked the child.

"I took it off my daddy when he were asleep, pissed. Only two thirds left..."

"Clever girl. Where d'you live?" I wus aware that if I gave her food in front of all the others, they'd follow her and steal it. She pointed down the track sculpted from trodden down rubbish and debris.

"Away with the rest of yuu." I let mae grip free of the thief and turning tu follow her. The crowd all still hung aboot mae friends, until Claudia herded everyone after me. We trod the street, our shoes clumping over the flat mosaic of rammel, my eyes avoiding the bones and the shite-smeared newspaper which squelched hideously under foot. We passed a group of cobbled together huts, all perched on the edge of a murky pond, the smell of which made me choke on mae own realisation.

"That's the nearest toilets," Flossie said casually.

A few minutes' walk brought us tu a brick hut, with an old iron gate serving as a front door, scraps of cardboard selotaped on, in a pathetic attempt tu keep the cold out. The girl unlocked the gate and let us in tu the small room, where I had tu duck mae heid. There wussa wee fire burning in a roasting tin in the middle. Though the building was full of holes, there wus nowhere tuu specific for the smoke tu go, so it hung in the air of the room, sneaking out here and there in search of oxygen. The girl's dad wus asleep on the floor and looked near unwakable.

"May we sit awhile and get warm?" I asked her.

She nodded. She had wisdom beyond her years. She neither wholly trusted nor distrusted us. We shunted in around the fire cheek tu jowl. I unpacked a selection of ten tins tu exchange for the whiskey.

"You said you only had ten tins all together," the girl said.

"A little white lie on mae part. What's your name, love?" I asked.

"Flossie," she answered. "Because of my hair."

Her hair was afro-curly, but looked reddish underneath the dirt, her skin freckly and olive brown, paled by long winters and weak light. She picked up a tin of soup and peered at it. She probably cudnae read, she wus likely a toddler when the Weathers kicked in. She took out a small knife with a blade shaped like a shark's fin and sliced a hole in the top, then held it in both little hands, tipped back her head and drank from it hungrily.

We all watched her with the quiet admiration you can only have for a child who has survived very bad things.

She took the remaining tins and hid them aboot, leaving just one in front of her Dad for when he woke up.

"Will he be angry you took his whiskey?" Claudia asked.

The girl shook her head and pointed tu another empty bottle of the same stuff.

"I just tell im he drank it all, he can't never remember. He thinks I just get us food from beggin."

"How is it, livin around here? A'ya tryin to gerrin'ta the Bubble?" Claudia continued.

"Alright," she shrugged. "Most people nice to me cause am lickle. Dad don't want me to leave im and go in Bubble. He not like what people say about it. They won't let im in, ees useless." She studied our faces, as shamelessly as children du, and we waited quietly. "There's a free hidey hole next door if you want somewhere to stay. Be bit small for all of you." She shrugged.

"Thanks," Claudia said. "We'll have a look."

Simian coughed as smoke swirled intu hus face.

"Why don't you free say much?" Flossie pointed at Roxy, Simian and Wolfgang.

Roxy shrugged and said nothing. Wolfgang, as if having been given permission tu speak, smiled widely leik a slightly frightening clown and said.

"What lovely hair you have, my dear."

The girl screwed her nose up.

"Err..." she said. "You're weird!"

* * * * * * *

THE OUTLAWS & THE OUTERLANDS

Roxanne Ratcliffe, Hertfordshire

Always boil the water before you drink it. My brain wrote this in lines, over and over.

We'd had no means to boil the water and we'd bartered it in bottles, assuming it was clean. We should've known better in the thriving shithole of the Outerlands. The water tasted like a poisoned peach dropped, tasted like the adrenaline shot of independence that drives me to be alone in a crowd. A throbbing, living mass, like grebs in a mosh pit. Or maggots swarming on a dead fish selotaped to a window pane. Sweat drips from them to me and soaks between us. A break in this image shows the ill crawling on the floor in a sewer of their own making. But my vision blurs and distorts again, they become Paula Rego's *Dog Woman* – carnal creatures on four legs baying and knashing, shoulder blades sharp to the sky, fur on end, lips drawn back. I cower back afraid, unable to escape through the treacle in my limbs. I struggle to crawl and twitch in my feverous sleep like a rabbit.

Struggling through mud to an empty, peaceful darkness that doesn't harangue my body with the ills of pain.

When I came to, I was cold in the face, but strangely clean. My lips were drinking clean water with undignified desperation. The taste of it. Nature's fickle liquid. One that could give life or deal death on a whim. Now it was cleaning my insides, giving me back the life it'd tried to take. We were in the back of a stationary pickup truck, amid strewn blankets and our bags, sheltered by a tarpaulin roof. It was Wolfgang pouring water into my mouth, his shaggy beard coming into hyper-real focus. I sat back, leaning my head against the wood. I felt nausea but this time it was clean. Country air rinsing my nostrils and soaking my brain with the oxygen the trees breathed into me.

"The Alchemist saves," Wolfgang said modestly, with an overstated bow.

"How did we get here?" I looked out of the back at the woodlands, a tussle of evergreens and birches.

"I had to flee us away from there. We had all shitted and vomited a little too much in that hell hole."

I shut my eyes to try to block out the images and the stench of the cramped room, which'd been our home in the Outerlands for barely more than a day.

"Guess Wolfgang's stomach is a tad maire resistant than ours, luckily," Claudia suggested begrudgingly.

"We're more than lucky. Fook knows what diseases all that sewerage is causing... Dysentery, Typhoid... Jesus fookin Christ." Charlie stared blankly ahead in horror.

"We're clean," I said.

"I dunked you all in the stream, when the sun came out. You might want to change your underclothes to warm up."

"Whose truck is this?" I asked.

"The traffickers. I bartered our passage. Don't think they'll take us much further, but the chap said he dumped a Volvo further up the road here. A little mechanic know-how might get the thing started again. But they want something in exchange."

"What have we got left?" Simian asked.

"I've still got some money actually, might they accept that?" I asked.

* * * * * * *

BROKEN YOLK

Wolfgang, Hertfordshire

In the wilds, people are clutter. Noisy, messy, polluting clutter – with their homes and cars and shops. Suckling like piglets off urban clumps where they can earn and spend wads of insignificant paper. They don't have the dignity of the wild things, only the neurosis. The Wild Rumpus nothing but cackling hens and mooning stags, shooting Aftershock and copulating in greasy dark corners.

An angry man had once fired a gun at the car we rode in – a beaten up, nineties Volvo with a spoiler on the back. Maybe he was angry that Volvo had strayed from boxy estates and streamlined something. But the joy of the car was its geek glamour. I digress. The bullet hole in the windscreen and the spider legs that stretched out from it, forming the cracked framing of the appearing village and the wilds.

Claudia yanked the car to a halt. Charlie muttered something under his breath about her style of driving wasting precious fuel, but he couldn't bring himself to be a scold. We sat and peered around at the clutch of houses nested amongst evergreens.

I was feeling drippy and dozey now.

"May I stay and sleep?"

The others had mostly rested to the purr of the car, but Claudia's driving made me queasy. They gave insignificant shrugs and exited the vehicle, clambering out the folded seats, through the two front doors, which slammed in unison. The waves of chill air that'd entered in moments held back abruptly by metal and glass (save for the one smashed window, repaired with a bin liner and gaffer tape).

"*Even the evergreens will have their autumn,*" I muttered to myself, as I began the slow sink, starting with thinking and dreaming at the same time.

In the flicker of my eyeballs beneath my eyelids, I dreamed too closely of the evergreen trees. Of their many plights and sufferings, as though I were in the beating heart of the forest. I feel the summer fires which turn whole hillsides to rows of spindly twigs. I watch the pine beetle eating them from the inside, and leaving them a strange shade of red, like wooden blood. I observe the loggers chewing away like beavers at the landscape. But buoyed by the winds and the rains, and the kindly sun, I feel myself inside the trees as they recover and repopulate. Drinking from the forest floors left fertile by dead trees and ashes. In the fresh, harsh winter the beetles perish, and I stare like a face from heaven as the trees grow before my very eyes.

Still stuck between thinking and dreaming, I was woken by a car door creaking open and the chill (beetle-killing) air that swam about my shoulders. I pulled my cheek away from where it had been rested too hard against the seating, giving me a pink tweed cheek.

Claudia's face (which had lost its smoky-eyed mask of make-up, since we left dear Yorkshire) looked like that of a doll left under the bed for several years. Dusty and forgotten by the sun.

"Fookin yokels." She climbed in and slammed the door.

"Nothing displeases me, quite so much as a broken yolk," I said agreeably.

She snorted in deriding humour.

"If thev got petrol, they don't want us ta have it."

"Looks like a one-horse zombie town to me." I squinted from the window, at what little I could see of crumbled garden walls and solemn-looking homes.

"Wish it were. That'd be maire interestin. They don't have one hoarse between them, jus stubborn, Southern prejudice."

"Have we met any cannibals yet?" I enquired.

She twisted around and sat sideways in the driver's seat, propping her feet over the handbrake onto the passenger seat.

"D'ya pay any attention to real life?" she asked suspiciously, but didn't leave room for an answer. "I don't think humans tekk too easily to cannibalism, at least not in this country."

I nodded.

"The English are too stoical for that sort of thing."

She snorted again.

"Yeah... just too damn polite to eat the neighbours!"

* * * * * * *

IN THE FOG

Bryn McLarey, Hertfordshire

There wus sick in mae beard. I had little choice. There wus probably all sorts of crap tucked away in there also and no shampoo tu dislodge it from living in mae face. So I wielded a razor and did the gentlemanly thing. But now mae face felt terribly cold and naked. I could feel the angry little hairs pushing back through the skin, leik itchy irritant pin pricks. I didnae miss needing tu shave at all.

The only time I'd done it every day wus at university, trying tu pretend tu be a fop.

Claudia had instigated the torture. She'd returned from the village shop (not unlike the shop in *The League of Gentlemen*, they didn't take money, but were happy to accept two litres of goats' milk) with cheap razors, a pair of scissors, tampons, a box of tea bags and five bruised apples.

"Yar beards still smell a'that skank hole," she'd told us. Even Simian with his strawberry blonde, patchy facial fluff. He wus the first tu cave, with a careless shrug.

"The smell is in everyone's hair tuu," I said.

She nodded, waving the scissors.

"Bit nippy to be shavin our heads though, in't it, Charlie?"

Wolfgang refused by claiming he'd not been without a beard since he wus twelve and a half. But he agreed to chop it right back.

"The forests will grow back from the devastation," he said solemnly.

Claudia now led each of us tu a nearby tree stump and briskly hacked off our hair to within an inch or so of scalp. We looked leik a strange androgynous gang.

"Still no petrol though?" Simian asked.

The Volvo wus running on empty, just like us. We sat inside the car and ate our apples in thoughtful silence. We didn't even know where we were heading now. I hadn't been able tu pick up the trail of the anarchist group and the Outerlands had robbed us ruthlessly of the health and energy we'd gotten from eating regularly. A thick fog had begun descending on the village, making it difficult tu know what time of day it wus. At first it snuck misty fingers around the car, then it set us intu zero visibility like a clay mould. The three in the back of the car shifted and elbowed each other restlessly.

I stared hard intu the fog and saw shapes and things that weren't there, tiny little darting sparks that were actually on mae eyeballs, leik sperm dashing around, crashing intu one another. But a lamp wus glowing somewhere, drawing nearer doon the road, and the tread of suspicious feet. I half expected it tu be one of the villagers coming, tu tell us we weren't even welcome tu park and sleep there.

A bulbous red nose, marked with a bulbous, pink wart appeared at mae window. A man knocked very politely on the glass. I rolled it down, wondering that the fog might climb intu the car.

"Ah, hellooo," the man said, wiggling his fingers as though he'd been offered a tasty treat. "I hear you chaps and ladies are in need of petrol?"

"Yes sir, we are," I said with wry graciousness.

"If you would like to follow me to my cottage?" he suggested, waving eagerly down the blind, scraggy road he'd metamorphasised from.

We exchanged wary glances, but as usual we had little option than tu follow the music of whatever eccentric piper chose to play tu us.

* * * * * * *

HOUSE OF GIN

Simian Thomas, Hertfordshire

My mind was littered with post-modern cultural references to the point of absurdity. Each misadventure feeling more like an episode of *The Mighty Boosh* (each character more similar to the Hitcher or the Crack Fox).

But I was unable to get away from the fact that we ourselves were not like Howard and Vince, nor Scooby Doo and the gang. We wouldn't narrowly escape the worst fate by the skin of our teeth every time.

The man, who introduced himself as Phillip Lloyd-Roth, seemed like another harmless weirdo, but I wonder where the crunch point is when the weirdo becomes harmful – something that had *always* bothered me about Wolfgang. He licked his lips a lot, and peered at each of us with piggy eyes. We'd followed him in a line through dense fog to his ramshackle thatched cottage and it now occurred to me I had no idea of the way back. We had turned left at some point off the main track. For all I was able to see of the surroundings, we might've been right in the woods.

It was warm inside, as there was a wood-burning stove. The small windows were like blank faces of smoky grey, peering in. The most noticeable thing in the place though was a transparent tank and a series of tubes, like some bizarre chemistry kit, bubbling away.

"Sit! Sit," he ordered cheerfully.

We wedged onto the sofa, three on the seat, one on either arm. The one Roxy perched on was slightly loose, so she hovered awkwardly next to me. A sizable brown rat ran across the nearly-nothing carpet and scampered up Phillip Lloyd-Roth's leg to sit on his shoulder, with a leisurely drape of its long pink tail. I hoped it was a pet rat. It squinted at us, sniffing the air.

"I used to have a country pile," Phillip explained hastily, as though we were judging him in terms of poverty. "But the Weathers, and what not. It all went to pot! Now here!"

He waved his walking stick around. (He didn't seem to need the stick, it looked antique, the head was bulbous, rather than curved and looked like it might be made of ivory.)

"Gin?" he asked.

"Excuse me?" Roxy said, as it seemed to have been directed at her.

"Would you like some gin? I make it myself." He seemed terribly proud and it suddenly occurred to me, quite drunk.

"Oh, that's what this is?" Charlie pointed at the tank and tubes.

"Yes, yes. All the lovely botanicals, turned into lovely gin. One must have some purpose in these sad times."

"D'yuu drink it by itself?" Charlie asked.

"Gosh, you're terribly Scottish," he said suddenly, as though it were exotic. "No, it's a little harsh for that. It's no Tanqueray! No, no, I have homemade ginger beer, and lime cordial. Plenty of sugar to preserve them!"

"Well yes, I think we can all dabble in that," Charlie affirmed.

Phillip disappeared, leaving us in bemused silence.

"He's like Toad of Toad Hall!" Wolfgang whispered excitedly.

"He's leik the queer auld chap in *Withnail and I*," Charlie added. "I think he might jump mae bones."

Phillip Lloyd-Roth returned with a tea tray of coloured, plastic tumblers filled with some murky-looking concoction. He clambered on a stool and selected an unmarked bottle of clear liquid from a row of maybe twenty of the same. He poured a slug in the top of each cup and carried the tray to each of us.

The gin was floating on the top, so my first mouthful was a little brave. It certainly wasn't Tanqueray. I tried to swill it around to mix it, but it was a little full. I stirred it with my finger and then sucked the drips off the end. The sweetness and the tart bitterness attacked my tongue at once. But it left a glow in my throat which was numbing my worries at least.

"So, d'ye have any petrol we might buy off you, good man? Or can we run the car off this stuff?" Charlie quipped, with gruff enthusiasm.

"Golly," said Philip, belching after his own drink. "What's the rush? Is there a rush? Where are you going...?"

"Stevenage," Charlie said, pulling a decision out of thin air. "How far is it? D'ye know?"

"Oh," Phillip said. "Let's see... not too far. Will you be staying the night, though? It does get terribly lonely around these parts. The others are a bit stuck in their ways... Stevenage, hmm. Now something *very* bad happened there a while ago. A meteorite or something I heard." He sucked his lips in thoughtfully. "I've an old map though, I'll get you the map." He disappeared again.

"I've changed my mind," Claudia said. "I think he wants ta eat us."

"He's just lonely," Charlie said. "Just a lonely old queer."

"Stop been a homophobe," she chastised.

"I'm not!" Charlie said. "I'm just stating the fookin obvious."

"I won't be able to sleep here," I said nervously.

"Few gins, you'll be out fa ther count, Simian. You won't know what's hit you. Or slid in you for that matter," he added crudely.

"I don't want to be..." I stopped mid-sentence as I heard Phillip returning.

He spread the battered old map out on the floor, with a weary sigh. Charlie leaned over and looked at where his stubby pink finger was pointing.

"You are... here... and um... Now let's see... Old Stevenage is... here! But it's a wreck of a city."

"A meteorite, you say?" Wolfgang asked. "How fascinating."

"Well," said Phillip dubiously. "There was a big ball of fire in the sky and I *heard*, but you know, hear-say and all that..."

* * * * * * *

BLIND TIGERS

Roxanne Ratcliffe, Stevenage

We were in an illegal drinking hole, named Bin Ends, in what used to be Stevenage. The city certainly looked like someone had thrown a fucking big rock at it, but it could've just been storm and flood damage. The local reaction to the rumours we'd heard in the village were rolling eyes and mutters about superstitious boredoms.

"Blind Tiger," Simian noted excitedly. He'd found an old book about the American Prohibition era, and begun relating things.

A blind tiger was apparently an illegal bar. It was ever more common that pubs were refusing to pay the strict new liquor licenses to the government that was willing to deny that we were alive, yet still wanted money off landlords. We sat in a dark, smoky corner and supped shit beer. Illegal brewing hadn't quite taken off yet. Cheap imports brought by traffickers via the Bubble were in.

"Hooch," Simian added, pointing at my bottle.

"This isnae illegal beer, sae it's noo 'hooch'," Charlie said contrarily.

It was in this dirty little drinking hole we heard rumours of a character called Toby Roe. It was implied to us that he could promise a future life for outlaws. An old man who'd joined us at our table introduced himself as rather wryly as Sid Arthur.

"Aye, I recognise the name," Charlie muttered with heavy sarcasm (he explained the literary reference to me later). "I think yuu used tu supply dope to friends a mine at the turn of the century."

Sid chuckled softly and warmly. We all peered curiously at him. He was the oldest person we'd seen still alive outside the Bubble. Erratic weather and lack of sustainable living circumstances had forced most elders to pay to cross over, or die with their principles (or poverty). Sid was a picture of aged health, like an advert for olive spread. We seemed to be a subject of happy laughter inside his brown eyes, more laughter than any of us could muster at that point. Except Simian, who was slightly delirious from both lack of sleep and having found a temporary source of espresso coffee.

"You're looking for 'another life', young things? Your anger has failed you – your atlas is turning away from the battles. You must seek the settlers of the North. Tobias Roe and Haydn Antoine, Logan Jeffers and Adam Griffiths, Maya Floss and Jacob Frith, Jessica Smith and Vincent Moon."

"Tobias, brother!" Wolfgang exclaimed, looking to Charlie.

Simian was furiously writing all the names onto his arm in biro.

"Doesn't 'Siddhartha' mock the worship of false idols? The creation of prophets?" Charlie asked, rubbing his hands together in an irritated way.

"Did I say these people were idols? Prophets?" the old man asked. "I said they were settlers, no more. They are re-establishing old living, encouraging the success of species, of animals and vegetation. They aren't your 'anarchists'. They believe in peace. To leave be the misguided who've fled to the Bubble, drawn by fear."

There were many lights going on in each of our heads. I didn't realise this until later.

"Why did you mention them in pairs?" I asked.

He nodded that it was a good question.

"They were one group, but they've split off to better spread the way of life. They're a tiny part, but I know them, and to know them is to have faith, I suppose."

"Will there be dogs?" Simian's eyes misfocused and darted around the room as though caught by movement of light.

Sid smiled.

"You've seen already, young man."

"We left the North," Charlie flailed a hand. "It wus in ruins."

Sid nodded slowly, looking quietly and intently at Charlie, as though reading a page, noting the language used.

"You were born in Scotland, weren't you?"

Charlie narrowed his eyes suspiciously and nodded.

Sid continued.

"The Scots living up in the Highlands away from the cities, or far out on blustery little isles. Have they not survived harsh climates, developed a way of life that suits?"

"There are harsh climates and there are *harsh climates*," Charlie sneered sceptically.

"The storms are a matter of the changing climate of the country, the dislocation of parts of the North Atlantic Drift. We believe it will settle down. Our climate will be more like Finland, Norway. Maybe the worst is already over." He gestured, "the people of the North are more ready to withstand the great Tempest, to adjust and rebuild. Others flee south, they may even flee the country.

But overseas territories have different problems. You don't want to flee to a drought, to murderous outbreaks of wildfires that destroy whole cities." He swayed as he spoke, probably from drink, but he hypnotised us like a dancing snake.

"And what of rumours we're entering the next Ice Age?" Charlie asked.

Sid gave an exaggerated shrug.

"You can't flee an Ice Age. You can learn to live with it, maybe..." he drifted off.

"Why a'you down here, instead of up there wi' them?" Claudia asked him, having been quiet for some time.

"My time is almost up. I'm recruiting. It's noble enough for me."

"And Haydn Antoine... is he blonde?" she asked hesitantly.

The old man nodded.

"You know him," he affirmed, and then smiling cryptically he added, "the Cloud follows the Sun."

"This all seems a suspicious coincidence," I said. "I think I know Toby Roe."

"You're of a certain generation, of a certain region, of a small country, of a certain mindset. I could go on."

"Didn't Maya Floss write a controversial book a few years back?" Simian asked.

"Exactly," Sid said. "Why have you heard of that book?"

"I read about it in an e-zine called The Chronicals."

"Devised by one Aiden Antoine," Sid said, with cosmic awe. "Like attracts like."

* * * * * * *

SILENCE & BROKEN THINGS

Wolfgang, Hertfordshire

"What's this drizzle for? I have no use of it," I said. A humid pause. "Where I'm from, the sun always shines."

"Where's that? Cloud fookin Cuckoo Land?" the Kaiser sneered.

It had drizzled for hours, and we had walked in it for hours. It wasn't a dangerous weather, but one that weighed gradually down on you. With each additional drip, our row of faces each mirrored the expression of a disgruntled cat left out in the rain. Our clothing and hair was soggy and sagging, extra baggage on top of the baggage we already carried.

We spotted with relief the ragged platform next to train tracks. They'd seen better days, but would hopefully carry us back to the North, however haphazardly. The steps were missing some, we scrambled and bundled each other up on the raised concrete, and then hastened to shelter. The incessant rain had left most silent, sick of one another. Sick of me, for I still chattered like a loon.

"You know, Mr. McLarey, I'm so glad I came upon you. For years, I used to get these voices in my head telling me what a piece of shit I was. A crazy, smelly piece of dog shit. And when I answered them back, people would stare. And they drove me sideways and upwards and inwards on myself, so I tried to cut them out... But since I met you, you've always been there to fill in the doubts and nastiness. So the voices felt a bit obsolete and went away again... So gratitudes for that."

Claudia for her part cackled at this.

"Don't mention it," the Kaiser drawled in deadpan Weegie.

Simian Ape, however, looked a little startled. I pretended not to notice. I understand he's frightened of madness because he's frightened of his own. Charlie noticed and patted him reassuringly on the shoulder.

"Neh worries, son, we've discussed this before. Schizos only pose a threat tu Daily Mail readers. They smell funny."

The windows of the platform waiting room had long been smashed, but the metal cage remained. We stepped one by one through the blank space of the automatic slide door, which remained stationary.

"They never recognise me anyway, as I have no soul," I remarked, but I don't think anyone knew what I referred to.

Roxanne Rat sat down on what might've been a seat. "What do we do now?" she asked quietly. "Just wait?"

"One supposes that's what a person does in a waiting room," I said ominously.

It was becoming unnervingly apparent in their faces that they'd selected a companionship of beings that could only now be separated by death. We were a pack, a skulk. Personal dislikes could not alter this, we must suffer one another. And they would all suffer me, like the annoying child in the back of the car who cannot simply be quiet.

I stared at the room and its echoes of a past civilization. A cracked, dusty television screen that would've once shown arrivals and departures, now just a grey face, a murky fish eyed mirror that only reflected movement. There was an old vending machine, the glass long smashed and the contents missing. There was also a hole in the floor which looked suspiciously as though someone had hacked through it with an axe or something. A ratty nose pokes out and he looks at me and says *"Don't be silly, I'm long gone."*

I looked up to see if anyone else noticed, but they hadn't. I wondered what the rat meant, but I quickly got bored of the thought. The waiting room was picture-perfect banality, as it always must've been. Now instead of being duly over-used to grey walls, flickering screens and repetitious announcements, we'd become accustomed to silence and broken things.

Feet scuffed the ground outside and a man stepped in from the drizzle, one of the bulky railwaymen that still clad themselves in bright orange vests like days of yore. He removed a flat tweed cap and shook the rain off it.

"Ello," he said, with a cheerful red face. "Saw you lot on cameras." He paused, waiting for our surprise that the old CCTV worked. Charlie stood up and shook the man's hand with strange formality.

"Hi, we heard there were still some trains running? Is it true? We were hoping tu head up north."

"Oh, aye," the man said, slightly woodenly, with the same enforced cheerfulness. "Bit of silly weather don't stop us! It'll take a while, mind. Days. Maybe weeks. Bit more of a challenge, but we do what we can. What you goin up there for? Ya bloody mad. We mostly bring people t'other way."

"We're trying tu find an old friend," Charlie said. "Haven't you heard of settlers up there? Trying tu make a new life, off the land and so on?"

The man laughed.

"Aye, but I've heard of Robin Hood, too. Was never too convinced it wasn't just a nice yarn to keep chins up!" He winked at Roxanne.

"When will there be a train?" Charlie asked.

"Well now, sonny. There's one due a few days ago, whats not come yet. I can't guarantee nowt, but I'd say she'll be along in this week sometime. You can sleep in the station office if ya like, nice 'n' safe wi'cameras, you know when thez dogs abaat!" He rolled his sleeve up to show old, pink bite marks. "Now, I don't mean to be a capit'ulist, but how you payin us...? We gotta eat, see."

We all looked at one another. We'd looted and scrounged whatever we could, but our bony faces showed it wasn't much.

"We have sum tobacco," Charlie said begrudgingly. "What else do yuu have in mind?"

"Well that's a start," the man said, he thought for a minute. "There's a pond out back with frogs, I've not been able to master catchin, but they're meant to be a bit tasty. And there's a dog what comes every night sniffing round, wants to eat my dinner and me. If you can kill er, you got yourself a ride, though we'll be needing more further up."

Charlie nodded thoughtfully.

"How do you know the dog is a she?" Simian asked doubtfully.

"She don't cock er leg when she pisses on yer!" the man replied with a hearty chuckle.

* * * * * * *

A REAL LIFE JACK

Claudia McLeod, Hertfordshire

"Did yuu ever meet Toby?" Charlie asked me.

The question formed a suspension in't air. A kinetic spider web which held the weight a his agenda. He was attemptin to sound casual, but I knew he'd been mutterin furra while. He doesn't seem to know that he mutters to hissel. He stared at his cigarette and the ashtray it hovered above.

I stared at him, waiting furrim to look up, but he didn't.

"No, Haydn jus mentioned him a lot. Most a his friends were dicks who spoke bollox and took too many drugs." I 'membered Rufio wi' ruthless affection and felt immediate regret for this remark.

"Not Toby?"

"No, I mean, I dunno. He jus seemed to have loads of respect and admiration fa Toby and that. It's weird, I never even thought about this til now."

Simian returned from the kitchen area of the station house cradling three odd sized cups decorated with paisley flowers and gold leaf.

"They only had Earl Grey," he murmured in a muddle, spillin tea over his fingerless gloves and cussin softly.

"Fookin typical," Charlie rasped, he stubbed his cigarette out and lit another he'd already pre-rolled.

Simian sat down and took a definitive sip.

"Little honey and lemon would've been preferable to UHT but beggars we are, and choosers we ain't. So Toby you were saying..."

"Ears leik a cat," Charlie muttered.

"He played guitar, I 'member that," I said thoughtfully.

"Well, he must be fookin Jesus, then," Charlie said.

"I mean, I dunno about findin this bloke, what difference it'll mekk to owt, but I really miss music, even jus listenin to it. I hope he still has a guitar."

A shiverin voice echoed through the rooms below, hauntin through the auld brickwork.

"*Where are you...?*" it sounded lyke a lost child.

Simian's face paled.

"It's ok Sim, I heard it too," I said. I'd been gettin't feelin Simian'ud been seein and hearin alotta weird stuff in his head of recent.

Our faces crossed't room to the CCTV screens which showed only flickerin ghosts a grey an white images anyway. Charlie and missel turned back tu't table, to one another, but Simian stayed poised, his jaw turned, presentin us wi'a profile, wi'a protrudin Adam's apple, wi' eyes rolled to one side.

Charlie handed him his roll-up and pushed the tea t'wards him.

"Stay busy, kid."

Simian settled a bit, shakily tekkin a drag and coughin a little, then suppin tea to suppress it. He looked at me. He always minds me a'tha lone kid in the movie left to deal wi'stuff he can barely compre'end – lyke the boy in *The Shining*. The door creaked open and Wolfgang came in, grinnin nastily tween his beard and scraggy hair. A real life Jack furrus, his teeth and eyes looked 'specially black t'day. He didn't need to say owt and neither did we. He sat down and took Charlie's brew from him, downin it lyke whiskey. He muttered something and laffed quietly to hissel.

"Where's Roxanne? Ya were meant to stay together," I said.

"She's barely a ghost anyway," he replied with unusual callousness.

We all waited quietly, Simian shiftin guiltily in his seat. Roxanne padded in through the creaky door wi'the train worker, Freddie. They were carryin sackin, she placed hers on the table. There were mice inside mostly and a young, scrawny rabbit.

"Are mice bones small enough to eat?" Simian asked.

Nobody answered. Freddie showed us where he'd cut a chimney in't ceiling, so that we could have a fire to cook over. He left us to our own devices and we stared at't meat we were meant to mekk a meal of.

"No frogs then?" Charlie said.

"I think frogs hibernate? He's got a bunch of traps set up already for rabbits and stuff anyway," Roxy explained. "He's being pretty generous."

Later, once we'd shared meat scraps (gnawin at mouse kebabs pretendin they were chicken wings), wi' no carbohydrate to fill the grindin hole in our stomachs, Roxy also brought up the subject a Toby with me.

"Did you ever meet Toby?" she asked.

"No," I answered, wi' a glance to Charlie.

"I dunno if it's the Toby Roe I met, I'm sure it's possible there's more than one. But I doubt there's more than one Haydn Antoine, who also goes by the name Aiden."

I nodded. Agenst my better judgment, I felt a saughey happiness that Haydn were alive.

"Whas all the fuss about this Toby person anyroad?" I asked, not jus to Roxy, but to Charlie and Wolfgang an all.

"There's no fuss," Roxy said, shrinkin into her secrets.

* * * * * *

GHOSTS IN THE ICE

Simian Thomas, Hertfordshire

I studied the map of train lines on the wall. It was not a simple coloured map like the ones they used to give to passengers. It was layers of information typed and scrawled onto the landscape. The original gradients and the positioning of signal posts, crossings, bridges and sidings were inked in by a printer. But on top of this were hand-written notes, and scruffy shading in blue pen to show where rivers and lakes had swelled, black and red describing bridges collapsed and lands slid.

It was unnervingly possible to see our route southward in many months previous – the great flooded landscape we'd traversed on that shitty little narrow boat, the suburbs where we'd lived in the commune and looted from wrecked buildings, the harrowing sprawl of the Outerlands. I was unable to decide which village we'd stayed in though. With that strange little man who'd fallen into a gin stupor so shortly after nightfall, and left us to peacefully chatter around his lovely wood-burning stove. But there were the craters of Stevenage, and a few finger steps up was the Victorian station house where we now slept and waited, and hoped.

The wind buffeted and rattled the windows, and I wondered how this building had stood the many tests of time. I was still seeing glimpses of past faces in every dark window pane. But I'd begun to adjust to these images, some were even familiar to my past self – a drowning child in the Indian Ocean reappeared again and again, drowning in icy fog or the winter drizzle. Floating like debris in my damaged psyche.

The fact that this was an image that I'd actually seen made me feel better. I could know it was a creation of my mind. Others ghosts confused me. It amazed me that I could imagine them in such detail, feel warm breath on my cold face, fingers tugging at the lengthening tufts of my hair. They followed me with their absence, and re-emerged wailing distress calls across damaged lands.

The station house had its own ghosts, as well as mine. A cold history imbedded in the bricks and mortar, which meant the rooms were never silent. They'd seen so many changes, so many different faces, that they chattered on like cold teeth, in ritual madness... As though it was a mind riddled by dementia, with so much wisdom to impart, but no rationale left to form sense and reason.

The arched windows, with decoratively carved eyebrows, looked out on the station platform, consumed in night-time sleet. It must've been mid-evening but it felt like the small hours, being so empty of civilisation. Across the tracks, which failed to gleam without moonlight, there was a steep bank and then the woodland, fraught with dense hawthorn bushes that were too late in the year to fruit. My eyes got lost trying to focus in the vague dark world. They got distracted by the face reflected in the glass, a candlelit boy looking terribly maudlin. He coughed pathetically, and I coughed back, my chest vibrating to a hoarse whisper.

The snow fell in a thick layer like icing that evening, and then it rained, and the rain froze over the top of the snow. It was icy and treacherous, humans rendered comedic mannequins, thrashing to keep their balance. I stayed in the station house again. I watched on one of the spooky little televisions – the she-dog sniffing around the station at dusk, crouching to pee as Freddie'd said she would. She looked to the camera and captured me in her empty gothic stare. We could barely hunt the birds and rats. Killing a real predator seemed impossible. I looked at one of the other screens with the usual grimace – it was the waiting room, but in the gloomy monotone image, the objects seemed to form into the shape of a hanged-man. The head of the man was frozen limply at an odd angle. The worst thing about it was that the man looked like me. I tried to avoid ever looking at that screen, but my eyes were drawn again and again to it... waiting for the dead me to wake up.

* * * * * * *

THE PAIN THRESHOLD

Roxanne Ratcliffe, Hertfordshire

I had a strange feeling it was Christmas. We'd lost all sense of the Western calendar by this time. Days had passed erratically into months. We could only note the rising of the sun and gradual turn of the seasons. Now it felt like the grim long months of winter, and there was no chaotic pagan festival to distract from the darkness and the cold. Staring glumly at the thickly frosted fields, I had a feeling that in the Bubble, the new micro state of England, they would have a tree dragged in from the cold, trussed up in red and gold. I'd never enjoyed the desperation of the maddening crowds to (shop and drink and cackle) make it all so special for themselves. But in deep midwinter, with a feeling that spring was far off, I could see the appeal of a quiet, rural Christmas with family and friends.

I moved on quickly. My feet crunched over the frost-encrusted grass, displacing its carefully sculpted lines. I could feel the chill air on my cheeks, movement breathing adrenaline and life through a body that was numb on the outside. We only had a few hours of daylight to move around and search for food, and they seemed to pass so quickly. The sun would drop hastily over the grey line of the horizon, twilight turning to dusk without a pause for breath.

Today at least, the sky was blindingly bright, giving everything in sight a crisp edge. I happened upon a small lake which was partially covered by a fragile sheet of ice. A flock of inland gulls had been teetering on this, but now as I watched they all took off and circled indecisively over the frozen water. The action doubled poetically in the reflection below. There was a small pier stretching onto the lake, greened over with frosted moss. I watched the birds, like a frustrated cat inside a window pane. I had no means to make them into food. And yet I let the light fill my eyes, ignoring my howling stomach which had probably alerted every animal nearby of my whereabouts. As with any day of beauty, back when I was worried by trifles, I let the sunlight fill me with pious optimism. I looked at my brittle hands rested on the fence, held together with frayed gloves that would soon expose pink fingertips to the elements. They still grasped things, still worked as hands should. They still reminded me, in my abstract states of mind, of the very miracle of life.

I looked up and around, ears and eyes alert to find a way through the trees and catch up with the others. We'd toiled endlessly, way beyond any capacity I'd thought we had. When I was ill and achy and alone, it was easy to feel sorry for myself. Like bedridden days off school, bored and sleepy, red-eyed in a nest of snotty tissues. But we were all ill, all exhausted, and all slightly delirious from lack of proper hearty food and sleep. It was the knowledge of this that kept us going. Nobody wanted to be the first to break, the first to admit a defeat that would've meant – if alone – a meek walk towards death.

PHASE FIVE

In which the North calls them home on a train & they learn a few tricks in self-sufficiency

PROMISES YOU MADE WHILE YOU WERE YOUNG

Bryn McLarey, Hertfordshire

The distant sound of a train trundling down the tracks... a beckoning hand, an awakening heartbeat.
  I'd been cynical that a train would ever come. I'd half believed the auld station house would become our home, and nice-guy Freddie our landlord. Promising the world, but delivering only rodent suppers.
  Snowflakes as big as my hand-span had been falling, whirling down tu become a hat on mae head before breaking on mae face, crumbling in slow motion. I'd been shuffling through the woods in search of food, peering intu burrows where lucky animals hibernated and slept out the cold. I clambered back up the bank which separated the forest from the train tracks, the hawthorn tugging at mae clothes and tangling mae ankles. I scrambled through with a child-like excitement.
  An ordinary auld passenger train wus appearing at an easy gait. At its nose wus a detachable wedge-plough, leik the ones used by trains I'd seen in Switzerland. The falling flakes had eased off as it hissed and squeaked tu a halt at the platform opposite. I dropped down the bank with a satisfying crunch of boots on fresh snow, and walked over tu its mighty head. It continued tu purr furra few

moments afore the driver turned the engine off. I'd always been more of a motor geek than a train spotter – but mae eyes examined the vehicle with uncertain glee. Noting how it'd been roughly remodelled for a new age.

Freddie wus on the platform already, his rosy cheeks glowing with fatherly pride.

"This is Boudica," he announced.

I hitched maeself up ontu tha platform, looking around for the others, but there wus no sign of them. Freddie waved tu the driver and he sounded the horn, the sweet sound echoing over the valley.

"We've failed tu pay for our travel," I said, regretfully. We hadn't gotten near the wild dog he wanted rid of.

"Well you seem brave enuff and smart enuff to sort me ahht further up. Gonna get Dougie to stay 'ere and mind the station, and I'll be travelling north with you lot." Freddie shrugged.

"Thanks," I said, whole-heartedly, hearing excited voices in the distance.

* * * * * * *

VITAL JUNK

Claudia McLeod, Hertfordshire

The carriages a the train were not lyke they used to be. The electric doors had been ripped off and replaced wi'the old style, where you had to pull down't window to let yissel out. They'ud each been rearranged in identical form, wi' four bunks attached tu't walls at one end creatin a gloomy claustrophobic space, wi'blinds tugged down. The bunks looked sturdy and auld, as though they'd been salvaged, maybe from the Navy. They had grey-blue wool blankets on too, wi' tattered sheets aneath and a duvet on top. Each duvet had a different patterned cover on, bringin an uneasy mixture of clashin colours that sat badly wi'the austerity a'tha bunks.

The middle quarter of the carriage was as it would've been, nearly, each side havin a plastic table wi'four cushioned seats facin on and coat hooks jus below overhead luggage storage. The final quarter a'tha carriage had a mekkshift cooker an kettle over one side (though Freddie quickly informed us that energy use was rationed), and a water storage tank wi'a tap comin off it. On t'other side was another table attached tu't wall wi' an auld radio on, an a series of shelves above it stacked wi' books, maps and the odd vaguely useful object – a blunt butcher's knife, a rolling pin, an empty plastic bottle, a torch that had no batteries.

There were three carriages in total, the one containin the driver's cabin was marked 'B' for 'Boudica'. Freddie cheerfully introduced the other two carriages marked 'A' for 'Annie' and 'C' for Clarabel. We were to stay in Clarabel, at the back.

"There's only four bunks," Charlie said politely.

Freddie shrugged amiably. "Annie has empty bunks at the moment, if one a you wants to sleep in there. Or there're the seats."

"Why's the driving train called Boudica, not Thomas?" Roxy asked.

"A very important question," Freddie said, as though addressin a child. "Thomas had a bit of a serious crash. Boudica's a far superior model, suited to the tuff environment. Just soes you're aware, we'ull be travelling *very* slowly. There are regular blockages t' the tracks, the snows and storms create havoc. We'll be asking you to help clear debris from time to time."

We all nodded, he 'd repeated this information several times afore the train had even arrived.

One of the original toilets wedged between carriages still existed, in the middle carriage for us all to share. The others'd been converted to store fuel and things. I once would've held on, to avoid such a skanky hole, but these days it were a fookin luxury even to be sharin wi' so many men unable to hit't target.

We grabbed our belongings from the station house (glad we could stow them as we'd accumulated more vital junk in the past few days), and moved into our new home. I took a last look at the bleak, broken platform before sinking inta the draughty hub a'tha carriage called Clarabel. Wolfgang'd adopted a double seat as his territory to sleep, scribble and witter. A stack a notebooks were ready as an elbow rest. He shifted his bum around, disturbin dust, as he tried to mayke a comfortable dent. Roxy nested in a bottom bunk, fillin the small window dent wi'her own necessities. Simian chose a top bunk, ta be further from the bogeymen hidin anneath.

It were an hour or so before the train set off wi'that reassurin jolt to life. The feelin of movement pulsed in ma veins, no longer stuck in the same weak footsteps. The rhythm began as the train gained a very steady pace, a rhythm that shimmied from side-ta-side, but always forward. Travellin home to the North.

* * * * * * *

EVERY CAT WILL HAVE HER DAY

Wolfgang, Bedfordshire

A Frenchman stole my hat. I'm still bitter about this. It wasn't my favourite hat, but it was definitely *one* of my favourite hats. I do enjoy provenance. The fact that an object can have so many lives, so much history, that you can lose it and someone else reclaim it. But did I trust him to love that hat? No. Did I trust him not to toss it in the dustbin when the weather warmed up?

This might *not* be a subject that ought to keep me awake at night seven years later... *but it does.* The hat is long dead. Probably the Frenchman is long dead. *But it's the principle!*

It was daylight now, the train chugging along – gifting through its windows on the world the stunning bright views, in cold morning sunlight. I was sleeping in the worn carriage seating. I'd let the others have the bunks. I always slept better in a chair, as grand old men do. Was I a grand old man yet?

I wrote in my book.

'I have no more words left to describe the frost and snow...'

I stared out, blinking, staring at the audacious beauty of the white, the blue, the yellow, the pink. I thought about how the Inuit have so many different words to describe different snow. I suppose we will conceive more, with it in such abundance.

'Sparse, stark, stricken, cruel... the landscape cursed with a bedding of fluffy clouds. Like Heaven arriving on Earth in all its quiet brutality.'

I paused, chewing the end of my pen, looking at the snow and the page.

'Blinding and blanching... the winter light... the strange haze which clots in patches on my eyeballs, congealing and sinewing into my brain.'

We passed a place where the plants in the field had been snowed on, then begun to melt and frozen again mid-melt creating incredible sculpted fingers of ice. We'd passed on from them in moments, and I repressed the need to jump from the moving train, to run back and investigate this natural art.

I had to learn to let go of things. Like my hat. Like my pet ferret. Like Cuan. It's okay to possess things purely as memory, I told myself sternly.

I miss that fucking smelly ferret... he looked a bit like Cuan. The bin lorry ran him over when he was chasing the neighbours' cat. The cat was cleverer, leading Fursty the Ferret to his doom – hiding behind the wheel of a stationary object, knowing from experience that once our wheelie bins were emptied and returned, the lorry would move on with its loud beeping. Fursty had a cat's tail between his teeth, paying no attention to the noisy slow-moving vehicle.

* * * * * * *

LAST TUESDAY AT THREE THIRTEEN

Roxanne Ratcliffe, The Midlands

I remembered I'd pushed the books and scraps of the week off my bed. They tumbled to the floor, and Herman Hesse's *Steppenwolf* slid under the bed to greet dusty neighbours. I'd then crawled under the covers to drown myself in neuroticism, to escape from commitments to literature and personal growth. Another book I'd never finish, another plotline stuck in time, unable to resolve itself. Endings are the most difficult because they don't really exist. We begin several times over but we don't know how to end.

My relationship with Toby was always stuck in the time frame of the beginning. Because it never fully began, it could never fully end. I had nothing to base any closure on. I just tortured myself with disbelief that it would never happen, that we would never accidentally run into one another. And it would be no accident in the end. Fiction loves the lie of the 'soul mate', of so-called destiny. As though fixating on someone you've not seen in years is anything other than fucking damaging.

The truth is that the choices we make are all half chance. We cannot comprehend all the chaos of multiple lines that lead us to any outcome. Or how things might've been different if we'd chosen to drink coffee instead of tea last Tuesday at three thirteen.

For every happy ending, someone dies lonely and confused. Where was their fated soul mate?

So it was no accident. I didn't even intend to resolve the relationship as such. I just knew that a future existed within the home of Toby Roe. That we could have the chance to do what we'd been afraid of even before the Weathers, and settle down. As vagrant as the migrating buffalo wandering the cold wilderness, the vagabonds searched for food and shelter. They sewed patches on the elbows of their long black coats and haggled fur from a passing huntsman, begging also for a lucky rabbit's paw. Each winter demanded more flesh to strip from their cold bones.

Dear Mr. Frost, could you spare me this morning? My hand is stuck to the milk bottle.

On the train I had time to daydream again. To process thoughts, to be the armchair philosopher staring at the passing sky, accompanied always by the rhythm of the tracks. I would sit and gaze – at passing trees, at smashed up farmsteads – with Wolfgang sat opposite writing his unreadable scrawl. But then the train would stop again, and the peace would be broken, as Freddie would herd us off to help move another fallen tree. And then we'd go exploring another pocket of the countryside. Hoping for fortune in finding something to eat, claiming the best bits of wood to make fires or carve into weapons, salvaging old chicken wire in the hope we could build traps. And all the time the voice of the train or the rustle of the trees whimpered *'Toby...? Toby...?'*

Way back in the warm cocoon of my book-less bed, I'd dozed and dreamed. Of pretty white winters, of worthy tragedies, of a small bearded man hiding away amongst the ruins of a nation.

* * * * * * *

A PORTRAIT OF THE ARTIST AS AN OLD BEAR

Bryn McLarey, The Midlands

'Would you walk by, on the other side? When someone calls in vain. Would you walk by on the other side? And would you be afraid? Cross over the road my friend, ask the Lord his strength to lend. His compassion has no end. Cross over the road.'

This is what rattled in mae head, in a choirboy's soprano, over and over. Mocking me with my own sarcasm. Every time I saw some mad vagrant, there wus never any question I would help them. There is a time to be a Good Samaritan, and it's when you have the *means* tu be – when yuu yourself are not living a hand-tu-mouth existence. Still... I wear mae guilt like a badly fitting hat.

It wus Flossie, the child in the Outerlands, who kept me restless at night. We should've taken her with us. We shouldn't have left her in a hole with a useless drunken father. I'm no sucker for kids. I'd never adopt any old howling, whinging brat. But she wus exactly not that. She wus already resourceful, already a born survivor.

I closed mae eyes firmly and tried tu sleep, but could only see her face. Meybe her dad would drink himself tu death, and she'd get inta the Bubble. Or meybe she'd be kidnapped and sold intu child prostitution. I wus good at thinking the worst. I tried tu remind maeself that I'd had no control over events, that I'd been sick as a parrot when we'd left the shanty town, unable ta conjure such logic. But it wus this lack of control that dogged me – the weakness.

I should've returned, once I'd recovered. I should've gone back and now I'd lost the chance. Now a train carried me north.

I rolled out of mae bunk, dropping quietly tu the floor. The train rocked gently beneath mae feet, the murky shapes of the carriage moving in and out of shadow. There wus just a small paraffin lamp lit, on one a the tables. On the opposite side Wolfgang wus slumped in a chair, snoring leik an old man. I sat down with the light, and I stared hard from the train window intu the darkness, trying tu see something out there, tu even know if it wus city or country we rolled through. But all I could make out wus a faded painting of maeself – heavy dark eyes, beneath heavy dark brows, hair growing back down over mae collar, a lazy beard. I looked leik pictures of mae father from the late seventies. He'd already looked old then – booze did that tu you.

I hadnae spent all mae time on the train sae far worrying about important things. Mostly I thought about sex, how long I'd been without it, and whether or not this wus damaging. It certainly did nothing for mae mood swings. I wus turning intu a teenage boy agen, the vibrations of the train often sending me tu hide in the toilet and knock one out... or meybe it wus just the novelty of having the privacy.

Mae internal wrath reminded me often of the ham of stage acting. I tread the wooden boards, I'm stood near the wings, cap in hand staring out at the barely lit audience. Juliette is suspiciously absent, and yet I've spotted her ex, Cameron, brooding in the third row. I've no lines in this scene. I must merely maintain a backburner of rage, which is never a problem.

I fix on Cam, thinking.

'Why is he like me and I like him?!'

Moody, arrogant, over-confident tu the point of being a farce. Both born tu be in a spotlight that they hate and relish equally. But the theatre wus an outlet for mae conceited anger at least, and a way tu meet women. Now what did I have? An unyielding bad mood and a desperate dick.

* * * * * * *

NO ONE GETS POINTS FOR STATING THE OBVIOUS

Simian Thomas, The Midlands

The train pulled into a village station early in the morning. Inside my half-waking brain I heard Freddie tell us we'd be there for a few hours. Still I couldn't wake up. The bunk was warm and cosy, swallowing me up. It was barely light outside yet. The winter failed to tempt me outside, tapping icy fingers on the glass.

But we had no food and I wasn't going to get away with being the lazy slob.

"Oi," Claudia poked the covers with an accusing witchy finger. "Get the fuck out of bed."

She said it in that deadpan voice that she uses most of the time, so you're never quite sure how serious she is. She can change from joking to angry at the flick of a switch. But I know I need her jokes and I need her anger, because I feel so void of emotion sometimes.

I was busy thinking this and still forgetting to move.

"Oi," she said again.

I sat up, pulling the blankets and duvets up around my shoulders. They put the heat fans on twice a day on the train, for very short periods. Once was in the morning, but it was still so cold to get out of bed. Everyone was kitting themselves out to go hunting, and it was surreal watching them. Claudia had an old police baton, complete with a clip to attach it to her belt. She pocketed various other tools – knives, nets, sacking – and put on an old pair of horse riding gloves, that were worn through at the finger tips.

She shot me a look – the definition of sultry. Claudia doesn't need to be intentional with this. It's just there. I rolled from my bunk, dropping with a thud. Socked foot meets vinyl floor. I imagined slipping through the lines in a vinyl record, as it spun. Lost in a language printed imperceptibly – an engraving. What would future archaeologists make of those discs...?

I was at liberty again. Able to have drifting, elusive thoughts and sleeps.

"Simian, wake up!"

I'd sat down to put boots on and slipped asleep again. I dreamed in black and purple vinyl. I looked up, wavering like a drunk.

"Whah?"

"Food," Claudia said sternly. "We need ta find food."

The others had left already, the cold outdoor air rushing into the carriage. I put on a coat, scarf and hat, scrambling through my pockets for gloves as she pushed me outside. I stood staring around. The concrete platform was littered with branches, stones and signs of a camp fire in the past, leaving an ashen black nest behind. The village was ruined, looking as though it might've been the same a hundred years ago. There were only remnants of snow left now – raised puddles of ice in despondent formations. I concentrated on where I trod as I followed Claudia, down across the train tracks which gleamed coldly.

Even with the icy air scratching my cheeks, I still felt sleepy. My companion was energized with a fresh, feisty determination. I trudged after her, wondering how, even if we found some animals, we would hunt them. The light was still weak as southern tea. There were even a few fog patches hovering wistfully about the trees and hedgerows. We were soon into fields, probably old livestock pasture, the grass glazed with unspoilt frost and the odd smidgen of snow.

Claudia stopped in her tracks and I nearly bumped into her.

"There!" she said softly, motioning with only her eyes so as to create as little movement as possible.

I peered out over the ridge of the field. Rabbits, loads of them, hoppity hopping, pawing at the frost to nibble the grass. Twitching and listening.

"How?" I asked.

Claudia crouched slowly, motioning me down too, and pulled something out of her pocket, that I had no idea she'd come by. Pub darts. I was shuddering awake now, hunger giving out a primordial growl.

"You won't be able to kill one with a dart will you? Won't it just hurt it and then it'll run into its burrow?" My brain was abuzz.

Her brow was furrowed.

"We could put nets on't burrows. But in doin so that would scare the rabbits off and they might not come out agen."

"Don't poachers use big nets to catch rabbits? Stretched across a large area of field?" I asked.

She nodded.

"I think we'll need some maire pairs of hands wi' this scheme. If we can catch several rabbits..." She drifted off, lost in thoughts of stews and dumplings.

* * * * * *

THE BRAINS TO PRESERVE YOUR OWN HIDE

Roxanne Ratcliffe, The Midlands

We'd carried a narrow log onto the platform and set it down next to our campfire, so that we might sit close and eat. But those at either end were too cold and had succumbed to sitting cross-legged on the concrete, in front of flames which danced and sparked inside my eyes. The brightness of them, their vivid colour, only served to make the abandoned village look bleaker.

Freddie and the other railway men – Smithy, Robbie and two others I hadn't picked up the names of – had leant us a kind of metal spit, and a large pan to hang from it over the fire. They'd also supplied onions, potatoes, cabbage and Bovril from their own supplies, so we could stew whatever rabbit meat we didn't barbeque, and make enough food to share between all ten of us.

The rabbit skins were discarded in a pile – the beautiful soft neutrals of the fur contrasting with streaks of brutal crimson where the insides showed.

"D'you know anything about how to treat animal skins, so we can use the fur?" I asked Freddie.

He beamed and shook his head. "But I know a couple what do. Been meaning to drag you lot to 'em today, to sort your footwear out." He removed his woollen hat, ruffled his dark blonde hair and put the hat back on again.

"Our footwear?"

"I can tell by the stench in that carriage someone 'uz gotta little trench foot, and the amount you lot have walked in boots, I'll bet you're blistered and bloody."

I nodded, maintaining a curious face.

"A bloke and his wife live here in the village, got a little set-up goin. They used to run a Cobblers shop before the Weathers. Now they've seen a great gaping hole in the market they've expanded their expertise – looking into the production of leather and so-on. Making things from scratch the old-fashioned way."

"Brilliant," I said, feeling that weight of dumb luck again.

Though a pessimistic Roxanne would've thought it was coming a bit late, given she'd already nearly lost a toe. I'd finished eating, and poked my head in the cooking pot. There was still some stew left to offer this couple, though I doubted that was much payment for what we were asking.

It was late afternoon now. The rabbit hunting and cooking had swallowed most of the day. I remembered the sack-full of wool we had from when we'd killed a sheep. We hadn't known how to make shearling so we'd cut the wool from the skin and thrown the skin away. I brought some of this as along extra payment. Claudia carried the rabbit skins with a wrinkled nose. Despite the wall of disgust I'd need to hammer down to learn this sort of thing, I felt quite excited. The idea of using every part of an animal killed (like Native Americans did) appealed to me. We could no longer afford to waste valuable resources.

We walked the village as we had done earlier, unable to see any signs that it was still inhabited. It lay mostly in ruins, already weathered away to the barest essentials. Some homes were merely foundations outlining where they used to be, the materials having been looted and taken away (possibly by the railway men themselves). The place was as grey and blank as the sky above it, standing solemnly in mute grief.

"It was like Pompeii or sommat when we first got here," Freddie said. "Nobody alive, just lots of stuff."

Ahead there was a wall about eight feet high. In the middle of the wall was a single lone door. It was wooden, but greened with moss. We'd passed it by before, and I'd looked at it, but it looked like an old front door used as a gate rather than a door to a building. Freddie knocked. (Even his knock had a cheerfulness to it.)

A woman answered. She had woolly grey hair and a face that had a leathery quality itself. I wondered if being around substances used to treat leather did this to you. She smiled at Freddie, but said nothing, waving us inside. Once in, we stood cramped awkwardly in a workshop space crammed with tables and tools, boots and tack for horses, and materials in various states of preparation for use. It smelt at first just leathery, but then an indescribable smell hit the back of my throat which was something else entirely. I couldn't pinpoint it, deciding it must be a combination of noxious substances.

A man was busy working in the shop and simply glanced at us as though we were disturbing him. Freddie acted like a tourists' guide, explaining how they'd salvaged all this stuff to set up the workshop, and how eventually they hoped to have a mobile cobbler and leather shop inside a train carriage, to travel the country selling wares. I was too busy puzzling over the various objects and tools to listen to the particulars. The woman stood watching me, blinking with the slow patience of a cat.

I gave her the wool, and took the open metal container of stew off Simian and gave this to her as well.

"We've some rabbit skins and I was hoping to learn how to treat them, so they may be used for lining or sommat," I said to her.

"How long are you stayin?" she asked.

Freddie shrugged.

"We're leaving at nightfall. The weather's good so it makes sense to keep going."

I looked back at the woman hopefully.

"It takes a lot of time, dear. It would take days, probably weeks to show you because it's cold." She paused apologetically. "Derek, can she 'ave that book you've got? You're done wirrit aren't you?"

The man looked up at me, unsmiling, still grumpy at having been disturbed. He had a beard and red nose and looked a bit gnome-like. A grumpy gnome.

He sighed.

"We'll keep one of your skins in exchange. You won't learn it quick either! It's a lot of trial and error."

"It's a lot of trial and error, dear," the woman repeated. "The number of hides I've ruined learning is no odds to no one. But they're only little skins and you're only using them for lining." She rummaged around some shelves and pulled out a scruffy book. "Now different animals, different skins. Some are tougher, some gentler. This book is mostly about making leather, so be careful. You don't need to lime them, liming takes the fur off! If you're not working on them today it's best to salt them. Have you got salt?"

I was frozen to the spot, trying to commit to memory everything she was saying. I shook my head. She shuffled off and came back with a bag of salt. The grumpy gnome glared at her.

"Now then, dear." She left a hand resting on top of mine and I noticed her old lace fingerless gloves and the shawl that draped down over her arms. "Use the brains of the animal to help treat the skin. With leather you soak the whole thing, but fur I think you have to keep pasting it in layers and scraping it off again. You'll need lots of clean water all the way through the process, so I would stay by a stream to do it."

"Brains?" I said, a lump forming in my throat.

"Yes, dear. You can use eggs instead, but you've killed an animal, you've got the brains there as a ready resource."

"It's a no-brainer really!" Freddie quipped. I was too stunned to even smile.

"It's all in the book, dear." She tapped my hand which held the book.

The book was titled *Traditional Tanning and Treatment of Animal Hides*. The cover showed a sepia image of a Native American, with an animal skin stretched out inside a frame.

"Right, on to the business of feet!" Freddie announced.

* * * * * * *

A SERIES OF IMPLAUSIBLE COINCIDENCES

Wolfgang, Dreamscape

I draw, with blind fingers, the eyes and teeth of a dog. He's snarling at the sky. An emotional reaction to the brutality the world inflicts upon him. Drips of saliva spray from his mouth in little love heart shapes. Miss you like a maelstrom.

I put a record on, real vinyl. Remembering that old gramophone playing out Spanish blues to the ruins of a German city. Dresden, your heart is mine. Or maybe just a little spit – nothing concrete, no lifelong commitment.

The song I play in the present is *October* by Jackson C. Frank.

"Prepare for the depths of your heart to sing to you," I say.

I paint their faces Max Beckmann-style in the gloom. Watching me with black holes for eyes, cheeks painted rouge to cover the grey white pallor. I dream of cabaret... or of the circus.

I try to tell things in the order that they happen, but time is slippery as a fish in the human conscience. Fingers on the strings. They listen in a silence already over.

"You like this miserablist music, Wolfgang?"

I nod and grin manically, like a deceased man strung up on puppet strings.

"I can't deal with music that isn't a little bit miserablist," Roxy says.

I realise today that she is indeed a little witch. She's looking at the cover of the book I write in, jagged black and white pattern, a little tweedy if you know what I mean. She lifts those pale blue eyes to me, with that little ghostly face.

"Dog tooth," she says. "It's my favourite pattern."

'Dog-tooth,' I mouth the words silently with new meaning. Little Roxy snaps her fingers and the worn brown seats of the carriage are all of a sudden the same pattern – black and white and grey teeth gnashing one another, grinding away in their sleep.

"Now I shall keep losing my book, little Roxy," I say.

She nods with quiet conviction. How shall I commit thee to paper? How shall I remember to speak of Dresden, of ruins, ruffians, brutalities and all my favourite themes? Of dog teeth chewing on the pages of photographs and drawings of the dogs themselves, of postcards written and never sent?

"Toby Roe is dead," I say. I see the grey bearded dog lying down, smiling; his eyes slowly close with the knowledge that he is finally alone, as every living creature.

"You can't kill what was never real," Roxy says.

Little Roxy snapped her fingers in front of my face, but this time was not for magic. She was trying to wake me from a waking dream, my eyes were doing R.E.M, even though they were open. Folks have mistaken this for a fit before. I try to think of it as a party trick I have no control over.

"Are you dreaming, Wolfie?"

I paused meaningfully, looked hazily around the carriage.

"I'm a dreaming man."

"You said Toby Roe was dead." Roxy's bottom lip was stuck out.

My eyes focused on her and drew the real world around me, filled in all the gaps and put her into context, of the time as well as the space and all that had already happened.

"The dog, not the man, the original Toby Roe. Don't worry." I pawed her shoulder. "We'll find them, we seem to be lost in a series of implausible coincidences."

"*Them?*" Claudia said suspiciously.

"Toby and the other one...?" I looked over to Simian who was lying on the seat looking glum and useless, he quickly found his little notebook and searched for the names he'd copied in.

"Aiden Antoine!"

"Yes that one." I looked at Claudia. "You mentioned before that you knew him, the Blonde Adonis?"

"It's *Haydn Antoine.*" Her face was contorted subtly with the strange anger of someone who felt they were losing grip on reality. "How d'ya know what'ee looks lyke?" Her voice was cold.

"I saw him in my mind's eye. He's very handsome." I said.

Roxy put her arm around Claudia in an attempt to reassure.

"Are you psychic?" Claudia leaned away from Roxanne doubtfully.

"All blind men are," I said.

"Yar not blind."

I reached up with a dirty yellow finger to poke myself in the eye, as if to find out. "Oh." I paused, a little confused. "Don't you feel like we've a collective subconscious by now anyway?"

I should just keep my mouth shut. But in all the confusion I tend to forget what I'm supposed to know. Besides, there was a flicker of admission in their faces at the final statement. We all meet in each others' dreams.

* * * * * * *

DOLLY BUZZARDS

Claudia McLeod, The Midlands

Part a'tha hillside had collapsed. From a distance it looked lyke an ugly face openin its mouth very wide and spewin mud and debris. A great mudslide'd tekken place at some point. It was visible where the railway men'ud dug through this before, but rains an thaws between passages had caused maire mud to slide. I could read the frustration in their fizzogs, as they wearily unpacked spades and buckets and wheelbarrows.

I admired their endless determination to maintain the East Coast Mainline. Freddy hadn't exaggerated about the slow progress a travel. Sometimes we would help clear the tracks and half a mile on around a bend, haffta stop agen and do the sayme. I appreciated how they'd set thissels this endless task, and seen possibilities in't ruined landscape astead'a bein weighed down wi' the impossible (like soo many).

Robbie stood next t'me leanin on a spade and stared at the mud on the tracks.

"We built a bit of a wall last time we cleared this bit. That was a waste of time, eh?"

I nodded, not really knowin what t'say, puzzlin over a useful strategy.

"We were hoping that it'd been so cold since the last time, the ground would stay frozen. Looks like the rain the last few days was enough to fix that. When snow melts it just waterlogs the ground, everywhere's saturated." He smiled wearily.

"Oi, Robbie, gerra wriggle on!" Smithy shouted. "No time for chattin to the dolly birds now, work to do!"

"Sorry," Robbie said t'me, probably knowin from my fayce I weren't too happy wi' the term 'dolly bird'.

Robbie considered hissel the civilised one among the men. He had a bulky frame, and judgin by't way his skin sculpted raggedly around his features, had probably been on't tubby side afore convenience food became extinct. I lyked all a'tha men really though. Smithy jus enjoyed bein obnoxious and livin up to the white-van-man stereotype.

I pulled on a pair a cellar gloves which I'd looted from't Red Deer 'fore we left Sheffield. I began helpin shovel muck inta'a wheelbarrow and separatin bricks and bits a wood off into other piles. I glanced over at Charlie, who was workin wi'a shovel several metres away. His back was still hurtin him from the beatin he took in Milton Keynes, and I could read the constricted jars of pain innis fayce each time he lifted't spade. It were a waste a words to tell him t'go easy though. He had to prove ta'tha men he were worth his weight.

It began to drizzle again and my fayce felt proper parky. I kept workin steadily to keep wahrm, squelchin across the mud and man-handlin the wheelbarrow as it tried to slide off the wrong way. I grunted and swore and gritted ma teeth, and Smithy smirked at me, but said nowt.

Findin the railway tracks beneath the muck felt akin to discoverin precious metal, but we were still a way off finishin, as we needed to mekk sure the section was passable. Charlie'd already started diggin a foundation for a new barricade – sinkin upright logs, and attachin chicken wire – when it began ta piss it down wi'rain.

"Break!" Freddie shouted.

We walked back tu't train, and sat inside dryin off and watchin the rain ruin the work we'd done. Roxy, Simian and Wolfgang arrived back, draggin between them a sodden, clarty sheep carcass. They dumped this just inside't door and came through ta the engine carriage where the rest ayus were sat nursin tea and lookin glum.

"The sheep was already dead. D'you think it'll be okay to eat?" Roxy asked.

"Depends what killed it. Might be diseased," Charlie said.

"It's got a broken leg and was part buried, so we think it got caught in a mudslide," Simian explained.

Smithy sipped his tea, listenin.

"Proper little scavengers, you lot," he teased.

It was easier for them to get food the traditional way, through tradin. We knew they rarely carried much meat though. It were hard to come by. Simian mayde the face he mekks when he dislikes someone, like he's mentally buryin them.

"Should I wait for it to dry off before I skin it?" Roxanne asked.

"Ay up, she's already eyeing up the skin for booties," Smithy said.

"Stop bein a piss artist, Smith," said the bloke I think was called Dave. "They've been dead useful recently. This one worked like a trooper today," he nodded ta me.

"Aye, she swore like a trooper too!" Smithy said quickly. They chuckled and not knowin a better reaction, I shrugged proudly.

* * * * * *

SCENES OF MILD PERIL

Bryn McLarey, The Midlands

The Earth rumbled, echoing in the landscape around us. The sound passed through rocks and hillsides, sweeping through woodlands. The ears of rodents and rabbits would be flickering in warning as they dashed from open fields tu burrows tu tremble and feel the storm inside the bedrock. We'd experienced this tuu many times in our lives now – storms that felt more leik earthquakes.

The light wus dimming, sae I knew the train would stop soon anywhey. It'd become tuu dangerous tu travel after dark, as nice-guy Freddie and his crew had passed this bit a longer time ago. They were less sure of the stability of the line.

But the train continued steadily, and the threatening horizon blackened and purpled in fury. Then we were swept intu darkness, and I realised we'd entered a tunnel in the hillside. There the train stopped. Freddie came inta the carriage.

"Sounds like there's a storm coming," he said in understatement. "To protect the train, it's best it stays in the tunnel. But as I'm sure you're aware, there's the risk of the tunnel collapsing for whatever reason. So if you want to seek shelter elsewhere, that's up to you." He paused, tu see if we had anything ta say.

"I'm not sure anyone fancies going outside in this wind and building a shelter that may also collapse in the night," I said.

He nodded.

"Afraid we can't risk having the lights on or owt, so a few candles only, and please be careful with them. Setting your carriage on fire is really *not* a good idea at this point!"

He retreated back towards carriage B again.

We lit a handful of candles set inside a small saucepan on the table, and huddled around. It wus probably only about five o'clock in the afternoon. It would be a long night holed up there. Roxy got out a pack of battered playing cards, of which we all knew the Seven of Hearts and the King of Spades were missing. We started playing Black Jack all the same, tu pass the time.

The winds still whistled down the tunnel, rattling the windows, causing the flames tu flicker and falter. I pondered our similarities tu the rodents – huddling underground, hoping for the best. As the carriage rocked on its wheels, I imagined how much worse it wus outside. I wondered whether there would be a blizzard, or hail, or rain, or quite possibly all of them at different times. I tried ta give an image tu every sound that moved through the earth and bricks around us – old trees wrenched from the hillside, their roots exposed and vulnerable, debris whipped up in the wind and slammed against the bank. But I could only speculate. We might've been blocked in already, and wouldn't know it until morning (or worse until we realised we were running out of air).

We pretended tu concentrate on the card game, but nobody really was.

"If the hillside does cave in, will the roof hold?" Simian asked, morbidly.

"Depends on the ways and reasons the hillside collapses..." Claudia said. "But they've reahlly reinforced this train, lyke a bomb shelter. It's survived this long, after all."

Later Robbie brought some tinned tomato soup through for us tu share. We opened the tins and propped them over the candles tu warm them up a bit, and then as we were wearing gloves anyway, ate straight from the cans, cradling them tu warm our hands.

We were getting weary now, the heavy darkness and the candle light causing eyes tu blink with sleep. Though we dared not fall asleep, because we were scared of being buried alive. We stayed crammed in the seats for warmth, and readiness ta move if we needed tu. Roxy rested her head on mae shoulder, I stroked her hair absentmindedly, but I could feel myself slipping away. The carriage still rocked with the wind, and the earth still shuddered around us, but it lulled me, and mae dreams began ta merge with the carriage. Mae eyes kept opening again, from time tu time. I wus convinced I could see the roof collapsing on us in slow motion. But in the paralysis of sleep I couldnae move tu save us, and wasn't sure how real it wus anywhey. I wus vaguely aware of the scenario repeating itself over and over.

There was a sharp crunching sound, sometime later, and I opened mae eyes. Only one candle wus still lit, and it wus almost deid – fading – unable tu illuminate anything other than its wick. Apart from that there wus only blackness and emptiness, as though we were hovering in a great void. Roxy's head wus still rested on mae chest, the reassuring weight pressed against mae heartbeat. I kissed her forehead and closed mae eyes.

In a half-dream state I accepted death.

I woke tu Claudia swearing, which in itself wasn't unusual. She had the torch out, which we only ever used in emergencies, due tu not having a ready supply of batteries.

She had the window of the carriage door open, letting cruel air in. I guessed she wus trying ta open the door, but it seemed tu be jammed or sumthin. I cudnae exactly make out what she wus up tu in the gloom, only highlighted in strips as the torch jerked around frantically.

"Whas going on?" I asked.

I realised Roxy wus gone from mae side and the spooky shape of Simian wus slumped against the window opposite me, possibly just asleep.

"I jus reahlly need the fookin lav and someone's in it!" Claudia said, as though I ought tu know this already.

I sighed, smiling at the mundane. I clambered from mae seat, and walked down the passage precariously, shins exposed in the poor light tu any number of blunt objects. I reached the door, and Claudia stepped aside grumpily. I poked mae hand out, grasping the handle and at the same time kicking the inside of the door in a precise spot. The door creaked open.

"There's a knack tu it," I said ta Claudia.

The door often went stiff in the cold, she knew this of course, and me patronising her (however jokingly) did nothing tu cheer her up.

"Dick," she said.

I smiled cheekily tu maeself, glad she probably couldn't see. I stepped down carefully intu the tunnel after her, following the figure with the torchlight as it bounced around. There wus a second track in the tunnel, which I nearly decked it on. Then I found mae feet between rails and followed the sleepers out of the tunnel inta the feeble daylight.

The damage tu the world outside wus meybe less than I expected. I squinted at the landscape. The direction of the ferocious wind wus visible where the collected debris wus strewn and caught up. Previous storms had already picked off most of the weak spots in woodlands though.

The only real sign of the terribleness of the storm showed in exposed trees caught by lightening – twisted black and silver like some Gothic art.

The high-vis orange vests of the railway-men were dotted around, as they surveyed the damage with a more professional eye. There wus a'course, plenty of rubbish on the train tracks ahead that would need tu be cleared.

Dave appeared, ambling towards me with a grin.
"Get to try the blowers out today."
"The blowers?" I asked.
"We salvaged an old litter-cart," he explained. "You know how they blow rubbish in a certain direction so the sweepers catch it?"

I nodded.

"We gonna try to attach them to the front, to blow the litter off the tracks as we go. The smaller stuff anyway. We was workin on it last night, for sommat to do to pass the time."

* * * * * * *

DEAD MAN'S BOOTS

Wolfgang, The Midlands

Ideal hands make laughter work. My life is like a bucket of jokes being kicked down the stairs. I gazed from the train window down into the flooded woodland where trees grew out of the water. Like in the Amazon, but a tad chillier.

'*Chilli = Hot. Chilly = Cold.*' One of the language exercises Brian taught me.

The hum of the train, like being inside a giant bumble bee, one who purrs away and bee-lines towards pretty flowers who drop their eyes coyly.

I missed the flaxen autumn, the dry bracken that cracked and crunched underfoot as I strolled through the woodland, collecting berries. The autumn has a sense of expectation about it, an optimism matured in white oak barrels. The winter expects only the worst. More ice, more rain, more empty bones.

Something about riding trains always quietened me and made me feel alone with my thoughts. And here we were on a train for days on end, and I was still captured inside of my thoughts, though they spilled out of my overflowing teacup onto the page. My mouth moved and I made small noises, eyes turned and pondered the noises that'd formed language. I was writing in German and thus speaking in German. I'd slid in my quietude, back into thinking in the mother tongue.

"Wie gehts?" Cuan asked.

But then I remembered Cuan was deceased. It was some other schlank creature with cheekbones sharp enough to hang your hope on.

We'd stopped. The sun was spectacular here where the train had pulled into an old station to refuel. I was given pause to stare out beyond, where the tracks curved into my vision at the end of the crumbling platform. They stretched away into the distance in neat, ordered lines turned electric white by the sun, and set against all those subtle neutrals – greys and browns – with the hazy backlighting behind branches. There were even a few vulnerable leaves clinging to the trees.

"Shit," a voice said.

It was the Kaiser, pointing. There was a body on the platform, half concealed, lying idly under a broken bench. Barely noticeable, like the furniture.

We'd all seen many dying and dead in our recent lives. But something about the casual nature of the body was still disturbing. It must've been the cold. Most vagabonds that froze did so hidden away in some hole they chose, to sleep and dream and never wake. Maybe he'd collapsed from exhaustion, or had some injury, or maybe he waited for a train that never came. Waited and waited, and then lay down and waited some more.

Kaiser arose, walked to the door and wrenched it open. He stepped purposefully off the train with that ruthless look. He rolled the body over, swept fingers over the face to close the man's eyes, and then turned his back to us as he dropped his chin and made the sign of the cross.

He returned quickly to cold, hard motives, checking pockets and socks and returning with his loot. In fact he even took the boots of the man, which were in good nick (not to be sniffed at when you've walked miles with toes poking out of holes).

"Size 9, I think?" he said, back on the train.

"Bitte!" I raised a hand.

He plonked them on the table in front of me. I examined them – combat boots, good soles. No blood at least.

Other items were laid out on the table: a whisky flask (a third full); a pocket knife; a hand gun; some ammunition; and a very battered old postcard from Sea World, Florida, headed *'Having a Whale of a time!'* Roxy picked this latter object up and began trying to read the scrawl on the back.

"Shouldn't we bury him?" Claudia asked, still staring at the body.

"How very Christian..." the Kaiser said.

"It's maire a hygiene thing."

"Is he still fresh? I expect dogs or foxes will find him soon," Roxanne said.

The Kaiser nodded. "I think he probably died in the night. He doesn't smell tuu bad yet, but I suppose the cold's preserving him... And it's not leik many people pass through here anywhey..."

I continued looking at my new boots thoughtfully. The cobbling couple we'd met a few days before had recommended moccasins for walking long distances in the future. In fact the little woman (who'd reminded me of Mrs. Tiggywinkle) had rattled off a list of footwear we ought to be wearing for our travels. We couldn't of course afford to buy moccasins from them. Freddie had bought them for us, but was keeping them for a time when we could pay him for them. Nor could we afford galoshes to go over the moccasins if it was wet. The woman had suggested a separate pair of seal-skin moccasins would be ideal for wetter weather also, as this type of skin was easy to waterproof and didn't go brittle in the cold. But she and her husband had no current access to dead seals, being stranded inland and all.

All in all it'd felt a bit like having a carrot being dangled in front of you and then being told all you could have was a knobbly bit of wood painted orange to chew on. The donkey wouldn't be happy with that.

The Kaiser was also examining *his* new toy – the gun.

"Have you ever used a gun before?" Simian asked.

We all expected a yes, regardless of the truth.

"I went clay pigeon shooting a couple of times, back in the Oxford days." He made a skewed smile. "It's not exactly the same though, is it?"

* * * * * * *

CINDERS

Roxanne Ratcliffe, The Midlands

Grey yellow faces and eggshells treading soft footsteps.
 Tread softly, you tread on my deeds. Bad deeds resolved with ashen colours, smudged greys into tiny dots of red, two red eyes glowing in the dark, like two cigarette ends. But there was no tobacco left today and a sense of dread was building, the slow tension of a film that lets you know something awful this way comes.
 Simian was suddenly at my shoulder like some skinny meek shadow. As though littlest Roxy might offer some protection from the smokers unable to smoke. He whispered in my ear, attracting black-eyed glares from Charlie.
 "It's Wolfgang I'm worried about. The other two are predictable, they'll just be mean and grumpy."
 I nodded conspiratorially.
 Wolfgang grinned a black grin from across the room as though he knew our fears. He rose to his feet and left the carriage. Charlie and Claudia shifted restlessly, dragon breath puffed into the air.
 "Well! Speak! I hayte this fookin silence, ya soft beggars," Claudia said.
 Simian giggled and shrunk further behind me.
 "Whatever, Simian. You wouldn't laff at a smack'ead doin cold turkey. *I feel so ill.*"
 "I'm not laughing at you."
 Wolfgang returned and sat in the same dark corner, next to the water tank on a stool. He sat with his leg poised angular, ankle disjointedly resting on the other knee. He had a pipe. He held it by the bottom like an old hand, tapping the mouth-piece against his teeth. The other two looked at him with a fast-fading question. He had no

tobacco, only the pipe. He sat and tapped and when he did speak he waved it in the air emphatically. It was something to busy his hands.

Simian left my side and Claudia immediately slipped in and replaced him.

"I know you don't have a sexual appetite or owt," she whispered. "I'm gettin a bit... y'know?"

"Desperate?" I suggested.

She shrugged as though it was an agreeable enough description. I looked at the men folk – Charlie cracking his knuckles and thinking murderous thoughts, Simian giggling skittishly like he might loop the loop, Wolfgang far beyond the loop.

"You're not getting *that* desperate, are you?"

"Fucking whispering," Charlie's voice growling like a storm threatening to break across the mountains.

We would both jump startled as the wind caught the open window and slammed it into the wall. But the windows were not of a building. The train trundled into a tunnel and there was no storm. Only the icy dusk outside.

I paused over the strange slips between realities, supposing it was just exhaustion. I'd felt that way for a while though. Poor diet doesn't lead to a lively brain.

Simian hovered, waiting to sit by me again, offering some of the Scotch he'd got in exchange for an old mountain bike he'd found. I was dumbfounded that he'd not exchanged it for a pair of comfy, warm moccasins.

Claudia decided to let him have the seat but not without spitting fur.

"Why does she get some?"

"Whisky is for comrades not enemies. Maybe if you asked nicely." He cowered.

She snatched the bottle from him. I imagined her swallowing it whole, opening her mouth and gullet like a snake. She just took a slug and then shoved it back at us.

"Do you think we should've kept the bike? Might've been more use in time." I asked.

"Nah," Simian mumbled without explanation. I supposed only one person could ride it and we all planned to stick together.

"Look me straight in the fookin eyes fa once," Charlie said.

Was he talking to me? Yes, it seemed. I'd been avoiding his gaze, but then I often do. I looked at him very closely now, reading his intentions. In the dimness his black irises dispersed their blackness into the whites. I saw only loathing for himself which he seemed to want to see reflected in my eyes. But I refused to mirror his negativity. I absorbed some of it instead, this didn't satisfy him.

"Why d'you always look at me like that? What have I done wrong?" he asked.

"You're the one glaring at me," I said.

I could feel Sim breathing at my shoulder. Charlie looked sorrowed and frustrated. It was all getting a bit too intense at times, us all being around each other so much.

The yellowed vacuum of the evening crawled slowly onward once the train had stopped. We waited for the ashen dawn. Wolfgang tap tapped his pipe. He was the picture of nonchalance, not out of step to any other day.

"Why a'ya not sufferin?!" Claudia asked.

He grinned his black grin at her.

"Cold turkey, my little chicken, is just another form of madness which has long since possessed me." He picked up his hat and placed it at a crooked angle on his head, eyes turning glazed as they grinned on into some other violent abyss.

* * * * * * *

SKULDUGGERY

Bryn McLarey, The Midlands

"Tell me again about your dream," Wolfgang says.

His face is warped by the fiercely cold wind, whipping around us in predatory circles. I see strange clarity in each crease that maps out his face, the stringy skin around his jowls, the crows feet that shuffle in the corners of eyes sae chillin'ly blue. Like the blue inside ice.

"There were dead bodies everywhere, like there had been a war or atomic bomb or sumthin... We were living in a shelter made of corrugated iron. The only food we had wus when rabbits jumped in the windows. We were slowly dying of rabbit starvation..." I want tu continue but the wind is sae harsh, ripping twigs off trees and dashing them at us. It picks up a ragged cloak that wus caught in branches and throws it over our heads. Everything turns black.

I wus right underneath the blankets – that much I could gather. My body wus straining tu filter the oxygen. I must've fallen asleep reading about *Brer Rabbit* outwitting the fox and the wolf. I wriggled around tu try tu find mae torch, it wasnae there. Meybe Mum'd found me asleep and turned off the torch and put the book on mae bedside table. I felt annoyed. She wudnae'v marked the page I wus on, I'd have tu find it again. I poked mae head out from the covers and the daylight made me immediately aware of bein inside mae adult face. I'd aged nearly thirty years in a heartbeat. The compression of everythin that'd happened in those thirty years deflated around me.

I sighed the heavy sigh of age and cynicism. I wus the only one awake, but the train had stopped. At least I thought I wus the only one awake, but when I slid from mae bunk I saw that Wolfgang wus crouched on his haunches in his seat, like some sort of gargoyle on the eaves of a Gothic building. He wus staring at his blank, open notebook. Outside wind and drizzle were battering the window – the weather had probably transcended mae dreams.

"What're yuu doin?" I asked Wolfgang.

He didnae seem tu register that he wasn't alone, but after a pause, still staring at the page, he said.

"I had writers' block sitting down. I thought crouching might help."

He tipped hus heid tu one side. His hair wus strangely immobilised, as though the dirt and grease held it as firmly as vile Eighties hairspray.

"It doesnae look leik it has," I said.

I longed for music tu greet mae mornings, music and the smell of bacon.
Wolfgang flicked his jaw-line in idle concentration, the sound of his finger nail hitting the bone seemed strangely loud.

"Christ, I'm ravenous." I slumped down in one of the seats opposite.

I looked about fa mae boots. At least I had a gun now. Hopefully that would make it easier tu hunt things, although I'd have tu get pretty close. I tried tu think how many metres away it would be effective from, and measure the distance visually.

"Remember in Belfast when that ginger kid pointed a gun at us?" I asked Wolfgang suddenly, chuckling tu maesel. "I fuckin bricked it!"

"When did you go to Belfast?" Roxy peered over sleepily, from one of the lower beds.

"I think it wus the same summer of the first Sheffield floods," I said. "Or wus it the year after? Pissed with rain most a' the time anywhey!"

"Why were you in Belfast?" she asked.

"Wolfgang kept winning holidays, jammy fooker," I said.

"I entered four hundred and twenty-three competitions that year," Wolfgang said. "I won three holidays."

"It wus a BB gun in the end," I said, going back tu mae story. "It wus on Falls Road and everythin."

Roxanne tipped her head over the side of the bunk tu peer at the floor, making sure ta keep the covers up tu her neck, sae as not tu let the chill in. Her mousey hair flopped tu one side, showing the smallness of her skull. I marvelled at its petite-ness, the same way a person might hold a baby bird and marvel at how small a vertebrate can be.

"Where are my shoes...?" she mumbled tu herself.

There wus a muffled screaming noise from outside the carriage. Looking up I realised the train wus parked in an exposed manner, causing the ferocious wind ta whip and whine around it, knocking on windows and moaning about Monday morning blues.

"Not even sure I want tu go out in that." I tugged boots onta painfully raw feet. They'd long shriveled inta deep wrinkles, from all the walking we'd done in wet, cold weather. While much of the blistering had healed sum, from resting on the train, taking the boots on and off wus still the most painful part of mae day. I ground mae teeth and the vibrations continued through mae skull.

As though realising I might be of use tu break his writing block, Wolfgang tapped mae shoulder across the table.

"Tell me again about your dream," he said.

* * * * * * *

A DISTORTED REALITY IS NOW...

Roxanne Ratcliffe, South Yorkshire

The train chunters along the track, its back and forth movement singing *'you'll never go back, you'll never go back... go back, go back... you'll never go back, you'll never go back'*. Once you hear this pattern a first time, you will always hear it over and over. Sometimes it drives the pulse of madness in your ears, sometimes it's a comforting familiar, pushing you to slumber.

The landscape altered mood and movement. The horizon dipped and slipped away revealing the drop next to the tracks. A vertiginous image emerged of fragile mists tumbling to acres of backbreaking rock, a bloody-knuckled landscape of ice and crags and blue shadows. A fleetful glimpse captured a lone man with his hood up, pondering the pages of a map. I pressed my forehead to the window. It was cold. A cold frame writing a visual story of the radically changed landscape. Click... click... I'd run out of film for my camera, but I continued to perform the act of taking photos with it. It continued to focus images and make that satisfying noise which claimed the moment lost.

We'd been living in the railway carriage for days turning weeks now. The distance of our journey would once have taken a few hours at the most, but like everything, bits of the old lines had become broken, or landslides had caused blockages. So the train would shunt to a halt and the railway men in orange vests would get out and investigate, deciding on courses of action, repairing rails and removing blockages. Sometimes we moved on in a matter of hours, sometimes it took a day or two. When the train moved, it did so slowly because there were so many hazards. We constantly faced the danger of crash or derailment.

One day there was a great shudder through the skeleton of our home. A noise began ahead of us, racing through the carriages, which sounded like metal screaming. We clung to the seats and the walls. I fainted momentarily from shock, and woke dribbling like a rag doll in Simian's one free arm. The train had stopped. The driving carriage seemed to have attached itself between two trees which'd prevented it careering fully off the tracks and crashing someplace worse. Freddie came climbing through into our carriage, tutting and shaking his head as though this were a mild irritation.

"We all alreet?" he gruffed.

We glanced to each other's minor cuts and bruises and nodded.

"Fraid you'll have to all gerroff, folks, while we fix t'all. Thes an old stationary carriage on a siding, bout half a mile away. You can live there fura few days, and we'll come fetch'y when wev worked out whassup."

"What's up?" Charlie muttered when Freddie had left. "The train is in a fucking tree, that is what is up."

We wrapped ourselves in every coat and blanket and scarf we had, like a crew of bag ladies hunchbacked by their clothes and possessions. We stepped out into the wind, which pinched cheeks with its cruel nails, whipping hats from heads and taunting the hair set free. We stepped carefully along the tracks, which were surrounded by a tunnel of bare forest. Stark branches that should've given way to views gave only more branches, gnarling and twisting every which-way. The tracks descended further into the woods and became more sheltered, the wind lessening its seedy whispering in my ears.

I looked to each face as we walked in silence, considering how we'd all changed over time.

Simian, always the skinniest, looked more deathly than ever. His hair was brown but had an unearthly auburn sheen. His high haughty cheekbones made him look like Bowie playing the alien Tommy Newton, and as with the character, he had a habit of not returning looks, sometimes sentences. He almost seemed to ignore communication for long periods, as though it was just white noise and images merging to static.

An increasing ruthlessness seemed to possess Claudia. She'd learned the *'law of club and fang'* all too quickly and easily. As though the brutality of her environment had to be met with her dead calm gaze. Her faded blonde hair, which crept from each corner of a fur-lined hood, did nothing to create a deception of innocence.

Charlie... a sense of powerlessness churning inside his catharticism. His eyes, coldly black, swallowed the whites. His curly dark hair which, growing again, made him look more like a tortured romanticist poet than an angry vagrant.

And Wolfgang. Wolfgang hadn't changed at all. He was born for this life – the life of the uncertain broken society and world flipped onto its back (legs in the air kicking like a frantic tortoise). Nobody would've looked at him twice now, no eccentricity assumed from his dress sense or hairy odour. No pretentiousness assumed from his philosophical nonesensities, or fearfulness at his apparent madness. Everybody was a bit mad these days.

He felt my eyes, and turned to me whispering. *"Our brains ache in the merciless iced east winds that knive us... wearied we stay awake because the night is silent..."* He left a long pause which let me shiver and find space to hear the quiet wind, and note that it was not night, and yet it was silent as it ought. *"But nothing happens..."*

We reached the carriage. Charlie, ever alpha, pointed sharply at the shape amongst the mangled trees. We climbed haphazardly through brush with all that we carried, muttering and swearing. Charlie dropped his things and began to wrench debris from the doorway where the truck sat alone on a scrap of track overgrown on either side. It looked forever trapped and tied to the forest, burying foundations into wet rotting wood.

His sweat soon brought us a way into this oblong home. It was like stumbling into someone else's abode. Some of the old seating was already moved to line the walls with narrow bunks. The shelves, once designed for luggage, contained stacks and stacks of old books and here and there the odd object – a slide projector with a missing lens, a once decorative hookah now nearly crumbling. Objects that no-longer fitted their names because they could no longer perform their use.

In cinema, the characters stand staring at the strange room. Their entry has unsettled dust that billows like a momentary sand storm, sticking in throats and eyes, catching bits of low light and twinkling. Dust is mostly human skin. The scene fades out.

PHASE SIX

In which they are stranded in the woods & Claudia meets a horse & a pig.

NERVOUS SYSTEM

Simian Thomas, Yorkshire

It is cold. It is cold and I am afraid.

I once wanted to mostly be alone. After my Cassie died I wasn't sure if there was much point in the rest of humanity. I'm still not so sure. It's callous to feel this, I know. It may seem egocentric too, though I'm not sure that I'm worth anything either. I've spent a lot of time with myself and I discovered I'm not so fun to be around.

With these belly-button-gazing thoughts, I lay in the darkness. It was proper darkness, not like the kind I used to know living in the city. We were in the middle of woodland that had maybe been there hundreds of years. I visualised its slow growth in steady fast forward and this articulated my smallness – a mere vole, poking his nose out to check for danger.

The moonlight was so much more powerful when not competing with the false glow of street lights. But it failed now, the tangled canopy of trees and curved roofing of the carriage let little light down. When the sky clouded over, the darkness was close and let nothing in.

I heard soft movements and breathing in the darkness and it was reassuring. But it was a comfort repressed by fear, by a hand around my throat, a silent contorted scream that dissolved inside me.

I must've been halfway between sleep and wake. I longed for music. I used to play it loud, to block out everything in my head. I tried with slow concentration to hear a song, the layers of notes approaching me at different angles, a tiny voice stuttering to be heard.

I also longed strangely for artificial light – the ambient lamp. I used to be able to flick a switch and be reassured of where I was, of the objects sleeping around me, of the reality I inhabited. Without it I was placeless. I lay in a dark cold space, and the darkness and the coldness might last till morning or until next week.

I shifted inside my sleeping bag. The rustle of my own sound was both reassuring and disconcerting. I wasn't sure if I was real and could make movements so the sound might not be me. When it was this quiet a person might even hear noises of a higher frequency than usual. These noises puzzled me alone as a child. I wish someone had told me it was my own nervous system instead of letting me dwell on my irrational fears.

I remembered the classically simplistic ghost story of dreaming that you wake up and switch on the light and a man walks in. He sits and smokes and stares at you. Nothing happens, he's just there. You wake the next day, knowing it was just a dream, a strange unnerving dream – but your light is on and there's a little ash dropped on the table.

The man is Wolfgang, an elongated sneer spread on his face. He's no actualised threat, not wielding a chainsaw, not making a mask from human skin. He's just there, like the cold hand on your shoulder which causes you to shudder.

I drifted to dreams, and I'm staring out onto the inner city street bathed in the insomniac orange light of the street lamps. A still image of emptiness, movement is an illusion, nobody walks and no shadows are cast for me to escape inside of. I dream that I cannot sleep and I am inside a game which is on repeat. I forget the rules and apply them badly and my fingers miss the right notes. I woke again to the Blackness. Someone was fighting in their sleep.

Little demon fry my brain, make me wake and dream again. Make me slack as in a noose, cut my hopes up fast and loose, let them drown in a river bag, teach their wisdom to a hag, drag the flies from in my brain. Make me wake and dream again.

* * * * * * *

BAD FISH & GOODS 'SHROOMS

Wolfgang, Yorkshire

Somewhere between dragging my whisky soaked body from the bed and starting my working day, the two rooms have blurred. The sink of the restaurant kitchen has replaced my bedside table. I tip out some whitebait from a bag to defrost under running water, but find it contains scraps of seaweed and (what the devil?) a live sea snail that crawls out and peers at me with his little horny-horns.

"How are you not frozen?" I ask him, before feeling that tell-tale tickle of some creepy crawly on my hand.

I leap like a lord a-leaping, batting myself in deranged manner – suddenly surrounded by aphids, unseen swarms in the air but I can hear you and feel you. Even if you only exist in the scaly swamps of my subconscious – I know you're there!!!

451

I spasmed from sleep to my bedroom, wrenching my wretched self from the bed. But dawn told me that this was not my bedroom, I was in an old stationary railway carriage and my dream was of a lost past in which I was haunted by the ordinary.

"What's up?" Our Kaiser was sat, elbows on knees, chewing on an old pen casing with much self-loathing. Nothing to smoke.

"Bugs... aphids." I glanced around myself suspiciously. "Where is everyone?"

"Foraging. Or whatever."

"Ah... hunter-gather," I murmured. "Why are you still here?"

He shrugged in a bored, apathetic kind of way, like a teenager asked why he was sat inside on a sunny day.

"Do we still have tea?" I asked hopefully.

"A little, have ta wait til they get back with the firewood though."

I shook my head. "Ah, no. Amongst *Stig of the Dump's* collection I found this..."

I hastened to where I'd left the object, which looked not unlike a clay oil burner with a teapot seat on top. I had had tea made for me by an Indian fellow with one, once. Had it been in Mumbai or Stockport? I forget. With my clumsy blackened fingers, half covered with hobo's mittens, I inserted on the lower level the dregs of a candle. This I then lit, from a soggy pack of matches, before filling the teapot with water from our supply and returning it to the upper level.

"How long will that take?" Kaiser asked.

"Not so long." I warmed my hands around the object.

"It's funny," he said, "how we stick tu old habits. The water by itself is good for you – we add tea, a diuretic."

"But," I said, "but, but, we don't know how safe the water is to drink and to boil it is the oldest way to make it safe. How tea-drinking no doubt came about in the first place. And feeling better is as good as being better, or some such wisdom."

"I don't think we have any cups."

Strange, such a ruthless survivor, the Kaiser seemed quite defeatist on this day.

"I also found these little china egg cups."

I showed them to him, a mismatched collection, but a collection none the less. One had a chintzy butterfly on, another Scooby Doo, my favourite was a simple green cartoon owlet with big eyes.

"How many are there?" he asked.

"Well I've found twenty-two," I said. "I think Stig had a little obsession."

"Where the fuck do you think this bloke got to, that collected all this? D'yuu think he's deid?" His voice trailed out strangely in a sorrowful sing-song tone.

"I hope not, I'd like to meet him, a rather resourceful fellow. The Weathers seem to have left over a fair few of these people. Hidden gems. Like that Sid chap, I could get on with him."

"How long will I wait fa the promised tea?" Kaiser grunted impatiently.

I tested the pot, which was near too hot to touch.

"Another minute, maybe. Better add the tea."

He rooted around and pulled out a bag of loose tea and a tea strainer. At that moment the other three travelers clambered and clattered into the far end of the carriage. Simian and Roxy were giggling. Claudia smirked and set down a bag of firewood.

"Just in time for a shot of tea." Kaiser waved an egg cup in the air.

"We found dandelion leaves," Roxy announced, stepping carefully towards us across the rickety floor and obstacles of bags and junk. "Need to wash them though, I guess."

"With water that we don't know is safe tu drink," Kaiser muttered.

"I found some weird mushrooms too," Simian said. "Anyone got any idea how to tell if they're safe to eat?"

"Yes!" I said. "Test them on the youngest!"

He gave me a bemused look.

"Pass them here," I added.

He moved over and handed them to me, bagged up in a handkerchief which I carefully opened on a table top. They had a honeycomb-like top. I turned one upside down, and checked that it was hollow inside. Simian stood at my shoulder as I peered at them, as though he might pick up how I could tell, which was largely guesswork anyway.

"They look like morels. I used to cook with these, very tasty. I'll try one, I'm probably immune to actually dying from poisonous 'shrooms. But if I start vomiting, having fits etcetera, maybe you chaps should skip them."

"When did you cook with them? Did you pick them wild, then?" Simian asked.

"No, no," I said. "I was a chef when I lived in Amsterdam for a bit. Morels are the most prized wild mushroom used in cooking. I've been mushroom-picking before with my friend, Herman. But we were after hallucinogenic ones then – silly naive young men, thinking we could make a fast Mark. We completely fucked ourselves for a month or so. I'm not sure my brain or body has been the same since. Casual mushroom folklore is *not* a good guide to safe picking."

"A'ya sure it's a good idea to risk eatin these? Could they kill you?" Claudia asked, and they all peered at me with eyes that spoke of slight concern.

"No, that's highly unlikely. Might get the shits and the vomiting, get banished to the woods for a few days. I don't think killer mushrooms grow in this country. I may be wrong. But no higher risk than eating food from a dirty kebab house, which I'll bet you've all done."

"So is this our food stuff for now? Flowers and dodgy mushrooms? I feel full already," the Kaiser said.

"Well you go set some home-made traps, caveman," Claudia scathed.

He pulled the stolen pistol out and waved it in the air. "Like... duh."

"Dandelions are terribly good for you," I said to Roxy, with helpful enthusiasm. "Full of vitamins, and potassium, and calcium!"

She nodded happily. "We could make dandelion soup."

* * * * * * *

OATMEAL STOUT

Claudia McLeod, Yorkshire

There was a horse mired in the midst of a water-logged field. He were stout and rugged, maybe a little Shire breeding in the mix. It'd been a while since I'd seen a horse and my heart leapt up like a bantling faced with the same problem, with no thought except heroism.

The animal looked at me with liquid eyes, from under a haughty fringe. He wasn't the highly-strung frighty type, he weren't strugglin and sinkin. He just looked proper grumpy. I shouted for t'others, but there was no answer, I'd walked too far away. Had I known back then what locals could be like wi' strangers, I wouldn't have tottered off alone. I looked about. The field was part of an auld abandoned farmstead, still cluttered wi' semi-useful stuff, which was what'd drawn me to start with.

Twenty metres or so from the horse I found some strips of auld wood fencing, half buried. They were bigger than me, but I wrangled one free and began the knackerin task of dragging it, bit by bit, across the soggy field into which I, too, was sinking some. I were mullin over how feral the horse might be and the difficulty of whether he'd even *let* me help him (these days we were as likely to hunt a horse as rescue it).

I was so busy doing this, I din't notice a bloke approachin across the plain, til I heard him shout.

"Geoffrey! Again?"

The man paid me no heed whatsoever, instead standing lookin at the horse lyke a mardy dad. He was wearing a coat patch-worked from any and every useful material, both manmade and animal. He had a woollen hat, wi'a peak, pulled over grey-brown hair. I carried on draggin fence, while he tutted and mumbled cusses at Geoffrey. I stopped a few metres away, catchin my breath and gawpin at the man's dog. It looked at first as though it'd been mauled in the face and chest, until I realised with a chuckle that it was a greyhound (or sommat close), wearin a fur coat fashioned from some other fluffy breed. It stood well back from any mud atop a hillock, shiverin on lanky legs.

"Scuse me?" I said.

The man turned slowly, as if surprised that I'd spoke to him. He looked at me suspiciously.

"What?"

"That your hoarse?"

"Aye," he said.

"I were gonna try an' free him. You gonna give me a hand?" I asked.

"Aye." The man shrugged.

He took hold of the other end of the fence and we tossed it intu't mud. Geoffrey the horse watched, boredly.

"I think we need another," I said.

"Aye," he said.

In silence we trudged back to the junk pile and wrestled more wood free and then lugged this back agen. We stepped ontu't first bitta fence which wobbled about and chucked the new piece intu't mud. It landed a foot or two from the horse, splashing him in't face – he snorted at us.

"Come on, you muppet! Climb aboard!" the man shouted.

He tip-toed across to the animal, slop seepin 'tween the gaps mekkin the surface slippy.

"Hup two." He leaned forward, beckonin. I stayed back fa fear a sinkin the mekkshift bridge.

The horse yanked a hoof free and lifted it forward, then another and another, 'til the fence were at his knees. The man grabbed hold of a scrappy head collar, buried in thick fur, and pulled at the chin. The horse chucked his head, snorted and hoisted himself ontu't wobbly boards, which sank further, but then seemed to rest. Carefully, man and beast escaped to firmer ground, and stood, the man pattin, the horse optimistic'ly nuzzlin pockets.

"D'you live around here?" I asked.

"Aye," he said after a pause.

"By yissel?" I asked.

He looked at me and then motioned ta'tha horse and the dog, to show his preferred company. I nodded.

"Okay, bye then."

He waved a hand to stop me goin and opened up a sack that were perched next to his cross-dressed dog (still shiverin obediently). He handed me a carefully wrapped parcel and then waved that I could go.

"Ta, love," he grunted.

I frowned and went on my way, hikin back over fields ta'tha woods and clamberin back through undergrowth until I spotted the coloured rags in branches which led me back to the carriage. Once inside, I unwrapped the package to curious faces.

"Eggs!" Roxy picked one up and examined it. "Duck, I think? Where did you get these?"

"Long story," I said.

"You're awfully muddy..." she added.

* * * * * * *

SOME HUMANITY, MAYBE

Roxanne Ratcliffe, Yorkshire

'Maybe if I wait here long enough the sun will come out. Maybe if I wait here long enough the old bricks will crack and begin to tumble down, revealing some passageway to an underground tomb.

But it's not the dead that dwell here, catacombs piled high with skulls. Things live and move and breathe and have some humanity, maybe. Their feral eyes rolling back to some time when they were only troubled by the emotive and the practical. When a world of bricks didn't weigh heavily upon their heads.

The sun burns my eyes so I develop a perpetual squint, my skin burned ruddy — a cowboy's grimace. He knocks the whiskey back, staring out across a landscape that may or may not be part of the

Earth. Be part of my dreams which sink like sand, slowly filling the gaps in the rock, in my nostrils in my mouth in my shoes.

I wake and stare to the light again, glinting across the rooftops of an entire city sprawled out. The roof is warm like tarmac beneath my back. The sky is vaster than the ocean. There's a boy here with me, amid the pebble-dashed houses. A pebble-dashed boy. A thousand different coloured stones inside his irises, little flecks of gold, aching to return to the earth that made and then eroded them, like tiny specks of glass.

I know that inside our bodies we're all sand. All filled with tiny specks of glass that sink and fall through the gaps in my fingers, each grain reflecting back something different to the next. Some other sentence I forgot to say.'

I read the passage several times over, feeling as though I'd written it and forgotten and lost it. But it was scrawled in a stranger's notebook, one with a shiny emerald cover with pink threading sown into the edges. This was the only passage in the notebook, which had been started and then forgotten.

The words reminded me dreamily of a house party I went to after work one night. It was a rainy summer, but that week was so hot. At seven in the morning we climbed on the neighbour's flat roof, through an attic window, and there was that vast sky, without a cloud and already warm. I was silly-drunk and had danced all night. I waved to Cuan to come out and join me, and waited patiently the way we do for the right moment, when we're shimmying like the birds of paradise. Trying to seduce without sophistication or cliché, just the sweet exchange of eyes and the carefully chosen word.

We talked and sat and then just lay and looked at the sky so that it was all we could see. A blank blue canvas on which to sketch a tentatively positive future. After a while it was just us two. I rolled on my side and gazed softly at Cuan's profile, his long lashes squinting in the bright light.

He felt my eyes and turned and looked back at me shyly.
And I knew if I wasn't brave, and didn't kiss him then, I
never would.

The wind rocked our lonely little carriage and I glanced
out of the window, almost expecting an oceanic sky, but
the glimpse I could catch above the stark canopy was pale
and greying with age.
   "Who wrote this? You?" I asked Simian.
   "No, no, Cassie of course. It was in her bedroom at
her parents' house. I found it after she died. She used to
go and sit in the General Cemetery and write in the
summer. I'm pretty sure she wrote that there, because it
mentions catacombs. I kept it because it was all by itself,
and it's got a timeless quality, I think?"

* * * * * * *

BEESWAX

Wolfgang, Yorkshire

I listened hard – the night was unearthly silent outside of
the carriage. There was barely a swish of wind in the trees,
and no sound of mousey scuttles or screech owls to
reassure that the world was still alive outside. Inside were
the usual rumbles of sleepy heads: Kaiser's muttered
apologies to God in his slumber; Simian's occasional
spasms as he dreamed wild of moons, birds and monsters;
Claudia – always the soundest, quietest sleeper – breathed
her heavy soft breaths...
   And what of little Moomin girl? I sensed wakefulness,
and listened firmly against the other human noises and

heard a little sniff, followed by a snivel. I lay quietly for a while, waiting. Some time passed and maybe she slept again and wept only in her dreams, but then there was a rustle and a faint glow of light growing at the far end of the cabin.

I hesitated and pondered upon my capabilities as a comforter, which I am somewhat doubting of, but alas I remembered little Roxanne once saying *'The worst thing about insomnia is it's so lonely. You feel like the only person awake in the whole world.'*

So I slid and shuffled from my seat into the aisle, and peered down the carriage between the lumps and bumps of slumber. She was sat crossed-legged on the floor, a candle next to her leaving bits of face and elbow illuminated, gazing tearfully at objects in her lap. My footsteps crept down the passage and she looked up unstartled by the hairy figure growing in size. I sat down next to her on the floor, my older bones creaking – I am not so old as a tree, 'tis true, but the cold does make them creak – feeling a bit oversized and clumsy.

She wiped her button mushroom nose with a hanky and looked at me with wide tearful eyes. I looked at the private objects, some scrawled writing in a hand I'd known well, and a photograph of a lost boy.

"Is Cuan dead?" she asked me.

Her sorrow for him had been boxed up and kept from the others, but maybe she knew I felt love lost also. I pondered quietly for the best words.

"I think so, little Roxy, I'm afraid to say. But... I think it for the better."

The woeful question in her eyes prayed me continue.

"He was quite brilliant, but the brilliant are cursed much like him. He saw through everything and it weighed him down with a great apathy?"

I hung a question mark in hope she was following my words in understanding. I'm often too hasty and leave people behind. She nodded quickly.

"He was cursed to find everything ultimately meaningless. Especially extremes of emotion such as love. He knew them to be neurotic and narcissistic, he condemned them in himself as weak and pointless in a way. He was numb," I said carefully.

She sobbed again and tried to repress it back while it stuttered forward. She blew her nose. Her eyes were lined red and weary. I felt a sliver of guilt. Maybe I'd said too much. Cuan was only numb when he hit the bottom... sometimes, often, he was a kite.

"Do you think everything is ultimately meaningless?" she asked me, her voice quavering, restraining more gushes.

I shook my head profusely. And not because I wanted to reassure her but because I was firmly against the idea.

"George Lakoff... a cognitive linguist –" I waved my hand to indicate I couldn't be bothered to explain "– once wrote that *'Meaning is not a thing. It involves what is meaningful to us. Nothing is meaningful in itself.'* A painting has no meaning to a cat. He cannot eat it, it won't keep him warm, it won't show him affection. Likewise, that painting can have little meaning to one human, be boring, be mere decoration. Yet to another it has great meaning. It may've altered that person's whole way of thinking, excited some new idea in them. Everything is meaningful to someone or something. The trouble with people like Cuan is they search for *some great truth. Some great meaning in all things.* But there are only small meanings. In looking for the meaning of everything, he found the meaning of nothing," I paused poking my tongue to check it was still working, "I'm speaking riddles."

"No, I think I understand," she said. "Do you think there's a reason things have come to this? The breakdown, the destruction?"

"Civilisation will always destroy itself. Look at the fall of the Roman Empire or some such... I'm not so good on my historical facts, too much of a theorist. Everything happens in cycles of birth and destruction and rebirth. Eventually the sun will self-destruct and the universe will have to be reborn."

"You don't believe we're being punished? That it's karma, or God?" she asked.

"People believe these things to believe they're important."

"That's what Cuan used to say," she said.

"Exactly. People need to believe they are important to feel their life is meaningful. In a way we're being punished for being power hungry. We tried to control nature and take over too much, and Mother Nature is taking the power back, for she created us and thus her power is greater. But she has no consciousness. She's a natural force. She doesn't say 'bad human, I will punish thee.'"

Roxy nodded, almost laughing. "I always thought that, but increasingly I doubt what I know is real. I have visions and I feel things differently. Sometimes it feels like there's more going on. Like there are spirits around, like we are watched. I feel like I'm going mad, like we all are."

I shrugged the shrug of a man who knew his own crazy demons. "Grief and trauma make madmen of all of us."

I felt another pair of eyes on me and the ears of the walls a-cock, wanting to note my wisdoms and snigger them down. I turned my head up to the nearest body a few feet away, wrapped tight in many covers, a little nose poking out. The candlelight was just able to catch a tiny point of reflection in Simian's open, listening eyes.

* * * * * * *

THE SIGNIFICANCE OF UNANSWERABLE QUESTIONS

Simian Thomas, Yorkshire

I returned from the woodland toilet to find only Roxanne and Wolfgang sat in the carriage. They were talking conspiringly again, as they had taken to doing often since we'd lived in trains. Roxy let Wolfgang wear the robe of wise old man very easily. I had an inkling this was something to do with Cuan. He seemed to allow Roxy to grieve more than the others, myself included.

Roxy was stripping down sticks to make arrows as she talked, and she broke off as I entered. They had a pile of sticks ready, so I picked one up and sat down next to her, beginning to strip the notches and uneven edges off with my own pocket knife.

"Don't mind me," I said.

Roxy looked at me, with a face that hoped always to make amends. It occurred to me that moment that her large eyes were actually colourless, like water, and only appeared to have colour in what they reflected – blue, grey and green in the open landscape, but here deep in the forest they looked tawny. The room was bright and her pupils were small, leaving more room for the irises.

"I was just explaining cod philosophy," Wolfgang announced, in a tone that suggested he'd witter on for a while, so I concentrated my attention on the physicality of the wood in my hand.

"You see, the cod is not aware of *Being*, at least we think not. And even if he or she is aware of Being, they are surely not aware of their significance to the human. As the favourite fish, the over-fished fish, etcetera... and who knows why? Mister cod just tastes like white fish to me."

Roxy listened humorously, as though beneath the nonsense lay some profound truth. Wolfgang was silent now, reading my face across the table and I felt as though they were waiting for me to say something. Whether or not it should be tasting notes on fish I didn't know.

"Didn't you make Cuan mad with your *'Philosophy of Brian'*? Don't you worry you'll do the same to the rest of us?" I asked.

Wolfgang didn't flinch, but I somehow knew I'd hit a nerve.

"He did get a bit obsessed with Heidegger in the end..." he murmured regretfully. "He was obsessed with *'the Nothing'*, he thought it would bring ultimate clarity. Instead, like so many, he fell into it."

I remembered Hex obsessively watching *The Never Ending Story* and wondered if the same was true of him.

"But do you even know who *Brian* is? Before you bandy him about as some proof?" Wolfgang continued. I remembered his sad walk, to lay his friend down in the graveyard.

"I seem to remember he was a pigeon," I said with what I hoped was a deadpan delivery.

Wolfgang looked shocked at this, as though I had second sight. As though he was wracking his brains to know where I'd gotten this idea from. "He was condemned to the body of a common city pigeon, in order to know the ultimate meaning of Being," Wolfgang said. "He was not always a pigeon."

I looked sideways at Roxy, hoping she would read that this was proof of Wolfgang's ultimate madness. Just in case she hadn't noticed already.

"I'm trying to understand where Cuan got lost," she said to me, as though wandering around in the endless tunnels of Wolfgang's psyche would help.

"Probably by reading Nazi literature," I said.

"Now that's a sweeping generalisation. Heidegger wrote *Being and Time* before he fell into that murky pond," Wolfgang said softly.

"He still became a Nazi though, didn't he?"

"It's a strange one. I find a great sense of equality between all beings in his writing, but that is my own reading," Wolfgang murmured, and then raising his voice with firm conviction he announced. "How so many of my countrymen fell to the hideous ideology, that prescribed heinous medicine, is a painful labyrinthine mystery... But you must understand the place of *'turning a blind eye'* in the whole saga."

He looked on the verge of tears for a moment. I wondered how many times the English had dogged him about the issue, unable to separate his homeland from its history.

Roxanne had chopped one of Claudia's darts up and was attaching the sharp point to one end of her arrow and the wings to the other end, using wire to secure them. It was a trial object which we needed to test, though we had yet to successfully make a bow with which to shoot the damn things.

Claudia had already fashioned a kind of spear from a larger branch though, sharpening the wood itself to a fierce point. She was apt at being a wild thing.

I stared out of the window of the carriage at the dense rows of birches and the way the light slipped between them. I sighed heavily, letting something escape from within me, the heaviness of doubt and cynicism. Wolfgang was not malicious, I told myself firmly and he was no more or less at fault for Cuan's downward spiral than anyone else. He wasn't trying to poison Roxanne, he was trying (however haphazardly) to help her. It was nice, for a few minutes, to see outside of the paranoid frame. To see only a beauty in the world outside, untarnished by my own preconceptions.

"A penny for your thoughts, young ape?" Wolfgang asked over-curiously.

I shrugged and motioned with a slightly effeminate wave to the world beyond the carriage.

"It's a nice day out..."

* * * * * * *

MORE ANIMAL THAN THE ANIMALS

Bryn McLarey, Yorkshire

I jerked awake from a dream, not sae much wet as sodden. For a moment mae eyes were open, but the imagery in mae dream wus still painted on the room in monochrome. She uz either a siren or a monster. She is both.

I sat up in the bed, which wus basically an old low-backed double train seat parked adjacent tu the wall, with mae feet sticking off the end. They were not a fookin comfort ta sleep on after the bunks in the main train. I automatically rustled around for the means tu roll a smoke, but it hit me again. No tobacco. It'd been days now, technically we were free of that vile addiction, havin been through the sweats and the madness. I ground mae teeth together loudly. I preferred havin the choice when it came tu givin up mae bad habits. What does a person do in this moment, withoot a fag? How may I sit quietly in *disgruntled* contemplation, and mull o'er my dreams?

I surveyed with quick jealousy mae sleep-soaked companions. The fact that I could see owt utall must mean it wus a very clear night outside. Clear and probably cold as fook. Ney point in extractin maesel for a quiet walk. It'd mean forcing boots unto mae battered feet again, sumthin I tried tu minimize tu once a day. I pulled the covers up around mae shoulders, hunched in the darkness, cussin like a hoodie.

I felt an aching regret. Not for noble things like love lost, or good deeds I should've done. In mae involuntarily chaste and smokeless situation, I felt nothing but a callous regret for all the women I'd never screwed, and all the cigarettes I'd never smoked given the opportunities I'd once had. I could pick them out from the dredges of mae memory... Juliette had said she wasnae feelin too well on mae birthday, but she'd still do it if I wanted. (By which she meant lie there motionless, putting up with the sweaty humpin beast that wus weighing her down.)

I'd said, 'no dahrlin, you get sum sleep now'. Now I'd give mae rotten left foot tu be that sweaty humpin beast. And the time that smarmy thespian called 'Horatio' had offered me a toke on his spliff at a party, and I'd said no because of mae rule about *never givin maesel reason tu be grateful to a prick*. Also I wus still pretending to be a good boy at the time and wus worried it would send me off the rails.

I'd give mae rotten right foot tu be off the rails right now. I'd have no way of walkin by maeself. But I'd have drugs and women, and quality single malt tu ruin mae brain with. I wuduv made that deal with the devil right now – aye. But the only Satanic form of being wus in mae chest and I doubted hackin my aen feet off would result in a skulk of pretty whores tu come weaving through the trees (clothes shredded from the brambles of course, carrying a hundred pack of Lucky Strikes and a 2 litre bottle of 16 year old Lagavulin...)

'*Lagaluvlin*', Juliette used tu call it, like some sort of dyslexic poetic justice. I smiled wearily tu maeself, and then hit mae palm against mae head in frustration. How could I have given up on the Devil so quickly, and returned tu idolizing a woman I hadn't seen in sae long that I'd crafted the highest pedestal from which she shone. She reaches a hand down towards me, but she is way up amongst the clouds and I'm far below in the middle of an enormous, black mire.

I jerked mae eyes open again. I'd dropped off still sitting up, chin drooping tu chest. Nothing about me now but the stench of mouldy feet and a human sweating out his worst fears. I tried tu concentrate again on memories of lust and shallow pleasures, but while mae body throbbed with sexual hunger, the images of busty babes were still corrupted by Juliette's laughter at how predictable I was. All those times she tried tu trick me into slipping out of an English accent, by pecking at all the things that got mae goat – like golf, and pretentious facial hair and *grown men who were incapable of carrying three pints of beer at once.*

And so I thought of busty babes in Princess-Leia-gold-bikinis, with ringlets of red hair, like an ever-young Cassie Siddal, and at the same time I hummed and murmured mae entire knowledge of Dire Straits' *Romeo & Juliet*.

It's possible a tear pricked in the corner of mae eye, but the darkness is a veil over such secrets. In the same way no one must ever know mae weakness for Dire Straits, or sentimental wanks.

    I continued to murmur familiar lyrics, in love and out of key. Inside this puss of romantic cathartism expelled from mae hardened shell (the age of the armadillo), I passed through every lilting gaze that'd made mae heart beat faster: from teenage lust on muddy football pitches; tu Janine's translucent white-trash tops, and the pink bra showing through; Juliette's fingers tracing mae collarbone in the wee hours; a girl called Sally pinching mae bum while her mother wasn't looking; Jenny's sweet, sad eyes when I came home with another black eye; Cassie dancing on the utopian sands of Phuket in a turquoise summer dress; Roxanne dripping wax onto mae arm and letting me believe for a moment that she would ever let me kiss her.

    These days mae heart wus dull and heavy, it beat only in fear or anger, or with some glum nostalgia. I wanted tu howl with the pain of loneliness, leik a dog left chained tu a kennel, without even a smelly pig's ear tu gnaw on. Had the God who I'd mistrusted and mistreated left me tu this? Left me in some purgatory where there wus neither hope of love and consummation nor a definite fiery hole for me tu step into with conviction.

    I lay back down on the wonky, unforgiving bed. I closed mae eyes firmly on the dark world and asked the Sandman tu at least grant me mercy.

* * * * * * *

EXISTENTIAL TRAIN WRECKS

Wolfgang, Yorkshire

I sat scribbling in the note book, pausing to itch my shoulder. A hairy shoulder. The hairy likes to sit on my shoulder, whispering sour nothings in my ear. He likes to aggravate the itch so that I cannot write.

Her pale eyes addressed me carefully, and I looked up knowing this silent communication, knowing beautiful little Roxy was sat in front of me with her precious petite Moomin features. (How a Moomin may be petite I don't know. I seem to remember some likeness to a hippo.)

"You won't write about me, will you?" she said with quiet awe.

I stifled laughter. As though to be penned to some paper is somehow more dangerous. As though knowing something in writing of someone's perception of you is too much. As though it doesn't mystify their perception further. I hastily found a new page and scrawled the words *Roxy doesn't want me to write about her.* I tore it out and handed it to her.

"Quickly eat it before anyone sees what I've written!"

She held it and looked dejected and misunderstood.

"You're our muse, little Roxanne Ratcliffe. Nothing you ever do or say is not already admirably noted in the blank pages of the mind. Your fear of being written is no different to another's fear of having their photograph taken. The photograph is already taken! The eye takes a picture and engraves it on the memory. Am I write or am I left?"

She gazed around the carriage, her eyes scuttling over the old books stacked on every surface, and our own debris sitting atop these little platforms – a stray hat, a claw hammer. She settled on her majestic old 35mm camera, which had found a home on top of some Byron poetry. She almost wanted to rush and pick it up. She looked back to me slowly instead, leaning forward across the table top, glancing at my notebook and then to my face.

"The photographs I've taken of you have never come out."

I nodded in agreement.

"That is because I don't exist."

She pursed her lips in thought. I lingered on her pale eyes, waiting for the words.

"How come they can see you too?" She motioned to the human shadows in the carriage. The cloud, the primate and the fucking Kaiser.

"They too, have eaten too much cheese. It makes you see all sorts of things. Or maybe the camera is mad and you're all sane? Are cameras not known to pick up images of ghosts sometimes?" I suggested.

I could see one of the shadows trying to eavesdrop on the conversation. They worry my disease of the mind is contagious, and Roxy is contaminable.

"I don't have any pictures of Toby," she confessed. "I was too embarrassed to try to take any."

"But you've written him in your soul, he exists as a picture in the mind's eye?"

She suddenly looked awfully fearful and her voice that'd been a whisper, drew barely to a breath.

"I can't see his face," she said with genuine upset.

I nodded. I didn't tell her that neither could I.

I looked to my hand paused above the page, holding a pen not in readiness to write, but in readiness to think about writing.

"You know I write the *Philosophy of Brian*? Not about actual people? Not like a story or a journal, more like *theory?*" I spit over my shoulder at my own word, but have not been able to find one to better describe.

"It's still about us though? In some way…" she muttered with attempted perceptiveness.

"Everything is about you, Roxy. The world's axis would collapse if you were not in existence," I said.

She looked annoyed.

"Very funny, there's no need to be mean."

"How do you, or I, know that it wouldn't, though?" I asked her.

I repositioned my pen and hesitantly wrote the words *'existential train wrecks'*. She watched. Does she know that a person can't write what they would write with another watching? In the same way they would never be as they are, if they know a camera is watching.

"I've never understood what 'existential' means," she said.

I nodded agreeably.

"Nobody knows what it means. It's just a term people bandy around to make themselves sound clever, or to be ironic."

This train carriage was Roxy's favourite because it was stationary. It would never go anywhere. It would never see the sea or the Pennines. It was the comfort zone, the womb. The safe place to hide from a world that changes too fast, from an ocean that was flooding the land with wreckage that ought to be at the bottom of the sea.

* * * * * *

THE ROOM THAT TIME FORGOT

Simian Thomas, Yorkshire

I had cobwebs in my hair again. The carriage had so many cobwebs, they almost formed net curtains. Feather duster longing resurfaced as I sat picking the bits of stuff out. I'd considered cutting my hair, but it seemed pointless. It kept me warm, after all.

The light was just beginning to dim outside, so I lit a candle, enjoying the warming sight of the light dancing into the gloom. Whoever had left the carriage as it was had installed an ancient iron wood-burning stove, with a narrow chimney to let the smoke out. I shoved some of the scraps of dry wood I'd collected inside the stove and lit the tinder with a match. It was a relief to have a small supply of matches for once. There was nothing quite as tedious as the inexpert trying to create fire by rubbing bits of wood together.

I realised with immediate grumpiness that I'd wasted a second match – I could've lit the fire from the candle. I blew softly on the tiny flames growing inside their nest. It was quiet in the little train car. I enjoyed the moments of peace before the others would return to clutter up the chaotic space further. There was a large selection of badly maintained books in the carriage. I'd begun trying to escape into them in the evenings. I would peer into pages for some myth or curiosity written decades before.

While the books were an obvious luxury, everything else in the space seemed to have been left for a reason. The reason being that it was junk. We'd made use of very little of it, yet it still sat there in the way. Maybe we ought to chuck it outside in the bushes, but it seemed like it wasn't our place to do this. The lost little cabin felt as though it'd been intentionally left there, to shelter lost souls from the ravages of the wilderness. The collection of oddities and literature brought a certain forlorn homeliness to it.

I picked up an old rag and began dusting a little, and shoving things into corners. It was difficult to distinguish the belongings of my friends from other junk though, so I gave up fairly quickly. I neither wanted them to return and find me tidying up like a housewife, nor did I want earache for moving people's stuff around. I reorganised my own little bit of space instead, a little corner of order which would quickly be ruined. I was covered in fluff and dust, like everything else in the room. I was only moving it around, after all. Without a Hoover it was all in vain. I sneezed loudly, startling myself.

I sat close to the stove and warmed my hands, peering out through the windows for signs of life in the woods. Now that I had light inside and it was dark out, I felt that vulnerable feeling that eyes outside could see me, but I couldn't see them. (Especially not through the dirty, webby windows.) The forest bristled and sighed in the breeze, but there were no tell-tale cracking of twigs underfoot. I began to worry that in the dark, the others wouldn't find their way back. But surely the light would be visible from a way away, even through the dense undergrowth. I envisioned un-particular threats weaving through the trees towards the light, irrational fear filling my throat.

"Evenin' Simmo," a voice said from the door.

It startled me, but I immediately realised that it was one of the railwaymen – Robbie. How a man of his bulk was so light-footed I don't know.

"Hi," I said uncertainly. "What are you doing here at this time of night?"

He climbed through the doorway and lumbered into full view. A stack of books teetered over in his wake.

"Whoops." He half kicked, half shoved them out of the gangway. He settled himself down in a seat opposite and removed his woolly hat as though he was about to impart bad news. "One a' your lot did their ankle in. We've put her back on the main train, they're gonna stay there tonight. I volunteered to come and tell you what was goin on. Don't want you worryin, or tryin to go off finding them alone in the dark."

"Who? Roxy?" I asked.

Robbie's mouth set flat in embarrassment that he didn't know all our names.

"The slightly taller, pretty lady," he said hesitantly.

"Claudia," I said.

"That's it," he said. "Couldn't quite think of her name. I knew it were a ghoul's name, was gonna say Morticia!"

"A ghoul's name?" I said.

"Claudia's the name of the little girl vampire in that film... with Tom Cruise an that?"

"Oh." It clicked in my head. I smirked. "I'll have to tell her that."

"Ah, please don't!" he grinned wryly.

An odd silence settled, during which Robbie fidgeted with his hat and looked around the carriage in bemusement.

"Funny fuckin little pad, in't it?" he said after a pause.

"Yeah," I said.

I still wasn't sure if he was intending to stay or not. I weighed up the worst case scenario between an evening of stilted conversation and one spent all alone. For once it was the latter.

"Do you want some tea?" I asked.

"Aye," he said, warmly. "That'd be grand. Right funny little place this," he repeated still in awe. "Like the room that time forgot."

THE SWAMP OF SADNESS

Claudia McLeod, Yorkshire

Oh the fookin irony. One day y'help some gadger rescue a horse stuck in mud, and then a week or so later...

I'd climbed a tree that arched over a mossy mire. I were armed wi'a spear and some darts, and wharra hoped was a large dollop of patience. I sat proper still and quiet on that branch for hours. I even seen Charlie and Roxy pass by (on the higher ground), bickerin quietly. I tried to overhear what they were sayin, but it was lost in the mizzle.

I became almost a part of the tree, not spiritually like, more physically, cos my arse ached and my limbs felt dead as rotten timber. But I kept a keen ear to all the birdsong, and began tryin to learn which was which tweet, if only t'pass the time. I were frozen, but if I kept rayte still I couldn't feel how cold I was. The coldness, and the numbness and the deadness wouldn't help little miss huntress though when it came to the crunch.

This was sommat I discovered when, after hours of waiting, I saw sommat better than a wood pigeon. It were the size of a biggish dog, but had an oddly butch shape, movin around in the undergrowth far below. I tried to twist round to watch it, without mekkin any noise. I were slightly frighty that I didn't know what the fook it were, and twisted my neck all I could. It was still just a rough, dark brown shape rustling in the bushes. It worra big brute. Had I been on the ground I would've climbed the nearest tree to get away from it.

It was gettin nearer. The drizzly wind was shakin the tree a little, so I shifted slightly at't same time, tryin to disguise my noise. Closer, closer, snuffling, snorting. I held the spear in the air, anticipatin the force I needed on a creature that big. It crossed the very bit of ground I was hopin for and I thrust the weapon through the air wi'all I had. Despite my other hand holding onto a branch (numb with cold), the force of my throw, threw my stiff torso outta the tree entire'ly. The leftover kinetic energy of the angle I'd aimed at mayde me proper somersault and haddah bin a cat I would've landed neatly on my paws.

I were not a cat though, I werra cack'anded human. A pain shot through me ankle, and I suppressed a yelp, tears pricking my eyes in shock. I were flounderin in muck, I stopped movin – realisin I'd landed in the swamp. In some ways the clarty slop had softened my fall. I peered over at me ankle, but it were down in the mud. I decided it were only sprained, but I was stuck all the same. Stuck in the mud lyke a grumpy horse. I wiped dirt from my eyes, but my hands were mucky too. I looked around. There was no sign of my quarry. Thank fook.

I laid there for a little while, calming missel, until I were able to think. The whistle, I had the flashing whistle in my jacket pocket somewhere. I wriggled a little, wary that every wriggle sunk a bit more of me. I fished in a pocket – nowt. Fished in another – a hanky and some darts which pricked my fingers. Inside pocket? This was a struggle but at last I found it.

The sound of the whistle as I blew it hurt my own tabs and echoed eerily in the woodlands round about me. There were scared rustles and the sound of wings beatin, as the nearby wildlife evacuated. I blew the whistle til I ran out of lungs. And then lay pantin, listenin for sounds of people, lost in the melancholy dampness of a woodland swamp.

Later, after Charlie and Roxy had dredged me out wirra string a nets and carried me to the main train (which was nearer than the lonesome carriage), I told my story.

"I think it were a warthog," I said. "Are there warthogs in this country?"

Blank faces answered.

"Maybe it escaped from a zoo or sommat," Dave offered. He'd cleaned my ankle and wrapped a bandage. My clothes were proper ditched and my hair was lank and mucky. Smithy'd made me a brew and offered me his last two paracetamol.

"It's alright, ta. It don't hurt too badly now," I said.

He placed them firmly in my hand.

"Keep them. It'll ache in the night. You won't get no sleep," he said.

"D'you think you might've hit the animal?" Dave asked.

"I've no clue," I said. "You didn't see my spear did ya?" I asked Charlie.

"I'll go back and look for it," he said sulkily.

"Take someone wi' ya. Don't want you gettin stuck an all," I said.

He shot me a look to say that he wont as daft as me.

"Is the train nearly fixed?" Roxy asked. The men had used one of the trees to lever the carriage back onto the tracks.

"Nearly," Smithy nodded. "We'll be able to move on soon..."

* * * * * * *

DUSTED OFF FETISHES, CORRUPTED BY NEUROSIS

Wolfgang, Yorkshire

Already the dust had settled a little. The forlorn objects of the carriage whispered quietly of our absence – of the claustrophobia of a library of memory. We are all (in part) a little bug trapped in that library, knowing only a contained moment that stands still, fixed by page or image. We don't know the moments we live now. The transient, the forgettable.

I pay close attention only to fetish. Everything else is gone, changed, disintegrated – had 'memory rubble' swept over it, as Günter would so cleverly have put it. It is unhealthy to give too much time over to neurosis, so instead I try to block this with fetish. Everyone knows and understands fetish. They just don't understand the word. They think too much of sexual peculiarities, when really I understand it as the nuance of enjoyment. Some like clean things, minimalism, order. Others (such as myself) fetishize clutter and chaos. Some prefer the elaborate and fantastical, others the gentle streak of sunlight upon an ordinary kitchen sink. Stripy cats or fast yellow cars, money and power or anarchy and rebellion – the little personal pleasures, however at odds.

The neurotic being is that which makes us sick as 'human'. That concerns itself with its own petty image. As though it could ever begin to comprehend the ever-changing nuance of any other neurotic's opinion. Know the truth silly id! Nobody will ever love you, or admire you. They will only love some little fetish about you, admire some little fetish about you, and probably only because they think it reflects positively on their own sick human ego. Love is just a collection of fetishes and, hopefully, requitement (read that as compatible fetishes)! This will merely add another layer to the wafer-thin transparent skin-like curtain of your self-esteem. Love is just an illness of the ego. It is not something you need, you can never even love yours*elf* despite knowing it all too well – you can only fetishize it. But do my friend, by all means. I do myself. Love thyself in this manner. Try to fetishize the good bits. The human condition is to fetishize the bad. The bones, the greed, the notches on bedposts... the ability to drink that fat old Labrador under the table.

So I took a last longing glimpse at the friendly carriage we'd called home for a little time and stepped back out into the brutal British landscape (so much more Dante than Constable). The rough wind batted at me like a playful bully boy. He tugged my scarf and I tugged back. I told him he can beat at me all the way home, but I am *intrepid*, I will reach home.

"Who are you talking to Wolfie?" Little Snork Maiden's urchin face poked out from layers of scarves and hoods.

"Why the wind, sweet pea," I replied. And she smiled sweetly and I enjoyed her smile because I knew she fetishized my loopy nature at this point.

"Are you intrepid, Wolfie?" she asked.

"Indeed, little pea, indeed I am intrepid. I think we're all rather intrepid. Do you not think so?" My voice was turned into layers of song, as the wind attempted to pick it up and whisk it away from us.

She smiled again with meek affirmativeness. "I hope so."

"Have we not already come rather far?" I asked of her, trying not to enjoy the companionship my ego painfully hankered for.

She sighed. A gentle, barely legible sigh that the wind swallowed hungrily. For a sigh is too subtle for him. We stepped out from tangled undergrowth and onto the train tracks. They stretched both ways, far off to two distant horizons, to distant question marks of future memory, of chaos and clutter and sudden epiphanies. Donald Judd would not be content with so much *clutter*, I thought, shaking my head gravely.

* * * * * * *

LOVE OBJECTS

Roxanne Ratcliffe, Dreamscape

'*Nether Ed is crouched on the pavement, chalking out letters in some other language. Some days he feels quite small, a thumb sized man inspecting the drains as though they are the great open chasms at Lady Bower, watching the spiders drown. Other days he swells and grows like Alice. His arms harden like brittle dry stone walls, the fillings in his teeth crumbling away like old cement. He tries to grin but something in his face is sad and lost and ignored. He is such a giant that they don't notice him. With genial nonchalance he sniffs and rubs his nose.*

There's a ladybird trapped between two window panes in his house. He's seen it a few times, flying around. It must've crawled in to hibernate and, now woken, cannot find the escape route.

If I was smaller, I could sneak in and find you, thinks Ed...'

Charlie tips the book and shows me the image, a few lines and scribbles depicting the character – a bald man with a slightly crooked nose and sketches of a beard on his chin.

"Who does that remind you of?"

I feel a pang of fear. Or maybe love.

"Cookie and Haydn thought he were real. They thought they'd seen him," Claudia murmurs. The carriage rocks gently along the tracks, steady as my nervous system.

"That makes no sense," I say. "Haydn knew Toby. Why wouldn't he associate the image?"

"That's not so much the myst'ry. How'd they know about Nether Ed at all if this artist died before any work was published? And Nether Ed, if he existed, lived in Sheffield. Haydn and Cookie were in Derby."

The hours creep on the back of my neck, picking up each hair, on the clock ticking on the wall, reminding of half believed rumours as a child.

"Have you asked Haydn?"

"Of course, he doesn't remember. It dun't seem significant to him," Claudia says.

I nod and examine the book. It has a ghostly reflection of age, the later pages blank – telling of death, of absence of the hand that put pen to paper.

"Why d'you have the book, Charlie?"

"She gave it to me," he answers.

"She hadn't finished."

"I was going to return it to her."

I see the book in the water, the slow erosion of salt on the pages, floating.

"We put too much emphasis on love objects," I murmur.

I remove my Casio watch and lay it on the table. It's been broken for years, the numbers somehow still existing on the screen, stuck in another time.

Wolfgang snatches it from the table, pressing it to his face, breathing on it. "This is Cuan's watch." He clutches.

"No, Wolfgang. You just want it to be. It's just a watch like any other." I say.

"It's funny," he points to Cassie's book, "Roland Barthes wrote of *The Death of the Author* as a metaphor to explain that all works are open to interpretation. He said *'the death of the author is the birth of the reader'*, or some such. You're all readers, interpreters of the story, the telling. As she *is* dead – some literal rendition here?"

The landscape outside the window looks like tea stains.

"Wolfgang...?" I ask.

"Yes."

"Adolf means wolf in German?" I ask.

"Sort of."

"What does wolf mean?"

"Wolf means wolf."

The train juddered, and I opened my eyes, squinting in the window which had returned the yellowed land to white and blue and every shade of grey. Charlie glanced over at me. He was the only person not napping. Being back on a moving train was making us all sleepy. He yawned widely like a donkey.

"D'you still have the book Cassie wrote? About that Nether Ed character?" I asked. He looked at me in disbelief.

"She fucking drowned, Roxy. I suspect the book is being read by squid at the bottom of the sea."

I nodded agreeably, somehow liking it better floating down there.

"And d'you know who Roland Barthes is?"

Wolfie suddenly jolted awake for a moment and haphazardly raised a hand. "The man is a complete fucking genius. I'll tell you later."

He fell back to sleep, his whiskers twitching over vital half-dreamed philosophies from times gone.

"I do know who Roland Barthes is," Charlie said.

"Eh, look at all the sleepy heads." Smithy shoved through into our carriage with Robbie in tow, and the other one who only ever grunts and laughs, and never speaks. I looked particularly at *the other one* now, thinking it was strange that we'd gotten to know everyone but him. He acted like the kid on work experience, who just did as he was told, laughed at the jokes, but never seemed to think it was his place to comment.

Simian'd just woken up, narrowly avoiding Smithy poking a grubby, oily finger in his mouth, which'd been slightly open while he slept. He scowled.

"You know where we're headin next?" Smithy asked, in that attention-seeking way "Newcastle." He nodded meaningfully as he said it.

A few years ago a massive tidal wave had hit the coast around Newcastle. I remembered the news reels with a shudder. I remembered someone telling me the power of the wave breaking on South Shields, would've ripped limb from limb any victims in its path.

"We're gonna stop in 'bout an hour and cook some food though," Robbie said. "Lookin forward to a squirrel kebab."

* * * * * *

THE AUDIO LANDSCAPE IN A HEAD FULL OF PAIN

Simian Thomas, Durham County

It is a morning dream. The waves are crashing against the windows of the train, portending their strength. The train crosses sand banks that sink as fast as we pass over them, like wet sand beneath feet. It threatens to suck the train into the Earth. I try to grip the sides of my bunk, but I'm paralysed, I can barely move my eyes. Eyes pinned on the ocean, mistrusting how peaceful it looks, knowing with the fear that knows my subconscious-self better than I, that the sea will rise.

It's flat-lined on the horizon. I have no memory of the Indian Ocean rising up to swallow me. Maybe I never saw it. Maybe I was napping when it swept me up. But I can imagine the sea rising – the horror of a great wall of water speeding towards me and the collective panic of the people. I wait for it to happen in the dream. I stare at the flat line of the sea, waiting for it to swell higher. But it doesn't.

We were going to Newcastle, a city that had felt that weight of water. I should be used to this kind of disaster zone, but Phuket was like a dream now. I wasn't sure if it ever happened. It didn't seem real. I was glad the train was still moving as it meant we weren't there yet. I hoped we'd never get there. I slipped out of my bunk and sat down by the eastern window. There was no sign of the sea. There was a droning noise in my head. I shook my skull, trying to expel it.

"Is that a no?"

Someone was talking to me, that was the droning, an exterior reality.

"What?" I said, maybe a little rudely. My eyes focused. Claudia, ever impatient.

"Tea? D'ya want some fookin tea?" she asked.

"Yes, please." I looked around and felt slightly startled.

Everyone was up and sat about. When I'd slid from my bunk it'd been like nobody was there. Just an empty sleepy train. Just me and my horrors. Charlie was rolling a cigarette.

"I thought you didn't have any tobacco?" I said, trying to prove to myself I could still put things in chronological order.

"Negotiated sum rations with the men folk," he answered mysteriously.

"Wouldn't it be better to just give up?" Roxy asked.

Charlie laughed and said nothing. I looked out of the window again at the steadily passing banks and trees. I almost hoped there would be a blockage on the line, so we'd have to stop. It was a bright day, the low sun creating hypnotising webs inside my eyeballs every time it peeked over the bank between the trees. A cup of tea was planted in front of me, nearly spilling over the side. It had milk in. I had no memory of us getting hold of milk. Maybe Charlie had negotiated milk and tobacco. I took a sip. It was still too hot and tasted odd. I looked at Claudia, and she looked back at me. That dead pan gaze.

"It's sheep's milk... remember?" she said.

"Oh," I said. I didn't remember, but I failed to think it mattered. I stared off into the haze, listening to the vibrations of my stomach telling me I'd not eaten in many hours. The empty, rocking motion like a ship on a sea inside a bottle – back and forth, back and forth. A storm of dissent threatening to rumble and roll. That noise again as well, droning, like an insect inside my head.

Roxy touched my arm. I think she'd been talking. All I could hear was the sea inside the seashell which was my ear. I met her quiet eyes and wondered what she saw in mine – a confused mist of time which had no structure. She'd given up asking me if I was okay (or maybe I could no longer hear her), but she remained quietly patient, as though she could will me out of part-catatonic states.

Things were better when I didn't have time to think. Things were better when stuff just happened and I had to deal with it or face the last nails in my coffin. It seemed very odd that I was alive at all. I was fascinated by a body that continued to function. As though I was separate from it, as though it wasn't mine to destroy. Rather it owned me – it carried me to safety when the world became threatening, it sought out food and warmth and shelter. I'd made no conscious decision to walk into the Red Deer all those months ago, beneath a sarcastic rainbow. My conscious decision would've been to stay in the doom all day and wait for death to put me at peace.

* * * * * * *

AMATEUR THEATRICS

Roxanne Ratcliffe, Newcastle upon Tyne

We reached Newcastle with a sense of apprehension. The sign in the railway station stating our place of arrival felt alien. This was no longer the 'Newcastle' of our youth. While so many cities reduced to ruins were unrecognisable as the places they once were, a sense of noble grandeur still hung about here. Freddie bumbled into the carriage as it pulled to a hesitant stop.

"Well, chaps and chapettes, this is the nearest thing to a tourist stop," he said brightly. We looked glumly expectant. He pointed to some steps leading up off the platform. "If you go up there and follow the signs for 'viewing point', about a 10 minute clamber and you'll be able to see the city as she is now. Nice enough day fer it an' all!"

"Is there much chance a grabbin some belly-timber?" Claudia asked.

"The greatest population of living things round here is rats. No surprises! Stay the fuck away from 'em. Country rats is sometimes okay. City rats has been in our sewers, they'll carry all sorts. Take a bat with you, try to shoot 'em by all means. But they're not food for us, we're food for them. Now there's a fair amount of pigeons and sea gulls around. The nifty bit is killing them without them dropping into the water!"

We nodded dubiously. Charlie counted how much ammunition he had left.

"D'you know where I can get more bullets?" he asked.

Freddie nodded.

"We could get you a proper shotgun, we could get you bullets, but it don't come cheap."

"I'll swap a Claudia for a shotgun," Charlie muttered, but Freddie was already on his way out, whistling *Sloop John B* with a purposeful air.

We collected what weaponry we had to defend ourselves and left the carriage beginning the steady, mysterious climb, following the handmade signs.

"It's weird that they've bothered to do this," Simian said. "Why make the signs? It's not like they can get anything in return. It almost feels like a trap."

I shrugged, my eyes worry-weary. Any fear in us had become almost familiar. Besides, we trusted the men now, they weren't like Gaz. I concentrated my attention on my feet climbing the steps, listening uneasily to the chatter of rats in the walls.

It took a good twenty minutes to clamber through the maze of corridors, stairs and funny gaps, but finally we reached the top and shuffled outside onto the roof of the building. The light was fantastical in contrast to the number of days spent under gloomy, cloudy skies. But without the cloud cover it was distinctly colder, and a chill finger ran down each spine.

We stood silently side by side, staring down the river. Most of the city had been destroyed when the sea came in, but the great iron bridges on the Tyne still stood, gleaming giant in the white winter sun. Man's feats of engineering surviving in a place where he had perished. The city echoed with the jeer of herring gulls, which seemed to have grown to pterodactyl proportions.

There was also, more quietly, the coo-coo of another bird humanity deemed vermin. Our ears invisibly perked toward this sound, for it was collected somewhere nearby. Charlie, stood ahead of us, raised a hand to tell us to be still and quiet. He pulled netting from his pocket and crept like an oversized cat towards the sound, slowly peering over into a brick alcove formed from weather damage to the building. He reached either side and snapped the net across the escape route. At the same time the pigeons panicked and flew straight into it. Three of the four caught in the mesh, which he swiftly twisted so they couldn't escape. He aimed to execute each one with his bat, then they lay in a bloody, twitching heap. The sound of gulls screaming overhead reached cacophony as they announced a late warning of our threat.

We looked on pathetically at the dead birds. I no longer held any remorse for our murders, only regret for the meagre rations. Pigeons again, and these weren't the nice plump woodpigeons, but the scrawny city types. They triggered in Charlie a certain memory though. He stepped up to the edge of the roof. Silhouetted against the skyline, he sparked up his last cigarette and let a harsh rasp of theatrical laughter escape.

"It's the pigeons I feel sorry for. What did they ever do tu deserve this?" he gestured wildly to the landscape.

"They had it made, living in the cities, easy pickings and all. But we polluted them. We watched them be turned slowly black and dirty, from our dirt, and then said what dirty mangy flying rats they were! Fucking pests, leaching off our society, our clean, white linen society."

He stepped down solemnly, and gave a half bow.

"From that play you were in?" Claudia said, remembering.

"*Pigeon Politics*," Charlie smoked and nodded. "The ethos, I feel now. Thank fuck for all the fucking vermin. They're all we've got left tu live off."

"It's like Toby once said," I agreed. "Vermin are just an overly successful species – like people."

"Toby, Toby, Toby. What's so fucking special about this bloke?" Charlie teased.

I looked away over the city filled with giant puddles, bits of old buildings sticking out towards the sky, concrete icebergs that would never melt.

"I dunno. Toby had this vision, this strange kind of... optimism? That went beyond everything. He saw the big picture. Not only that we're just a drop in the sea, but that every drop in the sea matters, not to themselves, but to the final outcome. Something a person did a hundred years ago might affect how we act today without us knowing it."

"Optimism?" Charlie said coldly. "You think he still has optimism?"

"Optimism isn't as simple as saying everything will be okay."

"You leik people who spout big truths." Charlie said. "Like Cuan... and look what happened ta him."

For a fleeting moment then, I glimpsed his regret at driving Cuan away.

After spending a short spell of time musing on the fantastical landscape, we returned inside the maze of conjoined buildings with our kill. We trod carefully down the first few icy steps, which threatened to toss us to bags of bones at the bottom. We descended to the first corridor and peered in the gloom in order to follow backwards the signs from the station. As with the route up, there were the scuffles and squeaks of ever present (yet invisible) rats. Something felt wrong though and I tugged Charlie's arm ahead of me, assuming he would sense the same thing, but he seemed casually oblivious.

"My shoe lace..." he muttered.

He handed me the bag of dead birds and his looted pistol, both of which I held awkwardly. The scene progressed strangely in front of me like a dream. Dread filled me beyond rationale and I took the safety off the gun and turned quickly to where our backs faced a barely lit corridor. We were hunted. A huge pair of eyes and jaws were already nearly airborne. The gun went off in my hand like a knee-jerk reaction and the huge dog plummeted past my shoulder knocking me to the ground. I'd sufficiently injured the animal to have diverted its attack, but it was still thrashing, jaws frothing with unspent rage.

I was reminded of the silly artificial wolf in *The Never Ending Story*. My mind suspended, my body curled into a defensive ball and there was movement around me. A pack of animals closed in to defend one of their own.

And that was that. The dog was dead and we gazed dumbly at it. The brutality that we as a species inflicted on the world was now real blood on our hands. My face was close to the floor, on the same level as the dead animal, its facial expression stifled in the confusion of mortality. No-longer were animals kept in pens and disposed of for our convenience. My body was engulfed with adrenaline and strangely in my throat I felt actual bloodlust, brought on by the anger at being preyed upon.

Claudia scampered down the corridor with the policeman's truncheon raised readily. She scouted for more danger, but instead found a nest of orphaned puppies. Simian gave me a hand up and we followed to where she was stood. A gaping hole in the brickwork half hid three scruffy, scrawny little things – old enough to be weaned off milk and on to whatever their mother scavenged or killed.

"That's soo typical," Claudia said. "She were defendin her pups."

"Or feeding her pups." Charlie rolled his eyes.

"One dog dun't hunt five people," Claudia said.

"Desperation, either way, probably pretty hungry," Wolfgang muttered.

"Anyway, it's only humane tu put them out of their misery?" Charlie said.

The old world echoed in us as empathetic humans, who wanted to save, to heal and to rehabilitate the lost.

"Practically, we could keep one and rear it." Wolfgang peered at the three bundles, old enough to view us suspiciously, crying for mum.

We were all silent for a bit, listening to the whimpers and yips.

"If we're starving we still have to kill it though," Charlie said.

Everyone nodded in strange agreement.

"And which one gets to live?" Claudia said.

"Survival of the fittest," Simian said.

We exchanged looks. We'd all had to kill to live so far, but this felt different. Still, even he'd reached a new decisiveness. He took the bag of pigeons Charlie had reclaimed and placed it a few metres from the hungry pups. They sniffed the air and began a miniature fight with one another to first get out of the hollow and then head towards the meat. It was always obvious that one was stronger, braver, more dominant. He wasn't the prettiest, the fluffiest, the one you would pick to take home and cuddle. But he was stout and gutsy – tearing at the sack with tiny teeth. I picked the puppy up and peeked under the tail.

"It's a she," I said.

Charlie let a quick, soft laugh escape.

"You're such a feminist."

* * * * * * *

ZEITGEIST... & A FLYING PIG'S EAR

Wolfgang, The North

Memory tries to shuffle its cards in the right order, dividing the black from the red, the hearts from the diamonds. But a joker springs up in the middle and he throws everything into chaos. Why the joker is in the pack in the first place nobody knows. The nonsensical exists precisely to be nonsense...

Tap, tap, of pen on the page. I can write such revealing sentences. Yet I complete no essay and no novella, finally or easily, because I struggle with structure like George struggled with the Dragon. Myth is easy because it never really claims to be exact. It's just a fucking story; don't believe a word of it.

"I never knew you were from Nottingham, Roxy?" I mumbled, to prove I was half listening to the conversation and not completely immersed in my hobnobbled psyche.

She nodded quietly, tracing condensation on the carriage window. Claudia had a cheek rested on her other shoulder, listening dozily, occasionally adding a memory to the pile of rubble they were all eagerly building a ramshackle house with. The light was dimming outside, painting the moving landscape into deep purple.

"Robin Hood and his Merry Men? I always liked the little green hats," I mumbled.

Roxy shook her head gently.

"So many people I've met thought it was *actual* history. Yeah, like they all lived in one tree."

Naivety lost. There's much lost by memory, like the stray dirty playing cards Cuan used to pick up in the street. I pursued a memory of this character – we remember best our infatuations.

I recalled laughter and the scene cross-faded to Cuan reading the guidelines for how to get a first in Fine Art.

"Are you radical?" he said, poking his rodent nose in my face.

"Sorry?"

"*It actually says to qualify for a first in fine art your work must be radical!*"

"Oh," I said. "Golly"

He bristled with the incredulity of bright youth.

"How do they *mark* work for being 'radical'? How do they define 'radical'?"

"They reach up their arses and pull out the first thing they can get a hold of!" I quipped.

He laughed, flipping beer mats with casual panache. It's possible I remembered that wrong. Were we even in the Red Deer pub at all? We usually were. Most good ideas were sparked in a pub. I skimmed through options and set the backdrop, hastily arranged the mis en scene. I would like *Dog Days Are Over* to have been playing, but that was definitely the wrong era by a modest few years.

Besides we *were* still dogs lapping at the feet of the Art School Institution, which holds its pupils in a perpetual state of both awe and apathy. (I could write a thesis on exactly what I mean by that because I find it so curious, but maybe you should just go to art school, then you'd understand.) I returned to the conversation with Cuan, his gaunt elfin features exaggerated to beauty by my warped memory.

"How do they know now that we are 'of our time'?" he asked.

He was genuinely upset about something, I think, and thus plunging into great rants in order to purge the blues, or some such.

"I know we're of our time," I said decisively. "But I'm thousands of years old and have seen so many things that I can feel a beat."

He was drunk enough not to question this. Or maybe he never questioned my immortality. Immunity baby.

"Why?!" he spluttered. "Are we radical?"

As though he believed there was no such thing.

"No no, we're completely un-radical. We've lost the ability to be radical, us Western folk. We're too cynical, too apathetic. We've witnessed too many failures of the radical... communism, etcetera." I waved a hand around dismissively. "That's precisely why we're of our time; we lack a generational rite of passage. We're unable to grow up because we're already too jaded for the nine-to-five job and the 2.4 children."

Knowing we had our teeth into something he nipped to the bar and purchased some single malt whiskies. He took a thirsty slug of his.

"You keep saying 'we', how are you of *this* generation? You were there when the Berlin wall came down!"

I'd never told him this. He'd speculated the fact so much that he himself thought I'd told it. I paused thoughtfully.

"A generation is not marked by age, but by mindset." I coughed and laughed. "No, no, that's the whisky talking. That's the sort of thing an art lecturer would say."

We laughed heartily and Cuan pretended to fall off his chair, then gave an exaggerated clownish apology to the bar staff (who clearly didn't give a flying pigs ear).

"It's such a fucking circus that course." He tossed his curly hair.

"Anyway, you're a child of the Thatcher era, but you're planning to vote Tory?"

I meant this to be relevant, but it manifested a diversion instead.

"Only to piss my dad off. He's too fucking liberal. It's all I can do to annoy him. What kind of parent lets their kid study art, for fucks sake? Does he think I'm gonna paint watercolours to pay for his retirement? So anyway, that's about the level of political engagement you'll get from my lot."

My memory is always tied to a specific person or place or both. I tend to remember when I was most happy, and to the other extreme the times I was least happy. Waking up drunk amongst bin bags with some youth pissing on me. Things I don't care to recall, but if I try, they're so very vivid. The vividity of my memory is what makes me a chosen teller of tales (like the man in *Le Jetee*, who they made absurd use of). The trouble is I've a little tendency towards drifting off on a tangent. Because there are so many little memories and some so gloriously mundane. I'm like an excited child at the fair torn between the Fun House, the Hook-a-Duck and the Waltzers. I was glazed and lost in this prettily lit image when I realised Roxy was peering at me curiously. I supposed I was mumbling to myself again.

"What do you remember about Sheffield?" she asked.

I paused and coughed a little to clear my throat of cobwebs.

"Well. It was certainly colder than L.A," I started hesitantly. "Blustery, it was blustery a lot. It didn't rain as much as Manchester or Plymouth though... or Seattle."

"How d'you remember anything, when you've been so many places?" she asked.

"My brain is like an archive, but it's unregimented. I cannot order what I find there, but there's a lot." I snuffled into my hanky for a bit.

Roxy remains youthful in her curiosity. The pursuit of knowledge keeps us young, maybe. The awareness that there is always more to know. Most lose this (at least visibly) after two or three decades of living, which is silly. Have you the wisdom of a hundred year old turtle?

"Where were we?" I asked.

"Sheffield," she said patiently.

"Ah, Black Sheep, Pale Rider, Moonshine. Beer is a good method of remembering a place, particularly in fair England. And more revealing, yet still related, to the weather. Even the pale stuff would cheer a grey day. I remember the Red Deer, but I spent so much time there with the Kaiser, and the Red House as well to be fair, and Dulos. And that smoky low-ceilinged bar on West Street that sold Tuaca for £1.50?"

Roxy smirked. "I worked there!"

"Oh yes, so you did. There was that girl with curly, red hair, she was *very* pretty. And the Australian-Polish girl who drank a lot. I liked her. She never judged me for being a smelly old tramp."

Claudia cackled. "I did," she said affirmatively. "I still do a little bit."

The ace of clubs clouted me on the head. I fell down like a cartoon bandit.

"Anthropology..." I mumbled.

I drifted back to Cuan in the pub. The silly shapes he pulled with his elastic face, the gestures of skinny elongated arms and the rings around his eyes that told a secret history like the lines inside the trunk of a tree. That intense look he would give me often, that swallowed my immortal stinking soul.

Just like Roxy, he'd once spoken of his fear that I (the author, the sneak, the eternal observer who must be mistrusted) would commit him to paper. He didn't know that he was already tattooed on the inside my eyelid. Just the one mind you, I'm not *that* obsessed.

"Wolfgang?" Roxy tapped me back to the present.

Here in the rickety train, the faces of those who'd thus survived in this century, perishing neither in their misspent youth, nor The Weathers that shortly followed. I smiled, knowing these were my comrades whether they liked it or not, that their faces were more than blurred and faded photographs, shuffled amongst the cards.

The door which led to the front carriages was rattled open by nice bloke Freddie. He cheered and planted a bottle of Tobermory in front of Roxanne. (There was only a third left in the bottle, but we appreciated the sentiment.)

"Sweetiepie!" He leaned drunkenly into her bemused personal space. "That mutt tasted better than mutton. Good kill sweetart! Av some juice to celebrate."

He veered back off down the carriage, stumbling and singing in snatches.

"How much is that doggy in the window? Woof, woof."

Roxanne shrunk down in her seat and glanced sheepishly at the orphaned puppy fast asleep in my lap. I laughed heartily and snatched up the first swig from the bottle. Claudia and the Kaiser were already closed in on us but I passed it quickly to little Roxanne. She held the bottle which looked oversized in her tiny hand.

"Tell me about your Sheffield," I said to her.

She swigged sweet, grainy whisky. The taste wrapped her tongue around with its own memories of peaty earth and salty seas that crashed around the Hebrides. She remembered lying in the attic room next to Cuan, the wind howling and baying around the rooftops.

"My brother, David, told me to go to university in Sheffield," she began. "He said I wouldn't like it straight away because Nottingham was full of great architecture, but the centre of Sheffield was blitzed," she paused. "The steel factories made propeller blades for the war planes. So there were lots of ugly post-war buildings. But I'd grow to love it, because it was tatty and modest. I'd make life-long friends there."

"He predicted all that?" Claudia asked, reaching out for the bottle of whisky, which Roxy passed to her unpossessively.

"Well, not exactly, but near enough. I did everything in Sheffield, it was my city. I fell in love and got my heart broken, I got a degree that was of no use except as an experience, I worked in bars and lived the lifestyle I wanted. I felt true grief when I left."

"You came back," Kaiser said, his face remembering with equal joy and loathing.

"Well, Claudia moved back and I only had superficial friendships left where I was. I was too late already though – some of my favourite places were gone. The Art School was sold off for demolition, some pubs and bars had closed down because of the recession. There were a few people still there, but *it* was gone. And The Weathers came and pretty much destroyed the remains."

500

I remembered, like a photograph, the city swept away, the pools of scum not washed clean from the streets. I remembered being sat stunned, reading the last book I had left at the time. I forget most of what I read in it, except for when it explained that the word 'cynical' had come from ancient Greek, meaning 'doglike'. I had sat next to a dirty puddle in which a grubby Westie lay belly up and dead, reading that bit over and over .

And I thought of Cuan, my zeitgeist for a generation. I thought of him and his bitter cynicism, and it was him lying there belly up to the empty skies. Skies that echoed with the vulnerable mortality of all this... which was memory.

PHASE SEVEN

In which they search for Riddlehamhope & their wildest dreams come true at the foot of the Cheviot Hills

INSECURE LUMPS OF ROCK

Simian Thomas, Northumberland

I had never been so cold in my life. I was convinced of this. Even when I got stranded on a rock in the sea as a teenager, in the dark. This was a different kind of cold. It was very still and quiet. It penetrated my clothing and skin and bones and snuck inside my head, between the squelchy bits of my brain, so all that I could think was – 'I'm cold'. Though this alternated a little with – 'I'm exhausted'.

    We'd walked for hours through the bleak Northumbrian landscape, sticking to the scrawny pastures still marked with dry stone walls and broken fences that leaned drunkenly into the wind. We'd walked with energy and determination at first. (It must nearly be spring after all. We must've survived colder weather than this?) But the track had grown longer and longer and the cold persistently followed us, a pack of hungry wolves waiting to gobble us up. We were at a shuffle now. We knew if we stopped we'd never start again, our bodies failing to stutter back to life, like the engine of an old banger. We knew if we stopped, we'd die out here in next to nowhere, exposed to the skies and the volatile weather of the nearby moorlands.

So each of our brains spoke softly to itself – 'I'm cold... I'm exhausted... if I stop I will die.'

It was frightening that a big part of you thought giving up was the best option. It was the only way to end the torture. If I'm dead, I'll no-longer feel this pain. But then the cold was already a painful cold, we were numb but with pain. I felt like a frozen piece of meat, defrosted enough at the joints for rudimentary movements like some crude puppet. The cold was pain, and to wait to die was to wait for more slow pain. How long would I take to even lose consciousness properly? Maybe several hours. I saw these thoughts echoed in the faces of my friends, though I could barely put them into focus.

I opened my mouth to speak but there was nothing there. My brain couldn't handle the multi-tasking. Charlie lumbered forward suddenly and clumsily pointed ahead. There was some sort of building, maybe an old farm house, nestled between the ruins of other buildings reduced to mounds of earth and stones. Hope switched on a light in our heads and we moved like enthusiastic zombies (maybe not any faster than before). We clambered over insecure lumps of rock. Roxy slipped. My reactions were too slow to reach out straight away, but then I grasped her arm and helped her up. We looked for an opening to the building which had survived the Weathers remarkably well. Had we had good working eyes to see, we would've noticed places where it'd been skilfully reinforced and repaired, stacks of sandbags forming strange architectural features.

The first door was locked, but a little further round there was another which Charlie tried and it opened. We scrambled inside and found that it led straight into a farmhouse kitchen and a fire already burned in the hearth. I felt such relief that the place could've been inhabited by vampires and I wouldn't have cared a jot, so long as I could sit near that fire. The five of us crouched in front of it wordlessly, rubbing our hands and staring into the flames which seemed to be gloriously blinding in colour, after the barren grey of the endless track.

Charlie muttered clumsy thanks to God. As we began defrosting and our awareness returned, we peered around the room. A mug of something hot was sat on the table steaming and a woolly jumper was left on the back of a chair. Some recently deceased rabbits were strung up from a hook in one of the beams, the odd little blood spot dripping down on the worn wooden floor.

"It's like the Mary Celeste." My voice quivered back to life.

The kitchen was full of organised clutter, useful objects collected and placed. There was a loud grinding noise and part of the floor moved to one side to reveal a hatch. We all stared on, dumbstruck, as the crown of a head poked through. His hair was black, with flecks of silver and a large pale patch on one side, though he was only maybe in his forties.

"Ah," Charlie said quietly. "A badger."

The weather-beaten face emerged followed by broad stocky shoulders. He heaved himself out and closed the hatch, looking as rugged and fearsome as the wilds.

"Well, here's a bunch a' lost souls. Thowt ah heard people." He spoke with a local accent. He picked up the mug from the table and sipped some. "Did I ne lock the door? Dinnae geht many aboot these parts but they tend te scavenge everyfookinthing..."

Charlie stood up now and shook the man's hand. After all he hadn't asked us to leave.

"The door was unlatched. Sorry for the intrusion but they're near death with cold. Mae name's Charlie, who are yuu?"

"Stig!" Wolfgang exclaimed, pointing to a row of eggcups on the mantel.

"They caal me Brock," the man replied. "I sposes ye're ahl hungry?"

We nodded.

"But firse, some hot water wi'a dram a' whisky, I think."

"I lyke this bloke," Claudia muttered, sleepily.

I stared at the egg cups and tried to remember their relevance but my brain was too hazy. I was defrosting too quickly and the fire felt so very hot. Yet parts of my body remained cold. I was shaking almost into fits and then my body failed and I crumpled to the floor. I drifted in and out of consciousness as warm liquid was put to my lips and hands lifted me and cocooned me in blankets somewhere. I was tucked away to sleep dreamlessly and wake to live again.

* * * * * * *

LIKE A BADGER CAUGHT IN A THUNDERSTORM

Wolfgang, Northumberland

From the hug of an armchair I watched the Stig-man who called himself 'Brock', a term for a male badger. He was indeed of badger character. An earth dweller, a digging species with huge hands like a mole. Badger has not the sleekness of other hunters, but he's both bold and cautious, stout and swift. He has a bloody-minded nature, he does not give up easily.

Brock scratched his thickset neck, which looked tanned from the layers of dirt. His hair was mostly black, but speckled salt 'n pepper here and there, then on one side, to the back, a large strange patch of silver-white, not in keeping with his age.

Upon polite asking from Roxy on this strange marking, he'd grinned toothily, with the face of a man who likes to tell tall tales, and pronounced that he'd been struck by lightning, some time ago. Little Roxy is not so naive as her face would have you think. But as it was a polite question, she did not question the reply, and neither should I. For there is what is real and physical and there is what is told, and when the real and physical within a moment of experience has passed, there is only what is told. And we tell ourselves as much as we tell others.

Brock looked at me then and I realised I'd been muttering quietly to myself, in German at least.

"Noo then Deutsch-bag, what's on yee mynd?"

He had the raw, rustic accent of the locale – a kind of dialectal bridge between Scotland and England. I peered back at him and tried to remember another time and another person who had idly nick-named me the same.

"Where does the phrase 'nick-name' come from?" I asked. "It reminds me of the slang 'nick' to steal... a stolen name?"

He smiled wryly as though his wisdom could never be words.

"What are yee *on*, Jerry? Yee think tee much. Less think, less yammer – more do. That's how ye'll survive this shit. It beats me hoo the fook yee intel-lectuals huv lived s' lang."

"It beats me. An American phrase, I think." I dragged my mind off the delights of language "I know useful things too. That's how I've gotten by my whole life, that and the ability to exist on the very meagre." I shrugged.

"Av gotten them oot of most messes." The Kaiser was dredging up his Scotsman's growl, struggling for alpha status, despite being in helpless admiration for the badger.

"Yeah, ya carried us all the way here." Claudia glowered. She turned to Brock, "and why d'ya think I'm a fookin 'intellectual'?"

He shook his head silently, as if to say *'women'*.

There was a sense of safeness in the company of Brock, however. As if should danger threaten, should a hungry cougar come a-prowling, he'd wearily shake his head as if to say *'Can yee pesky kids ne look after yissels?'* Then save us, whilst remaining nonchalant.

There was a water butt fixed onto the wall of the farmhouse kitchen. A drainpipe crept in from the roof to feed it. Brock turned the tap on and filled a cup with some water, hairy nose close to the surface to gauge the appearance and soak up the bouquet.

He sighed.

"I thunk thes sommat deid in the system, have tu gaen clean it oot."

He dragged a battered ladder out from the cupboard and disappeared outside.

"Stig," I said with hopeless admiration, "he never rests."

We'd been steadily recovering from our death walk through the barren North. Our bodies gradually coming back to life, in order to tell more stories of woe. The new moccasins protected our feet from fresh blood and blisters, but old wounds had reopened. Kaiser's trench foot had doubtless worsened and when he removed his shoes, the plastic bags and his sodden socks, the fungal smell made me want to retch. And I myself am a smelly wretch.

Simian was out for the count, bundled in blankets in a chair closest to the fire. Roxy sat quivering like a cold little ratty. I pondered how the two of them, with their delicately bred bones, had not perished. Although had their feet failed them, Kaiser would've carried either a fair way rather than discard the weaklings. I myself still had another handicap in my pocket that I'd near forgotten.

I produced the bundle of fur. She'd wriggled at the beginning of the journey, but now was completely still, in a ball, like a clenched fist that refused to open. She'd been in the pocket close to my beating heart and body warmth, but doubtless still had suffered for her lack of movement to keep blood pumping. She seemed to be in hibernation. I sat cross-legged close up to the fire and rubbed her with my sleeve. Her little nose emerged, her eyes squinted up like a new born. There was a teeny whine.

Brock clattered back into the room, a chill of air following him before he slammed the door. He sniffed a loud sniff and looked down at the pup.

"Crikey, tha thing alive?"

"Just about," I answered, rubbing the critter again to further whimpers.

He put a dab of lard in a small iron pan and held it over the fire for a moment to soften, then got a small chunk of bread, and dipped it in the fat. He crouched down next to me, his frame filling the space so that I was shrunken. The puppy sniffed the morsel, licked it and then keenly clamped it into tiny jaws.

"Ya've bread? Where from?" Claudia queried.

"I mak ut," he said. "I aenly huv yeast, flour an water though, ne salt so it doesnae taste tuu canny."

"May we have sum, or is the pooch the priority?" Kaiser asked.

Brock looked at him with a blunt expression.

"Withoot the survival uf animals we'd probably ne last lang. We'ud be eating each other and wearing human skin," he muttered with dark resolve. "I've ne much meat around, but ahv plenty a broth from boiled bones. Ah'll heat sum up for yuus."

"What about the rabbits?" Claudia asked.

"Well, yee're a grateful bunch, aye. The rabbits are fer feeding mae prisoners in the cellar."

We exchanged looks to create a census of whether this was gallows humour, or the raw uneasy truth. I resolved if he had prisoners, at least he had the decency to feed them juicy rabbits. He picked up a great black cauldron and hung it on a hook over the fire, adding a little more wood to the flaming mass. I watched the sparks and demons leaping in the air.

Soon enough we were sat around the table, dipping bread in lard and broth in a greedy fashion, with only the noise of lips slurping and knashers chewing. But Roxanne broke the quiet with her humble curiosity.

"Can I ask what you're doing here? Out in the middle of nowhere. It doesn't seem a very suitable place to settle."

Brock nodded.

"I think ye just asked, sweet pea. Well, this isnae mae only home. I've several places dotted aboot. I've several 'occupations' if ye will, one of whuch is mekkin detailed assessments uf the changing landscape – where the floods are happunin, which landmarks are likely tu survive a few years. Some friends of mine make new maps based on auld maps, which we can then exchange for various commodities. It also gives us sum idea on a small scale of if an' when the Weathers wull settle doon, and what our climate will be leik when they dee."

"Gosh," I said. "So you do think they will settle down?"

He shrugged.

"They huv already for the time be. The North Atlantic Drift has gone te fook, thas what majorly fooked this country. The whole Gulf Stream hus probably had her wicked way aroon the wold. Our climate'ull continue tu be a lot less wahm than it used te. But all the storms an floods, an sae on, were like a *big* tantrum. I think she'ull calm doon and we can re-acclimatise."

"She?" Roxy said.

"Mother Nature," he said with gruff humour. "Geyts a little huffy from time te time."

"These friends who mayke maps, da they breed dogs an all?" Claudia asked.

"Aye," he nodded. "Haydn and Toby, they'll be who yee're affta..."

"How did you know that?" I pursued.

He shrugged.

"I heard word. Sid Arthur?"

We puzzled over how long it'd taken us to travel North, yet word had somehow gotten there faster.

"These other 'abodes' you have dotted around?" I asked. "Is one an old railway carriage?"

"Yeah, thas a favourite. The train men ne doubt showed you that one. I've many dealings with them. We ken one another. They sent you this way, aye? Away from Alnwick an the mentalists?"

"A series of invaluable coincidences..." I mumbled to myself.

"Ye can stay furra few days here to reboot," Brock said. "Then ahll point ye in the right direction and it's up to ye."

"How can we repay yuu?" Kaiser asked.

"With the dog," he said, without hesitation, as though it'd already been decided. "Ah need a pup to train assa tunnel dog. Been waiting for Toby to gimme one, but he's sae faddy aboottis dogs and what age he'll gi them up. I need a bellikin."

"What's a 'tunnel dog'?" Roxy asked.

"Mae other 'occupation' is the building and upkeep uf a network of tunnels, reinforced in places liek bunkers. So thes a sayfer wey te travel during bad weather. Ah need a dog thas used te bein dayhn there ahl day (s'well as ootdoors). S'often risky where the land's unstable. Dogs are canny ut alertin ye to danger. It's dark as fook dayhn there."

Little Hobo was crouched on a stool next to me, lapping from a saucer of broth, oblivious to the conversation. I sighed a weighty, remorseful sigh. I was reminded of the great mine in Günter Grass's *Dog Years*, and the black shepherd dog that seemed destined to live down there. My pup was not all black, she was not proper shepherd either, there was something else in there I suspected.

"Whas her nayme?" Brock picked her up and examed her, like one might do to a prospective purchase.

"Hobo," I answered.

"It's a she," he said.

"Hobina," I shrugged.

He laughed a hearty Northern laugh and little Hobo wriggled in glee.

* * * * * * *

GUILT HAS NOTHING TO DO W'IT

Claudia McLeod, Northumberland

It were snowin again.

"It must be fookin April b'now." I stared out the window. It were once a pretty bay window. Now it was covered with a heavy tattered curtain which were coloured wi' dirt. Me and Roxy were sat between the curtains and the pane, on't window seat. It was a bit nippy, but we could get a picture round abouts the house. It was bleak as fook outside. It looked as hostile as it'd felt when we trudged through it a few days before, wi' barely a hope a not dying out there. Now the emptiness was turnin white.

"I remember it snowing in April in Sheffield once," Roxy said thoughtfully. "Bobby came to pick me up from work and we went to the chippy." She was rambling. Pissin out idle mem'ry, one of them stories that went nowhere. "Golf ball sized snowflakes were falling outside. By the time we got to Bobby's car it was covered. Gone by morning though."

I didn't answer. I wasn't in a great mood. I was fairly sick of hearin Roxy talk about Bobby. Bobby was lyke Cuan, and Rufio, and Cassie – a cold, dead face that should've been forgot by now, but some people refused to be scribbled out in time. I'd thought far too much in recent days about Rufio, rememberin how he seemed t'hold me and Haydn's relationship together. Lyke the gaffer tape on me auld boots.

The snow was settling thick and fast, soon we could barely see past t'other side a the pane through the falling flakes. I imagined it continuin until the whole farmstead was buried.

"It snowed lyke this just after I had the abortion," I mulled, without thinking what I was saying. "I 'member cause I saw Kate Jackson from The Long Blondes in Wait'rose. Ordinarily I would've gone up and spoke to her. But I were soo sad, I could never'uv found t' words."

I frowned, still staring at the snow, still findin my eyes tried to focus and refocus on fallin flakes, so that when I looked around it looked as though Roxy was growin. I studied her fizzog and realised I'd never even told her.

"You had an abortion?" Her forehead creased in question.

"Oh, yeah. It was when you moved back to Nottin'ham furra bit." I sighed, realisin there was all the explainin to do.

"Haydn's?"

"Jody," I answered.

"But you were with Haydn then..." She drifted off, did a little thinkin.

Roxy's a *naturally* monogamous person. I'm *naturally* a selfish bitch. The grass is always greener an that. Jody had a new girlfriend, so obviously I wanted to screw his brains out and remind him that nobody could ever measure up to me.

"There's a small chance it were Haydn's, but I'd put my bets on Jody. It woulda turned out ginger, questions woulda been asked." I sighed again.

My brain hummed an auld song that reminded me agen and agen of the livin thing inside me that refused to die – the fooking guilt.

Roxy was bein very quiet and sweet so I rambled on, tryin ta fill the gaps.

"Snow mekks me feel broody. And feelin broody reminds me that I'm a cold-blooded murd'rer."

"Don't be daft," she said. "Everyone should have a choice."

"I could've had it adopted though," I said, "but that woulda been harder. To know your kid was growin up wi'out you, that someone was doin a better job."

I pressed my forehead to the cold window pane and imagined I was lost in the flurry of snow.

"I'd rather not yammer on about it anyroads," I muttered. "Shit happens."

"Rather not talk about what?" Charlie poked his head through the curtains.

"Rather not talk about what a disgustin, ugly, irritatin human being you are to purrup with," I answered.

"I understand," he said with that annoyin smile. "Girl talk? I'll stay out of it."

If killin unborn babies counts as girl talk, I thought. Even though Charlie already knew about it, I couldn't be bothered with dredging it all up again.

"Go and sort yar feet out, you smelly greb," I said.

He laughed. "Thanks McLeod."

Brock had insisted outtah all ayus that Charlie stayed inside over't next few days to dry his feet out. This worra'course frustratin him. He disappeared again and left us in our quiet little snug. Roxy yawned.

"I've been having very strange, vivid dreams since we got here. Have you?" she asked.

I shrugged. "I don't really dream."

"Everyone dreams!" she insisted.

"Well, I don't remember them." I shook me head.

"Oh," she looked at me lyke I were a very strange form of human. "I can't imagine what that would be like. Anyway, I dreamed last night that I was carrying myself. There were two of me, so I had to give one a piggy back. The city looked beautiful though. I was stepping down this path and could see all the way over. It was a mud city, with little shining lights gleaming in the puddles of dirt."

"Love'ly." I wasn't sure what I were meant to make of this.

"You don't ever dream strange stuff like that?" she asked, as though she didn't believe me. As though I was just tryin ta avoid talkin bout my dreams because they were that dark and bleak, they should never be spoke of.

"I never remember stuff I dream," I repeated.

"Wev enuff wahm watter for the next bath," Brock called. He poked his face into our cold booth, eyes full of gravedigger's mischief. "Who's next?"

"I think am the last one," I said.

Brock had the capability to heat water for baths, but it worra slow process and he worra busy man, so it'd tekken this long for us all to get a turn.

"Aye," he said. "Afta ye, I mayht chuck the smelly German in agen. The firs one dinnae seem te make much difference."

I nodded.

The bathroom were freezing compared to the downstairs rooms, which had fires maire regular. There was an auld fitted bath in't corner, but the plumbing no-longer worked so it were used for storage. But Brock had reclaimed an auld roll-top bath from somewhere. (How the fook he'd gorrit up there is anyone's guess.) He could heat great pans of siphoned rainwater or melted snow to fill it, and then it had a basic drainage system. The steam was rising off the surface of the water proper fast. It were mistin't air so I became a blurry smear as I quickly undressed and stepped carefully into the warm water. The careful sinkin of each body part into it worra akin to sex at this point. I hummed happily, finally sinkin up to my neck. The water clouded and turned almost black in seconds wi'the quantity a muck which must've collected on me. All the washes we'd had soo far involved cold dips in rivers, usually we were only brave enough to splash our faces.

I lay there, alone with my thoughts. I stared at my toes poking out at t'other end, reflected below thissels in the murky bathwater. Lyke some sort of fleshy, mutant butterflies. In the blurry, mesmerisin heat my troubles and memories became loose and careless. They drifted up ta'tha mossy, muswebbed ceiling where the cracks formed landscapes, cross'atched by dirty, peelin paintwork. I'd stay there until the water was luke warm and my fingers looked lyke Charlie's feet.

* * * * * * *

ALIEN NATION

Bryn McLarey, Northumberland

Underneath the ground is a different world. Mae soul is lighter sometimes, but noo it feels heavy. The entrance is marked Hades and guarded by a blonde boy. As though it were some canny joke at the expense of mae subconscious. Some days the stone tunnels drip-drip with nature's fickle liquid. Other days icicles form like stalactites hanging doon from the roof. But these here were the ruined tunnels, unlived. The tunnels where Brock worked – rebuilding and restructuring so that we might keep our future. He maintained the stores of food and materials. There were even rooms people could live in furra wee while, with the simple pattern of heating bricks and the slow release of heat back intu the caverns. It reminded me of all the strange science fiction where humans were forced tu live underground like worms. We weren't all the way there yet, but I wondered if Brock thought sometime soon we would be.

"Sae long as we caen burn, we caen heat," he said. "Still ets shite furrus that since the last Ice Age we'uv killed off all the beasties whose skins kept us wahm. Wolves and bears used to roam these parts." He sniffed and rubbed his grubby nose. "But ther a many wild dogs aboots," he motioned tu the fur blanket he carried. "I cannae work in these materials of course, leather es sae invaluable. It lasts sae long. But to sleep in..." he nodded wisely tu hissel. "Ye'll notice most of our short haired breeds have died oot. Ets all the wolf coats that survive and they're happier in this climate. Pity – used to have a Staffie, miss the critter."

There was no tone of remorse in his voice. He wus un-emotive. You cannae work every day in these cold corridors and stay emotive, neh self-pity survived here.

But he wanted tu evoke the emotions of others, most of all he was a teller...

'All the best stories are just interesting lies', a wiser chap than me once wrote. In Brock's stories the real and the exaggeration merged seamlessly. It didnae matter if he knew which bits were true anymore. What mattered wus the eyes watching, the ears listening, the lips slightly apart in canny surprise. This wus where his humanity wus. When he spoke, he recalled every great story teller that yuu knew, that I knew, that someone once spoke of. Mae Grandpappy (a naval officer) sprung tu mind. The smell of whisky rising up through the floorboards, leaning on the wall in the darkness tuu intoxicated tu walk. The stories of a drunk were how it all began, he could never remember, mae pet, *what really happened...*

An ego and a beer equal an exaggeration.

For sum reason a memory flashed tu me. Brought on by the smell of wet mud and rotten things, I thought. A memory of clearing out the leaves of a wintered pond (one of mae odd jobs being the skivvy to a landscape gardener). The body of a frog, bloated and frozen in death, floated tu the surface.

I followed Brock doon the dark tunnel. He wus silent now. As silent as the Earth which wus all aroond us, an if I listened gently I could hear mae own wee heart beatin. A small sense of panic emerged in mae absent emotions. An old claustrophobia, as though I wus trapped, buried. But I relaxed, for death cannot make harm of me. The asphyxiation I willnae notice, as am tuu busy smokin.

* * * * * *

AN ABSTRACT NOUN

Simian Thomas, Northumberland

We'd been snowed in at Brock's farmhouse for a few days. He had an underground tunnel in which it was possible to travel, but it didn't connect all the way to Toby and Haydn's house yet. He was also a bit vague about whether or not some bits might collapse on us. After a while the snow cleared some, and the sky looked less like it would chuck up a blizzard at any moment. Brock stood on the mossy rubble outside the farmhouse with his nose in the air, closing his eyes and reopening them, appearing with all pretention to be tuning into the wild, and listening for the weather.

"Fookin bullshitter," Claudia muttered. "He's tekkin our welfare in't snow as a fookin joke."

"It's better that there is snow. It won't be too cold. And if it starts again we can bury down in it to keep warm," Wolfgang said.

"Aye, it's a tuff choice deciding which mentalist to have faith in," Claudia added. "If we're gonna goo let's not beat about the bush. We're going into't wild and the weather is shit."

"What is the 'wild' anyway?" Wolfgang said. "Nothing if not an abstract noun..."

Claudia made her eyes wide with a sarky, fear-inducing stare. She kept this intense stare at Wolfgang to make him shut his gob and stop spouting pretension. Philosophical theorising wouldn't keep us warm and safe after all. This felt like the precipice and yet stepping off into thin air, without guarantee of a safe foothold, felt inevitable. And so we readied ourselves as best we could and set out again on foot, armed with a scribbled map of current landmarks and the advice to head roughly northwest. We were looking for a place named 'New Riddlehamhope'. Yet Brock had assured us there would be no signposts and if we asked locals they would send us south towards Durham County.

"It's a bonny pet name," he explained with an unreassuring wink. "Ask fe the Breamish River if y'ask. My advice is daen't ask. Best to look leik ye know where y'gannin."

We put our layers of clothes back on like old friends – hats and jumpers and double hoods, extra socks stuffed into moccasins, our coats the final layer, a frayed protector. We were heading into what used to be designated as Northumberland National Park and Brock'd explained this place was at the foot of the Cheviot Hills, on the banks of the Breamish. As we began walking, the apparently endless pastures disappeared. They were replaced by wetland bogs, wild gorse and heather-patched hills, all forming a landscape that'd looked so desolate and characterless just a few moments before. But as quickly as the fields were gone, they seemed to appear again, and we were regimented back in between the dry stone walls, which seemed to have outlasted most buildings and roads. These seemed the only constant in the everchanging North, reminding that every bit of scrub and scramble was once owned by someone. The snow still lay in fair patches, but wasn't thick enough to disguise things too much. Brock had set a particular path to avoid the swampiest areas, though he assured us most of it would be nicely frozen over still.

We were mostly walking on old farm track, or damaged roads. The hardest navigation came when we left these, clambering stiles and following footpaths. The snow was beginning to thicken on the ground in these places and Charlie stopped several times to scrutinise the map and swear a bit to himself. He was getting the most tired too, from ploughing out our path, so Roxy suggested we kept swapping who was walking at the front – as wolves (and soldiers) apparently do when travelling in snow.

It was with relief that we entered woodland for a bit, giving a feeling of shelter for a short period. But this soon turned back to scrubland again and I lost count of stiles and gates and broken down gaps in walls that we'd clambered through. Wolfgang, who was at this time leading, stopped dead all of a sudden. We all bumped into one another, as those at the back had forsaken concentrating on anything other than putting one foot in front of the other, following the person in front.

"Angel of the North!" he said.

We all looked upset for a minute, thinking we'd somehow meandered towards Gateshead. But he was pointing to the ground. In an unspoilt patch of snow ahead of him, a bird must've taken off, leaving the beautiful marks of its flapping wings in the white. A proper snow angel, I thought. We decided this was an appropriate time to rest and drink some of our water stash, seating ourselves on the omnipresent remains of walling. We all gazed with relieved hypnotism at the snow angel in the centre of the prettied landscape, where white touched more white and even the sky seemed a similarly peaceful shade.

"It's a good omen," Wolfgang announced, matter-a-factly, pulling his hood back a little to get a better view.

"You're a bad omen," Charlie said, merely finding any old excuse to insult any old friend.

I nibbled on some of the tasteless bread Brock had given us to snack on, looking for life in the emptiness. The odd few birds were about, hob-knobbing with neighbours about the vagrant people sat on the wall, legs dangling in casual jauntiness. Finally I spotted a couple of men on horseback in the distance. They paused their horses and looked at us for a bit, discussing something with one another, shooting wary glances about. Eventually they disappeared and we took this as the time to set off again.

"Do we seem to be on't right track?" Claudia swiped Charlie's map.

"Yes!" he said, playfully shoving her ahead so she nearly fell in the snow.

The sound of careless laughter was a relief. The big wilderness today seemed just a playground; the weather was holding back its worst.

* * * * * * *

THE FOREST OF HIDDEN RUNAWAYS

Roxanne Ratcliffe, Breamish Valley

The snow on the ground seemed less and less as the day wore on and we reached lower land again. After walking between a series of patched woods, which gave us cover and shelter from the chill fogs sneaking from the hills, we eventually saw lights in the distance. Maybe the flicker of a candle inside a lamp? My heart skipped with little tremors of hope. We'd been on the verge of giving up for the day and building a shelter in the woods. We were approaching a settlement, but it seemed to be all in ruins. Empty, old farm sheds, made from breeze blocks and corrugated sheet metal, seemed to be the only thing still standing, and most of those had gaping holes in the roof. They loomed about us, promising little protection, making rusty creaking noises. We stuck to the woods. There was probably an old road around somewhere, but it was all too overgrown to know.

Wolfgang lost his top hat in the hands of the trees. He growled as he dragged it free. He'd been terribly excited to find it in Brock's attic.

"This is a cursed forest." He looked around suspiciously. "I feel it."

The woodland indeed seemed to get even denser the closer we got to the small plot of land that we were aiming for. Everything that appeared to be a path soon turned back into undergrowth. The sky was turning indigo as darkness stalked us, but there remained a half-light as we reached the garden. The lights of the house had disappeared as though to deter us. But we stood stubbornly staring up at the blank windows. The large beam of an old torch suddenly fell on us.

A small figure approached hesitantly and I recognised the way he moved. As the light caught him I gazed dumbly on. He was completely bald now, his chin highlighted by a scruffy beard, wide grey-blue eyes swallowed us with an unthreatening gaze. Charlie stood a foot from him, looking down with a furrowed brow. The rest of us stood behind like mystic shadows, our coats billowing in the evening breeze.

"Please leave," the man said calmly. "There's nothing here for you."

Charlie snorted.

"We're nae leavin. We've come a long fookin way."

"I've dogs..." the man said carefully.

"I've a gun," Charlie replied.

"You can't stay," the man repeated firmly.

Charlie seemed angered by his lack of anger. He snatched his collar, leaning over so their eyes were level. His two fiendish dark irises reached inside two warm orbs wide with question, both unflinching, reading in each other an opposite.

"Let him go." I pushed to the front.

Freed from the beastly grip, the man found himself instead trapped in my eye line. Charlie's words drowned out by the silence in our heads.

"Roxy...?" he said with slow disbelief.

"Toby." I returned.

"This is Toby?!" Charlie spat.

Another figure, taller and skinnier, had also approached from the house. He was carrying the lamp which lit the scene, the beam jerking frenetically. A black dog shadowed him with glinting eyes. He had a youthful shock of pale hair. Spectacles framed the gaze of a boyish face beneath a man's beard.

"Claudia?!" He spluttered in delight, weaving obliviously through the crowd to hug her.

I broke my uncertainty and hugged Toby, just to see if he was real. He hugged me back as though the world was ending – which it probably was.

* * * * * * *

HALF CUT

Haydn Antoine, New Riddlehamhope

The images that contorted to our reality were more than surreal. Fistfuls of minutes earlier we'd suspected strangers were afoot and blacked out the house. We'd stood between closed curtains and the window pane, peering through, shivering our breath in ghosts on the glass.

There were sometimes beggars around the area, destitute skeletons wandering like the undead. Sometimes we played the Good Samaritan and helped them, but these times often turned drastically bad. A lot of people left around had serious mental issues – their numbers were dwindling though, gradually massacred by the winters which worsened each year. Those that did survive were part of clans. They were the locals and we the aliens, our accents betraying us. Betraying that we had no hoard of henchmen to retaliate crimes committed.

We were numbed to the sights and signs of death by now. We'd chosen the bleak, wild, crippled landscape instead of becoming pawns to the new Southern government. It was at times a lonely sense of exile, but it was free. We toiled steadily to keep the house in one piece and live off the land. We'd formed a plan between ourselves and some other friends who lived further along the base of the valleys.

But now there were people on our land, treading on the cabbage patch. Toby sighed and handed me the emergency torch we sometimes used to stun wild animals. The twilight was threatening to die into darkness as we exited the house.

"Keep the dogs in," Toby murmured.

I shut them in, except Fidel who shadowed me, a calm guardian offering protection from the uncertain. I followed Toby down the steps at a hesitant distance. Five people were stood, one clad in a long black woollen coat, I suppose only seeming so surreal as he wore a top hat over the top of his hood. Not the most practical attire for the Weathers, recalling some strange Victoriana. He looked like a hobo magician. I couldn't help but stare at him, and was thus clobbered with a flashback to a dream in which he holds my collar and presses his face close, speaking in a foreign tongue. His eyes are close to mine but he's blind. It's like staring into a pool through a layer of ice.

One of the men in the group spoke threateningly to Toby as I snapped back to the present. He closed a fist on Toby's collar. Fidel growled a quiet warning growl. The man was tall and well stacked with muscle and an intense sense of unprovoked anger. He had dark hair and was heavily bearded, a stout face with a Roman nose. I'd learned, through too many predicaments, to read people and situations quickly. He had a Scottish accent, rather than Northumbrian. I felt he was neither deranged, nor likely to hurt Toby. Just trying to intimidate. I looked to the rest of the group and my eyes met with a familiar face. My heart thumped and skipped to life, as though it had previously been in hibernation.

Claudia McLeod, that past love of hauntingly, beautiful cynicism that'd ultimately led to the demise of the relationship. Our paths had turned in different directions and the world had gotten in the way.

We dashed to hug one another. Cynicism melted like the icy pond into which past children had fallen. I was breathless and without a word able to form, amongst some flood of Shakespearean sonnets and Byron poetry that filled my muddled brain. We stood close, breathing icy air into each others' faces with big stupid grins. Even in these days of darkness a beacon of light can penetrate the frosted land. I no longer had to wander lonely as some Heathcliffe-like creature. I turned and looked to the man who I learned to be Charlie and saw Heathcliffe himself. Two black eyes beneath a lowered brow, swallowing into himself my leftover loneliness.

Isolated in the big old house with Toby and the dogs, my only media had been musty old books, classics, eternally relevant stories I'd previously lacked the patience to read. But looking at Claudia now, a past flooded back that I thought I'd lost. Of spontaneous nights and morning hangovers, of hip-hop and drum and bass and dancing like an idiot. Of lying on the sofa watching endless films while Rufio made tea. Of afternoons sat in the pub trying to motivate myself to go home and do some work. Of enthusiasm for things I could no longer comprehend – ridiculously priced clothes that didn't protect me from the weather and made me look like a fashionable clown.

The Byron quotations left me and I looked adoringly into Cloud's eyes and said with utter Englishness.

"What's up, dawg?"

She smirked and shook her head almost shyly.

"It is wharrit is. It is. What it is."

* * * * * * *

FERAL CHILDREN IN THE MOON'S ORBIT

Wolfgang, New Riddlehamhope

Hippy paradise beckoned to us wily men of the forest, in the form of glowering light, which asked that we fellows ascend these steps and enter the open door.
'*Riddlehamhope*', Brock had called this place... riddle... ham... hope.

The night was not the coldest nor bleakest we'd yet found. I didn't need to break icicles from my matted beard. Yet the warmth of this house made me feel like I'd somehow come home. The Moomin one was rejoined uncertainly in the arms of little-man-Tobias, who maybe had all the answers, and Cloud had re-found her boy toy, the Adonis, in the same place. No coincidence, no improbability, no fate. Do not question the story, the story will only question you.

I feel a new philosophicality growing in my cracked bones, and again I jump from saying I felt to I feel, which every tail-tale should do. Everything is happening now and yesterday. Time is incoherent. It measures the immeasurable; it tries to trap memory into truths.

The house was old and narrow. It'd once been part of a small hamlet, but abandoned. The cold weather had gradually rotted everything, and the woods and gorse-riddled undergrowth were swallowing the houses into ruins. How long does it take for the Earth to swallow our bricks and cement? (Less than a century? The time it takes for a prince to come galloping by?)

The mossy air was heavy with realities. Here, besieged by the wild plants that waited to consume them, were allotment plots, using the fertile soil to grow food while the Jack of Frosts took a holiday. The inside of the kitchen had a door that lead down into a typical townhouse cellar, yet a mysterious hole in the wall led into another cellar, and then another. While Russian vines and wuthering storms had dragged the walls of houses to the ground, the cellars still existed beneath the soil forming the maze of tunnels that Brock had described. And these too, eventually connected with disused sewer channels and the old flues from lead smelting. A giant badger set was evolving beneath the beclarted northern county.

With this cellar below, the kitchen was elevated above the garden plot. The house stood on a slope down to the back from which we approached. There was a door to the cellar in the back garden, but also these steps (that we ascended) leading up to the kitchen door. The kitchen itself was a huge L shaped room with a long wooden table fit for a feast, a huge roaring wood fire in the middle, as well as an old cast iron stove at the back.

As we climbed the back steps leading to this orb, I contemplated the black shepherd dog sat in the doorway, intent on meeting the gaze of every Being that passed over his threshold.

"Are you Harras or are you Pluto?" I whispered beneath my breath, for he was surely *one* of Günter's creations.

"The devil's dog," Kaiser hissed softly. "Look in his eyes."

Roxy removed a glove and extended the bony white fingers of her hand for the dog to sniff, before roughing the ruff of thick fur and muscle round his shoulders.

"What's his name?" she asked Tobias Roe.

"Fidel." He smiled quietly at her.

"IN-fidel!" I shouted rather loudly to the night sky.

"Would you mind being quiet outside?" the Blonde Adonis asked with utter politeness. "We don't want to give away our position."

I gave him a comraderous pat on the shoulder.

"Damn right, soldier!" I said in a hushed growl. "There's a war goin on..."

Claudia smirked the way she does when she's tolerating me.

"This is Haydn," she said. "Haydn, this is Wolfgang."

"I shall call you Adonis," I confided to him.

"Then I shall call you Amadeus," he shot back with all the pluck and strut of a young cockerel.

We'd begun invading wonky wooden chairs around the great table by this time. Kaiser took a pointed seat at the head of it, silently fuming away at the small, insignificant man who seemed to have the heart's possession of his Roxy.

"You both have composers' names." Toby turned to me.

"I haven't heard of a composer called the young Adonis," I said quick-wittedly.

"My name should be pronounced Hi-den according to the name-sake," Haydn explained.

"Adonis it is then."

Toby was looking thoughtfully at me, turning over every sentence in his head, as though I would somehow make sense to him if he paid close attention.

"Are you all hungry?" he asked the group in a voice that showed reluctance to lead more than a donkey.

"We're always hungry," Simian murmured, "livin the life of gypos."

"Nomads, brother!" I corrected proudly.

"Wouldn't say no to a big fat bloody steak," Kaiser said, possibly sensing some vegetarianism amongst these bohemian gardeners, but he was judging by old rules. Homo Sapien took up hunting during the Ice Age after all.

"Don't know about that, boss," I murmured. "I've not seen anything bovine in months."

"You'll eat whatever is purron ya plate and be grateful yar not sleepin rough tonight." Claudia said with her usual avid charmfulness reserved for Kaiser's contrary moods.

"I've a few rabbits ready fer the pot," said Toby. "It's not much between us. We'll catch more tomorrow."

As if on cue, another dog (a daft-looking cross breed, all mad fluff and Jim Henson puppet ears) was let in the kitchen door with an ex-bugs hung from his jaws.

"Do we get free dog dribble with our food?"

The dog actually dropped his catch at the master's feet and I laughed aloud at the wonderland lunacy of dogs feeding humans. But then I recalled the so-called feral children, and Romulus and Remus, and Toby would've mentioned Shaun Ellis if he'd had a wire on my thoughts. I stopped laughing rather abruptly.

"I've plenty of bread if yer fussy," Toby said with dry Yorkshire humour.

He disappeared into another room to prepare some bunnies, ready in rigor mortis to be eaten. He would no doubt skin and hang the fresh kill for later.

He stewed the meat in a big pot with various vegetation over the fire and served us all great bowls full, with homemade bread to dip. It was no feast for Kings, lacking wild boar and peacock and so forth, but it felt the luckiest we'd had in so long. We gobbled greedily. I thought of the Saxons and the Celts, and the Baltic races of yore. Of fur hoods and stone walls that ached with a history of such meals gladly eaten – with all the poor manners of the boar itself.

* * * * * * *

THE BLACK SHEEP IS BITTER

Bryn McLarey, New Riddlehamhope

We were sat in the kitchen – just the three of us left and the dying fire the only source of light. Dogs were laid out on the wooden floor, motionless and hairy, leik so many authentic rugs in a huntsman's lodge.

Toby Roe. A name which'd developed infamy among us. And yet here he wus like half a pint of watered-down Abbeydale Moonshine. Small and pale, prematurely bald, and cowardly seeming. Meek. That favourite trait of mine.

"Is there a particular reason you've come *here*?" he asked hesitantly. He was still pawing at a mug which'd turned cold and empty a while ago. "I mean all of you. I assume Claudia came looking for Haydn..."

...*And Roxanne for me*. That's what he wanted tu believe.

"You should know," I said bitter as a pint of it. "We came on some mysterious search for *you*."

There wus a long silence, during which he looked at me carefully with those wide meek eyes.

"I don't understand," he said.

"This is our *Heart of Darkness* and you are our Mister Kurtz." In saying this I realised it wus an upside down concept. Unless Toby wus cursed with madness and genius and we'd sought him out to kill him. But I wus avoiding answering questions, because I wusnae really sure why we'd come all this way for this stupid, insignificant, little man.

Haydn looked blank at mae remark. He glowed with a youthful sense of ignorance, despite only being a handful of years younger than us. And he wusnae ignorant I supposed, just not well-read. How I liked tu perceive a human being as 'well-read', as though they were the book with a cover so worn and tatty, from being held so many times and shoved back on the shelf between so many other books. I digress.

"Have you seen *Apocalypse Now*?" I asked him.

Haydn nodded. He wus a media junkie Claudia'd said, way back when she disappeared off to Derby.

"Same story, pretty much. A journey intu the jungle tu find the damned Mr Kurtz – the same tale played out in a different era." I sunk mae heid so it wus virtually bathed in shadow for dramatic effect. "*The Horror.*" I uttered the words with quiet drama.

Haydn half-laughed uncertainly.

"Horror has a name and a face," Toby mused, staring intu the bottom of the mug, as though looking inta the jungle.

"So... have yuu any original words of wisdom tu share with us?" I asked. "Since we've travelled so fucking far tu find you."

"Knowledge speaks, wisdom listens," Haydn put in matter-a-factly, as though the authority of this saying could constitute an argument in favour of Toby's careful silences.

"You seem tu have neither, mae son. Where does that leave you?" I was still thinking about him as a mass produced book, stacked in the front of Waterstones, waiting for some idiot tu buy him for some light-weight holiday reading.

As I'd said those last words Simian had slid quietly intu the room with Claudia in delayed tow.

"You think he's a 'gap year brat'?" Simian said tu me, with that delicious shitty smile he always gets when he's got one-up on me. Some days he reminds me of Cuan in this way, remembering tiny little remarks from sae long ago. "You know there's no such thing anymore? Every person here has seen worse things than your Glasgow council estate could ever offer."

"They don't seem tu scuff though," I answered, rather pathetically.

"*You don't see the scars!*" he hissed melodramatically, pointing his two fingers at his own eyes.

Claudia wus nodding and smirking away, and Sim broke into edgy laughter, squeezing mae shoulder the way I do tu others when I'm winding them up. Claudia wrapped her arms around Haydn's shoulders. I don't get them either. I always thought of her as being rather leik me, but then look at mae taste in women. Meybe she likes a doormat. Meybe they all do. Nice guys get the girls and the meek shall inherit the Earth.

"I thought you'd all gone to bed," I said.

"And leave you ta bully these two?" Claudia asked.

With a bit of murmuring and indecisiveness, Toby trundled off upstairs, hopefully ta look in the mirror and find a voice. Claudia dragged Haydn off, for puppy sex or whatever. Meanwhile Simian used his well-honed scavenging skills tu sniff out some whisky in the kitchen. It wus a fucking cheek indeed. The stuff wusnae easy to come by. He poured us both a small measure in our empty cups and sat himself at the table near the fire.

There wus a patter of claws on the wooden floor and the black dog Fidel appeared on the chair at the head of the table next to Sim. He looked tu both our faces with those intense eyes. Sim sighed precociously and went off and found another cup, pouring some whisky into it and placing it in front of the dog. He'd seemed calmer and a lot more humorous since we'd arrived at the house. I resented this. That some strangers seemed tu give him more piece of mind than old friends.

"We're all the devil's dog," I murmured again, looking intu Fidel's eyes.

He looked back at me with an even gaze. As though he wus indeed the master of everything, the voice Toby Roe would never find. Except he wus silent tuu, possessing all the answers yet knowing they were more than he, and tu divulge them and save himself would mean nothing.

* * * * * * *

THE GIRL WITH HER HEAD SCREWED ON

Claudia McLeod, New Riddlehamhope

Listenin to Toby chattin, that first evenin in the house, I'd begun to realise how little we still knew. We'd relied (while foragin, huntin and scroungin) moastly on luck to put food in our gobs, through the hardest season a'tha year. Toby was lyke an oracle of self-sufficient livin. He knew what were available each month, where it wu' likely be, and how it ought be cooked, or preserved for the later, leaner months.

In contrast to our piss-weak fayces, he and Haydn looked rayte healthy an ruddy (as Brock'd also done). Toby knew how to put together a proper diet a grub. He knew how to use an animal 'nose-to-tail' wi' no waste. He had lottsa different mini-larders all over the house to store different types of food – smoked and cured meats, pickles, chutneys and jams, dried mushrooms, herbs and fruit. Most impressively he'd also installed and adapted an old solid-fuel Rayburn cooker, so it could heat five radiators and a water boiler.

Our homemayde weapons looked childish, next to his hand-crafted crossbows – which he favoured over guns cos they made less noise and the ammunition could be mayde rather than traded, and often reused.

Toby and Haydn's time was carefully planned and used. They'd nuff food stored, so they could mostly occupy their time with other things during winter. He hadn't a course predicted the arrival of five more mouths to feed. While Brock seemed to have got wind of us from Sid summow, Toby and Haydn were oddly taken aback. In fact it felt as though, if we had all been total strangers, they would'uv turned us back out int'ut hills.

Spring were creepin in though. Even if layte frosts kept comin back, in between we could benefit from new food sources. Toby was in a rush to educate us. If we sat down for an idle durin't day, he would shove some book under our nose to do wi' seasonal foragin, or how to tell which mushrooms could be eaten, or migrant habits of the animals.

The large kitchen had several shelves of books, moastly on useful subjects, but Haydn increasingly collected old novels and had begun tellin me bout them in the same gushin linn he'd used once t'ramble about music and films. The room had an original fireplace, which they used for heat and a little cooking when they didn't have the stove on. Lyke Brock's homes, the place were cluttered wi' objects that looked like they might be useful. The walls had a few paintings on them, salvaged at some point, and pots and utensils sat on shelves mayda driftwood. Survivors of the Weathers seemed to be all hoarders by nature. We slept that first eve on makeshift beds, among stacks of junk, but Toby rearranged it all the morrow.

In part of the cellar, below the kitchen, there was a meat larder or butchers area – where animals were hung, gutted, and plucked or skinned. It generally smelt fairly horrible, though not rotten. Just that smell of dead, raw meat, which gorrin the kitchen a little bit even though the cellar door was firmly shut to keep the dogs out. Toby and Haydn had a whole pack a dogs and besides the musty wood smell and any cooking smells in the kitchen, it always smelt reassuringly doggy. Particularly on damp daays.

    I understood immediately why we'd been drawn here. Even if we couldn't stay livin withum, we could learn how to live properly agen. Havin the auld knowledge over the landscape gave the power of survival that could pass down generations. Because Toby had most of the knowledge, he quickly became the manager of our time. This would bug the hell outtah Charlie, I thought, who was trying hard to be patient and vaguely humble, but it wussa constant battle.

    The others though were takin to Toby and Haydn like ducks that hadn't seen water in a fair while. Simian seemed almost smitten by Haydn, which were funny. I knew if he'd met him back in't day he would've dismissed him as a badly-dressed, coke-sniffin scenester. Because that's what he were. But Haydn liked to be very much in the niche of time, and the niche of time no-longer involved cocaine-nose jobs, or all-night rayves. It involved sawin up animal carcasses and mekkin nettle soup. Bygones. He carried the same energy and enthusiasm that he'd always had, even if he'd lost the public school innocence.

    Wolfgang liked both of um. Probably due to some deranged thing about havin met them in his dreams afore. During the first evenin he stared at them both soo much I wanted to punch him. He were lyke a child sometimes, so unaware of himself and how rude he was. Roxy seemed t'turn back into a shy schoolgirl, which worra bit daft for a woman in her thirties, but I spose it's endearin or sommat.

Suspicious as I am, I tried ta find a grudge against me in Haydn, but it didn't seem to be there. I still held grudges gainst people I'd dated when I was thirteen – he seemed to have forgiven me all the shit overnight. He was always lyke that though. He'd not seemed bothered when he'd told me his brother stole his first real girlfriend – it wassa funny anecdote. More importantly he'd forgiven Cookie for knockin an entire bottle a red wine onto box ful'a rare vinyl. I would've slapped the clumsy bint to Hull an back.

* * * * * * *

DIRTY BLUESY BASS LINE

Haydn Antoine, New Riddlehamhope

Without a computerised library of music and film I was an empty vessel. My brain echoed only the music of the wilderness. But I was not entirely without media. All of a sudden stuck in the house with an unusual scrap of free time (not spent digging the allotment, foraging, hunting or planning stuff) – I took to reading books again. I'd not read with such verve since around the age of twelve or thirteen, when I lost my library card and started spending all my allowance on CDs. I also turned a fair amount of my alone time to playing GTA and looking at my brother's porn magazines.

But now it'd become the best way to spend the latter part of dark winter evenings, after we'd cooked and eaten dinner and I'd played tug with Rufus until he was tired out. Brock always brought us books when he came across them. So we'd already amassed quite a collection, although anything of lesser quality generally ended up being used to help get the fire going if nothing else was available.

By the time Claudia and her friends arrived, I'd read everything we had, and my favourites two or three times. On the first evening the angry chap, named Charlie, mentioned a book called *Heart of Darkness*, upon which *Apocalypse Now* was apparently based. My blood buzzed. I'd always loved the connections between media. Intertextuality. My favourite word to bandy about as a journalist. The arguable basis for all post-modern media – the homage, the in-joke, the cultural reference. It'd always helped fuel the addiction I had. If Simon Pegg made some Sci-Fi reference I was unfamiliar with, I'd hunt it down like a dog with a scent rag.

I'd not felt this feeling in a long time. I needed that book. I wished I had a phone to ring Brock that minute. I wished I had the internet to look it up. Brock did have an old computer and router stored away in one of his hideaways where he had access to a generator. We'd checked out of curiosity to see if the internet was still being used (we couldn't abuse vital resources regularly for something that was trivial to our new existence). And it was. Our connection was exhaustingly slow of course, pretty much unusable in fact. But it pleased me that this heavenly body, this invisible monument to progress, was still there. They probably still used it down south in the New State of Greater London, which Claudia's friends referred to as 'The Bubble'.

I wanted to dig out Toby's encyclopaedia before bed, but it was my first evening with Claudia. The draw of her long-lost scent and touch was naturally more powerful than the words of Joseph Conrad – I looked it up first thing the next morning.

A week or so later, Brock made one of his appearances. Arriving from one of the tunnels that joined the cellar. He had a half grown dog with him, which he picked up as soon as he got up to the kitchen. The only other animal in the house was Ana, our big mama-dog, a typically pretty black and tan Collie-Alsatian cross. She stopped short of greeting Brock with the usual charm, instead sniffing the air at this canine intruder and murmuring a barely audible noise that was not quite a growl.

"Tsss." Brock held up a hand up to silence her.

She looked up at him with trusting eyes, waiting quietly. He dangled the puppy's bottom towards her nose, so she could sniff it. The puppy whined and wriggled. I couldn't help giggling.

He put the pup down on the ground and Ana circled it snuffling around, poking her long nose at the creature with matronly authority. Once satisfied, she licked its face, and wagged her tail at Brock.

"Where did you get that?"

"From the German," Brock said. "I tek it thev arrived."

"What's it called?"

"Hobina." He smirked.

"Is that a Native American name or something?" I asked.

"Is the feminine of Hobo, apparently."

I thought about the mad German and it made sense.

"I'm trying to track down a book, Brock," I said, maybe too quickly.

He rolled his eyes in that way that makes me feel like a young upstart.

"Forst things forst. Gerra mash on," he said quickly.

But once I'd filled the kettle, he pulled a present out of his bag. It was the sheet music and lyrics for one of the later Eels albums – *Shootenanny*. I grinned the widest grin, flicking through it, my memories of the music suddenly so clear.

"Can ye even read music, Mr. Music Hack?" he asked.

"I know a dirty, bluesy bass line when I see one!"

* * * * * * *

A PINE MARTIAN

Simian Thomas, Breamish Valley

I was awake in the slipstream of conscious experience. A flock of birds twirled and disappeared over the trees, the low sun pouring amorous light onto whatever surface it could reach. I was spellbound by the day, by the feel of my feet in the snow. I'd even almost forgotten that I had the snivels, save for the fact I kept snivelling and the cold made my face produce extra terrestrial gunk out of all orifices.

My brain was also befuddled by the phlegm of knowledge which Toby was trying to push inside it. Brain just wanted to enjoy the simple pleasures of aliveness, not cram for an exam in survival. It was my first real outing with the oracle of the wild and the first thing I noted was that Toby rarely wears a hat, despite his lack of hair. I assume this is in order to be at one with nature (hear and see better). But the combination of this bald globe, the wide pacific eyes and the type of scarf he wraps in layers around his shoulders – all these things gave him the air of a wise monk.

He was talking. He was telling me learned things, and all I could absorb was his likeness to a monk.

He was saying something about deciduous forests – that much I could gather. I wasn't sure I even knew what deciduous forest was, but I didn't want to look really stupid. His voice was extremely pleasing to listen to, when he did speak. It was all easy-going North-Yorkshire with a slight up-note, which he must've developed from all those years in Canada.

In this strange morning light, the fresh musical curves of the snow meeting the banks of rocks made it look almost like sand dunes. There was a single trail of prints through the unspoilt snow.

"What was that?" I asked him, trying to engage.

"A fox, I should think," he answered. "One a'the tricks to recognising tracks is that only very particular types of ground will give you clear prints. Certain types of snow, mud or sand. But you can often tell by't way the animal moved what it were. This snow is too deep to show a distinct paw print here."

I nodded, imagining the fox trotting over the bank at dawn. We followed the track further up.

"And you see here there's a change uf movement?" Toby pointed. "The payce has changed a'sudden. Either the animal was scared by sommat, or maybe it set off chasin prey."

The tracks disappeared over the rocks and into the trees.

"There's a spot further over which often gets reayht good tracks," he enthused.

We trudged through the patch of woods and came to a clearing, the ground dipped slightly.

"The snow's too deep today," Toby said. "But you can see a lot'ta life has passed through here. I don't just look at tracks for huntin either. I record whas here to see how well the eco-system is doin, what animals are surviving."

He produced his recording device – an old school book full of graph paper onto which he'd sketched life-size examples of tracks. It was also full of notes on the number of times he'd noted individual species and so on.

"There are loads uf animals you never actually *see* living round-the-doors. I've found the tracks of pine martens, wild boar, all sorts of odds an sods."

What the fuck was a pine marten? I thought. I didn't even know if that was an animal I should be afraid of encountering. I'm cursed with a mind that creates every worse-case scenario, like always thinking wasps will fly into my ears.

'Ooh, silly boy. Make sure your ears are free of jam,' Cassie once said.

So stood there looking at the criss-crossing marks in the clearing, scribbling one another out, I was overwhelmed with irrational fear of the unknown – imagining every tiny creature all ganging up together and swarming at me with their tiddly claws and teeth.

"You do get wild boar here, then? Claudia thought she encountered one," I said, getting a mild grip on myself.

He looked excited at this.

"Yeah, yeah."

He flicked through his book to show me a sketch of the tracks, which looked a lot like all the other tracks to a novice. (Especially when you put in all the varying factors he'd remind me of – like different speeds and the texture of the ground.) "See how the wild boar has cloven hooves, lyke a deer. But unlike the common deer their dew claws are much lower down, soo you get these indents..."

I looked at the sketch of a hoof which looked like the ajar tips of scissors and the two marks behind them that he pointed out.

"You get similar marks wi' reindeer," he explained. "But they're loads bigger. I've not seen any wild boar here in't flesh, but the fact that they seem to be thriving is dead exciting. They survive all over the world in very diverse climates. All the ones in this country probably escaped from captivity. They may'uv even been breeding with domestic pigs that've gone wild."

He studied the snow for something he could make an example of.

"See now these tracks here. This were a type of rodent wi' a long tail, probably a rat but they're not clear enough to tell the size." He pointed to the line following the footprints.

I remembered waking in the night in the Gin House, with Philip Lloyd Roth's rat sat on my chest peering at me. I shuddered. Toby sensed my unease, I think.

"Are you okay?" He furrowed his brow.

"Yes... um... It's a lot to take in, all this," I said a little doubtfully.

He nodded. "I think, to master tracks, the best thing t'do is to sketch them when you see nice clear ones and then compare them to images in one a'the books back at'house." I was silent, so he then added, "Don't worry about all the different rodents and squirrels, concentrate on sizeable animals that are either a source of food or possibly danger."

I maintained the look of glazed doom. Wasn't it bad that I couldn't already recognise dangerous tracks? I decided to change the subject.

"How come animals are doing so well despite the Weathers?"

We turned and continued walking through the woods, the trees casting long shadows on patches of white and sheltered browns.

"I wouldn't sa'much say they're doing *well*." He performed that philosophical fleeting smile of his. "But most are fairing a lot better than the humans. I'm sure several species have been wiped out, I can only gather information from round abouts, not the whole country. But the rapid change in climate, the difficulties this creates, will have been at least slightly offset by the disappearance of us." He paused his speech meaningfully, though he continued a rhythmic walk, with which I tried to keep step. "The wild is claiming back the island now the issue of our overpopulation has been addressed."

He looked sideways at me as though to ascertain if I was someone who could handle the idea that *we* were vermin. I wanted to reply that few who'd ever worked in the service industry would fail to agree with this, but it was a silent question. I pulled a scruffy rag from my pocket and blew my nose loudly into it, maybe too loudly. It echoed it's displacement through the trees.

"You've got a cold?" he asked. "I'll make you a remedy when we get back tu't house. What did you do before the Weathers?"

Was this a change of subject, or was he asking about cold remedies? "What did I do?"

"Your occupation?" he asked.

I snorted. "Not sure I had an occupation. I worked in a shop. I flopped university. I failed at travelling."

"Oh," he said. "You seem very bright."

I looked doubtfully at him, we reached the other side of the trees and sat down on a log, with a view of the snowy hills. Toby seemed to be multi-tasking keeping an eye out for wildlife and counselling me.

"Nobody thinks that," I said. "I can barely hold a conversation most of the time."

He looked away firmly, as though trying not to be too intense.

"Well now, you'uv been through a lot."

"Who said that? Roxy?" I asked, maybe a little too narked.

He looked puzzled. "No, I can tell." He said this softly, carefully.

"We've all been through a lot," I said.

"I don't mean recent history," he said. "I mean yer formative years."

"I was a spoilt brat!" I exclaimed.

Toby was quiet, letting the landscape speak, letting the wind pronounce words that had sat unpronounceable on my tongue for so long. I could almost see myself welling up and crying. I've not cried in front of another person since I was about eight.

"Tell me bout yer friend, Cassie," Toby said quietly. "You mentioned her last night..."

The wind now seemed quiet. I could just hear my own heavy breathing in my head, sounding desperate, almost asthmatic. So when I began to talk I did so only to silence this noise. The words poured out from me, uncontrollably. This had never happened with friends or family, despite so many offerings of kind ears. I somehow needed a stranger, like a confession booth with only a blank screen and the vague knowledge of a person beyond it.

* * * * * * *

OUR ENDLESS NUMBERED DAYS

Roxanne Ratcliffe, Breamish Valley

As with much of our travels, our new found existence at Riddlehamhope (or what Charlie referred to as 'the dog house') was spent active. And so there often appeared little time for talking, or even quiet reflection. This frustrated me. There was so much I wanted to say to Toby, but all the conversations I wished I was able to have with him over the years melted away in my mouth.

We'd wake early and Toby and Haydn would allocate various tasks for the day. I felt an immediate need to be of use, rather than to just sit around watching how things were done. As with our hunting and gathering trips in the past, much of the day was taken up with exhausting and often rewardless tasks. Though at least we were adding to an existing food stock, rather than specifically trying to get things to feed ourselves the next day. We would arrive back, usually just after dark, cook and eat dinner, and then go to sleep within a matter of hours so as to be ready for the next long day.

I even found that out on the trail with just myself and Toby, there was little time for conversation. To maximise potential for food it was important to be constantly alert to the landscape and make as little noise and disturbance as possible. While he was obviously keen to advance our skills in the hunt, I couldn't help feeling like a burden on him. Like the new kid at work.

Gradually though I began to adapt, and remembered that verbal conversation wasn't everything. During summer holidays as a child, I spent endless days with my brother and became practically mute, to the annoyance of our parents. The games we invented together were beyond verbal language, and often the only sounds in the house were my giggles, and the occasional breakage when David lost his temper. I remembered also that Toby was relatively fluent in basic British sign language – which came in use out hunting, when we did spot something of interest.

Most of the real talk was done around the tea table, as in tradition. But like with my extended family, any serious chit-chat was quickly high-jacked by the loudest voice. I liked Haydn Antoine immediately though. He had that elusive ability to take things seriously but not be serious about it. He was charming and polite and thoughtful. I realised I'd missed these qualities in people I met.

I must've seemed particularly frustrated a few days into our stay, having returned again with nothing to contribute to the week's food.

"Don't fret it, little Rue," Toby said quietly. He had a strange ghost of a smile, which dimpled for a moment, then disappeared. "It's gonna get a lot easier soon. Spring is on't way. We'll be less reliant on meat."

He sat next to me, hands spread on the wooden table top, which was marked with lines. He had the whitish graze of a scar crossing his hand from between his thumb and fingers.

"How did you get that?" I asked.

"I was working in a wolf sanctuary," he said. "Never panic when a wolf has his teeth on you. That's the worst thing you can do!"

I nodded.

I daydreamed of Spring, of the abundant plant and animal life that would re-emerge. But Spring was showing a certain reluctance to take hold. There would be mild, sunnier days, and we would go out and find wild flowers and seasonal mushrooms. And then a bad frost would come and it was all gone again. And like the seasonal change, our conversations still didn't come to fruition. Toby was holding his cards very close to his chest – I started to think that it wasn't me that was struggling to talk. I was in an invisible box, pushing at the sides, stuck in what felt like loveless infatuation. I seemed to have induced cosmic fear in the object of my affection. Either that or after all this sprawl of time, he just didn't feel the same way about me anymore...

"Why's it called Riddlehamhope? Is that the old name?" I asked.

He shook his head.

"New Riddlehamhope. I took it from the name of an abandoned farmstead I once visited years ago. It were further south on't border wi' County Durham, I think. I just lyked the name a lot. It seemed apt."

* * * * * * *

DAMN DOG

Bryn McLarey, New Riddlehamhope

I stared at the dogs and they stared at me and I stared back. I hadda commitment tu confront sum aspect of Toby Roe that the others were infatuated with. Yet it wus the dogs who whispered confrontation. Neh violence, just eye contact, body language, a sense of stature – gauging the threat of The Kaiser. Fidel spoke no words tu me, uttered neh growl, but he appeared from nowhere often. He'd just be sat looking at me, leik a mirror.

He wus an all black German Shepherd dog with a King's robe of gleaming fur, a proud chest and a noble face. He wus top dog alright, with his mate Ana, a black and tan cross-breed. Within the pack they had two grown-up offspring – Rolf and Rufus, who were both on the cute and stupid side despite their good breeding. There were another two who were unrelated, a Husky-type cross called Otto, who wus white and blue-grey, with the odd bit of ginger. And lastly a much smaller, light-footed female named Cujo, who looked leik a fluffy whippet and had fur which looked either black, grey or auburn depending on the light. They'd had problems with her, Toby said. She didn't quite fit with the others and sometimes she'd disappear for days on end. He worried she'd get pregnant and Ana would go apeshit, because only alpha females get tu have pups.

I turned away from the watching eyes, and mae double reflection in each, and looked at Simian.

"Grumpy, Happy, Sleepy. It's like the seven dwarves," I said.

"That one's definitely Dopey," he pointed tu Rolf, smiling.

Haydn looked up from the papers he had spread on the table. He stood up and walked over tu stir the broth on the stove. The dogs' eyes glanced briefly ta him before re-fixing on me. Makes you feel kinda special, aye.

"There's only six," Haydn murmured.

"Toby's the seventh dwarf." I gave a wee chuckle.

"You're a bit of a cunt, aren't you?" Haydn said.

He didnae look up from the pot, but tossed his tousled blonde fringe a little. I suspect he is leik Samson. If ye shaved hus head he'd wither away like a weak flower. Vanity is an armour like any other.

We'd turned this house on its heid. The foundations murmured uncertainty aboot us bein here. Had there been stone gargoyles in the eaves (Wolfgang imagines there are) they'd wake from centuries of silence and mutter dissent tu one another, scowling better scowls. The floorboards creaked tuu much with the weight of boots treading the passages. The worn, peeling walls were burdened with the extra shadows they must carry.

Simian moved and sat next ta one of the dogs on the floor, and touched him on the snout. Rufus, the camp one, one ear up one down, paws too big, oversized and comedic. He lifted one uber paw and placed it on Simian's arm as a mark of ownership.

"This is my favourite." Sim grinned haplessly.

"He's my favourite too." Haydn glanced sideways at me.

"Maybes ye should both fight over him," I said.

"Fidel's your favourite," Haydn said.

"Some sort of poncey gay fight, meybe with pillows. What makes yuu think I've a favourite? I prefer women tu dogs, thanks muchly."

"Is his cuntishness affectionate?" Haydn asked Simian.

Simian made a knowing face that seemed ta internally swallow some thought and regurgitate facial sarcasm in replacement. "Maybe."

He stared out of the black window at the blackness. A pale movement passed it and the kitchen door unlocked and Toby entered. We all looked tu him, his paleness, and eyes that'd been expanded in the darkness now shrinking quietly back. He held an authoritative pause and the dogs waited with baited breath for acknowledgement. They seemed tu be producing some invisible energy that made the room buzz.

He acknowledged the top dog first.

"Fee," he said.

Fidel moved forward and sat proudly in front of him, pushing out his chest in the usual regal fashion. Toby laid a hand on his head and passed him some titbit. The other dogs bustled forward around his knees.

"Tsss!" he said and they all settled calmly in a circle, ears forward.

Master of the Universe, tell us what we should do next.

He gave each a titbit and a little attention. Cujo hung back from the others. Meybe she wus more stubborn, or meybe she just didn't want to get trodden on.

"Simian likes cruelty," I said, returning tu the conversation petered out.

Haydn sat down opposite us, but close enough tu where Toby'd now sat that their sleeves touched. (Allegiance brother.) He looked at Simian with interest. I think the two will get on. I think they'll all geht on. Except me. One day I'll walk out inta the dark and nevah come back. Noo, noo, I cudnae leave Wolfgang. He'd revert tu psychosis if ah left him, then the whole house would be damned. I would huv ta stay and keep the damnedness to maesel.

* * * * * *

WAIFS & STRAYS... THE VERMIN & THE FERAL

Claudia McLeod, Breamish Valley

Toby was a small, bald man wi' a short beard that never seemed to get any longer. Compare that wi' Charlie and Wolfgang, who wi'out constant shearin resembled yetis. He'ad an aura of calm that Simian likened to a Belgian monk – sumone who spent his days brewing strong beers and caring fa bees. It were strange to meet a person who had so much myth surrounding um. My memories of him as an absent friend to Haydn (a voice through distant telephone lines) had blurred over the past year wi' Roxy's quiet confessions, and Wolfgang's chaotic projections of hope.

Now alone wi'him I felt a strange feelin, as though all the muscles in my body were soughin and gently easin into place. But superficially this only mayde me feel tenser. I war convinced the reason I'd survived this and that was my inability to let my guard down. As we walked down't track I kept snatchin glances at him. He were too busy tunin into't woodland to notice. Ana was shadowing his heels. I was keen to appear apt and useful to huntin and stuff, I didn't want us to feel like a handicap ta him and Haydn.

I concentrated on the quietness of my footfall and the movements of the woodland, strainin my ears and eyes. But Toby had an easy advantage, furrit were Ana who'd hear things and see things before either of us. Hunting wi' the aid of a dog was new to me, but I quickly realised how much of an advantage it were. She'd stop, so we'd stop and then her ears and nose and eyes would all point in the same direction. Toby's crossbow proved a far more efficient weapon than owt we 'ad, so the huntin was better.

Further through woods, wi' me carrying the bounty (the only way fer me to be a'use), Toby led me to climb up to the first bough of a huge auld tree. It were arched over to one side as though depressed, mekkin it possible for Ana to follow us up and sit proudly next to him, wi'her tongue lollin out. Trees this age seemed unusual round these parts. Most a the woods on t'hills had been carefully controlled and logged, afore it all went to pot. Only now were they spreadin beyond their order'ly lines.

The hills sloped down beneath us and we were greeted with a view of the landscape, the rolling pasture and the stoney banks of t'Breamish river, which were strewn with the winter's debris.

Toby brought a flask of tea out from his bag and I smirked at the Britishness of it.

"What?"

"Have you brung jam sandwiches an all?" I joked.

"A gud brew's grand owt, as me dad used to say," he said. "It were the only thing I missed when I lived proper out in the wild."

I nodded, acceptin the plastic cup he handed to me and taking a small sip.

"Is this goat's milk?"

"One of our friends keeps goats. There's a bunch of feral goats that 'av roamed these parts since afore the Weathers and he caught some kids and domesticated um."

"Brock said he knew folk breedin Highland cattle, an all?"

"And reindeer," he added. "We've a series a breeding programmes along the border. But it's not like farming. It's more encouragin species in the wild. We recon that's more sustainable. To encourage wildlife that's able to thrive despite the changing weather conditions. We can keep a piddly amount of domestic animals for milk an that, but it's not yet practical to keep them for meat."

I nodded thoughtfully.

"And wild boar? One a them scared the shit outta me one day when I were huntin. It war the last sight I spected to see. Are there many about?"

"Yeah, there was a certain amount of them already running wild and I think more've escaped old farms since. They can be rayte dangerous, but they're such a strong species."

"It's all very clever, what yu'v been doing. All we've managed to do s'far is stay alive."

"Well thas pretty important too, to the survival of our species," Toby said sweetly.

"D'ya have a breedin programme for us an all?" I joked.

He shrugged philosophically, and then changed track.

"Haydn says you did a lot of horse ridin when you were young?"

"Yeah, loads... Why? Is that useful?"

"Well, they're the most appropriate means of travel now. My friends Adam and Logan 'av a bunch a horses. I can ride a bit, but we could do wi'someone experienced to teach everybody proper. It's one skill to sit on a horse when it's walking. It's quite another to get control back when it's bolted from a wild dog."

He spoke from experience, I could tell from his face.

"I don't have a huge amount of natural patience," I said dubiously. "But I'll girrit a go, by all means. My dad were a horse trainer. So I like to think I know what am doin!"

He seemed quietly enthusiastic about this, as though it opened up soo many possibilities.

"Grand. I'll get on t'Brock about it."

"D'you think we'll all be useful?" I asked (with, I hoped, a certain tact).

"Yuv all been useful to each other. I don't see why not. If I wa' unfriendly to begin with, it were because we've had bad experiences wi'people coming to us for help and then rippin us off, stealing supplies and so on. There's a certain type of folk who've survived purely through being ruthless and selfish."

"I'm sorry if Charlie makes an atmosphere. He's the usual macho type. He wants to be the hero."

I broke off as Ana's eyes and ears perked up all of a sudden and we followed her gaze down't valley to a figure clamberin over a ruined bit of dry stone wall. There was sommat about his body language that gev me bad jeebies and Toby bristled with silent anger. Ana gave a low growl but Toby shushed her. We all kept still and quiet in't shadow of the tree until the man had disappeared in a different direction.

"Gmork," Toby said eventually, his voice quivering. "He stole one of Ana's half grown pups. I think he beat it to death when it wunt do what he wanted. He's lined his coat with the pelt anyroad."

"Speak a the ruthless and the fookers rear their ugly heads," I said. "Is Gmork his real name?"

"Haydn named him that. It's the baddie wolf from *The Neverending Story*. I think his real name's James."

I laffed a little, as we clambered down from't tree.

"Typical Haydn, still views the world as a fiction."

He nodded. "It's one way of dealing wi' it."

"Does he live by himself?" I asked.

"We thought so to begin with, that were why we helped him out. He likes the reputation of lone wolf, but he has a clan alrayht. They consider thissels to have a certain territory and if they think you're invadin they won't be very nice to ya."

"Oh, well. That can be Charlie's project, protectin't fold."

Toby looked at me with soft, hopeful eyes. "I don't want a civil war."

"I'll keep him on a leash," I promised.

* * * * * * *

DOMESTICATION OF THE WILD THINGS

Haydn Antoine, New Riddlehamhope

Riddlehamhope was quiet for once, save for the fire crackling in the hearth and the bats flitting two and from the roof. Ana turned her pointed face around the kitchen, absorbing emotions, expressions and haunted eyes. She let her fluffy head fall to the floor between her paws and emitted a great sigh. The sigh spread to each of the other dogs. They readjusted their dozing positions, eyes quickly scanning the room before reclosing, ears flickering briefly.

"I love a good dog sigh," Wolfgang announced. There was a questioning pause. "They just seem to expand and spread through the room." He put his hands together and then spread them apart. Toby smiled. "It's like," Wolfgang hesitated, "something big being weighed out against something *very small.*"

I was glad of these words. Glad he occasionally hit a note of poignant philosophy, instead of rambling on about boring, mad shit, like a doped-up conspiracy theorist.

There was quiet again and ears searched the space left behind – human ears and dog ears. Eventually the floorboards growled. It was Otto. His throat was still pressed against the wood but he'd picked up footsteps. His growl was insecure, wanting reassurance. Ana raised her head again as Charlie came in – she watched him cross the room to the huge old mirror, scarred and misted with dust. He leaned briefly towards it, his profile reflected, the Roman nose and grizzly beard. Fidel followed him into the room without a sound. He paused next to Charlie, rising on his haunches and putting his paws on the base of the mirror, so that he, too, looked into it. So that his profile was reflected beside Charlie's, black snout and eyes, mocking the human's vanity.

"Black dog on mae shoulder," Charlie muttered.

Scruffy curls were rearranged to equal scruffiness. Fidel watched him in the reflection, like a younger brother picking up the other's moves. Charlie growled at him. Otto growled again and Wolfgang laughed.

"It's a dog's life, in the doghouse. With the fucking Kaiser and *Comandante*?" He pointed at Charlie and Fidel.

Charlie sat down and took one of Wolfgang's roll-ups. "Ruhe, bitte." He lit it on a candle. The kettle on the stove hissed a little and then began to whistle. All the ears in the room perked towards it. "The kettle's boiled," he said dryly.

I watched Claudia slip out of her seat and step over dogs to the stove. Rolf rolled to his feet and followed her hopefully. She'd aged in movement since I'd last known her. Her hair had lost some of its youthful gold. I pictured a normal domestic scene. A woman making tea in a kitchen, a pet getting in the way, pale English sunlight coming in through the window. She'd never have been a housewife anyway.

The sky was grey and low outside. Dusk was settling. I remembered grey days when we'd go to the park and play football in the mud. The cold didn't matter then. When we were tired there was a pub to go to. We'd go and watch some shite bands play and she'd drink more pints than me.

People grow up when they have to. It was hard to be young now. I tried to remember the words I used to say, the objects I used to value, the hundreds of films and songs I consumed that I've now forgotten and will never find again. Claudia placed a mug of tea in front of me. She leaned her arms on the table so that she was down level with me, eyelashes and lips close to my cheek. She whispered the opening lines to *Witness the Fitness*. I smiled. It was her new game to remember. To remind me of what I'd left behind on the computerised memory in the very back of my brain.

* * * * * * *

MAN HUNTS WOLFGANG/WOLFGANG HUNTS MAN

Wolfgang, Northumberland

It was hard to stay dry and alert all in a once. My hood was saving me from water down the back of my neck, but it blocked the sounds of the woodland – the Douglas Firs playing Chinese whispers in the caverns of my ears, which were soggy with wax (or brain poo, as I like to think of it). It also impeded my vision, pushing lank hairs forward to bother my face.

It wasn't hard rain, just spittle, consistently falling, only varied by the wind. I had to peer about me 45 degrees to get panoramic sound and vision. To hear what the wind was telling the squirrel in the birch tree. My eyes played tricks and etched faces into the knots of trunks. The track was broad and stoney, once well-trodden and wide enough for land rovers.

I was exposed on this track though, so I snuck off down a muddy, meandering subplot, taking small pleasure in the tangled roots and uneven rocky terrain. Here I pulled my hood back down, the patchy canopy providing some relief from the skies.

But after a short walk, before me in the mud I happened upon tracks which chilled my blood a little. It was surely the imprint of a feral dog, but what a size. It must be an awesome beast... and there, with it, some smaller tracks too. I tried to size up the better odds (for me) – a behemoth mother dog, angrily trying to protect half grown pups, or a pack of mixed sized mutts on the hunt together.

I decided angry momma would be worse. I stopped and listened, sniffing the air for that wet dog smell that might reveal a waiting assassin. The wind was blowing neither towards nor away from me, rather nipping back and forth in all directions. I couldn't think how to tell how fresh the tracks were. Certainly likely to have been laid in the last twenty four hours. Migrant animals could cover a great distance in that time, but if mum had pups she was likely still nearby.

I was just before a blind corner and didn't want to 'do a Farley Mowat' and accidently come nose to nose with *Canis Lupus*! I was also reminded of a fiction of a mortal game between a huntsman and the last wolf in England. The book had been amongst those in the confines of my library. The story thrilled in the jumbling of predator and prey – man hunts wolf / wolf hunts man.

My breath was tight, feeling keen eyes watching me and the salvation of tongue on teeth. In a moment of clarity the trees roots and rocky terrain were no longer a nicety but a hindrance. I thought of tripping and tumbling. The blind corner awaited me, like a half dreamed harbinger of doom.

No wolfish face greeted me around the corner, but that of a dirty hairy old tramp, with a sharp accusing look in his eyes. I jumped and so did he, I yelped and the forest answered me in an echo. It was a mirror. Around a blind corner in the middle of a darn forest, some dirty coyote had hung an old mirror from the branch of a tree, swaying there in the wind. Bringing my image to me, scrawled in the lines of age deepening in my reflection...

I braided my damp hair Hussar-style, announcing "Bidandengero... we meet again."

* * * * * * *

CHARLIE DON'T SURF

Bryn McLarey, New Riddlehamhope

I rose early, unable tu sleep in the bedroom, which felt alien in its cosiness. I wus well used tu being crammed into a roomful of people, but for a while it'd been a series of draughty train carriages. The need for the body heat of others had outweighed the need for silence.

Now I craved silence and solitude, so I snuck downstairs tu the kitchen with a candle casting leaping shadows on scant wallpaper and scuffed banisters.

The brick-walled kitchen wus reassuringly cold. The dogs lay in a big pile in order tu stay warm themselves, a nose or a tail poking out here and there. Eyes opened some and watched me in the shadows, but they barely stirred. I sunk in the armchair next tu the fire. It wus near dead, the odd tiny ember still glowing. I pulled a blanket up ta mae chin and stared into the gloom, shivering a little. I could hear the rhythm of the nearby river outside, in continuous conversation with the sky.

A short time passed in which I wus still wrapped up in restless, repetitive thoughts. These seemed a luxury after the many nights when I'd fallen asleep purely from exhaustion, without a crumb of reassurance that I would even wake the next day. Now I heard soft footsteps coming down the stairs. I hoped it wus Roxanne for some reason, but it was the other runt. Toby slipped through the door, sidestepping snoozing canines and then paused meaningfully as he saw me.

"Oh," he said. "I didn't know you were down here. Sorry to disturb you."

I didn't believe him – he'd probably heard me rise and didn't trust me pottering about by maesel.

"Ney bother," I answered.

"Trouble sleeping?" He wus hovering a little awkwardly, as though he wasn't sure whether or not he should sit down.

"Aye," I replied.

He nodded and then continued his business, putting some more wood onto the fire and stirring it back life with some dry bracken. He peeked through a heavy floor-length curtain at the grey light appearing outside.

"How come *you*'re up so early?" I asked eventually.

"Lots to do." He filled the kettle up from the tap off the water tank.

"Where does that water come from?" I asked.

"It's filtered rain water. Often it runs out and we have to go tu't river."

"I see."

We were quiet again. He made us strong, black tea and sliced some of the bread loaf off, handing it tu me on a handmade wooden plate. He sat down at the table and began eating and supping, sae I followed suit. The chewing and slurping soundtracked Toby's procrastinating.

"What did you do furra livin, afore the Weathers kicked in?" he asked in that amiable Yorkshire lilt.

I snorted. "I wus an actor and technician in the theatre. And a bartender tu pay tha bills." It seemed a bit ridiculous now. The long lost luxury of a creative job.

"Oh." He was evidently a bit surprised.

"What?" I said bluntly.

"Didn't take you for a thespian," he mumbled apologetically. "Hopin you might've done carpentry, or built things." He shrugged.

"Is an oaf leik me more use as a manual labourer? Of course I've done carpentry and built things."

The dogs were awaking now the fire'd warmed up. Rufus and Ana sat in front of it wavering sleepily. Rufus made an undignified whining noise and Ana licked his face in a motherly fashion. He saw me lookin at him and wagged his tail dopily, coming tu rest his muzzle on mae knee. I patted his head.

"Mommy's boy," I chided. "Does this one ever kill anythin or is he just a pet?"

Toby didn't answer this. "Our friends are building a log cabin up north. Would you be interested in helpin?" he said instead.

I rubbed mae fist on Rufus' muzzle and he squirmed happily.

"Is tha the future? Log cabins? Is this place gonna fall tu pieces eventually?"

"The upkeep on houses like this is tuff in freezing winters," Toby said softly.

"I did wonder," I said. "How far up north? And why not here?"

Toby began putting out ingredients for bread-making on the table with a very old, scratched plastic bowl. I tried tu remember where yeast came from and how he might have it, concerned romantically with the idea that I might brew beer at some point.

"We need to be able ta move about and stay in different places, 'cos other animals do. Migration. It's not that far though, still along the border."

"I'd be happy to help with it." I nodded.

Toby set a mixture of yeast, sugar and luke-warm water near the fire and began stirring salt and fat inta bread flour in the big bowl.

"Could actually make pizza," I mused. "That would feel very odd. Assuming yuu have tomatoes?"

He shook his head.

"I need to mayke a greenhouse to grow that sorta thing. I think I have some very auld tinned tomatoes stashed somewhere, mind. I've got cold frames outside to help defend veg from't frost. But I 'aven't even tried tomatoes."

I decided not tu mention I had no idea what a cold frame was. Rufus wus sniffing around behind Toby. He stepped back and trod on a paw, evoking a squeal from the daft mutt, an nearly knockin the bowl over as he startled himself.

"Shit, sorry Rufee! Cookin by candlelight really in't a good idea." He lit another candle, which didn't make a lot of difference.

Otto, with his white muzzle and odd-coloured electric eyes, was leaning forward to stick his snout in the yeast mixture. I pushed him away gently with mae foot.

"Do they need taking oot for a walk or sommat?" I asked.

"Oh, you can just lerrem out and they'll catch thissels breakfast, hopefully," Toby mumbled.

I stood up and walked ta the door exclaiming a slightly high pitched.

"C'mon!"

They all rallied excitedly towards the door, shoving, sniffing and gently nipping each another, letting out short sharp barks of glee. I opened the door just enough for one animal tu slip through at a time and they dashed out in a line, nose tu bum, tails wagging in each others' faces.

* * * * * * *

THE BARKING OF RUMINANTS

Haydn Antoine, Northumberland

Although our conversations were littered with nostalgia for what the Weathers had swept away, I don't think any of us completely regretted the loss. The people who really couldn't live without computers and cars and disposable fashion items were probably dead. Or in the Bubble. I assumed the Bubble had these things. Sometimes I dreamed out its composition, wrote the blue prints for the architecture. I imagined it to be like what was once proposed for the moon, a literal bubble of oxygen in which humans could stay safe in Space.

On the surface there would be a great dome, with some sort of weather shields that could be activated during threatening periods. Beneath ground surface there would be a network of places and passages like a gigantic rabbit warren, including the old Underground train system. It would be like living in some kind of shopping mall, soulless and overpopulated. I tried to fathom every institution, every school, abattoir and bar all crammed into this thing. The only people who ever went in and out were lower ranking members of particular trades – the traffickers, huntsmen, the maintenance people whose job it was to look for flaws in the shields and make repairs.

A part of me wanted to visit it just for a day, out of morbid curiosity. In my imagination it was like a certain type of hell. My biggest fear was that if I went there I'd want to stay.

Staring down at the dead man beneath the ice, I knew he belonged in the Bubble, and I wondered why he was so far north. Brock said a plane had crashed in one of the lakes last year. Maybe it was here. I looked around for other signs of this, but could only see the flatness of the snow on top of the ice, with a series of animal tracks running through it.

"I know him," I said to Claudia. I found myself giving her a weird, uneasy smile. She looked at me with icy blankness.

"Don't be daft. You can't even tell."

The man was a smear, but somehow I knew who it was. And it reminded me, for all my pathetic longing for the internet, and digital music, and late night cinema, I didn't want to change a thing. In that environment Claudia and I had failed – because the world got in the way, because in that shallow, self-absorbed society, relationships were just another disposable commodity. Even if I hadn't moved to London, Claudia would've got bored and moved on, because she's like that. She might even still do so in time. She's just less likely to meet someone else out here in next-to-nowhere.

We walked back slowly through the lingering snows, hand in hand. Passing the woods I pointed out where a whole series of trees had been stripped of bark, all on one side at the same height. I walked over and traced the shredding and tooth marks with my gloves. In places it looked like etches of flames.

"What's done that?" The wind whispered through Claudia's hair and brushed her lips as she spoke.

"Ruminants... barking," I mumbled, not realising how cryptic this sounded.

"Eh? What kind uv animal?" she asked.

"I don't know *exactly*. Toby could tell you. It'll be deer, or sheep, or goats."

"And they bark?" she asked with cheeky humour.

"Barking means tearing the bark off..." I began weakly. "Some types of deer do actually make barking noises anyway. I think its red deer though and I don't think there are any red deer around here. Can't you stop letting me witter on now?"

"Stop witterin on." She kissed me on the cheek.

We continued back to the house, savouring the cool sunshine. We kicked snow off our shoes and stepped into the kitchen. Wolfgang, Charlie and Roxanne were all sat by the fire defrosting after the morning's adventures. I filled the kettle and hung it over the fire, warming my hands, staring at the flames.

"We saw some dead bloke in a lake. Haydn thinks he knew 'im," Claudia announced.

"Hugo?" Wolfgang asked.

He gave me a devilish grin which chilled my bones. I'd assumed he was a harmless old nutter, ignoring his irritating habits up until now. I stared at him coldly, wondering how the fuck he could have known the man's name. Had he been involved in the plane crash somehow? If it had been that...

"You were mouthin the name to yissel," Claudia whispered in my ear.

I had been, I realised, saying his name over and over. I felt a wave of relief.

"He used to play rugby with your brother," Wolfgang said.

Claudia assumed this was random speculation and ignored it. I felt a strange panic grip my mind, as though I wasn't sure what was contained. I wasn't sure if I was making up memories according to spec. Or forgetting some conversation in which I happened to have mentioned my brother and his rugby mates. I didn't give Wolfgang the gift of agreeing though. In fact I looked away, glazed and thoughtful. The kettle was beginning its initial hiss, before it belted out the full on whistle.

"Who wants tea?" I asked.

* * * * * * *

MAN'S BEST FIEND

Simian Thomas, New Riddlehamhope

"The metaphorical dog endures his fate with wry acceptance that things will always be a bit shit. There will always be a weight on his dog shoulders... a dogged look in his eyes... He will always be in the doghouse... any fleeing in the hope of a better life will land him in 'Dogville'. And his time will always be measured in dog years."

Worn out clichés written in the dirt...

Roxanne was in a feverish sleep, twitching like a half-dead android in the chair by the hearth.

"Should we move her upstairs? She's spooking the dogs," Haydn said diplomaticly.

Tobias Roe nodded, making no move himself – he was busy. We were meant to be busy too, but were waiting for instruction.

"Will you give me a hand?" Haydn asked me.

I half jumped in my seat, so used to Charlie taking on any kind of action that was needed.

"Yes, certainly." I find myself responding in such polite Englishness to Haydn. He reminds me of chaps from my youth, proper chaps, those alien creatures who were always so damn *nice*.

He scooped Roxanne up and I walked ahead of him, opening doors and other such vaguely useful things. Ana the she-dog followed us with a matriarchal air that said 'what this child needs is a motherly eye'.

Up in the end bedroom, I pulled back covers on the bed and Haydn tucked and tidied Roxy in. The room was unexpectedly warm due to the angle of the windows, which let the white sun poor in and somehow filled the room with an unreal angelicism.

"It's nice in here." He seated himself by the window.

I sat opposite. Ana sat and looked at Roxy's drowsy face for a while, before settling down on the carpet. Haydn pushed his glasses up his nose. I noted they were broken on the nose-piece, but had been taped back together so neatly that it was barely noticeable. It was this exactness that I cherished in Haydn Antoine. That and his name – I should no doubt send an email to Cassie noting the perfection of his name. She would understand, but no, another conversation I couldn't have.

"What were you saying about the term 'dog'? Before Wolfgang interrupted?"

I let a wry smile pass. It *would* be Wolfgang that'd interrupted. It was apt. I repeated my analogy of the metaphorical dog, with each careful reference to Wolfgang's obsessions.

"Do you think you've arrived in *Dogville*? In the sticks where everyone's paranoid and has an agenda?" he asked, as though thinking about the locals, the other locals.

I was surprised he knew the film reference. Few had the patience.

"No, I think I'm more afraid that we are Dogville – and you and Toby are the sufferers. I'm afraid the little clan I've travelled with are all fucking mad. And our instability is contagious." I glanced towards Roxanne, her eyeballs busy writhing in her head, stuck inside images she couldn't forget.

"I shouldn't worry," Haydn responded thoughtfully. "It's just post-traumatic stress disorder, isn't it? We all have a little of that flying around, particularly without a concrete future. I feel like Toby and I've at least found an idea for a future – it may not be the profound answer that Charlie was looking for." He shrugged.

"The metaphorical wolf, though," I continued in a trance of my own making, "is very different to the downtrodden mutt. It's more a mysterious and ominous danger."

Haydn tipped his face slightly to one side, he leant forward with his hands clasped over his knees.

"Is Wolfgang a mysterious and ominous danger?"

"He's certainly unpredictable. But, no. I was more pondering some analogy of survival – to survive, we must be more like wolves than dogs?"

"Hmm," he thought for a bit. "I think they're two sides of the same coin..."

* * * * * * *

VELVET WHICH CLOTHES THE BONE

Roxanne Ratcliffe, Dreamscape

Nether Ed is watching me. He's sat on his haunches amongst the crags, gnawing on a bone like a wolf-child. His eyes are huge in the technicolour light. Day is breaking across the mountains, pink clouds and luminous rays expanding inside his irises. He points down and I follow the simple language of his finger. Bobby is sat further down among the rocks, half concealed in summer heather. She is wearing ceremonial clothing like a Native

American Chief. She watches me from beneath a haughty fringe. She's dyed the tips of her hair again, the natural black-brown contrasting with maroon ends as though dipped in ink. I admire the well-tanned hides she wears, the immaculate caribou-fur trims. I reach to touch her headdress which forms antlers, perfect in their symmetry. To caress the velvet which clothes the bone. They turn to dust beneath my touch, blowing away like ashes...

"You can't touch me, I'm dead," Bobby says, with the usual bossiness. She brushes ash from her hair.

I lie in the heather and absorb myself in the comfort of her company – watching her face above me meditating, cast in bronze skin against the mauve sky.

But my coolness is quickly being replaced by a sweaty inner heat and the sky above us clouds with thunder. As the first thunder rolls away and leaves rain drops behind – Bobby dissolves like ice-cream, the colours of her clothing streaming away down the valley.

I'm in a heady panic now. I know things are taking a turn for the worse. I return to stand beneath Nether Ed. He seems to be my guide in this other world.

"What should I do, Nether Ed?" I ask him.

I've brought a big bumble bee from the heather flower as a token of appreciation. It crawls up my wrist and then bumbles into flight, making a higgledy piggledy line towards the dreaming man. Ed smiles and gives a tiny cocktail umbrella to the bee, to shelter him from the rain. Nether Ed likes the invertebrate creatures particularly – he feels more akin to them than the beastly human race. He wishes, as his birthday present, for his own exoskeleton to replace his easily torn outer-skin.

He sighs at my question. The rain drops are getting larger by the second, falling into the creases of his face like giant tears.

"A Yorkshireman can't give the answers of maire Northern climes. I know not the molten origins of these hills; I cannot hear their histor'y for it's written in't local tongue."

I stare at the dark rock, feeling the tectonic shift that had forced it through the surface.

"*Whin Sill*," he whispers with a comedic hesitance, trying to form the word. "*Whin Sill.*" His eyes are closed. As he opens them again to the rain and the heather, they become wide with shock. He points again, like a monkey.

I peer down the mountain through the mist that is sweeping in from a distant shoreline. The rain itself is also clouding the atmosphere, which still feels unbearably muggy, though the origin of the heat seems to be my own body. The shape of a figure is stood on an outcrop. He starts small but seems to grow in size. His face emerges – it's Wolfgang maybe, but not quite Wolfgang. His eyebrows and ear-hair have grown completely out of control, twisting out and growing into immense, dark forests, his nostrils flared in anticipation. He looks how I imagine the Norse God Thor would look, and as though knowing this he opens his mouth and begins to blow a mighty gale. I cling to the rock, but the bumble bee and his brolly, and Nether Ed and I, are all picked up by this mighty gust of wind and forced whirling up into the sky.

I woke with a bump. I was disorientated, expecting the railway carriage, expecting the dusty books stacked up, the sound of the wind in the trees. Instead, a strange room, and the eyes of a dog. Ana licked my face with a steady, excited gaze, wiggling her back end. I pulled back a little. *What lovely teeth you have, my dear.*

I still felt horrible and dizzy, and in need of something – water, and fire. I'd suddenly turned cold. The sun had dimmed outside. The curtains were open on the darkness but I felt too weak to close them. I climbed from the bed and struggled with the door, then stared in horror at the length of corridor to the stairs. Ana nosed me encouragingly, and hanging onto the banister rail I edged along. The sight of the stairs spun in vertigo. I half closed my eyes, and used my feet to feel my way down the staircase.

I nearly fell through the door to the kitchen, startling the occupants, but somehow Ana's body was there to stop me toppling over. I staggered to the chair which I'd fallen asleep in several hours ago, and collapsed.

Everyone was looking at me – Toby pensively, his nervousness contagious, so that I suddenly felt a flock of butterflies unsettled from my insides. They began whizzing in a circle like a moth around a lightbulb. Then they grouped together and came flying out of my mouth. I gaped so as not to spoil their pretty, delicate wings.

"What's the Whin Sill?" I asked.

Claudia sat down on the arm of the chair I was slumped in and stroked my hair in a maternal fashion. My face felt cold with sweat.

"She'as funny transitions from dream to wake," she murmured in explanation.

I coughed, possibly from my seasonal bug, possibly the sufferings of a second-hand smoker... but most likely a stray butterfly. I kept looking at Toby, disbelieving my eyes. Disbelieving that I was awake, disbelieving that the future had become the present – that my obsessions had somehow materialised.

I felt a bit of loss. What could I obsess about now? The fact that he might be a pale shell of what I wanted. He brought water to me, as though I'd somehow asked him for it.

"The Whin Sill is a geological feature a'tha local land, runnin from't coast and into the Pennines. It's mayde of volcanic rock," he explained.

My brain tuned into the heat of the fire, the sparks that spat, molten magma. My thought train on runaway tracks, without breaks, without visibility of what was ahead. I sipped water and then nearly dropped the cup. A hand propped it on the table top too far away.

I hummed the song *All I Need*. I remembered another bit of a dream in which a face fell to pieces. All the scrawny Radiohead fans I've ever loved. Skulls that smile and then break promises they never intended to make. And all the dogs, gone to the dogs, emotional meat-scraps recycled as food. I closed my eyes again because the room hurt them – the fire torched the surface, the eyes pressured with questions. If I shut my eyes they'd leave me to sleep again and then I could just eavesdrop.

But I was deposited somewhere between dream and wake, worrying that I was late for work and needed to put the washing on. Worrying I'd forgotten to brush my teeth and buy my mum a birthday card. Worrying that a brolly wasn't effective protection from an active volcano. A dog was whining. I knew he shared my worries, just like Nether Ed and the bumble bee. We were all in the same leaky fuckin boat.

* * * * * * *

SOMEONE ELSE'S OFFSPRING

Haydn Antoine, Breamish Valley

The long winter finally relented. The snows and frosts which'd been plaguing us intermittently disappeared completely overnight, and the cool, sunny spring emerged. The single blossom tree left in Riddlehamhope turned pinkish white (reminding me of suburban springtimes). Wild daffodils sprouted in spectating rows and the call of the first cuckoos sounded through the trees. The world around us which'd appeared so resolutely cold and barren for so long suddenly gave birth to colour.

The days felt immediately longer, as the clouds didn't create false dusks in late afternoon. We spent every moment of daylight outside, gathering fresh foods and enjoying the buoyant atmosphere.

The sheep that'd always grazed the moorland re-emerged in great numbers, looking terribly pregnant and burdened by their overgrown coats which were beginning to malt in clumps.

"Ever sheared a sheep?" Claudia asked, as we stared at the flock of white faced Cheviot sheep. They seemed unflustered by our presence, chewing on grass and staring at us in that mindless way they do.

We only had a sharp flat knife. Claudia's technique involved straddling the shoulders and clinging to whichever animal. Several of them pushed her into the muck. But being Claudia she just laid there laughing and tried another one. Once securely pinned, some of the sheep seemed to begrudgingly accept their haircuts and after a couple of hours we had five fleeces. We sat on a brae and drank from a flask of tea, watching the first lambs interacting with their mothers. A stream meandered down the hill before us, heavy with melt water and recent rains, collecting silt and scraps of plants which leaned too far over its tiny banks.

"Well, that were a jobsworth." Claudia watched the long-eared lambs tottering about. "Y'know thes a missin link in this survival thing," she added suddenly, a little self-consciously. It was that tone of voice she uses, when she's going to say something out of character. I furrowed my brow in anticipation.

"We need to have babies," she said.

I nodded. She meant 'we' as a clan, but I knew what was coming and while it filled me with the overwhelming fear of responsibility, it also felt kind of right. She shielded her eyes and looked down.

"Who's that?"

I followed where she was looking downstream, to where a woman and a teenage boy were attempting to cross. The woman had very black hair, but the boy was much fairer. They looked like something from olden times in their ragged clothing. Maybe we did, too.

"I don't know. Maybe it's Gmork's missus," I paused. "We should get out of living in this area. I don't feel safe with them around."

Once they'd crossed the river, they disappeared further down. We finished our tea and packed our sacks full of wool.

"Fooks sake," Claudia remarked drolly. "I'll have to learn to knit now."

"Sommat to keep you occupied while you're pregnant!" I teased.

"Who said owt about me gettin pregnant?" she asked.

"We'll have to get a spinner first," I remarked thoughtfully, still enjoying the thought of her sat in a chair, knitting grumpily.

* * * * * * *

THE DISMEMBERED PARTS OF OTHERS

Wolfgang, New Riddlehamhope

The new season had finally sprung. The dim lurking shapes of the ruined settlement seemed like a sudden haven – a secret garden. Wild flowers poked up between piles of bricks, and birds fluttered about gossiping with one another, pecking greedily at insects and worms.

Away from easy sight of the house, I found a sunny, secluded spot and sat down with my notebook. It was a broken bench I think, though it'd become joined into part of a collapsed wall. Only a panting dog found me, the dopey noisy one called Rolf. I'd brought some whittling with me, should someone come and ask what useful task I was committing myself to.

"You know what we need Rolf?" I asked the dog, who was all black, with spots of tan, and a white patch around one eye. "A bloody good skive."

He licked his lips, dribbled a bit and lay down at my feet, as if in agreement. In the distance I heard the practiced whistle of Toby, like a shepherd's whistle. Rolf perked his ears up but didn't move – maybe he knew the whistle wasn't for him. Maybe Toby had a different whistle for each of them, or maybe Rolf just wanted to skive. He lolled his back end over to one side, squashing purple crocuses with his bum. I tutted like an old lady.

It had been so long since I'd had the time to sit secluded and *write,* yet disappointingly nothing much was coming out of my pen.

Dog squashed crocus, I wrote.

Feeling no philharmonic ditty coming fourth, I decided instead to document things of interest – for the benefit of future anthropologists or some such apologies. Gazing ahead of me at the old foundations of buildings, which had become potato beds, I noticed how one strand of lopped fringe was caught in the light. In my misfocused gaze it created a minute rainbow. I wasn't sure quite whether this would concern the anthropologists... but who was I to assume?

Rainbow in my hair
The old foundations used as potato beds
Old windows made into cold frames

I added the second two, to give them some image of my surroundings – the list was starting to look like an odd poem though. I do hate poems a bit. Unless they're mind-fuckingly-good. But once I get the idea in my head that something is a poem, I can't unform it. I stared at a small pile of stones on the bank and wrote '*Cairn*', as they reminded me of the stone markers up on the hills. Then I thought this might be confusing so I put in brackets *(Stones, not the dog... The dog is a shepherd, as is God.)* Cairn is a type of terrier too, you see.

A tiny fly buzzed past my face, like a little dry currant with zippy-fast wings. He disappeared into a stack of old tractor tyres, which were filled with earth and covered in fine mesh. Nothing seemed to be growing in the tyres. I looked for evidence of what'd brought the neighbourhood to ruins, and spotted a favourite menace/deity – a buddleia plant. He was living inside old walls, wriggling roots between the bricks and cement to loosen and weaken the structure. But Mr. Buddleia and his unashamedly purple displays are a favourite for the bees and the butterflies. And life without bees and butterflies is a mere trifle.

Buddleia = menace slash deity (life without bees & butterflies a mere trifle!)

I was happier that my little bracketed notes were disturbing any similarity to the form of a poem.

The Buddleias couldn't have taken the whole village though. And why had our house survived, standing grandly above the rubble and ruin? There was definite storm damage to the area, a certain directional flow of debris. In the sunlit chirpy afternoon, I envisioned the great storm wreaking havoc and in the midst Toby stood solemnly at a window, a witness to the howling chaos. Witness to the wind huffing and puffing and blowing the other piggy houses down...

He probably hadn't been here during the storm, I reasoned. He'd probably found the house afterwards.

One house survived the storm.

And rearranged the dismembered parts of others to form its own kingdom.

Toby appeared all of a sudden, man and dog strolling through the kingdom. I dropped my book and pen and hastily picked up my whittling. Toby almost walked on past me but stopped and turned.

"Ah," he said.

Rolf sat to attention. His mother Ana sniffed him and made a face that said 'I can smell you've been skiving, son!'

Toby didn't say anything else, so I said, "A nice spot for whittling, this!"

"Yes," Toby said. He stroked his beard, looking wisely at the ground. "What're you writing?"

The book lay open at my feet, pen un-lidded... tattle tales.

"Some notes and things. Well, in general I write a kind of anecdotal philosophy, but I've lost my flow, sir."

"I see," he said, as though he didn't.

"Anthropology," I added, thinking this might bear roots.

He performed that trick where he decides I'm talking nonsense and changes the subject. "I don't know whether it's worthwhile building some more hutches and things for livestock." He looked about thoughtfully. "Or if I should wait until we move."

"We're moving?" I asked.

His mouth set in indecision.

"Probably, it's difficult to sustain the house in cold weather."

"But all the work you've put in here," I said. I was already in love with Riddlehamhope. I wanted to put a name on the door, carved in wood. "Riddle, Ham and Hope are three of my favourite English words."

He furrowed his enigmatic brow and nodded.

"I'm tempted to keep it as a Summer house. It would be more economical to live in log cabins in Winter, more compact, easier to heat." He looked at the sky, avoiding my gaze. "But I don't know if this place would survive the Winter without constant attention."

"What livestock are you getting?" I asked.

"Ducks maybe, for eggs. Goats for milk, or maybe some sort of cow if I can get hold of one. There used to be wild white cattle up at Chillingham." He looked at the other bits of buildings that as yet had no porpoise, mentally constructing porpoise for them.

Rolf, bored with appearing interested, had rolled on his back and was pawing his mother in the face, to try and entice her into a game. She nipped him sternly, but this only seemed to encourage him. Toby looked down at the dogs, with wry amusement.

"Anyway," he said firmly, so both dogs sat up ready for action. "I'll leave you to your... whittling."

* * * * * * *

IN THE DOGHOUSE

Bryn McLarey, Northumberland

Fidel stopped abruptly and refused tu go further. I berated him and called him ta heel but he refused, skulking back in the shadows. I turned around and bang out of nowhere a tall savage-looking bloke wus stood in front of me on an outcrop of rubble. He had the scarred face of somebody who picks fights in pubs and thinks a bottle is a noble enough weapon if his fists are failing. He wus dressed up in strips of leather, with a black fur pelt around his neck. He wus multiply armed, most noticeably with a machete, which his hand graced meaningfully, while he grinned a hideous grin at me.

"Top uf the morning," he said in a rusted, lowland Scottish accent.

I met his gaze squarely, mae lip curling a little in apprehension; I knew this must be the infamous Gmork. I said nothin, considering mae game plan. How wus I to *not* bring trouble knocking on the door of the dog house. I wus at least three or four miles from there, which fell in mae favour.

"Thas Toby's dog." He continued grinning. "You a matey wit that fookin cowardly piece of shite?"

I snorted. "Ah stole the dog. I dinnae ken who I stole him from."

"Fook off! That dog is devoted tu the wee man, like a bitch is devoted tu her pimp."

I shrugged. "It's a fookin dog. They'll do owt for, say, a slab of reindeer meat."

Fidel gnashed his teeth and growled a blood-curdling growl like none I'd ever heard from him.

"You itchin furra piece of me, pooch?" Gmork said to the dog, raising his knife. "You got reindeer? I'll trade yus." He slavered a little. A diet of rats and mutton can make people pretty desperate.

"I think he wants yer balls. He doesnae like the idea of scum liek you bein able tu breed," I said.

"Damn fookin right. But I'll slice the fooker in halv afore he sinks his teeth in me." Gmork gnashed his teeth back at Fidel, who was frothing with fury, and I realised he wus only waiting for the right word or action from me tu launch at the man.

"Easy fella," I said calmly.

Fidel didn't look at me, but he quietened down and simply fixed Gmork with the evil eyes.

"Was hus nayme gen? Sum silly commie name itus?" Gmork asked.

"Ah dunno hus nayme. I call him Fella. Thas his nayme noo." Mae accent wus thickening as I conversed, a defensive weapon.

"Yoo no settlin here wi' these fookin peace-lovin gardeners then?" Gmork asked, appearing tu buy mae guise hook, line and fucking sinker. (Though I wudnae put it past him for it tu just be a trick. He wus thug alright, but meybe not so stupid as he wanted me tu think.)

"Are you havin me fur mutton?" I exclaimed. "Did you never read *But n Ben a-go-go*? England is fookin sinkin, mah man, and tha better for it! Ahm gannin North. The seas are risin but the Highlands are high. The ocean will be swallowin this land ahm tellin yeh. No long now until the English all droon, an it'll be a better world fur it."

He grinned.

"Aye," he said. "Meybees you're right, Weegie, meybees you're right."

We went our separate wheys and I continued huntin, though I knew he followed me for a wee while as Fidel'd sniff the air and growl quietly as though mutterin curses tu hissel. He might have been hopin tu track down a stash of reindeer meat or foil mae lies, but I wus oot an aboot for several hours and eventually Fidel seemed tu've relaxed and refocused on finding scran.

We arrived back at the house and I set down the days kills, holding one up meaningfully.

"Mountain hare, Toab! You were right, they're spreading south."

He wus sat at the table with Roxy, making somethin out of bits of neatly chiselled-down wood, he nodded and kinda smiled. Since he wus relatively underwhelmed by this, I went for the emotional jugular.

"Met your mayte Gmork t'day." I left this hangin in the air, while they all looked at me. I just grinned and winked and filled the kettle pot with water and hung it over the fire.

Fidel wriggled up tu Toby, renewing his allegiance. Claudia gave me a shove uf annoyance fa being ambiguous.

"What happened Charlie? Fess up."

I shrugged modestly.

"I might've just managed tu rid him. He's a Celt after all, feed them a bit of folklore about the Lowlands sinking."

"The low lands are sinking," Wolfgang said.

"Well, technically the sea's gettin higher, rather than the land actually *sinkin*. But saime difference, I spose." I chuckled.

* * * * * * *

ON THE HOOF

Haydn Antoine, New Riddlehamhope

Adam and Logan were delivering our horses the next day. Claudia was ecstatic, the rest of us probably more apprehensive. Horses were big, unpredictable, and a lot of work. The dogs largely looked after themselves and each other. We were part of their pack almost. While it was reassuring that Claudia knew what she was doing, I wondered who'd take the lead if she was weighed down with a baby.

Mentioning this only opened me up to the usual abuse.

"Agreed, I'm loads more useful than you. You carry the bayb'y, sit in a chair all daay an eat for two. Yu'll enjoy it much maire than me."

"Horses are a lot of work, right?" I asked.

She snorted. "Fook yeah, they takeover ya fookin life."

"D'you think that's a good idea for us?"

"Course I do, I'm biased. Think of potential an that, how much ground we can cover. It's an investment. It's lyke ownin a very pretty but stubborn car."

"Is it?" I said, with a little sarcasm.

"Or three," she added.

Brock had built stables into the cellar. There were old barns close by, which could've been repaired, but we were wary of thieves. He was now trying to make the space habitable for the horses. He'd brought us a barrow-full of dry grass and bracken.

He was a hoarder of skills and knowledge, as well as objects. He had the advantage over Toby in that he regularly visited the other settlers and incorporated their strengths and specialisms into his own. This made him a little bossy and self-important at times. Claudia's technique for handling this was to change everything she didn't like as soon as he was gone. He set off back down his tunnel at nightfall, muttering about other stuff he had to do.

"Well that's fookin bollocks for a start," Claudia began moving stuff around.

"Can't you control your woman?" Charlie said as we stood well back, watching by lamplight.

Rolf and Otto were excited something new was happening, running around exploring what was essentially just wood, bricks and straw. He'd said it totally straight-faced but I was pretty sure it was a joke. I'm not sure he wore the trousers in their friendship. He couldn't very well expect me to wear the trousers in our relationship.

None of us liked to tell Brock he was wrong about anything. He was the circulation system among our strung out community. The glue, the knowledge bank, the supplier. And he was definitely capable of holding a grudge. I said as much to Claudia.

"Yeah, I've worked with his type afore," she mumbled grumpily. "Indispensible til you knock um down a peg. But ya can't know best about every'thin, full fookin stop. Deal wi'it."

Charlie laughed. "Such diplomacy, McLeod!"

She grunted, peering at the supply of horse care products. "Sithar! A fookin body brush?! That's fa indoor horses who barely see rain. Takes all the protective oils outtah their coats. If I see any of you use that..." She shook her head ruefully.

"We'll get a clip round't ear?" I asked, in a bad Yorkshire accent.

Charlie chuckled. "Such gratitude, McLeod."

"I am grateful," she said. "It would just be appreciated, if he lyke, y'know, gevva shit about what I know?"

* * * * * * *

THE APLOMP PARADE

Claudia McLeod, New Riddlehamhope

Adam Griffiths and Logan Jeffers had arrived on't back of two a the hoarses they were gee'in us. They were leadin a third behind 'em. I wasn't clear on how they were gonna get back wi'out the hoarses, but I assumed someone had thought of that.

Adam was first to dismount, wi'a friendly grin beamin from behind a big, black, bushy beard. He shook everyone's hand wi' enthusiasm, while Logan lingered reluctantly with the hoarses. Logan were more feral looking – suspicious and distant in his mannerisms – so it often felt like Adam was compensating furrim. I gradually picked up a tight bond 'tween em though. It were either a very intensely close friendship, or maybe more. They would exchange looks often, as though they knew each other's thoughts.

I examined the hoarses one by one, running me hands o'er um, buildin an immediate firm trust. Logan watched me careful'ly. Little bits of auld knowledge began resurfacing, brought on by t'smell an feel of um. They were maire hairy and rugged than many of their recent ancestors, the cobs and huntin breeds bein better equipped for the weather.

Adam were chattin away to Toby and Haydn, eager to fill in the months since he'd last seen them. I ran a hand down the first hoarse's leg and turned up his hoof. He were wearing shoes, sommat I'd wondered about.

"Do you shoe em yersells?" I asked Logan.

He nodded expressionlessly.

"When are they next due fur change?" I asked.

"A few weeks," he answered.

I'd wondered if they would just let their horses go barefoot, rather than bother wi' the shoeing process. (They needed changing every six weeks or soo, dependin on how fast the horse's hoof grew.) But there was doubt horses used for ridin and so on, could develop tough enough feet naturally in a damp, cold climate.

"I've never done it befarr," I said. "I've watched many times though. I can probably pick up the skills quite easily."

He nodded with healthy cynicism. Why should'ee assume I knew what I were doin, afta all?

"I'll be back to help," he said. "If you can keep an eye on them, and just remove them if they're looking loose."

I showed him intu't stables and he looked around them silently. Then one by one we led the hoarses in and un-tacked them. They had food and water ready, which they plunged eager noses into.

"Where d'you get the tack from?" I asked.

"We mekk it," he answered.

I got out the dandy brushes Brock had gi'en us and we gave the horses a quick rub down. Adam had two lean looking dogs wi'him and they sniffed around the stables themselves before laying down in the spare hay furra rest.

Dusk was fallin and it'd begun to drizzle, refreshin the stale air. Through the stables we joined the cellar and clambered up tu't kitchen. Having visitors we were allowed the whole heating system on and the house felt dry and comforting. Haydn'ad made a curried goat stew and a large batch of fresh warm bread. Logan lurked close to Adam, seeming reluctant to sit down, but Haydn ushered him tu't table, where he were sat next to Wolfgang. I was too quick to judge this as a bad move – Wolfgang heroically introduced hissel, an afore I could pick up my knife and fork Logan had launched into a muttered speech about the wonders of Germany.

Sat at t'other end uv the table, I could catch little a what he said though. Haydn whispered in my ear.

"Logan thinks he fought in the First World War," he paused. "On the German side."

Not wantin a whole whispered discussion on this topic, I just arched my eyebrows at him. I could feel Adam's gaze on us.

"Where did you two meet?" he asked.

"Oh, um... Derby?" Haydn asked me.

"I think it were Birmingham," I said.

Adam looked puzzled.

"Before the Weathers?"

"Oh yeah," Haydn smiled cheekil'y. "We're old friends."

"Are you from Derby, Claudia?" Adam asked, spoonin green gooey goat stew into his mouth and gerrin a fair bit in his beard. He were one of them people who used people's names very often.

I smiled. "Do I sound like I am?"

"No, you sound a bit Yorkshire actually. But then I'm not sure what they sound like in Derby."

I nodded.

"I used to live in Whitby maeself," he said. "That's where I met Logan actually."

"You don't sound Whitby," I said. He had a more local accent, though it weren't very strong.

He shook his head. "Sunderland. I gotta job doing the ghost tours in Whitby. I used to be a bit of a Goth, well not exactly Goth, a metal-head though!"

I nodded agen, unable to talk as I was too busy tearing at garlicky meat.

"It's funny to talk about stuff like that now?" he continued wi'a chuckle. "Like having a past life."

"Claudia used to be in a band. That was how we met. I scrounged an interview," Haydn explained.

"Oh right," Adam said "What kind of music was it, Claudia?"

I stared into my food, a little dazed. It seemed bizarre, being asked that question *now* that I'd been asked a thousand times. I could barely even 'member my re'earsed answer. "Um, quite an eclectic mix – blues, funk, electronica and owt in between real'y." The same old phrase fell breezily off me tongue.

"Wow... no thrash then?" he quipped.

"Actually I played in a thrash metal band when I were a teenager," I said. "I had plenty a issues to vent."

Clearly I no longer looked 'like the sort', as he seemed dead surprised.

"Where in Yorkshire are you from, Claudia?"

"Ripon," I answered.

"Don't think I ever went there. I heard it was nice though."

"It wasn't," I said with affectionate derision.

He nodded.

"I met Toby when I was working at Ponderosa and we stayed in touch for years."

Adam and Logan seemed tu falter in enthusiasm afta dinner, their journey tekkin its toll on them, an they retired to bed. I decided to tekk an early night an'all. I felt like a little girl wi'er first pony agen. All excited and full of enthusiasm for all the borin tasks like shovelling shit and polishin tack.

* * * * * * *

THE BEST LAID PLANS OF WOLVES & MEN

Simian Thomas, New Riddlehamhope

Not everyone was ready for Toby's in-depth ideas on dogs and men. But I lapped it up, feeling like I lacked something, and wondering if he could fill it in with either knowledge or cement. I felt a bit like I was joining a cult sometimes. But Toby tried so hard not to preach that I had to push him for information, dressing it up in part-true guises of my doubts. I'd tell him it unnerved me when dogs got all wound up and frenzied. After all, the human mob in a frenzy was nothing to be happy about. I knew that much from local derby days in Sheffield.

"Thes order in a pack a dogs," Toby would say. "Every member has a rank, a particular job to do that's suited to their character. It's a common assumption that the Alpha dog is the moast aggressive dog, but thas wrong. The Alpha dog is the decision-mayker, the fittest animal boath physically and mentally. This animal dun't put itself at risk unnecessarily, that task is delegated the Beta dog."

I thought of Charlie's recklessness in Milton Keynes. I'd always assumed he was our Alpha dog.

It was nearly time for bed. Adam and Logan had already turned in. Their dogs were sleeping in the stable, being used to horses and not so used to other dogs. Toby'd asked if I'd make a last check on the horses. I wasn't sure what I'd be checking for, since I knew nothing about them. I went down into the cellar which joined into the stable block, holding up a paraffin lamp like Florence Nightingale, light and shadow jumping and dancing. I called softly to the dogs to put them at ease. They'd already thoroughly sniffed me earlier in the day, reading my life story in smell no doubt.

"It's the job of the Beta dog to keep everyone in their place," Toby had continued, *"to dole out most of the discipline, to be the bouncer. Thas why Otto is always first to greet strangers and why he's always growlin and nippin t'others."*

Adam had just two dogs, the horses being his speciality. They were both a bit more leggy than ours. Toby said there was some Lurcher or Greyhound in the mix with a long-haired breed. They both padded across the brick floor towards me, tails wagging with gentle curiosity. I gave them both a quick pat and let them sniff my hands again, so they could know what I'd eaten in the past few hours and also pick up the individual smells of the dogs upstairs.

"If it's a big enuff pack, there's usually a Tester," Toby said. *"This dog is responsible for quality-control. Mekkin sure everyone is caypable of doin their jobs. When Fidel's around, Ana tends to do this, but if he were suddenly gone for sum reason, she'd prob'ly tayke over as Alpha dog. In fact it's maire common to havva bitch as the Alpha dog; they're bett'er thinkers and bett'er hunters."*

I held the lamp up over the wooden fence that penned the horses in, and spoke calm greetings to them. Two of them (the black one, and the brown and white patched one) were sharing the larger stable. They looked over at me briefly and then turned away with cat-like aloofness. The third horse – which was brown, with a white stripe down the centre of his face – leaned his head over and poked his nose around my pockets, sniffing. It occurred to me I probably should've brought carrots as bribery. I tried to shine the light around to check the stables, though I'm not sure what for, but one of the dogs was still getting in the way, probably smelling female dogs and getting all excited. And the friendly horse was determined that I wouldn't have come down without a present. He butted me gently with his head.

"The lower ranking dogs or wolves tend to be more nervy and subservient. They either perform the task of Lookout, or the lowest rank, the Omega." He paused thoughtfully. "Thas why nervy, shy dogs will often bark a lot, to warn you that sommat is going on. And the Omega dog is actually a very important role. They keep the peace between t'other dogs, they try to absorb any tension in the pack."

Omega. That was me wasn't it? And Toby was counselling me that being lowly and subservient was an important role. I studied the rest of the stable, and noticed near the door in the pile of hay an object which looked strange in the light. I thought it might've been a tool we'd dropped, which was best to remove, in case it was sharp and might harm one of the animals. I stepped forward and reached a hand down for it.

"Wolves method of communication wi'one another is at times violent," Toby explained. "They form these tight knit packs and must have absolute order – to maximise the chance of survival. Wolves don't shout, so when they reahly mean business they'll bite an snarl an pin each other down. It's their language. But they won't cause severe harm unless they reahlly need to, or if the victim suddenly panics and acts lyke prey."

As soon as my hand touched the object in the hay, I realised it was a bone. And before I even had a chance to digest this information, there was a pair of dog jaws clamped on my wrist and a terrible growl vibrated through the room around me. I'd let go of the bone again slowly, but still those teeth clamped onto my own skeletal wrist and I could feel the hot heavy breath on my skin. It's very easy to listen to wise words on how to deal with dogs, of how to not act as though you're afraid. It's a whole other issue when you have a feel for the power of those jaws which could splinter through your own bones at any minute.

He shook my wrist, with another growl, the strange sensation vibrating through my nervous system. *Puppy not prey*, I mouthed to myself. I whimpered – it was an easy noise to make given the situation. The grip loosened a little, but he was still pulling me into an odd angle, so, against my human instincts, I slowly lay down on the floor. I continued whimpering a pathetic apology. I'd somehow kept hold of the lamp in my other hand, but it was the wrong side and I could hardly see the dog. He loomed over me, spittle gradually dripping down in heart-shaped blobs.

It was probably only a matter of seconds before he let go, the thumping clock in my head keeping no time. I felt the strange adrenaline of freedom, paused for a moment stunned, and then holding the lamp in front of me I began a steady crawl towards the door. I thought it best not to suddenly become tall again. The horses watched with unconcerned curiosity. I suspected if they were capable of snooty giggling, they would've been. I crawled into the corridor which led to the stairs, knees grazing along the rough brickwork. When I reached the bottom of the steps, out of sight, I got shakily to my feet. I felt silly and embarrassed now. I wasn't sure I should even mention it.

But of course the dogs upstairs knew something was afoot, bristling with kinetic energy. Toby was already at the top of the steps peering down.

"Everythin okay, Sim?" he asked.

I grunted feebly, clambering back into the warm womb of the kitchen. I sat down at the table and the dogs bundled around me, to make a quick examination. To them I'd been in enemy territory. Maybe I was a hero.

Toby poured me a dram of strong, sweet elderflower wine and waited for me to speak.

"I accidentally picked up his bone," I said gravely and emitted a howling chuckle as the weight lifted from me. I pulled my sleeve back and Toby looked at it quietly. There were the teeth marks clear as day, but he'd not broken the skin.

PHASE EIGHT

In which Nikolai arrives & Charlie visits the house at Driskel.

MUCKLE FLUGGA

Wolfgang, New Riddlehamhope

I dream of the Arctic wind, so harsh in its carriage of shards of ice, it literally rips at the skin on your cheeks. Beard frozen, the frozen hair joined to the frozen snot that tries to drip from my nose. Sinuses confused in their want to shoo out the contents of my brain. The cold begins to get inside and I fear it freezing up all the goo inside my head.

The raw words of the local land – the brae and the burn – make sense in the winds that knife. Make sense when I'm stood at the foot of a glacier, feeling the physicality inside me of when it carved the glens and gullies, the cleughs and crags. Scratching out meaning in the rock and earth, sculpting the sights that put knots in our throats and beats in our hearts. A slow-moving glassy-eyed monster with more power than maybe even the ocean. Or are they one and the same...? When the glacier melts it joins the sea, the sea evaporates to the atmosphere which snows down on the mountains and freezes in compacted layers...

I was woken by a hammering on the door down below, shaking me from slumber like a dog with a devilish master. At first, in the dark, I thought I was back in a Sheffield squat, with the landowners' heavies knocking down the door to beat my addling brain and body. I peered around the room, and by smell I knew I was among fellow outlaws, in Riddlehamhope.

There was movement into the room. A liquid shadow slid by and slipped between the thick heavy curtains, to peer out of the window. I could smell uneasy fear. The same feeling most of us would feel with someone banging on the door in the middle of the night. It never bodes well. If it isn't bad news materializing itself, it's a messenger of bad news.

"Who the fook is tha?!" The Kaiser's voice came from somewhere in the blank recesses of the room. I wasn't sure if he meant the banging or the shadow that'd entered.

"Gmork." Toby's voice came soft and distinct from behind the curtain. "He's got someone with him. It doesn't look like one of his clan though."

Having never set my own eyes on Gmork, I could only imagine his hideousness, like something from the *Evil Dead* trilogy. (One of my first introductions to American film, due to my phobia of cinema spaces from a young age – it'd taken the advent of the video cassette for me to become film-literate.) And beyond his hideousness, I could only speculate at the person with him, as I listened to the dogs in the room below barking in frenzy. Some madman found wandering the wilderness, brought to curse our doorstep? A woman kidnapped and abused, with whom he wished to exact our pity to get us to open the door?

"Shall ah go and teach him it's rude to wayke a sleepin man?" Kaiser rasped hatefully.

"I thought you were tryin not to give yersel away as an ally?" Toby said, still soft and clear.

There were more entering the room, the other three dwellers in the house, hovering uncertainly. The banging had stopped for now. We were all quiet – waiting, listening with keen ears for any tiny noise. The dogs were quiet too, all listening, eyes wide in a world that replied with the same blank, dark gaze.

"He's gone," Toby said.

"What about his companion?" I asked.

* * * * * * *

COLLATERAL WISDOM

Roxanne Ratcliffe, New Riddlehamhope

"D'you know the meaning of '*Butterflies & Jelly*'?" I asked Wolfgang, one day when it was dogging me. I kind of knew, of course. It wasn't a reference to long term love. It was that initial buzz. We were in the butchery plucking a couple of Canadian geese, bagging the downy feathers for insulation and the largest feathers for arrows. Why dead birds reminded me of the subject, I can't really say.

Wolfgang smiled nostalgically. "Meaning or origin, little Rue?"

"Oh, origin I spose," I said.

"Do you remember Devlin?"

I nodded. Devlin was an Irishmen who'd haunted the nightspots of Sheffield (with what Cuan once described as 'collateral wisdom'). With curly, dark hair and warm brown eyes, he'd always looked how you'd expect a handsome man to look after years of hard drinking. He had a wily charm, but so far as I could tell used it purely in persuading others into mutual ruin – an evening spent on a cocktail of whisky and class-As was common enough.

When he had plenty of money he would buy round after round of drinks (a fresh one appearing on the table before you'd made two thirds headway into the last). When he ran out of money, he'd sit in the pub with the people he'd spoiled with his generosity and let them top up his glass. This was the only 'safe' time to be around him, I'd always thought. There were times (recalling savage hangovers) that I'd walked into a pub and walked straight out again, because he was there.

"What's it got to do with him?" I asked.

"Ah ha," Wolfgang said, like a magician about to reveal his magic. He paused, then shrugged. "Didn't you ever see him play?"

On top of his occupation as a health hazard, Devlin was also a folk singer and guitarist, and by no means run-of-the-mill – I'd been vehemently assured this by everyone I knew.

"No," I said. "I always intended to, but I was always up to sommat else."

Wolfgang nodded.

"It was a lyric in one of his songs, something along the lines of – *'the butterflies in my stomach and the jelly in my knees'*."

This explained Cuan's insistence that I go to see Devlin play. But I never had.

We'd plucked the easy fatty bits of the geese now and moved onto the tough areas which required broad tugs – filling the air around us with a snowstorm of feathers, the remains of fallen angels discarded on the brick floor. This and the repetitive movement made me think of some sort of ritualistic dance. It was hard and frustrating, but at least the surreal state of the room made us smile a bit. I'd only plucked ducks before this, so had no idea what to do with the long, black necks of the birds which snaked limply on the table.

Later when we sat around the table, me massaging the knots out of tired fingers, I pondered on something else.

"Wolfie, do Germans play cricket?"

A huge map was laid out on the table and Toby was moving around it with squirrel-like attention, pawing bits and stretching over to press his face close to regions of interest. He would pause to look at scrawled notes Brock had made for him.

Charlie and Wolfgang were seated at the table. Charlie was staring blankly at negative space, his gun rested on the table in front of him, his knuckles curling and uncurling hard-bitten nails around it. He was in a bad mood. He'd used all his ammunition and Toby had suggested it was pointless getting any more. Wolfgang was using a steak knife to remove bits of food from his teeth. As I spoke he continued, head tilted, eyes roving toward me like a suspicious hound chewing a bone.

Eventually he removed the knife and set it down.

"Cricket? Yes, but it's not the same as your English cricket. It involves hiding in dense undergrowth making clicking noises, but throwing your voice so a person cannot find you. Jimmy Cricket."

"Why d'yuu ask him questions and expect any sense Roxy?" Charlie asked, through tight teeth. "Cricket wus only played in the Commonwealth, I think."

There was a scratching noise at the window. It was foggy outside, right up to the glass, but a wolf's face had emerged through it, pawing, big eyes swallowing the light inside.

"Let the dog in, Roxy," Charlie said.

I was annoyed by his tone. "Stop being a pissy fucker."

"The fog will get in!" Wolfgang said.

I got up and regretfully opened the kitchen door, shivering as the cold air swept in, carried on a rough, hairy coat.

"Ana!" I tousled the she-dog's head. She spun in circles around me making a happy coughing sound.

A whole pack seemed to be pouring through the doorway, as though falling out of the fog itself. A mass of black-tan-grey-white bodies suddenly filling the empty space. I recalled Dracula's hounds of death, red eyes in the black.

It was Hobina's first trip out with the other dogs. Brock had decided she needed to be 'socialised'. He entered last with Hobina – a clumsy rush of too long legs and over-excitement, running to each of us with excited barks. She seemed to have forgotten I'd shot her mother, leaping up to plant mucky paws on me and trying to lick my face.

"I'm pretty sure thes sum Akita in that dog," Toby said thoughtfully. "She'll be bigger than the others."

"What's that?" I asked.

"They originated in Japan," he began. "You'll recognise them though." He scanned his shelves for a book of dog breeds and flicked through it until he found a picture. "They were quite popular among irresponsible owners in this country, cause they can be quite fierce."

I stared at the picture.

"Yeah, that does look like her mum. I thought it was like a big husky, because of the tail."

"They dinnae leik other dogs much," Brock said, with gruff cynicism. Looking at Hobina interacting with the others, I couldn't see this at all. "One set on my old Staffie once, he were only bein friendly. Had ta bop it on the snout to gerrit to lay off."

"Well, you can mayke peace wi' the breed now," Toby said wryly.

"Wus jus sayin," Brock muttered, looking at his dog with a wary eye, as though she'd turn at any minute. "Wait til she gets big."

* * * * * * *

THE TIRED SOUNDS OF THE COYOTE

Simian Thomas, New Riddlehamhope

It was the middle of the night. The world outside was a sheet of black, disturbed only by the restless nocturnal spirits. For once everybody was awake, sat in the kitchen around the great table, which itself told stories of the fall of a mighty tree. Cut from the centre in one chunk, ingrained with the histories of bugs and beetles and birds. A thousand dinners eaten from the living tree. Now dead, it sat in the brick-walled kitchen and witnessed more dinners, more gossiping birds, more small dramas that would make mini echoes in the surface of time.

"What's ya nayme?" Toby asked presently, after reviving the fire and making the child hot goat's milk and honey.

The boy, who Gmork'd left on the back steps, cradled the cup and looked suspiciously at our faces with heavy-lidded eyes. He was so quiet and unresponsive I wondered if he spoke human language at all. Maybe he'd been raised by friendly badgers. The dogs were padding the room back and forth, eager to sniff the boy, but every time one came near him he looked so terrified that Toby pushed it away.

"Nikolai," the boy said eventually.

Otto tried to sneak past under the table to sniff him, but Toby caught him gently in the curve of his ankle.

"Tss!"

Otto retreated over to Haydn for reassurance. The boy, who must've been about twelve or thirteen years old, looked very weak and malnourished. His hair was pale, probably blonde, but looked almost grey from lack of sunshine.

"Why'd he leave ya here?" Toby asked.

Gmork'd given up banging on the door and strode off into the night, leaving the bundle of bones in a heap on the cold, wet ground.

"James..." Nikolai drifted off.

"Why did James leave ya here?" Toby repeated gently.

"Ahm ill," Nikolai said. "He said ah'd die if I stayed withum. He said you werra doctor, man."

"I'm not a doctor," Toby said.

Nikolai looked close to tears, barely able to focus on the people. He seemed only aware of the dogs circling him.

"D'ya wanna go to bed and we'll talk maire tomorrow?" Toby asked.

The boy nodded feebly. Toby made dandelion tea and put some bread and fat on a plate and helped Nikolai upstairs to one of the bedrooms. He returned after a few minutes and sat down at the table.

"D'you think it's a trick?" Haydn asked.

Toby shrugged.

"He's genuinely not well, but Gmork may've starved him on purpose."

I was filled with an eerie sense of horror at this.

"I think we saw him a few weeks ago, wi'a woman," Claudia said.

Toby nodded.

"I don't think he's their son. He dun't look like um. Either he became ill so Gmork wanted rid of 'im, or it's sum deliberate trick. We'll just hafta wait and see." He paused tiredly, rubbing his head with both hands. "He might not even survive. All I can do is give him rest and tonics and hope fur't best."

We sat in empty, thoughtful silence for a few minutes. Eventually Toby got up, glancing sadly at Roxy as he did so.

"I'm gonna try an get sum sleep." He sighed and left the room.

I thought about sleep, but I still felt wide awake, full of a million questions about these baddies, trying to fathom the motivation of ruthless people. I'd led a fairly sheltered early life, able to give a wide birth to the skag heads in Sheffield train station having a domestic argument about him fucking someone else. But even then I could see the motivation behind the blind rage – sex and love and narcotics. They could be placated in moments with a drug that relieves ill will...

I reasoned simply that all we were to this other clan was competition for a limited food supply. Why should they feel any empathy for us?

* * * * * * *

THE SANDS & THE SNAKEHEADS

Claudia McLeod, the New Northumbrian Coast

The dunes stretched well inland formin an other-worldly scene. Rollin humps a sand an grasses created small hills that looked lyke bleached woolly mammoths, dozin in't afternoon breeze.

Where the dunes proper'ly began and the land ended was not clearly marked, as the mighty ocean had thrown several hundred tons of the sand at the coastline. Fish'd been seen in't trees and sea shells were still foundt'wards the base of the Cheviots. The locals referred to it as the 'Borderland Tragedy', but they spoke rarely of the old bonds torn open by tha sea, and the resculpted county.

Once off horseback, it were hard graft leggin it about the dunes. They mayde me feel lyke a kid at'beach agen, but the thought of all the dead bodies buried beneath mayde my feet feel heavier. It were grand ridin though. Our hoarses were well used to the area, an when we came to an open stretch they side-stepped, snorted and tugged til we lett'em gallop. We had to slow up agen quick, though. There were no point knackerin them out yet, when we'ad work to do.

There was endless potential on the coastline – rock pools where shellfish and seaweed could be gathered and the strand could be combed for useful objects to salvage. But our biggest hope wa'that we might catch a seal. Asides the enormous quantity of meat, the skin was one'a the best types ya could get hauld of. It could easily be waterproofed and didn't wear down, crack or go brittle in't cold and wet weather, the way other stuff did.

For these reasons we'd brought an extra hoarse to help carry back any excess weight. We wont too optimistic, though. The trip were more about explorin potential. We'd only just gotten the hoarses and were still workin to train them. Toby was riding the skewbald that Adam and Logan had naymed Legolas. He were probably descended straight from domestic stock (maybe gypsy) and he were what my auld ridin teacher would've described as 'bomb proof'. I was riding a dark bay stallion, called Aragorn, who were a little more spirited. His origins were unknown, as he'd been caught as a foal from a group of feral hoarses. Aragorn worra handful, sae it were just as well our pack hoarse Gerald, an eight year'ol bay gelding, was calm as a cucumber.

We took turns leadin Gerald, but Toby was still tryin ta master controlling the one hoarse, wi'out havin to fret about another. Lego might've been easier to handle than my ride, but he were still stubborn at times.

We'd not even reached the actual beach yet, but we'd found a strange seawater pond in a patch of hard ground. Wi'out the tides refreshing it, it probably wouldn't contain owt good, but we stopped to investigate. It were easiest if Toby got off, while I held the hoarses. Aragorn danced impatiently, so I chatted to him. His ears flickered indecisively. Then he flared his nostrils, tossed his nose and rolled his eyes. I realised Gerald was spookin too and I looked around.

Wi' careful observation I spotted several pairs of ears and eyes peerin from different spots. It werra young, unruly packa dogs. They couldn't have been too wise at huntin together, else we would never'av even known they war there. They were eyein the hoarses wi'a mixture of hunger and suspicion. A bunch of scrawny little beggars skulking around lookin more nervy than fierce. "Can ya hold Gerald a minute?"

Toby'ad spotted the dogs and remounted. He nodded and took the lead rope off me.

Aragorn war by now dancing barmy on't spot wi'adrenaline. I pointed him at the nearest dog and gev a little squeeze. It were lyke ridin sommat shot from a canon. He charged at the dog and as it scuttled to safety, I spun him round nippy and aimed fa't next one – toppin sand dunes and hoppin dips. A sandstorm a' fury an hooves poundin close to the par dogs ears.

As I spected they retreated to safer distances, but still loitered. They'd follow us now, hiding and seeking – waiting for a sign a weakness.

"We can't hunt seals with this rammel on our tail," I said narkily as we set off agen.

Toby gave a glum nod.

"I should've brought Fidel wi'us. He'd av mayde short work a' them."

Finally we came over a hump and there was the sea. It wussa cloudy day and the water stretched out, barely distinguishable faraway wi'the skyline. The ocean winds tossed manes and tails in fizzogs and at times whipped sand in my eyes. There were no cover now fa'the dogs, so they hung bout ten metres be'yind us, watchin and waitin. We travelled along the water's edge, paddling in't surf. The hoarses wanted to dash off agen, but Toby and I war tryin ta forage. I knew alotta shellfish tended to be just below the sand. We'd brought a small rake wi'us, but it was a matter of lookin fa feedin seabirds in order to find the right spot.

"Whas happened to Lidisfarne?" I asked. "And Bamburgh Castle, is that roundabouts here?"

Toby looked out onta't blank water.

"Some'a Lidisfarne is still above sea level, but all the people there at'time were swept away. Bamburgh's now an island. You can see it from further down't coast."

'Ventually he settled on a place to stop and dismounted. He began rakin, turnin up clams and cockles. I held ahl three hoarses and faced the dogs. They hung self-consciously in a line. Just like a gaggle a' teenage lads, knowin they ought to be posturing... they inched forward one by one, bodies close to't ground lyke they were shepherdin. The waves were sweeping in close to us, repetitive lines formed below in't sand lookin like tiny snakes. As though faced with an army a' tiny snakes

Aragorn reared up a bit and smashed his hooves down, flingin wet sand about. It was a warning to the dogs, but they were too blind-stupid with hunger to pay attention.

I were feelin a little vulnerable by this point. Controlling one mental hoarse I could about deal wi', but hangin onto't other two at sayme time weren't fun. I looked to Toby. He'd set down his bucket of shellfish and wi'a calmness that was well-rehearsed he pulled his crossbow off his back and shot dead the nearest dog. In case they didn't realise this werra good time to leave, I handed him the two spare hoarses and agen aimed the equine rocket at them.

This time they had nowhere to hide and the pack split apart in fright, dashin chaotic'ly t'wards the nearest cover far up the beach. I picked on one and followed'im, imagining the pounding heartbeat at the feel of hooves on the sand behind his tail. He dodged and weaved this an that way and eventually I dragged Aragorn to a halt. I faced the fleeing animals til they were ahl totally out of sight and then returned't Toby.

I hadn't realised how far I'd gone. By the time I pulled up next to him, he'd filled his bucket wi'shellfish and various seaweeds and already skinned the dead dog. He packed the pelt away, leavin the remains on the sand.

"I spect his hungry friends will make short work of him. Or, if not, the gulls will." Toby's voice were dark.

I nodded.

He pointed out'ta sea and passed me his binoculars. On some rocks away from the shore, there were a handful of seals dozin.

"I'm not shar they come ontu't mainland at'all. I haven't seen any drag marks along the shore. They probably stay on't islands. We'd need a boat and probably a harpoon to even think about catchin one." He looked up and down the beach. It stretched for miles either way, wi'no sign of owt other than the sea birds that occasionally dotted the shoreline.

"We can't really stay long, can we?" I said. "Need to get back by nightfall, an it took a couple of hours to gerr'ere, din't it?"

He nodded, reluctant that we'd travelled ahl this way for one dog skin and a few cockles.

"I don't know what time it is wi'out the sun." He shielded his eyes and looked up at the fine layer of cloud.

I handed him some water from our supplies, he slugged it greedily and then passed it back.

"Last time I came here it was wi'the dog sled. There were snow on't beach... it were magical." He readied the hoarses, and remounted Lego.

We sat for a few moments admiring the view and then turned in't direction of home.

* * * * * * *

FRAILTIES & LOYALTIES

Bryn McLarey, New Riddlehamhope

The boy Nikolai had stayed in his room for sum days now. Individuals could go in, but he didnae come out. He wus apparently much better now, but wus still afraid of everything. Thas what they said. Toby visited him most often, with a soft voice and social worker's eyes, though he confessed he didn't think he wus great with children. Claudia'd been up there that morning, no doubt thinking about her own future brood and whether she had the patience.

She came back down with a wild scowl set intu her fine-china face.

"What's the little shit up tu now?" I asked.

"How he's survived. I'm flamed if I fookin know."

"What did he say?" I asked, meaning about his background, about the clan. We still didn't have much of a story.

"He just whinged and whined and dodged questions." She stuck her bottom lip out grumpily.

"Y'should all stop panderin tu him. Leave him alone, don't feed him much. He'll soon get bored and hungry and come out," I suggested.

"Maybe," Claudia said. "Anyroad, bes go sort the hoarses out, try an teach Sim to ride. Can't fookin wait."

We'd agreed that Nikolai shouldn't be left in the house alone, in case his motives weren't innocent. Havin spent ahl week oot and aboot, leavin the baby sitting ta others, it wus mae turn. Toby'd left me a list of things tu do in his worn brown notebook, though I could barely read the scrawl. There were books to look at, maps to examine, a broken curtain rail ta fix... all of it dull and pointless when the sun wus shining outside and the sky wus wide and blue over the hills.

I watched Claudia from the window, leading the brown horse out intu the yard below and tying him up tu a hook she'd put in the wall. Simian wus stood awkwardly around, patting the horse's neck and trying tu pay attention tu what Claudia wus sayin. I could hear her voice lilting through the air but no individual words. Sunlight picked out wee hairs on their heids, awardin the scene a peaceful, timeless quality.

The house felt empty and airy now that we could open windows and drive out the stuffy dampness of winter. There seemed tu be ladybirds everywhere, they must've hibernated inside and now woken up. I'd never thought ladybirds could swarm, but they did. I counted seven on the wall and twenty three on the window pane. The light turned them inta black spots with a red tint around the silhouettes.

The stairs creaked and I immediately snapped out of idle daydreams. I made maeself motionless as a hunter in grass – becoming part'a the auld brown furniture, mae breath merely the flutter of insect wings. Nikolai wus sneakin alright. I could hear him trying very hard tu avoid makin noise on the stairs. As he got tu the bottom he paused and waited, listening, probably trying ta peer through the jam in the half-open door for any movement. He poked his head around and I gave him a big, evil grin.

"Oh," he said.

"Hi," I said. He'd not seen me since the night he'd arrived and probably would've preferred to run into someone else, someone he'd already sussed out a bit.

"Feeling better?" I asked.

He hovered in the doorway uncertainly.

"Sit down." I waved tu a chair.

He paused still, counting his options, considering being the little piggy going wee, wee, wee all the way back to bed. Reluctantly he moved a chair and sat down quite far away from me. The scrape of the legs on the kitchen floor broke the quiet of the house. I felt a wee bit like everyone else had been good cop tu the boy and now it wus mae turn to be bad cop.

"Who named you Nikolai?" I asked.

I don't think it wus anywhere near the question he wus expecting. He shrugged, but I decided not tu accept the shrug as an answer. I waited, looking at him expectantly, piling pressure up in the room.

"I dunno, me mam, I guess," he said eventually in annoyance.

"Who's your mam?" I asked.

He shrugged again, so I repeated the saime routine.

"I dinnae know, man," he said eventually. "I cannae remember."

"You can't remember much by the sounds of things," I said. "Had a bump on the head or something?"

I wus bein careful tu speak with an English accent. If he returned to Gmork mentioning a Scottish bloke, he'd know it wus me.

"Ye lot ask alottah questions," he mumbled.

"I know, it's awful. Why should we be so curious about a strange boy appearing in the night?" I said.

"I'm noo a boy," Nikolai said.

"You act like a boy."

We sat in silence furra while, him avoiding eye contact, fringe flopping stubbornly doon to hide his face. His hair still looked oddly white. Meybe it wus jus that colour, leik the boy at mae school we used to call 'lightbulb' because of the shape and colour of his heid, and tha fact that he wusnae the brightest crayon in the box.

"Now you're better, are you planning to stay here? Or go back with that Scottish bloke?" I asked eventually.

"James..." he said, ne lookin up, the nayme spoken loaded with meaning.

"Was he nice to you? Did *he* treat you like a grown-up?"

"No," he said. (Though to which question or tu both, I cudnae judge.)

"Do you want to go back?" I repeated.

"It's easier here," he said.

"We do everything for you? You'll have to pull your weight if you stay. And get over your issues with the dogs." I stroked mae beard thoughtfully, a habit I'd taken tu, ready to be an auld man already.

"The black one bit Sophie," he said.

"He'll bite you too, if you seem to be an enemy. He's protecting his pack."

"Thas noo very reassuring!" Nikolai lifted his head and narrowed his eyes at me.

I looked back at him with even calmness. "*I'll* bite you if you turn out to be an enemy. Don't be a fucking enemy."

The door to the yard steps swung open and Claudia came in with Simian. She wus mid-conversation but stopped when she saw Nikolai. He jumped to his feet and scuttled back upstairs. They both stood and looked at me expectantly – I smiled a smug, nonchalant smile.

* * * * * * *

ONLY BILLY HAS THE ETHER

Roxanne Ratcliffe, the Cheviot Hills

The sky was a meek grey. It seemed to be clamping the cold down on the land and there was little wind, so the air remained icily still. Occasionally I thought I felt the odd raindrop, but it seemed to stick to my face and form spots of ice. There were two wood pigeons up in a tree nearby – they were sat motionless with cold. It was the only tall tree in the area. I wondered what the birds were doing so far up the slopes.

"Cushat," I mouthed quietly to myself.

I edged around the foot of the round topped hill, finding a worn dirt path. It was hard to tell if it was a footpath or a sheep path. Sheep paths generally led to nowhere. (Maybe I'm doing the sheep down, though. They probably led to good grazing.) I was on the more northerly Cheviot Hills, which were covered in a newly budding carpet of heather, creating shades of fresh young green and orange. Even on such an austere day, it still held onto a defiant beauty. Not one that could be easily captured with a camera, because the light was too poor, weakening all the colours and shadow. But it could still captivate my blinking gaze.

The path dipped sharply down and I could hear the burble of a burn before I could see it, half concealed among grass and clumps of gorse. I hopped over and continued over the damp springy turf around the path that ringed the next hill, heading towards the steepest face. I admired the scatter of rubble around the top – it looked like a particularly well-preserved old fort.

There were no sheep about here and I wondered if it was true the farmers still controlled their grazing. I hadn't known the sheep still belonged to people, assuming they were feral, until Brock began a seething tirade at Claudia and Haydn for shearing some. He said it would bring trouble for us, in a way just stealing a whole sheep and using it nose to tail wouldn't have. If a whole sheep disappeared, wild dogs could be blamed.

The heather was thicker and more overgrown on this side of the hill. I could hear small birds singing out to one another and occasionally glimpsed one flitting in the air and disappearing in another spot. There was movement far up the hill, of something much bigger. At first I thought it *was* sheep, two blurs of greyish white against the greens and browns of the new and old heather. But as I looked more carefully, I realised the movement was different. It was the feral goats who'd apparently roamed the Cheviots for years. They weren't, as I'd imagined, much like domestic goats at all. More like something from a Siberian mountainside maybe, with long coats that made them look as though they were floating over the scrub.

They had slender arching horns and effortlessly agile movement, all combining to make them feel mystical and ethereal. Like guardian spirits of the slopes.

I attempted to whistle down the brae to attract the attention of the others. The goats, if they saw or heard me, were unconcerned. The steep climb protected them – they could outwit anything up there. They were well beyond the reach of a crossbow and as I watched them, spellbound, I didn't even want to kill them, however good they tasted. I began to hope my whistle hadn't been heard.

Then I heard a noise. At first I thought the wind was making a peculiar sound, but then I realised it was something else, something alien in its distant familiarity – the hum of an aeroplane. I stared at the sky, but it was blank and expressionless. No dark spots showing through the cloud. I remembered the pause after the sight of an aeroplane before the sound arrived and tried to look ahead of the sound. But it was already fading. I tried to envision a world still existing in which people flew planes. I suppose people with money, people in the Bubble could still do such things. It felt bizarre though, this connection with a past civilization invading my present existence – in which I lived on these lands as people did hundreds of years before.

I was so lost in thoughts of planes and wild goats I didn't even notice Toby and Nikolai clambering up from my left. I swore at myself in annoyance. It was dangerous to become so unaware of what was about. They'd both spotted the goats by the time they reached me, though the animals were edging further away as they nibbled at young heather.

"Yeavering Bell," Nikolai said in his dense accent, made even less easy to follow by his teenage mumbles and grunts.

"Sorry, what?" I asked, for the twentieth time that day.

He looked irritated as always and he pointed at the hill.

"Ess caald 'Yeavering Bell'- means 'hill uv the goats'." He shrugged defensively. "Jus thowt it were funny, leik."

"Oh," I said. "Yeah." I tried to smile at him, but he was already staring self-consciously at his own feet.

Toby made an amused face.

"Yee cannae catch em. Specially no them wily feckin billys." Nikolai shook his head gravely. "Boaared else, enywes. Gannin hyem."

"You're havin nowt fa supper if you go hoame now," Toby said shrugging. "Up to you."

"Hadaway," Nikolai muttered at the grass.

"Did you hear the plane?" I asked.

Toby frowned. "No."

This seemed odd, they weren't far away when I'd heard it – I was beginning to doubt that I had. "...Thought I heard a plane fly over," I mumbled.

Nikolai looked up at me, dead in the eye, as though this was a big deal to him.

* * * * * * *

CAMOUFLAGE

Haydn Antoine, New Riddlehamhope

All eyes were on young Nikolai. Even when we pretended they were elsewhere. I found him somehow ordinary and extraordinary at the same time – he was a typically sullen teenager, seeming not to have much he wanted to communicate. It was that familiar period we all went through (yet had somehow forgotten) where you shut in on yourself, because you feel suddenly very vulnerable and self aware. It's often heightened in troubled adolescents and Niko was certainly one of them. But then who wouldn't be a bit messed up by the whole saga of the Weathers, at that age?

But between the lines written by the cardboard teenager (in grunt-speak) there was a whole lot more going on. Nikolai was pretty sharp and was so often quiet it was easy to forget he was there – and thus listening. Not that I thought he was a threat, really. If he had been sent as one, I doubted he had it in him not to feel grateful to us for all we'd done. But his perceptiveness was at times a little creepy, when he caught you off guard. Charlie had been speaking in an English accent since he'd arrived, but of course he eventually slipped. He loved showing off.

"Are'ye Scottish?" Nikolai asked all of a sudden, having done little more than grunt yes or no all week long.

Charlie carved a face of contempt and looked at him across the kitchen. Nikolai was crouched on his haunches, on a chair in the corner. Cujo was sat next to him. She seemed to have taken a shine to the outsider. He seemed to like how small she was. They were both good at hiding.

"Aye," Charlie said. "Does it matter?"

"Why diya speak leik an English ahl the time, man?" Niko asked, eyes wide.

"Camouflage." Charlie flashed a hand in front of his face, as though to disappear. He broke his accent into his Dad's Sunderland twang. "Tu escape iden-ti-fi-cation."

"Thas crackin!" Nikolai said. "Wishd ah could do that."

"Whas yer surname, Niko?" Charlie asked.

"Nikolai McLurg." He looked away boredly, biting his thumb. "Niko-Mac."

"I think McLurgy is a better nickname. In aulden times they wudha referred to yuu as 'a sickly child'," Charlie said.

Nikolai shrugged, but seemed sunk again – back into the protective pond of silence. It was odd that Charlie felt the need to fill in the role of school bully in Niko's life. As though that was the role model he was missing.

Maybe Charlie was just a bully.

But Nikolai himself was good at camouflage. Good at working himself into the furniture in the house. And when out and about with us, it was more like having a pet than another person. Flashes of confidence would emerge and he'd seem to come out of his shell temporarily, then just like the hermit crab – *zip* – straight back in again. I think sometimes Charlie read this as him duelling with his own conscience, trying not to accidentally become one of us. But I wondered if it was more complicated. While he was indeed sussing us out, I felt this tendency to be at one with the furniture was simply his age and shyness. I remember becoming very withdrawn at his age, the safety of primary school giving way to big school. Invisibility suddenly felt like a valuable skill, in order to avoid negative attention.

One afternoon out collecting firewood, with Niko dragging his feet and generally acting like the work experience kid – he disappeared. And it did take me a while to notice he was even gone, in the dutiful spring drizzle. I retraced my steps thinking he'd probably just stubbornly sat down for a rest somewhere sheltered. But no, he was gone. He'd become part of the landscape and, with a shiver, looking about me through the rain which fell so consistently in vertical lines, I had a feeling he was gone for good. Gone before we could know more than he was willing to give away.

I set off back to the house – it was possible he'd gone back. But no, it was utterly empty, everybody was out. I dumped the damp wood by the stove (still warm from breakfast), hoping it would dry out. I felt at a loss. Should I raise some sort of alarm? Was this an emergency? Were we in danger? I didn't feel panicked, just confused and lost. I mooched around for the next few hours, finding various unimportant chores to do at Riddlehamhope, waiting, just in case.

And then suddenly he was there, pale little face at the window, knocking on the glass. I unlocked the door. He was a blank page, giving nothing away. He was sopping wet and his clothes were covered in mud, but he'd brought a bag of firewood – far better quality, drier wood than what I'd collected. Without a word he stoked the fire and hung the kettle over it. He sat drying off and made us both tea.

The words 'Where have you been?' were stuck in my throat. I opened my mouth, and then closed it again. Eventually though, I panicked that the others would come home and I'd have to have asked him, whatever non-committal reply I got. I wondered if I was a weaker one, he thought he could take advantage of.

"Where did you disappear to, Niko?" my voice eventually quivered. In fact it almost sounded like it hadn't broken yet, as though Nikolai was returning me to my twelve year old self with a bump.

He pointed to his batch of firewood. "Ah jus knew a better spot."

I felt a glimpse of relief, but I continued to worry about it and it still didn't fit that this had taken him so long. Maybe the 'better spot' was far away, but I doubted he would've gone miles and then been bothered to lug it all back.

The others arrived back at the house in dribs and drabs. Nikolai had busied himself at the table, working on his own crossbow, with a composite prod and string from dried sinew. He was acting the teacher's pet now, asking lots of questions. Roxy had come back with Toby – she shook off her wet coat, with a weak sigh. She seemed disappointed about something. Toby also looked a little preoccupied, but I waited subtly and caught him alone when he went down into the butchery.

"Everything okay?" His brow furrowed perceptively.

"I'm not sure," I said quietly, with a half laugh that quickly dissolved to mud. "Nikolai disappeared for a few hours today. I didn't know if he was coming back at all. He said he'd just gone to a better spot for firewood."

The excuse seemed even dafter now it was coming out of my own mouth.

Toby scratched his beard thoughtfully.

"Tattling wi'the enemy?"

I shrugged.

"Okay, best keep it on the down, I think," he said.

I nodded, but then felt jittery again, because I knew Claudia would sense something was up and weed it out of me anyway.

* * * * * *

BETTER THAN BOVRIL

Bryn McLarey, Breamish Valley

I sometimes wonder how mae life would've been different now, if all this hadnae occurred. They're mealy, pointless procrastinations, of course. But I return tu them with unquestioning obedience, wondering where I would be now...

Would I huv a mortgage and a wife and all that shite? Would some woman finally have cleaned me up intu sumthin respectable? Would I be a sink-estate-success cliché? Sighthill just a blip on a past horizon? Or would I still be doing split shifts in a bar and smokin weed in a friend's attic? It's ahl relative. It's ahl just me staring through a dirty window pane.

The windows of the pub hadnae been cleaned in a wee while. The whole place wus grimy.

"Wev nae airs and graces here," the bartender'd assured me.

Only maeself, Brock and Nikolai had ventured tu the Plough Inn. It wusnae far from home, an I'd passed it many tymes, but it'd looked abandoned and forgotten – a genuine old country pub, authentically hauntin me with past joys. But sitting inside had finally left me with a bad taste in mae trap. The air wus heavy and intense, jus leik when you walk inta any dive pub where they dinnae know yuu. They knew Brock, but that wusnae enough tu settle five pairs uv scabby eyes back tu card games and beer. Only local accents were in currency here, so I wus playin mae daddy, in mae aen surreal script.

The room hadda low ceiling with black beams and a fire in the hearth, even though it wus a balmy spring day ootside. The walls had once been white but were now grey-beige with soot and tab smoke. There wussa dusty vase on the window sill, with a bunch of long deid dry flowers, soo in pieces that aenly stems and the odd stray brown petal remained. The bar itself wus short in length, but everybody sat or stood at it, including us. Except one lone man in tha corner, sat on frayed seating at a low table. He wus fortyish with faded ginger hair and smoked

a pipe. He supped sumthin from a jar that looked like
Bovril. I hadda feelin he wus someone special, someone
who didnae need tu watch his aen back. Every fooker else
in that gaff, including us, wus very aware of their aen
spine. The tuu on the far corner of the wee bar playin
Black Jack seemed wary even of each other.

I'd begun tu realise, as we settled into our wee rut at
the foot a' the hills, that the picture we'd had of the new
country as we'd travel'd hither and thither wus just a series
of Polaroid snaps. It'd seemed like mere fistfuls of folk
were maykkin ends meet, one way or another.
Northumberland had at first seemed barren, lifeless and
abandoned. But I now realised it wasnae soo. These
people were fookin hardy as their sheep and their ponies
after all. The settlements worst hit by storms and the leik
had been left tu ruin, but other villages and toons had
gathered up the locals. They lived in pocketed
communities, where they traded both money and goods.

The communities were mutually supportive to
members, but suspicious of others. And if a member wus
caught committing a crime against one of their aen, they
were outlawed – often 'marked' and run out of toon. But
they turned a blind eye tu members committing a crime
against another community – then *stealing* became 'lootin'
and *rape* became 'tuppin' or 'coverin'.

Brock had said the scorch mark on Gmork's bath
chap wus leikly a sign he'd betrayed a community. Meybe
even up across the border, rather than locally. Brock
thought his own way of manoeuvring wus the best way –
as a trusted trader, with a finger in many pies. Advice, tall
tales and a gruff, earthy cheer guaranteed him a warm
welcome *here and aboot*.

"Ah were a graveyard attendant in tyme gan. Could
tell ye a stroonge ghoul-tale or tuu," he said to Nikolai. He
shifted his arse on the narrow bar stool, leaning on his

elbows and staring at the empty whisky bottles behind the bar, before tekkin a peek in Niko's face tu gauge a reaction.

"Aye." Nikolai scowled cynically. One thing he wasnae wus gullible. Impressionable meybe, but neh gullible.

"Nae word uv a lie," Brock insisted.

"Aye." Nikolai swigged from his bottle.

"Cheeky bogger." Brock gave the landlord a cheerful wink – meybees tryin to break the atmosphere.

I could be stuck in a metal box, in a commuter belt right noo, I thought. Heading home in the midst of rush hour, to a healthy dinner of bean sprouts and pulses.

I'd chosen tu slorp the local beer, from an unmarked pump, referred tu only as 'Canny Brew'. It wusnae – sae far as I could tell – a canny brew. It wus cloudy and a little sour, but still on principal it beat the generic tasteless bottled lager imported from the Bubble. That was what Niko wus drinking. (Still, I was into Tennants Super and 20/20 at hus age.)

Brock wus also maire willing tu brave the shite beer.

"Cannae stand the bubbly stuff. Bubbles a fa Fairy Liquid, noo beer," he muttered. But Nikolai wus a teenage boy and teenage boys won't be told. "Ye slorp whatever ye will," Brock had said diplomatically. "Yer big enuff an daft enuff to make your aen mistakes."

(As though he'd fallen in with a bad crowd and started snorting cheap coke and fingering dodgy girls in bus stops.)

We endured the last sup of our beers and headed back out into the late, languid afternoon. The sun wus perched above us between tuu clouds, its rays visibly reaching doon over the brae, like in a Renaissance painting.

"By chuddy gum," Brock said withoot emotion. "Wi cloods sa canny, yeh could be forgiven fa believin in a Heaven abev…"

* * * * * * *

THAT'LL LEARN YA

Claudia McLeod, the Cheviot Hills

Nose to tail, we descended the narrow path, stones slipping forward away frum hooves which found their stubborn grip.

"Ya need to lean back more, Brock, to help balance the weight," I said in the brisk tones of a bossy hoarsewoman. "An try'ta keep your hands still and low. If you jerk them around it'll muddle him."

As the path flattened out a bit onta't heath, Brock pulled Aragorn to the side and told me, wi' camp drama,

"If ah wanted a lesson, Ah'd ask ferrit."

He were probably mostly narked that Nikolai was so obviously a better rider than him. And that I'd said he could only ride Aragorn, as the other hoarses weren't big enuff furrim. He looked clumsy and outtah place on't back of a hoarse. The cockiness he had on't ground were gone. He slumped there in't seat a'the saddle, lookin lyke a drunken toad. I bit ma tongue over this, I'd already told him to sit straight. There was only so much tutting I could be bothered wi' hearin.

We stood in a line while Brock peered at one'a his maps, looking fa changes in't land which wa heaped in clumps of moss-crop, lyke everywhere round abouts – hardly recognisable. The sun were up and bakin down from a clear sky. I rolled my sleeves up a bit. Lego stamped his hoof and swished his tail at flies.

"Hey Niko, look at us. Leik three cowboys, eh?" Brock said. "You wanna play cowboys?"

Nikolai, in contrast to Brock, looked a bit small and stringy to be riding Gerald, but he had the skills. He ignored Brock's jibe, smirking to hissel. Further along we came to a ruined building, some of which was still standing, though the windows had no glass and there was a chunk ripped out where the walls joined the roof. The outbuildings were piles of rubble already, wi' moss an nettles cuddled inta gaps.

"Careful noo," Nikolai piped up. "Sophie got caught in auld barbed wire, hereaway."

"Ah see ut," Brock said quickly. He dismounted and being careful to mekk sure his thick gloves were secure, he began tuggin the barbed wire from its hiding place, while Aragorn eyed it suspicious'ly.

"Who's Sophie?" I asked.

Niko blushed and shrugged.

"Your girlfriend?" I teased.

"Gi'us a break. She were more leik me mam," he answered. "Ye minded to huv a gander in the hoose?" He pointed at the building.

"Aye," I said, in a deep voice, as Brock would.

He smirked agen, and as though this had egged his confidence to express hissel he said, "In't it funny how sumtimes the bushes aen the trees?" He pointed out an example just beyond the boundary wall.

"Y'should try that one out on Wolfgang, he'll love it," I said.

We tied our hoarses to a gorse bush and left Brock outside picking the best nettle-heads. The house smelt'a plaster dust and had that starched, windswept look about it. Little history was given away of the auld inhabitants by the worn iron coat rack and ripped wallpaper (revealing different generations of patterns). In the main room, an ornate fireplace sat in ruin. Nikolai beckoned me into a side-room where an auld fridge sat. He tugged open the door to it, and the smell hit me before the image. There were a dead man contorted in the empty fridge – his skin as browned as his clothes, mangled hands coverin his face, the bones beginning to show through.

Nikolai's chuckle filled the house as I momentarily jumped back. I clouted him around the head. The man must've sheltered there from a storm and died curled up in it.

"Fors time I fun him, the door were propped open. But Ah closed it tu preserve him, leik," he explained proudly.

We climbed cautiously up the staircase, to the first landin, which had a window lookin ontu't wild moors. The middle a the landin floor were missin, wi'a gaping hole leadin down to bits a stone and then nowt. We perched on the edge and peered out the small window, the wind blew dust at me. My heart was still thuddin in my chest from the gruesome discovery below. Now I gaped in horror at another image, wonderin momentarily if I'd gone mad, or if this was a crazy dream. On a far off stile on the left hill, just in view, was Nikolai, as blatant as the day were light. I looked at the other Nikolai teeterin next to me and he looked near as shocked and shaken, as though encountering his own doppelgänger. Dumbstruck I waved a hand to beg explanation.

"Tristram," he mumbled. That was all.

I grabbed his wrist and dragged him back downstairs and out the door intu't sunshine. I could see the sayme stile from this spot, but the ghostly white-haired boy wa' gone. Brock was whistlin tunelessly to himself, preoccupied wi'nettles.

"Explain!" I were sick to tears with Niko's bloody secrets. I still had hold'a his wrist and was slightly aware I looked lyke a madwoman.

He cowered as though I were gonna belt him one.

"Noo sin'hem in years!" he pleaded. "He's mae brother."

Brock were payin amused attention by now.

"Where are ya parents?" I demanded.

"Deid!" he said quickly. "And Tristram an us got split up. He left me!" He were close to tears.

"...And!"

"And James an Sophie found me. They saw after me. Brung me up as their aen, til I got sick..."

"And!" I said.

"And thas et. I got dumped on ye lot," he said, in defeat.

"Kem on noo," Brock said faking boredom. "Stuff to dee."

We got back on our way and I tried to push all the other lit'le questions outtah my brain. Staring at the different shades of patched heather on't hills, broken by dribbled green lines formed by sheep paths or melt water. I noticed the heath-land close by had little silvery twigs linin the ruts.

"Do they still burn the heather?" I asked Brock, realisin it still looked as controlled as it had done back on't Yorkshire moors in ma younger days.

"Aye," he said. "Huv to keep it doon for the sheep grazing."

"I never see anyone about," I said. "Shepherds, I mean."

"Meybe they sees you firs," he grunted.

We got to a firm, wide track crossing the slope.

"Sha we huv a wee canter?" Brock said, keen to test Aragorn's speed maybe.

"Yeah," I said. "Might be bes to put Arro behind Lego though. He's easier to control if you put a tail in front of him."

Brock shrugged and let me tekk the lead. But as soon as we set off he did nowt to keep Aragorn from overtaking, which a course the mad-hoarse did, nippin off up the hill, while Gerald happily ran behind us. Then Aragorn pulled one a his lit'le tricks he'd turned on me a few times already – suddenly swerving mid flight at nowt. As though he were a boy racer on a motorway, switchin lanes. Brock was unseated, caught on one side wi' an ankle wedged in a stirrup so that if he did fall he'd be dragged. He were yanking on't reins, tryin ta slow down, but Aragorn had his head and were keepin it.

I dug my heels into Lego to spur him forward, though I were doubtful that I could overtake. Legolas didn't pay much heed so I swiped him wi'tha ends a the reins and he switched up a gear. The track were about to take a sharpish bend ahead, so I spotted my chance and aimed Lego so he would cut the other hoarse off by jumpin a ditch. We landed just ahead and I were able to grab Aragorn's reins and pull him into the side of Legolas so they both bundled to a halt.

Brock, scrabbled his seat back and slumped panting. For once, he looked his age. His face were creased with worry.

"Thanks," he muttered, with about the only bit of humility I'd probably ever see from him.

Nikolai pulled up next to us, a little too jubilantly.

"That'll learn ya," he said loudly.

The exact words I'd stopped from coming out of me own mouth.

* * * * * * *

AN ANTHEM FOR DOOMED YOUTH

Simian Thomas, Breamish Valley

If you ever want to make the wind laugh, tell him your plans. The words will be laughed from your mouth and caught in his breath, carried away across the land. The austerity of tawny grasses and cracked, steeply hair-pinned old roads all whizzing beneath. Emotions restrained by the wings of vertigo, in which you're fragile to the peaty bogs which seethe in the Earth. Black rock rises up in crags, where only scavengers sit and contemplate fools below. The laughing wind has battered the remains of built-up life into the land, so that stones and nettles and earth all sculpt strange, dead features – misshapen noses that can no-longer breathe freely, the empty eyes of windows without glass, hair follicles which mark the graves of so many.

    A caffeinated consciousness... something I've forgotten. How it feels to be medicated, as well; to be evened out like a rough edge, a mistake, a rut. In the pub one night, back in Sheffield, Roxy and I invented the perfect beer mat. On one side it had a ring for where the drink sat, with the words *'this will make you feel better'*. On the flip side it had the same ring and the words *'this will make you feel worse'*.

    I remembered this as I followed the length of broken fence that would lead me home to Riddlehamhope. Haydn was with me, like a dream figure that you're vaguely aware of. He wasn't used to the long empty silences, the dead space between two brains unable to articulate. He was probably making a concerned face, but I didn't look at him. I was absorbed in an internal world. Almost oblivious, like a special child in a special situation, too busy watching my feet try to avoid the potholes in the old tarmac.

    I tried to remember when I gave up the meds. It was before I had to. Before the wind lifted a van off the hill and dropped it on the doctor's surgery. And so I had even grimly smiled when I walked past that day and saw what'd happened. By which point, I was well beyond the indulgence of *'I hope nobody was hurt'*. When death is an everyday occurrence, a person begins to only worry for their friends and family. Everything else is just a number – twelve killed here, twenty-one there. Just a bunch of people as infinitely complex and loveable as everyone I know, but I don't know them.

    I had chosen a reluctant freedom; knowing it would come, knowing I would have to experience the worst part of my life magnified, in high definition. Like one very long, detailed replay of a kick in the teeth.

Now, I thought, now... What about now? No caffeine, no dope. Simian in the real world, with no cushion, no Perspex window. Out of the shade and exposed to the real heat of the sun and with such weak, pale skin. My feet on the tarmac were now still. They were rested on wooden boards, wet dog nose nuzzling an ankle and then licking something on my shoe. I don't know how I let these bits of time slip from my grasp. Gorse tea. The yellow flower which seemed to open all year long, trying to hide its ugly, shaggy stalks and twigs. Even catching streams of sheep fluff in an effort to conceal its gnarley limbs. I'm unfair to the gorse tree. It's hardy and resilient – a survivor. It had spines, more than one, which seems a little greedy.

    I sipped the tea. It was the only sign of my existence. Claudia was being allowed to try out the guitar Toby had made – even the dogs were enraptured. Toby had his old guitar as well, but it was becoming like some special antique that he no-longer wanted to use too often. We watched as she tuned the new one, watched her eyes and lips and her long-coveted touch on the strings. It was almost too much to hear music at this point. As though the nerves in my body had become desensitised to cold and pain, and dead things... yet music would overwhelm them. The fraught emotion shared only in a particular note. My ankles clung to the legs of my seat, my bones feeling the bones of the chair, through scant socks. I could feel a draught on the back of my neck as well, feel each individual goose pimple.

I didn't know the song that Claudia was playing – maybe it was one of her own. It had a timeless, placeless character. Her mouth formed sounds that had a haunting, beautiful, animal quality. Her voice connecting so well with the guitar and the air that few words could be distinguished. And like staring into the eyes of Fidel, the black wolf-dog (something I occasionally dared myself to do), I felt suddenly as though we were with the spirits, in touch with the primordial. Our very souls were on their knees – baying and howling in emotive unison at the overwhelming indifference of nature.

* * * * * * *

CLOSE HORIZONS

Roxanne Ratcliffe, the Cheviot Hills

It was always a gasper to get up into the nearby hills, but after the initial clamber it was more easy-going, up-and-down hiking. There was a strangely empty quality to the hilltops near Riddlehamhope. There were a few patches of conifer and gorse, but mainly it was scruffy bleached grassland and dry bracken flattened by wind or snow. On cloudy days the hills seemed endlessly nondescript, save for the ancient ruined hill forts which marked out peaks with grey rubble. Yet the empty sameness was somehow reassuring and peaceful, like being able to free up your mind from all the clutter and questions, and just let it drift idly on the breeze. I felt closer to the sky here, not because of the height, but because often when walking along the saddle between two summits, only close horizons were visible – maybe only ten or twenty metres away. As though if I walked straight up them I could reach up and touch the woolly clouds that edged slowly along the peaks like a flock of scruffy, stoned sheep.

Sometimes the same clouds would even sink down lower, absorbing me in a damp, claustrophobic fog. And then I was always disappointed that they were so ungraspable. Rather than you touching them, it was them that touched you, cloaking objects and people in a blind, vacant despair. But the clouds were higher today, revealing where they could, the rolling pastures below and the far off patchworks of heather.

Charlie broke into my musings, bored of being left out. "Where's that fookin dog gone?"

Otto was nowhere visibly about, and there were few things to conceal him. Unless he'd run over to the woods already.

"Shit," I said. "We're meant to be making sure he doesn't disturb grouse."

It was nesting time for many birds, so we were supposed to be trying to keep a respectful distance, to let them breed successfully.

"I think they nest in heather. I dinnae think they'll be here. And what kind of stupid bird nests on the fookin ground, anywhey? The only reason they've survived sae long is that they taste good." Charlie ground his teeth.

I smiled and attempted to whistle. I've always been shit at whistling though, no point even trying with my fingers in my mouth. Charlie laughed at my pathetic attempt and whistled himself. His was so practiced and piercing it hurt my ears to stand next to him. Otto appeared from nowhere, bounding up the hill towards us. He greeted us as though he'd been far away in Mordor (or Morpeth) for days, fighting for the greater good.

We continued along the green path, distinguished from paler grasses; I assume it spent less of the winter hidden from the sun by snow, wondered how many folk trod these paths on a regular basis. I'd occasionally glimpsed a sheep farmer, carrying an old crook, followed closely by a loyal border collie.

"Huvv ye heard I'm being re-stationed?" Charlie said with maybe a little drama.

"What d'you mean?"

"Toby wants me tu go and help build a log cabin, further north. At Driskel, wherever thattus."

"Oh, I think sommat was mentioned," I said. "I thought it was just temporary?"

He shrugged with intentional mystery.

"It's what some of their friends are working on, isn't it?" I asked.

He nodded. "Jacob Frith and Maya Floss. Get to meet more of the clan, I suppose."

"You'll be back," I said. "We wouldn't get rid of you that easily."

He stopped and turned to look at me, with a sentimental smile. Taking me by surprise he gave me a big bear hug, picking me off the ground for a moment.

"I'll miss yuu, you sarky little cow."

* * * * * * *

A PAINTING OF A PERSON WHERE THE PAINTER HASN'T MASTERED HANDS – SO THE HANDS ARE HIDDEN

Bryn McLarey, The Borderlands

I wus disappointed that they'd already built a log cabin. I'd wanted tu mayke the firs one, the auld man ego, the need tu mark the land. Toby suggested I travel up there on horseback, but Claudia insisted I wus too big for our horses, sae he'd borrowed a Shire horse from Auld Cruikshank the shepherd. It wus naimed Django Reinhardt and wus a slow and steady animal. Just as well as Ah'd never ridden a horse before. Truth be told, I wus nervy as hell, but Django plodded along at a pace that infuriated everyone but me. Toby'd decided the mileage we were tu cover wus a good opportunity ta get the dogs practiced in harnesses, pulling his homemade buggy (adapted with bike wheels for the less snowy times). As he wus only using four dogs and they weren't very used tu it, he mayde them rest often. But even so, they would race off whey ahead a me and then have tu wait ages for Django tu catch up.

I felt a strange pride at the sight a the dogs, runnin in organised formation. I asked Toby why he'd left Fidel, his strongest dog behind.

"Well, they have to run in pairs and Otto is better at it, cos uv his breeding. He's best to lead, but if I ran him next to Fidel, they'd squabble."

It seemed fitting that Otto and Ana ran ahead and Rufus and Rolf ran behind. Though it wus Otto's fault the cart crashed at one point, as he saw a squirrel in a tree and decided tu deviate from the road. I came plodding sleepily around the corner tu find Toby tangled up in gorse bushes, cussin leik a trooper. I helped pull him free. He wus covered in wee scratches, which Otto eagerly hoped tu heal with his slobberin tongue.

"Any serious damage, chief?" I tried not ta grin.

He smiled grimly and shook his heid, pushing Otto away frum him. I'd let go of Django without thinking, but luckily the greedy GG had simply buried his nose in the nearest patch of lush grass. I dragged the dog buggy back ontu the road and examined it, tightening the wheels back on and repacking our few belongings. Toby dusted hissen off and untangled the dogs from the bushes.

The other difficulty wus when we had tu leave the road and cross bumpy farm track, at which point Toby gev up tryin tu ride the buggy and just walked behind it, forcing the dogs tu go nearly as slowly as me and the horse. Eventually we rounded a corner and down below a log cabin wus visible, looking utterly out of place in the stoney landscape. It'd taken us an hour longer than expected tu get there, though I doubted they knew exactly when we were meant to arrive.

Once we were thirty yards or sae from Driskel, two figures appeared in the doorway to witness our haphazard entrance. The buggy arrived well ahead of me, with Toby joggin behind it. The dogs attempted tu greet auld friends while still in harnesses. Behind this chaos, Django and I kept our even, plodding speed. Making our dramatic entrance in slow motion. Maya Floss and Jacob Frith stood watching in amusement.

Maya wus very tall, or meybe she wasnae that tall and I'd just spent the last months of mae life with two female runts. She looked as tall as me mebbe. But I cudnae'uv confirmed this unless I stood next to her, and on entry tu the cabin I wus ushered tu a chair to rest. I wasnae sure what I wus resting from, though mae bum and legs were definitely not used to four hours in a saddle and I wus walkin leik Ah'd taken a good rogerin.

She hadda warm Scottish accent (Aberdeenshire, I would guess), which sat oddly with her bloodlines, which looked Asian and African all at once. This tallness – and mae inability to describe to maeself her origins – threw me, and I found myself compulsively lookin at her agen. She also carried herself with the kind of confidence I'm witless to the source of. Most confidence is false, a kind of thin veil over fragile human bones. But this hadda strange density tu it.

Jacob, on the other hand, was not unleik Toby. He wus possibly a bit rougher around the edges, though meybe that wus just an illusion created by his Northern Irish accent (which in its sandpaper blues always gev off the tough air of the possessor havin survived 'The Troubles').

He had long, curlyish ginger hair, which wus already faded and prematurely streaked with beige-white. He looked at me with the same quiet curiosity as Toby, and I had the feeling back in the modern, civilised world (that had crumbled behind me as I walked away), he wus what I would've termed a 'Yoghurt Weaver' – muesli-eating, sensible types, with shower-proof coats and a fondness for twee things like knitting and allotments.

He suggested Toby and he go and collect firewood – and no doubt discuss me. In fact I wondered for a millisecond if I wus being got rid of in some whey. This wus ridiculous paranoia, of course.

I wus thankful for the panting dogs, once the men had left. While most of them lay flat on the floor, Otto put his muzzle on mae leg, as though needing someone tu tell him what a sterling job he'd done out there.

"Good boy." I stroked his ears, glad of something tu occupy me.

I really wasnae sure how to start a conversation with Maya, so I thought it best tu wait for her ta start. The cabin felt a little Scandinavian in its economic use of space, and oddly minimalist in comparison to the domestic spaces we'd sae far occupied. But then it wus new (still smelling of recently chopped wood), so meybe clutter hadnae had time tu amass. The building wus open plan, apart from the bedrooms and bathroom. Maya had made tea rather reluctantly, as though she didnae want to welcome me tuu much. Agen, maybe that wus just paranoia.

"I'm sorry," she began, as she set the tea down and I mumbled thanks, "I've no idea who yuu are, or why you're with Toby?"

It wus almost noo even a question, but I thought it best to fill her in anywhey.

"A group of us arrived a few months ago..." I said testing the ice.

"Oh," she said. "Yes, I think Brock mentioned it. A German gave him a dog?"

"Wolfgang," I affirmed, adding with a lilt of humour. "The German, no'the dog."

She smiled politely and I felt that thing I feel when I dinnae think Ah'm charming tu a woman – the desperation tu charm the woman. We looked at one another evenly, letting a silence fall. Otto had at last collapsed on mae feet.

"Where are ye from?" I asked, trying to turn the conversation on her.

She arched an eyebrow.

"Aberdeen," she said. "My parents were from Mauritius, if thas what yu mean."

"I thought Aberdeenshire," I said quickly.

"I lived in Antrim for several years tuu. Thas how I came across Jacob. He grew up in Derry."

"Oh," I said (thinking, he's Catholic if he calls it 'Derry'). "Did he woo you across the Giant's Causeway?"

I hoped she knew the story of the giant and his Scottish love, but then I realised that I didn't know whether they were a couple or not and felt a little dumb.

She looked at me anyhow, not like she wus listening, but as though she was trying tu read my thoughts instead. *They're wholly impure*, I wanted tu say, but she wus probably a feminist and wouldn't appreciate this. The silence had been tuu long now and I wanted to move on from the last in what felt a long line of silly remarks.

"Ye think you have a bit of an Antrim twang, tuu? Mae dad wus leik that, a mixture of places. I grew up in Glasgow..." I got lost, unsure of where I wus going, realising I'd not taken a single sip of tea yet.

I took a sip of tea. It wus nice and strong, but had already cooled. How long had I been tryin tu create resemblance of a conversation? I gulped it all doon, wonderin whether the silence wus full of sexual tension or utter contempt. Mae leg wus completely deid now, with the deid weight of sleepin dog on mae foot. I needed the toilet but hadda feelin if I stood up, mae foot would give way and I'd end up face doon on a carpet of disgruntled canines.

Otto, stirred with a flicker of his ear, tu indicate the return of the men. The door swung open and the two entered, laden with sacks of wood. They both looked at me with the saime expression. I hoped it wus envy at my rugged good looks. More leikly it wus pity at the (almost) middle-aged letch shrivelling up on a wooden chair.

* * * * * * *

SUDS & DUDS

Roxanne Ratcliffe, New Riddlehamhope

The sun was out again, so Claudia and I decided we should commit the day to all the mundane day-to-day toil we'd been putting off. Hand washing our own clothes wasn't the highlight of the lifestyle we led, and we were ever concerned the blokes would start expecting us to do theirs as well. So we tended to leave ours the longest and filthiest.

Now it was warm enough, Toby'd strung up a washing line in the yard. It wasn't ideal to try to clean and dry clothes there, with dogs and horses around shedding their winter coats with enthusiasm. Still, as with all folk who keep more than a couple of house pets, we were well used to muck and hair being everywhere. It was the wash tub itself getting hairy that was bothering me, swearing to myself, as Claudia wrung stuff over the plants and pegged it out.

"Yuu'd better soap yer gob oot tuu, afta all that cussin," Brock quipped as he appeared out of the stables.

He must've come up the tunnel, though why he needed to in this weather I don't know. He liked appearing randomly.

"Hi," I said.

"Ay up," Claudia said, a bit too brightly.

I wondered if she and Brock'd made peace. He rested against the wall, smoking, his eyes creasing in easy contentment.

"Washin yer duds," he muttered.

"And no we ain't doin yours, fore you ask."

He made an innocent face. Then after a thoughtful pause said.

"You lassies gehting on alrate, then? Nae bother?"

"Should we spect bother?" Claudia asked.

"Yuu're a contrary one, eh?" He rubbed his eye socket, looking slightly out of sorts in the bright daylight, as though he belonged to darker, bleaker times.

There was a rustling and snuffling behind him in the stable. "Outtah there noo, Hinny!" he called over his shoulder.

Hobina shuffled out, tail awag. She looped around me and Claudia, shedding as she went. She tried to stick her nose in the wash tub and drink, but I shoved her away.

"Is it dangerous round here for us?" I asked, unable to ignore what I thought he was getting at.

He took a long drag, wrinkled his nose and looked off into the distance. "Ah used tu work assa groundsman, furra very auld graveyard, years ago," he began. "There used tu be an alleyway runnin next it. A short cut. Number of young lassies who'd walk up there on their aen at night." He shook his head and sighed.

"What's ya point?" Claudia asked a little narkily.

"Ah ken that yous want to be independent," he mumbled, as though trying to think of the right words, "and ah dinnae want tu tell you what yer can and cannae doo, but..."

He sighed again, waving his roll up in the air in hesitation and avoiding eye contact.

"Spit it out, Badger," Claudia said.

"Ah dinnae think these times are much mair, or much less dangerous, for *women*. Ah jus think you huv tu take sensible precautions."

I bundled a fresh batch of sopping clothes onto Claudia's pile to string out. We could no longer be accused of provocative dressing these days. Our hair was always unkempt, either hatted or knotted, and our clothes were baggy and practical. And yet that rarely spoken threat of 'tupping' still hung about. Would it still be our fault if it happened? Even without tottering drunkenly up an alleyway at night in a short skirt.

Neither I nor Claudia said anything, so Brock rambled on with unusual self-consciousness. "These folk are okay. They just have their way of doing things and you gottah mind ut and stick to ut, and then you'll be alrayte. You gottah mind that they're livin close tu the bone, leik yuu. This neck uv the woods, yer pretty sound. The Hills ahr seen as common land noo, sae lang as you leave Auld Cruikshank's sheep alane." He shot Claudia a glance.

"Is that the bloke I've seen wandering about?" I asked.

"Aye," Brock said. "Nice auld beggar. Wus proper understanding when I explained why his gimmers had thor hair cut! Poor boy had loads of rievers aboot in the winter. People get more desperate then. The white faced sheep with pink blobs on thor backs are hus."

"Only did about five sheep." Claudia smirked coyly.

"Yuu still owe him fur um though," Brock mumbled. "I've described ye, sae if he sees you..."

I continued scrubbing at a tough patch of dirt on a pair of jeans. They were wearing through at the knees.

"Ye need more jeans?" Brock asked.

We both looked at him hopefully. He pulled out a small notebook.

"Write name, size and 'jeans'." He handed it to me with a pencil. "D' ye ken the boys sizes?"

We both looked blank.

"Ah'll getta bunch. Easy to sell on." He paused as I scribbled in the book. "How's the cuckoo in the nest doin?"

"Nikolai?" Claudia asked. "Not slit our throats in our sleep and stolen the hoarses yet."

"Yous keep a rayht close ee, while Charlie's off elsewhere. He's frighty of Charlie."

"He'll be frighty of me, if he does owt bad." Claudia ground her teeth.

* * * * * * *

PASSIVE/AGGRESSIVE...
PROGRESSIVE/REGRESSIVE

Bryn McLarey, Driskel

Being a hare's hop from the Mother Country hud been making me feel a wee bit like I wus on some voyage of self-discovery. Sae far I'd discovered mae casual disregard for Scotland wus no sae dissimilar tu mae casual disregard for England, in that it didnae really exist. It wus a mere collection of words that automatically fell from mae mouth, leik an uncontrollable dribble, anytime somebody asked mae opinion of a place. Mae discovery essentially wus that I didnae want people tu leik me, so I'd say something I thought would piss them off. Leik 'the Highlands are fookin overrated, an listenin tu English sops witter on about them is coma-inducing'. Okay, meybe the last half of that sentence wus true.

After the first unveiling of Spring in the tweely-named Riddlehamhope (which I preferred tu refer tu as the Doghouse), I'd stole maeself the courage tu heid alone over the hills tu Windy Gyle.

Windy Gyle, along with having a fantastic nayme, sat right on the border tu Scotland. It wus still a little chilly back then, but the sun wus up in an empty sky, creating a bonny haze on the horizon. The hills of Scotland looked better than in any memory I had. They didnae look real. They looked leik a rose-tinted cinema backdrop. Meybe the way the sun wus falling on that side tuu, mayde them look far grander and nobler than the hills behind me in England. I must huv stood for meybe an hour or sae, in an emotional limbo, on the verge of tears (a few pints of Thornbridge Jaipur IPA would certainly have tipped me over the edge).

I wus thinking aboot this while settling over supper at Driskel. I'd spent the latter part of the afternoon getting a guided tour of the area from the benevolent/malevolent Jacob. His constant hair tossin and references tu impressive things he'd built and caught forced me tu equal him in sounding leik a twat. It's the male ego puffing its chest out at the sight of someone else's washboard abs. By the end of the conversation we mey as well huv wacked our dicks oot on the table and measured them against one another. What irritated me most aboot maeself is that, even though I know this pointless competing is precisely that, I cannae help joining in. In fact I join in with such vigour, yuu'd think I wus the chairman of the fookin Society for Pointless Competing (I bet that really existed at Oxford, an all).

By the end of the conversation I'd established that: we'd both taken further education further than anyone should (unless you're actually a real doctor); both read the top one hundred best books ever written; could both reliably look after a cellar full of real ale; and could both build a three storey house from scratch, without any help from anyone else, using aenly the materials found in a tuu mile radius. Oh, and les no forget wrestling wild boars. Sumthin neither of us had attempted, but we'd both of hudda bloody good go, given the chance.

All this made me feel very fookin English, as the aenly things I competed at growing up in Glasgow were drinking, fighting and sex. Meybe this wus why at supper, in some sort of meditative trance, I wus remembering standing at Windy Gyle, feeling very proud of the hills that gave birth tu me.

"So how are the new arrivals gettin along? Brock hasn't said much recently," Jacob asked Toby, as though I wasnae there. But this remark snapped me out of mae trance.

"I thought you had '*no idea who Ah wus, or why I'd come here with Toby*'?" I said to Maya, meybe a little accusingly.

"Oh I neiver talk tu Brock." She wrinkled her nose. "My bullshit detector hits the red zone any time he opens hus mouth."

She was bizarre, I thought. I mean there wus some logic there, but deciding such a severe resolution.

"I think the man is liquid gold for the very saime reason," I mumbled.

"Take no notice. She's obsessed with the truth!" Jacob said.

"Oh, Jacob. I mean, that story about how he got struck by lightning." Maya shook her head in disgust.

Toby and I exchanged a wry smile. (This didnae happen often.)

"Brock doesn't take too well to Maya's intellectual theories. That's the real bone between them," Toby said. "To answer yar question, Jacob, they seem to have tekken to it all pretty well."

"Well, I'm no brilliant with the ponies yet..." I put in, hoping tu sound vaguely self-deprecating.

"I think the trick with horses," Jacob said matter-a-factly, "is to realise they're more like cats than dogs. Expect stubbornness and arrogance, rather than loyalty and obedience."

"Well, I can certainly identify with that," I quipped.

Later in the evening, after I'd surreptitiously consumed as much booze as I could get away with (if

Mead even counts as booze), we discussed sleeping arrangements.

"There's only one spare bed, so one of us needs to sleep in here, on a pile of mats," Toby said pensively.

"Oh, I'll sleep here. Your back is worse," I said valiantly. "I belong out here with the dogs, anywhey."

"Thanks," Toby said. "Thas good of ya."

"Ney bother."

I wus bedded down in front of the open fire, which had turned tu embers, when I woke in the middle of the neet. I wusnae sure why I'd woken, jerked from a dream in which Maya and I romantically rode horses over a sea of shimmering shale. I hud the sudden feeling I wus being watched and realised the looming shadow sat at mae knees wus the real Maya. I thrashed an arm from the bedclothes, flexing a shoulder with what I hoped wus rugged nonchalance.

"You okay, lassie? Trouble sleeping?" I asked, trying tu keep the quiver from mae voice.

She said nothing in reply. She just looked at me with liquid eyes in the dark, as though ignoring mae words and instead reading mae impure thoughts.

* * * * * *

EARTHLINGS ON THE FLIPSIDE

Wolfgang, Breamish Valley

The Breamish trickles and tickles my ears close by. The ever-present sound of water, like when I lived in a house next to the Porter Brook, or the many times I passed out drunk on a bridge over the River Spree. And I may dream

I'm Ophelia, slowly sinking in madness. I saw a bridge somewhere about the country when we were travelling, where the passage of the river had moved by some change in the land, so the remaining scrap of bridge crossed ordinary ground and the river ran beside it. A bridge beside a river – something from a Surrealist's dream. I assume they dream always of bowler hats and melting clocks?

The Kaiser and I had been sat in a sheep stell one day. Not that there was anything to hide from. We were holed up like truants because I remain Mr. Kaiser's confidant, as he knows anything I were to repeat would be received with scepticism.

"... It seems they were destined for a happy-ever-after," he said with charmless jealously, throwing stones at grass. He was feeling like a lonely old goat maybe, surrounded by the youthful love of his friends, who if not yet exchanging kisses, were still in some romantic limbo.

"Homo Sapiens are only *destined* to breathe, eat, breed, sleep and die," I explained handsomely. Disappointed that I'd a made a list of five, instead of a list of three (which good men know is far more poetic). "Have you completed these tasks?"

The Kaiser nodded grumpily.

"Have you offspring?" I gossiped.

"Probably. Niever knew if the wee bairn wus mine." He stared off, but thus returned. "Huv you?"

"I've improper spunk." I flashed my canines. "It's probably for the best."

"It is."

The grey stones supported the boned backs of grumpy old men, grumping for the misplaced chances in their misplaced lives.

"You dinnae think God punishes me for mae ills?" he asked, knowing he could only be reassured by the answer of an Atheist.

"If *He* is looking down upon us, *He* has saved our necks many times. We have little reason to bear *Him* a grudge," I said.

"Yuu can take the piss all yer want. Nehbody knows what awaits us on the flipside," Kaiser said.

"Worms," I answered. "I think I shall enjoy being a worm... and if I get chopped in two, I can be two worms."

"It must be nice sumtimes, tu jus be fuckin loopy and no givva damn," he said.

"Giving a damn is what looped me in the first place, sir," I replied.

"Whatever happened tu yuu...?"

I looked at my arms – my sleeves had been rolled up ready for graft, like a ruddy faced farmhand, but in the shade of the stell, my skin had goosepimpled.

"Why are they named goose pimples?" I asked.

"Don't change the fookin subject," he said, though he was already too irritated to play the listener.

"Let us not enter blindly into the grizzly labyrinth of what ruined the greatest mind in modern Germany," I said firmly.

He laughed, a Scottish laugh. He laughs differently in English.

"Whas yer surname?" he asked.

"I have no surname, neither do I have a Christian name because I am not Christian. I go by the name of Wolfgang. That is all."

His eyes creased deeply as he smiled, wearing down his roughly chiselled face. We'd had the same conversation on many occasions over the years. But he would return to it as though one day I would tell him a surname and it would somehow unravel my past in all its blood-drenched glory.

I stood now, getting uneasily to my feet, for all the bones and muscles had crumpled in the crouch position. I leaned on the stell and looked across boggy rambles to the nearby track. I thought I'd heard an approach, but there was no one. Just two trees leaning towards one another over the muddy lines, like one gossiping lady leaning to whisper in the other's ear, conspiring their womanly secrets.

"Simian, yuu insipid streak of piss." The Kaiser gathered himself into a stance.

Simian had somehow snuck up in another direction. He was carrying six deceased grey squirrels.

"Nearly shot a cat," he muttered glumly.

"Should've done," Kaiser said. "Evil fookers."

"I like cats," Simian said.

Back in the present day, I awoke from my afternoon doze. Nikolai was stood in the kitchen staring at me.

"Yer don't half snore loud," he said.

"I wasn't asleep! I was dozing," I said. "I still had one eye on you, like a cat."

"Funny," he said. "Looked to us leik you was checkin yer eyelids fer howls."

"I've no idea what you're talking about," I said.

"You wudnae make a canny spy." He shook his head. "D'ye want a mash?"

"Excuse me?"

"D'ye want a brew?" he said.

"Oh, brew. Aye, bonnie lad. A brew would be grand," I said in my pathetically stilted accent.

* * * * * * *

THINGS TO DO IN DRISKEL WHEN YOU'RE DEAD

Bryn McLarey, Driskel

The devil is in the detail, sae they say. The plan wus tu build a similar log cabin next tu the current one, a replica of sorts, but I wanted it tu be bigger. The idea wus to keep them fairly compact, sae they were economic tu heat, but it seemed a waste of energy if we'd then have tu build another one as well, tu sleep more people. I also thought a butchery should be included in the interior. For the last one they'd built an adjacent hut, but this wus vulnerable tu thieves and dogs.

"And a butchery is surely better underground, tu preserve the meat?" I added.

"Yuu're suggesting we dig a cellar?" Maya said.

I thought for moment.

"Meybe we could dig something nearby, with Brock's help. We could make some tunnels."

"Ah," she said. "Brock and his rabbit warrens."

"And where do yuu get good enough wood from? Most of the pine aboots here looks leik it wus logged on rotation," I said. "Mae understanding is it needs to be aboot seventy year auld, in order tu have a tight enough grain, sae that it won't warp and split?"

They all shifted in their seats and looked at one another.

"Yuu made this place with shite wood?" I asked.

"We've no way of transporting better wood," Jacob said. "This place was kind of an experiment, to try stuff out and see what works."

"What's going tu happen when the big bad wolf comes along and blows your hoose of sticks doon?" I asked.

"Don't ridicule us, Charlie. It's no going tu blow down. It mey not stand the test of time. It's just temporary. We're working out the little issues," Maya said.

Little issues? "I'm beginning to think Brock wus right when he said this whole thing wus a shambles."

"Well piss off back tu him, if yuu don't wanna be helpful!" Maya said.

Toby looked pensive. He'd taken tu looking pensive a lot. Jacob looked irked, like a more rugged, hairy reflection of Toby. A heavy silence fell, the sketches in front of us suddenly void of meaning. I wus annoyed. I liked the cabin, with its Dutch-style roof and sense of space and woody smell. I didnae want it tu slowly get eaten up by the landscape, its skeleton twisting tu reveal gaps, which would gradually let the weather in.

"Does that shepherd that owns the big pony – Django – huv a wagon he can pull?" I asked.

Toby nodded.

"It needs repairing. But I'm not sure where the nearest auld forest would be, or how the locals would feel about us choppin bits down."

"Little issues," I said wryly. "If we wanna du this, we should du it properly."

Toby looked me firmly in the eyes and nodded, as though for once I wasnae spouting arrogant crap and sae he could finally be bothered tu listen.

"It's possible we could use something other than pine. Oak, maybe. But pine is much straighter, that's why it's the usual choice. I don't know enough about it really," I said.

"Well I've got some books on the subject. We could have a browse through them and see what we turn up," Toby said.

"I'll meyke some tea and then we can huv a gander at the bit of land yuu've got in mind for this," I suggested.

I wus met with thoughtful nods.

"Things tu do in Driskel when yuu're deid," I muttered as I stood up.

Toby chuckled. "Aye."

"Are you dead?" Jacob raised his eyebrows comically.

I looked at my arms and hands, which still seemed to huv blood pumpin roond them. I clenched and unclenched the fists tu test the muscles.

"No yet it seems," I said dryly.

* * * * * * *

THE MEANING OF BLUSTERY

Wolfgang, New Riddlehamhope

The winds were baying at the doors and windows again. Howling like ghosts for lost love and broken promises. Outside the upper storey of Riddlehamhope they whipped around in fury, tapping on the bathroom window and poking teasing fingers at the roof tiles. Fidel, Cujo, Ana and Otto all bolted out of the kitchen door when it was opened, sticking close to walls and thickets, as cats would. The other two dogs hid and I chuckled at them as I closed the door on the wind and sat down again. They were mortified by the sound outside – I looked deep into their inky eyes and read stories of previous trauma.

"A man who brainwashed people for a living once said to me, 'you can put in happy thoughts or bad thoughts. But if you ever want to reverse your work, *negative things are a devil to get out!*'" I was muttering to the room, really.

Haydn looked up from his morning mash, a hand rested on a mug, newspaper in lap like a gent. Brock had brought him a local paper. They weren't like the local newspapers of old, though – cats, A.S.B.Os and charity fairs. They were very strange indeed.

"Winds like this do make them frighty," he looked at the pair circling uncertainly. "Reminds them of bad things. Like our family dog when I was a kid, was terrified of fireworks."

"Reminded of the Blitz," I affirmed.

"She wasn't quite that old!" Haydn said.

"I think dogs have a certain collective memory, like we do," I said. "Toby says they live in the present, but they still sense what is passed down the generations. A certain uneasiness about things. Just because the older dogs braved the wind, they were still perturbed by it. Imagine Fidel, master of Riddlehamhope is scared? A lesser beast would certainly cower in the corner like a big girl!" I said the last few words directly to the dog under the kitchen table.

He gave an uncertain half-bark, it sounded like he was saying '*Rolf!*' The other wimp, Rufus, lay down across the doorway to the hall, so as to get in the way of people coming down to breakfast.

"I had a dream this morning I was drowning in silly string," Haydn mused, as though it were relevant.

"What is silly string?" I asked.

"That stuff people used to spray at parties," he said.

"String that is sprayed?" I tried to imagine such a thing.

"Someone kept spraying me with it in the dream, until I was so buried in it, I could hardly breathe."

Claudia stomped into the room before I could ask for further explanation. She sidestepped the doggy-obstacle with a melodramatic tut.

"Has anyone mayde me a brew?" She flumped down at the table.

"I'm afraid all the servants have come down with typhoid, princess," I said.

Haydn laughed.

"Don't encourage him," Claudia said. "He's written down several lines of speech that Charlie gev him to be said to me while he's away."

I rose from my seat.

"Never fear, fair maiden. I will mash thee a brew," I said valiantly. "Or should that be brew thee a mash?"

"Less talk, maire sport," she said.

I remained unsure of what she meant by sport, but I extracted myself from the table anyhow and put some water on to boil.

Haydn smirked and whispered something in Claudia's ear. She scowled at him.

"I think I kinda miss Charlie," Haydn said thoughtfully. "Even though he's a bit of a dick. I assume it's mostly sexual frustration and he's more agreeable when he's getting some...?"

"*Maire agreeable?*" Claudia sniped. "What is this? Jane Austen?"

"Jane Austen is very good," Haydn said. "You should read some."

"And I've no idea what Charlie's lyke when he's 'gettin sum', as that usually means he's suddenly not allowed to go out wi'his drinking buddies. As they're female, apparently thas weird!" Claudia's slanting eyes were reduced to slits.

"Ah," I said. "Jenny-any-dot, she was a bit of a madam."

"I mean don't get me wrong. I'm not sure Charlie was ever very monogamous, but he certainly wasn't fookin *us*. Daft bint," she added.

"A good point, well made," I mused. "Though I think it was him returning home stinking of '*booze and drugs*' that bothered her."

"Oh yeah, that were us." Claudia grinned, then she made a strange face and burped.

"A good burp, well made," I said, though it was on the prim side compared to her usual efforts.

"I just vomited half ma lyfe intu't toilet upstairs," she murmured grimly.

"Ah." Haydn looked taken aback.

"And yeah, I do blame you," she said to him firmly.

Rolf rested a nose on her knee and whined at her, wagging his dopey tail.

"Stop bein such a needy whinge-pup!" she said to the dog, but in a tone of voice he would hear as sympathetic.

The wind bayed at the door, calling the dogs to their doom, jeering and chattering around the stonework.

"Sum one tell the wind to shush," Claudia said.

* * * * * *

THE CHRONICALS

Haydn Antoine, New Riddlehamhope

By this time in my life, *The Chronicals – A Media Junkie's Survival Guide* was several doorstops thick. While it had begun life as an e-zine and been birthed in a world that strove towards a paperless existence, I'd eventually realised how fragile this made it. Or at least how fragile my ability to access it was. The first section was probably immortalised in cyberspace, but cyberspace was no longer such a tangible thing.

So with a heavy heart and a speedily emptying wallet I'd printed the beast, and when I travelled north to find Toby, it was one of the few things I took with me. I'd taken my laptop too, a sentimental lapse of judgement. It was sat in a box somewhere at Riddlehamhope, obsolete without electricity to give it life. But The Chronicals was still thriving in its own way. It had graduated from a collective reaction to the state of things into the steady documentation of a country in the middle of decline and then rebirth. And equally importantly, how we'd wrestled and mangled and rewritten our lives in order to continue them. The middle section was as much a scrapbook of newspaper cuttings as anything else, along with reaction from me and others in meticulously hand written pages.

There were gaps in time when I'd run out of access to a pen that worked, or when I was just too depressed and at a loss to carry on. These gaps wrote their own truths in blank-paged enigmas. I'd sometimes written a date at the top and then nothing.

Simian'd raised the subject of The Chronicals within the first few days of their arrival. I'd been so caught up in the whirl of things – and by things I mean Claudia – that it'd fallen out of my brain. But now I returned to it, what with realising I hadn't written anything for a while. It also occurred to me that some of Wolfgang's more comprehensive observations might be added to it, and better still Roxanne had a bag full of camera film undeveloped which'd captured much of the early destruction.

It was mid-evening and supper was on the way. I clattered up the creaking stairs to my bedroom and unearthed the project in its entirety. It consisted of several volumes stacked up, even though I'd had to pick and chose which bits to print with the initial project. I carried it all precariously downstairs and bundled into the kitchen, carefully propping it on the end of the table.

"Ye bugger mar! Whassat?" Nikolai asked.

"The Chronicals," I announced, with breathless pride, part from exertion, part from excitement.

"Oh, wow," Simian said. "Am I in there?"

"What d'you mean?" Claudia asked.

"I contributed to the *This is the Winter of our Discontent...* project," he mumbled casually.

I paused, gaping like a fish, sifting through my overloaded brain. "I don't know," I finally admitted. "I printed some of that stuff..." I shuffled through the segmented pile and found the section which would contain the project. I handed it to him. "Here, have a look. See if you can find it."

He took hold of it, like he was holding something sacred. A precious, ancient text.

"See, I was thinking," I began excitedly, "how amazing it would be if we could add Roxy's photos to it and any other contributions you all might have." I gestured to Wolfgang.

Roxanne seemed a little transfixed by my sudden burst of enthusiasm.

"How can I possibly develop them?"

I looked at Brock straight away – he scratched the white patch on his head, as though this was the useful part of his brain. He shrugged. "Bound tu be an auld darkroom round the doors. Either in a college or an auld camera shop. I dinnae ken aboot gettin the right chemicals, though. But Ah'll certainly get on the grapevine and see what I can turnnup." He paused. "Itull not be cheap, though."

"Here it is," Simian muttered quietly.

I took the page off him and read it, the passage flooding back to me. I was back in the cafe in London with Aleks. I felt a wave of nostalgia and grief, even though it'd probably been the loneliest period in my life. I gulped, holding back a tear that wanted to escape the duct and tumble out.

"Anyway," I stared at the page. "Better sort supper out."

Claudia squinted at me. "Bless," she said. "He's getting all emotional..."

PHASE NINE

In which they have a dinner party & Roxy finds a suitable conclusion.

TRAPPED IN PAGES

Roxanne Ratcliffe, Breamish Valley

The concave rock face was dark and pale in angular patches, but close to the water it was greened over with moss. Above the rock face, clumps of grass and tree roots weaved a moulded emerald frame. It seemed to clamber right over the edge, as though waiting to dive into the pool below. Water dripped from beneath this, down, down, drip, drip, into the dark pool. This liquid must've come from the spray of the waterfall to my left, which began about ten foot up and painted a straight white line down the thickly-mossed rocks. It felt like the water rushed inside my ears, falling at vertiginous speed into that quiet peaty brown pool.

Opposite the concave rock face, my legs dangled towards the pool. I felt not quite safe, as though any minute I could be knocked over the edge, to flail against sharp stone until the water swallowed me. It wasn't far down though. It was the effect of Linhope Spout tumbling next to my ear that disturbed my equilibrium. Toby was sat almost next to me. I could feel every millimetre of him pushing the air apart, without looking. My sinuses and fingers, my heart and mind all seemed to tingle as though waiting to sneeze. Without looking, I even knew the contemplative facial expression, each position of the hairs in his beard, the way a smile tried shivering to appear and then forgot its own existence. And the eyes as huge as a galaxy inside the sea, specks of colour in them rotating like dust particles in the air.

I had to say *something* to break the tension in my tongue, so the first thing I thought of, from nowhere, fell out. Almost drowned in the water...

"Toby... d'you like Radiohead?" I asked.

He'd think this was a random curiosity, not the weight of my soul resting on the question. Not that it would change things however he answered. If anything, a shrug or a 'not really' would be a relief. As though I wasn't always destined to chase the same entity.

"Yeah," he said. "We had a whole conversation about them when we met in Italy."

He'd never actually mentioned Italy before. I gulped. I suspected I knew what this meant. Toby was probably the origin of the issue, formed in my adolescent brain.

"The early stuff or the later stuff...?" I continued casually.

"Both," he said. "I couldn't favouritise. It'd be lyke choosin b'tween my children."

I was relieved to feel my face break into a smile, and I looked at him and he was smiling too.

"We're gonna have a swim," Claudia said from behind me. "Are you joining us?"

It was certainly warm enough, but the pool was so murky. I was afraid of what my feet would find at the bottom.

"I'm not," I said. "Is water that dark okay to swim in?"

"I think the peat is good for the skin." Haydn was stripping down to his boxers.

"I think I'll go for a wander," I said.

Claudia was removing clothes, too. She kept a vest and pants on, but it would be pretty see-through once wet. I wanted to get Toby away from Claudia's boobs if I could. He'd politely look away of course, but they'd still be there. They had an overwhelming presence.

We began walking down beside the stream, and hearing behind us the splashes, yelps and giggles of the other two, I had the feeling it was better we were out of the way anyway. They'd only be getting all amorous, sooner or later.

"Are you okay?" Toby asked, as we negotiated the rocks and roots at our feet.

"Sure," I said vaguely.

"Is that an actual yes?" he asked.

"Sometimes it feels like you want to get inside my head."

"I do," he said. "You're very enigmatic."

We found a quiet spot next to the stream and sat down again. I crossed my legs and faced him, tugging at a patch of grass. "There's really not so much to know," I said.

"I've missed out on about fifteen years of your life. I think there's quite a lot to know."

I kind of cringed. I'm not sure why. Ordinarily, sat there with him, with the sunshine and the water, I would've almost expected him to kiss me. But for some reason it felt as though the air in between us was a vacuum, a dead space that couldn't be crossed.

"It was your choice." The stubborn teenager was speaking from somewhere inside of me.

"You were too young," he said.

"I know." I ripped at grass, chucking it towards the stream for no reason.

A small, brown bird with a white chest flitted to a rock sticking from the water. Its body bobbed about as it peered at us with beady eyes. Toby took one of my hands in his and traced it with his fingers – I stared at my own hand too, barely breathing. I looked at the nails and the lines worn from age and hard work. It didn't even look like my hand – it looked like my mum's hand. The realisation of this made my body vibrate with grief, not for lost youth, but for a lost mother. The faces of people who'd once been my whole world passed my eyes like ghosts. I'd often have half-wake dreams, early in the morning, that Mum, or David, or Dad were bringing me a cup of tea. But mainly Mum. And I was always paralysed there, hearing their footsteps on the stairs, feeling them enter the room and move around the bed. Even my eyes were unable to move, so as to see them properly, to articulate their faces.

I was crying. Toby stroked strands of once fairer hair from my bloated red cheeks. The sound of hooves came from up the hill, so I knew it was Brock arriving as promised, to interrupt our delicate moments. I wiped my face with my sleeves and giggled that maybe Haydn and Claudia were going at it, and would be even more disturbed by Brock's timing.

"Oh dear," Brock said as he pulled up, clearly confused by the fact that I seemed to be crying and laughing at once.

* * * * * * *

MAXIMUM EFFICIENCY

Simian Thomas, New Riddlehamhope

It seemed to be a big deal, having visitors coming. I felt like my mum used to make me feel when she fussed around, plumping pillows as though anyone would notice.

Not that we had pillows to plump or that anyone was fussed about the appearance of things. These were dead concepts now, not things you admitted to being concerned with. We had to only care about noble things, not petty distractions.

I missed petty distractions. I wished I didn't, but I did. I'd always been quite happy to bask in my own roll-top bath of vanity and consumption. Two concepts which Maya Floss believed to be the downfall of humanity. I had read *some* of her book all those years ago, but then I'd let the modern world distract me too much and it'd fallen by the wayside. The preparation for these visitors was more a matter of putting things in order, of making the household look like it was running on maximum efficiency. Although according to *Broken Planet*, her diatribe on modern living, maximum efficiency was also a *bad thing*. Trying to run a planet on it had led to, well, *this*.

Either way, I felt like a child again. I felt like Toby (and Charlie for that matter) wished I'd run along to my bedroom and play on my own for the evening. But no, I'd stay and eat the food we'd saved for the occasion. I'd be utterly in awe of Maya. She'd say clever things and I'd feel like I'd been educated.

As with my childhood, while I waited for the guests' arrival, I occupied myself with the trivial. I sat on the floor and played with the dogs, which were also in everybody's way.

When Charlie and Toby had returned from Driskel, I'd asked Charlie what he thought of Jacob and Maya. Though I'd really just meant Maya.

His eyes had lit with secrets. "Well," he'd begun, "Jacob is a big, ginger yoghurt-weaver. He seems pretty sound though. I've nae bones with the bloke."

"And Maya?" Claudia'd asked.

"She's a real piece of work." Charlie was unable to stop smirking to himself.

"Spill!" Claudia said, sensing drama.

"She's tuu intelligent for her aen soul. And very spirited, in many ways. But also a pain in the ass." His expression as he spoke was full of a thousand more words he wasn't saying.

"You've soo got the hots for her." Claudia transformed into a gossiping teenager.

"Better than that." Charlie raised an eyebrow.

"What?!" Claudia said.

"She totally pounced on me," he answered casually.

"I thought she an Jacob were a couple?" Claudia said.

Charlie screwed his face up and shrugged in confusion. "I just don't know. I cudnae even work out if they slept in the same room. There were three doors, but one might've been a cupboard. And I slept in the main room."

"She might jus be fookin wi' you," Claudia said, a little protectively.

"She can fuck with me ahl she wants." Charlie was trying to sound his usual callous self, but the doubt remained chipped into his shoulders.

And so I sensed everyone was a little in awe of the evening, what with the high expectations of the food and the company. We were already mostly seated around the table when they arrived. Jacob walked around shaking everyone's hand with easy charisma. He gave Haydn and Toby manly bear hugs, and nearly did the same to the six dogs who were very happy to see him. Maya seemed less at ease with the occasion. She was tall and filled the room with an awkward energy. She slid into a chair opposite Charlie and immediately seemed more elegant and radiant. They only half said hello to one another, avoiding much eye contact. Claudia looked at me across the table and winked.

There were only two spots left for Jacob, at either end of the table.

"Who should I sit next to?" he mused.

"Sit next to Roxanne." Charlie flashed a quick smile. "She's much cuter than me."

"I'm inclined not to disagree," Jacob said charmingly.

Roxanne blushed and shrank in size. Nothing embarrassed her quite like a compliment. The trouble with Roxy was that she always attracted compliments, because people assumed she had low self-esteem and needed a boost. But this was an illusion. She had more self-confidence than I ever had. She was just shy and modest and smart enough to know that these were qualities not weaknesses.

I looked quickly to Toby, who was putting finishing touches to the food. He looked a little forlorn that he'd be stranded at the end of the table away from Roxy. So far as I knew, nothing had fully materialised between them, despite the constant feeling that it should.

I'd lost myself in the milieu of things, too busy thinking and day-dreaming and forgetting to listen to the conversation. So it was a shock to come to, and realise Maya had already launched into some in depth discussion about something. I'd vaguely gathered the subject of Brock, of why he'd declined the invitation to the supper. From what I could gather, he and Maya tended to lock horns over everything.

"As the supposed 'intelligent species', we should be *custodians* of the planet, not *users*. The world is not simply a resource for us to exhaust!" Maya took a long sip of her wine and looked around the table, as though we were an audience.

"Do yuu think humanity is *capable* of that?" Charlie asked, finding his feet quickly. He enjoyed a good argument, after all. "In the saime way the nature of a cat is tu be aloof and independent, in the saime way the nature of a rabbit is tu fuck a lot. Humans are egocentric, power-hungry, bloody-minded. No event in history has ever taught them tu be otherwise."

"You're picking traits to suit your argument, though," Maya said quickly. "I know it's easy to be cynical. I'm cynical. But humans are also hugely empathetic animals. Do you think your little group of friends would've survived this long without any help from other humans?"

"Empathy has never won out against greed, though." Charlie gestured calmly.

"I'm not sure greed has ever won either. It usually destroys itself somehow." Maya took another sip of wine.

I tried to work out which one she'd picked. The elderflower, I suspected. I wasn't sure why I thought it was important. "You and Toby, and all your clan are still 'using' the planets resources anyway," Charlie argued. "These neat little niches you've developed up here, with the dogs and the goats and sae on – it's still a kind of agriculture. It's still playing around with nature fa your aen benefit."

"You can leave any time you want, Charlie," she said.

"I'm not the one bein high and mighty aboot what we should and shudnae be doin tu the planet! It's easy tu talk about principles. It's a lot harder tu live by them when food is hard ta come by."

"We're developing a style of living that is more in tune with nature, like the Native Americans, the Inuit and the various tribes of Africa and South America." Well-rehearsed words rolled off Maya's tongue.

"I don't think they had breeding programmes, or tried tu speed up evolution in species their survival was reliant on."

"Anyway!" Claudia interrupted abruptly. "It's lovely for Charlie t'have someone to argue with. But you've got your lives ahead a'you to continue this argument, so could we jus purrit aside for now?" She gave them both that sultry smile that said 'we all know what this is really about'.

Charlie laughed softly, almost to himself. Maya looked unperturbed.

"Supper's ready," Toby announced meekly from the stove.

"Genesis," Haydn chuckled, but I didn't know what he was referring to.

He stood up and began dishing up the food. I was salivating at the thought of the meal, knowing how much of the good stuff we'd put aside for it and how many hours Toby had spent cooking that day...

* * * * * *

DISEASE ON THE WING

Roxanne Ratcliffe, New Riddlehamhope

I shifted uncomfortably in my seat and stared at the food. Moments before it'd been a well-earned feast, but harsh reminders lurked on my plate, between the grouse and the goose, who spoke silently to one another. I selected a piece of tender fowl with my fork and put it in my mouth, but it tasted like ash. My guts twisted inside of me. I thought my physical rejection of food was a long-lost foe.

A symptom of the modern life which itself had become dated and void of meaning.

"Can we not discuss this whiles we're eatin?" Claudia said firmly. For a moment I felt an image in which she and Maya were eyeball to eyeball, weighing each other up like two feral cats.

"Okay," Maya said. "I'll leave it there. But with the threat of Avian Flu getting ever nearer, I advise you mostly avoid birds as a food source. That's all."

Claudia was sat close on my right and I heard her say beneath her breath.

"Get out of yer own arse."

I couldn't chew the meat in my mouth. I swallowed it with a gulp and could still feel it as though it was sat in my throat, squatting like an Adam's apple. I felt as though the only social choices now were eating or speaking and I could do neither. I found myself smiling self-consciously. When I smile like this I feel like people can see my skull, the crawling nerves winding beneath my skin.

I sipped the strong, sweet wine and moved food around my plate. I put a small mouthful of potato in, but couldn't bear to taste that either, swallowing too quickly again. On my left Jacob was sat. He was talking in that lovely, rough North Irish accent. He seemed suddenly hyper-real. I could feel the vivid detail of his hair which was every shade of gold and auburn, giving him the look of a lion.

He was like Aslan, and wasn't Aslan meant to represent Jesus? I concentrated on his throaty purr, glancing now and then regretfully back at my plate, which wasn't getting emptied fast. The gravy looked like an oil slick.

"What did you do before the Weathers, Roxanne?" he purred. I probably looked very vague and distant so he was using my name to pin a verbal reaction.

"I worked in a bar."

He and Maya had probably done many grand things. I'd forgotten to listen properly. Maybe he'd been a freedom fighter – I remembered watching the film *Hunger* about the first hunger striker among I.R.A prisoners. Bobby Sands... his body turning to skeletal rack and ruin. The thought of the bed sores and grey-yellow skin didn't help my appetite.

"You all seemed to have worked in a bar," he said with a cheeky smile. "People who worked in bars after being a student always struck me as people reluctant to grow up."

"I wanted to be a photographer," I added, no less pathetically.

He nodded.

"My friend was a photographer for National Geographic. It was tough to get into."

I'm shrinking to thimble size. If only I could eat, maybe he'd stop trying to have a conversation with me. I put a small chunk of vegetable in my mouth, I didn't even know what vegetable. It tasted of nothing. The nothing made my tongue want to spit it back out.

"You're not eating very much," Jacob said after gobbling a good forkful himself. "Aren't you hungry?"

Panic seethed in my brain like water touching electrics. Back in the dated modern world it was easier to make excuses like 'I had a big lunch'.

I shrugged in a non-committal way. I knew it wasn't like eating birds was likely to give you bird flu. You were more likely to catch it handling the raw carcasses. My body was rejecting food for the wrong reasons. I was overwhelmed by the sense of sadness that we could learn to be self-sufficient and live off the land but we had no defence against a pandemic. We could all be wiped out in a matter of months. I'd let the idea soak through my whole body and fill me with dread.

I looked over at Toby and he was watching me intently, with those big sad eyes. My body felt empty, craving loneliness, or maybe just craving that the room was almost unpopulated. That I could discontinue unhinged conversation. I could feel tears welling up. I took another big slurp of the wine. Drinking seemed to hold back sobs and self-pity, but without the help of food it was beginning to make me feel light-headed.

Sometimes I can continue participating in a scene, but I mentally step back. As though I'm also a camera, filming. Inside the camera lens everything means something. Peoples' body language and facial expressions are there to denote some aspect of the story, some aspect of the characters relationships developing, or worse, falling apart. I did this a lot before Cuan and I broke up, sat back and watched us, and asked questions. The more I did it, the more I wanted to put us out of our everloving misery – like a terminal pet, or a gangrened limb in need of hacking off.

I was a camera now, looking in on the scene, watching Toby watching me.

* * * * * *

SURPLUS CABBAGE

Bryn McLarey, New Riddlehamhope

I wusnae tuu sure Maya was going down well with the table. She wus a bit preachy. She meant well, but I had tu admit that Toby's guerrilla-technique of turning people around tu his ideas seemed more effective. But Maya had made many a speech ta roomfuls of eager intellectual ears about her theories. This tends tu fill a person with unnecessary self-importance.

The food wus amazing anyhow. A roast ta die fae, with three different meats, proper tasty gravy, potatoes cooked in dripping, massive Yorkshire puddings, carrots and kale, and some other cabbage. There seemed tu be a lot of cabbage aroond. I gobbled greedily. It'd been a long day and I'd been looking forward tu the meal all week. I had tu remind maesel tu slow down and savour it.

The conversation at the table moved swiftly along. Before food wus served we'd tackled M. Floss philosophy, and the Avian flu fear-mongering raised its ugly head again. Now it patched up intu the ends of the table. Jacob seemed tu huv taken a shine to Roxy, which amused me. I almost wanted tu cheer him on. A yoghurt-weaver with some fooking balls, Roxy! Surely thas yer dream man? Sure he's ginger, but they're better suited tu the climate!

Predictably Toby wus looking on at this a wee bit forlornly.

Claudia, leik me, wus busy tucking into the food. She's neh one for idle chatter until the plate is empty, and I respect her for it. Haydn wus distracting Maya from serious subjects by repeating how much he thought she looked like a Scottish musician called 'Soom T'.

"I know, Haydn," she said. "Yuu told me that time you were drunk!"

"She wasn't your sister, was she?" he asked eagerly.

"I don't even know who she is!" Maya said, though she wus obviously quite happy with the attention.

"She was from Glasgow. Sexiest singing voice ever... Apart from Claudia, obviously!" Haydn said.

"Oh you're a singer, Claudia?" Maya asked.

"Uh-huh," Claudia grunted between mouthfuls.

"I didn't huv any family in Glasgow. I don't think I ever even went there," Maya remarked thoughtfully.

I raised an eyebrow.

"Yuu told me you'd been."

She looked blank and thoughtful.

"Oh yes, I did a lecture at the university! Noo chance fer sight-seeing though."

For some reason I felt suddenly protective of mae city.

"Not a Charles Rennie Mackintosh fan then?" Haydn asked.

"No, who is that?"

"One of the greatest designers of the early twentieth century. He created the Glasgow School of Art and a bunch of other places," Haydn said.

"I didn't see the art school," she said.

Haydn shook his head.

"My nanna would have had a fit at an educated lass not knowing Mackintosh. She was from Edinburgh, but she lived in Durham when I was little."

"I didn't study *design*," Maya said.

"Yeah but he was more than that. It's like saying you've not heard of Dylan Thomas, cos you've never studied literature." Haydn chewed food as he spoke.

"I'm not really familiar with Dylan Thomas either," Maya said. "I find the arts quite frivolous. It's just intellectual entertainment. It's not something you should take seriously."

"Wow. My nanna would be on you like a cat right now," Haydn said.

I laughed, nearly coughing out part-chewed spuds and gravy. Maya stared at me with a modicum of horror, before looking away again. Somehow the threat of a long dead elderly lady had killed any controversy in her argument. And I wondered if all she wus actually after wus controversy. She wus an odd fucker – I've never met someone so intelligent that considered high art *frivolous*. I wus starting tu wonder if she even had a sense of humour, like meybe humour wus tuu silly and trivial for her as well.

* * * * * * *

THE LITTLE GREEN STICK

Wolfgang, New Riddlehamhope

It occurred to me at the dinner table, so I had to excuse myself and scrabble in my coat pocket for my notebook. The damn pen was low on ink as well, so I practically engraved it into the paper.

The sparrows are the proletarians of the bird world. They don't need flights of fancy, peacock eyes or the colours of paradise. Just a prickly hedgerow and a mask of happiness that enjoys the small detail and demure hues of Mrs. Sparrow.

"What are you writing?" the Jacobean lion asked me. I was probably elbowing his mate (was she his mate?) who'd not yet finished her greens, being too busy listening to the sound of her own voice.

"Specifically about proletarian sparrows, in general the philosophy of Brian," I said breezily.

One has to learn to be breezy and economic in explanation when talking about one's *art*. More than a sentence and I see their faces begin to glaze, like hot glass. In the cooking pots before me, in the great healing jug of broth-like gravy, I'd thought of Günter and his *nail and rope soup*. Some are happy with their lot, some don't need *nail and rope soup* to realise the potential of their own existence – able to not dwell on Dad removing his belt and exacting his own horrors on a new generation. Some can forgive, or if not forgive, live beyond forgiveness or forgetfulness. Some can.

"Who is Brian?" Jacob asked.

"I'm afraid that's the wrong question," Simian piped up suddenly. I realised how quiet he'd been, but now maybe the wine had gone to his head. He smiled a broad knowing smile. "You can't apply a logical question to the work of Wolfgang. Well, you can, but don't expect the answer to enlighten you."

"What is the answer?" Jacob asked, but he was asking Simian, not I. Simian knows us all in his gut, not in his logic. That is his skill.

"Well, eventually Brian was condemned to the body of a pigeon. But apparently it's a mistake to say that he *was* a pigeon," Simian said.

"You're right," Jacob searched Simian with his eyes, as though he had overlooked something. "I don't feel very enlightened by that."

Simian blushed, and I wondered what his gut felt then, about the Red Lion, after whom so many pubs were named.

"Did your father die young?" I asked Jacob. It'd come to me from somewhere, from the single strange dot of black in the colours of his irises – a fault on the lens.

"Yes and no," he said, in that full throttling accent which was winning my heart, like those of the others. "Why d'you ask?"

"An inkling. I like to inkle," I mumbled.

"You mean you like to speculate."

"That too!" I said.

"They say my father died young, but my father died in 1972, in a famous bloody massacre. I wus born four years later... You can see the problem with the logistics of that?" He grinned.

"You were illegitimate?"

"That's one word fer it," he quipped.

"What were your thoughts on the Troubles?" The Kaiser butted in. He'd been eager for the subject, I suspect. Our exploration of Belfast city, all those years back, had stayed knotted in the Kaiser's sinews.

Jacob looked at him with a quirk of his mouth. "My aulder brudders were in the Irish Republican Army. Because of ma dad, it was personal." He paused. "I liked tu think I was above it all, but nobody is above it all when it's your family and friends. I went ta university and studied my arse off to get out of it. To find some purpose in my life beyond upholding a hundred-year grudge. But it's tough. People are sympathetic now to the civil rights movement of black people, but this was still viewed as some petty religious squabble." He waved a hand in the air. "Bygones. Let's not dwell in our past lives."

"Here, here!" I said. "Doing so only ever made me insane."

Maya gave me a sideways look over her last neat forkful of food. "Yes," she said, after she'd admirably chewed and swallowed. "It's funny how quickly we slip into talking about the past. Isn't the future much more exciting?"

I chuckled and she looked maybe annoyed. "Homo Sapien is the most nostalgic of all beings," I mumbled wisely. "So, Mus Floss, I take it you're living the dream, rather than living the nightmare?"

"Of course," she said. "For me this is what is meant to be. Which are you living?"

Her attention on a person weighed very heavily, I thought, whereas Jacob's attention was light as goose pimples. "I'm living both, but then I always did," I said.

"Cuan fookin said that once!" Kaiser grinned, intentionally stubborn towards nostalgia, to rattle Maya's bones in more ways than one. "He wus pissed ta fook, and ramblin on about how we live in both a *utopia* and a *dystopia* all at once. Mental little fooker!"

"Thas the nicest thing you've ever said about him," Claudia said with her droll, heavy-lidded eyes.

"Of course!" Kaiser spluttered with happy laughter. "He used tu upstage me all the time! You know what an ego-maniac I am…"

And there it was. Forgiveness for the hundred year grudge. Some can forgive, though I can't say they can forgive their father. Some can ignore Iago's whispers in their ear, green eyed rumours spread like coughs and sneezes – cured only by the sea. Some can walk the road of tears and search only for the little green stick, on which a wise child inscribed the secret to happiness. Some can. Which reminded me of something we'd missed and made me ponder…

"Where is young Nikolai?" I asked.

* * * * * * *

TRIFLES

Claudia McLeod, New Riddlehamhope

Havin heated a basin a' water and mixed in Toby's homemade soap, I sunk my hands into the warmth and began scrubbing the dishes that were soaking beneath the fine bubbles on't surface. Holdin up an old rag, Maya arrived at ma shoulder, overshadowing me by several inches.

"I'll dry, if yuu can tell me where things go."

A surreal situation, I thought. A domestic dinner party, too much wine, and little dramas unfolding around't table and now the kitchen sink. I knew this bird had an agenda, I fookin knew it. But I still didn't spect ta hear what came outtah her mouth.

"So have yuu and Charlie ever slept together?"

Maybe it were meant to sound light-hearted and gossipy, but it didn't. I stopped whar'ah were doin and looked at her and looked across the room to where the others were chattin among thissels oblivious'ly.

"Given we're boath massive slags, surprisingly no," I said.

"Curious," she said. "Yuu huvva certain chemistry."

"Wev bin friends for bout ten year. We get on." I was doing nothing to encourage conversational flow.

"What about him and Roxanne? Have they ever had a thing?" she persisted.

"What is this? A'ya hopin to compare notes with sumone?"

She frowned innocently.

"Why? What's Charlie said?"

"Are you and Jacob a couple?" I asked. "Nobody seems to know." Hit her on the break, I thought.

Agen she frowned innocently. She were quite pretty when she made that face. Though pretty was the wrong word, I meant sommat less girly, more passionate. She were either oddly unaware of herself, or an evil genius. I hadn't decided.

"No, well, we've had our dalliances in the past. We're both free spirits though," she said.

The mind boggles, I thought. "Fraid I'm too dumb to know what 'dalliances' means," I said. "D'ya mean that you're fuck-buddies?"

She seemed unflustered by this remark. "I like you, Claudia. You're very frank. I think we'll get on."

"I'll let ya know when tha feelin's mutual."

She took this as a joke and laughed. That were always one a'tha joys of havin a fairly monotone voice. I could let other people decide when I was and weren't jokin.

"Where does this go?" She waved a gravy jug.

I pointed vaguely to one a the shelves. Toby would probably re-home it aal later anyroads.

It irritated the fook outtah me when Charlie sidled over to us. He were probably worried about the sorta thing I would say to Maya. "What are you ladies talking about?" he asked.

"Your sexual history," I replied, quick as a cat up a tree.

"Oh, Claudia." He pinned me around the shoulders in a friendly rugby hug, the type he uses when he wishes he could only control ma mouth. "You are a joker."

I untangled missel from him. "Definitely got a few Charlie jokes up ma sleeve." I raised an sunk my eyebrows, as I pretended to concentrate on the plate I were washin.

"Anywhey, we're havin pudding nae, if you want tu rejoin the table and retire from yer mud-slinging," he said.

"*PUDDING!*" Haydn said loudly to me.

"*PUDDING!*" I replied.

"*Oh, Brian, you are funny,*" Haydn said.

"Why are we talking about Brian again?" Maya asked. "Who is Brian?"

"They're quoting from a television show. Ignore it," Charlie said.

"Irony is built on a hierarchy of understanding," Wolfgang began.

Maya looked a little baffled.

"Excuse me," she said, and left the room, but she returned a second later holdin Nikolai by't scruff offiz collar.

"Who is this?! He wus hiding in the hall," she asked.

I laughed. "That's Nikolai, our slave boy. He were probably snoopin round to see if we were talking bout him."

"Whatever, man," Nikolai said. "Yullot dinnae notice if am here or noo."

Maya let go of him, rolled her eyes and disappeared again, presumably tu the toilet. But Charlie also disappeared a moment later.

"You hungry now, Niko?" Toby asked. "Want sum food?" He gestured tu't leftovers.

Nikolai nodded.

* * * * * *

THE YOUTH OF MAN

Roxanne Ratcliffe, New Riddlehamhope

'Mother Nature is tender. She believes ultimately in good, despite all she has witnessed to the contrary. She will one day drown the kittens who have devastated her planet, who have lived faded, ignoble lives where industry and invention and convenience have become the primary objectives.

I lived in the industrial heartlands of the north, where the community required a regeneration of the soul, but were instead given a face lift. Nip and tuck. Sweep the toxic waste under the carpet and nobody will know any better.

All will be forgiven and forgotten when the endless rains come to wash us clean of the blood on our hands. Mother will reprimand the Youth for the damage he did. She will discipline fairly, she will take like for like...

Cassie Siddal'

Skimming through Haydn's book – The Chronicals – I'd come upon the name. I read the passage and stared, incomprehending.

"Simian...?" I said. "Have you seen this?"

He held the worn brown cover in his arms and peered at it. He looked only numb.

"Yeah, I remember when it was first posted on the e-zine. I had a small heart attack. But there was a note afterwards saying that the person who posted it had found a book with this passage hand written into it, and the signature."

Simian passed it back across the table to me. Toby leaned over my shoulder to see what we were talking about. He read it carefully and thoughtfully, his breath quiet.

"Was that your friend?" he asked Simian.

"Maybe," Simian said. "I'm sure it's possible there are other Cassie Siddals in the world."

"Is it like the sorta thing she wrote?" Toby asked.

"The style is, a bit," Simian said doubtfully. "But she wasn't one for writing about 'issues'."

Having given up his own seat to the hungry Nikolai, Toby had an excuse to pull up a stool and sit next to me. Nikolai was stuffing his face and ignoring everybody except Cujo, who was trying to curl up in his lap, despite being a little too big. Jacob watched him for a moment and then turned to Toby.

"So where'd this boy come from? Did he come up from the south too?"

"He got left on our doorstep in't middle a the night. He war ill," Toby shrugged.

"Ever the Good Samaritan, Toab," Jacob patted him on the back. "Have ya heard from Jessica and Vince, by the way?"

Toby shook his head.

"Not for a while…"

Jacob nodded, with a grave look in his eyes.

"Vince's still very ill," he said. "I don't know if he'll make it."

They looked sadly at one another for a few moments, in a silent exchange.

"I told Jess she can come and live with us, if she needs to," Jacob said at last. "That's if she can put up with Flossie."

A wet nose touched my hands and I looked down to see Ana. She was snuffling over me, as though trying to find out something. I wondered if she smelt my fear.

"Hey, babby." I stroked her ears.

"She's one hell of a dog, that one," Jacob said. "You get me one just like her, Toab."

"There's sommat I've been meaning to ask you," I turned to Toby, in a fleeting moment of bravery.

He looked at me very calmly and intently, as though I was about to propose marriage or something.

"Where did you get the names Otto and Ana from?" I asked.

He just sat there looking at me quietly. His face quivered with a thousand thoughts, and once again it was as though the whole world was scribbled out around us and there was just me and him and nothing else.

"Wasn't it from that film we watched years ago?" Jacob said, as though Toby needed reminding.

"*Lovers of the Arctic Circle*," Toby said breathlessly.

"Thas the one," Jacob said. "It wus a bit on the twee side, but overall quite sweet and beautiful."

"Sounds lyke a description of our Roxy," Claudia said.

"Can I talk to you in private a moment?" Toby whispered.

"Okay." I was unsure if my limbs were working.

"What's happening with pudding?" Wolfgang asked.

"We're waiting for Charlie and Maya to reappear," Haydn said.

"Be waiting a while." Claudia chuckled.

"What d'you mean?" Haydn asked.

Toby led me out into the hallway and we stood in the darkness almost under the stairs. I waited for him to speak, barely able to see his facial expression. I could just hear his breathing and almost his heartbeat, like a rabbit in a headlamp.

"I've sommat I need to say..." he said, barely coherently.

I waited, the seconds ticking over.

"Roxy," he began again, then silence.

Gradually I found my eyes were adjusting to the light and I could make out his features. I reached out and touched his fuzzy jaw line with my fingertips and then I decided to be brave and kiss him, because I was so afraid that if I didn't do it now, I never would.

We were tangled up in a fierce embrace still, sometime later, when a thick Scottish accent spoke from the hall behind me.

"Aboot fookin time," Charlie said, and then abruptly disappeared.

* * * * * * *

THE OLDEST SHAGGY DOG STORY

Wolfgang, Dreamscape

It's one of those fucking great nights. The sky so clear and crisp, the air so very cold that your mouth looks like a chimney every time it opens, belching out fog into the air. We huddle inside this strange room which feels like a long low ceilinged cave, except for all the plastic and metal – we nomads are destined for the cave, destined to be feral again.

We have a few candles dotted around the carriage, and a wood fire. The previous occupant had made an actual metal chasm of a chimney from the junk he'd collected. I remembered now *Stig of the Dump*. I think it was the third English book I read by myself. I look at the way he's insulated draughty corners with bits of old carpet and bin liners and wonder if it *was* Stig himself that'd lived here.

The room warms up quickly, extinguishing our foggy breath marks. I spread the love by pushing a bottle of Scotch around the room. What have I bartered for whisky I cannot recall?

"What have you learned today, Homo-Sapien?!" I shout, to the shadowy faces surrounding me. The kiddies around their campfire, wrapped in blankets, cuddling mugs, only they contain the devil's water instead of milky cocoa. I laugh grimily.

Kaiser glares at me, his torso enlarged and bearlike, knuckles locked for reparation. Should know better than to upset the Kaiser, me, but I don't know better. Wolfgang the brave. Wolfgang the stupid. Truth be told, I'd spent so long not speaking while we'd rolled along the mobile railway that my tongue was too full now and words couldn't spill out fast enough.

"Stupidity doesn't matter anymore. Human intelligence has led us not to distinction but extinction. Discuss?"

Snork Maiden flutters her pretty lashes, pretends to understand me in her rational little head.

"We're all gonna die." Simian Ape looks bleak.

"Much will unfold yet, much, before a creature could really say whether I was right, or whether it was merely speculation. But I do like to speculate."

"Do we have tu talk sae much?" the Kaiser scowls.

"Thou would rather we sat in dark silence, contemplating the doom!" I suggest bravely. "Homo-Sapien, your time is almost up. What will you do with the remaining time? Be a moody old goat, or make a last bid to understand that our demise is just another twist in the stream? Realise, *Christian*, that we're a fucking insignificant species?"

I'm not sure I believe it all in the self of mine, but it's nice to be controversial – nice, indeed, especially when there's an Authority figure to rile up.

I was born in East Berlin fourteen years before the wall came down. That's what they told me, anyway. I have no memory of being a child. I'm not sure I believe I ever was. I think I was born a half-grown adult. I've no opinion of communism, as I don't remember experiencing it. And yet I feel I've lived in other places, through other times. A youth counsellor (with whom I was drinking in a bar, I had no such personal luxury) once suggested I had a syndrome with a funny name – that meant I empathised so deeply with characters in books and films that I felt their life experience was also mine. But that's just the sort of half-baked theory a sceptic or Atheist (or sceptical Atheist) would suggest.

Anyway. I was living in an artists' commune on Oranienburger Straße before I met Kaiser. He walked into the Stadt Garten one day, where I was sat painting ponies onto a burnt-out Volkswagen bus. Oh those were dreamy, carefree days, my friend, my brother of apes!

He pressed a pistol into the side of my head.

"Follow me," he said in English.

"Are you the fucking Kaiser?" I squawked in a disgruntled fashion. And so our kinship was born.
The Simian Meer Cat raises the bottle of Islay Single Malt aloft to toast, but forgets his lines. I think him even drunker than I; I can see the whisky clouds in his eyes.

"So... ladies and germs. What is the plan from this day forth? Once we get in a train that moves." I say.

Everyone settles into some sense of concentration and porpoise. They search the cave for a leader. I'm the leader of chaos, that goes without saying. But chaos is not always what the world needs. At least that's what they all seem to believe.

The Kaiser usually leads, that's why he is the Kaiser, but he leads with the fist... or the bullet. Which ever witch is most appropriate. Yet, my little Bambino, sometimes neither is appropriate nor appropriated... In which witch case, there may be an invisible tussle in the mud, between the quiet witch, and the loud witch, in their witchy outfits. Yet alas I'm off on such a tangent, even I don't know what I speak of anymore.

Roxanne Rat is a little tearful. I like her tearfulness. I hope one day for her to cry so much we will all wash away like rodents. Kaiser stares wide-eyed at her, like a child just told that Santa is suffering chronic obesity and might die soon.

The fire crackles on the silence. Each face blanked like a pandas with the eyes in shadow. The panda sits confused by this strange new world. He munches the bamboo and ponders what he did that was so wrong. Why does he deserve this?

I awoke with a jolt. The death of my dream self, the birth of my living self. I'd been napping at the dinner table like an old gent. I wasn't sure how much I'd missed of the conversation; my subconscious had probably been listening anyway. He does that.

"Eisbär," I said in the throatiest German I could muster.

Maya Floss, a lady of Amazonian stature, looked at me with a certain haughty Britishness. The peculiar thing is, I think she would identify so with my thoughts and dreams and incessant scribbling in notebooks, and yet she hasn't the patience to give my 'yammer' the time of day.

"Wolfgang is a little eccentric," Toby said. I almost think there was a note of affection in his voice. Certainly not derision. Monks don't do derision.

"That's the understatement of the New Century," Jacob Frith remarked warmly. Fritz the Cat, Frith the Lion.

"He's started a Northern Dictionary," Toby continued. "Yorkshire and Northumbrian phrases and pronunciation and where they crossover."

"One has to make sense of things somehow," I affirmed.

"Were you dreaming about polar bears?" Simian asked.

"Are you a polar bear?" I asked. "You were in my dream. I suspect you were drunk."

Simian had his elbow rested on the table and his chin in his palm, his hand hiding his mouth. But his eyes smiled, arching into half moons and crinkling in the corners. Who knew Simian had smile lines?

"Are we having pudding now?" I asked. "Now everybody has stopped courting one another and so forth...?"

"Ye lot are leik a bunch a horny rabbits." Nikolai shook his head. He seemed already to be growing into his odd face, the pointy chin and pointy cheeks and thick eyelids with fair eyelashes that were barely visible.

"Oh!" Claudia said "I think I forgot to tell everyone.

Nikolai hassa twin. What d'ya say his nayme was Niko?"

"Tristram," Niko said. "Him an me wasnae twins. Hus jus mae brother."

"He looks just lyke ya," Claudia said.

"Tristram and Nikolai, eh?" Charlie said. "They dinnae sound like very local naymes."

"Whatya sayin, man?" Niko asked defensively.

"Were yer parents fans of *very long books* by any chance?" Charlie asked.

"I dunno. They died when I worra bairn. Are we havin pudding noo then?"

* * * * * * *

CLAUDIA & THE MISTAKES

Haydn Antoine, New Riddlehamhope

Some evenings feel weighted down with such enormous feelings of joy and sadness and latent potential that they're almost too much to bear. Quite often these are the evenings we drink ourselves into the gutter, so we can forget we ever felt something so vivid, yet so intangible. This was one of those evenings. I felt furious love for my friends, and yet the pain of death and betrayal also ran through my veins in crimson energies.

Vincent Moon was right now on his deathbed, the colour fading from his cheeks as each day ticked by. Jessica Smith, the love of his life, would be sat by his bedside with the patience afforded to those who know every moment is another bit of sand draining away. She probably hadn't eaten properly in weeks, her chestnut hair lack-lustre and limp from the weight of its curls. They were old friends of ours, close friends – Vince and Toby went to school together in Huddersfield. They once squabbled over the same girl, who ended up going out with the captain of the football team instead of either of the nerds she sat with in chemistry lessons.

Tomorrow we'd doubtless set off to their farm, which lay the furthest north, several hours journey away. I hoped we wouldn't be too late to speak to Vince. I was insistent that he'd know all the time he'd put up with Toby obsessing about some girl he'd met over a decade ago had finally, unbelievably come to fruition. It nearly made me cry to see Toby look so happy as he did this evening and yet whenever our eyes met they only spoke one thing to one another, and that was '*Vince*'.

We'd finally finished dinner, and were sat around the fire. Claudia had the new guitar, and Toby had his old guitar, and they were attempting to jam something together and laughing as it went wrong. The sound of music floated out over Riddlehamhope, travelling up the Breamish River and on up over the Cheviot Hills, which stood silently and majestically in honour of the occasion.

Otto suddenly set up howling and all the other dogs sprung from their dozing spots and joined in – wanting to be part of the carnival of noise and food and celebration. We all sat and listened to their voices for a while, a shiver collecting on all our spines in awe of the ancient music of wolves. But as quickly as they'd begun, they were silent again. They all turned and looked at Claudia as though questioning why she'd stopped her music.

"You play," Toby said to her. "Your voice is better than mine anyway."

And so she began – the unnervingly familiar opening chords of *White Girl Blues*, the song that'd seduced me all those years ago. And yet, without the electric landscape of the band, it sounded almost like an old, old song, passed down generations. A song about how the white people stole all the good music from the black people, a song about how insignificant our hopes and dreams and personal problems are, in the greater scale of things. And yet we still howl on about them, because that's all we can do.

She'd confessed to me last night that she'd slept with Jody. That the abortion she'd had happened when we were together, not shortly before. She said she wanted a new start now, a slate scrubbed clean through honesty. She didn't want to feel guilty for her lies as well as her deeds.

This too was weighing on me. This too was making me drink the wine a little too quickly. But if I was honest with myself, I'd probably already guessed the truth years ago. I'd probably used it as a lever to remind myself, when I moved to London, that I was better off without her. Without the furious dramas, without feeling like I was on a runaway train rolling on down the hill into utter oblivion.

And I didn't feel like that anymore. I was beginning to feel somehow safe and secure with Claudia, as though she would look after me, as though she wanted only to make up for all the years she'd spent being a bull in a china shop.

The fire crackled in the hearth. The dogs were snoozing and Roxy, too, was dozing in Toby's arms, looking delicate and peaceful. Charlie was rolling a smoke, Simian was reading through more of The Chronicals, and Wolfgang was muttering to himself as he poured out more booze. Nikolai was perched up on a stool in the corner, trying to be invisible but coughing from trying to drink his wine too fast. Jacob was sat with his elbows on his knees, stroking his red beard and listening to Claudia intently and meaningfully. I looked over at Maya, who looked a little bored – maybe she didn't appreciate the music. She felt my eyes and looked at me, and then she jumped in the air all of a sudden, clasping her hand over her mouth.

"I totally forgot! I brought some grass with me!"

Everyone, even the dogs, turned to look at her in surprise.

"I knew there wus sumthin missin," Charlie said, returning calmly to his rollie.

* * * * * * *

NEXT TO NOWHERE

Roxanne Ratcliffe, Scotland

The glacier has a blue spirit trapped in its icy walls. Icy walls that split open into deep chasms – cravasses – that roll on down the slope and flatten out, crushing the gaps back together. The spirit is warm. It presses insistently at the near-opaque glassy walls. It needs no oxygen to survive in the ice caverns; it spins like the ribbons of a ballerina down the dangerous mill wells that form from moraine and whirlpools of melt water.

The glorious crags climb cruelly towards a heaven where you may be sun-burnt, frost-bitten and altitude-sickened all in one hour. The sun sidesteps a little and smiles her radiating smile, which blurs vision and draws out freckles. Nothing smells fresher than ice fields and evergreens on a crisp, cold, bright day – a smell they could never successfully package.

It was nearly autumn. Toby and I had travelled many miles up into Scotland, in pursuit of a rumour, a bit of folklore that may or may not mean something drastic for our future. And now sat among the mountains – with the horses grazing nearby as though they hadn't a care in the world – we stared in awe. There before us, way up in the mountains, was the beginnings of a glacier. I hadn't really said anything about this elephant in the room. I'd been too mesmerised by its beauty. So Toby had rattled out a mixture of hearsay and knowledge about it.

"It doesn't necessarily mean another Ice Age," he said carefully. "It's only small at the moment, and in places lyke Canada, they have huge glaciers. I visited one that they said were bigger than Vancouver. They just stay up in't mountains if the conditions are rayht. So it may jus be that, a small glacier, not even an ice field. Nowt to worry about…"

We couldn't fully fathom the alternative – the fact that there might be another Ice Age coming, sooner rather than later. It was best to not worry about sommat like that, until you were sure it was happening.

I had plenty to distract me in terms of little issues. I was mad with love again, and this disturbed me; the saged human inability to love like you've never been hurt, to repress the scarred canvas of past endeavours. But among the mountains I was able to free the feeling and let it drift away. The future could wait. All that mattered now was the sunshine and the cold alpine air, which spread through me like some meditative force. I wondered if this was what Wolfgang was talking about when he rattled on about an awareness of 'Being'. Instead of some pretentious thing a person came up with from thinking too much, maybe they just meant this – when you just feel completely humbled that you are alive and able to experience such colossal beauty in the world.

I hoped this was how Cuan felt before he died – somehow at peace, despite everything.

"What're you thinking about?" Toby asked.

I realised I'd been quiet for some time. I'd always resented this question before – my thoughts were my own after all, even if nothing else was. But he asked it in that sweetly curious way, as though I'd drifted away from him and he merely wanted to share the moment.

I tried to remember what I had been thinking, but the only thing that wasn't abstract was Cuan. "I was just thinking about someone I used to know," I said, with a coy smile. We exchanged a look, which took in the expanse of life we'd been apart, the experience we couldn't share.

'Meaning is not a thing; it involves what is meaningful to us. Nothing is meaningful in itself,' Wolfgang had once said, quoting someone again. Then he'd said something about cats not appreciating paintings. In my tumble of thoughts, this in turn reminded me of my brother's note: *'If a tree falls in the woods and David's around, does it make a sound?'* Sound had no meaning to deaf people, except in its absence. I felt this was rather profound and was on the verge of trying to share it with Toby – but the words refused to form.

"What happened to yer brother?" Toby asked. "Ya used to talk about him a lot. You were very close."

"He went to Cuba." I thought of what the word meant to me – the worn grandeur of sun-drenched buildings, Mojitos, music and dancing. It was probably very different now.

"Sometimes tryin to getta conversation out of you is lyke tryin ta bleed a stone." Toby smiled. "Ya thinkin too much, you keep forgetting am here."

I remembered suddenly, with strange clarity, a dream I once had. As though a jigsaw piece had fallen into place. I'd been trying to write my photography dissertation at the time, and getting very stuck. In the dream I was staring at an empty page, trying to think what to write, and then somehow I went inside the page. I was just moving through this white blankness, full of light, and I looked down and realised I was walking on snow.

There was someone else in the dream who came towards me through the snowscape, in which the sky and the ground were inseparable. It was someone I loved. He had a stubbly chin and he kissed me on the forehead. I tried with all the force I could impose on my subconscious to remember who the man was – but the face was lost and no other distinctive feature could unmask him. It could've been Toby, or Hal or Cuan, or all three merged into one.

I felt somehow like I was back at my beginning. And I knew it was the quiet little death sigh of the last page. I held Toby's hand and stared mistily at the great glacier, expanding on the skyline, beckoning to a possible future. The empty white world bleeds away.

END NOTES

3. The jaguar is a reference to a short story by Jorge Luis Borges called *The God's Script* (*Labyrinths*,1964, New Directions). Though sometimes in the story the jaguar is a tiger. The ceiling of lightbulbs is from a film called *The Bothersome Man*, 2006, Jens Lien.

9. *'dangers untold & hardships unnumbered'* is from the film *Labyrinth*, 1986, Jim Henson.

22. *Tim and Tobias* were a series of children's stories by Sheila K. McCullugh.

23-26. This passage contains several references to the film *The Shining*, 1980, Stanley Kubrick. Including room 237 and the quote *'Put the bat down, Wendy. Stop swinging the bat, Wendy'*.

29-30. This passage has gentle references to the film *2001: A Space Odyssey*, 1968, Stanley Kubrick.

32. The paraphrased Tim Burton quote is from *Burton on Burton*, edited by Mark Salisbury, Faber & Faber.

36-38. The Mother Black Cap is the name of the pub in the film *Withnail & I*, 1987, Bruce Robinson. There is also a brief scene in the film where a character is eating takeaway food in the bath.

38-40. *An Anthem for Doomed Youth* is a poem by Wilfred Owen, 1917, *'the shrill demented choirs of wailing shells'* is a quote from it.

40-43. The discussion here concerns the film *In America*, 2002, Jim Sheridan, *'...It's the stairs Johnny'* is a quote from it.

45-49. *'The steed is vanish'd from the stall'* is a quote from a poem called *The Giaour*, by Lord Byron, 1813. *'The only liquor so good they named a colour after it'* is a quote from the film *Death Proof*, 2007, Quentin Tarantino. *'When you cut open the body, the heart looks like a fist. A bloody fist'* is paraphrased from a film called *Closer*, 2004, Mike Nichols. Further quotes are from *Labyrinth*, 1986, Jim Henson.

62. *Disasters of War* refers to a series of prints made by the artists Francisco Goya. The mural mentioned genuinely exists in Belfast.

79. *'Well look at this morose mutherfucker right here!'* is a quote from a film called *Chasing Amy*, 1997, Kevin Smith.

111-113. This passage references a short story called *The Metamorphosis* by Franz Kafka, 1915.

124. *'Mister Duck and the Bitch'* is from a novel called *The Beach* by Alex Garland, Viking, 1996.

131. The *'city of the immortals'* references a short story by Jorge Luis Borges called *The Immortal* (*Labyrinths*,1964, New Directions).

146-149. *'You're not crazy; You're just a silly little girl who is making herself crazy.'* Is a quote from a film called *Girl, Interrupted*, 1999, James Mangold. The chords and cotton wool clouds reference the film *The Science of Sleep*, 2006, Michel Gondry.

158. *Brand New Second Hand* is the title of an album by Roots Manuva, 1999, Big Dada.

162-163. The quote beginning '*And what if we dare to forget?*' is an extract of writing by my esteemed friend Daniel Morris.
168. The *Rufio* song is from the film *Hook*, 1991, Steven Spielberg.
175. '*Mine is a long and sad tail!*' is a quote from the children's book *Alice in Wonderland*, Lewis Carrol, 1966, Bancroft Classics.
180. There is a reference here to a description of *Mister Duck* from *The Beach* (Alex Garland, Viking, 1996), of '*skin hanging of a coat hanger*'.
183-184. The quote beginning '*Girls like guys with skills...*' is from the film *Napoleon Dynamite*, 2004, Jared Hess.
187. '*Drop, drop, drop... Tomorrow and tomorrow and tomorrow*' is a quote from a novel called *Brave New World*, Aldous Huxley, 1932, Chatto & Windus.
194-199. *Hairy McLarey from Donaldson's Dairy* is a children's book by Lynley Dodd, 1983, Mallinson Rendel Publishers. '*You must know that a cat should have three different names*' is a quote from T.S. Eliot's *Old Possum's Book of Practical Cats*, 1939, Faber and Faber.
209-211. '*Dust is mostly human skin.*' Is from the film *Sunshine*, 2007, Danny Boyle. Although the imagery here of the bride echoing Ophelia is eerily similar to that shown in the film *Melancholia*, 2011, Lara von Trier, I wrote this passage several years ago.
215. The phrase '*The thrill of waiting up for the end of the world*' came from the film *I'm Not There*, 2007, Todd Haynes.
218. The quote beginning '*Sorry am late. Went furra piss...*' is courtesy of Dan Layton, a greater comic talent than I.
224-227. '*In the same way he is me & I am all men*' is a reference to the short story *The Shape of the Sword* by Jorge Luis Borges (*Labyrinths*,1964, New Directions), where he is quoting Shopenhauer '*I am all other men, any man is all men.*' (Here we go down a rabbit hole of homage.) The quote '*Beware of enthusiasm and love. Neither last very long*' is from the film *I'm Not There*, 2007, Todd Haynes.
232. '*The Tracks of Mae Tears*' references the song by Smokey Robinson & The Miracles, 1965, Tamla.
248. A reference here to the film *The Bothersome Man*, 2006, Jens Lien.
252. *Waking Life*, 2001, Richard Linklater.
254-256. *Badger's Parting Gifts* is the title of a children's book by Susan Varley, 1984, Andersen Press.
270. There is a reference here to the death scene in the film *Into the Wild*, 2007, Sean Penn.
281-283. The film described is the opening scenes from *Don't Look Now*, 1973, Nicolas Roeg.
283-286. '*It can't rain all the time*' is a quote from a film called *The Crow*, 1994, Alex Proyas. The quotes '*If we don't try, we don't do; if we don't do, why are we here on this Earth?*' and '*This train carries people to where they don't want to be. It is a sad train. Burn it.*' Are from the film mentioned here *Shenandoah*, 1965, Andrew V. McLaglen.

286-289. *The Youth of Nature* is the title of a poem by Matthew Arnold, 1852. *The Lady's not for Burning* is a play by Christopher Fry, 1949.
296. '*All she wants is constant affirmation. Everything outside of herself is ruled out. But Art, my friend, cannot be ruled out!*' is quoted from the novel *The Flounder*, Günter Grass, 1977, Luchterhand.
297. There is reference here to a poem called *Voodoo Girl*, Tim Burton (*The Melancholy Death of the Oyster Boy & Other Stories*, 1997, Rob Weisbach Books).
299. *Wolf Like Me* is the title of a song by TV on the Radio, 2006, 4AD.
323. 'Barguest' is apparently Yorkshire slang for an unwanted ghost, 'padfoot' is the canine equivalent.
330. *Kind of Blue* is the title of an album by Miles Davis, 1959, Columbia.
338. '*One day the rain is gonna come and wash all the scum off the streets.*' is a quote from the film *Taxi Driver*, 1976, Martin Scorsese.
346. *Dust of Ages* is the title of a song by Eels from the album *Blinking Lights and Other Revelations*, 2005, Vagrant.
377. *A Bottle & a Friend* is the title of a poem by Robert Burns.
443-446. '*The law of club and fang*' refers to a theme in the novel *Call of the Wild* by Jack London, 1963, Scholastic Magazines, Inc. The quote beginning '*Our brains ache in the merciless iced east winds that knive us...*' is from a poem by Wilfred Owen called *Exposure*.
459-463. *Of Moons, Birds & Monsters* is the title of a song by MGMT off the album *Oracular Spectacular*, 2007, Columbia. The quote beginning '*Meaning is not a thing...*' is from a book called *Women, Fire, and Dangerous Things: What Categories Reveal About the Mind* by George Lakoff, University of Chicago Press, 1987.
483. *The Death of the Author* is an essay by Roland Barthes, first published in Aspen, 1967.
516. '*All the best stories are just interesting lies*' is from a poem called *All the Best Stories* by Drew Robey.
529-532. '*Horror has a name and a face*' is a quote from the film *Apocalypse Now*, 1979, Francis Ford Coppola.
544. *Our Endless Numbered Days* is the title of an album by Iron and Wine, 2004, Sub Pop.
547. *Damn Dog* is the title of a song by Manic Street Preachers (written by Jacob Brackman and Billy Mernit) off the album *Generation Terrorists*, 1992, Columbia.
555. *Black Dog on my Shoulder* is the title of a song by Manic Street Preachers off the album *This Is My Truth Tell Me Yours*, 1998, Epic.
556-558. The plotline mentioned here is from *The Cry of the Wolf* by Melvin Burgess, 1990, Andersen Press. '*Bidandegero*' is a mysterious character from the novel *Dog Years* by Günter Grass, 1963, Luchterhand.
558. '*Charlie don't surf*' is a quote from the film *Apocalypse Now*, 1979, Francis Ford Coppola.

588-592. The theories described here by the character Toby Roe are loosely taken from animal researcher Shaun Ellis, particularly one of his books - *The Man Who Lives With Wolves*, 2009, Harmony Books.

595. I should note though Devlin wasn't based on a real character, there was a folk singer in Sheffield known as 'Shea' who sang something similar to this if my memory serves me.

610. The title is a reference to a quote *'Only Lily has the ether'* from a film called *All About Lily Chou-Chou*, 2001, Shunji Iwai.

626-628. *An Anthem for Doomed Youth* is a poem by Wilfred Owen, 1917. *'The overwhelming indifference of nature'* references something Werner Herzog says in his film *Grizzly Man*, 2005.

669-672. *'The little green stick'* and *'the road of tears'* refer to the life of the writer Leo Tolstoy (particularly to some content in the documentary *Imagine – The Trouble with Tolstoy* aired by the BBC in April 2011). *'Nail and rope soup'* refers to an idea in the novel *The Flounder* by Günter Grass, 1977, Luchterhand.

674. *'Pudding!'* is a quote from the sitcom *Spaced*, Edgar Wright, Channel Four, 1999-2001.

675. *The Youth of Man* is the title of a poem by Matthew Arnold, 1852, the words *'faded, ignoble lives'* are quoted from it also.

688. The quote beginning *'Meaning is not a thing...'* is from a book called *Women, Fire, and Dangerous Things: What Categories Reveal About the Mind* by George Lakoff, University of Chicago Press, 1987.

Lightning Source UK Ltd.
Milton Keynes UK
UKOW050644200912

199321UK00002B/16/P